TIDES OF CHAOS

CHRISTOPHER BRAMLEY

A World of Kuln novel

SANCTUM

First published in the United Kingdom in 2022 by Sanctum Publishing

A CIP catalogue record for this book is available from the British Library.

ISBN 978-0-9931273-7-3

Published, Designed and Set by Sanctum Publishing
Set using Pfeffer Mediæval/Cinzel Decorative &
Adobe Garamond Pro 10.5/13
For all enquiries please email: info@sanctumpublishing.com
www.sanctumpublishing.com
All images, maps, and other media Copyright © Christopher Bramley

Foreword and Acknowledgement

It is said of momentous, earth-shaking events that you always remember where you were when you heard the news. When I heard of the death of Sir Terry Pratchett, I was waiting to board a plane to Manila via Hong Kong. I had been scheduled to run an intensive course, followed by my first holiday for ten years, involving beaches and coconuts and time to get on with starting Book Two. I was trying to recover from serious burnout, and I was very much looking forward to it.

The news was a sudden shock. I had known of his battle with his illness for years, and admired the redirection of anger and frustration at it into his books. In a world where many of us struggle daily to put our thoughts coherently to paper, Terry Pratchett was faced with a far harder struggle - one which affected him profoundly, and yet which he appeared to resoundingly re-channel, judging by the continuing genius of his books.

I don't know how I felt most when I saw the news: regret, that I will never read his new work again, and that I never managed to meet him and tell him how much I admired his work; sadness, that a man of such vision had to struggle so hard to do something he so loved. Admiration and respect, for his character and his genius, his fortitude and stoicism, his wit, for making me laugh freely and be absorbed into such cuttingly defined worlds with their underlying social commentaries. Sorrow for his family and friends for their much more painful loss. And last, melancholy... and a shard of pure selfishness that there will now never be a chance that he might read one of my books, that I can never say to him: "See this? All this was only possible because of people like you. *Especially* you."

My holiday is to relax and recover... but it will now be tinged with sadness, and - since I am also getting on with the messy business of writing this book you will be reading - a driving urge to pour even more of myself into it and say: *Here. Here is a book that perhaps Terry might have enjoyed, one that could never have existed had he not been. One that pays homage to one of the greatest.*

The other point that is equally powerful for me is that of my very close friend, Michael. The first book - The Serpent Calls - was dedicated to his memory, and I hadn't really planned on this, but he kind of ended up in this book. I think my idea was that he would have left our world and ended up passing through Kuln... yet, somehow (as he ever did!) he has charmed his way into being more integral to things, into becoming a pivotal figure. With the kind permission of his family, one of the characters has ended up being partially based on him. I would like to point out that he is not entirely this character, nor is this character entirely him; both have said (or done) things the other might not do. Still, they share certain things in common, and in some small way it helps him live on... perhaps to continue, somewhere else. People should know about Michael; he was an incredible, complex, simple, intense friend, with a cruel streak and a noble heart. He Got Shit Done, at maximum output. Life around him was unnerving, alive, and fun - sometimes terrifying. His legend deserves to be known, at least in part.

So, as befits a darker sequel, this book acknowledges two strikingly different but extraordinary people of exceptional achievement, without whom the world is a markedly lesser, bleaker, darker place.

They will not be forgotten.

- CB, en route to Hong Kong, March 2015

Addendum:

Since this was written, many things equally earth-shaking have happened. A TEDx, a pandemic, irriversible life events, finding out that I am unquestionably very autistic (and in a typically atypical way, natch), and dealing with a number of other struggles - including mental health - have been a few waypoints.

I wrote the above in 2015 as I wrote my first words for this book, in a state of shock; this addition is from an older, possibly wiser, and certainly more learned self to acknowledge how much more has influenced the book and changed me since then.

And lastly, more than seven years on... I still feel Michael's loss as keenly as ever.

But I am kintsugi – and my purpose continues.

- 2022

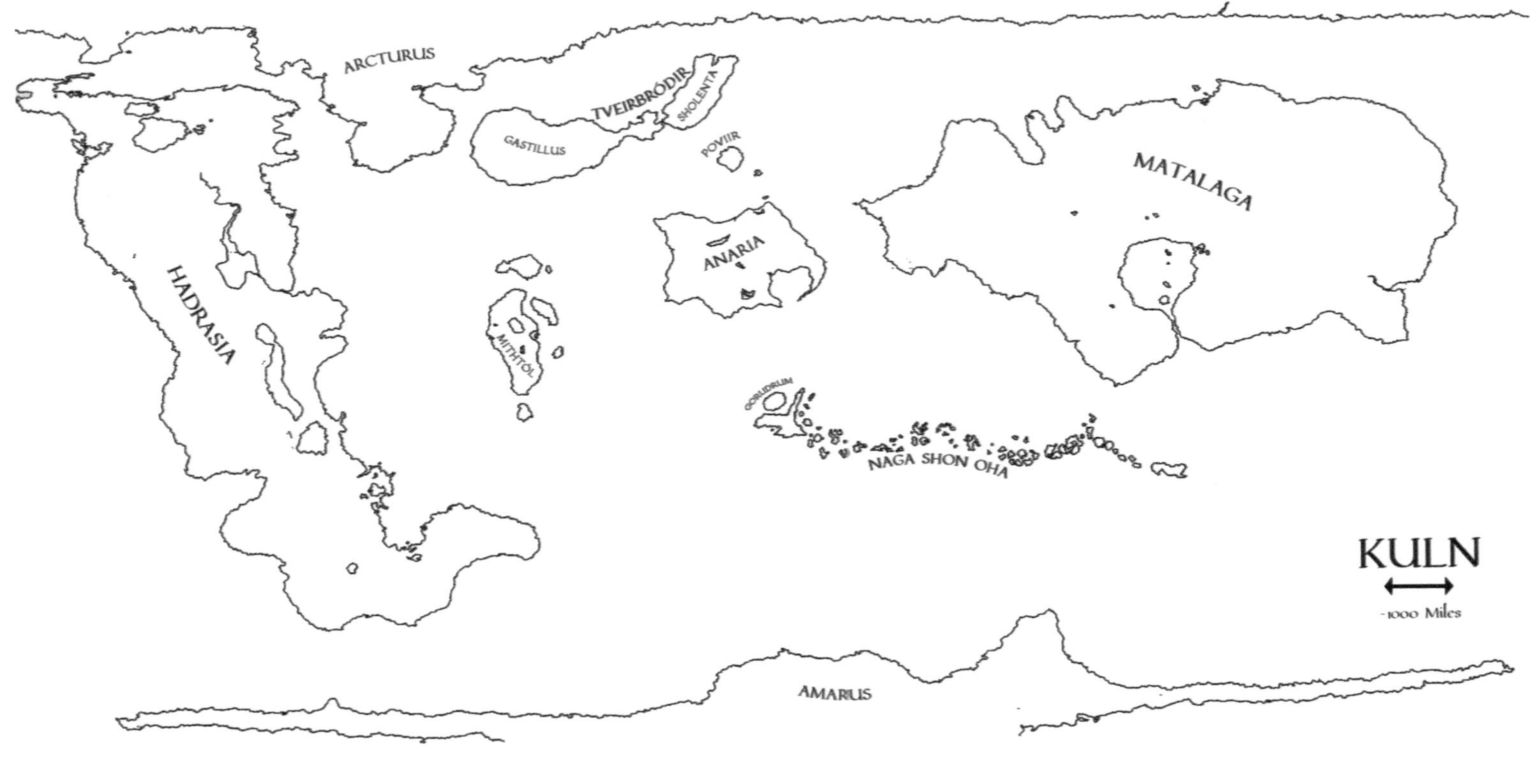

ARCTURUS
TVEIRBRÓDIR
GASTILLUS
SHOLENTA
POVIIR
MATALAGA
HADRASIA
ANARIA
MITHTÓL
GORUDRUM
NAGA SHON OHA
KULN
1000 Miles
AMARUS

ANARIA

ANARIA
~100 Miles
LODNOR
UNITED TERRITORIES OF MEYAR (FORMERLY HANÁ)
NASSMOOR
ARKON MTS
TERENDON
FOOTHILLS OF NASSM.
FOOTHILLS OF RHE
LAKE MERIMAKEA
EYOTSBURG
SOLTSVAR MTS.
RELDENHORT PLAINS (ORK TERRITORY)
STORAKTAR RIVER
PUNSLO
CAPSLIM
THE PIT OF KHARNOK
DIMN
SKYREACH MTS.
SERGOTH PLAINS (HUMAN BARBARIAN TERRITORY)
GORRINOR
IGNAT
DARKENSPIRE M (DWARF TERRITY
SKYREACH MTS.
NOVIN
ACHENOR
BANISTARI EMPIRE

AEGLAND
KINGSPORT
WORLD'S CREST MTS.
NORDLAND
LAKE NORDLING
NORTHING WOODS
SUDSLOTHIAN
TAMISMUTH
THE CROFT
HOEVEN LAKE
GLEADSMOOR
FORDLIN'S RUIN
DAROST
EORÐELAND
SUDLAND
(DWARF TERRITORY)
THE HALINAX
DRAKEHOLM SOARING
IRILVIEW
IRIL ENETH MTS.
DELVING
LÉOHTSHOLT
(ELF TERRITORY)
TABANOR
VALESRUIN
IRIL ENETH MTS.
IRIL PASS
DIMNESDAIR
BANISTARI EMPIRE
VALE
KIWIJÁNMJI
KANAK
CZTERSPOSOBY
MORLAND
G'BOKUN NYUMBA
JEDOUM
ABDINA AL MORZE

This book is dedicated to two people:

My wife Grace, who refused to help me with it because "the story was too exciting to spoil". We've been through fire together, and it's broken us more than once, but I will always love her profoundly and I'm very, very proud of her. Mahal na mahal kita forever, asawa ko, come what may. Thank you for the skinpigs and hippotatamus.

And of course, to Sir Terry. Thank you so, so much.

'There are many more domains to existence than simply those of Good and Evil. Order and Chaos are far more profound, concepts more definable yet less tangible to our own minds; yet even then there are domains within domains – not nested within, but as entangled as a thicket of brambles.

Not all which is of Order is beneficial, in the same way Good may do great Evil in the name of a Greater Good; not all which was born of Chaos is Evil, in the same way life will mutate and evolve erratically to avoid destruction or take unexpected new paths to success. I have heard many debate the morality of Good and Evil, but they remain as subjective as anything created by - or innate to - mortals.

But Order and Chaos... ah, even Universe itself and all the Gods therein bow to these laws, and both are necessary for our reality to exist. They do not care for truths, or lies, or opinions. They simply are.

For Universe to exist requires, of course, a balance of some sort to be struck between them... and therein lies our current problem, the definition of that state. There is only one thing that lies between them, and one being outside these laws; and although I believe both exist, that does not mean we will find salvation.'

- Excerpt from the writing of Aldwyn Varelin

ONE

The beast breathed heavily as it squatted on its haunches in the brush at the edge of the farm. It could smell the animals upwind within the small barn, and yellow eyes gleamed with anticipation.

Its flesh - now impervious to the ravages of time and lasting damage - still ached with the transformations it had recently undergone. Fleeting memories were lost in the swirl of hatred and desire for blood. A predator's focus meshed with cunning, and old intelligence seeped through slowly, perceived here and there amidst the desire to kill and maim.

Eager to feast, to drink, the beast bayed, head back and eyes screwed shut. Clawed hands closed convulsively around the nearest bushes and branches, shredding them of leaf and bark, and powerful muscles bunched under rough fur.

Sharp hearing picked up the sudden frantic clamour from the barn, and the panicked reactions from the farmhouse beyond. A figure appeared as the front door was thrown open, a crude weapon in its grasp. Flickering light spilled out, and then was cut off as the door slammed. The faint sound of a bolt being drawn came, as other noises signalled windows being secured.

A growl rumbled up its throat. Livestock were good to kill; anything was good to kill, as long as it sated its hunger. But nothing was as good as men. Their fear, their knowledge of what it would do… the sport.

There was hatred for those that it was, yet was not, could not be.

Hatred for their pathetic little lives and their arrogant stupidity, their dependence on each other.

Hatred for their measure of what it had lost.

Triumph in what it had gained.

All of this was dim, hidden behind a haze of brutality, a red sheen in its mind. It bounded from the trees into the steading, racing for the barn. Roaring, it slammed against the doors, the beam holding them shut. From within terrified lowing erupted, and the whinnying of a horse. It finally regained enough sense to wrestle the drop bar from the brackets and pivot it around.

Chaotic murder seething through its mind, it flung the doors open and leapt in, tearing into the first creature it found.

The small horse tried to kick in agony and fear, but the beast was to the side and it missed.

Sinking its claws into the hindquarters and the back, it leapt the stall edge and slammed the horse into the other side, sinking its teeth deep into its shoulder. The horse screamed, and the other occupant began to smash against its stall. Reaching down, the monster clawed into the horse's stomach, and then crouched and savagely tore with its teeth, snarling in the wash of blood. It was not experienced, and the horse fought for some moments, catching it hard in the temple with a leg before sinking, quivering, its life trickling from the ghastly eviscerating wound in its belly.

Dropping the dying horse, the creature jumped out in front of the second stall where a cow had snapped the lock on its gate. Unsteady from the blow to the temple, it leapt at the cow but was not prepared for the large creature to swing its head into line so fast. A horn pierced its side and it howled in agony. The normally placid cow pushed in panic and anger, sensing an advantage, and rammed the unnatural beast back into the opposite wall. The thick hide and folds of the cow's throat were preventing the claws from having deadly effect, and the beast was snapping in pain. It slashed across the cow's eyes, then pulled itself from impalement as the blinded bovine half-reared back. Quickly, the blood already slowing from its dreadful wound, it grabbed the horns and wrenched with all its might. The cow fell to its knees and toppled. With a howl of triumph, it tore into the throat again and again until the cow had stopped moving. Blood from the ragged gash began to form a huge pool.

The abomination paused, chest heaving after its exertions. Its fur was a sodden mess of blood.

Such power it had! The tearing agony in its side had become a dull memory already. And yet, it felt hollow. Hungry, still it did not feed. It moved to the barn door, ignoring the chickens squawking and flapping in the dark barn, its yellow gaze fixing on the farmhouse not far distant.

There. There it would find satiation. Living, thinking, frightened beings, young and old. Easy prey. *Deserving* prey.

This was not a hunger born of stomach, but of delight. It could smell the fear from here and bayed again in bloodlust.

Running in a crouch, it covered the ground quickly and slammed against the main door. The old oak held and was barred solidly. In rage the creature attacked again and again. Finally, the red mist receded enough for thought to form, and it backed away, casting its gaze from side to side.

Around the house it moved, clawing at any ingress it found, eliciting cries of terror from within which only fuelled its bloodlust. All the windows were solidly shuttered, until the second to last.

Badly hung, it allowed a clawed hand in around the edge, and the creature tore it off with a heave. Panting with effort, hearing shrieks within, its bloodied lips drew back from its dagger-like teeth in something not quite a snarl, not quite a smile. A rumbling chuckle growled from its throat, and it climbed through the window into the farmhouse.

ତ୍ତ   ଞ

Leona rose from her crouch, her senses alert. She was weary in spirit; for months now she had been fighting chaos and death across the sparsely populated lands north of Novin with her brethren.

If anything, Night's warning hadn't been dire enough. Although part of her nature was raw and primal, in tune with the red and bloody cycle of Nature, it was a normal part of things - the cycle of death and birth, and balance - but what she had encountered here was madness. People and animals had been butchered and ravaged at random with no rhyme or reason, the very land wantonly soaked in blood and the stench of terror and death. It was more than an affront to her and her fellow Druids; *Gaia* itself cried out in protest.

The summons from the other Druids had been enough to tell her that this was urgent, but she hadn't realised the extent until she had arrived in the vast darkness of Grunsholt, the great ancient forest stretching from northern Novin to the southern bank of the mighty Storartar estuary. The one small city-outpost of Kisholding in the north had closed its gates, and in the lands around it she had seen farmsteads ruined, villages razed to the ground. Even some towns had been overwhelmed. The inhabitants were scattered or slaughtered, and they were often the lucky ones. Few survived the attacks, and some of those that did suffered a terrible fate. Livestock was trapped and killed, with only some eaten. The creatures preferred human flesh and sport. Even the wildlife was run down, torn apart and left to rot. A wave of death and cruelty had flowed into the west, and they struggled to stem it.

Before she had joined them, the Druids had slowly pushed them northwest with incredible effort and loss, away from populated areas. Within the endless sea of trees, they were harder to find, harder to fight. Now they prowled the woodlands to the east and west of the northern tip of the Skyreach Mountains, the remaining foes the most cunning.

The most dangerous.

3

If even one escaped, it could all begin again.

She had travelled up northwest through the plains once Night had left her, moving quickly and silently day and night, pushing to exhaustion even for one of her kind. Nearing the southern Stonestride, the semi-natural arch crossing the broad waters into the island-city of Eyotsburg, she had begun to hear rumours of war, of terrors in the night. At first, they had merely been whispered stories of fearsome creatures that delighted in slaughter. As she had journeyed west, they had solidified into reports of people going missing, of violent deaths. The further towards the mountains she had travelled the worse it had become, until the stories stopped being whispered. Through and around the range of stony peaks, people were fleeing en masse.

She had followed the trails around the peaks, seeking her brethren. Before she even reached them, she ran across her foes. The monsters had fallen after a fierce battle. She had been lucky – they had been many, but young and easily outwitted. Once she found other Druids, their bleak news had confirmed that the situation was grim indeed.

Moving out of the cover of the trees, she looked east to the mountains that bordered Novin and trailed south to circle Ignat. Her nose twitched, her heightened senses catching a faint whiff of smoke and blood, and she sighed. It seemed that was all she could smell these days. For the first time in millennia her order faced an overwhelming threat from the chaotic abominations they had sworn to protect nature from. She had lost friends and kin, some of them trapped and torn apart by cunning and aware foes that hated them with every fibre of their being. Hated what Druids were, what they represented, above all else.

Leona had little time to reminisce these days, but she did occasionally think of her erstwhile companions, left behind outside Punslon. She had known them such a short while, yet she had grown to care for them all.

Deeply wise and gentle Aldwyn hiding behind his distractedness, although she could also smell his deep fear; yet he showed the most courage, continuing despite understanding what they faced.

The boy, Karland. There was something about him she could not define. Something special.

His friend, the girl Xhera; quiet, intelligent, strong. As much as she had ever felt that a normal human could be a little sister, she had felt protective of her. She sensed the girl was also special, in a different manner to the boy.

And then there was the ork.

Remembering his huge form and quick temper, his loud laughter and sheepishness after his rages, she smiled briefly. Beneath his broken Darum and rough behaviour, he was one of the noblest beings she had met, with a surprising complexity to him.

Her frown returned as she contemplated the last of the group, the enigma of a man named Rast Tal'Orien. She felt a curious attraction to him. He was striking, hugely built and as powerful as a panther; noble-featured rather than handsome, but he moved with animal grace and was quiet and calm, as a deep and mighty river flowed unhurried through the hills. He had the manner of a king and the aura of a master. People knew his name in many places, and his deeds were always honourable, yet he was a supreme fighter, a dealer of death; the *Banidróttin*. His skill was tempered by a nobility of spirit and unwavering loyalty to doing what must be done. As close as she was to nature, she understood and admired him for that as much as anything else. Nature was gentle… but it was also bloody.

Remembering that last night in Punslon, Leona saw their faces again as they bade her goodbye. She had travelled a little way with Night before he left her to continue his own search for answers. Being alone had allowed her to move far quicker than she otherwise could have.

She felt some guilt at having left them at the fringes of the Dimnesdair, but if anyone could get them through those fell woods alive it would be Rast. She hoped they had survived and found what they were looking for. When - if - she could leave, she would search for them again. The Druids were too busy stemming the tide to seek their source for now, but that would have to be dealt with too. The one small comfort was that comparatively few of the creatures survived their birthing.

The abominations were difficult to contain. Some moved in packs, some moved alone. There were many more than there were Druids, and even though her fellows had great powers and cunning, they were still losing irreplaceable lives. She was considered powerful among her kind, but it only took one mistake to be lost to the ravening horde.

The last farm she had found had been sickening, even for one used to blood. The animals in the barn had been rent asunder and blood had splashed up the walls as they flailed in their panic. The family must have been terrified, cowering in their home and hearing the agonised screams of their livestock, but that had not saved them; the beast had crashed through a window and killed them all in an orgy of death. It had eaten more of them than the animals, and probably not waited until they were dead. The last to die had been the youngest child, gutted and then left hanging armless on a hook in the pantry.

She knew it was one creature, large and powerful. She had tracked it for days, hatred driving her. It was young and cruel, new to its power, and would not be thinking as wisely as she, but they were all cunning, all as capable of some thought as men. Its trail smelled of death and blood and corruption and a terrible twisting hunger, and it led somewhere into these woods.

She threaded her way deeper into the gloom, silent and swift. Her presence brought a brief peace to the woods around her, the woods responding to a keeper of the land. She felt the slow beat of the forest, the natural chaotic order of the creatures within, and her soul responded silently. Creatures moved around her boldly, knowing she was no threat, sensing some protection in her shadow. In the distance a great woods elephant acknowledged her passing with a subsonic rumble.

This was what she had wished to show Karland. The slow-beating heart of the woods, the synergy of all the life within; the ebb and flow of nature, both death and nurturing. Many woods had a darkness on them now; she remembered the deep Northing Woods near The Croft and the growing shadow she had sensed on them. Creatures that should not be moved there these days, but still the heart of the great forest was as enduring as ever.

These woods in northern Novin had become tainted with the blood spilled by monsters that knew no boundaries. They sullied the natural order with their presence. Theirs was not the unpredictable chaos inherent in natural order; it was raw, unhinged, untrammelled. She needed at her very core to destroy them. It was her reason for existing.

The peace of the woods moved with her for many hours, comforting and taking comfort in equal measure. The day drew closer to its end, but she was not concerned. Druids had senses to match their foes, even in the dark.

She skirted a large section of gar-woods, silent and grey. There were no animals there - only bones sucked dry of flesh and blood. People had fled into pockets of the deadly trees in their fear and found their doom.

After a time, the animals around her grew scarcer, more timid, and eventually they vanished. The peace grew less in her heart and in the trees, and when this finally failed, she knew she had found her enemy. The woods around her held a preternatural stillness, and as the sun set, shadows between the trees became ominous.

Leona approached a mossy mound of rocks that rose amongst the silent trunks, the silence prickling her. Her eyes pierced the gloom with ease. She saw nothing out of place. There was no movement around her, but she felt hostile eyes watching her.

This was where the creature waited, knowing it was hunted. Her ears twitched; a faint rasp of breath reached her, deep and ragged. She could not tell where it came from.

The stench of the creature lay thick, underlaid by the coppery smell of blood. The scent was everywhere.

Her hand crept to her worn club, willingly given from a solid root, but she knew against this foe it would be of limited use. She would need to draw on other powers to prevail here. Slowly she crept forward along the side of the mound.

A roar was her only warning, talons scraping on rock as her foe launched itself from the top of the mound at her back. She flowed underneath the huge creature as it sprang, spinning and lashing out with her weapon. As it struck with her full weight behind it, she yelled. The air shimmered and distorted unnaturally around the club's impact.

Although many times her weight, the monster was smashed brutally aside by her augmented strike as if it was a child, and she whirled upright, ready. She had dealt a blow that would have killed a bear, but that would only slow it for a few seconds.

The creature had tumbled fifteen feet, slamming into the mossy ground. It twitched, then rolled with frightening speed to its feet to face her. A heavily muscled torso heaved with great wet breaths. The clawed hand rose to its damaged side.

The stink of it filled her nose, a raw and feral musk. Its eyes were terrible lamps, oversized fangs dripped with saliva beneath as it glared at her through bright yellow irises. Taloned appendages that were neither hands nor true paws clenched in anger. Young as it was, it was powerful. It did not know why it hated her; only that it did.

It roared in challenge, a terrible sound.

Fury and a terrible aversion swept through her. Dropping her club, she cast her robes wide, ready for battle. She needed more primal powers for this enemy. Her vision filled with red as hate that matched and overmatched the terror in front of her erupted within, and her answering snarl gave the beast pause.

Leona summoned her powers and leapt.

଼   ଼

Ventran entered the dark mansion quietly through a window. He had every right to be here, but the habit of not being seen coming or going - and years of training and experience in places he shouldn't have been - made him wary. Something felt… wrong. The air was still and the quiet of the house seemed oppressive, but there was a sense of anticipation.

There was a feel to empty houses. This was not quite it. Something tickled the back of his mind, dead and cold, skittering madly and breaking his thoughts up, as if a shadow passed not only over him but through his substance. It was discomfiting.

He slid up the stairs, placing his feet silently, feeling for loose boards under the carpet. His hand strayed to the knives inside his jacket, and a twist of his wrist loosened the throwing knife strapped to his right forearm. The feeling was gradually receding, almost as if the darkness was absorbing it back into itself, but the house still did not feel empty. Normally a mansion of this size would have servants, a butler, people waiting or working at most hours.

Not this house.

When the Master was away, it was deserted.

Now there was a feeling of waiting, of a presence that had not been there before. His heart hammered suddenly. Usually, he was the one who gave fear; it was rare for him to feel any fright, but for the first time in a long time he was feeling the thrill of it.

Moving down the corridor towards the main study he dropped the throwing knife into his hand, feeling the keen edge nestle as his fingers caressed the flat of the blade. He cracked the door open and peered in, his eyes well suited to the moonlight and dim shadows. He scanned the shadows, the shapes, watching for the hint of movement with the patience of a hunter.

All appeared as it should. He waited for two more minutes, breathing slowly and shallowly, his ears straining for movement, sound, the breath of another living being.

Nothing.

Confident that he was alone, he moved into the room silently, ready to investigate the bedchambers beyond.

'Ventran.'

The rasping voice came from near the cold fireplace. Without hesitation he whipped his hand at a ragged shadow that, even half-glimpsed, seemed somehow *wrong*. There was a flurry of movement and the shadow chuckled with a sound like sand being shovelled over a grave. Two pricks of red glinted in the darkness before a candle flared with no obvious source of flame to ignite it, wax trickling from the localised heat.

The hand came down from in front of the face with the blade held cleanly between a cracked, damaged finger and thumb.

'Greetings,' whispered Sontles harshly. The balding head was criss-crossed with dark putrid lines, as if his substance was barely holding together, and he was even more hunched than usual. Blackness flaked off his normally neat clothes. His eyes burned in the low light from a face that looked charred, by something other than fire, and the slight fringe of hair that had ringed the back of his head was gone.

Charred by shadow, thought Ventran, oddly. No wonder he had heard nothing. Sontles did not breathe. *Silent as the grave, indeed.*

His master moved painfully towards him, his movements jerky, coughing slightly.

'*I need blood,*' the cracked voice said. Ventran drew back warily, and even in evident pain Sontles grinned, light flashing from a fang. '*Fresh, warm, vital. Young women, men. No alcoholics or addicts. Bring them alive.*'

Ventran relaxed and nodded. The black flakes looked like dried blood and skin, he thought. He wondered what could damage Sontles. He had seen what the man was capable of, once he had finally been persuaded to believe that he was what he appeared.

Sontles had been missing for a little while, gone when he returned bearing news of his hunts. He had taken up what affairs he had, and relaxed, returning to the mansion every so often. Tonight had felt portentous, although he did not subscribe to superstition as a rule. Nevertheless, he had felt it time to check again.

Looking at the damage done to his master, Ventran could not keep elements of horror and curiosity from his voice. 'What happened to you?'

A sigh came. '*I released a bound God.*' The vampire coughed. '*Such power flowed through me! Such beautiful chaos! It almost consumed me. Were I mortal, I would have been destroyed.*' The wheezing breath sounded awful. '*I must heal... it will take time.*'

A bound God?

Sontles was not in the habit of exaggerating, and Ventran did not like the sound of that. Powers were coming into play that eclipsed him, and he felt a sense of awe as a prickle of discomfort ran through him.

If he was lucky, Sontles would finally tell him more of what they worked for. If he was very lucky his master might even perish, leaving him holding the reins of power.

Sontles sank into a wingback chair in the shadows near the fireplace, and clenched his fist at the nearby candle, which guttered and extinguished. Ventran bowed slightly and left, already planning where he would go past midnight to find fresh victims.

The privileged young of Lodnor tended to congregate until the small hours around the bazaar, smoking Banistari hashish and drinking. Most of these were well-to-do young rich, the few percent left in a land ravaged by inequality and misrule. They did not care for the woes of the vast poor as long as they had their riches and their influence. The problem with the elite was they would be hard to reach, harder to entice, and doubtless full of drink or drugs. Besides, many of them were offspring of political allies it would be unwise to anger or destabilise at present as they worked towards the disenfranchisement of all but the wealthiest in the land, but they invariably had many servants with them to mind them and see them home.

It would be easy to take a few of those. They would be assumed to have run away.

He had already had his own fun tonight, leaving another ruined and gutted victim in a gruesome puzzle to be discovered in the poor quarters. Ventran was still wary of being caught, as he had no official status and the guardsmen might simply kill him on sight rather than hold him for questioning, despite his symbol of Terome. The law was a faint voice in Meyar in these times unless you were noble. More than once he had almost been cornered.

The commoners rightly thought there was a demon loose in the cities he visited, little suspecting the demon was a man, but there were always some that ignored the curfew. If he came upon one of those, he considered them fair game.

Now he would add some disappearances of servants to the terrors of Lodnor. The city, foremost among all the states of Meyar, was filled with rich and privileged who enjoyed untold wanton pleasures while the majority of the people in the realm scrabbled in poverty and fear under crushing rule. The relatively peaceful king, who had been fair and just as kings went, had been overthrown more than ten years ago, and the Prime Alderman had stepped in, promising the people to rid the country of serfdom and royalty. Serfs had rights, but they wanted to be freemen. The people seethed as a volatile mass, and he redirected their anger, soothing them, turning their rage from the nobility - who by and large had not been as oppressive as people thought - and instead blaming outside religions, other nations. Decadence, greedy foreigners, the failings of heresy, these were the problems. The people needed to come together as one, regain their prominence.

They could make Haná great once more - as Meyar.

He said what they wanted to hear, a man consumed with passion and mindless rhetoric. It was astonishing how people would ignore lies and immorality under their very noses as long as the one in power agreed with their complaints - complaints that had been fomented and amplified by the very men promising to solve them. Fear, greed, and bigotry were easy levers, especially to the less educated.

It was not Ventran's way, but he loved watching it in action.

With one hand you shake theirs, telling them what they wish to hear, even as with the other you remove their rights, their freedom, their power from behind their backs.

People are so stupid.

Little by little, those rights once held as citizens of Haná were removed, until the country groaned under a fraction of powerful ex-nobles living like emperors, and the commoners living and dying at their behest. It could not last, but Ventran knew it would carry on for long enough to grind the wealth into the coffers of the nobility.

It suited him.

The nobles would quickly replace those he took, and his victims would find a true treasure: a desperate love of life. Far sweeter to his blade than a victim wishing for an end.

Nothing sweeter than hope. He grinned. *Nothing more bitter than hope denied at the last.*

Even as he smiled to himself at the thought of the play of blades through the flesh of the unwilling, his thoughts turned again to his master and the gruesome state he had arrived in.

Where had he arrived from? What had he been doing? What could have harmed him so?

Ventran hadn't tried to give his reports. They would take time, and his master was clearly in neither state nor mood to accept news of his partial success. One thing however was clear: the times they had planned for were coming. He would be at the crest of the wave of blood and death, at the right hand of power.

Given free rein.

He chuckled quietly and padded into the night.

TWO

Darost sprawled behind its yellow-white walls in the near-WinterBirth daylight as summer approached, the waters of the great river sparkling as they made their way through the city. To the west lay the Greatway, the western road, sweeping southwest towards the plains and the Arkons past the borders of Eordeland. To the north, the Nordsrud rolled through the fields towards the huge Lake Nordling and Boreamere, and beyond that to Kingsport. To the east the Merrad road swept to divide Nordland and Sudland before falling south around the northeast tip of the Léohtsholt towards Taranor, past the sprawling ruins of The Halinax.

The Run Wash river split from the River Nassing west of Gladsmoor, curving up and over it before running past Fordun's Run down towards Darost. Several other waterways crept out of the Northing Woods and surrounding hills to join it after Fordun's Run, where it deepened and grew strong and fast into the Eaofer, once slang for the growth of Darost on the riverbanks. East of the great city it deepened and widened further with the help of other rivers into the slower-flowing but powerful Tamis and wended its ever-more majestic way to the sea. In the farthest east, at the southern foot of the World's Crest mountains, Tamismuth lay at its wide mouth.

It was a rich land, tamed across rolling green fields outside the wilder woods and hills, farmed for more than a thousand years. The new green was still speckled by the starkness from the month of Grima to the south, remaining darker green in the Northern forests where there were more evergreens. But despite its foggy peace, a peculiar tension underlay the land.

Once free and uncaring, now people outside cities were wary at night. Strange creatures were seen, and orcs, once legend, were now a very real danger.

The cities remained much the same. Darost itself carried on, rebuilding from the horrors of Yosgaloth and the sacrifice of the great red dragon Györnàeldàr. Despite this and other warnings, as ever, human nature prevailed; many had forgotten the lessons learned quickly, and others dismissed the dangers, preferring their own comfortable stories to the harsh truths that lay outside the walls.

The Sanctum, half a mile across and hidden behind walls, tradition, and the city, carried on as usual.

Eordeland lay complacent still amidst its long contentment and ordered life.

Outside, the first faint howls of chaos could be heard.

଀   ଁ

It had been several weeks amidst the mayhem after the battle with Yosgaloth before they had found time to honour their friends, but none of them had forgotten. It had been far easier to forget that they had journeyed less than four months in their hasty travels across the continent.

The loss of Györnàeldàr had been fresh, and immense, but less personal. She had been their friend, and Karland had cared for her as much as any mortal could for a dragon, yet they had known her only a short time. She had been so overwhelming, for all that there was a definite person inside the scales and fangs. She was also still somehow in this world, in some vague and not quite understood way.

For the death of Aldwyn, Karland had found some closure at least. Rast's threnody and the succour of the travellers of the Nassings had helped them to begin to come to terms.

The death of their noble friend the great ork Grukust had been the one left undealt with. There had been no body, no way to mourn him past a pile of pale stones on a cliff and his dwarf-forged axe, which had been passed to his brother. Their plans to wait for evening and hold vigil had been thwarted with the release of Yosgaloth, and events had moved quickly after that.

To Karland, who still thought of those he had lost quite often, it had felt as if the great warrior was restless, waiting for his friends to honour him.

One grey evening, Karland, Xhera and Rast had moved from the flurry to The Sanctum's private graveyard, quiet with watchful headstones and the solemnity of ageless repose. There, before the entrance to the catacombs, they had built a cairn of laboriously found pale stones again, and added to it another cairn of normal darker stones and a much larger cairn which they decorated with red flowers from bushes nearby. It was the closest they could get for the dragon.

Into the evening they sat, Rast lighting a candle for each small pile as darkness fell. The faint bustle of the city had receded, and each had been alone with their thoughts of those fallen.

'Am I boring you, Master Dresin?'

13

The lecturer's voice cut through the class. Karland jumped, realising it was aimed at him, and lifted his head from where he had apparently been staring blankly at the doorway. Several heads turned to him in amusement, others in condescension. He could see Xhera out of the corner of his right eye, and swore he saw an eye roll. Two rows down a leer from a good-looking and haughty Novinian named Aran made him sigh inwardly.

'Well?'

'No, Master Darfin. Of course not.'

'This is quite complex, you know.' The middle-aged man - not only the lecturer for this class, but the Master for this section and level of students - peered at him, and his voice was peeved. He knew Karland was not stupid. 'Can you please repeat back to me the essence of what I just said about the basis of the two types of healing?'

Karland briefly considered boldly making something up, but he couldn't face it. 'Um-'

There was a snigger.

'Perhaps it would behove you to listen a little more carefully.' Darfin's voice was also cutting, and Karland reddened.

'Sorry.'

'Hm. Come to my office after the class.' His black eyebrows, one striped with white, bunched. 'So. We have looked at why herbs and tinctures may help a body heal, and we have talked about the natural symbiosis - that of animals and plants feeding each other cyclically. But what of understanding how it works? How can we understand a living being to a cellular level, and even beyond, and how can we sense and even manipulate the energy within to achieve greater things than the body can do alone? This is where a certain talent comes in - that of sensitivity to energy. Yes, yes, stories call it magic, but it is simply another sense that very, very few are born with. Even fewer are born with the ability to truly tap into it, to manipulate it.

'With it, if you are sufficiently trained, you can enhance your healing skills in many ways. You can sense much further down into living structure, persuade the body's energy to do things it would not normally, even use energy to preserve what can be preserved. We are all connected to it in a small way, as we are to the air, to the earth under our feet. The body is capable of great things, given energy and understanding. The sensitive healer simply provides it that fuel and knowledge in a crisis. The body remembers and responds better to healing afterwards for similar ills. A quite remarkable machine, the human body.' He looked around the room, his gaze sharp. Karland was writing this down, as was everyone else, but he had already read much of this in Aldwyn's notes. He meant no disrespect to Master Darfin, who was one of the rare semi-sensitives who could heal outside Morland.

In gratitude for services rendered, and in honour of their sacrifices, Karland and Xhera had been enrolled on scholarship into the University. It had also been a wish of Aldwyn, he learned. His half-formed ideas of becoming some sort of world-shaking mage had been dashed when he had rapidly found that even getting used to sensing power took a great deal of time, and that was only if you were Sensitive, Talented, Gifted, Aware, whatever a race or nation called it.

Only if you could even sense it could you then begin to learn the nuances of it, and they were limited by your capabilities. Whilst they did get a little better if used, you would have, more or less, that general sensitivity for your whole life. You could learn more efficient use, but you never had more power.

Karland finally understood what had upset his master so much about healing on a practical level, not just in his notes. Aldwyn could sense and manipulate energy within a body to help heal on a very limited basis, raising the effectiveness of medicines used fourfold, but he couldn't perform miracles. Apparently a very few could sense and even manipulate down to a cellular or even molecular level. There were rumoured to be three of these last in the whole of Eordeland, and two were in The Sanctum, both Morlanders. They were far too busy to generally lecture, and no one would receive teaching unless they held a similar level of sensitivity.

The classes on theory and energy flow were also popular, but there were no practical classes. In the whole of Anaria, perhaps ten people in each generation had any serious abilities. Of those, likely none had true power.

His mind wandered again as he thought of how quickly dragons healed and wondered if it was possible to transfer that ability to people. Perhaps he could have healed Aldwyn if he had known how, or at least kept him alive. Sighing, he shook his head and turned back to the lesson. He doubted it, and anyway, it was done. His friend was gone.

He knew that the dragons could sense other energies, including living energy, from some distance. Could they heal each other, too?

His pencil drifted from words to doodles once more as his thoughts ambled.

Half an hour later, Master Darfin finished the day's teaching, and motioned to Karland as a reminder. Sighing, Karland collected his notes, shuffling the rough paper into order. He exited into the hallway and moved slowly through the students, thinking about the impending talk. It wasn't the first, and wouldn't be the last.

'You should listen more closely,' Xhera's voice said reproachfully.

Karland turned and shrugged, a little irritated. 'You might be a perfect little student, Xhera, but I have other things on my mind. Remember Aldwyn's work?'

Her dark eyes flashed, and her pale complexion reddened. Her temper tended to flare more than his did.

'I'm not a 'perfect little student,' you idiot,' she retorted. 'I just pay attention. I thought you loved learning? And don't you dare suggest I have forgotten-'

'Why don't you two love-birds take it elsewhere,' drawled a lightly-accented voice. Aran stepped into view, his usual crony Fron trailing him. He was a year older than Karland and Xhera, though he looked three, and never let anyone forget that he was Novinian nobility; polite to the Masters, he was a trial to everyone else, and had picked Karland as a victim soon as he had laid eyes on him. Fron was a natural sycophant and follower, smaller and less bulky, with a rangy whipcord unpleasantness and a mean streak. 'I don't even know why you bother coming to these classes,' he continued as Fron snickered. 'You're clearly not suited. Common birth, common mind. You can't even pay attention.'

Karland opened his mouth as Xhera turned on the older boy.

'Why don't you get lost?' she suggested. 'He's brighter than you'll ever be.'

Karland winced. That wasn't strictly true. Aran had been schooled by some of the pre-eminent Novinian scholars, and had been at the university far longer. In fact, half the problem was the boy resented the fact that the two of them had joined the classes at a younger age, and without going through the careful selection process that he and all the other students had had to go through. A gifted mathematician, he ran rings around Karland most of the time, and always had something biting to say which left Karland unable to reply without sounding stupid. Being bigger, older and stronger didn't help, and he was formally trained in several forms of combat, as all Novinian nobles were. Karland had come to realise that however far you got in life, and whatever you did or said, you would always find a Ben Arflun somewhere along the line - a bully, child from his village or otherwise.

'I hardly think so,' said Aran, smirking. 'He's an outclassed runt. If I had my way, he would be run out of the university. And as for you-' his eyes swept her figure, 'you'd be better off using your mouth to *other* purposes.'

Fron waggled his eyebrows, cackling, and Karland felt his anger begin to rise. He and Xhera might bicker - well, *did*, constantly - but with what they had been through, and what they knew, all these little power plays seemed frustratingly petty, even more so because he still didn't know how to deal with them.

Instead of losing her temper as Karland would expect, Xhera ostentatiously rolled her eyes. 'Is that honestly the best you could come up with?' she asked derisively. 'I thought you had *some* brains.'

'I've got more than a brain for you, you little-'

'That's *quite* enough, thank you.' The voice of Master Darfin made them all start. The man stood to the side and behind Aran and Fron, his gaze stern. Aran opened his mouth and the teacher cut him off. 'I am surprised at your bearing, *noble* son. We had always considered you above reproof. It appears we were wrong.' His gaze bored into Aran, who flushed. 'It is not for *you* to determine the worth of others here. You will not insult another student in my hearing again, or we will find a suitably laborious punishment for you.' His brows beetled. 'And if I hear you but once more speak so lewdly and unbecoming your station as you did to Xhera, shaming our faculty and yourself, you will be up before the university masters.'

'I am not some peasant-' began Aran, his cheeks red with anger and shame. Darfin's piercing voice cut him off.

'No. You are a *student*. You will show respect if you wish that to continue. And if you think you are only here to learn facts in the classroom, you are not the student I thought you were.' He turned his back deliberately and the boy's eyes glared daggers. 'Karland.' He gestured.

Xhera's eyes were sympathetic as she left. Aran adopted his usual swagger and left in the opposite direction, Fron trailing sullenly.

Karland knew there would be problems ahead with him now. Never before had Aran been caught by the faculty, many of whom believed him to be almost faultless. There was little doubt as to whom would be blamed. It took the edge off any jubilation.

Master Darfin blew a breath and shook his head. 'You're disruptive, boy, but it's not all your own fault.'

Karland shrugged, not really knowing what to say. Darfin motioned with his hand and headed off around the corner towards his nearby office, Karland trailing him dispiritedly.

It was odd. Despite everything he had been through, his stomach still sank when he felt as if he were in trouble.

Everything had seemed so right when he and Xhera had joined the classes by Council decree, but gradually he had felt shunned, ostracised even, despite his stature with dragons and the Council, and the fact he actually got on with everyone. He was a little too different to mesh completely. Slowly he had realised that the people who didn't like him went to some effort to ensure others didn't either. He got on well with most, but he avoided getting drawn into circles of friendship. Being a loner didn't make you feel less lonely, even in the midst of a city.

Xhera had similar issues, to a lesser degree. She constantly took people by surprise with her intellect and sudden temper, but generally stayed hidden where his own more outgoing character made him an easier target. She was stronger, too; she didn't care about being well-accepted, just wanting to fit in on her abilities alone, but Karland was both apart and wishing to be a part.

Once he would have been any bully's main target - the small unsure boy, the class joke - but his time in the last year and more had hardened him. Apart from a couple of notable exceptions, bullies tended to ignore him now. He had a projected confidence that only a few seemed to see beneath. For the first time in his life, he wasn't worried exclusively about shame, or pride, or losing; being hurt or beaten. Most of the time it all paled in comparison to orcs and assassins.

To Dragons and Demons.

But it seemed everything was relative. New confidence had developed from experience; he knew the world was not as he had once seen it, was wiser now. His innocence had faded rapidly, and he stood on the verge of adulthood.

And yet...

Why do I still feel unable to answer Aran? Why do I have no voice, no argument? Why does he ignore what I have done, who I am? Why do I feel no worth?

Underneath it all, he still felt the weak and often lonely boy from The Croft.

'Karland.' Darfin's voice snapped him back to the present as they entered his office. 'Please sit.'

Karland sat with a sigh, the feeling of dread in his midsection. It really *was* amusing. He had come through fire and loss and horror, yet the quiet tone of his teacher asking to talk filled him with guilt-laden worry.

'You seem distracted a lot, Karland. You don't always get work done, you don't listen, and you can be quite disruptive. Not deliberately, I think, but still.' Darfin shook his head. 'Normally, I'd leave you to get on with things and drop out, but there are several problems. You are bright. You ask surprisingly incisive questions, you take your tutors aback with answers. *Sometimes.*' Darfin raised his eyebrows. Karland shrugged. He was of the opinion other people were usually much smarter than he was.

'You can be exceptional when you actually engage with the work. You often take in information as well as any other student, and read as if a scholar of thirty years. You and Xhera joined late at the express orders of the Universalia Communia, including some of the Council of Twelve. This means I cannot just ignore you and let you fail at what you are taught when I know you can do better. Eyes are on me as well as you. Do you understand my frustration?'

Karland nodded. 'I do, master. Honestly.'

'Then what is it, boy? I know something of your experiences, but Xhera usually excels in her studies in most areas. I suspect there is something else with you both, but why are *you* especially having so many problems, do you think?'

To Karland's surprise, far from being accusatory Darfin's voice was laced with genuine concern. His intent to mutter something and get out as quickly as he could with the least damage done vanished, and after a moment he tried to put it into words.

'I will try and explain, master, although I'm not sure I know myself completely.' He stared into the corner, marshalling his thoughts. 'I don't work like Xhera. She's smart, organised, studious… all the things I'm not, I guess.'

'Don't be deliberately self-deprecating, boy,' said Darfin disgustedly. 'Half your trouble is you won't admit your capabilities. You give too much credence to what people say about you.'

'Right,' agreed Karland. 'I can think quickly, and piece things together. I can read faster and remember more than even she can. But I just can't sit down and force myself to slog through all of this work, day after day. My mind wanders after a while. I start thinking of my friends. Master Varelin. Not being able to save him…' he trailed off. Even now, thinking of that traumatic moment brought back the gut-wrenching fear and loss.

'I thought a prime focus of your studies was that you swore to learn enough to carry on his work, to ensure you could help others in future?' said Darfin gently. 'I know what happened with him, and what he meant to you. I met him many times. He was a good man. It is one reason I am making allowances for your distraction.'

'It *is*,' said Karland in frustration, 'but I already *know* a lot of what we are doing! And he taught… well. Differently,' he finished lamely. 'And, well.'

Darfin looked at him steadily. 'Go on. Spit it out.'

Karland sighed, and took the plunge. 'He already taught me a lot of these things. He could… tell when something wasn't grabbing me, and would present it in another way that did. I can't just sit and remember things that bore me, Master Darfin, but when I'm interested, it's like a- a fire. I just… learned a lot faster,' he finished lamely.

Darfin nodded slowly. 'Hmm. And you need the fire lit. I think I understand, Karland. He was *mentoring* you, something he could afford to do with two students. I have thirty-seven students in this class alone. Some of my colleagues have more.' He blew his cheeks out. 'You are not the first - and nor will you be the last - to have difficulty learning this way. Some students need inspiration and interest to go and do it all themselves. Some are built to study and will learn day in, day out, although they may not be as intuitive. Others need to be led by the hand. Still others have to be pushed, and some simply cannot be taught. I believe you belong to the first, especially looking at the results when you *are* interested in what we are doing. You've led the class several times in discussions, but only when you can be bothered.' He shook his head. 'If I could combine your interest with Xhera's studiousness I'd have the perfect student. You have been frustrating all of your teachers, boy. Not just me.'

He leaned back and steepled his fingers, frowning in thought. 'I can do something with the learning, but you will have to deal with your distractions yourself. I know you lost several friends. I lost a few myself from the fall of Irilview, although I grant they were not killed in front of me. We are all distracted, but you must focus that keen mind of yours better. You could fly through every class if you could apply yourself.' He rubbed his chin thoughtfully. 'To extend your analogy, you are one of those students that requires a fire of interest lit, rather than a bucket filled with the water of knowledge. Students like you are often capable of great things, but are… hard to teach with everyone else.'

'It isn't just that,' said Karland, wondering if he could even explain himself. 'It isn't just Aldwyn. It's what we went through. Battle, demons. Grukust, who died to save us. Györnàeldàr, who died to save this city. And then I start to think of everything Aldwyn talked of, of what may be to come, and I can't help thinking - what is the point of all this? Don't we have bigger things to worry about?'

He stopped, shaking his head. There were things that he was not supposed to discuss outside the Council and his friends.

'I didn't *want* to be part of all this, but I am. We all are. Why does it feel like no one listened to the dragons? Why am I sitting here learning when there might not be any point?'

'I… see.' Master Darfin sighed, and stretched. He oversaw hundreds of students in the Academia Esoterica, Karland knew, and his specialty was what the University called Energistic Theory, lectured at varying levels.

'I can't say I fault you, Karland. I have been told not to press you both on certain events, but I also know something of what is going on. We are on the verge of war, and we have seen results at first hand; I believe you were even involved in that assassin attack after the Meyari Ambassador was expelled, and I can see there is more you haven't told me. But you mustn't give in to despair.'

'It's not despair so much as… oh, I don't know. The feeling we should be *doing* something. Master Darfin, I have seen more than Yosgaloth and a single dragon. I feel if we do not do something soon we will fall - perhaps even if *we do* act.'

'We *are*, boy. But nations, and Councils that decide the fate of nations, do not move quickly, and although for you it is clear-cut there are a plethora of other things that must be considered at each step for a whole country. Meanwhile, we must continue on with our lives. We are taking small steps so that Eordeland might take large strides. Don't lose sight of the large problems… but focus on smaller tasks at hand and complete them as you can.' He stood, shrugging his shoulders and swinging his arms to loosen them. "I'll help you as I can; speak to other lecturers, see where we might let you forge your own study. Focus on what you feel you must to be engaged. You know the syllabus and what we are covering, so use that to learn to your advantage in your own way.' His voice held a note of warning. 'See that you get the work in on time. This won't help your popularity with some of the others. They will see it as preferential treatment. I know some are already offended you dropped in halfway through this year's course and will take any excuse to further ostracise you.'

'I know,' said Karland, 'but, honestly - I think they are the least of my problems.'

'Let us hope you are correct,' said Darfin without a smile. 'At least there is some balance. Some of the class also believe you to be some kind of chosen hero for your companionship with dragons. That was a sight I think I will never forget.'

Karland nodded uncomfortably. He hadn't realised Master Darfin had seen him speaking to the giant immortals, but almost an eighth of the city had seen him with either Györnàeldàr or Körànthír. It had brought him some unwelcome attention from a number of people, and some strange adulation from others, although seven months without miracles or further signs of being some sort of dragon lord had it mostly forgotten.

'I'll try,' he promised. 'It's just that we also have a lot of extra studies from Master Varelin's notes, and the Libraries to research as well, plus I have to train with Rast every second day, and we have the City Guard training with the others-'

'That I was not aware of,' said Master Darfin, almost ruefully. 'Even in The Sanctum - *especially* in The Sanctum, in fact - communication is not always good. Students usually have *some* downtime. I'll work on something for you and Xhera. I've been told in no uncertain terms you are not to be ignored and left to struggle, which annoyed me at first, I'll admit, but I begin to see why.' He moved to the door and opened it. 'I'll see you in class tomorrow.'

'Master,' nodded Karland, rising and moving out.

He felt a little relieved, and grateful. Master Darfin was a person, after all. He was not in real trouble, and perhaps would find things easier from now on.

That only left him people like Aran to deal with.

oz   so

Two days later they had a rare moment to continue the studies they had sworn on behalf of Aldwyn.

Karland had given up pestering Rast months ago for more access to Aldwyn's notes. He glumly realised that he simply wasn't important enough in the University to enter more than the Librariums. Still, they had many of his recent books themselves, and he was the only one with the key to the Library of Thingos where many more lay.

The day was grey and rainy, and there was nothing better than to be in the Librariums with their huge multi-story windows and the soft white glow of library lights, the strange almost-globes glowing for twelve hours before fading. Karland had believed it to be magic when he had seen Aldwyn's, but it wasn't. It was a chemical mixture that absorbed sunlight and did not release it until it was strongly agitated after dark. They could be used as a lantern or a table light, or played with in the hand. The special glass was extremely tough; he had never known one to break.

Their current subject was Gods, something Aldwyn had been very interested in.

To their despair, they had quickly realised that there weren't only a few Gods, but literally thousands of references to deities both major and minor, possible half-deities, and other, half-whispered Gods. The Gods of major religions were there - Terome, Delmatra, Isha, and a score of others - but there were many, many more. Aldwyn's notes casually mentioned book after book.

They worked for another hour, and then Karland dropped his pages and notes with a sigh.

'What's wrong?' asked Xhera, looking up.

'I can't stop thinking about earlier. It was just, I don't know. So *unfair*. If I could just make him see my side-'

'If you are waiting to prove yourself to someone like Aran, then good luck. You'll be waiting forever,' said Xhera pragmatically. Karland knew she grew frustrated with his lack of ability to focus. 'He doesn't like you. You can't change that. Just accept it and move on. The only reason he pretends to respect me is because he wants to master me in some way, even if it's by getting into my underwear. That, and the fact it's beneath him to answer a girl who taunts him. You're another matter. You have a quick mouth and he hates being made to look foolish.'

Karland blinked at her frankness. He didn't want to think of anyone getting into her underwear.

'So, what - I should let him act how he pleases? He's the only person allowed to get annoyed about anything, to say and do things?'

'Well, no, but you do tend to have a strong opinion on things, and you tell people straight out. He doesn't like that, especially when you use logic and reason. The more you give him proof he is wrong in something, the more he will adhere to his viewpoint - unless he has evidence to drop you off the mountain.'

Karland laughed quietly to himself and shook his head. He knew any amount of people, Aran and Xhera included, who defended their own opinions at least as aggressively.

'You should've seen me in The Croft, Xhera.' He thought back to the countless times he had been in trouble with parents and peers alike. 'I used to always give in so as not to cause problems. I didn't want to offend. I hated arguing. Still hate it. I always tried to see everyone's point of view.' He shrugged. 'I've spent most of my life trying desperately not to argue, to be logical and fair, and getting rolled over by people who shout louder. These days I don't let that get in the way of what I know is right. I can't not speak up for the truth, you know? It's... like it hurts if I don't.' He shook his head. 'All *those* people were at leisure to tell me their thoughts. To dictate to me what was right. None of them ever hesitated to tell me their opinion or to be honest with me. But now if I do the same, *I'm* opinionated? *I'm* being too honest? It works both ways.'

Xhera sat for a moment, watching him with her serious blue eyes that saw so much of him, and then smiled. 'You are one of the kindest people I know, Karland. You're honest, and fair, and smart. You have unwavering integrity. Not everyone is like you. Perhaps they envy that.'

'I'm nothing special, Xhera. I've failed at most things I've tried to do. I haven't made much of a difference, and I feel like a fraud half the time. I study, I train, I do all these other things and I still feel like I'm fooling myself, and one day someone will notice that I'm nothing in particular and I'll be back where I was, only this time I'll have been right the whole time. I don't like feeling like that, even if it *does* mean that, for once, I'm right.' His lips twisted in a wry grin.

'You think you haven't made a difference?' she said in astonishment, shaking her head. 'You fought someone who bullied you your whole life for me. You attacked armed men for me. You fought *orcs* for me. You've faced every danger at my side, been there without fail, and you *haven't made a difference?*' She looked angry, but then seemed to realise he honestly meant it. Her expression changed. 'Oh, Karland. How can you feel like that? I don't know what my life would be without you. Why can't you see that? Just once?'

He shrugged again, not knowing what to say. It would be wonderful to allow himself to believe it all. He was quiet for a long moment.

'I just can't. When I sit and think, I doubt myself more. It was better when we travelled, even though we were so close to death... I just had to do things, I couldn't think and mull it all over. I only know that what other people see of me is different to what I see of myself. But then,' and he smiled, 'I'm not you. And the fact someone I... care for... so much believes in me *does* make it better. You've spent most of your life feeling trapped. I've spent most of mine feeling worthless. Give me time.' He caught himself before he managed to say too much about his feelings.

Her face twitched, as if she would say something profound - he didn't know what - but then she hesitated and the moment passed.

Instead, she said, 'You're an *idiot*, Karland Dresin. You are the rock in the desert of my life. If you continue to overthink everything, I'll slap you.' Her face grew troubled and her cheeks heated slightly. 'I still remember what I said after... after the Portal. I still don't know what the purpose of the visions was, but I was wrong. After Rast spoke to me I was angry, but I thought about his words. I realised there were others who have nothing at all, that I had a good life compared to them. But since I met all of you, I feel like I've had everything. You helped me to see the world, to become myself. You just don't know what that means to me.'

Karland smiled, his eyes tracing the faint freckles on her nose.

Gods, she is beautiful, he thought. Sometimes the way she moved or spoke sent a tingle straight to his stomach.

If he truly had the courage she believed he had, he would have spoken his heart to her, but the beauty of their friendship sat squarely in the way. Once those words were spoken, he knew, things would be different forever. He couldn't risk that for the answer he knew he would get.

'I don't think your sister could have caged you forever,' he said truthfully. 'Aldwyn said we both had a part to play in what comes. You're more of a real scholar than I am, and you're more organised, better at getting to Aldwyn's answers. We're... a good team. I sometimes feel we were meant to meet.'

'We were,' she said without hesitation. 'We were always meant to be there for each other, Karland.' She rose as his heart started hammering.

What did she mean by that? he wondered.

Not what you think, said another sly voice, and he cursed inwardly. He wondered if everyone else had these niggling voices that cast self-doubt all the time.

'Come on, you idiot. Let's get some food,' she grinned, breaking the moment. He nodded, brushing his depressing thoughts aside for the moment, and followed her, his mind on her words.

THREE

Later that night, Karland sat thinking on a balcony on top of the Cuneus Pinnacle. Like all students, they had lessons in each of the twelve segment's classrooms weekly. One day they would qualify to choose a major Academia, then a sub-Academia specialty.

Their room was several stories under him, down the winding staircase that connected the rooms each side of the Cuneus tip facing the Dodecagon. It was a mark of high favour that they had not been assigned to the dormitories, but instead given a small room above the Cuneus Librarium on the third floor in the Academia Linguistica, overlooking the Garden of Green; their small balcony had a view of the Dodecagon Tower, and the suite had three rooms and indoor jakes. It was highly luxurious.

The bridge arched from the Pinnacle over the dark gardens a hundred feet below, curving towards the side of the Tower and the locked and guarded door there. Each Cuneus - what they named the segments of dome - had one. It allowed Councillors and dignitaries to reach the chambers without walking through the rest of the building and gardens, and provided a shortcut to the Bulb, the Councils' secure meeting quarters at the top of the Tower.

There was no sign of Xoth, thankfully. Danger and horror always seemed to be higher when the small moon was bright in the sky; people were learning to associate the fast-moving poisonous green with evil.

There was some silver light, but not much. Tonight, Lunis was a sliver and the night was shadowed.

He was well-wrapped - it wasn't too cold, but there was a stiff breeze that came and went. He wasn't really meant to be here this late, but the guards knew him well enough, and most were unlikely to tell someone they had seen speak to both Council and dragons that they couldn't sit and watch the stars. Karland guessed at least one kept an eye on him, but otherwise he was mostly left alone.

He remembered clearly back to the magical time when he and Xhera had hidden on top of Hendal's roof, looking at the stars and talking quietly. Although Xhera often sat with him here as well, it was never quite the same. That night, in the silence, without light, they had shared a closeness - a bond of souls, pure and uninfluenced by previous friendship.

Here, there was always the city, always light and distant sound. They were both so busy. So much had happened. Deaths, momentous events; neither were the children they had been then. They verged on adulthood.

Tonight, he was alone by choice. He was thinking of their lost friends again. In the seven months since they had returned to Darost, the ache had eased, and he and Xhera had regained their determination to continue Aldwyn's work.

It wasn't simply a case of doing it for his friend. They had spent enough time with Aldwyn, and seen enough, to know that there was something monumental happening. He knew the Council only half-believed, even now, and he wasn't sure how much he believed himself despite everything. Xhera, on the other hand, was quietly convinced.

Rast, well; it was hard to tell. He had grown even more taciturn than usual recently. He was spending increasing time training the Guard on orc and Meyari tactics, the latter of which he seemed to know a lot about. He also spent a lot of time with the Council.

Karland wasn't really sure where his giant friend was from originally. He spoke Darum without a trace of an accent, but half the continent had a common base with Eordeland, and Darum was a widely used trade language - the widest across Kuln, in fact. Major cities on three continents used it for much of their trade, and certainly in Anaria many people spoke Darum variants as a primary or secondary language.

Karland was growing to realise that despite their education and their advantages in a progressive and advanced society, the people of Eordeland were relatively lazy. They did not face the strife many others did, and most of them spoke only Darum. In fact, many didn't even consider distant lands; the rural areas were very closed in, as Karland and Xhera knew from their homes.

His thoughts drifted back to Rast. Since he and Xhera had accepted scholarship places at the University in recognition of their valour - a rare honour, he knew - Rast had stayed longer. He had sworn to protect them. But there was more to it; Ulric relied on Rast, and they were a grim pair when they discussed battle. The two men found a kindred spirit of sorts in each other.

Slowly, Rast had found himself taking on more and more, until he was busy every day. There was always their training with him, although this was now every second day. Karland knew he wished to collect the horses left at Deep Delving, and they had spoken of journeying to find Aldwyn and bring his remains back, though that was dangerous travel now. Rast had even mentioned travelling to find Grukust's body if he could - not to bring to his people, whose custom was to let remains lie where they would, except on the great plains where they would build a pyre - but to mark his fall better than the simple pile of white stones.

Karland wasn't sure exactly what Rast believed, and he didn't think the big man would say prayers over a grave, but honour and respect were important to him. He had also been quite clear that if he went, it would be too dangerous for Karland and Xhera to accompany him. Once into the mountains had been enough; it was still wild country, and it was unlikely a dragon would be there for them this time.

Xhera didn't want to go back anyway, that was certain. It held too much pain for her. Her past; the loss of Grukust, the memories of their time with Györnàeldàr. He wasn't so sure he wanted to go back himself.

As it was, all three of them had unwillingly become involved in events. Karland had assumed - with some relief and perhaps a little annoyance - that he would now be excluded from momentous happenings, but that was not proving quite true. He and Xhera still had the best recent knowledge of Aldwyn's work, and the key to - and the location of - the Library of Thingos. Since the Council currently had more important things to worry about than cataloguing a hidden library from scratch, so far only he and Xhera had continued their reading of Aldwyn's journals and other texts.

It appeared that what they had learned from Aldwyn on the quest had only been a scratch on the surface. There was a lot of hidden meaning he had been unsure of the relevance of, and much that he had guessed at required correlation. There, the Librariums of the Cunae had helped, and that was as far as they were permitted.

The deeper Combic Libraries were secure and well-guarded. The texts within were said to contain dangerous or forbidden knowledge; ancient scrolls pressed between thick glass plates, the rarest of books and parchments, inventions and blueprints and mention of terrible secrets. There were rumours of even deeper lore.

Since the accident more than a year ago, where one of the highest-ranking Librarians had mysteriously burned to death along with several extremely rare and suspiciously relevant works, no one went unaccompanied, if only to ensure the bright blue-white library lights were used instead of any flame.

Being caught with flame in the Combic Libraries carried a harsh sentence, and immediate expulsion from the University as a minimum. Ever since the betrayal of Politikus Belen and the infiltration of assassins and traitor guards resulting in multiple deaths, including one of the Council of Twelve itself, the Welcomers had lost any reluctance to punish. It had been a terrible blow to the pride and the record of the Onyx Guard, the elite Guards of the Council; never in their history had any of the Welcomers defected, and doing so to a foreign power was a source of immense shame. Background checks and investigations had gone to the highest level, even to the Council and Captain Jekob himself. This had rippled out into the Eordeland Guard through Captain Dorn, and a few more soldiers and almost twenty Sanctum staff including the sub-Steward of the Academia Historia had been tried and convicted as a result. The depths of Kingsport Dungeon held them now. Two had killed themselves.

A few had been paid large sums of money, and one or two held records of deposits in the banks north of the river. This led to more captures when the banks grudgingly allowed a search for similar deposits. Others had been otherwise bribed or threatened. In the case of several Guards, they had been blackmailed; one had lost his daughter to Politikus Belen, who had spirited her away. Tearfully he had pleaded with them to do anything they might. Jekob had promised what aid he could, but Belen had proven resourceful. The girl had vanished for good.

It was certainly a time of unrest and suspicion, much different to the first time Karland had stayed. Gone was the sense of the complacent city unaware of anything but itself. In place was an underlying tension, a fear, a realisation that things were more serious than the usual political bickering.

Against that were set groups of dissenters, either business, political, or simply those who did not believe the claims that had leaked out despite the Council's wish for low-key dealing of the situation. There were groups in the city right now petitioning and rallying against the governors of the nation 'conspiring' to withhold information, and others who chanted that they did not want war and the Council sought to expand their powers.

Most of these groups did not look at the reasons behind the Council's actions, and word of mouth made it worse. Karland found it hard to believe, but then Aldwyn and his own innate sense of fairness had taught him to work based on fact and truth rather than supposition and cherry-picked information. That was something he shared quite fiercely with Xhera.

His thoughts turned to his friend. Their relationship was hard for him to define. They were so close, yet he was very worried about overstepping the bounds of their friendship. He wondered if the friendship would be the same if he did and was afraid to find out. They cared for each other; that was enough.

For now.

Xhera was asleep below, exhausted from her work. She had been spending much time in Aldwyn's notes, more than Karland. In many ways, he was better at the intuitive leaps that Aldwyn had made and she was better at searching out puzzles.

Together they made a reasonable attempt at emulating Aldwyn's own studies. That difference came out in other ways, as well.

Xhera was eminently practical where Karland's mind was always analysing. They spent many late evenings learning lore, looking at archived works of Aldwyn in the Cuneus Libraries, seeking anything to flesh out the notebooks Aldwyn had here.

It wasn't enough. The Library of Thingos held the bulk of his recent works. Thus far they hadn't surrendered the keys to the Council. Karland wasn't sure he wanted other people in the home from home he had shared with Aldwyn. It was a very personal place, and the thought of scholars tramping around and moving books was… well. Upsetting. Certainly Aldwyn would have been indignant, glasses probably askew in outrage.

He chuckled to himself. How many times had he seen, even provoked that?

The stars looked beautiful tonight as they peered through the covering cloud. Guards were visible here and there, moving in the shadows and patrolling. Since the assassin had been thwarted by Rast, and the attempts had been made on Council members, security had been tightened tenfold. The five scholars in the whole Sanctum who had enough sensitivity to detect falsehood with any degree of accuracy were working in shifts to screen people in sensitive roles. Karland didn't envy them their faint talent. One was only a novice.

He took a deep breath, breathing through his nose, tasting the tang of the night air. It was cold; DeepWinter edged toward Efnniht and WinterBirth, but he still had to wrap in his travel cloak to sit long.

His faint discomfort returned, a tingling itch at his core over someone who made him feel worthless, tongue tied, and weak.

Aran.

It was as if his energy was sapped when he was near the Novinian. He couldn't stop thinking about him.

Aran was the middle scion of the House of Telemer, one of the Noble Houses of Novin. Under them lay the Common Houses, and above them lay only the House of the King, currently Yoris. House Telemer was also the progenitor of Stag Company, a decorated and powerful mercenary company which was seventh in line from the King's own.

Aran was proud and haughty, a favoured son who knew it. He was quite pale, and vocal about it; Novin was a surprisingly wet and cold land for being so far south, subject to lush summers and winters that blanketed the land in snow and bitter cold. A chilled major sea current from the north ran down the western edge of Anaria, and Novin was mostly much higher than the plains and deserts to the east and south, sitting on the Western Plateau that ran up the western side of Meyar as well. The nobles there cherished the lack of skin colour, considered a badge of not working outside like a peasant.

Xhera was as pale as Aran, apparently a mark of many from Valesgate - Valesruin, now - but Karland was darker. By most standards he was quite light-skinned, but somewhere in his family history was different blood, and Aran would not allow him to forget it.

It wasn't just that, though. Karland would have given much to look like Aran, sound like him, move like him. He was almost beautiful to look at. Most girls sighed at him, even women his senior tried to ingratiate themselves. He was privileged, entitled, deep-voiced, and moved with a natural grace, picking up most of the physical training with ease.

As if that weren't enough, he was a head taller than Karland. His shoulders were wide and his posture good. A well-chiselled face with prominent cheekbones and an almost unfairly defined jawline sat above a long powerful neck. He was habitually clean-shaven, and his blue eyes were darker than Xhera's. His dark blond hair usually swept back to be held by a leather thong, but on occasion he allowed it to fall and frame his face to each side, which it did with annoying grace and style. His arrogance was well-founded.

Under other circumstances Karland would have envied him, but there was something repellent about him. He was sly, smart, unpleasant, and totally self-centred. Aran had utterly no remorse or care for others.

Naturally charming, he was quick witted and could talk his way out of any given situation with authority. His recent slip with Master Darfin, as far as Karland knew, was the first time a faculty member had been witness to Aran's true nature. Where Karland would panic and stutter with his voice slipping higher, or having plegm suddenly in his throat at the worst possible moment, Aran was urbane and smooth, and it astonished Karland how many of his quite obvious lies went unheeded.

Aran had taken an instant dislike to him. Perhaps, thought Karland glumly, there was an aura about him which impelled people like Aran and Ben Arflun to loathe him on sight. His difference made him a target, he was sure, and if there was one thing Aran liked, it was an easy target.

Aran was also the only other student not to be in the dormitories. He was afforded some private quarters overlooking the Academia Mathematica atrium. Not only was Karland also in private quarters, but his faced the main tower and Gardens.

Aran did not like being seen as less deserving, especially than Karland.

Thinking of someone he disliked so intensely had certainly changed his mood from melancholy to a thrumming semi-anger, so Karland was unsure for a split second when a furtive motion caught his eye.

He glanced over three Cunae and his breath caught. Unmoving, he would be hard to see in the shadows, but any movement was easy to spot for him. Frozen in fascination, the adrenaline surging into him, he could see something horribly familiar in description.

A large dark shape, blurring somehow into the shadows, seemed to glide across a section of roof towards him. He blinked. It had looked like a trick of the light, but it had moved with purpose. He leaned forward, mouth dry and his heart beating faster, eyes and ears straining.

A guard nearby coughed and he cursed softly. Another movement, a little nearer, suggested spread wings for an instant, and then there was nothing. If he hadn't been looking for it specifically, he would have never seen it. He wondered if he *had* seen it. Perhaps that had only been what he had expected to see. It seemed the guards had seen nothing.

He slid quietly to the edge of the balcony, peering over with only his eyes. He made little noise, breathing slowly and deeply; his time with Rast hadn't been completely wasted. He heard the guards moving on patrols and frowned. There was nothing. Surely, they would have seen it?

He nearly shook his head.

Idiot.

Stories of demons, thinking of terrors appearing as if sprung from the shadows, and then seeing a shadow that was probably nothing more than his imagination.

He peered back over again, and as he started to move away, back towards the door, he caught motion from the corner of his eye.

'YAHHHH!' he yelled in shock and heard a soft *thwap* as if something had leapt away. Scrabbling backwards, his eyes searched the darkness frantically. Seconds later, guards appeared as if they had sprung from hidden doors, torches casting dancing light everywhere. He definitely couldn't see anything now.

'Hold!'

'What goes?'

'Lad? Is that you?'

He held up a shaking hand, waving it. 'I. Um. There was something there. It moved fast.' He waved his hand where he thought the movement had been.

Welcomers peered around, moving in twos to cover the balcony. One by one, they shook heads.

'You sure, lad?' asked a Sergeant kindly. Karland felt his face grow hot.

'Yes, sir. I have been taught to trust movement in dim light from side vision. Something was there.'

'Best do a full sweep, just in case,' the Sergeant said. Karland could almost hear his thoughts: the boy was tired and had perhaps dozed off up here, jumped at shadows.

'Sarge… if I'm honest, I reckoned I saw something too,' called a tall guardsman named Virn. 'Thought maybe I was seeing things. Like a huge bat, maybe. Could have been a bit of cloth blown loose, I s'pose.'

A huge bat. Karland's mind blossomed with suspicion again, and he rose.

'I… I think we have seen something like this before. Well, heard of it.' It sounded pretty weak to his ears. 'There was something in Fordun's Run that attacked people, like a demon in the night. Since the breaking open of the Dimnesdair, there have been some dangerous creatures loose.'

'That there have,' said another guard Karland didn't know except by sight. He thanked the gods that he sounded like he believed him. 'My granny lives down south, near the Irils; she was damn lucky to have been missed by that hellspawn as it came to Irilview, and them orcs.' He spat and made a blessing to Isha. 'Village too small to be worth the eating, I guess. She said that a couple months ago, some creature came through and trampled three fields and a barn flat. Ruddy great thing it was, higher than a house, stumbling about like it was lost. Guess it didn't like the villagers waving torches around. Ran off into the forest, knocked a few trees over. Miracle no-one got hurt.'

Karland thought of the great forest elephants he had seen. If it had been one of those, he was astonished no one had been killed.

'Pull the other ear,' suggested another guard. There were a few grins.

'Nah,' said a woman. 'Three month ago my man said a dragonfly big as a child landed and tried to take his brother's cat. Died in the end, like it was losing strength, couldn't breathe or summat. That were east of here.'

There were mutters of derision until the Sergeant snapped them back in line. 'That's enough, you lot. Split and search in twos, staggered coverage, standard pattern.'

'I'd best go and find Rast,' Karland said. 'He tracked the other thing we heard about. It might be the same.'

He left the guards moving warily in a search pattern and walked back to the doorway down. With one last look around, he swiftly entered the staircase and ran down the steps to the room.

Rast was standing on the balcony looking outwards, the doors open. His grim face was turned to the night, still with the short beard that had grown during their time in the Dimnesdair and afterwards.

'What is it?' he asked softly.

Of course he would know that something was going on. Sometimes it seemed that Rast had a sixth sense.

Karland told him and Rast shook his head.

'It's possible that it's the same creature we heard of in Fordun's Run,' he admitted. 'Or at least, another one, whatever it is. It makes sense it would be more easily seen by someone here; there are many more people in a city. I will help the sergeant look.' He lifted his grey cloak from a chair and swung it around his shoulders, then padded up the way Karland had come.

Karland sat on the sunken cushioned seats. He was sure he had seen something, and if anyone could discover what it was, Rast would.

‘ ’

Two days later, Karland was still nervous about the evenings. Rast had found nothing, but he dismissed any suggestion that it had been a coincidence after tales of something that had swept through the docks and one of the poorer areas, leaving a trail of broken bodies. Something had badly injured, frightened, killed or maimed. It was too similar to the unknown demon that had frightened the folk of Fordun's Run.

The stories were told and retold for days, starting as whispers of information and quickly becoming rumour. It was a vampire. It was a demon. It was a giant bat. It flew, it walked, it just appeared from the shadows. It killed and drank blood; it had killed no one, but left many crippled. It had butchered men, women, and children indiscriminately; it had only attacked those involved in misdeeds. People had been torn apart by talons, people had been killed surgically with weapons, people had only bruises and breaks. People died of fright without a mark on them, their souls torn from their flesh. People had vanished, dragged through the shadows to one of the Hells. It was of the spirit of Death come to earth for everyone; it was a judgement on those with evil in their hearts.

About the only thing people agreed on was that it wasn't human.

Contradictory whispers flew, mostly muttered in horrified fascination at third hand. The Eordeland City Guard stepped up patrols, and people were more cautious city-wide about going out at night.

The rumours had spread like wildfire. According to the people who knew - Councillors Holmson and Brókova, Captain Dorn, Rast and a few others - two had died, seven men and four women had been maimed or partially crippled, many more had been injured.

The other alarming thing was the number of people who had started calling it judgement on the wicked. It appeared that quite a few had been saved from the illicit attentions of criminals by the being. Some of the more radical in the city were calling it a creature sent to purge Teromens, despite there being no evidence of the victims even being religious; in response, the Teromens pointed this out, and referred excitedly to a passage in the Book of Terome saying that his representative, an Angel of Darkness, would scour the wicked from the light and take them back to Its realm when His people were at their most desperate hour.

'A bloody headache, is what this is,' said Dorn sourly to Karland and Xhera three days later. He had finally given in to the questions, mainly because they were the only other people who had prior experience apart from Rast, which allowed him to question them in turn. 'The Teromens seem to ignore the fact that what is happening to them in Meyar is far worse than here. If anything, the damn thing should have shown up there to plague the Assembly of Aldermen.'

They had spent some time talking about what had happened in Fordun's Run. Dorn had asked astute questions, seeking to find a pattern. He looked thoughtful several times, thought Karland.

Even Rast had been unable to find no trace of it despite hours of searching. It was odd to find that he was, in fact, still just human; it was the same dissonance Karland had felt after Rast had been badly injured in the Dimnesdair.

That was the trouble with being so capable at everything. People had expectations of perfection.

'It's strange how it has followed us here.' Xhera glanced at Karland, half mischievously. 'Well… you. *I* wasn't there the first time.'

'Has it, though?' asked Karland, although he had thought something similar. 'It could be coincidence. After all, the last time I knew of it was seven months ago in a town only a little northwest of here; if it was following us why wasn't it here before, or in Punslon, or your tuns or The Croft?' He felt quite pleased with his leap of intuition.

'That's true,' Xhera said thoughtfully. She shivered. 'I'm mainly worried you saw it in The Sanctum. Or you think you did, anyway. It could be anywhere.' She looked at him appraisingly. 'Maybe it has always been there and you just didn't see it.'

'As to that, don't worry,' said Dorn. 'Jekob has stepped up the Welcomer Guard to full strength anyway, given the current situation, and reserves are in for the more basic duties. Patrols are increased, torches are now lit all night on all stations. And I have a captain investigating the attacks in the city.'

'You have other captains reporting to you?' asked Xhera curiously.

'Over two hundred. Actually, my formal title is Captain-General,' grinned Dorn. 'Captains of Companies report to Majors of Battalions, who report to Regimental Colonels, who report to me in Darost, Jekob in The Sanctum, a Major-General in the field, or the General-Marshal. In Darost, Captains of the City Guard report directly to me, as Darost falls under my stewardship. Apart from The Sanctum, of course. Technically, I'm in charge of tens of thousands of soldiers across Eordeland, not including the Welcomers.' That explained Dorn's long travels every few months, realised Karland. 'There are far less of them, but they have more intensive training in diplomacy, specialised weapons, close quarters combat, and security. Then there are the Onyx Guard, who make normal Welcomers look like privates. Some of our own guards graduate into them.' He sounded proud.

Xhera looked surprised.

He grinned at them. 'It's all bit of a mouthful though, so people tend to stick with *Captain*. It's also not too overbearing for civilians, and my Welcomer counterpart especially is very public facing. Of course,' he reflected, 'there *are* times overbearing is precisely what is needed. And I'm not as diplomatic as the Welcomer ranks. Never had the training and doubt it would stick.'

Karland thought back to Captain Robertus.

Captain-General Robertus.

The young man had been even more brilliant than he had realised, rising on his own merits to Captain-General. He had had no idea. He wished fervently he had known him better before he died.

'But... he said you were in charge of the city-wide militia,' said Karland. 'Not the whole country!'

'Well, he wasn't entirely wrong, although it isn't a militia. The guards are actually rotated army troops. Keeps them fresh, flexible, anchored in the people they protect.' He smiled a little. 'Neither Kel Robertus nor I used the full title except formally, and you looked like you were having enough trouble as it was. Anyway, both Captain-Generals report to General-Marshal Colcos. He's typically the one referred to as General.'

Karland thought back to how awed he had been about the Dodecagon the first time, and his nervousness at meeting the Council. Realising the two men casually chatting about cards were two of the most powerful military men in the country definitely would not have helped his composure.

'Today, for once, I have a little time free,' said Dorn. 'I thought perhaps I could show you some dual weapon techniques, see how apt you might be. Rast tells me you are both learning well.'

'I'm pretty sure I will be awful with two weapons,' said Karland ruefully. 'I am better with my left hand since I broke my right arm, but that is about as far as it goes. My right still knows it's the favoured side.' He looked at Xhera's small serious face, which was set in concentration already, and stifled the laugh he knew would annoy her. She never stopped challenging herself. She looked so… serious.

Dorn led them to a practice area and set them thrust and parry patterns with knives. He was quickly forced to agree with Karland. 'Mostly, it is a matter of practice,' he said, 'but if you aren't truly ambidextrous you will reach a limit for the weaker hand. You are very good with your main, however. It would take much work, but you could be competent with two weapons.'

Competent, thought Karland regretfully.

Xhera was better.

'You show some good possibilities with knives, especially throwing,' Dorn observed. 'I think you could use a parry and main to great effect.'

Karland bit back a jab when he saw her face break into a heart-melting smile that nearly dazzled him. She *was* better, he admitted ruefully.

'Remember, even a master will not often use two weapons. It is usually not practical except as a last resort,' warned Dorn.

They were practicing patterns to aid muscle memory when there echoed the sound of rushed feet, and a guard ran in, out of breath. He saluted and spoke without waiting for acknowledgement.

'Captain Dorn - there has been a tragedy. An attack in the markets.'

Dorn sheathed his beautiful silver-inlaid longsword and shortsword at his belt smoothly. His hands remained hovering near them, heavily callused palms half-cocked in anticipation.

'Details?'

'Three fanatics armed with Ignathian repeating crossbows, swords and Meyari trident daggers managed to get into the merchant's district with their weapons unchecked and attacked families buying food in the mercantile market. They killed and maimed men, women, children.' He sounded like he was in shock. 'The bolts were tipped with something the healers are finding hard to counter. It seems to infest the wound, causing infection and preventing clotting. It may yet kill from blood poisoning. There was no logic behind it, no cause. The guards were forced to kill them. They were shouting that it was done in the name of Terome.'

Dorn cursed volubly, his hands in fists. 'Who were they?'

'We don't know, sir. Meyari, from their skin and words.'

'This is the third incident this year.' Dorn looked suddenly tired. 'The market's locked down? Good. I'm on my way.' With a quick nod to Karland and Xhera, he left.

Karland looked at Xhera, He felt as shocked as she looked; her face was bloodless.

'Children, too,' she whispered. 'What's wrong with people?

Karland shook his head.

'You know what this means,' he said. Xhera looked at him questioningly. 'Anti-Terome feeling will rise. People will retaliate. Whether it's deliberate or not, people are becoming divided.'

'It doesn't matter if these men represented all of Terome or a part, does it? The whole Church will wear the blame.' Xhera looked despairing.

Karland recalled something Aldwyn had once said.

'I guess it's easier and quicker to generalise,' he said. 'Aldwyn always said Truth takes too much effort, that people are lazy enough to *want* to be misled.'

Xhera's voice was sad. 'The Gods help us if *that's* the truth.'

ℳ   ℴ

Marcus Andragostin sighed, looking around the hastily convened Council in the Tower. It was late afternoon, and a detailed report of the latest incident had come from Dorn. From the Bulb they could see the traffic of the city winding through the streets, each merchant and traveller a corpuscle in the great heart of the city.

'These attacks are more and more frequent,' he said. 'Over the last ten to fifteen years they have been growing. More and more in the name of Terome. But it makes no sense. Terome was a peaceful religion, an offshoot of the Booklore of Delmatra.'

'Maybe a thousand years ago, it was peaceful,' muttered Eremus. 'You forget it has the most expansionist religious policy of any Anarian religion since then. What about the Southern Crusades, the Barbarian Enslavement, the Wars of the Eyot? The Nassings Subjugation, the Banistari Encroachment?'

'The Encroachment failed spectacularly,' Nessa Contemus pointed out.

'Only because they had no idea about desert fighting or tactics - and they found the Emperor heavily guarded. If they had managed to take him as he travelled and convert him-'

'The plan was doomed to failure from the outset,' said Jamus Holmson. 'There was never any chance they would take the Emperor, and the drugs they planned to use would have needed constant application.'

'They also thought an empire of warriors *must* be inferior if they were infidels,' another voice muttered with amusement in its tone.

'Seven hundred years ago, all Anaria was less stable and more embroiled in war,' said Mira Lyss thoughtfully. 'Religions change over time, whatever their holy texts might say. We have found more peace between realms, more acceptance, in recent years. Politics and territory are the main reasons for disputes now, and even that is subject to the Anarian Pact. We have diplomats, treaties, trade. I had hoped we had entered a more enlightened age.'

'Well, it appears that Terome wants to drag us kicking and screaming back a thousand years,' answered Brandwyn Tarqas. 'They still butcher Nassings, and eye Eyotsburg keenly.'

'Until the borders closed in the last year, all the reports we had actually indicated that the common people of Meyar, the Eyots, and the Nassings have suffered far more than we have in attacks,' said Jamus Holmson. 'The entitled and noble kill and enslave with impunity, and set bizarre demands on people too poor to fight back. They are far more oppressed under this new *democracy* of the Assembly than they were under the old monarchy.' He sighed. 'It was hoped as the only other non-monarchy that Meyar was a progressive step. Instead, they leapt backwards, and inwards.'

'But do the common people see this? Or only what they are told is the truth?' Aurelia Brókova mused.

'I don't care about Meyar,' interrupted Whyll Regus. 'What is the purpose of the attacks *here*? They can hardly be fighting for freedom if they strike down children in the hearts of our cities.'

'I don't believe they are really adherents to the word of Terome,' suggested Augusta Andragostin. 'They say that they are following the true word, from what I hear, but a large part of any faith is interpretation. There are two major sects of Terome-'

'Three,' muttered Daffydd Gusta.

'-three, and only one of them says all other peoples must be converted to the worship of the one true god; but this is the one people here believe *is* Terome. I think they do this to stir anger against the other two. They might not even be true followers.'

'There are some that would argue that this fanatical core *is* the truth of Terome, and the rest are not true followers,' said Gusta wryly.

'But Terome was a follower of Delmatra!' exclaimed Marcus. 'He was a man, a disciple, not a god! We still have some of his texts in the Combic Library, for Delmatra's sake. He preached peace, not war.'

'Since when has religion been required to make sense?' snorted Daffyd Gusta.

'I think we are moving off the point here,' observed Mira Lyss. 'In recent times Terome has disavowed violence and preaches to be a religion of peace once more, yet attacks still continue in its name. We are told that this is not the fault of the Church. The fact is that whilst these attacks are occurring in many realms, including Meyar itself, more and more target cities in Eordeland, especially Darost.'

'This could not come at a worse time,' rumbled Ulric, finally breaking his silence. 'We are dealing with a crisis bigger than any we have seen for centuries.'

'Agreed. Talk of war, refugees, the upcoming Anarian Summit in Banistari in nine months… we are stretched to breaking point. Civil unrest has sprung up internally in every city, much against Meyari,' said Jamus Holmson.

'And now religious hate on top of it,' said Tarqas. 'What can we do? With tensions as they are, if we're seen to be siding with a supposed enemy… we're having enough trouble with people disputing us now. Already we're blamed for allowing 'other religions' to flourish, of accepting outlanders to live here. Not two years ago it was a mark of some pride to be the most accepting realm of other peoples and religions. Now, refugees have been helped, but we have also had Darostans refusing sanctuary to Irilviewers! Things have started breaking down from being part of a nation to being part of a city. Refugees from another city *of our own realm* are being treated like vermin by our own people.' He looked around the table. 'This is not us, my friends.'

'It is a sign of the troubles of the times,' said Councillor Contemus cynically. 'People who wish to keep their privileges draw borders in their minds for their cities, their families. Outsiders are suspect. If things get much worse, there will be riots, enforced curfew, and martial law, and we know how that will go. We can't risk internal street wars.'

Augusta Andragostin thumped the arm of her chair. 'Well, we need to do *something*. Teromens have been killed and treated like animals. Eordeland refugees robbed or threatened by their own people. None of the people in the street - and there are a surprising amount of them in Darost alone, by the way - seem to have done anything other than attempt to carry on with their lives, yet of the thousands here, already scores have been attacked, abused, or threatened.'

'I have reports of even people here in Darost eyeing neighbours with suspicion, not just newcomers. Many of the Teromens here are Eordelanders too - and gods above and below help anyone from Irilview who is a Teromen. Someone is spreading the rumour that Yosgaloth came to cleanse the purge of Terome from our streets.' Holmson shrugged, his face pensive. 'We can at least thank our fates that Teromens are from many backgrounds. If they were all conveniently and obviously foreign, we'd have cultural and racial segregation as well. As it is, a Church of Terome here in Darost has had firebombs thrown at it, even before this latest attack.'

'Someone tried to set a *Church* on fire?'

'Not just any Church. The *Cathedral.* With children in it, during worship. The Teromants poured out and butchered a score of the attackers, and the rest fled, but it almost devolved into a full-scale battle. People are frightened.'

Ulric rumbled back to life. 'Captain Dorn's men are investigating. People are very good at forgetting that they are attacking other people who aren't always doing anything wrong.'

Mira Lyss sighed. 'It is so easy to see the people a thousand and more miles away and say, 'all of them hate us. All of them are of an accord." She looked around. 'You only have to glance around this room to see that agreement is not something that comes easily, even to the wise. If we can't agree with twelve of us in a room, how likely is it that the entirety of the United Territories of Meyar do? I would guess that the majority of people there are like those here; scared, easily led, and believing that the enemy are less than human.'

'This has become more than serious,' said Ulric. 'It's exactly what fanatics want… On *both* sides.' He shifted his gaze to Eremus. 'You still believe this will not end in war?'

'The Prime Alderman rules, not the Church. A few fanatics do not answer for the government, and they have sworn reparation to our coffers with the new Politikus. Besides, no one would field an army to march a thousand miles to certain defeat.' She sat back.

'We assumed war when their Politikus murdered one of the Council,' said Nessa Contemus.

'It will not come to war,' snorted Eremus firmly. 'Their new Politikus is on their way here even as we speak. The debt promised will pay for a large amount of rebuilding Irilview. And don't forget, war was voted against.'

'I do not discount an attack,' remarked Councillor Tarqas. 'The reports we have had are shocking. Poverty is rife, the population is suppressed. Drafts into the Church and military are high. They can draw on a much larger percentage of the population than we can and their Teromants are truly fanatical. Defeating their attack would cost us in lives, money and land. They know we have an uneasy peace with Banistari. It may be madness, but if they do not care, they can cause great harm.' He shook his head. 'Don't forget, as well, that I believe they are induced to this for higher stakes than our outlying towns and villages. If what Aldwyn and his companions said was true, it is a first move in an attempt to destabilise the entire continent.'

'I'm inclined to believe it,' drawled Marcus Andragostin.

'Well I am not,' said Eremus sourly. 'And neither is the Universalia Communia. May I remind you that this Council accepted a vote four months ago to salvage this through diplomacy? They took a binding vote against Eordeland moving to war.'

'A vote taken *without* the knowledge of this Council-'

'Nevertheless.' Her voice was conceited. 'The Communia voted. We are bound by their decision.'

'And what if they *do* send an army?' snapped Ulric.

'I hardly think Meyar will send their entire army after us,' she said acidly. 'It would be suicide. But I move we begin corralling Teromens - for their own safety, of course. Perhaps they should be moved outside the city walls. There *is* an established township there by the western gate.'

'That way, if they do attack, they will not kill their own,' agreed Regus sagely.

'What?'

'It's a temporary town for traders!'

'A shanty!'

'Shame!'

'This is madness,' said Tarqas coldly. 'Being Teromens won't stop them, Eremus. Have you not listened? They could well be slaughtered out of hand. You are talking about wholesale sacrifice of our citizens. Do you want that on your conscience?'

'They won't attack.'

'Where does this end?' asked Jayleen Woodhearth, the newest member of the Council. 'How do you propose this? Do we remove Teromens, or Meyari, or both? What about their families? What if their parents or grandparents are Meyari, or Teromen. How far do we go in our persecution? You are proposing more problems, not a solution, Eremus.'

'And what of it if we cut the canker out more deeply?' snapped Eremus. 'It would lighten our load, which is heavy enough. The houses left would be used for refugees, not foreigners-'

'*Foreigners?*' Councillor Brókova said softly. 'Citizens who *own* those houses? So it is not merely Meyar, now, but anyone different? What of those like myself, with mixed Morlandish heritage? What of Augusta and Marcus here, with Banistari features? Or Ulric, with Poviiri in him? Will you take our houses, too? Where is the divide? Is it blood, or skin, or birthplace, or religion? What of the darker skin of west Eordeland and the paler of the north and east? Will that too become a divide?'

'You speak as if an attack were a foregone conclusion,' said Eremus hotly, flushing. 'This is not just about our city. This decision will affect our entire country.

We are the economic and trade centre of the continent, by the Gods! Call in their debts! Listen to diplomacy! But do not be seen to make ready for war. If we do what you suggest, we will badly damage that status. Our nation is founded on equality. We must do what we can to keep our people safe.'

'Then *listen* to me!' shouted Ulric, slamming his huge fists on the table with a boom. Eremus jumped, as did several other Councillors. Holmson put a warning hand on Ulric's arm. 'I tell you, an attack is coming! You voted for me to prepare, told me to make ready for war - and then you hamstrung me behind my back! *How is this keeping our people safe?'*

'The situation was re-evaluated by several sources for an *official* vote,' snapped Councillor Regus. 'Violence is always our last resort.'

'You seek to embroil us in a war that may not come… perhaps for personal gain, or to make us seem greater,' added Eremus in agreement. Her face was smug. 'Advisor, since Councillor Ulric cannot control his temper, perhaps he should be removed until he calms down?'

'Ulric.' Mira Lyss's voice was calm, warning. He was glaring, breathing heavily, but after a moment relaxed a little, scowling. She turned to Eremus. 'I will be the judge of what is appropriate, thank you, Councillor Eremus.'

'I seek to keep us safe,' Ulric growled, sinking back. 'There will be no second chance if you are wrong.'

'They have denounced Belen, with an offer to send him back as a prisoner if he is captured, and the new Politikus will arrive inside the month,' said Eremus confidently. 'I applaud your ideals, Ulric, but they are an overreaction. It would be insanity for them to attack. We would hold their Politikus prisoner and destroy their force.'

Councillor Regus nodded. 'Meyar is more than a thousand miles away. It has an inferior force, inferior weapons, and they are heavily in debt to us. Their Prime Alderman alone has loans we could call in at any time guaranteed with the banks. They would forfeit all their considerable assets here.'

Eremus nodded.

'So perhaps you can tell me what else Meyari troops were doing deep in the Dimnesdair, more than a thousand miles from their homeland?' Holmson's voice held no small amount of acid. Eremus ignored him and continued.

'We have only the word of Tal'Orien that they have allies. He could have mistaken what he saw. Humans with orcs! Really.' She ignored Ulric's growl. 'The *fact* is, Councillor Ulric, the Universalia Communia voted against a war footing. Preparing for war and being seen to prepare for war would be in direct violation of that decision. We will let diplomacy take its course, as we will let democracy stand.'

'And who decides? You? Will you let them stall us until they are at our gates?' demanded Ulric.

'You are past the personal glory of battles now. We have not had full war for seventy years. We have entered a new age of prosperity and peace. You would jeopardise that.' Eremus's voice was cold.

'It began when *Meyar* tried to assassinate several members *of this Council!*' snapped Ulric.

'And there we have it,' added Holmson dryly. 'Councillor Eremus was not personally threatened, so it cannot be real. Besides, who wants a war that could affect our personal fortunes? I wonder how different this story would be if your family had diversified into weapons instead of money?'

'How *dare-*'

'Councillors! Please,' said Mira Lyss.

'We took a vote. Your side lost. Democracy has spoken.'

'This isn't about *sides,* you witless-'

'*Councillor* Eremus,' interrupted Mira Lyss, her voice cutting Ulric off sharply, 'that decision is not yours to make. Remember democracy is about having a *voice,* not once, but forever. There can be subsequent votes. Things can change as the situation warrants.' She stared in warning at the Councillor, then turned to Ulric with a sigh.

'However. Advisory interjectory: Councillor Ulric. Councillor Eremus is correct. The vote was cast from the Universalia Communia according to our laws. We cannot force another vote without more evidence or majority request from them. This Council weighed the warnings, but the vote suspended all war preparations until we have attempted diplomacy again. Any instability now could spark off continent-wide aggression. We cannot risk that.'

'I am telling you; they have begun it already. If we do not at least prepare, the deaths of all those following will be on your heads. It is the worst kind of insanity to have no contingencies! At least allow me to *prepare* for a major attack. Relying on diplomacy alone is madness.'

'Casting diplomacy aside against an unsubstantiated attack by Meyar is worse,' Eremus said. 'All eyes are upon us.'

Mira Lyss stood. Her voice rang out. '*Advisor interjectory.* Councillors. Please. This is not reasoned debate. All opposing viewpoints must build a case for moving forward after we meet with the new Politikus and have it put to a vote. I remind you that in matters ecumenical to The Sanctum, the whole Universalia Communia must be involved. This Council can vote on wars and make executive decisions; but these are laws and the people that we are talking about.'

She beckoned a Welcomer over. There were no scribes to take notes and minutes; a Welcomer was designated to the duties as required, unless it was a meeting held in the Bulb high above where there were no minutes ever taken. She tasked him to note the movement and draft it for her as a template to be sent internally within the week. The silence was broken only by mutterings and hushed conversation.

Despite her intervention, the tension was palpable. Not in living memory had the Council argued so strenuously about such a divisive issue.

Ulric heaved himself to his feet, like an avalanche in reverse. He glared around him. 'I am done here. Let me know when you all see sense.' He glanced at General Colcos and then left.

'Well! How rude!' muttered Whyll Regus.

Mira Lyss looked around. 'I suggest we all break here. This Council has become divided. The law says we may not meet formally unless a full circle, outside sickness or death. Ulric is now absent. We must seek to consider the choices with open minds and reconvene.'

Until the majority of the Universalia Communia thought otherwise, Dorn thought, there was little chance of them being any more productive.

He hoped for all their sakes that Eremus was right.

FOUR

'*This* is the Eordeland Recurve bow! It requires much less draw than a Novinian Longbow to deliver a similar blow! You *will* still need to develop skill and control to use it!'

The words were delivered in a clipped, practiced manner, backed by lungs like bellows. The bellower was an older, rotund man with an astonishingly huge moustache, and crinkled eyes in a weathered face. Sergeant Rennal Erwhist was one of the most decorated bowmen in Darost and had been a Master for two decades as a ranger in Troubadour Company. His form looked portly, but he was tall, and his paunch was as solid as the thicklycompressed buttes they were loosing at. His powerful shoulders and hands made the archery look easy, and Rast had told them he was exceptional. A lifetime in the military, however, had left him with little patience, a brusque attitude, and a voice that could startle birds from the trees at a quarter of a mile. This was their first lesson with him, near the southeast gate. Before, it had been simple practice in their spare time under supervision, but now the Sergeant was to take classes of all Sanctum students in hand. If Karland were to guess, it might be to do with the hints of war on the horizon.

'Note the outward recurve of the bow and the stiff tips! The Eordeland bow is composite. That means it is made of many layers of material. The limbs are what we call working limbs, this means they will move! It adds power to your shaft, but you must draw fully!'

He took a breath, and a little of the volume left his voice, although it remained ear-shattering. He continued.

'Standard draw on our bows is *heavy* per two-foot of arrow wood,' he continued, watching them all carefully over his bristling brown-pepper brush. It stretched to each side, curving down thickly then up to a point. Karland wondered how he drank soup.

'*Your* bows are light draw weight, on account of you being juveniles or youths.' He glared at them as if daring them to suddenly become adults. 'When you draw, you will pull hand to cheek and draw fully. It *will* be hard. It *will* get easier. When it is your turn, select arrows of differing sizes. In battle you may have to work with what you can salvage. Today, we are loosing eight arrows at the buttes, fast as you can. I don't want to see showboating at fifteen a minute, half draw. Full draw! Aim. Eight arrows a minute at twenty yards! When I blow my whistle, you *stop*. Anyone touching shaft to string after that time will be in shit deeper than they have ever been before. Nobody moves until it is blown twice. Is that understood?'

'Sir!' Their voices rang out. Today there were seventeen of them clustered around the buttes, great circular foot-thick compressed hay bales.

'Good luck today, Dresin,' murmured Aran as he walked past. Karland felt a little warmth; it seemed he had misjudged the older boy.

At his turn, he moved to find his tab, which they were all using. Gloves were given when you could put six of eight arrows into the bullseye from fifty yards two times in five - recognition of your elevation to true Eordeland Archer.

He reached into his pack and felt nothing.

What?

He rummaged, carefully testing at first, then more frantically. He was aware that everyone else was readying up, and he was looking around vaguely, confused.

'Where is your protection, boy?' barked Sergeant Erwhist from in front of him. Karland jumped. The old man had a military cane he kept under one arm most of the time, apart from when he was using it - none too gently - to correct form in weapons training. He was tapping it on his shoulder now.

Karland's heart fell. His bracer and the leather tab to protect his fingers from the string were not anywhere he could find. Looking up, he saw Aran's smirk and suspicion washed through him.

Everyone dreaded coming down on the wrong side of the Sergeant. Old he might be, but he was one of those men who seemed to dry out and get tougher with years. He was of average height, but he seemed to loom over everyone, and had a habit of barking at people out of one side of his mouth.

Even veterans kept out of his way, but there was no question as to his effectiveness at training recruits. He didn't care that Karland and Xhera were there part-time; they were treated like everyone else.

'I, um. Put it in my bag,' said Karland. 'Sir.' He furiously searched his mind, convinced he had put them in the pack. Xhera caught his eye briefly, shaking her head as if he should know better. She wasn't wrong.

'Really?' Erwhist's eyes widened in mock astonishment. 'And yet... it ain't here! There's a bloody good reason you use those things, my lad.' He glared at Karland, as if affronted by the very sight of him. It was no consolation to know that Erwhist likely didn't care about him one way or the other, having seen thousands of recruits in his time. 'Tabs and gloves save our fingers, bracers save our arms! You're bad enough with a bow already. Now you'll see how much worse you get.'

'I could run and look again-' offered Karland. He was cut off by the Sergeant.

'You'll do nothing but what I tell you, boy. Today you'll be regretting your slackness. The rest of you, mark him well. If you forget your protection, you'll get the same, and you won't do it more than once.' His eyes swept around. 'Pick bows and line up!'

Xhera sidled up to Karland. 'Come on, let's try to pick you a forgiving bow.' She shook her head again, tutting. 'How could you forget? You heard what the Sergeant is like.'

'Honestly, I swear I put them there last night.' He shrugged despondently. 'I don't know what happened.'

'Well. Maybe it won't be too bad.' Xhera didn't sound hopeful. She spotted Aran laughing and narrowed her eyes. 'I'll wager tonight's meal that pompous idiot had something to do with it.'

'No bet,' said Karland morosely.

They lined up and began loosing arrows on the Sergeant's mark. Everyone had a bucket of thirty old arrows, not designed to be totally accurate, but the point of this practice was for muscle development and memory. The army bows were much harder to draw, and Erwhist stalked along the ranks, slapping people stingingly into good form with the tip of his cane.

It didn't take long for Karland's fingers to start aching. The bow felt more than forty pounds to draw, and after a few minutes his aim was wandering noticeably.

Karland noticed Aran, larger and stronger than most others, drawing a full eighty-pound bow, one designed for light infantry. His grouping was decent, despite the mismatched arrows; clearly, he had experience. Karland could hear his derisive comments about these fragile-feeling recurves, boasting that real men used longbows when Erwhist was out of hearing. Novin was proud of its longbowmen; some of them drew more than two hundred pounds.

Karland's fingers grew worse and worse, and eventually he missed the target altogether. The string was slapping inside his wrist with a sting every time, but it wasn't until he lowered the bow, unable to fully draw the string with his fingers, that he noticed the horrifying lump on the inside of his left forearm. It was swollen like a small egg, pink and purple. Pressing it, his fingers hurt, and he turned those over; dully, he noticed all three large fingers were swollen badly from the tips to the joint, with bruising already evident.

'Who told you to stop?' bellowed Erwhist, marching over. Karland held up his hand, and then pointed to the arrows that had plainly wandered left as he had tried to compensate for the pain. His face was flushed with pain and embarrassment, and the unfairness of it all. The Sergeant looked grimly satisfied.

'I can't continue, Seargeant.' He had to fight to not burst out, but instead showed the injury to make the man apologise. Surely this wasn't what he'd wanted.

'You will if I tell you, boy!' shouted Erwhist, disabusing him of that notion immediately.

Karland noticed other students sniggering behind the Sergeant as they watched, all cronies of Aran. Aran himself was watching, his eyes glittering with malice, and Karland had a flash of intuition. He was sure he had put the protection in his locker, and now he was equally sure Aran or one of his minions had stolen them. Aran solemnly slapped his bracer solidly, gestured in insult with two fingers up, then turned back to nock another arrow.

Suddenly his usual embarrassment vanished, and Karland glared back at the Sergeant. 'I can't continue, Sergeant! I'm not even hitting the target! And you've made me do it when someone else stole my protection from my locker. *Sir.*'

'Let me see those fingers, then,' snapped Erwhist. He straightened them roughly, and then nodded, his tone dropping. 'Made my point, Dresin?'

'Sir, they were in my locker last night-'

'Don't matter. I don't care if you dropped them in the latrines or the Council themselves thieved 'em. They're *your* responsibility. There's no excuses in battle, and laying blame don't help keep you alive.'

'Yes, sir,' said Karland sourly. There was responsibility for his gear, and then there was malicious theft. He knew there was no point voicing his suspicions. Erwhist had had years of students making up stories. He wasn't likely to believe him.

'Unlose 'em,' said Erwhist. 'Don't play me for a fool, Dresin. Go and stow your bow, rest these up, and don't you dare turn up without them again. And secure your locker.' He sighed and raised his voice.

'All of you - look at this.' He turned Karland so they could all see. 'Dresin can't loose the bow any more, and it's been not even an hour. Don't try to be a hero. Use a tab or glove, or this happens. One day you may have to go without, but only a fool does it by choice.' He tapped Karland's other arm, a painful jab right on the large round welt that had raised. 'And that is why we wear a bracer. Won't forget again, eh?'

Karland winced. 'No, sir.' He ignored the mocking laughs that arose from a few of the others.

'Good. Get on with it. And you lot! Back to targets. You've an hour yet!'

Karland unstrung the bow using the twisted rope stringer and sighed. His fingers throbbed badly, and his forearm felt numb, if anything. He could feel eyes on him and knew that many of the other students now weren't his friends. It didn't matter if he tried to be nice to them or not - some people were simply bullies, and delighted in tormenting those they saw as below them. They might have been indifferent if it were not for Aran. Once you were singled out, you were a victim.

He had been fooling himself, he realised. The other boy had never done anything overt like this before, but it was now clear Aran acted with impunity. Karland didn't deserve to be here, in his eyes, either in The Sanctum or the training.

He would have thought that knowing and training with Rast would have helped; the others held his friend in awe. Instead, it seemed to engender disgust, as if he had filled some position that others deserved more. That was Aran again, he suspected, filling their ears with poison. He knew the Novinian despised the fact he was - in his own eyes - less worthy than Karland of recognition.

He got on well with a few of the students, of course, but Aran was the popular, charismatic leader. Boys hung off his words, and he never seemed to have to *do* anything. Gradually, he was ostracising Karland.

He watched the rest of the practice glumly. Xhera looked at him in sympathy and left to stow her own gear with the rest. Karland sat for a moment, lost in thought, listening to his classmates fade into the distance. He finally stood and walked out, still thinking about what had happened, swearing he would not let it happen again.

Barely thirty feet from the entrance to the buttes he heard someone snicker. His hand and arm throbbed badly, and he gritted his teeth. He should have known.

He stopped and spoke without looking back.

'I know you took it,' he said quietly. He glanced back to see Aran perched on a wall with a smile Karland was rapidly growing to loathe on his handsome face. Fron and another boy Karland didn't know were there.

'What did you say?' Aran sprang to his feet, glancing around for other people. His voice had the clipped quality that Novinians often took with Darum.

'I know you took it,' repeated Karland. 'You're the only one who would.' He faced them, heart thumping. As always, any kind of confrontation filled him with mild panic, the feeling of weakness.

'Watch your mouth, vermin,' said Aran dangerously. He was still smiling but had taken on a stillness that spoke of violence.

'So you didn't?' Whatever he said, Karland knew would be a lie.

'You'll never know,' Aran retorted. Then he smiled. 'Be careful what you leave unguarded. You never know what could get... taken.' His eyes flicked in the direction Xhera had left in.

Karland gritted his teeth. 'You had better pray to every God you know that you never touch her, Aran.'

'You threatening me, runt?' Aran moved closer, his eyes boring in to Karland's. He moved in so that they were almost within kissing distance, and butted his forehead solidly into Karland's own, pushing his head back. 'You telling me how to live my life?'

Aran's two companions moved in, boxing Karland in. This was turning into a distinctly unpleasant situation, and Erwhist had moved on. Karland, his heart sinking, realised that he was alone with them.

A flicker of movement caught his attention, and he glanced sideways. He saw his friend Bradwr lurking nearby, watching, and waited for him to say something. All it would take would be a witness, and they would leave him alone.

He hoped.

Bra drew back, and then took off with a fearful glance. The young man was an excellent runner, and his slight form vanished quickly.

'All alone, Dresin. As usual. Don't get the message, do you?' Aran stared him down, his eyes threatening. '*No one likes you.*'

This was getting out of hand. Karland shook his head, moving backwards, and shrugged noncommittally.

'You snivelling little coward. You're not getting out of this that easily.' Aran moved in and pushed his shoulder. Karland almost stumbled. Aran poked his chest, and he batted his hand away. Aran's hand flashed out in a hard punch to Karland's shoulder. It hurt. The move was efficient, and practised; Aran was trained to strike, very well.

'You dare touch me, peasant?' Aran's eyes flashed. Karland moved back slightly, seeing the larger boy's feet set. Aran lunged, grabbing for him, and Karland grabbed the wrists as the hands went for his tunic and jerked to the side and back. Aran was yanked off balance, and he grunted in surprise as he went headlong past Karland. He landed in a heap and leapt back to his feet in rage. The two boys with him closed in on Karland, who realised he was going to have to fight, whether he wanted to or not. Aran feinted, and Karland ducked straight into a fist from the boy on his right. He staggered, his eye flashing white in pain.

A shriek of anger interrupted them, and everyone paused.

'*Are you so feeble, Aran?*' Xhera flew into view, her face flushed with rage. The look suited her, thought Karland detachedly; it wasn't blotchy, as it had been when she cried, but her cheeks flushed passionately, contrasting against her pale skin. As she faced Aran, she glared up at him, and she looked magnificent. 'You're no *man*. Three of you against one? Are you frail?'

Aran seemed unsure what to do now there was a witness. After a moment of hesitation, he smiled at her, like a man looking at a prize horse he was buying, and lifted his hand to gently cup the side of her face. It was oddly possessive, and she slapped his hand away with far more force than he had expected.

'Touch me again, I'll smash your pearls to paste,' Xhera snarled. Karland stared at her in astonishment. 'And then I'll drag you before the Council of Twelve.'

'Look at that, *boygis*,' sneered Aran, using Novinian slang for *boys*. 'Has to be saved by a *girl* again.' He ran his eyes up and down Xhera, pausing to eye her breasts and hips, and then turned and left with a leer, slowly, as if it was what he had planned. The other two followed him, expressionless.

Xhera linked her arm in Karland's, looking at his eye. 'I saw Bradwr running as if Yosgaloth were after him. He called something about you as he flew past.'

'Glad he actually bothered to help,' muttered Karland.

'This has to stop,' she said softly. 'What did you do? Why didn't you fight back?'

'I know Aran took my tab and bracer,' Karland said. At least the sting from his eye had made his fingers throb less. 'I didn't want to dishonour Rast. And... well. After Ben, when he hit you, you were so angry with me, so disappointed...'

Xhera shook her head. 'Idiot,' she said softly. 'I didn't realise, then, how bad it had been. I never had this kind of treatment. You can't let this get worse. Aran will continue to torment you if you show weakness, even if he doesn't realise it's really strength.'

Her words made him feel better, and he stood straighter, wincing. His eye was swelling already; it had been a solid blow.

'I'll talk to Rast,' he said. 'Aran I could maybe take, but as soon as I do anything, his friends start in as well. I can't fight them all.'

'Oh, Karland.' She touched his face gently, her expression concerned and her eyes taking in his.

It was *almost* worth the pain and humiliation for this.

'I don't know why they do this. I had the same in The Croft. I generally get on with everyone, but some people just... push. And once they do, so does everyone else. I didn't do anything to deserve this.'

'You're just different, Karland, and they know it. You're not weak, but something about you makes them *want* to push. And you don't push back, or you do, the wrong way.'

Karland laughed in disbelief.

'No, seriously. You're very firm about your morals. Some people might, I don't know… feel inadequate. But none of them have been through what you have. None of them have accomplished what you did. None of them have faced orcs or demons, befriended a dragon, have spoken to a *god*. None of them have been taught by Rast and by Aldwyn.' Her face was serious and impassioned, and she took his face gently in her hands to look into his eyes. 'None of them attacked Hoge and his men, alone, to help me, without fear for themselves.' Her eyes searched his face. ' You are my best friend. You are *unique*. How many of them would have survived where you did? *They don't know you.* You shouldn't let them bother you.'

At that moment, gazing into her startling blue eyes, seeing the faint freckles on her skin across her nose, being so near her, Karland's last barriers to his internal truth dissolved, and in a flood of emotion, he knew that he loved Xhera. At the same instant it was tinged with a welter of despairing unrequited feelings, something he was familiar with, and he knew he had to be careful not to come to idolise her, to lose who she really was.

He shook his head slightly to clear the thoughts and winced. Xhera let go and he almost stammered in his haste to change the subject.

'I know… but surely I should be - different or something? Better, changed? How can I still feel so defensive, so threatened, so… *worthless*? For the first time I don't have to be a victim. But still, I am. I never asked for this.'

'You have worth, Karland. You just won't let yourself believe it. And if you won't, how will they? You still act like a small boy who is beaten by everyone. Being strong isn't just about what you can do. It's about how you show that you can do it, too. Stop listening to the voices saying you are ugly, weak, stupid, have no worth. They are *lying*. Listen to the voices you value who tell you that you *aren't*, that you *do*.' Her blue eyes searched his face. 'You say you value the truth so much. *See it.* '

He marvelled at her then; so fragile, so dainty, yet with a strength of will he suspected he could never have, like the finest kid glove leather over a steel bar.

'Thank you,' he said softly.

'You're a good person, Karland, however much you won't believe it yourself. But your emotion drives you and you try to hide it behind logic. Others won't understand that.' She sighed. 'As for Aran… sometimes, well. People just don't like other people.'

'But I did nothing wrong to him,' he complained.

She shrugged. 'To someone like him, that doesn't matter. Come on, let's get that eye dressed up.'

'Sounds stupid, but I don't want to hurt him.' He considered his eye. 'Or get hurt, really. Be careful, Xhera. I don't think he'd stop at words if he could get away with striking you.'

'He's Novinian, remember; they're funny about women. He can't be seen to strike a woman in public. Much more shameful than me hitting him. Worry more about yourself. If he didn't like you before, he hates you now. I can see it in his face.'

෮ ෯

Karland couldn't shake his depression. He couldn't understand how other people could put so much effort into making other people's lives miserable and delight in it.

Xhera had tried to cheer him up, but he felt so inconsequential at the moment. Yes, he'd been through life-changing events, but he was still who he had always been, if a little sadder and more experienced. He felt himself changing, slowly, and knew this must be what it was to grow up, but still doubted himself almost as much as ever - if anything, more, in new ways - and now that they had returned, everything seemed to have slowed down.

Karland found the city both fascinating and depressing. It held more than half a million people, something he couldn't even begin to fathom. He constantly saw new faces full of mystery, beauty, stories. Karland was, at heart, an optimist. He rarely saw a truly ugly person, because there was almost *always* something beautiful about everyone.

In fact, at times he felt surreal as he moved through the mass of people, more than he had ever realised could exist in the whole world. Seen from afar, a city containing so many was astounding, but you could take it in after a while. Yet, once thrust viscerally into the arterial heart of the city as one minor corpuscle amongst hundreds of thousands, Karland found his attention constantly grabbed by everything he saw. He had an eye for detail, unlike Xhera, who was often more abstract, and he *noticed* things. Sometimes the observations felt overwhelming.

The main thing that he found hard to deal with was actually a simple fact that, apparently, no one else even considered.

Every single person around him was a complex, individual, living breathing person.

He could see scores of men, each one with their own concerns and stories, from merchants to guards to thieves to men he couldn't pigeonhole. He could see scores of women from old to young, scraping roughly against his burgeoning awareness of his own sexuality.

They had hopes, dreams, desires of their own. They thought their own thoughts. Each one slept, ate, breathed, loved, crapped, laughed, felt, and cried the same way he did in every bit as complex a fashion; each one, an individual life. Each one with something for him to learn.

It might be intrinsic, like a smile or eyes or a story; it could be in the form of a lesson to learn. Almost everyone had something worthwhile to teach him or show him.

The thought threatened to upset his equilibrium at times, because with so many, just in one city - let alone one country, one continent, the *world* - he would never, *could* never, meet everyone and experience that thing from every single person, even if he had a dozen lifetimes.

It was awe-inspiring, depressing, alarming, hard to grasp. The thought sometimes seemed too much for his head. There were too many people in the world to consider as individuals, but that is what they were, nonetheless.

Sonder, Aldwyn had called it.

The one time he had tried to explain all this to Xhera, she had looked interested, then alarmed, and then finally waved her hands to stop him.

'You can't *think* like that,' she said, shaking her head. 'You'll go mad. I feel like I'm going mad thinking about it now.'

'I think about things like that all the time,' he had responded glumly.

'Gods,' had been her reply. 'I'm off to do something lighter, like read some of Aldwyn's books.' She had only been half-joking.

He had come to the depressing and overwhelming realisation that even if he had an entire lifetime, he could never experience the lessons every person here had to offer him.

His real companions were Xhera and Rast, and Bradwr. This was enough, mostly, but not always. He felt lonely, surrounded by people, and even the recognition that most of them were too wrapped up in their lives to think the same way didn't help.

He had escaped a life he felt limited by and trapped, knowing that he needed to expand and become himself. Yet now, after seeing such fantastic things, and being a part of world-changing events, he was once more… just a boy. No-one particularly special, he thought ruefully, but someone lonely despite not being alone.

His depression came and went. Some days he was fine, and his time with Xhera cheered him. They were closer than ever, although he had experienced a few heart-wrenching moments when other boys flirted with her, and he couldn't tell if she was responding. But then, he reminded himself, they weren't together. He held no claim to her heart. He was her friend, and that didn't seem likely to change, which was both good and bad.

Other days however, he felt like he was suspended over a yawning pit with nowhere to go but down. Invariably these days involved Aran or one of his cronies, but they also coincided with the amount of times Karland himself managed to do things wrong, which was distressingly often. Hardly a real hero, he thought ruefully. On days like these his positivity vanished, and all the cajoling in the world about his past achievements and his studies could not lift his mood.

In an effort to distract him, Xhera took him to one of food halls that dotted the inner Sanctum instead of eating in their room as usual. Each Cuneus had its own, running across its segment on the ground floor - apart from the Academia Legalis which was on the first, over the great Council Court.

The Cuneus food halls curved along their lengths, three hundred feet and more along their longest wall and forty wide. Banquet-style long tables with benches ran in rows down the length. Academia hangings lay along the walls, showing the history of each Cuneus and its focus, helping to deaden the furore of hundreds - sometimes thousands - of voices. The middle of the longest wall held the large kitchen and serving area, and there was always a Welcomer squad somewhere. The ceilings rose to twenty-two feet, with windows each end, angled mirrors to reflect light, and high torches even in the day. The hall was filling for lunchtime, with more than a hundred already there.

Karland and Xhera stood scanning for a seat on the near benches after collecting a tray of fresh hot pie with vegetables and a cup of the half-ale permitted to students under their sixteen majority. As sponsored scholarship students, they paid no rent or food. As part of their extra work on Aldwyn's notes, they even earned a weekly stipend from the University, enough for a little spending money.

To their surprise, Councillor Daffyd Gusta was seated with another man perhaps ten years younger than himself, talking quietly. He waved them over.

'We don't want to interrupt,' said Xhera politely as they moved over, her voice raised over the increasing murmur of voices. The elderly Councillor smiled, and gestured to the Welcomer Guard behind them to stand down. They didn't look at all welcoming, and had a discreet armband of black. Karland realised they were the Onyx Guard; personal bodyguards to the Council. Karland saw other Welcomers around the hall; they were everywhere these days.

'Please. I do not eat here often, and it would be nice to talk outside the more… formal settings we normally see one another in. I was just people-watching.' He turned to the man next to him. He was a little shorter and stouter than Daffydd Gusta, and still had some colour left in his hair, but his face was lined. Two kind eyes that looked sad because of a downward slope to the outer brow sat above a clean-shaven face with a ready smile. If Daffyd Gusta looked like someone's grandfather, this man looked like a kindly uncle.

'Jonnal; meet Xhera, and Karland. Two young people who have achieved more than their years would suggest, and are currently studying here.'

Jonnal half-rose with a slight bow, and spoke in a light, smooth voice. 'Charmed. I have heard your names, although I don't get many other details.' He shot a jibing look at Councillor Gusta, who smiled back at him, and turned to Karland and Xhera.

'This is Jonnal, my husband,' he said.

Karland blinked. 'Husband?'

'Come now, I know The Croft is in the provinces, but surely you have similar marriages out there?'

Karland remembered the smith in his village had a male partner. There were quite a few same-gender couples in the area. Most had seemed to think little of it, although it was never overt; it wasn't until he had come to Darost that he had realised some people took a dim view of same-sex relationships. He had never heard the smith refer to his partner as his husband.

'Yes,' he admitted. 'I'm not shocked - I just never heard of two husbands. Or wives, I suppose. And, well. I suppose I hadn't really thought of any of you as… married.'

'You mean, having lives outside the Council,' smiled the Councillor, his eyes twinkling. Karland half shrugged, not willing to challenge that.

Xhera giggled. 'One of the farms near us is run by two old wives. We all knew they were basically married.'

'Eordeland isn't like Novin, or Meyar,' said Gusta. He patted the hand of the younger man next to him with a smile. 'We've borrowed some acceptance from Morland, I think. There, it's commonplace for couples of any gender to have a commitment. Sometimes more than couples, if I hear correctly. They are often quite… publicly open-minded about relations there, as long as everyone involved is in agreement.'

Karland was left with some interesting mental images and tried to keep a thoughtful look off his face.

The Councillor looked reflectively at the ring on his left hand, a twin to the one on the other man's. It was a polished silver band with a bright blue line of some precious stone down the centre, quite different to the large green and gold ring of Scholarship of the Sanctum on his right, the same Aldwyn had worn. All Papered

Scholars - including the Council - had one. It could be used for seals and had the stylised embossed symbol of a scroll before a flame.

'We're not *quite* so open in Eordeland. A bit more formal. Still, we have many religions here, and a rich heritage of traditions from many cultures that sit alongside our own. You hear some say that we're losing our national identity, but it's not true. It's still there, and we take the best of others and add to it. With religions, too. Although some like Terome will not marry couples of one gender, others will, even out in the provinces. And Delmatra has never forbidden any kind of love.'

'Meyar and Novin believe that anything other than a man and a woman in marriage is an abomination,' said Jonnal. 'Teromants quote the scrolls, proclaiming that it says a 'man and a woman', and 'progeny'.' The younger man shook his head in disbelief. 'Most people here have grown to understand that marriage is about love and respect, not just producing children, and it's not limited to one religion, either.'

'There are more voices arguing now,' remarked Gusta.

'Rast said Terome has changed a lot,' said Xhera, nodding.

Jonnal shook his head.

'Terome has always preached that homosexuality is a sin,' he said. 'Mostly it's disapproval and words. Becoming a pariah, abuse, that sort of thing. Not pleasant, but it's much worse in Novin. There you are seen as less than a man. They seem to ignore women who like other women, but then they seem to ignore women in general.'

'Cleaving to the same sex openly carries a death sentence there, for men anyway,' said Gusta, sadly. 'It seems the further west you go, the less accepting people are.'

'What about Banistari?' asked Karland. 'I've heard they also have some... interesting views.'

'On just about everything,' laughed Jonnal. 'Men are warriors, but the women must be answered to in the home. They forbid marriage within one sex, but have no problem with open liaisons. Some men think that being with other men is simply more manly, and doesn't affect their relationship with women. It's not even considered intimate. And as for their rulers, well.'

'I heard about that,' said Karland. 'Are they really brother and sister?' He blew on his forkful, still very hot from the bronze warmers. The steak and ale pie was excellent, once he managed to swallow it.

'Yes,' said Gusta. 'The current rulers are. It's hereditary, from within a vast family, so they can almost always find close relations to sit the thrones, and *technically* they are married as we know it... but they produce no offspring. Marriage is one thing, but it is strictly forbidden for them to have sex, even if they are far enough removed to do so.'

Xhera's face showed what she thought of that idea. 'That's disgusting. Why are they married?'

'To keep the power and hierarchy strong, within one family. It promotes loyalty, and they have a complex intra-familial system of advisors. Family is very important to Banistaris, and it removes a lot of mayhem that would otherwise ensue, although I believe veiled murder and framing are not uncommon in the lower ranks. The higher you go, the more focused the gaze, so the upper ranks are usually relatively safe - remarkable, as in most monarchies, it is usually the opposite. They are an interesting people. I have been to their court and found them to be both quite extravagantly lascivious and politically shrewd.' He raised his white eyebrows, and took a swallow of his ale, his throat moving a little like a tortoise's. 'They can have as many lovers as they like, as long as the lovers do not also interbreed. Strict records are kept to prevent inbreeding becoming a problem. The punishment for incest is death, or sterility and exile if it involves High Royalty.'

'*Isha*,' exclaimed Xhera.

Karland took a sip of his drink, wondering what it must be like to live in such a strict society.

'Not much like Novin,' snorted Jonnal, taking a drink.

Gusta laughed shortly, and without humour.

'Yes. If you want a hotbed of intrigue, intolerance, murder, rape and incest, Novin provides them all in abundance, especially in the nobility.'

'Astonishing they have any left, when you think about it,' muttered Jonnal.

'They have more than eighty Houses, twenty-six of which are Noble, and the families are large,' pointed out Gusta. 'Even noble women are barely considered above chattel by some, and if you are born a peasant, you may as well accept a short, brutal life and a horrible fate, unless you are promoted to high military rank. Novinian nobles are often cruel and aloof. They abuse people however they wish. '

Xhera looked uncomfortable. Karland knew what the conversation had triggered, and truth be told it recalled a certain forest witch to him as well, but before he could say anything, Gusta changed the subject. He was a politician, and Karland knew he had read their discomfort quickly.

'Anyway. A quick history of the lands. And just in case you are wondering which one of us folds the clothes, we take it in turns.' He winked.

Xhera smiled, relaxing, and tucked into the rest of her pie. Karland followed suit. The half-ale they were permitted was not bad, but he couldn't wait until next year when he could legally order anything.

They chatted a little longer, Gusta and Jonnal being very interested in tales from when they had journeyed with Györnàeldàr. They carefully avoided anything related to Council matters, and Jonnal vanished to bring more drinks. It turned out that he was a scholar in musical affairs in the Academia Artem, and although he said he was at best a mediocre singer, he knew the history and development of most of the differing styles of music in Anaria.

'You'll find that we're all just people, doing our job,' said Daffydd eventually. They were all quite relaxed, but Karland still felt slightly strange to be sitting chatting to a member of the Council of Twelve. All of them except Ulric had always been very formal, and Ulric was closer to a force of nature than a normal person. 'I was sorry that Aldwyn Varelin never formally stepped into the Council as Arbitrator, but that isn't to say we aren't effective as we are. Some of us are better suited to some areas than others, but we all vote with the good of our realm in mind.'

'Even-' began Karland before he could stop himself, and then paused. He caught Xhera's eyeroll out of the corner of his eye and flushed slightly.

'Ahhh. You don't like Councillor Eremus, do you? She's a prickly one. And given her attitude to Aldwyn and yourself, I cannot blame you.' The old Councillor studied his knuckles for a moment. 'Joy Eremus provides a necessary function for the council. She is not well liked by everyone, and occasionally overuses her power, but she provides a vital service in Council meetings in several ways. She acts as what I like to call a reality test. Councillor Eremus is the voice of dissent we may expect from many people in Eordeland - especially those both privileged with money to lose, and some of the people who do not wish to understand the politics of things and see a more... *simplistic* view - and we must be mindful of that. She keeps us grounded, and reminds us that purely thinking in terms of the abstract is not always a good idea. She also acts as a demon's advocate, not always unwittingly either. I think she truly does want the best for Eordeland. The majority of the Universalia Communia clearly agree, or she wouldn't have been elected, but she never learned any tact, that's for damned sure as mustard.'

Jonnal laughed into his ale, almost choking, and added, 'You should see her at formal events. Always looks like someone added too much extra lemon juice to her drink, yet her husband is one of the most affable men I have met. I feel he may be a little henpecked.' A warning look from his husband sent him grinning back into his tankard. Karland chuckled. He liked Jonnal and his sad-looking eyes.

'We all have our suitability, Jon,' said the Councillor reprovingly. 'I know my value lies in caution and an ability to see strategies, a bigger picture, but ask me to focus on detail and I can get lost in it. Someone like Mira Lyss is needed to stop us all fighting in the chamber; everyone respects her impartiality, and one voice is better for speaking to the Communia than many.

'Ulric, well. He looks like he enjoys a simple life of hitting things with those bear-paws, and perhaps he once did, but he is also one of the most astute men I have met, for all his accent and demeanour. Very good at strategy and tactics.'

'I like Councillor Tarqas,' said Karland. 'He reminds me of Aldwyn.'

'Poor Brandwyn is the voice of reasoned thinking, although he has not been heard as much of late.' Gusta sighed, and Karland remembered how drawn the old man had been last time he had spoken to him. After losing Robertus and Aldwyn, and nearly being killed by an assassin, the Councillor had been somewhat muted. The events had taken their toll.

'What about Councillor Novas?' asked Xhera. As usual, she had been quite quiet, content to listen. Karland didn't know how she marshalled the most pertinent questions, but she usually did. 'Who will replace him, and his role?'

Councillor Gusta looked at her sharply for a moment.

'Clever girl,' he said approvingly. 'We were indeed a Council of Eleven.' He bit his lip thoughtfully, and then sighed. 'Well, this is nothing you won't find out soon enough. We have just finished the process of another internal election to replace him from the Universalia Communia. Only the most suitable, senior and capable members are even considered, and there must be a proven track record of no corruption and evidence of selfless work for Eordeland, amongst other things. The new Councillor will not take over the role of, um-' he shot a glance at his husband. '-liaison for the wandering scholars. Councillor Holmson has already proved invaluable in that position.'

Karland supposed *liaison* sounded better than spymaster. Draef Novas had not only been contact for wandering scholars of the Universalia Communia, in itself an exalted enough company, but he had also secretly used them as a network. Even more covertly, he had a further hidden network of Darostim amongst them, the ancient scholar sect that had sworn to safeguard the knowledge of mankind against disaster.

'What about the, uh-' Xhera clearly realised Jonnal might not know of the Darostim, and looked for a way to finish the question. Gusta picked up on it quickly enough.

'Our other friends? *That* matter requires much further thought and discussion before we reach any decisions.' Jonnal cocked an eyebrow. Gusta shrugged in apology. Jonnal smiled without rancour. He was clearly used to certain things not being discussed.

'Do Councillors have houses in the Hoard? I was thinking to visit one day,' Karland asked hopefully, keen to visit the estates and banking towers north of the river where the wealthiest lived.

Jonnal chuckled and Gusta crowed with laughter.

'Ah, lad. Did you not know that the Council are limited? The Universalia Communia set the terms for elevation to the Council. It is a position of great power in the land… but to gain it you must lose equal power elsewhere, if it exists. We draw a decent stipend, eat well and have quarters any noble would envy, but any holdings outside are kept or sold for us while we are in power. We cannot hold businesses or interests, and the money we earn is not perhaps what you might think.

'No, the Council is about governance, and intrigue, and knowledge. No entrepreneurs end up in our ranks, not for long. Councillors are usually set until enfeeblement or death, but they can be removed with a majority in the Communia, or they may retire. You would be most welcome, but we have neither palace nor manse amongst those houses of stone and gold.'

After a little more discussion, Gusta and Jonnal rose, bidding them a good evening. As he rose to bid them farewell, Karland caught sight of Aran sitting many benches away, watching them intently. He wondered how long he had been there. Aran was casting furtive glances at him, and talking to several of his cohorts, who were smirking.

Karland sighed inwardly. The abuse he would get for 'sucking up' to a Councillor was inevitable, he knew, and it would be pointless arguing otherwise. It was an odd attitude; Aran himself placed great stock in who he knew.

He guessed glumly it was because he was not born a noble, so it simply wasn't the same.

Councillor Gusta had certainly cleared up some understanding of the arrogant boy's attitude, especially where Xhera was concerned. He resolved to try and react less to the needling. It was clear that for whatever reason, Aran did not like him, and about that he could do very little.

It wasn't until they had returned to their apartment and Xhera had paused and turned to him very slowly, and asked in disbelieving tones, *'Joy?!'* that they both burst out laughing.

Rast appeared in his doorway with an eyebrow raised before vanishing again.

Karland and Xhera only laughed harder.

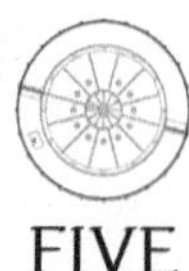

FIVE

Ventran sat clouded in thought. He had an urge to drink - something he did not often do - and to be alone. He had placed a reasonable amount of coin behind the bar in The King's Crown, a throwback to the monarchical glory days of Haná, and had made it clear that he expected regular drinks and no disturbances. He sat in a dim corner in view of the fireplace, drinking slowly, flipping a dagger absently in his left hand.

Tonight his thoughts were not on the play of blade on flesh, or on victims; even on his ambitions in Meyar.

The orphaned street urchin he had been had had many worries. After years of training with some of the best assassins in all the realms and free rein to practice his skills as his urges took him, the merciless young man had merely swapped old concerns for fresh ones.

But not tonight. Tonight, only two things bothered him.

Sontles had healed, slowly, a pile of drained corpses being dealt with by his minions. Once he had recovered, he had summoned Ventran and demanded a report.

Ventran winced, remembering his master's eyes boring into him. He had blurted nearly everything under the powerful gaze, his will broken down. He had word of success or failure back from all his bands of killers, the hired and the conscripted from the Teromants. All except one - the last one that had gone after the Darostim scholar Aldwyn Varelin.

He managed to hide this from Sontles with supreme effort, but couldn't hide the fact that they didn't know where the pendant Sontles desired was.

He had rarely seen his master angry. Sontles had carved furrows in the ancient oak table with nails as hard as talons, and the hiss and bared fangs had frightened Ventran, unlocking a primal fear within him. He had hurriedly assured Sontles that he would rectify it, that it was not his failure. The vampire's last words followed him out, carrying the weight of threat.

'Find and kill whoever has it. Use any resources you need. Do not disappoint me again, Ventran. If you cannot do my bidding, I will find another who can.'

Varelin had escaped. The pendant was hidden.

The problems were likely one and the same.

It troubled him. From all reports, Aldwyn Varelin was an old man, but he had still avoided death several times.

Ventran remembered back to the kill of that first scholar, the first of the Darostim. He had failed to take the pendant his master's spies had said Kelpas Withy had, but he had redeemed himself by hunting anyone tied to him, and the trail had led him through some very unexpected victims to one girl, barely a woman, who had given him a gift in her tortured, dying insanity.

Names.

Somehow, she had known of many Darostim, and they in turn had given up more. Although he was sure he had not weeded out every one of the bookish society, more than fifty had died at his orders. None of it had done any good. The old fool had sent the pendant to Aldwyn Varelin, according to spies in Darost.

The pendant was more than an old necklace. It was a key of some sort, that allowed access to - something. Another place, power of some kind. The details were vague, and sounded frankly dubious to Ventran, but it was not for him to judge what was fact and what was mere tale. After all, he had once thought vampires a myth.

Sontles sought it to help him dominate all of Anaria. There was something more to it than that, though.

Ventran wasn't stupid. He disdained normal social limitations, had no care for the suffering of others. It even interested him, excited him, but he felt nothing for anyone or anything outside himself. He had no real ideas of social etiquette, personal boundaries, what he should or could not say or do, and he didn't care. He was very good at emulating those around him, but it was a game he only played at whim or necessity. People often assumed he was touched in some way as a result, but he didn't see it as something broken inside him. It was strength that was missing from other people.

Weak fools.

People deserved to be used and abused if they didn't have the wit to notice or prevent it.

Ventran was extremely wary of Sontles. He knew first-hand that his love for death was shallow compared to the sea of what his master was capable of, revelled in. A steady supply of slaves went in to his master's mansion, and none ever came out of the basement. He had never entered, but he knew the tang of fresh blood, and it was powerful, pervading the house. There also seemed to be a lot of macabre decorations subtly arranged around the mansion these days.

Yet… he had a nagging feeling that there was more.

Sontles stood to take control of the Church of Terome, but for the powerful Holy Voice. Even now, he was cautious. Their political and theistic enemies had followers and were dangerous, but Sontles had plans in place for them. Eventually, even the Prime Alderman would be cast down, leaving Sontles in charge of both a powerful Church and the United Territories of Meyar. He already controlled part of the military arm of Terome, and few people knew of the wary emissaries from the orcs that had slipped over the border from time to time.

Almost fifty thousand of the creatures waited near Eordeland, ready to do the bidding of the Church. His master had told him they lay hidden from an ancient demon that Sontles had released. He had hoped it would destroy Eordeland, but somehow it had survived, the demon driven off by drakes.

The Prime Alderman was charismatic and powerful, and had done much of the work in the preparation for war against Eordeland. He believed the orcs would aid him; Sontles believed they were his. Time would tell which of them won, no doubt at the cost of the other's life.

Ventran's money was on Sontles. And after that, Anaria would be ripe for division and conquest.

If they could crush Eordeland.

Another beer arrived. He drew on the fresh foamy head thoughtfully, swilling it around his mouth and enjoying the hops. He noticed a single large ant on the edge of the table waving antennae over a small spill of beer. Odd to see one out alone, late at night. It didn't look like a normal ant, and in the dim light appeared bright blue. He casually crushed it with his thumb and wiped the mess off on the bench, considering.

Politikus Belen had been in Darost to receive stolen information from their spies, one of whom was highly placed, and had seized the opportunity to slay Aldwyn Varelin. He had failed, despite one of his 'servants' being an *oibrífola*. Ventran had been surprised; Ignathian wetworkers were the best blade assassins he knew of.

Belen had been lucky to survive on his return; his idiocy and arrogance had confirmed Eordeland's suspicions of mercenaries within their borders. Worse, they now knew exactly who the enemy was. But Belen was still powerful and had managed to blunt Eordeland's focus by pretending to be a new Politikus offering diplomacy and goodwill whilst using his deep knowledge to good effect. The fools had backed down from war.

Ventran was unsure if they knew of the orcs, but he doubted it mattered. If they struck at the same time, no realm could likely survive.

He turned the possibilities over in his mind.

Eordeland had an army that was a match for any in Anaria. They were highly trained and backed by excellent leaders, tactics, and weaponry, and they had technology other armies could not match with those damned scholars and their science. No one was sure what they were capable of, but the rumours were enough to make most men blanch. Only a fool would send an unprepared army against them. Their defences were excellent, their country was strong and ruled by a united Council. They were matched only by the Banistari Empire, which had superior numbers of fierce desert warriors and cavalry. They had an uneasy alliance. Only the Iril Eneth and the vast forests and plains in-between had prevented there being more clashes.

The other lands were different. Morland was old and powerful but didn't have a large army. It was said that to attack them was to court death - as the world-bestriding Kharkistani Empire had found a few thousand years ago. They usually ignored the squabbles of other realms.

Novin was feudal and mercenary, full of fierce noble captains who owed main allegiance to their lord's banner, then the crown. The lords swore allegiance to the king. All of them swore allegiance to gold. Some were men of honour, but not many. The king himself had the Knight-Captains, lords who were loyal to him alone. Without them the country would have relapsed into warring island-cities centuries ago. Novin had thousands of mercenaries already pledged to Meyar, and once pledged they did earn their gold. Most of their constant warfare was internal House struggles, clashes with Sergoth Barbarians, and attacks against Ignat.

Ventran sipped reflectively, feeling the warm ale fuzz faintly under his tongue, the heavy hoppy taste following.

Ignat was… odd. They lived in their stone towers, sniping at Novin and constantly fighting to prevent annexation. They generally kept to themselves. Belen had been lucky to find one willing to work for pay outside the country; it didn't happen often, although they accepted acolytes from time to time. Those that were spies tended to end up picked clean as a pile of bones in the RavenSpire, the tallest tower in Ignat.

He didn't even consider the tribal savages. Half of them weren't even human, and none had loyalty to any land.

He sipped again, satisfied.

Eyotsburg was the only other ally Eordeland had, and without their navy and fortress they were pitiful. They couldn't send aid a thousand miles across land if they were under seige.

Alone, Eordeland was doomed. Mighty, rich and proud… despite the treaties, if other lands saw them weakened, they might also attack to claim some of its wealth. As long as Meyar did not make any major mistakes, victory seemed assured if they could only draw them out of their cities.

Eordeland had vast tracts of arable land and many defenceless towns and villages; the huge cities relied on trade to survive. Their army was strong, but their land was soft. If they stayed in their cities, they would see their prized land destroyed, their trade cut off. They had come to rely too much on the peace of both, and if they were drawn out, they would be hamstrung when their major force was crushed.

If Darost fell, the other cities would fall, one by one.

His thoughts returned to Varelin. The old man nagged at him like a worrisome tooth. Everything was falling into place, except for that one old man. Blast the pifing old fool! After the failed attempt in Darost he had sent a full unit of Teromant Chaplains. Fanatics, believing in their holy duty; skilled killers. They had picked up the trail outside Darost, heading south, and then… nothing. No more reports. He was forced to assume that somehow the whole elite unit had been wiped out.

All those Darostim the girl had spoken of were dead. All but Varelin.

Not only was it irksome in the extreme, but Varelin was the most important of them all. Hamstringing the Darostim, at least temporarily, hampered their responses to the coming war, but Varelin alone had the key that old fool Withy had sent him.

Sontles wanted that key.

Ventran just wanted Varelin dead.

And actually, now he brought it to mind, there *was* something else that bothered him, something he had been pushing from his mind. He drew a longer swallow of the bitter ale, hardly tasting it this time, and his brow furrowed.

Tal'Orien.

This warrior. This *legend.* His name was known in many lands, and people spoke of inhuman skills in battle. Big, fast, strong, smart. Gifted.

Damn freak of nature, he thought sourly.

Perhaps he could see a way his unit had managed to fail, after all. The madman had reportedly attacked twenty or more insurgents in The Sanctum and somehow survived. Many of them hadn't, although the number he had killed himself was vague.

What was known was that Tal'Orien had killed the Ignathian, as well. That had been no mean feat. The man had been an expert, someone Ventran had been wary of himself.

He couldn't help admire the man's skill, in his own twisted way, but he envied his power, and the warrior was bloody annoying. He hung around the old sod like a bad smell.

Either get the old man away from him, or take him down. Wish we could hire a Morlander. Tal'Orien can't fight poison.

There was a thought. He might not be able to source a Morland assassin - they generally worked to an annoying and specific code of morality - but wetworkers also knew their venoms, usually coating *lovar* tips in them before each job, and they weren't the only killers who knew herbs. Perhaps that was something to consider.

Either way, the old man and Rast Tal'Orien were at the top of his corpselist. Sontles had demanded the scholar's death. He knew far too much. If anyone could find this keyhole for the pendant, he would.

He couldn't rely on Chaplains again. If they failed… it was his head.

If you want someone killed right, do it yourself.

Ventran tossed back the last of his third pint. He would find this old man, end him personally.

With any luck he would see how accomplished Rast Tal'Orien really was.

The barmaid approached again, seeing his tankard empty, and he gazed directly into her eyes and flashed a charming smile, which she hesitantly returned. She had skinny hips but full breasts, and a red birthmark around one eye which men probably did not look at much, given the bountiful view they had lower down. It didn't make her ugly, but Ventran couldn't care less about minor physical defects. Perhaps he did feel like some fun tonight, after one more drink.

Then later, perhaps some *real* fun.

Ⓒ   ⓈⓄ

Karland was brooding again that evening, unable to thinking about the growing isolation he felt. He tried to explain it to Xhera.

'I sometimes feel very lonely,' he admitted. 'I know you often feel the same way, and you're more withdrawn with people you don't know, but I get on with nearly everyone. And yet… I never feel part of anything. I get forgotten, left out, ignored. Like I'm just - inconsequential.' He shook his head. 'Maybe people just don't like me.'

'Oh, Karland,' Xhera said, putting her hand on his cheek. 'It just seems that way. A lot of people like you. But some people are just always outsiders. You have always wanted to belong, but are too different, too… yourself… to fit into a group. You're more of a leader than a follower, but aren't much of that either unless you have to be. You go your own way. You'll always be yourself. Don't regret that. It doesn't mean you have to be lonely.'

Karland felt the warmth of her slender hand on his cheek and fought to keep from blushing, from closing his eyes and just feeling it. Her beautiful eyes were on his, and he didn't know what to say, or if he should say anything.

Finally, he managed something.

'And what of you?'

She smiled, and withdrew her hand. 'I am content. I have a few friends. I have our work. I have my best friend.' Her eyes held his and his heart warmed. 'That's enough. I don't need to feel part of anything more. You're more social than I am; you believe in people more. Maybe that's why it's harder for you.'

'I suppose,' he said. He was grateful for this serious girl that had stolen his friendship and his heart. The talk had helped him feel better. He changed the subject. 'Aran was there earlier, listening. Looked like he's plotting something.'

Xhera snorted.

'When *isn't* he plotting! I don't know why you let him bother you. If you want my opinion, he's envious of your training with Rast and that you're closer than he is to the Council despite not being noble.'

'But that doesn't even make sense. The Council isn't noble. We haven't had nobility here for hundreds of years.'

'I never said it was logical,' Xhera said. 'The Council is still the seat of power here. He's insecure and jealous, and not a good person.'

'Well, I mostly ignore him now,' said Karland, drawing a disbelieving look from Xhera. 'Well, I do. It's only when he pushes me that I react. I can't help thinking that maybe it's just his upbringing. That maybe deep down he's all right.'

'He's not going to change. You can't judge everyone else on your own moral code. Some people are just shit.'

He sighed. 'I know. It's just…'

Xhera saw the expression on his face, and shook her head. 'Karland. Don't let it change who you are or how you are. Just… just be careful with your emotions. One thing I respect about you is your heart. Your empathy, your care. Don't lose it. Just don't… let it interfere with your head.'

He exhaled slowly. 'You're right,' he admitted. 'I'm glad you're here to remind me when I question myself.'

'Which is every day,' Xhera said. She looked a little sad. 'Do you think you're the only one? I'm just a farm girl. I keep catching myself thinking, am I really here? Am I really doing these things, seeing these things? Sometimes it's all so surreal.'

Karland laughed. 'If there is anything you aren't, it's 'just a farm girl'. Aldwyn said that we were special, meant for more than, well. Mundanity. I look at you, and sometimes... I know what he means.'

Xhera looked down, her cheeks slightly flushed. She looked as if she did not know what to say, her mouth slightly opened. Karland couldn't look away from her lips, from the tip of her pink tongue peeking between the sharper tips of her white teeth. He fought down a sudden desire to kiss her.

Snap out of this, he told himself again.

Better to have a soulmate than risk losing her by forcing something that she didn't feel.

A knock on the door was a mixed blessing. It distracted him from his eternal dilemma, but it intruded on the intimacy.

'I will see who that is,' said Rast from somewhere behind him. Karland jumped, flushing slightly. How long had the big man been there? He could give a stalking panther lessons in silence.

As if in answer, Rast smiled slightly.

'You have heart, boy, but you must learn that the only way you can be friends with everyone is if you lie and manipulate them. If you are true to yourself, someone somewhere simply will not like who you are, and that is fine. Don't be so permanently altruistic, boy. Accept that some people want to live a lie, and be done with them.' His eyes were serious. 'Aran is one of those people.'

Karland flushed slightly, then nodded. 'I... I know.'

Rast nodded and dropped a hot hand on his shoulder before moving to the door. He opened it carefully, and then swung it back and bowed slightly.

'Castellan.'

Castellan James bowed, gaunt and severe in the light from the hall. Karland had not seen him, except at a distance, since the last time he had been in The Sanctum with Aldwyn.

'Master Tal'Orien.' James straightened. 'I apologise for bothering you in the evening, but there is a matter which has come to my attention.'

Rast shrugged very slightly. 'Never a bother, Castellan. It must be important to require your notice.'

'I have been asked to personally escort you to a small gathering. The location is not public. I understand you have been quite involved as of late.'

Karland had heard that the Castellan was probably better informed than Novas had been, about matters within The Sanctum at least.

'I am ready.'

Castellan James nodded, then looked at Karland. 'Master Dresin, an aside. I have brought you someone whom you may be acquainted with, upon his rather *insistent* requests.' He moved to the side and motioned his head, and a trainee Eordeland Guard entered the room.

Morlandishly dark-skinned in contrast to Karland's own slightly dusky tan, he was broad-shouldered with fine, even features that held delicacy and hinted at the exotic. Under his helm he looked familiar. Karland stared, his brain taking a second to click in delayed shock.

'*Seom?*' He rose and moved to the door.

The guard's face broke into a white-toothed grin that swept all doubt away. ''Master Dresin'? What happened to 'Karland'?'

'Impertinent youth,' muttered James. Seom snapped to attention.

'Sir! Sorry, sir!'

'At ease, recruit,' replied James dryly. 'You are on leave this evening. Carry on.'

'Thank you sir,' Seom said, and saluted.

James acknowledged him and held the door for Rast, who nodded to Seom and slipped from the room with his customary grace. As the door clicked, Seom turned to Karland.

'So *that's* Rast Tal'Orien. He's *huge*. And *you're* his companion!' He shook his head. 'All the Guard vie for the chance to train with him, and here you are, lounging in his quarters. I think we have some catching up to do-' he noticed Xhera, sitting near the fireplace on the sunken seats and stopped.

'Hello; what have we here?'

His manner changed abruptly, becoming the silky smoothness that used to both amuse and annoy Karland.

'Seom, meet Xhera. Xhera, Seom.' He said nothing else, curious to see how they would react to each other. He was already fairly certain how Seom would act faced with a pretty girl, but he hoped his old friend would see through the skin and discover how much more there was to her.

Xhera stood and nodded to him. Seom crossed over and stepped down to her level, pressing his lips to the back of her hand. She quirked an eyebrow at Karland, and he cursed himself inwardly that he had never thought to do the same.

'Xhera. What a beautiful name. You truly belong here in The Sanctum, where the treasures of men are guarded.' Xhera raised an eyebrow and turned the grip into a handclasp of welcome, and Seom looked surprised at the firmness of her grip.

Karland rolled his eyes. 'Give it a rest, Seom.'

Xhera laughed, and they all relaxed a little. Karland noticed Seom sat facing Xhera, a little closer than he was comfortable with.

None of his business, he reminded himself.

That didn't stop him feeling slightly sick. Already little butterflies of panic fluttered through his guts.

He remembered what Seom's dark good looks and easy manner had gained him amongst the girls of The Croft, and changed tack, trying to shake the thought off.

'Seom - *what* are you doing here? I haven't heard from you for, well. Two years? I didn't know you were in Darost. And a Guard!'

Seom laughed, his eyes on Xhera. 'After father moved us away, I decided I wanted more than remote villages and trade. He gave me his blessing and sponsored me to travel here. I don't think he expected me to stick out the training, but I made it in.' He looked at Karland and then seemed to flush slightly darker under Xhera's calm blue gaze, which was probably not the same as the admiring gazes he was used to. Karland smirked inwardly. If Xhera confused other boys half as much as she did him, it would be interesting to watch.

'Actually, I'm still a trainee. I won't be a guard for two years yet,' he admitted ruefully. 'The age limit's seventeen for active duty, though you can start training earlier and learn specialties. It's a good way for the Guard to get fully trained soldiers in bulk. There are programmes set up to test if you're suitable. I'm looking to join the Welcomer Guard, and there are written tests and everything,'

'I can't see you having too much trouble,' said Karland. 'You always were smart. You could write, unlike Arflun.'

'Arflun,' snorted Seom. He grinned. 'That arse. What's he doing with his life?'

For a second, Karland was about to fall back into the easy routine of insulting his childhood nemesis, and then shook his head slightly. He felt Xhera's eyes on him, and knew these two were the only ones who really understood what Arflun had once been to him.

'He's changed, Seom. The Croft was attacked by hundreds of orcs. Many people died. He stood with the young of the village, protected mothers and young children. He's kind of a hero.'

'I heard of the attack. Is that admiration in your voice?' said Seom, wonderingly.

Karland shrugged.

'I've made my peace with him. He nearly died. Somehow everything we used to have between us means so little now.' He grinned. 'He's probably still an arse though.'

'What Karland didn't say is that he knocked Ben Arflun on his backside protecting my honour, then saved his life in the attack. If Karland hadn't been there, they might have all died. *He* led the counterattack against orcs inside the town centre.'

Karland blinked. He hadn't planned on mentioning that; it was a little too much like boasting. Xhera grinned at his discomfort. Seom looked at him with scepticism. Karland blew out a breath.

'I realised he was just a stupid little boy who liked having his own way,' he said. 'No one should die on an orc's spear in front of their family for that. It put things in perspective. And it was only luck I didn't die either. Rast's horse did the real work.'

'Hold on,' said Seom. 'Go back to the part where you knocked him on his arse. Since when could *you* do that?' He coughed, and grinned. 'Sorry. That sounded bad. You know what I mean.' His eyes took in Karland's frame again, and his face changed as he really saw Karland.

'Guess I can now,' said Karland. He shook his head. 'Probably always could. He was so shocked. All it took was enough reason.'

Seom's eyes slid sideways to Xhera and his lips twitched. 'Reason enough.'

'I've been training with Rast for nearly a year,' said Karland. 'I'm not quite so bullied these days.' He thought about Aran. 'Mostly.'

'Deadking's balls, I bet not,' said Seom.

Karland tucked that away for future use. It was logical that the military tended to call more on him than Delmatra or Isha. The Iron King was the god of the dead. Seom coughed and looked abashed.

'Sorry, Xhera. You, ah, hear a lot training with the veterans.'

'I bet,' she murmured.

'You train with Master Tal'Orien, you said. That explains a lot,' mused Seom. 'He's something of a legend to the soldiers.'

'He fought on the walls of The Croft, and slew the orc leader in one blow,' said Xhera. 'He went through them like death on the wind. He has earned their tales.'

'He's fought in a lot more than that if you listen to the stories,' remarked Seom.

'You look fit and strong,' Karland said, changing the subject. It had been a long time since he had seen his friend, and they could talk about Rast later. He couldn't help adding, 'I bet you've cut a swathe through the ladies here.'

Seom's gaze flicked to Xhera. 'Well. I can't help it if ladies like a tall dark stranger.' He grinned, his eyes on her.

Karland felt a little annoyed.

'You always were the tall, dark… strong, handsome, popular one,' he said, trying not to let envy creep into his voice. He was surprised when Seom burst out laughing.

'You should look in a mirror these days, Karland. One of the glass ones here, not a metal one like we have out in the sticks. In case you hadn't noticed, you look me in the eyes when we stand, and you're as broad shouldered as I am. You look stronger than I ever thought possible. I've never known you so confident.' This time the look he cast to Xhera was serious, devoid of flirtation. 'Karland has this bad habit of not realising his own worth, in case you hadn't noticed. That's why people always run over him rough-shod.'

'I had noticed,' she said, smiling. She was watching them both intently, seeing how they were together. In a way he realised this was a bit of competition for her as well; he had told her of his old best friend, but never expected to see him again. He was unsure if she would be jealous or not.

For himself, he was delighted to find that it was as if they had never been apart. Seom had always been as a brother. He felt as if he had finally found some stability again in a world full of change.

Seom turned to her and smiled. 'That's a good point. I'd like to know how you came to be lumbered with this lummox's company... sharing the burden along with the rest of us.'

'Get poxed,' retorted Karland. Seom laughed, and Xhera followed. She sobered quickly, however, and Karland knew why. Even now, she had the occasional nightmare about the experience with the Novinian Plains Walker, Hoge.

She described their meeting, how they had recognised a common yearning between them, a shared loneliness. Seom nodded; he knew exactly what she meant. Karland knew he'd always despaired of his friend's deeply restless soul. 'Sounds like you two needed to meet,' he said, and Karland knew he meant it. Seom was genuine and emotive. He could charm birds out of the trees, but he was also far blunter than Karland. He had often envied his friend's apparent ease of dealing with any situation.

Xhera quietly told of her kidnap and abuse. She didn't go into detail, but Seom wasn't stupid. He looked horrified, then furious. His sense of justice was one thing he shared with Karland. When she described Karland's attempt to rescue her, he clenched a fist.

'*Yes!*'

'Um... I failed,' Karland reminded her a little bitterly, his memory of it still painful. 'Rast had to save us both.'

'Idiot,' snapped Seom. 'If you hadn't gone back, Rast wouldn't have followed, she wouldn't have lived. Take some damn credit.'

Point, Karland's traitor hindbrain said.

Shut up, he replied silently.

Seom hung on the description of the fight between Rast and the bandits. Karland took over this part, telling him everything he could remember. Seom marvelled at the details. 'Eleven bandits, and he took them all down, unarmed?' His finger stabbed at them. '*THAT* is what I am doing this for. That level of training, of skill. I hear he trains some of the veterans now. One day I'll train with him too, I hope.'

For possibly the first time ever, Karland detected envy of him in his friend. He hadn't really thought about how prestigious training with Rast was. He remembered the number of times he had tried to avoid it.

'I can ask if you like,' Karland said. Seom looked almost hungry at the prospect. 'Maybe you could join my training. I can't promise, though. He's pretty busy with General Colcos.'

'Would you? That would be amazing.' Seom shook his head again. 'I can't believe you train with him. I've heard about you and the Council, and Rast, and the General. I heard a lot of stories, actually. None of them seemed like, well.' He shrugged, a grin on his face. 'You.'

'Thanks,' muttered Karland.

Xhera slapped his arm playfully.

'Well, it doesn't,' protested Seom. 'It wasn't until I heard your surname that I realised it was actually *you*. I had to bug people non-stop to get to see you. I don't get into The Sanctum that much; the trainee barracks are in the city. Got put on report twice. I think Castellan James and my Sergeant are quite annoyed with me, but I had to see if it was really you.' He grinned. 'I've heard everything from you travelling to fabled lands lost to time to you knowing dragons. It'll be good to know what really happened.'

Karland and Xhera carried on their story, intertwining the tales. The journey to Punslon following the remainder of the orc raiders, the ork tribes, the Dimnesdair, and the death of Grukust. Xhera nearly wept again talking about it.

Karland glossed over the forest witch details, uncomfortable. They spoke of Drakeholm Soaring, and then sparingly of the Darkling. That was something else that still haunted them - the experience of being in its presence even for a few minutes still touched their minds with darkness. Karland still sometimes felt cracks in his mind, limned with jagged red nothing, as if his mind might still shatter with the right blow.

They described the portal and the Greater Dragon and finally Yosgaloth and their race to warn Darost. Karland choked up speaking of the death of Györnàeldàr, but Seom had been in the city and seen some of what had happened. When they finally finished, and he had run out of most of his questions, he shook his head in wonder, quiet for a long moment.

'If I hadn't seen some of this for myself, I would have called horseshit. Of all the people least likely to have all this happen-'

'Yes, yes,' said Karland. 'If you keep saying that I'm going to get offended.'

Seom laughed. 'Sorry. You *have* changed, though. For the better.' He leaned forward, a serious, almost wistful look on his face. 'I'm glad you're safe, my friend. Glad you're better for it. I can't say I don't wish it hadn't been me, but who knows if I'd have even lived? Sounds like half the time only luck kept you alive.' He smiled. 'I told you all your bad luck before was saving the good for something.'

Karland laughed in turn.

Seom stood.

'I should get back. I don't get much time off, but we can meet up when I'm free? I can send word.'

'That would be great,' said Karland. 'I've really missed you.'

'You, too.'

They walked to the door. If the hug goodbye Seom gave Xhera was a little more protracted than he would have liked, Karland chose not to notice. Seeing his oldest friend again felt good.

He was elated that they had all got on so well. It had felt like more than the sum of the people there; both his friends in different ways. He hoped the twinge he felt when he thought of Xhera - and Seom's flirting with her - didn't grow and disrupt things.

He clasped hands with Seom and noticed to his surprise that his grip was definitely at least as firm as the rangy recruit. Seom had always been much stronger and surer. 'I'll let you know about the trainings, all right?'

'Thanks,' said Seom. He grinned widely. 'I'm so glad to see you again… blood-brother.' Karland laughed. He remembered the childhood oath they had made, and what had happened. A thought occurred.

'Wait.' He waved his hand. 'I thought you hated the sight of blood?'

'I've toughened up a bit,' said Seom. 'Now it's only my own I hate seeing.'

Karland punched him affectionately on the shoulder. 'Idiot.'

'Well. See you soon.' With a last lingering look at Xhera, Seom left.

They closed the door and sat. It was getting late; they had been talking for hours, and Rast still wasn't back. Xhera stretched sleepily.

'I'm glad you saw him again,' she said. 'I liked him. A lot.'

A lot? thought Karland. *What did that mean?*

He nodded, smiling happily and tried to ignore his overanalysing brain. 'I'm so happy he is well. He really is like a brother.'

'I have to make three classes tomorrow,' yawned Xhera pointedly. 'You have four, if I recall.'

Karland cursed inwardly. He was glad she'd remembered. He hadn't.

'Night, then,' he said. Before he turned to go, Xhera gave him a sudden hard hug, then stepped back looking abashed.

'Good night,' she smiled.

Karland went to his room and drifted to sleep, feeling almost ecstatic - not from the words, but the tone of her voice.

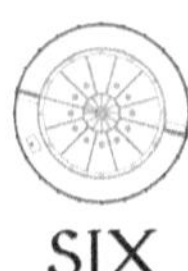

SIX

Five cloaked figures met late in the night, flanked to the foot of long stairs by stern-faced Onyx Guard in dark garb. They climbed to the top of the Academia Entitas's Cunae Tower, stylised with suggestions of Ignathian archicture. It was rare that any notaries from Ignat came to Eordeland; thirty years at the last count. They were a reclusive people.

The tower summit held a hint of the RavenSpire. A high tower peak, it was lined with glass and stone inside, though of course there were no corvid residents. The particularly large and intelligent breed from the Ignathian mountains was not common in the lowlands, although they travelled far and wide when the urge took them.

The peak was kept maintained but had fallen into long disuse; it was rare that anyone visited bar the servants who dusted. There was only one winding staircase up to the tower summit.

What better place to hold a hidden meeting, thought Dorn as he nodded to the Guard and moved up the stairs.

A smoked sphere of glass let out a dim candescence, enough to see faces at close range but not to shine out of the tower, should anyone be watching at this hour. The light was enclosed in a way that would quickly snuff a flame, but the Library light inside glowed steadily.

The Captain-General of the Eordeland Guard observed from the shadows, part yet not part of the clandestine meeting. Dorn's counterpart awaited everyone at the centre of the chamber with General-Marshal Colcos, the former in black formal armour and the latter in his customary crisp grey uniform.

General Colcos glanced around under austere brows. He stood ramrod straight, his hair brushed back from his gaunt temples and his hands clasped behind him. In the dim light his face had hints of a skull, but the glint of intelligent and alert eyes gave it animus. He nodded to Jekob, who left to secure the staircase, taking the Onyx Guard with him.

'Councillors.' He nodded as he greeted them. His voice was very educated, his enunciation precise. 'You doubtless know why I have called you here. You have all shown great support for reacting to Meyar's attack. Deliberations over a war footing took the Council nearly a month, and further prevarication removed any sense of true threat. Then the Universalia Communia voted against war, in favour of recreating diplomacy with Meyar, despite assassins and treason in our ranks.' He sounded disgusted. 'I believe it is still imperative that we move to a war footing. I shall speak frankly.' His voice was brusque.

Dorn remembered back to his own surprise at the vote. It had seemingly come out of nowhere and caused no end of clashes in the Communia and Council at the worst possible time. The vote had moved to disseminate troops across Eordeland to guard against the threat of rogue orc bands, which was directly opposite to focused planning for external conflict, and step down all war preparations in favour of renewed diplomacy. It had carried with a narrow margin.

'Make no mistake; relying on diplomacy shall not save us. The words of many of the Council are, if not lies, then half-truths.' His gaze bore into them all; uncompromising, unafraid. 'Some do not believe in the threat represented by Meyar, or these orcs that Councillor Varelin's party stumbled upon. Others seem to be treating this as some petty by-play, politics as usual. Let me assure you that it is not.'

There was something almost bird-like in his quickness and poise, thought Dorn. He highly respected the other man's strategy and judgement; in their discussions together, Colcos had impressed Dorn as few other men had. He had seen him sparring with short spear, too, unafraid to face his own veterans despite his age. He was very good.

'There are certain signs that precede a war. I saw them; I believed it was clear the Council had seen them, too. They continue to mount. Councillor Eremus's leading of a negative vote caught me unawares. I do not know what game she plays, but this is a critical juncture for Eordeland.' He cleared his throat and straightened his uniform. 'I would be remiss in my duties if I did not place the welfare of Eordeland above all else. Even the will of the Council. Even my own career.'

There was a faint susurration of whispers.

'My choices are clear. I resign my commission and act as I can to spread the awareness of hostilities… or I go against the vote cast and make ready for war in any event, whatever the consequences. What I cannot do is sit idly by.'

His face was calm as he delivered this news. Dorn was surprised, but not overly so. Colcos understood his duty.

'What is it you ask of us?' asked the huge form that could only be Ulric. He must already know, Dorn reasoned, but wanted to be persuaded along with the others.

'I ask that you consider supporting me to make Eordeland ready for war, despite the vote.'

'You ask us to go against our own voted decision, our own laws,' came the voice of Mira Lyss. Dorn was surprised she was there; if there were anyone he thought had to be objective, it was her. 'I cannot be part of this. I am the Arbitrator.'

'I know, Councillor Lyss,' Colcos replied with a curt nod. 'I invited you to bring rationale to our... discussion as you would any council debate.'

'And if I feel I must bring this to the attention of the full Council?'

'You must do what you feel is right, of course.'

'Mira, you know this is madness,' rumbled Ulric. 'Voting on going to war was one thing, but Eremus slipped in the clause to include even preparations at the eleventh hour. I am not suggesting we go *to* war. We have been *at* war since Draef Novas was killed.'

'Preparing for the worst is simply common sense,' remarked Jamus Holmson. 'It was ridiculous to propose that it would escalate matters. This new Meyari Politikus whom Eremus has such high hopes of has still not arrived, and all we hear are excuses. All reports from the travelling scholars and my other sources say that it is already too late. Are we to have no defences at all?'

Mira Lyss said nothing.

'I have since found how far Eremus bribed and manipulated to force the vote through during the months of chaos after Yosgaloth,' added Holmson. 'The Council was distracted. She planned well. Her manipulation could invalidate the result, Mira.'

'We must respect the will of the Council,' said Mira Lyss. 'And of the Universalia Communia. Our realm depends on following our law. The vote was formally cast. If democracy is ignored Eordeland will be weakened, badly.'

'Even at the cost *of* our realm?' replied Colcos to Mira Lyss. 'Councillor Lyss, the vote was not true. The Universalia Communia were pressured into taking it in haste before you had even selected a replacement for Councillor Novas. They were told half-truths and lies. This is not true democracy. There is no point in bowing to the bidding of the populace if it destroys our realm! The Universalia Communia did not truly know what they voted for. If they had, it would not have been as it is.'

'But it *is* as it is,' she said. Regret tinged her words. 'Any amendment to the vote requires a recast.'

'Hypothetically the Council can ignore the vote of the Universalia Communia. It *is* considered advisory,' remarked Holmson slyly.

'Doesn't it require a unanimous Council to do so?' asked Brókova.

Mira Lyss raised her eyebrows and shrugged regretfully in acknowledgement. 'It is true, but even if we ignored it, the Universalia Communia could cast a vote of No Confidence and attempt to remove some or all of the Council. They might even succeed. That would cost us at the worst time for either war or diplomacy.'

'How many times has the Council ignored this advisory vote?' asked Ulric.

She sighed. 'Never.'

'Eremus covertly influenced a large number of Universalia Communia with lies and promises, enough for them to pressure their Councillors against this so-called precipitous move,' Colcos replied evenly. 'There must be mitigation for this, surely?'

'Does no one else find it suspicious that her family's fortunes are bound up in finances owed by Meyar?' asked Brókova acidly. 'Or that the Guard sent to protect remote trade routes would keep their goods safe?'

Colcos waved his thin hand.

'*Why* does not matter to me. My only concern is the safety of Eordeland.'

'We never even thought to do such a thing with the Universalia Communia,' Tarqas admitted heavily. 'We were so sure we had consensus.'

'What do you think, Captain Dorn?' Ulric's voice rolled towards him like an avalanche of bears.

Dorn considered carefully. 'I understand the need to maintain the laws,' he said. 'If the highest in the land break them with impunity, they are no laws.' He rolled his neck, thinking. A vertebrae popped quietly. 'But it comes down to a choice; are you willing to gamble the fate of everyone in Eordeland on political manoeuvring? This is the first time in decades we have been faced with an invasion. It would be madness not to be prepared when we have the chance. And what of the orcs? Reports have come in over the last few months saying a huge force preceded Yosgaloth and vanished somewhere south of Irilview.'

'It is too much to hope that creature ate them all,' remarked Ulric sourly. 'Eremus refuses to believe they exist, either. What about you, Tal'Orien? You are the most objective of us here, without ties or influence from politics.'

Dorn blinked as the deep voice of the huge man fed into the chamber from near the door. He hadn't even seen Rast standing further back in the shadows. From the starts, it was clear others hadn't either.

'I can only advise on what I have seen and believe. Eordeland is not my land, but she is the closest I have. I have seen the threat we face. I have seen unrest across the lands. You risk the lives of all your people if you do not prepare for the possibility of war.'

'I do not propose that we act as rogues,' said Colcos. 'I merely propose that we bend the restrictions quietly where we can, to ensure we are not defenceless.'

'Eremus and her allies would be able to twist that into more than it is,' warned
Mira Lyss. 'They have already incited the populace against Teromens and outsiders.
The people are directionless, angry. Councillor Regus says what the people wish to
hear. They have more support than you do. It would not be hard to swing public
opinion against your actions in the short term.'

'What are the alternatives?' asked Colcos rhetorically.

'You realise this is dangerous; we could be held to account, even exiled from the
Council,' said Holmson. 'That might not be successful, but it would achieve its
purpose; to split the rule of Eordeland and weaken it further.'

'Damn her!' growled Ulric. 'Why does she do this now?'

'It was easier to react immediately after the arrival of Master Tal'Orien', said
Aurelia Brókova. Her dark skin reflected little light, and she looked mysterious. 'He
brought dire news, and it was proved right in part soon afterwards. He is respected
and trusted in many lands, and we had learned to our cost that orcs exist and are
terrible. A horde of them could topple a country if it struck unawares.' Ulric
grunted. 'And we could hardly ignore a Dragon. But most people cannot sustain
emotion long, my friends. After the fright and anger wore off, and nothing
happened, the focus shifted. Preparations cease to be the priority against the refugee
crisis. We have relied on diplomacy for so long we find it hard not continue even in
the face of attack.'

'Eremus made herself very popular diverting the blame onto Teromens,' said
Holmson. 'Whyll Regus is her staunchest ally, and nobody can persuade as he does.
The Academia Linguistica is adept at communicating to the people at large. I never
expected his skills to be turned against others in the Council to push an agenda. And
the Sub-Academia Communica is how people gain news throughout the city,
especially our own scholars. It did not take much to taint the information to sway
them, I think.'

'We have grown complacent,' said Ulric almost ruefully. 'We thought we were of
an accord. And what of the orcs? To leave ourselves defenceless is madness!' He
hesitated. '…is Eremus a traitor?'

'I think not, for myself,' said Tarqas, 'but she will happily watch us all burn to
achieve more power for herself. Joy Eremus has long waited for a situation she can
use. Her views are not tolerant, but in times of unrest they are echoed by more
people. We have grown too reliant on plain truth. She speaks what people wish to
hear. It is not always the same.'

'If the Council was split, she might be able to call for a recast of members herself:
a vote of No Confidence. She could even assume temporary full control,' said
Holmson.

'But that is insane!' snapped Brókova.

'Perhaps she truly believes that Meyar is not a threat; that the orcs don't exist. It would certainly explain her reasons for doing this at such a delicate time.'

A moment of silence was broken by Tarqas. 'It is a risk we must take, even at that cost. You know my secret. The Sanctum stands to preserve the knowledge of men. Simply because a political structure has grown up around it of people manoeuvring for power, it does not mean we can forsake our primary duty. A duty, I remind you, that has lasted two thousand years! It is the highest priority of the Darostim.'

'And if the worst happens? If we are cast out? Do we Invoke?' asked Jamus Holmson quietly.

There was a startled silence. Dorn had not known Holmson was Darostim; clearly, neither had the others.

'Are you mad?' hissed Tarqas. 'That would destroy Eordeland as we know it! Things are not *that* bad.'

'Invoke?' asked Mira Lyss. Brókova cocked her head. Colcos was also quiet, his eyes darting between the two members of the Darostim.

Tarqas spoke up reluctantly.

'We ask that what you will hear is not repeated again-' he looked at them in turn, 'Mira, Aurelia, Dannon, Dorn. Ulric. It could damage Eordeland irreparably.' He took a long breath.

'Written into the foundations of The Sanctum and Eordeland Lore is an Edictum which can be invoked in the utmost peril. It has been long ignored, but it is there. It breaks our laws, destroying the power structure in place if needs be, and exposes the Darostim, handing control of everything to them. The Darostim who are wandering scholars are but one part of the whole. There are others, trained to other tasks. The intent is that in the gravest peril, the Darostim may rise to protect the knowledge guarded for men by any means necessary.' Tarqas looked around at their dimly lit faces. 'In such terrible circumstances there would be little left to destroy. To do it now is unthinkable!'

'But the Darostim are already exposed!' protested Brókova.

'Not so. The Council has been made aware that they still exist. A myth, a cabal of old men, many of whom have already been murdered. That is all. No one knows the breadth of the Darostim, and few still know it even exists bar the Council.' He looked around under weary brows. 'You know I am one; you know Draef Novas was one, as was Aldwyn. You now know Jamus is too. I have been Darostim since I was thirty.'

'And if you *invoked* this Edictum?' asked Mira Lyss. Her tone left it impossible to tell what her thoughts were. Dorn wondered if he was watching the breaking of the Council here and now.

'Invoking could destroy our whole society,' said Tarqas. 'Once exposed in all their power, the Darostim would need to assert themselves immediately to survive, potentially using forbidden knowledge. It could never be undone. Current political and economic structures would deny the claim, knowing they would lose their power. Chaos would erupt. Eordeland would break and would never be remade, the laws cast aside or broken as needed. If they won, the Darostim could become a terrible force which might have to destroy entire realms to survive.' He shook his head. 'We exist to keep the hidden knowledge of men for our darkest hour of need. If it isn't the darkest hour for men, where chaos already reigns supreme? I fear once unleashed, the power could be easily abused. The world could fall under one conqueror. It would be beyond imagining.'

'Deadking's balls,' muttered Ulric. 'Let's not do that, then.'

'Should not all Darostim then be removed immediately?' asked Colcos. His tone was curious more than threatening.

'No one knows who we all are; that attempt could itself precipitate retaliation. But make no mistake: we have never been here to rule. We are merely here to safeguard the last knowledge of men should the world collapse,' said Tarqas sadly, 'not to ruin our land. I am an Eordelander. A Councillor. While I still draw breath, I will defend our realm and our ways.'

'How would such an ancient clause be enforced?' asked Brókova. 'Could it be ignored as you suggest?'

'It is written in the Arcanus Sanctus, the great tome of Eordeland. Our own Council Edicts are drawn from there. Only the Council of Twelve and a few others know it as the core of our government, refined and referenced for a thousand years and more. How often has it been read in the last fifty years? It is the only copy I know of, and shielded by the lives of the Onyx Guard. To deny it would be to render the root of all our laws meaningless. To obey it would destroy the government. Either way lies anarchy.'

He walked a dangerous path, thought Dorn. If those here felt this to be a large enough new threat, they would try to remove the Darostim. If what Councillor Tarqas said was true, that could cause a civil war that would make the currently impending one look like a minor disagreement.

He wondered if any others here were also Darostim.

'And if Eordeland is conquered?'

Tarqas shook his head. 'Unlikely. Better for us to seal the Combic Libraries and all die than face the terrible consequences of Invoking the Edictum, if it is not the end of everything men know. Better that a million of us die than that. The Combic Libraries possess the knowledge to break the world.'

'How can you say that?' asked Brókova in horror. 'Those are our people's lives! Men, women… children! As well give the city up to that hungry devil lurking in the Arkons.'

'The knowledge is held in trust for a day that humanity itself might not survive. What is the greater evil, Aurelia? That people may die now, or our whole race ceases to exist?'

'That is an impossible choice.'

'Quite - which is why I hope I never have to be the one to make it.'

All gathered were silent again.

Mira Lyss finally spoke. 'I have much to consider I should not have known. I *cannot* be here. I will not speak of what I have heard, and I suggest we all forget any talk of the Darostim. Agree what you must, bend where you must; but if I am made aware that our laws have been broken, I will call the Council to session. Those responsible will be held accountable; Darostim or otherwise.' Her outline turned to Ulric. 'Be especially careful, my friend. Eremus hunts your head.' She turned and left. The sound of her descent faded.

Ulric's voice rumbled after a long moment. 'Are we agreed then? Now is the time to say no.' He paused for a long moment. No voices came. 'Then we make ready, against the wishes of Council and Communia. Quietly. And hope we are not discovered.'

'Eremus will tear us apart if we are wrong. She could end up leading the Council. Become voted Advisor.' Brókova's voice was low.

'She might find less power than she wishes, whatever happens. And she would not hold power forever.'

'And if we are not wrong?'

Ulric sighed.

'I pray we are. The fate of Eordeland depends on it, in more ways than one.'

ଓ ଯ

Rast dreamed.

He sat, cross-legged in *dônaethar* trance, memories dancing through his head, crystal clear around the centre but blurring at the edges.

It was not the same as the reverie of the elves. They slipped into the trance as easily as they breathed, resting with their eyes open even as they did things. Elves never truly slept. For a human to achieve the trance took years of practice, study, and focus.

The concentration was immense. Sweat dotted his brow and forearms. The trance accelerated healing, allowed a full night's rest and recovery in one to two hours. It was difficult to split attention; it had taken many years for Rast to learn to concentrate and still listen out, after spending almost that long again learning to achieve the trance itself. He'd reached the point where he could stand watch at night and rest only an hour or so, alert and recuperated, but he believed it was the utter limit of what a human could achieve. It was like a deep daydream which allowed certain things to filter through from the waking world.

It approached midnight. The distant murmur of The Sanctum reached him. He sat on the balcony, hearing the footsteps of guards several floors below, the chirping zz-zz of crickets in the inner gardens, voices from hallways. A regular light almost-snore came through Karland's closed door, though not Xhera's. She slept with her mouth closed, but despite all the training with Karland to make him use his nose, once he slept his body rebelled.

His ears were alive; his skin tingled with the night breeze. But with his inner eye he saw a different scene, hard and sharp.

Once again, he waited, watched. Steam rose in the cold night air of the mountains, and snow lay strewn on the forest floor, fallen from clearings in the high pines. Much of it was churned up. Thirty feet away, a fire crackled. At its edge, a large flat four-wheeled wagon glowed and charred in different parts. Already two wheels had burned through and collapsed, the iron shod rims unable to sustain the weight, softening in the heat. The distant whinnies of the two large horses that had been hitched to it echoed from walls of rock and ice. Rast hoped they found sanctuary in this wild place.

More than others had found.

He was badly wounded. His body was much younger and slighter, barely older than Karland. The injuries from tonight and the last two weeks had taken their toll; Death's sweet lips were not far from his. He could feel her cold breath.

Blood dripped freely down his left arm from the shoulder, despite the makeshift bandage he had tied tightly around it. More blood had crusted from a rent in his left side, deep and horrible. Every time he twisted, fresh blood oozed.

His head hurt badly, a slowly crescendoing throb. His right eye didn't work properly, more from pressure in his head than the eye that was nearly swollen shut on that side. His legs shook with the chill, and it felt as if half of his ribs on the right were broken. He was very hungry, very weak. A slice across his scalp had the side of his head covered in yet more blood; he had lost much more than he could afford in this bitter cold.

He was powerful, strong, a gift of birth. Even so, he should be dead by now.

He would be soon.

He did not care.

Seven bodies lay around the camp, all that remained of the last of the three groups he had hunted down. One lay right at the far edge, his head at a horrible angle on his broken neck. One lay with his head stoved in next to another with a dagger in his back. Elsewhere another lay with a sword pinned through his ribcage to the dirt, his knees drawn up and hands near the blade. Two had become engulfed in the flames that had spread from the small campfire, and at the clearing edge another lay in a pool of arterial blood, eyes staring.

The last lay propped against the tree to his left, glaring at him. The noble insignia on his collar glinted in the light. The lump on his head must be agonising, and he seemed to have trouble focusing; Rast had possibly fractured his skull with the blow from the discarded log, ironic since Rast was certain he had an identical injury. A dark stain on his front spoke of another gash, but he was less injured than Rast himself.

The simple chain around his neck looped down and crossed behind the tree to his wrists. He couldn't pull his arms forward or disengage his hands without strangling himself. Given time, he could possibly work his way free, but Rast did not intend on giving him the chance.

The Novinian spoke, his voice raw with effort. 'I *know* you, boy. I thought you a ghost.' He spat, the bloody froth dribbling down into his stubble. 'Don't know how you still live. Don't care.'

Rast said nothing, trembling with the effort of standing and watching.

The noble's eyes narrowed, a cruel smile spreading on his face. 'She was the worst cunt I ever had.' He laughed, his voice cracking, until he fell silent, panting. With supreme effort he spoke again, the croak making him almost incomprehensible. 'So kill me, *boy*. And know you're not worthy of it.'

Rast did not speak. The rage within him felt distant, a bright nova a galaxy away in the darkness.

The man knew he was doomed. If he went free, he would seek Rast out and have revenge. Worse, he would continue do what he had done to more innocents. He knew Rast would never let him go, and goaded him for a clean, quick death befitting his station.

Rast waited, growing colder. He would have thought the man passing into a coma if the hate-filled eyes had not stayed locked on him.

He knew he would not have to wait much longer. Their voices filled the wind on this cold night where dark deeds had occurred.

They knew.

They came.

Rast had always been gifted many things; size, speed, strength, endurance. His hearing was keen, as well as his sight and smell, and he could almost sense when someone crept behind him, when he was being watched.

Times like tonight.

As his feeling of his own body diminished, it seemed to flow outwards.

A combination of a soft noise and feeling alerted him. At last, he took his weary eyes from his hated enemy and looked further into the trees, where they grew thicker.

Two yellow eyes reflected the firelight in an unholy dance, green at their centre. They were spaced wide apart, and he knew the creature was large.

They seemed to glow.

There was no emotion there. Only hunger.

He sensed others behind the eyes, hidden, and somehow knew they had not circled around him.

Not yet.

The eyes shifted and moved forward slowly into the edges of the firelight. In the shifting dance of shadows, Rast saw the hulking form of one of the great grey mountain wolves of the Arkon and Skyreach ranges. In winter, they travelled from range to range across the great plains. Unlike the smaller red lowland forest wolves, they did not fear men. They were smart, and even the orks respected their cunning and strength. He had faced them himself, once.

A pack could bring down a wyvern, with luck, or one of the great rinoks of the plains if they caught it alone. They matched the darker, short-haired dire wolves for strength and size, but were more intelligent and aggressive, if more wary. They also hunted in much larger packs. Even gar-wolves were wary of these predators.

The great wolf approached, sampling the scene before it. Rast felt its gaze take in the carnage, saw it scenting the fresh death. Wary yet, it glanced to the man against the tree, and then turned its attention to him.

They did not usually hunt men, but it was winter, and food was scarce.

He crouched, watching it with an unwavering gaze. He knew that it might take this as a threat, but also knew it realised his weakness and injuries. Hurt though he was, he would not be easy prey, and the wolf seemed to sense that. Something akin to acknowledgement passed between them, and then it dropped its head and loped over to the campsite. Its shoulder was higher than his navel.

As if at a hidden signal, the rest of the pack slipped from the trees, yellow eyes gleaming. Rast counted nine of the great creatures. A small pack.

Unbidden, he tightened his grip on the wicked dagger in one hand and hefted the long heavy branch in the other. He was not afraid to die; was even ready. But something within him would not willingly accept their attack without payment in kind.

They ignored him and sniffed around the near fringe of the camp site, nosing curiously at the destruction. One moved near the chained man, and he suddenly kicked his leg hard and yelled hoarsely. His rage had shifted to fear. His eyes flew to Rast, and he croaked.

'Please.'

Rast watched, his face impassive.

'Please!' Gone was the aloof sneer, the goading. Panic welled up.

The wolves were attracted by the spasm and noise, and moved closer, their hunting instincts kicking in. They would feed on the bodies as a matter of expedience, but they were built to bring down their prey and feed on fresh, warm meat.

The pack surrounded the man, watching him with singular focus. Almost curious, they crept forward. The largest lowered his great head to the large gash on the man's sternum and licked. A faint growl rumbled forth, and it calmly dug its teeth into living flesh, the huge canines slicing into the wound. It tugged its head brutally, powerfully, like a dog jerking a held branch.

'Please! Please! Please!' The man's voice broke into babbling screams, his legs thrashing. As one, the rest of the pack lunged forward, tearing into legs and stomach, powerful necks tugging at his looped intestines with sharp teeth, and his screams became awful.

Tearing sounds, growls, gurgling shrieks beyond agony that tore the already pained throat to shreds gushed out, a bubbling symphony of red death. Rast stood, watching, his face settling into grim lines that would etch themselves in coming years around his mouth.

The man juddered, eyes glazing in massive system shock.

The wolves tore his guts nearly to the backbone before one of them nosed up into the chest cavity and tore a hole in his heart.

Rast watched them tugging at the corpse, tearing it piecemeal from the chains. He turned his back and walked painfully to the burning fire, knowing the wolves would not willingly approach it. He collected supplies from the camp slowly, dragging what corpses he could to the edge of the light, and moving back. One man was not enough for the pack. Part of him hoped that they would not cultivate taste for human flesh and attack a stead in the future, but he did not even know if any steads remained here.

The noble and his men had seen to that.

Rast breathed deeply in his trance, remembering the smell of blood, of burning. The musky pervading scent of the wolf pack, and the sounds of them feeding and talking to each other in their own way. Of death visiting the man who had broken his life, changed its course forever.

He never even knew the man's name.

He did not care. But he had sworn that he would protect all he could from men like the noble. He had sworn to kill only when he must, but he had never hesitated to do so.

Of all his memories, why must this one remain so clear?

Better this than others.

Yellow eyes. He had seen them somewhere before, outside his dreams. They meant something to him. He knew he would see them again, but, wrapped in his memories, could not think where.

More than two hours later, Rast opened his eyes. During his meditation, he had automatically tensed and relaxed muscle groups intermittently so they did not become stiff and numb. He gave a low sigh.

Yellow eyes. The screams of the damned.

He rose, no stiffness apparent, his left knee faintly popping. Since the vision in the Portal, he had known that there lay a way, perhaps, of reclaiming some of what he had lost when his life had been set upon this path. There had been times when the desire to kill and slay had been overwhelming. After watching the man die, for a fevered time he had been consumed by a matching numbness to empathy, and a passion to slay all who perpetrated such acts. With the return of his mind and health he had controlled himself, and with his return to reason had regretted the torture the man had endured. However richly he had deserved it, it had not been justice. It had been revenge.

It had not been who Rast was. He should have killed the man cleanly.

Rast knew he had not been in his right mind then; the exhaustion, the rage, the injuries and the shock had been great.

He shouldn't have survived. He had nearly died, descending the mountain, and only by chance had he been found by a stead that had been spared what he had endured and nursed back to health. He'd worked hard to repay his debt once recovered, despite their protestations, and then left, unable to stay, seeking something more. It had been made clear to him what his calling was.

What he was good at.

He had travelled aimlessly, his mind as adrift as his wandering, his thoughts unable to focus past what had happened. What he'd lost.

When he had found the men, they'd nearly killed him, and it brought no solace.

Revenge was hollow. It brought nothing back.

It troubled him, picked at his soul. He needed something to fill the void torn within him.

In Morland, he had slowly been fully healed, his old injuries soothed and his body and mind renewed. He had realised the evil and chaos growing in the world made his duty clear: to finally admit his greatest strength and embrace his gift.

To learn how to truly fight; how to defend.

How to protect.

Something he hadn't managed with Aldwyn, the last in a litany of failures.

He knew intellectually that he could not have prevented his friend's death, but he would never forgive himself for it. He would never accept that it had been unavoidable. For all his strength, *because* of his strength, Rast endured whilst those he cared for died. He couldn't help it; he was a survivor. Even in those times he had not cared for his own life, his body responded on instinct. He had always emerged eventually victorious.

The perfect warrior.

The thought was bitter.

He looked at the great angry red scar on his leg, dark in the low firelight, and massaged it with his strong fingers. It was finally fading to silver, another token of a fate avoided. The crocodilian they had faced in the Dimnesdair had been overpoweringly strong, and faster than expected.

It had taken months for the full use to come back without pain, although Aldwyn's healing had been extremely quick. He shook his head, remembering. The solution Aldwyn had used to flush the wound and then laced around the stitches had been agony and had left a yellow-red stain for more than a week. Rast hadn't complained; he knew that the stained area meant no infection could live there. The old man hadn't had the skill the Morlanders had, but his small affinity for healing and his vast knowledge of herbs had convinced Rast's body to heal the awful gash to a usable - if very painful - level in a matter of days. Without that, they would never have escaped the Dimnesdair. Even with Aldwyn's *persuasion,* more than once it had bled anew. Without the skills his friend had learned from Morland he would have burst the stitches, possibly crippled himself, probably died of infection in that hot place, but even so it had slowed him, blunted his edge. As it was, they had been so exhausted after fleeing that he had nearly fallen when they had been ambushed.

When he had failed Aldwyn.

Rast knew from experience that deep scar tissue would be an impediment for months until broken down. He had massaged the site as best he could every day, gently at first. Full range of motion and strength had returned. All he had left now was the ragged angry crescent to remind him of the tooth that had caused it.

Thinking of pain and scars made him glance to his hands.

He flexed them unconsciously, tracing the faint angry crimson across his knuckles with his gaze. The marks from the dragon's blood were strange; not noticeable in the way that a birth mark might colour or thicken skin, not as contrasted, but there, faint, unmistakeable. He could still see every crease, scar and print. It was as if it had sunk past the first layer of skin and glowed dully underneath it, as if he had been tattooed with a shimmering red hue from the hot wash of caustic blood from his dying companion.

His hands were stained from the fingers and thumb, across his palms to the wrists. The volatile blood had gushed up his hands over the knuckles. The angry sheen was least noticeable in low light, but in sunlight it stood out, almost shimmered, and more than one person had stopped and stared.

Rast the Red-Handed, some called him now. For the blood on his hands or the stains, it was hard to say. He wasn't sure it mattered.

The dragon's lifeblood hadn't just marked his hands; it had burned him, and never stopped. He remembered the growing pain, the feel of it eating into his frail human flesh. It had burned and stung like acid, but he had ignored it, trying to give Györnàeldàr what comfort he could as she died. No wonder the ancient stories told of their blood eating into the edges of weapons.

It had certainly damaged his boots.

The sensation was interesting, he supposed. Not like fire, destroying his flesh and bringing agony and scarred numbness, but a reminder he would never forget. It was nothing compared to other things he had borne in life. It had faded to a deep, dull, distant warmth; there if he thought about it.

Rast had found that heat did not increase it. In fact, where before he would have felt pain, he could now place his hand near enough to a fire that the danger of a burn was high, and feel only a tingling, as if it spoke to the fire instead of burning.

Györnàeldàr had marked him apart from other men.

Some had said that the blood of a Dragon was the mark of destiny, others the mark of a king; others still a death sentence. Some said it was slow and terrible poison.

A slight smile quirked the corners of his mouth.

Everyone considered him so immortal, so invincible, but he was as pervious to harm as any man. He had come close to death more times than he could count. Skill, luck, reflex, natural talent and experience all kept him alive, but they could not last forever. He only had to fail to evade her once; one day he would feel her cold lips kiss his.

Most of his life had been a dance with the dark maiden, and he had sent many to kiss her first.

For a rare moment he wondered what he would have been had his life not been destroyed. Then he shrugged, swirling his cloak around his shoulders and checking the spring clips just behind the blades of his *shirka* were secure.

Things were as they were. What was done was done. He would protect those who needed it, who tried to harm none and simply live, and he would hold to honour, to wisdom.

To justice.

To duty.

Out there in the darkness lay a city - and beyond that, a world - filled with people being harmed, persecuted, violated, slain. War might be coming, but it was yet far, and there were closer dangers.

The Council feared that assassins still crept the corridors of The Sanctum. Karland had seen what could be the night demon that had hunted in Fordun's Run here, in Darost.

Rast had rested, yet was restless. He rose and moved to the railing.

It was time to hunt.

SEVEN

Drufel moved around nervously, stacking the thick-walled packets of nighthaunt on the docks, waxed linen-wrapped packages the size of bricks. He knew that a buyer waited in Tamismuth. To his left and right Arfis and Ger worked away. Ger had a dry cough that made Drufel wince when he heard it. It was low but harsh, and Ger muffled it with the crook of his arm.

Drufel shook his head. Ger liked to smoke motherwort, and he smoked far too much. He'd heard it made you feel calm and euphoric, but the amounts Ger took it in gave him breathing problems and dried his throat out.

They were making ready to load a vast amount of the drug onto a ship bound for the east; Ger was replacing packets one at a time with packed flour, Drufel was checking the drug was sealed and stacking it into crates, and Arf was loading full crates onto the waiting ship. They were the last team to do this, while the well-bribed dock attendants distracted the crews of both ships. If all went well, no one would know what had happened until they made port in Morland.

It was simple, really. The old docks were patrolled, but with the recent issues the city guard had focused elsewhere. There were villages and towns all down the river. The drug was easy to use; expensive to buy, but worth its weight in gold.

So much for crimeless, perfect Darost, he grinned inwardly.

Any city had its lawless side and its own dark denizens. The new drug had hit Darost, and leaders of the shadow councils in the other cities and towns further down the river were interested. There was profit to be made.

Nighthaunt had been outlawed in Eordeland, but was permitted to pass through towards Morland, unopened and seals rigorously checked. He had heard that it was prized by their *daktarim* for nausea and sickness treatment. Some was shipped there by sea from where the plant grew, in the west of Meyar, but it also travelled east through the Nassmoors to the rivers on the borders of Eordeland. It was slower, but more reliable. Meyari ships were not the most seaworthy in Anaria. Sometimes the trumpet-shaped flowers came through the gates, but this was not enough.

The packets of creamy powder were going missing from the Morland-bound ship because shipments had stopped by sea. No one was sure why, but a limited supply was now coming overland via merchants and loaded onto boats further upriver, just outside the borders of Eordeland. The underworld couldn't hide its delight at the hike in price and limited stock.

Eordeland was an old and orderly land. Punishments were harsh, but just. It was very rare to be given a penalty of death. But there were always trees to fell, crops to tend, ships to row and mines to toil; hard labour for years was an effective deterrent. And for the intractably criminal, the dungeons of Kingsport Fortress were deep, a throwback to a less civilised age.

To be a brazen thief was to be a grass stem standing above its fellows, in danger of being lopped off by either the Eordeland Guard or the far more frightening Shadow Council. Unlike the relatively enlightened and civilised lawkeepers, the associates of the Shadow Council would kill you outright, and you would be lucky if you were not tortured first. The collective Guilds of Thieves had honour of a sort, but if you betrayed their creed, you would find no mercy when an assassin found you. Many rogues ended up haunting the shadows as hired assassins, unwilling or unable to apply their skills in day-to-day work.

Nighthaunt had fitted into this system perfectly. Originally used as a deadly poison, at some point someone found that if it was inhaled as dust instead of ingested it would induce powerful hallucinations, break down willpower, and make people very easily persuaded. Blown into a face as the victim inhaled, they became almost catatonically suggestible, handing over entire fortunes with no memory of the fact afterwards. This made solving the thefts next to impossible.

As a consequence, a new crime wave was spreading through the cities of Eordeland, from Darost eastward.

If you blew nighthaunt into the face of a merchant, he would dreamily open his own doors for you, even groggily help a thief load their cart with his belongings. It wasn't just used for material thefts, either. More than one woman had awoken unwittingly violated, even pregnant.

But it was fickle; too much and the damage could be permanent, or the victim's heart could stop.

It was easy to give too much. Many people had died. Thieves did not measure it medically. Lives were being horribly destroyed by its misuse.

That, reflected Drufel, was not his bother.

The Shadow Council took a dim view of the movement of the drug, although they were known to allow some shipments past for hefty cuts of the profit. But shipping to another realm was different to selling it here.

In concept it was a useful tool for their members. In practice it was too easy for mistakes to happen, and many of the higher Guild members believed that the art of theft itself was under attack from such easy enablement. If they caught you with Nighthaunt in Eordeland, especially Darost, you were likely to find yourself packed into a barrel filled with water and lye to dissolve into sludge.

If you really pissed them off, you might not be dead first… and you might find your loved ones in there with you.

Drufel chuckled to himself as he slung twine-tightened packages, pressed with a forged wax seal. The art of theft, indeed. As long as he made money and had what he wished he didn't care. This work was easy and rewarding and the Shadow Council believed that the teams were checking the seals, not replacing the product.

It felt good to play the players at their own game.

He worked for another twenty minutes before he realised he hadn't heard Ger cough for some time.

'Ger?'

A brief, faint noise like a sail flapping in the wind caught his ears. A low cough sounded.

Drufel looked around, a bag of the drug in his hands unplaced.

'Geram. That you?'

Silence.

He carefully put the firm package down, his hands dropping to his knives. Drufel had travelled in his youth, even into Ignat, and learned his weapons well. He had soldiered with Novinian Mercenaries and worked for hire as a Shadow Council hitter. He had an aptitude for knife work and had survived many street fights with his blades. He wasn't quick to kill, but once he drew, he usually sheathed them in someone, and he had no compunction about murder.

Drufel crouched, sliding his feet carefully along the cobbled dockside. He cocked his head. Water slapped the side of the ship next to him, and he shivered slightly.

Everything was shadowed and quiet. He looked around, beginning to feel the first pricks of fear.

Night, he reminded himself a little more forcefully than he should have to, was his time. He was its master, sleeping most days and working at night. He was a man of the shadows. A Hitter of the Shadow Council. If anyone was out there, they would be wise to fear *him*.

Fear me, whoever is out there.

Even internally it didn't sound convincing.

He moved towards the last place he had seen Ger working. There was no sign of the man. A package had dropped to the cobbles, a rip in the side spilling cream-white powder to mix with the filth of the muddy docks. The ground was wet, and Drufel cursed inwardly at the loss of a package. They were paid on exact count.

He glanced behind him. Arfis, a hulking brute of a man, was also nowhere to be seen. He was supposed to be carrying the large crates onto the ship.

'Bloody idiot,' muttered Drufel, gritting his teeth. If they had both decided to take a break, he would personally see that they lost more than one packet from their cut. He wasn't working his arse off alone to get other people money.

A faint wheezing sound distracted him as he cast around, trying to see if Ger was leaning in some corner. Following his ears, he almost tripped over the dark form lying face-down behind a palette.

He turned it over, knowing it was Ger. The wheezing was bubbly and loud. Ger's face was covered in blood, brutally damaged, as if he'd put up a fight. His left eye socket was broken, along with what looked like more than a few ribs. One of them might have clipped a lung.

Drufel dropped Ger and stood, flipping his knives blade-down. A rival gang, perhaps… although there had been no warning. Seven men were involved in this night's enterprise, and most were involved in distraction and scouting for danger. Either the lookouts were compromised, or some of them had been taken out, too.

For a second, he wondered if Geram had made the monumentally stupid decision to annoy Arf, who was known to put people through walls when he felt he was being made fun of.

A gasp made him look left. He glimpsed an urchin, one of the destitute scamps that hung around the docks and poor streets. Dirty and wide-eyed, the child sprang up like a startled deer and ran. The first rule of being a homeless dockside urchin was to not be caught by anyone, for anything.

Dru grinned to himself. It wouldn't be the first time urchins had ambushed a busy man in enough numbers to take him down, and it might explain why lookouts hadn't given a signal. The little rats could get through the most unlikely passageways. He couldn't see anyone else. It might be this worthless creature had simply been trapped, the last of a feral group. Really, they should all be dumped into the river with stone-filled boots.

He hefted his knife and threw it, spinning end over end to sink with a *thock* into the bony back of the boy. The pitiful creature screamed, a thin wail of despair as he fell to skid along the stonework on his face, skinny limbs bouncing.

Drufel glanced around again. Nothing. He sauntered over to the urchin, noting it was a boy; short, ragged hair muddy over fine features. His forehead was open to the bone from the fall, a lump starting, and blood poured from the wound. It was far less serious than the knife in his back, however.

It was right through a lung, Drufel noted professionally. A good throw. The brat wasn't long for this world. He retrieved the blade, hearing a bubbling crackling noise as air rushed from the collapsed organ into the pathetically thin chest cavity. At least he wouldn't attack any more hard-working men, Drufel thought with a chuckle. He'd have to find Arf and get him working double time to finish this shift, and then they could get Ger some help, if he lived that long. If not... more money to split between them.

The boy stared sightlessly into the ground before him, in shock, struggling to breathe and see as blood poured from two large wounds. They were only yards from the ship side, where the dock plunged ten feet or more to the river.

Drufel reached down to grab the boy's wrist and ankle. 'Soon be over, boy,' he grunted. A lot of shit ended up in the river; one more piece made no difference.

A soft noise behind him warned him a fraction of a second too late. He dropped the urchin and drew his knives in a smooth blur, whipping around.

The first knife crossed in only for his arm to slam into what felt like granite. He dropped the knife with a curse and ducked quickly, switching hands and slicing. The giant, flapping black form in front of him did not change in its movements, but he felt resistance on the point. Even as that happened the shape flowed away from the blade, and he found his arm held in a vice-like clawed grip. Something trapped his arm with his hand uselessly holding the knife against the dark form.

It resembled nothing so much as a gigantic bat.

Sudden fear shot through him. He'd heard stories of a supernatural demon that prowled the night, faster and stronger than a man, killing indiscriminately. He jerked his arm back. Nothing happened; he may as well have tried to tear down a tree. Dread lent power and panic to his moves. He jerked again, powerfully, lashing out with his foot.

The pressure disappeared, although he had not connected, and he staggered back, nearly tripping over the prone form of the dying street orphan. Drufel bared his teeth and shifted his grip on the knife but was simply not fast enough to avoid the savage blow which struck him full in the sternum, harder than he believed possible. His air blasted from his lungs heaved in panicked agony. The blow broke several ribs and lifted him off his feet. Drufel had just enough time to realise what had hurt Ger so badly before he hit the side of the ship with terrible force. His head cracked against the wood and he thought he heard something break as his vision went black, shot through with golden bursts of light. He didn't see his plummet to the water, although he shuddered in shock as its freezing embrace closed over him. Still unable to breathe, he jerked spasmodically as cold fire flooded his struggling chest, his movements growing weak.

A sensation, too fast to register, of unbearable, immediate and overwhelming impact.

Nothing.

ଔ   ଠ

The orphan vaguely felt himself lifted in a powerful grip to gaze into the face of Death itself. His legs didn't work properly, and his head was fuzzy, his eyes refusing to focus. Shaking in shock, heart fluttering weakly, thin chest struggling for breath, he reached out one small hand in a mixture of wonderment and vagary to the cowled head, tangling his fingers in the rough cloth, before his undernourished body simply could not take the punishment anymore. His heart stopped beating between one bubbling breath and the next, and he sighed almost in gratitude, strangely comforted by the spectre come to bear him to Isha to be reborn again.

He shuddered, hiccoughed, and slipped away, his view hazing towards white, a point of freezing emanating from his core, himself, Death, and the whole world turning to frozen marble-sheened statues for all time-

ଔ   ଠ

The Guard arrived at the docks not twenty minutes later, alerted by commotion and flames. People said they had seen a devil flitting between chimney stacks, making no effort to stay hidden.

They found a wanted man floating dead in the river, trapped and partially crushed between a ship and the dock. Two more unconscious men lay nearby, one badly hurt, and four others were discovered further out. Not all were asleep, but one babbled insanely about the judgement of men, clutching a shattered arm, with what looked like claw marks down his face.

They also found a ship full of registered nighthaunt and packets of white flour, and another ship nearby part-loaded with similar packets well under way to becoming an inferno.

'Arrest the lot,' sighed the lieutenant in charge. 'Crews, docksides, these sods.' He nodded to the injured ruffians in custody. 'Have to be a full investigation.' The paperwork would be awful.

'There's no saving that ship now,' reported one of his soldiers, her face stern. 'Must have been doused in lamp oil, Sir.'

He nodded wearily. From a cursory glance, it almost certainly contained crucial evidence. He'd just have to hope what lay on the docks told enough of a tale. 'Just

98

make sure it doesn't spread. Scuttle it carefully, let the river take the fumes, and quick, or it will hit half the city. Keep everyone back from that smoke, or we'll have soldiers doing what anyone tells 'em - or dead. We'll sort this bloody mess out tomorrow. Nothing goes in or out of this dock.' He looked up nervously at the rooftops. 'And make sure everyone stays in squads.'

☙ ❧

In the middle of the blazing pyre, unnoticed, a small shape was laid out like an ancient Povirii king in state.

☙ ❧

'The devil of Darost has struck again!'

'Men murdered on docks in dead of night! We aren't safe in our beds, I tell you.'

'I don't know about you, but my bed isn't by the docks,' a woman's voice said in some amusement. Other voices drifted past the tent opening behind Rast and Karland. They had called in for something Rast had ordered weeks ago. Karland cocked his ear to the snippets of conversation.

'If you can call *torn apart* murdered.'

'To shreds, you say?'

'Some was crushed, set on fire, tortured. Drained of blood. It's the end times, count on it.'

'I heard it's one of the Dark Angels of Terome. Disgusting religion. They're all devils.'

'No, missus, no, it's a judgement '*gainst* Terome. Them was all Teromens what was butchered.' The voice sounded satisfied.

Karland chewed his lip. Most of the talk this morning sounded like the usual idiocy, except for a traveller who swore that spiritual peace was spreading from a rough farming village in the east like a wave of contentment, but there was no doubt that whatever had been around Fordun's Run had arrived in Darost - or something very like it. He shivered to think of how close it had been to him in The Sanctum. No one had seen it again there, although Rast had searched and Welcomers patrolled the building and the high Sanctum walls every night.

Something like that could hide *anywhere* in a city this big.

He did wish, though, that people would use sense and reason and listen to the actual explanation given by the guard. According to them, only two had actually died - one wanted murderer, and a young boy who had hidden on the burned ship.

99

'I hope they catch it soon, Rast.' he said. 'You've not found any clues where it is hiding?'

Rast shook his head. 'The guard have found no sign, Karland.'

He sounded unusually frustrated. But then, Karland considered, he'd also not found this demon. It was rare for Rast to fail at something.

Karland himself was almost cheerful today. Reuniting with Seom had lifted his mood considerably.

'Got what was coming to them, sirrahs,' said the dark-skinned Banistari owner of the tent stall as he straightened with a wrapped pouch of objects and held it out to Rast. Tall and proud-looking, he was meant to be one of the best herbsmen in any market in Darost - one reason he had a stall in the main marketplace. 'They dealt in nighthaunt, so they say.'

'Oh.' Karland had heard about the drug and the recent plague of victims that had swept through the cities. Dorn had been especially bitter about finding it hard to trace the operations at the heart of it. It sounded like something had chanced on some of those involved, at least. Perhaps now they would find leads to others.

Rast took the bundle from the man and opened it, unwrapping a waxed paper ball to reveal a yellow-green rough orb larger than Karland's thumbnail that was crystalline and shiny. He chipped a tiny piece off with a knife edge and thoughtfully placed it in his mouth. The man watched, expectant. Rast nodded after a moment.

'How much *kof* extract?'

'Per lozenge, thirty grams of unrefined weight *klah*,' the man replied. ''Tis seasoned, not green, so it is more potent, especially as a catalyst with the other additives. You understand the risks?'

Rast nodded. 'I am accustomed to its use. Thank you.' He handed the man several Greats.

'What is that?'

Rast glanced at Karland. 'Rare ingredients, extracts of many stimulant herbs mixed with heated honey for quick effect. Expensive, and dangerous, so do not try to sample them.'

'What is it for?' asked Karland. Rast wasn't a healer, so he assumed they were to do with fighting.

'The mixture of herbs and stimulants combined with the rush of sugar gives you a huge boost in concentration and energy,' said the owner, sounding for a moment almost like Aldwyn. 'You gain increased focus, and your body feels fuelled. It enhances focus and reactions for a short time. Your senses sharpen, too. Very useful, but only to be used sparingly.'

'It sounds amazing,' said Karland with interest. 'Why don't they get used more?'

'Not many know the making of these, for one,' Rast said. The owner grinned at Karland and wiggled his eyebrows at this, four gold teeth flashing under a hooked nose. 'They cost a lot, for another. The ingredients are difficult to obtain and mix correctly. They are… addictive. You experience a powerful fatigue when the effects wear off, and they don't last all that long. And if you are not careful, or have a weak heart, they can harm you. People have died before, taking too many or at the wrong moment.' Rast shrugged. 'They also rot your teeth.'

'Oh.' Karland looked at the bundles. 'Everything has a price, I guess.' Possibly dying didn't sound worth the reward.

'Indeed.' Rast hefted them and moved off. The stall owner bowed to Karland, who nodded back and followed.

'Nighthaunt is a plague,' said Rast. 'I wonder how many innocents have been hurt because of it?'

This last was spoken softly, his voice sad.

'I know Dorn wishes he could scour it from the city,' said Karland. 'He said the last thing he needs right now is drug catatonia and a new wave of thefts.'

Rast nodded, his face troubled.

EIGHT

Karland relaxed in the quarters they shared with Rast, lounging in front of the recessed fire, slowly slipping away. Xhera sat nearby with her back straight and her feet together, knees bouncing as she looked out of the nearest window and pondered.

A soft knock at the door started him from his seat. Xhera rose.

'Come in,' she called.

Rast entered and paused. 'We have a visitor,' he said in his deep, soft voice, stepping aside to reveal a small, slender, nondescript man in faded grey and black robes. He was smiling thinly, his piercing blue-grey gaze like a shaft of sunlight off deep ocean on a cloudy day, even in the candlelight.

'Night!' Karland exclaimed, jumping up to greet him. Xhera laughed, and beat him there, giving the slight man a brief hug. Karland shook his pale hand warmly. Night's flesh was very cool, as if he had bad circulation, and his grip felt fragile but strong. He smiled his thin-lipped smile at them.

'Karland. Xhera.'

'What are you doing here?' asked Karland, grinning.

'I arrived last night. I waited some months in Eyotsburg, and eventually came looking for you all. I realised something must have happened.'

'The situation changed somewhat drastically,' remarked Rast.

'So I understand. I know something of Yosgaloth, and its history. It was worshipped by an ancient race called the *Kreel*, and nearly brought the old world to ruin before it was bound. And then there are the dragons you found... truly fascinating. You were saved by an incredible set of circumstances, and I am glad, both for you and the possibly the greatest collection of knowledge in existence was saved. The Sanctum, above all else, must stand. The wisdom hidden within the catacombs here is too precious to lose forever.'

Karland felt somewhat embarrassed. 'We sort of forgot to get word to you, with everything that was going on. Plus, well… Aldwyn was the main reason you wanted to meet us, anyway.'

'Not just Aldwyn,' said Night, his eyes on Karland. As before, Karland could not hold their intense gaze long. Night pinned his soul to the wall and bled his will. They were remarkably similar to a dragon's. He supposed it was a reflection of whatever power Druids held. 'You all have a part to play in what is to come. But I admit that I feel his loss sorely. I think we would have been two minds in accord. And I am sorry for the loss of the others, too. The ork was… unusual.'

'The Seeker has just come from meeting with the Council,' said Rast. 'He is known here to some, but it remains to be seen if they listen to his advice where they have ignored the advice of dragons, Druids and men.' His voice was wry.

'Seeker?' asked Karland.

'My formal title.'

'Oh. Seeker of what?'

Night smiled. 'Knowledge. Amongst other things.'

'Let him sit,' chided Rast.

Karland flushed slightly. 'Sorry.' They moved to the recessed chairs in the floor before the fireplace. Despite the warm room, he didn't remove the faded black robes, but came to sit with them nearer the fire. Rast poured them all water. Karland got the impression that both of them, in different ways, had seen everything there was to see with one glance around the room.

'I am afraid I cannot tell you all we spoke of,' Night said to them, 'but I feel you deserve some of the answers they received, and perhaps a little more about myself.'

'We also have a request for you, from the Council,' added Rast softly. Although his face was as impassive as ever, Karland had the feeling he was troubled. 'I think we should discuss that before anything else.'

Night nodded assent, and Karland glanced over to Xhera's worried face. Rast looked at them all, and then leaned forward, the firelight casting dancing angular shadows across his rugged features.

'The Council has much to do,' he said. 'They are co-ordinating the movement of refugees from Irilview to permanent locations in cities across Eordeland, but most are still in Darost. There is growing pressure in the city, and unease. Despite appearances, even an orderly city like Darost is not without its underside, and it is proving to have teeth. It is a troubling time for unrest to rise, but ever there are those who will use politics and money to their advantage, no matter the cost to the people.' He shook his head. 'The Council are being split too many ways, but they recognise that what we did is not meaningless either.'

'Finally,' muttered Karland. Xhera elbowed him.

'I don't believe they realised how much they were depending on Aldwyn. On all of us. That we brought back unclear visions and tales of demons was a blow, even though without us, they would never have known of the orcs. Of Yosgaloth. But they need to know more.'

'Aldwyn was onto something,' said Night. 'His studies had set solid ground; reasoning, fact, logic, historical precedent. It is unfortunate that even in the higher levels of politics, people prefer to listen to unfounded opinion over demonstrable facts, especially if it supports their values. I have seen some of his previous works. He knew a lot more than he told even us, I believe.'

'So - what now?' asked Xhera. 'He is gone. They still have a lot of his notes. Can't they learn something from those?'

'Perhaps,' said Rast. 'If they had time.'

Karland had a flash of understanding. 'Couldn't we help?'

Rast nodded, with a small smile of approval. 'Not just help. The Council has requested that you take over his work, both of you, and try to uncover his thoughts. You knew him recently better than anyone here. You are keen to learn. And most of all, you possess the keys to the Library of Thingos.'

'I had almost forgotten about that,' said Karland, feeling a little guilty.

'He has shelves of notes and observations there!' cried Xhera.

Rast nodded. 'Indeed. This would disrupt your University studies, but-'

'Of course,' interrupted Xhera in excitement. 'We have already been trying to do this. If we have time… maybe, we can piece more of this together.'

Karland certainly wouldn't miss some of his classes. Or classmates.

'So - what does this mean for us?' he asked.

Night smiled encouragingly. 'You are to think back to everything Aldwyn told you - especially you, Karland. You spent more time with him in recent years than anyone. You must both follow what his notes say he was looking at and try to interpret anything you can. It goes without saying that you will have some access to the Combic Libraries, where much of his deeper work is.'

Xhera clapped her hands, laughing. '*Yes!* The Combics, Karland!'

Students did not get access to the Combics. It was for scholars and apprentices only. They could find *anything* in there!

Through a flush of victory, Karland wondered how this would affect what the other students would think. They already sniped at their additional privileges, helped by Aran.

He couldn't help grinning, nonetheless.

'You will not have time to attend all your classes, but it has been promised your education will not be forgotten. And you will have guaranteed positions here at the University whatever happens.'

Karland hadn't thought about the long term, or what he would end up doing. He couldn't galivant about the continent on quests for the rest of his life, he supposed, and given what the last one had cost him, he had no wish to.

Before, it had seemed like a magical adventure. That had quickly changed. He would be quite happy to have no more. But he had no intention of going home and running his father's business, either. He wondered how Gail was; he had received a few letters from her and his parents, and she seemed to be growing up fast from the tone of them. Eight was young to be able to write, even in Eordeland. He had the feeling his father was going to lose both their children to the University - disappointing, at least in terms of his attire business.

'Well?' asked Night, smiling slightly.

Karland and Xhera glanced at each other.

'Of course,' enthused Xhera, her cheeks flushed with excitement. Karland nodded.

'I will inform the Council your agreement,' said Rast. 'Be sure you understand the importance of this. If Aldwyn - and Night - are correct, the fate of us all may rest on discovering what Aldwyn knew.'

Xhera spoke up, her face serious. 'We've found it hard to keep up with our studies and keep our promise to Aldwyn, to be truthful.'

Karland nodded. 'I agree. Before, all we wanted was to study at the University, but things changed as we travelled. When we lost Aldwyn.' He shook his head. 'We felt like we had hit a wall.' Xhera nodded beside him. 'I've been so frustrated, trying to piece together what he had been telling us from a few notes and keep my studies up as well.'

'You were here by special decree, as a reward for your services,' said Rast. 'Although you would have little excuse for wasting study, this would have been allowed for.'

'So what did the Council say?' asked Karland.

Night related much of what had been said in the Council meeting, interrupted by their questions. He was patient in his replies, no matter how Xhera or Karland pestered him.

Eventually, Night chuckled dryly. 'I'm no dragon to remember everything I have seen or heard or read. I can only hold so much before it gets replaced by more. Your friend was different. His reputation in intellectual circles is exceptional. He retained more than most, but it was his ability to make incredible leaps of intellect that set him apart. A truly remarkable mind.' He sighed. 'My Order believes that the Darklings wish to ruin Kuln. War and death are merely the mechanisms by which they can sow chaos; it matters not if we live or die. They seek to unmake this world. We discovered that Sontles is their agent.'

'Who is he?'

'A better question is *what*. Sontles is a bishop in the Church of Terome, but he is not a man. Not anymore. He has become dark and evil, with powers beyond other mortals. The Order of Illuminus hunts him, but he is protected in Meyar, in the Church.' Night shook his head. 'We will destroy him if we can. But I need answers first; I have agreed to stay and help you study Aldwyn's work, in return for your help with mine. They are closely aligned.'

'The Order of Illuminus?' frowned Xhera.

'I suppose I should give you some more information about myself. Since we shall study together,' he added. 'You remember I told you that we tend toward names of primal power?'

Karland nodded.

'*Erus ex Noct Nocti* is my given name, from old Darum… and before. It loosely translates as '*Lord of the Night*.' I find it a little melodramatic when I am not with my people. *Night* is as informal a name as I have, young friends. I am honoured for you to keep using it. My society is quite formal; one tires of the precision at times.'

'You're a *Lord*?' asked Xhera.

Night laughed quietly.

'All my people are named *lord* or *lady* at coming of age. We are like dragons in that respect. Seeker is my title. It describes my role for the Order, a Seeker of Knowledge.'

'So what exactly do the Order of Illuminus do?'

Night's burning blue-grey gaze, powerful as the hurricane sea, softened slightly.

'We stand in the shadows to face the light,' he almost chanted. 'We Illumine our Darkness with the flame of Knowledge.'

It had the sound of ritual. Karland wondered what it meant.

'You're like the Darostim?' asked Xhera.

'The Darostim are another shade of our Order,' said Night. 'They lie in the shadows behind the Universalia Communia, who themselves work for the good of Eordeland behind the Sanctum. Oh, they say their pursuit is pure knowledge, but it is knowledge that will conveniently benefit Eordeland.

'The Darostim, now: theirs is the purpose of balance and order in Anaria by any means necessary. They will do anything they must to protect the collective knowledge of The Sanctum's libraries and establish balance. But even they are subject to the whims of mortal realms and the hearts of men. The Darostim work for humankind.' His glance slid to Karland, and he once again felt the force of will from this otherwise nondescript man.

'The Order of Illuminus is not within any realm, however. It owes fealty to no one except itself and the First. We observe and record without interference where possible, unlike the Universalia Communia, or the Darostim, and we record knowledge for and of *all* races. We know of many more places than this endpoint of the webways.' He seemed about to say more, then stopped. Karland opened his mouth, and Night shook his head. 'You are not ready for that knowledge, Karland. Ask another.'

'If that's the case, why are you hunting Sontles?' asked Karland instead.

'By the decree of the First herself, we seek those, like Sontles, who are... evil. We seek to turn them from their destructive ways, or destroy them if we cannot.'

'An Order of Scholars? Hunters of monsters?' asked Rast, interested.

Night smiled his thin smile. 'Something like that.'

'You say he is no longer mortal.'

Night studied the big man, eyes hooded. 'He is a drinker of blood. Undead, evil. In Eordeland, you would call him a vampire.'

'Are you serious?' asked Karland. 'Vampires are real?'

'Yes,' said Night. 'Many things exist which men think myth.'

Karland had seen too much not to believe him.

'How can a scholar destroy such a creature?' asked Rast.

Night leaned back, and his pale face softened. 'A Scholar of Illuminus is not entirely without resources. We have access to much hidden knowledge. And we cannot let the world fall to ruin.'

'I would learn how to do this.'

Night shook his head. 'Their power is too great even for you, Rast. No mortal can face a vampire's strength and speed without powerful weapons.'

'Nevertheless,' said Rast. 'I wish to know what I can.'

Night shrugged and nodded. 'I pray it never comes to that, my friend.'

Talk slowly moved on to other matters. They spoke of what had happened after Night had met them. Of Leona he could say little; they had parted ways a little down the great plains road from Punslon, where he was travelling north-east to round the Arkons. She had struck out directly across the plains.

'If only Aldwyn had been through the Portal, had met the Greater Dragon. If anyone could have made sense of it, he could.' Xhera looked sad, and Karland felt a shaft of sorrow too. He knew his old friend would have been ecstatic to have done so.

Finally, Night rose.

'It is late,' he said. 'You must sleep. I shall see you tomorrow evening.' He moved to the door and opened it.

'It is good to see you again,' called Karland.

Night paused and looked back, then bowed his head slightly.

'Thank you, my friend. That means much to me.'

The door sighed softly shut.

NINE

Ulric stood gazing out of the window into the darkness, a large ornate comb in one hand and a sunstone on the ledge before him.

Rrrrt.

Rrrrt.

The sound repeated as his thumb ran along the tips of the strong teeth reflectively. His other hand was on a battered helm, somewhat conical, the kind of thing some men would itch to attach horns to.

'This comb was my grandfather's,' he mused. 'For the beard or hair of a man or woman of war. Made from whaletooth set with gold. Poviiri raiders are well-groomed and honourable, you know, not like the stories. They enjoy the finer things in life even on *vikel.*' His rugged hand rested on the evidence of the raids. The helm had also belonged to his grandfather and had been worn on *vikel* for many years. He traced its dents and lines with troubled fingers; he might be wearing this again soon enough. 'Cultured people doing brutal work, but they still have honour.'

He sighed and turned to General Colcos. The man was dressed in a smart grey uniform, as usual. Taciturn, with his gaunt frame and face and cold clipped manner of speech, he was much slighter than Ulric, but still a powerful presence.

Thinning hair was still dark on top, receding slightly to either side of a pronounced widow's peak, faded to an elegant grey at the temples. General-Marshal Dannon Colcos was the second most decorated military leader in the history of Eordeland, known in his youth for his charisma, his ability to get difficult things done ruthlessly, and his skill with a short spear. Men followed him naturally and respected him, though he was a hard man and brooked no nonsense from anyone. He was not above putting even Councillors in their place, but his loyalty and dedication could not be faulted. Ulric had served with him in their youth, even fought alongside him. No one was better prepared to deal with the upcoming crisis. He had earned the title many times over and would be well-supported by his Major-Generals.

'So,' Ulric said. 'Five skirmishes with mercenary patrols east of the Arkons in the last two weeks, some suspected Meyari troops. Banistari politely sniffs our southern border, and we cannot tell whether they are merely observing, aiming to provide help, or considering invasion. Up to fifty thousand orcs have *vanished* in the region of Irilview's ruins and could attack at any time. We have had to divert many of our troops to maintain the peace internally after the destruction of Irilview and the aborted evacuation of Darost. Looting is rife, crime has risen hugely, and we have a new cult called-' he looked down at his notes, his heavy brow furrowing, '-the *Sons of Havoc* stirring up hatred and discord among the people of Darost. Foreigners are being attacked in the street, trade is dropping, and we border on civil unrest. There are still bands of roving orcs draining our Guard. Even the *Iterscientiams* are attacked between towns, their books destroyed. You've sent two battalions to the northwest border to prepare for a serious strike from Meyar despite the vote, and more to the southern border just in case, and we could both end up imprisoned for it.'

He took a deep breath. Colcos remained attentive.

'We have lost contact with the delegation sent to meet the new Politikus and have no idea if they – or he – are still alive. The only good thing here is that we've heard neither hide nor hair of the orc horde again and hope that writhing devil swallowed them up on its way here. Does that about sum it up?'

Colcos nodded. 'Yes. I have recalled all reserves and we are drafting those willing in the populace into the auxiliaries. General Veirce is more than capable of holding the south and east. General Neider will cover the north-west. There have been no probes so far of our borders, and we've been shoring up defences on the border forts, but there is a lot of open ground out there. Meyar may begin using mercenary strikes along our borders over the next few months to distract from the true strike I feel is coming. It could land north of Gladsmoor, or it could drive south and then in East to the Greatway, which would better support a full army.' He pursed his lips. 'Two legions of mixed battalions would normally be enough to hamper the full might of Meyar, but I am concerned they may split their attack. And if these orcs that Tal'Orien spoke of exist, and attack as well, we are in trouble.'

'Would we meet them outside our borders, or at our gates? Darost has never been broken.'

'No, and she would not be here either... but much valuable land will be destroyed if we allow them into Eordeland. Many lives would be lost, and they could bypass us to towns, even other cities. That foul beast damaged enough land as it is.'

'Mmm. And the training?'

'The men have begun to bring up the strength of all reserves. They are drilled constantly, each squad with an experienced leader, and we have the cavalry, engineer and ranged reserves at full strength. The full complement of Eordeland infantry are ready. But it is slow work, avoiding the notice of the Council at large. The City Guard and Welcomers at least are at full strength. They are always kept at defensive readiness.'

Ulric laughed shortly. 'The Council doesn't argue *that*.'

'Mm.'

'What do you think of Rast Tal'Orien?' asked Ulric.

'The men speak in awe of him; if the stories of his prowess are true, he is a man to be cautious of,' said Colcos. 'He has honour and is a sound strategist and tactician. I do not believe him prone to exaggeration. The opposite, if anything. We should not discount anything he says out of hand.'

'You mean like Eremus?' asked Ulric wryly.

Colcos snorted. 'Eremus!'

Joy Eremus was a problem. She did not believe that Meyar would expend the resources to attack an ally from a thousand miles away, especially one so much stronger. It was madness, she said, and therefore would not happen.

Power brought a certain type of blindness, reflected Ulric. None of them had dreamed that the Council would find itself hamstrung by a sneak vote from the Universalia Communia, certainly not after almost four months of preparation for an attack and a formal Council move to war footing.

Eremus had been given assurances from an envoy that Belen was hunted, and diplomacy would rule again. She was backed by enough of the Council that the Universalia Communia agreed to a vote, little realising the Council was divided. Whyll Regus had presented the vote to them, after using his influence with the news spreading city-wide. He had been persuasive. They had decided against moving to war, instead voting to resolve it via diplomacy and focus on the internal battles with mercenaries and orcs. It had been triumphantly presented as a fait accompli by Eremus even as Ulric prepared.

The fact that it may have offered good trade deals for her family's holdings was dismissed by the so-called Peace faction. The Council's advisory vote was meaningless. Ulric, Holmson, Brókova, the Adragostins, and Tarqas voted for war footing. Mira Lyss abstained as Advisor. The others voted diplomacy first, believing the threat was not significant enough. The Universalia Communia held firm.

Unless the Council moved to martial law, giving themselves direct control, there the matter would stay. There was a very real danger that they would not decide before the attackers lay before the gates of Darost.

Now they debated further over the word from Night, but Eremus still held great influence with the Universalia Communia. Until the debate resolved, they would try peace before even giving the impression they girded for war… orcs or no.

Ulric suppressed his anger and turned his thoughts back to the General-Marshall as he continued.

'In light of the pending attack, Captain-General Dorn and I will co-ordinate the main defence. Captain-General Jekob will concentrate on securing The Sanctum, putting it on full alert and locking down the walls and access. He will also be taking interim charge of the remaining Eordeland Guard in the city, both for defence of the walls and for internal policing. We may have to consider martial law and curfew.'

Ulric grunted and chewed his lip. 'If we do that the vote is meaningless. We must be careful, however. Eremus knows this.'

'Generals Vierce and Neider will secure the southern border at Taranor and the internal patrols of Eordeland respectively.'

'Do you think Jekob is up to the task?' asked Ulric. 'He is a good man, but he does not have Robertus's flair… or the same respect of his men.'

'Give him time,' said Colcos. 'This was thrust upon him. He has had a lot to cope with.'

'Time is limited,' said Ulric. 'He will either cope, or not. Let us pray he can. We have no one else. Gardenson would do well, but-'

'We need him where he is more.' Colcos shrugged. 'There is always the Castellan,' he added doubtfully. Castellan James quietly held a non-military rank of Captain in the Welcomer Guard, but he was not a warrior. 'Perhaps he can aid Jekob.'

Ulric was quiet for a while, lost in thought. Whichever way he split it, Eordeland was in trouble, financially and militarily. The cost of succouring thousands of survivors of the horror of Irilview was a drain on a city that was also frantically trying to repair damage to its walls and deal with an influx of Nighthaunt. It had taken half a year to deal with the crisis and spread the shock of it; the extra refugees had put a serious load on the administration, and they were still coming in – although that meant more had survived than initially feared and was a star in the dark night at least.

'I am worried, Dan,' eventually he said, quietly. 'We ignore the warnings. We are slow to respond. And without full Council support, I am limited. They do not believe Meyar will come, even after hearing the Seeker. And we must prepare for the orcs.'

Dannon Colcos raised an eyebrow.

'There are too many things at once. We should have been ready, but here we are, barely preparing half a year after we knew war was coming.'

Colcos nodded.

'It is the price of everyone having a voice, Ulric.'

'If we are attacked on two fronts by such numbers, we can't protect all the borders and towns. Many lives would be lost, along with harvest and land. Starvation, disease, slaughter; these are all real threats. Already we are struggling to maintain the economy here and rebuild, and all the while the merchants are shifting their money out of our clutches as if all the demons in the hells had come to collect. If the Banistari Empire decided to stretch their borders north at the wrong time, the veteran reserves at the eastern south border could not stop them.' He let his breath out. 'And there is this deeper problem… this growing unrest that Aldwyn Varelin spoke of.'

'I regret his demise,' said Colcos. 'He was a good man, and I never doubted his resolve.'

Ulric recalled his fright and cowardice, then felt a twinge of shame. In a way, Colcos was right. Aldwyn had not stopped his studies even in the midst of his terror; in fact, had conquered it and gone anyway, to the death he had so feared. That was more than any other Councillor had done.

'If Eordeland falls, it will be the start of a new dark age in Anaria. We must know how to avoid these things, and if not then how at least Eordeland can survive. Above all, we must keep the people safe. And the Combic Libraries. It is the vault of knowledge for the world of men.' His words echoed the clandestine meeting in the Tower.

'All the more tragic if the world of men causes its loss, then,' muttered Colcos.

Ulric shot him a glance. '*Ja,*' he rumbled, falling back on his Poviiri ancestry for a moment. 'So. Give me numbers.'

Dannon Colcos pulled out a freshly rolled scroll with figures, opening it out but not bothering to refer to it, instead handing it over. He knew its contents.

'Our best estimates say Meyar cannot be here in less than eight months from now. In six months, out of roughly thirty-three thousand soldiers in Eordeland including city guard and Welcomers, we could field maybe ten to fifteen thousand, not including supply trains. The rest are taken in patrols – especially of the southern borders to Banistari – defence of the cities and larger towns that are not evacuated, and defence of The Sanctum by the Welcomer Guard. And, of course, illness, and – potentially – desertion.'

Ulric's eyebrows rose.

Colcos shook his head. 'We have to face facts, Ulric. We have not seen war inside our borders for decades, and with orcs being a reality-' he shrugged. 'We cannot deplete Guard across the realm. I think attrition will be low. Still, the training prepares them well, and we have agents in every city drumming up patriotic fervour.' His smile was a brief ghost. 'This all assumes, of course, we gain full Council backing.'

'And what do we face? Come on.'

Colcos rubbed his eyes. 'Meyar can field upwards of forty thousand troops. Since they draft men and keep them in line with fear and punishment from all reports, on a similar basis I believe they can bring perhaps thirty-seven thousand to the field. It depends on how far they go with their Church and conscription, and how they keep them supplied. They might bring more if they emptied their cities of defenders. This is an attack born of desperation. I cannot understand why they would do it, but it could cripple us both.'

'Thirty-seven,' mused Ulric, chewing his lip and frowning. 'That is huge, logistically. Hasn't been an army that size moving in Anaria for hundreds of years. Still, they cannot beat us on even ground. Even with nearly twice the number.'

'Normally I would agree. Heavy drafting gives them ill-trained and lack-lustre troops, but they have an alarming number of Teromants marching with them. The Holy soldiers of Terome are different, Ulric. From what I have heard, they *are* well trained, and fanatics are always a problem. But even with them, we have a strong position.

'What worries me are these orcs. Should they attack our border – well, we know little of these creatures bar tales and legend. Are they trained? Are they disciplined? Even if they are not, if there are fifty thousand of them, even Darost may not be secure. Fifty *thousand!*' His eyebrow quirked. 'If they are working together – and I have no reason to disbelieve Tal'Orien – our realm is in great peril. We would have to respond, leaving our western border vulnerable.

'And then there are the Novinians. I doubt the King, or his Knight-Captains, will take the field; but how many of the individual mercenary Captains have been bought? I would guess Novin's normal strength at around fifteen thousand, not including their blasted Plains Walkers. Our spies indicate that less than four thousand have taken contract to Meyar, but that is still four thousand more, heavy cavalry as well.' He sighed and shook his head.

'So, we face up to forty thousand in the west and another fifty in the south which could be bastard *orcs*.'

Colcos nodded, his face stony.

Ulric's brow was furrowed. 'We must choose the field wisely.'

'We simply do not know enough, Ulric.'

'Gods damn it!' snarled Ulric in sudden anger. 'If we meet them on the plains or the lowlands, we would be surrounded and crushed. We gamble with our land, Dannon. We cannot let orcs past our borders. They would rape and pillage clear to Darost! We are already to the point of bursting with refugees.' He massaged his temples with thick, powerful fingers. The pepper and grey in his beard stood out in the candlelight, and his eyes screwed shut in fatigue for a moment from their habitual squint.

'So we meet them in the field or stay here and watch them crush our land, people, and wealth.' He looked up, his face grimmer than before. 'If they trap us in Darost… we will be easy prey for others even if we win. That many could cut us off and attack the rest of Eordeland. We no longer have Irilview to protect the south. I do not know if she will ever be rebuilt. And they have as much time as we to conscript and throw a large army at us, build a supply line. That many men cannot move through wilderness without careful planning. I think you are right about the mercenary attacks before that.' He came to a decision. 'I will send south and west to prepare.'

'You could be removed. Even tried as a traitor,' pointed out the General.

'*I do not care!*' Ulric nearly bellowed. 'I will keep this land safe, *whatever* the cost!'

Colcos held up his hands in a placatory fashion. Ulric glared at him for a few moments, eyes squinting in his customary appraisal.

'What allies can we count on?' asked Colcos clasping his hands behind his back.

Ulric shrugged heavily, calming.

'Truthfully? Few. There are tales of internal troubles in nearly every land, not just ours. Orcs harry every human realm constantly. Tal'Orien spoke of fifty thousand in the Dimnesdair, but there have been reports from every land of large numbers gathering. They strike at outposts and homesteads, as they still do here in the northeast. The whole of Anaria is under threat.

'I'm waiting for the return of our emissary from Banistari, but I hold few hopes there. We will be lucky if they don't try to catch us with our arses out and annex half of Sudland. Morland at least has promised a few hundred healers.'

Colcos grunted. He would use any weapon given him, but he strongly disapproved of assassins and poison. Morland healers were highly trained, and some were as adept at killing as they were at curing.

'Anyone else?'

'We sought contracts of our own with Novinian mercenary Captains. None are free for months, and the King does not care. Our envoy was bodily thrown from the court. We hoped to persuade them to withdraw their support for Meyar; he was lucky to escape with his life.'

Ulric shook his shaggy head. The Novinians were strange. They prized coin for combat above all else, with even their lunatic King getting involved occasionally. It wasn't unheard of for the captains to end up fighting each other on two sides of the same battle. They didn't care, as long as they fought well and got paid, and it was all done in accordance with their Accords of War. They were skilled mounted fighters, and also had the Plains Walkers, elite ambush shock troops specialising in plains concealment and anti-cavalry manoeuvres as well as close combat.

Colcos continued the depressive litany.

'Eyotsburg is all but entrenched from the north. At the worst possible time, they have asked *us* for aid. We are honour-bound to acknowledge their plea; Eyotsburg is nigh-impregnable, but there are still points on either side of the estuary where their ships are in danger of siege engines, and their Navy is their strength. We cannot say if Meyar will lay siege to the island-city. I cannot see if they would risk it, for all it would lose us a powerful and well-situated ally. If Meyar *do* march on us, the Eyots will stab at them, given half a chance. They loathe Meyar.'

Ulric pondered. 'We could send a company of veterans to honour the alliance, though we can ill-afford them. Even Eremus must agree to that. I plan to use this to our advantage.' He tapped his hand's fingertips on the table as if holding an upturned invisible cup to make his points. 'I will propose a veteran company under a seasoned Lieutenant, or a Captain. Maybe even a regimental commander.'

'A Major?' queried Colcos. 'Is that wise, Ulric?' His tone was doubtful. Even a Captain was calculated risk with such a small company. To lose a Major, one of only sixteen regimental commanders, would be dire to morale and defence.

'I don't know,' said Ulric bluntly. 'Maybe not. But it would show beyond doubt we are still serious in our accord with them, and he may be able to offer strategy and diplomacy where a Captain could not. And, more importantly for us, he will be able to accurately judge whether an attack from Meyar is likely. His testimony would be taken by the whole Council as fact and would heavily weight a re-vote to step up to a war footing.'

'Yes,' said Colcos thoughtfully. 'The risk is worth taking, I think. I wish we had considered this before. Our priority is strengthening fully in case of attack, and we can only do that with full acquiescence from the Council. We are under-strength for a direct assault from anyone. The numbers of internal patrols alone have forced us to use village-level militia.'

'We must wait for the right moment to propose it. Or do it without telling the Council.'

'Don't wait too long, Ulric.'

'Ignat will not fight alongside Novinians, and disdain all alliances,' continued Ulric wearily, acknowledging Colcos's words with a wave of a huge hand. 'The good news is we should hear any day now from the elves of the Leohtsholt.' He hoped, anyway; the little-known and almost mythical elves were wise and agile fighters with decades more experience in combat. They were strange, seeming to almost talk to creatures and, with senses and reflexes men could not equal, were deadly in battle. There were far fewer of them, however, and they tended not to involve themselves in what they saw as petty human affairs.

Colcos shook his head. 'What of the dwarves?'

'No word. Every trade delegation we have sent for a year has been turned away, and in the last few months they have stopped even speaking to us. Deep Delving might as well be a solid, deserted mountain. No patrols meet us, and the gates remain locked. '

It was puzzling. The dwarves relied on trade. Eordeland was their primary human trading partner, and a close ally. They were some of the most dangerous close fighters in the world, stronger than most men and with great stamina, although not as powerful as the plains orks. What they lacked in brute force they made up for with weapons and armour unmatched by any forged elsewhere, and formation fighting with far greater cohesion than human armies. The brusque dismissal of trade and the ignorance of aid was deeply worrying.

'Did you ask the orks, or the Barbarians?' asked Colcos with little hope. The Barbarians of the Sergoth plains were aloof and nomadic, as likely to ignore or attack than greet, and the orks were not trusted. There had been many skirmishes between them and men, and they were fierce and independent.

Ulric shook his head.

'No, nothing formal. We sent word, but the Barbarians are unlikely to reply, and the orks have little use for humans.' He blew out a breath, trying to ignore the feeling of impending doom. 'Eordeland largely stands alone.'

Colcos made a moue with his lips.

'So we may, with great luck and allies from other realms, be able to field twenty thousand in six months if we drive now. Less than a quarter of the enemy we could face.' He unrolled a map of Anaria, placing weights at the corners to stop it furling, and indicated the land between the Eastern Arkon foothills and the western border of Eordeland.

'I anticipate a possible two-pronged attack, the larger from the northern route around the Arkons. The Novinians will have to attack from the south. I believe our best option will be to force them into attacking us here, in the eastern Arkon foothills.' He swept his hand left into their fringes. 'Aside from the enemy on the plains, if the orcs sweep up from the Iril Eneth they could be a serious threat if we were too far around the northern Arkons to stem the army there. Neither force can leave a better armed and trained army hitting them from behind as they lay siege.' His hands gestured as if to describe the attacks. 'They must know that if we catch them against our walls, it will be a massacre, despite their advantage in numbers. If they hit us together-'

Colcos rubbed his temples and blew out his lips. He looked tired.

'I tell you, Ulric... I have made my living – and won many battles – by always being able to anticipate what the enemy is thinking, what their options are and how to counter them, but this time... this time, old friend, I just don't know enough. Meyar cannot hold this far from their borders. If it were just an army of normal men, I could understand what drives them, but we also face fanatics, and perhaps even these orcs. I fear that we may be pressed back to our cities, and if that happens it will be a slow death by attrition and the razing of our fair green land. We would be vulnerable to any other attacks.' His eyes glittered as he spoke what they both knew.

'These armies do not come to conquer Eordeland. They come to destroy her.'

TEN

'Come on, Xhera,' called Karland. It was Endwice, the eighth and last weekday usually spent at rest by all students, often away from The Sanctum. Midwice - the mid-week rest day - was spent on their own study and rest in the grounds. Although he loved the vast University, and they regularly visited the gates and main market, there was still a huge amount of the city he hadn't ever seen. There were parts he had been strictly told to avoid; for all its seeming enlightenment, Darost was a large, old city, and the older, poorer parts could be very dangerous, especially the docks.

The Sanctum was a city within a city. The twelve-segmented dome was huge, around two thousand feet across, and held almost everything required for students and Scholars. Because the Cunae were aligned to the compass they were often unofficially referred to clockwise as a number, with twelve to the north.

Apart from the food halls there were a few registered shops, huge dormitories, halls, auditoriums, courts, and other quarters and stores. There were many passages off the inner and outer ringways, and each Cuneus held a soaring Atrium with a fountain along the inner ringway. Between each segment was a passage from the Central Gardens out, with long-unused barriers at the outer rim to seal the dome off in case of attack; grooves ran down each wall between ten of then, with fifty feet of metal-woven interlocking slabs of man-made rock held above like a roof by huge pins, and the two main routes to the city held thick counterbalanced ironwood gates that could roll across on rails.

It was capable of easily housing more than twenty thousand people, excluding Welcomer Guard and staff, although there were far less. It wasn't just the University; it was also the seat of Government, with all of the civil servants supporting them, and barracks for the nearly five thousand Welcomer Guard.

Alongside the twelve central gardens, fantastic in their diversity and carefully tended by the Academia Botanica, there were surrounding parks and trees along the perimeter that could offer privacy and wilderness. It was spoiled somewhat by the hubbub of the city not far beyond the grounds of The Sanctum, which had its own deep moats and high walls, and by the Academia Cuneus Towers which loomed above the trees. Karland still found the towers incredible. Each one had hints of unique architecture at the summit supposedly in the styles of different realms.

The gardens, however, gave only an illusion of freedom. The presence of guards was felt if not seen, and high walls patrolled by more hid beyond the artfully grown trees. Here and there were other signs that this was a citadel in its own right, and well defended.

Occasionally Karland felt the need to get out into the city at large. He and Xhera spent more of their free days catching up and doing extra work than he liked to think - the formal addition of the studies of Alwyn's work and the training with Rast left them few long stretches of time for leisure.

Although he and Xhera had been minor celebrities just after the attack of the demon and the dragons, most of the people who had seen them had been guards. When people did treat him as special because of it, it felt uncomfortable. Wrong. To people in the city, it was association with notoriety. To Karland, it was glorifying the deaths of his friends.

Besides, he thought, popularity was not the same as notoriety. Thankfully it had lessened quickly once people realised here was no gain from it.

He was eager to explore the fullness of the city more, perhaps even crossing to the northern bank. In all the time they had been in Darost, they had not yet visited the Mercantile and Banking district. To his knowledge, it was the only city in Anaria to have such a district, and it represented the monetary and trade power of Anaria in many ways.

Darost had been built in an interesting fashion. When it had been founded as capital of the realm, a fort had been constructed. The Tower of Jehennah had originally been twinned as part of a huge castle, the seat of the last King. The grounds had held woodland, game, and a powerful spring. Unbeknownst to the populace, it also hid a deep, vast system of caverns, some flooded. Now the old walls were part of other structures, the castle was gone, and the Tower of the old ruins stood alone, its twin torn down. As the line of kings had died out, The Sanctum had been built over the spring and the deep caverns the other end of the grounds from the Tower.

Around this new centre the city had grown up and expanded outwards in waves. If you knew where to look, you could see where the architecture had changed in uneven rings, old defensive structures left like tidemarks or absorbed into new buildings. As power had moved away from nobility, the divides and the once-segregated sections in the city had shifted and merged somewhat. It hadn't been until the rise of the Eordeland Merchant Gentlemen that a second part of the city had been built on the northern banks of the river, but the oldest areas lay upon the southern bank. Some parts of Darost were still slowly crumbling into oblivion after a thousand years and more.

They walked out of the Gate of Crowns, the main gate into and out of The Sanctum, waving to the guards on duty, and walked west into the mercantile district which surrounded the main Square. Along the side of this was a veritable warren of smaller squares and stalls in the narrow avenues of the City Market. This was their target for the morning. In the afternoon, Karland fully intended on following his plan of crossing the river north for the first time.

...subject to Xhera, of course.

He had experienced what she liked to call shopping before. It mostly consisted of moving at breakneck speed between stalls until wares caught her eye - seemingly at random - at which point he would watch her browse for hours, usually suffering in silence. Thankfully that was as far as it went; she was still a farmer's daughter, and although she appreciated it when he offered to carry things or was courteous, she also chided him readily if she thought he was considering her 'just a girl'. Her slight build was packed with more muscle than the city girls, although she still exuded a delicate air, and the training with Rast had only added to her athletic figure. She was more than capable of carrying them herself, and she didn't expect things bought for her, or even wish for expensive wares. She was far better pleased with a good deal.

As always, they both detoured as they entered the great square to pass before the gigantic statue of Györnàeldàr that had been erected here. It wasn't quite life size, although it was still almost two hundred feet long and took up quite enough room in the open space. It didn't quite look like her to Karland, who had known her so well, but it had enough similarity that it always brought her back to mind. The statue held the quality of being alive, somehow.

The sculptor, Myrl Bloch, was very talented, and had sat for long hours talking to Rast, Karland and Xhera in an attempt to make the sculpture as close as possible to reality, making sketches and asking for feedback on them. He was a very serious young man who lived somewhere in the Academia Artem and spent most of his time fulfilling contracts around the city. Owning a Bloch sculpture was both costly and considered a symbol of status, especially as he often refused commissions. Not only money could buy them.

He had portrayed her in the pose where she had just called both a challenge and a cry for help to summon her kin to combat Yosgaloth. Bloch had managed to also imbue a sense of fear into the proud features, and somehow a feeling that she had also just breathed a huge line of flame. The effect was convincing enough that people often avoided walking directly in front of the statue.

She hadn't breathed flame then, of course. It had been sound, but beyond human forbearance, both mental and physical. Karland would never forget that cry.

Underneath a large plaque read,

The Call of the Serpent Györnàeldàr
Saviour of our City and friend to our People

As he always did, he stepped over the boundary rope with a nod to the guard and laid a hand on the huge snout, feeling her loss. The stone was warm, almost as if it held a memory of her. Karland remembered Körànthír's words, that her spirit still dwelled on Kuln, and could almost believe it was here, in this statue. The Guards keeping watch on the market left him alone; they knew who he was. They watched for others, who were more likely to carve their names into the lovely work.

No matter how enlightened the society, some people never changed.

As he followed Xhera through the cacophony Karland kept his eyes peeled for pickpockets. There weren't many here - there were too many guards - but it wasn't unknown. There were cheaper stalls and more… interesting wares in the older parts of the city, but the cutpurses increased dramatically in number too. It was safest to browse here.

His thoughts drifted to what he wanted for himself. He'd had his eye on a large black quill for some time from a stall that did brisk trade providing to scholars. The ones in The Sanctum were perfectly fine, of course, but they were typical scholar's quills - fully stripped of barbs and mostly white or grey goose feathers. This quill was almost eight inches long, and - so the shopkeeper had assured him - from the wing of an Ignathian raven, long known as the smartest of birds. Karland had tried not to roll his eyes at this. He wanted that quill, though. It had barbs on both sides that were gracefully cut in a curve above the hand, and the shaft was neither too thick nor too thin. Bound in silver at the bottom and with a finely crafted steel nib, it sat well in the hand. If he was to continue his studies, he had decided resolutely that this was his tool for it.

Xhera had shaken her head over it. She didn't care what she wrote with, as long as it worked.

If it was up to Karland, he would have made a beeline for the stall, bought the quill - perhaps his own matching quill knife, should he have enough left for it - and then spent the rest of the day exploring city streets. It wasn't up to him today, and sigh though he might, he couldn't deplore a day spent in the company of his best friend.

It worried him, sometimes. Perhaps she would grow bored of him with so much time together. Perhaps she would never find that spark he hoped she might if they grew too familiar.

Perhaps she wouldn't find it if they weren't familiar *enough*.

The dichotomy infuriated him, made him nervous. She had clearly caught the interest of other boys, some of them less than desirable.

Well… all of them were *undesirable*, of course.

His thoughts flashed to Aran for a second.

He felt a tingle whenever he was near her. For him, there was another dimension to their friendship.

Agony in some ways though it might be, he treasured his days with her. With their experiences together he had thankfully never developed the lovesickness he usually acquired with girls. For the first time, here was someone he didn't need to try to impress. From the beginning they had connected completely and equally. She knew he would die for her, and she for him. It was a little unnerving, in a way.

He almost didn't know what to do about not having to worry about what to do.

On the flip side of that, of course, he didn't know what to do about the *rest*. He felt that he was on the brink of being able to topple into something more but had no clue how.

What if he asked her and she said no?

What if the asking changed their friendship?

What if she said yes?

Shaking his head, he glanced at her as she moved amongst the stalls. Sometimes his heart hammered to look at her.

As if she felt his gaze, Xhera lifted her head and her serious little face broke into the smile she had just for him before she continued poring over whatever she had found.

I will not fail you again, he thought again fervently. *Whatever it takes.*

His vow had, to his surprise, remained strong. He had promised himself many things in his life; done many things that had, at the time, produced powerful emotions and thoughts. He had once thought that promises based on those things would last for all time. He had been wrong, as most were who believed their emotions set things in stone, especially as children.

Time bled colour from emotion. Distance and experience removed urgency, anger, belief in some cases. He had decided that humans simply didn't have the energy to sustain decisions like that.

That had been before something worth sustaining had come along. Now, he couldn't imagine his life without that promise.

She could look after herself, but he would always be there for her, nevertheless.

Idly considering things, he realised that his tongue was pressed against his front teeth, and he was creating a vacuum in his mouth which was starting to ache his cheeks. Half-yawning, he looked around. His attention was caught by a flamboyantly dressed man, not an Eordelander from the look of him. He was dressed in noble attire, a little different from the luxury of the richer merchants - a little more formal, perhaps. He had a well-wrought sword on his right hip, marking him a westhander, intricately wired shut and wax-sealed.

When they had first come to Darost, Karland had been too full of the sights of the almost surreally huge walls and the throng of people to notice much detail, passing through the gates after an almost cursory check for arms. Rast didn't need any, and the scholar and Karland had had nothing past a basic utility knife between them.

The second time they returned, of course, they'd bypassed the gate by several hundred feet vertically.

Now he was used to the commonplace sight of bound weapons, or men who walked a certain way clearly missing a weighted scabbard at their hip.

Under Darost law, any large weapons or blades longer than ten inches as measured against the knotted string all the City Guard had on them were either taken and stored on entry to the city, or bound shut with wire and wax and sealed. Any unreported breaking of that seal resulted in immediate imprisonment, loss of the weapon, and a heavy fine, and City Guards were entitled to check anyone's seal at random.

The Sanctum was even stricter. Knives were completely forbidden, apart from utility knives with two-inch blades or less for eating and basic study.

Karland wondered idly why Rast was allowed to keep his *shirka*.

Supposedly, the only bearers of serious arms in the city were the City Guard and Welcomer Guard. They carried steel shortswords and solid extendable steel batons which formed effective close-quarters maces. There were units that also had hand crossbows and swordbreakers. Bows were no longer required practice for the entire populace - the requirement had fallen out of use several hundred years ago - but the composite wood Eordeland Recurves were less suited to the streets of a city than the city hand-crossbows, which were fired in a practised pattern in each unit to minimise re-cocking times. Full crossbows were usually only for battle.

Crossbow squads were known half-derisively as 'shortshafts', but it was a brave man who said that to the face of a guard bearing one. Respect for the law was enforced with little humour by the experienced soldiers rotated in from the army.

It had worked very well for nearly two hundred years. Eordeland needed its army to be kept in active condition but fought few major wars; their armies were so well trained and advanced in both tactics and equipment that they were more of a deterrent. There were always the usual manoeuvres and border skirmishes, or action against bandits - especially in recent years after the attempted penetration by Meyar - and there were now battles with orcs, but that wasn't enough to keep them all sharp, so entire companies would rotate into City Guard duty across the country from the garrisons. No matter how lawful and ordered a city, guards always found plenty to deal with.

Different rules applied, of course. Karland had heard guards referring to the difference between being 'on the job' and 'in unit '. One advantage of this from what Rast had told him was that the soldiers kept a healthy relationship with normal people, more or less. In many dedicated armies they could become segregated too easily, losing touch and having problems with violence and disassociation. By and large squads rotated out every six months.

One thing he found interesting was the interaction between City Guard and Welcomer Guard. It had been obvious when he had first arrived that Dorn and Robertus had a good friendship. Karland wasn't as sure about Captain Jekob; he was quite reserved and had little humour, though he was very efficient. Karland missed the easy friendship of Kel Robertus, whom he had liked so much but known only such a short time.

As always, he felt a pang at the loss of the smiling fair-haired man. He had visited his grave more than once; The Sanctum grounds held a graveyard for dignitaries and officers away from the crowded city cemetery. It was a singular honour to be laid to rest there; in time, Robertus's bones would be laid with reverence in a consecrated part of the catacombs that the Combic Libraries lay within.

Karland's thoughts turned to the vitriol he had heard in the city. Meyari looked similar to Eordelanders and spoke in a similar fashion, which made it a little harder for people to rail against them as there were fewer obvious differences. Yet the Cathedral of Terome had been vandalised, and people had been hurt, even killed. Karland had never seen anyone here worshipping Terome hurt anyone else. Most of them seemed to be very quiet people, quite pious for the most part.

But Meyar was the nation of Terome, and although the local Churches denounced the war, it could not be denied that the enemy country was also under its control.

There had been no trouble for a few weeks, though, and the day was bright and clear.

After thirty minutes, Karland had seen everything and was still following Xhera around. They had floated from stall to stall in the marketplace, where many unusual or interesting items could be found, and currently were in the middle of one selling different types of clothes that were piled high at random. Finally, he sighed.

'Are you actually going to *buy* anything?' he asked. Xhera picked up a laced blouse and shook it out calmly, judging the fit, and then draped it over her left arm and rummaged through a few more.

'I'm looking,' she said after a minute.

'You've been *looking* for more than an hour.'

'I haven't found what I want. Anyway, it's nice to just look,' she replied. She switched to another pile, pawing through clothes, then stopped, looking thoughtful. She hefted the laced top again and then muttered, 'Never mind,' dropping it on another pile. Karland rolled his eyes and caught sight of the stall owner, who winked at him and went back to watching the various shoppers carefully.

'I don't know why you go out to look at things and never buy them. I find what I want quickly and then get on with more important things.'

Xhera cast a sharp glance at him. 'Like what?'

'Never mind.' He looked over at a low wall nearby. 'I'll be over there when you're done. If we want to go to the North Bank today, you'd better hurry up.' He felt a little aggrieved; she *knew* he had been planning on going to the Hoard.

Xhera muttered and dived back into the clothing.

Karland sat on the cool stone, blinking in the sunlight. It wasn't that warm, and where the sun touched him, it was welcome. He looked off northwest to a few of the spires of cathedrals and temples, some of which rivalled the Dodecagon in height.

Darost was a heaving mass of people at the best of times. The City Market was buzzing under the watchful eyes of many guards. There were more at the Coin Exchange on the north bank, less in the dockside markets in the poorer sectors where the items were often less costly and a lot less legal, with the risks all that brought.

There were three safe sections of the docks where the great barges moved people and goods between the southern and northern docks of the city. The northern bank was connected to the south bank by a beautiful bridge spanning the entire river. A pinnacle of Eordeland engineering, it was a mixture of huge footings and tall pylons which leaned inwards from each shore, sending thick struts down to crisscross in the middle, each holding the centre up. The suspended bridge was wide enough for many people moving abreast and stretched at the highest point nearly a hundred feet above the waters below. It was the gateway to the banking district and the homes of the extremely rich. Eordeland, Darost in particular, had proudly taken on the mantle of 'friends of Dragons'. Some wits had begun referring to the northern bank as the Hoard. The name had stuck.

The Hoard was the economic centre of much of the continent. Eordeland had the most stable economy and taxes of any of the realms; anyone was welcome to have money, even excessively, but taxes were set accordingly. They had learned about the Great Decline where the rich had evaded ways to pay and even accrued more than allowed - causing soaring prices, starvation and homelessness, widespread rioting and a great divide from the few percent that owned most of the money. The laws had been quickly changed and strictly enforced, and the nobility had - supposedly - waned into irrelevance.

As often happened, Karland's drifting mind recalled facts in the semi-distracted tones of his lost friend.

In fact, it is interesting to note that it was here in Darost where the common practice of surnames on assumption of majority was first, mm, established, which was something many other realms tend to simplify as where people came from, or from trades. Many unique surnames in a populace however allow easier records and enforcement of a, ha, general tax for everyone over sixteen who earns. It is fairly handled for the most part, not that anyone will admit that... no system, though, is, ah, perfect. And one must have something to complain about, mm?

Karland had just over a year left before he, too, joined those august ranks. Adulthood.

Taxes. He blew his cheeks out at the thought.

Things had changed after the Decline. The Sanctum as a body owned many areas of south Darost, making the assets the rich could buy fewer, and there was a generous cap on personally held wealth set for everyone who wished to be counted as a resident of a city with all the associated benefits. The excess to this flowed back into the upkeep of the cities and infrastructure, and by and large this worked; Darost was - for a very old city - moderately clean and well kept. Although they constantly complained about taxes and laws, the residents knew full well for the most part they were privileged. There were no serfs or slaves in Eordeland. Not legally, anyway.

Even the criminal guilds in the cities were taxed. Karland had avidly read exciting stories from nearly six decades ago when there had been almost full-scale war between the City Guard and the various thieves and cut-throat gangs in Darost, Kingsport and Tamismuth. After riots, death and damage to many of the poorer areas, the Council had announced that unless the gangs curtailed activities and contributed to their cities, they would see a great purge to remove them all, city by city, sewer by sewer, using the full army and every reserve to do so.

The criminal gangs had come up with a compromise. They had formed one guild with what they called the Council of Shadows, comprised of the heads of all the major criminal organisations in each city, and elected to its head someone known only as the Shadow Scholar who ensured the guild kept within certain guidelines, and negotiated taxes relative to the value of reported crimes. This did not absolve criminals if they were caught, but it did ensure an uneasy truce between the sides.

The secretive Shadow Scholar had changed three times in the last two decades. It was a role many in the guild would be reluctant to take on. One at least had been assassinated.

Karland had quickly found that the more interesting areas of the city were often not to be travelled lightly. The Merchant district was fine, as was The Sanctum and its surrounds, of course, and the main thoroughfares and the Hoard and the surrounding manses were safely patrolled, but Darost had begun, as many cities did, as a settlement on a river, and some of the oldest areas were also the most dangerous.

Apart from a few areas, there was little segregation of rich, poor and in-between, although they tended to accumulate in neighbourhoods. He had always assumed from stories that cities were neatly divided into quarters, or sections, housing rich, poor, religious, traders, and so on, but Aldwyn had rudely disabused him of that notion. Karland smiled to himself, remembering his friend's avid descriptions of the city he loved. Aldwyn had been right, of course. In a city of more than half a million, there were areas with slums and shanties, and areas that only the well-to-do set foot in, but there were mostly just streets. Here, the drudges rubbed noses with the middle class sometimes in the same street, and they were interspersed with pockets of the destitute. The vicious and semi-criminal kept more to themselves in their own streets and the docks of the city. The Churches and temples were spread throughout, seemingly at random, although they tended toward the western side.

The upper classes deigned to brush shoulders with the middle classes at best. Few of the latter could afford the limited living space and high costs north of the river. Darost was not a city where money dictated everything, but despite having no nobility now there was a definite divide in the form of the river and its trade.

Darost's wealth flows through the city, went the saying.

Its shit drifts south, went another.

Karland had been fascinated with the rich history of Darost. It was like a mixture of an intricate clockwork mechanism and a heart, pumping trade. He still couldn't comprehend the sheer number of people in the city. As often happened when he thought about it, the overwhelming melancholy of *sonder* rushed through him, dissociative and pinprick-cold.

Something caught his attention and brought him back from the mental pit of thought he was once again carefully picking his way around.

Looking around for what had snagged his thoughts, his eye caught sight of a Welcomer Guard he knew from The Sanctum - Jonas, the man who had denied them entry with Aldwyn. It appeared to be his day off. He was talking seriously to one of the market guards, both of them peering around from professional habit.

Glancing back to Xhera, he could see her serious little face as she queried the stall owner, who had clearly realised this was no casual shopper. He jumped down from the wall and made his way over, catching something about some trouble at the Greatway West Gate. He waited for an opportune moment to speak, not wanting to appear rude.

'Morning, Master Dresin,' Jonas said with a nod, noticing him there. Since that first meeting, he had been unfailingly polite and friendly. Despite the dressing down, he had respected Robertus greatly, as all of the Welcomers had, and he knew Karland had been before the Council.

'Good morning,' replied Karland. 'I didn't mean to interrupt.'

'No interruption. Just some odd trouble,' Jonas smiled.

'Trouble?'

'Nothing major,' responded the City Guard guard on duty in clipped tones. He was not trying to be rude, but his attention was only half on the conversation. 'Some plains savage is stuck at the West Gate having an argument. Tried to bring a bloody great axe through, then argued when he was told he had to leave it. Said it was sacred and he wasn't to be parted from it, as if that made a difference.' He snorted. 'Sarge said word would go to The Sanctum, but no harm in making him wait a bit.'

'Rules are *quite* clear,' sniffed Jonas. Karland bit his tongue, remembering all too well how much the man loved adhering to the letter of the law.

'Even a bloody great green bastard should be able to work that one out,' the other guard agreed with a short laugh.

'Wait - an ork?' Karland blinked in surprise. He only knew one ork fitting that description, and his heart thumped hard.

That's not possible.

'Did you catch his name?'

'Not a bloody clue, lad. Grungo Bungo or something probably with these greenies.' He grinned, then stopped at the look on Karland's face.

'Rast Tal'Orien and I faced a company of foes with an ork. He killed an ogre and a gar-wolf to protect us,' said Karland coldly, his face heating. The casual denigration had triggered a flash of anger against a surge of hope that was painful. 'He gave his *life* for us. They are *people*. With *names*.'

'All right, lad, all right,' said the guard sharply, looking annoyed. Jonas shifted a little uncomfortably. 'They just ain't the same as us, that's all. No disrespect meant, I'm sure, but you can't tell me they ain't different.'

Karland gritted his teeth. He might be a guest in The Sanctum, and be given some respect as a Dragonfriend, but very few knew what their group had done. He was still only a guest. Rudeness to a guard might have unpleasant repercussions, and certainly would entail serious words with Rast or Dorn. Probably both.

'Maybe I'll go and see.' He moved away, all thoughts of the north bank forgotten.

'Maybe you should,' the guard called after him in unfriendly tones. Jonas said a few words Karland didn't catch which seemed to mollify the man. He seethed for a few seconds; Karland loathed unfairness, but the prospect of an ork distracted him.

He moved into the stall and tapped Xhera's arm. She glared at him; she had finished browsing the stall, but apparently decided it needed a second pass.

'Not now, Xhera. We need to go.'

'What?' She looked outraged. 'Look, you don't bring someone out shopping and then *interrupt-*'

'There is an ork at the West Gate,' he interrupted. Any other time he would have found her temper irksome, but not now. Surprise replaced annoyance on her face. 'The guard said there was an argument over the bound-weapon laws.'

Xhera dumped her clothes in a pile in the nearest free space. 'Oh! Karland, we have to go and see. I can well imagine an ork objecting to city limits.'

'That's what I-' He shook his head. 'Never mind.' He sighed again, the sound echoed by the stall keeper who picked up the crumpled clothes with a scowl and began to fold them.

'Sorry!' Xhera called back to the man as they left. He shook his head, but the scowl lessened.

Karland's sigh had been for something else entirely. He was, he thought ruefully, very unlikely to get to the Hoard today after all, especially if their suspicions were correct.

He shrugged. The Hoard was all very well and good, but orks were *interesting*.

ELEVEN

The main thoroughfare led straight to the West gate. Not much more than a mile and a half later they arrived, a little breathless.

Off to one side at the checking station there was a slight commotion. Karland caught sight of a group of guards. If you entered Darost with an obvious weapon - or if the guards suspected you might have one illegally concealed - you were politely directed over to the station, and there you stayed until they were satisfied you were clean - up to and including being stripped and searched if you made their lives difficult enough.

Very few did not understand the clear requirements for entering Darost, but Karland had never heard of an ork in the city either. Given their culture, being parted from their weapon was like an insult, and it wasn't as if it would prevent someone getting hurt if one lost their temper. He remembered Grukust in Punslon, and the uproar that had them chased by an angry mob.

There were Guards in a ring, all facing inwards. Through the crowd he saw a familiar back, the Dwarven axe rising up off it as of old. Karland went cold, a shiver of disbelief running up his spine.

The huge frame towered over those around it. The long black hair, pulled back at the top and loose lower down, fell between powerful shoulder blades as the head was bent down slightly towards a tall guardsman speaking patiently. Karland felt as if he had been punched in the gut.

He turned to Xhera. Her face mirrored how he felt, white as washed linen and eyes staring in shock.

'It can't be,' she whispered, barely heard over the hubbub.

Karland stared at the huge ork. He had seen Grukust go over the side of a mountain. His arm had been almost torn off, hanging from threads of tendons, hot red blood pumping, yet the skin was unblemished. How could he be here, alive?

He shivered, wondering if he were dreaming.

After a moment Xhera's lip trembled, and she blinked as if clearing her eyes. She sniffed and pinched the bridge of her nose almost like Aldwyn used to, but to wipe moisture from her vision, not in thought. With a shaky laugh, she nudged Karland.

'He truly does look like his brother,' she said, her voice a little shaky. The words sank in slowly, and then Karland recalled that they had given their friend's axe to his kin.

This ork had a ranginess about him that wasn't quite the bulk Grukust had owned; hugely muscled, but slightly leaner than Grukust. The face turned to them, perhaps sensing eyes on him, and although it resembled Grukust's, Karland could see that it was not his face. As his heart slowed its hammering and his eyes saw what was really there, he realised that although this ork was nearly of a height with Grukust, he was younger, with fewer scars on his face or chest.

It was Darus.

He stared at them for a moment, and then pointed to them and spoke to the guard. Other guards were checking weapons around them, and more stood watching the ork warily. It was obvious that the axe was his only weapon; in typical ork-fashion, Darus wasn't wearing much past a *rinok*-skin loincloth, with a wide leather baldric for the axe over his right shoulder similar to the one Grukust had worn, and a familiar-looking shoulder-slung pack.

Karland grabbed Xhera's hand and approached, wondering what to say. He noticed the guard was a Lieutenant, and the weapon remained unbound. Darus was very obviously in front of the checkpoint, and this discussion was about his axe.

'Darus,' Xhera said, bowing. Karland felt clumsy in comparison, but he banged his fist against his chest in what felt a laughable attempt to salute the green giant.

A broad grin broke over the ork's face, and he spoke, his Darum excellent.

'Greetings, friends to my brother! I am fortunate to see you here. *Kap*-bearer Karland. Xhera fair-skin. I had hoped to find you in this city, or Rast Tal'Orien; I feared that I had missed you. I had not thought how many humans might live here.' He looked around. 'I bring word from the Over-Chieftain, my uncle.' He banged his chest gently with his fist, and then glowered slightly at the Lieutenant. 'I am denied entry, however.'

'As I explained… sir, you must lodge the axe with us in secure storage until your business is done,' cut in the lieutenant. He looked tired and frustrated. 'I appreciate you are an envoy of your people, but you are carrying an axe the size of this lad on your back. Look around you. A city is not the plains.'

'You do not understand what you ask,' rumbled Darus.

'You are here to speak with Rast Tal'Orien?' said Karland. Darus nodded. 'And the Council, I would think. I am sure they would let you pass. Can we send word?'

'Karland,' Xhera said in warning. He grimaced to himself, knowing she was right; he could get into a lot of trouble speaking for them like this.

'The problem is lad, we can't seal an axe this big to a sheath, and he won't let us take it away. Either we store it, or he doesn't pass this point.' The lieutenant had lost some of his frustrated demeanour when Rast and the Council had been mentioned, and he seemed to recognise Karland, but was still adamant. 'If you ain't a diplomat on my list of entry, you're bound by common law, and even *they* get sealed. It's even stricter since Meyar made a mockery of our treaty. Far as I know - which is a fair bit - orks ain't covered under it anyway.' He shrugged.

Darus rolled his big shoulders, sighing. 'I understand, human, but this is the axe of my brother, the Champion of the Tribes. It is not a mere weapon. It is my legacy, legend to our people. I cannot just… give it to those I do not know. It is like handing you my brother's soul.'

'What if we could guarantee him?' asked Karland. 'We can go with him to The Sanctum.'

The guard shook his head regretfully.

'Sorry, young'un. More'n my job is worth. Literally.'

'Darus, what if we can guarantee you will have it returned?' asked Xhera.

'I told him he gets a chit for it,' said the guard. 'Didn't think that enough. What he thinks anyone else's gonna do with an axe that big is anyone's guess.'

'What if Captain Dorn or Rast vouched for him?' asked Karland, ignoring Xhera's warning motion.

The guard shrugged.

'If Captain-*General* Dorn took responsibility, I'd abide by it. Master Tal'Orien, on the other hand, has no legal standing here, however much I respect his skill. He's under the same obligations, matter of fact.'

Not entirely *true,* thought Karland.

'Not that it makes a real difference,' added another Guard. 'He don't exactly need a sword.'

'Have you *sent* to Captain-General Dorn? Or the Council? Lieutenant…?' enquired Xhera quietly. The guard shook his head.

'Pridall, miss. He just said he was here to see Master Tal'Orien and the Council. To be blunt, half the people passing this gate are here to see the Council, lass, and I already spent more than enough time on this.'

'But he is here as the envoy of his people - the united tribes of the Plains. Surely that's the same as a diplomat from another realm?'

Lieutenant Pridall frowned. 'Maybe,' he admitted. 'But that ain't the same. First ork I ever saw in the city. Must say, he's pretty well spoken for a tribesman.'

Xhera turned her solemn little face to the ork, her blue eyes steady. 'Darus…
your brother swore to protect me. He was my friend, and he trusted me. And we
trusted him, with our lives. You saw us in front of your council of tribes. We
returned your brother's axe to you, and we brought you warning of Yosgaloth, the
demon. Will you trust me?'

Darus nodded, his face grave.

There was something about her more and more these days that commanded
attention. Karland almost envied it; sometimes when he spoke, he found people just
ignored him, which upset him, as if he just wasn't important enough to listen to.
But when Xhera spoke, there was something about her that made them listen, even
when she spoke quietly. He tried not to feel bad about it, but occasionally it made
him feel inconsequential, although he had not yet had the nerve to pull someone up
about it. It just felt… unfair that others expected to be heard when they spoke, but
often ignored him when he did.

Right now, her words were reaching the right ears.

'I believe that the axe of Grukust will be cared for by this guard until word
reaches him from The Sanctum. What if he promised to send it straight there so it
was with you once he has it confirmed that you are a guest of the Council? You are
here to see them on behalf of your people, aren't you?'

Darus looked from her to the guard with his huge dark all-black eyes, and then
to Karland. His great chest and stomach rose and fell slowly in deep, even breaths,
and he looked thoughtful, driving home a noticeable difference between him and
Grukust. His brother had been quiet, gentle and loyal underneath a quick-tempered
exterior many had taken for stupidity; his Darum had been rudimentary at best, and
when annoyed he reacted before thought, although he had been remarkably
introspective at other times. Darus had much in common with his brother, in
stoicism, mannerisms and looks especially, but in other ways he seemed profoundly
different.

His Darum barely had a trace of accent, although the tribal cadences of orkish
and his tusks changed some words a little. Although he had the size and power of his
kind, they seemed to come second to his thoughts. He was slower to anger than the
others Karland had met and seemed aware of much more than just his own
emotions.

Long before now, Karland thought with bittersweet amusement, Grukust would
have had the guard by the throat. Darus, however, was as polite as any reasonable
person faced with bureaucratic obstacles.

More so than some.

'I mean you no disrepect, Lieutenant Pridall,' he said slowly in his deep voice. 'I understand duty. It is why I am here. Will you give me your oath that the axe of my brother will be delivered to me?'

'Soon as my shift here's finished, I'll carry it to Captain-General Dorn myself. Acceptable?'

Darus considered him carefully, and then nodded, looking relieved.

'Yes. Care for it as you would your child.' The ork tugged at the axe head, sliding the haft from the leather loops on the baldric. He held it carefully in the middle, deliberately non-threatening, and extended it horizontally in one hand. Pridall took it carefully with both of his, looking surprised.

'Not as heavy as I thought. Forged *titan*? These runes look Dwarvish. It must be worth a fortune.'

'It is beyond worth. My brother won it by right of arms from the dwarves,' said Darus with pride. 'It is a mighty weapon, and was wielded by one of their champions. It is a treasure of the tribes.'

'I understand,' returned Pridall. He turned and laid it on a large sheet of rough unbleached canvas behind him, and wrapped it quickly, binding it with white cord in a practised winding that would prevent tampering before pouring red wax from a small pot over the final knot. He hefted a city seal and pressed it firmly into the wax, blowing on it to cool quickly and keep the detail crisp. 'I'll deliver it personally later today. You have my word.'

Darus held out a huge hand for the guard, human-style, and after a second's hesitation Pridall took his forearm. He smiled slightly. Karland sensed all the guards around them relaxing.

'May I also welcome the first ork Ambassador to Darost,' the Lieutenant added.

Karland smiled. It might not be strictly accurate, but it was a generous thing to say. Darus half-bowed and saluted in the manner of the tribes, and then moved past the checkpoint. He waited for Xhera and Karland to precede him, and they started up the main road east to The Sanctum, trailed by two obvious Guards.

Darus walked with them, his dark eyes taking in the sights. There was nothing like this on the plains, thought Karland. People stared at Darus in astonishment, and a blanket of whispers lay in their wake. They parted before them like a stream around a rock.

'It's a bit overwhelming,' Karland said, remembering his own first visit.

Darus nodded. 'The size of the buildings. The walls and gates I had never imagined to be so big. But I have seen Eyotsburg and Punslon, Karland. I was taught the trade language of Darost there. I am not as… what do you humans say? *Green…* to cities as you might think.'

His dark eyes were slightly crinkled in amusement at the jest. Karland had a powerful flashback to Grukust's humour and smiled back. Xhera laughed quietly at them both.

'Sorry,' Karland said. 'I didn't mean to assume. But even then, everything here is so… old, yet advanced. Huge. So many people.' He shrugged. 'When I first saw Darost, I couldn't take it all in. Still can't, sometimes.'

Darus nodded. 'I have never seen so many together in one place,' he admitted, then snorted. 'And so many have, apparently, never seen anything like me either.'

Xhera reached up to brush her hair back, retying the loop she held it back with. 'Well. You stand out in a crowd.' He grunted. 'Take it as a compliment.'

'I take no offence. I find humans equally fascinating to look at. You are all so… *different* to us. So puny.'

Karland opened his mouth to object and caught a knowing look from Darus. He laughed instead, shaking his head. 'Your brother fooled me more than once. You won't catch me so easily.'

Darus chuckled, and Xhera caught on, smiling.

They reached the main square, leaving a trail of curiosity in the market. Darus gazed solemnly at the great statue without speaking. Karland was thankful they didn't see the guard who had disparaged orks.

At The Sanctum, Xhera stepped in before Karland or Darus could speak and introduced Darus as the orkish envoy to the Council of Twelve, and old acquaintance of Aldwyn Varelin and Rast Tal'Orien. As she was explaining, Captain Dorn arrived to meet them, Rast alongside him. Word had obviously preceded them.

'I extend the greetings of Darost to you, Darus of the orks,' he smiled. 'Captain Jekob was unable to greet you himself.'

Darus clapped his hand to his chest formally to both men, and then clasped Rast's hand Barbarian-style.

'Warrior Tal'Orien. It is good to see you again.'

'Well met, Darus,' said Rast. 'We had not expected to see you here. You gave me something of a shock when I first saw you.'

Darus looked puzzled for a moment, and then nodded. 'The resemblance was ever strong,' he agreed. He almost smiled, but clearly memories of his brother's loss still did not allow much light-heartedness. 'I was hoping to find you first, because I must speak with your Council on matter that concern my people as well as yours. Perhaps you can help me do so. But I do confess, I also wished to meet you all again. You have no idea how highly my brother must have thought of you, to have done what he did - even with honour at stake.'

'He was a cunning warrior,' said Rast quietly. 'And a good friend.'

Xhera had tears in her eyes at her memories but smiled at the young ork. Words that had been held back when they had seen him flowed now.

'It *is* good to see you,' she said. 'Even if you remind me so much of him.'

Darus regarded her gravely, and then placed a fist to his chest. '*Kunnia olen.* Your grief does you credit, young human. You must have cared for him very much.'

'He was our friend,' said Karland quietly, feeling sad. 'He died for us, and we would have done anything to prevent that.'

There was a moment's silence, and then the ork nodded, a small smile on his lips.

'*Hai.* I cannot fill the breadth of his shoulders, but I would like to spend time with you all. Hear more memories. Know his story after he left us, before he died. He was *mestari, sankari;* hero to our people, but he was also my brother.' He sighed. 'For all we argued.'

A slight throat-clearing reminded Karland that Captain-General Dorn was waiting. They turned to him.

'Allow me to welcome you on the behalf of the Council of Twelve, Envoy Darus.' Darus raised his eyebrows. 'The Council has suggested that you meet them tomorrow, after the lunchtime recess, since they have business they are completing now. Perhaps this gives you a chance to rest after your travels, and us a chance to talk more informally?'

Darus nodded. 'I am curious to see this *university.* And I am hungry.'

Xhera grinned at Karland, who returned it. He remembered Grukust's near-obsession with food very well.

È Ê

Darus sat in one of the chairs in his room on the lowest floor of the luxury suites facing the tower in the same Cuneus as Karland and Xhera, then promptly rose again as it groaned. He shook his head and moved to the recessed steps to the fireplace all the rooms seemed to have, then changed his mind and moved to the balcony doors. After opening these and all the windows, he came back and sat down on the stone.

'Feels cramped,' he muttered. Karland remembered well Grukust's reaction to close woods. It seemed that a life on the vast plains left orks a little claustrophobic, especially in a human building where everything was a little too small for them.

His room had been hastily arranged by one of Castellan James's Stewards. It was similar to, if smaller than, the room Karland had stayed in with Rast and Aldwyn when he had first visited, but much finer than their current quarters.

Darus spoke to Dorn, as blunt as his brethren.

'This room makes me uncomfortable. You honour me with it, but… I wish to go out there. To the gardens.' He pointed out of the window.

Dorn glanced at Rast, who shrugged slightly. He nodded to Darus.

'Of course. I appreciate this is very different to your normal quarters.'

Darus rumbled in slightly nervous laughter. 'My normal *quarters* are the wind, the sky, the plains, and in the winter, a *tipi*.' He referred to the conical tents made of skins over long lashed bones his people used as they moved about the plains.

'Come, then. Let us move outside,' said Dorn. He spoke quickly to the guard outside the room, and then led the way down and out, through the corridors. Darus visibly relaxed when they emerged into the light and the garden out of the warren of stairs and passages behind them. Dorn muttered quietly to the guards stationed nearby. They began to move onlookers on. Darus ignored them all, as he had in the city.

They moved to a spot in the middle of the short grass a little to the side of the Tower entrance in the aptly named Garden of the Plains, away from the shrubs and bushes lining the edges, and sat in the sunshine. There were few clouds and the garden they were in was quiet; despite the murmur of activity from the corridors of The Sanctum, and the fainter but unending bustle of the city beyond the walls, the day held some of the timeless silence that breaking sunlight seemed to bring when there was no wind with it.

Darus squatted, rather than sitting cross legged, or lounging like the others - all apart from Rast, of course, who stayed standing and silent. The ork seemed quite comfortable. Karland sat next to him, watching the play of sunlight on his features and eyes. His skin was the matte mid-green of healthy temperate bushes. Karland had never noticed before, not even with Grukust, but deep within the large dark orbs of orks' eyes there *was* an iris. Although they were almost black, the sclera matching the colour of the iris - as in many creatures apart from men, dwarves, and elves - the iris had a threadlike gold filigree, and were, perhaps surprisingly, as expressive as human eyes.

'I bring word to your Council of troubles in the Tribes, and what has happened in recent times,' said Darus. 'But I also owe thanks.' He breathed a great sigh. 'Thank you, all, for returning my brother's *snagka* to me. Our last meeting was brief and had other… distractions… that were more important.'

Along with the return of the axe and Darus's great upset at the death of his mighty brother, a two-hundred-and-fifty foot dragon had cowed the combined tribes and shamed Brukk, bringing warnings of an ancient enemy loose from the Dimnesdair. No wonder he hadn't had the time or inclination for polite words.

'I feel a great shame, humans,' Darus continued, his gaze distant. 'I am expected to live up to his legend. I have been given the axe of a champion, and I have not even gained my *kap*. Many of the tribes do not think I am worthy, that it should go to someone else, despite the laws of my people. One is a great chieftain; he may not challenge me for a gift of my family until I gain my *kappanim*, and I fear he would win. He was one of the greatest warriors in the tribes beside my brother. He also wishes to combine his leadership with championship; become chieftain and Champion of the Tribes, perhaps Over-Chieftain. It has always been tradition that they are not the same. He disagrees. Long has he waited for a chance to cause dissent. Now it is here.'

'What of the tribes?' asked Rast.

Darus shrugged heavy green shoulders. 'For now, nothing. We have much to concern us. When you brought your warnings, you and that great red beast, we debated long, until Brukk brought his hammer down upon the talk. Runners were sent towards Punslon, and as we awaited them, he said that despite his dislike, we would be wise to heed your warnings of the orcs, and the demon. Too much was unknown, and in our pride perhaps we grew too reliant on our strength to the detriment of our young and the good of our people.

'Some thought him weak for it, and he was challenged. My uncle is still powerful. He made his point known in blood. For now, the tribes are one again. For now.' He shook his head slowly. 'I cannot say how long it will last. He was not challenged by this chieftain, but I fear he only bides his time. Too much is new, changing. The tribes journeyed north-east from where you met us, to the lowlands east of the Great Lake and west of the *Ruoho-piikkari*, the Plains Spikes.' He used the orkish term for the Arkons.

'The foothills of Rhé,' said Captain Dorn, understanding him. 'A good place to regather.'

'We kept watch for our runners. Few returned. Those that did spoke of seeing the demon from afar. They spoke of fear.' He managed to keep most of the scorn from his voice; it seemed inbuilt for orks to despise weakness, however much they understood it. 'I do not believe it found many, if any, of our kin. But orcs did.' A growl had entered his words, and Karland and Xhera found themselves leaning away slightly.

'Brothers and sisters were overwhelmed by thousands, mutilated, strung up. Such numbers the survivors said moved! Almost, we could not conceive. Our plains were blackened for miles. They swept through the pass ahead of the demon and headed east and north along the peaks. We do not know where they went, but it is possible the demon followed them. Rabble! If they had come against us, we would have been hard pressed, even united, but they ran in fear of the demon. If only it has taken them all. *Goruc'cha urch!'* He spat between his knees, his lips drawn from his teeth in a snarl at the thought.

Dorn's expression mirrored him for a second. '*They* led that foul beast to us! They have much to answer for.'

Karland shook his head numbly. Their flight on Gyornaeldar must have bypassed the exodus of the orc horde before the ancient demon. If Yosgaloth had chased them - and given its drive to consume all life, the urge to follow so many would have been powerful - then it was partially the fault of the orcs that Yogaloth had come east. How many lives would have been saved if it had not come upon Irilview in the night?

Rast's soft voice calmed his thoughts. 'It might have come east anyway. It was the clearest route to one of the largest cities on the continent. Darost would have been a powerful lure. My concern is where they have gone to ground.'

'What about the people in Punslon?' asked Karland, remembering their cold reception.

Darus shook his head.

'No one left there lived, Karland, although many have now returned. *Grikkala* willing the young escaped.'

Karland looked at Xhera and saw her pale expression matching his own shock. They had tried to warn them. He fervently hoped that they had sent at least the children on, but even on the road southwest to Capsum, the largest mid-plains town - more like a small free city-state, and the nearest main settlement to Punslon - they might have been overtaken, by orcs or the ancient demon. He felt sick.

As they talked more, it seemed from what Darus was saying that the orks were growing restless in the hills. They were unused to being forced to one location, and uneasy away from the plains.

Anti-human sentiment was spreading amongst the tribes, and the ugly rumour that humans were aligning themselves with their most hated enemy was hastening and embedding it deeper. For most orks, rarely meeting humans, this simply meant all men were evil. Pale skins and weak frames were becoming synonymous with *orc*. It was only a matter of time before they started killing any humans they found, and if the tribes took to war, they could wreak havoc in the centre of the continent.

Even Brukk, dismissive though he was of humanity at large, drew the line at this, and apparently made his point quite forcefully. Orkish politics sounded spirited at the least, mused Karland. But Brukk was growing old. He was nearing his forty-sixth summer, and although orks did not lose power as they aged as humans did, their bodies did begin to fail. Powerful as he was, he might be deposed, and if that happened, there would be major trouble for anyone trying to cross the plains.

'Why does Brukk have two *kap*-runes?' asked Karland curiously, the thought occurring.

'My uncle was once Brukus,' replied Darus. 'When he defeated the other chieftains to become Over-Chieftain, he earned his second *Kap*-rune, as only the Over-Chieftain may have. The family ending is lost, to indicate that he is now of all tribes. So my brother would have been Grukk, if he had ever desired to take the role; but tradition is that only a chieftain may challenge, and he would no longer have been Champion.'

'So he wasn't meant to challenge when we were before Brukk?' Xhera asked.

'It is... frowned upon. It would not have made Grukust Over-Chieftain if he had won - and he would have won. But it would have destroyed Brukk as our leader, cast us into turmoil. Whatever you may think of my uncle, he holds the tribes together in difficult times. My brother risked much for you... but he was ever one to do what was right over what was easy.'

'Where is the axe now?' enquired Dorn. Xhera explained, and he nodded.

'I will ask you to leave it in your room, Darus Brukk-kin, but you may keep it here unbound. I will have it sent immediately, and I will also name you official envoy from the orks and pass the word.'

Darus shook his huge head.

'Thank you, Captain, but I prefer to sleep in these gardens. I do not like the rooms. Keep my brother's axe safe for me. I will trust your word.'

Rast laughed quietly behind them. Dorn's eyebrows jumped in surprise. He looked as if he would object, then shrugged.

'I will put in a... strong request to Captain-General Jekob that he post guards and allow you to sleep here. Are you certain?'

'I have my bedroll, the stars, and the grass,' replied Darus. 'I will be at rest here.'

Dorn nodded. 'I know what the Welcomer Captain will say; he is a stickler for regularities and does not often see the humour in things. However, he is a good man. I don't think it will be a problem, unusual though it is.'

Karland wondered if Dorn knew what an honour it was for Darus to say he was worthy of keeping his most sacred possession.

He liked this ork. Although it was a little bitter-sweet, as Darus constantly reminded him of Grukust, he was different enough, and even more open than his brother had been.

A Welcomer moved up and spoke to Dorn quietly.

'Please excuse me,' said Dorn. 'A shipment of Nighthaunt was seized recently; it looks as if we might have found a lead for the ringleaders. Exciting stuff.' He grinned in anticipation. 'Rast? Would you come as well? You might be able to advise us on the… other matter.'

'I will help if I can.' He stood smoothly. 'I must speak with Ulric anyway.' They left, moving with purpose.

Karland knew Rast still sought this demon. He was also heavily involved with helping analyse the possible moves of the orcs, how they fought. Of all of them, he had the most experience with the creatures.

They sat for a while with Darus as light grew dim. Food was sent out for him, which they shared. Darus ate a very rare steak, muttering in delight over the unusual taste of cow. His manners were considerably better than his brother's had been, but Karland still wouldn't want to eat with him anywhere more formal than a food hall.

They spoke for some time about their journey, and what had happened. He seemed to stop breathing when they spoke of his brother's final battle, and Xhera cried a little recalling it.

'So many,' Darus breathed finally. 'He truly was mighty. An ogre! It is sad that our kin are so dangerous. They will kill even orks in foul temper, though they will not eat us. Once, they were not so misguided.' He sat for a moment, pondering. 'And a Gar-wolf. We call them *kuolema jalat; death on legs*. They are powerful foes. A pack of them once killed half a tribe before we slew the last. They are one of the few creatures we and our *rinoks* fear.' For once, he didn't sound disdainful. 'They have some compact with *urch,* though I think they are loose allies at best. They have tracked and slain our children before now.'

'I've never seen anything like it,' said Karland. 'It looked the size of a pony, with bone plates like armour.'

'That, above all, places my brother firmly in history. He defeated one unarmed; weaponless, cast it from a mountain! At the cost of his life. And you say he killed the ogre with one blow, by *throwing* the axe? It is not a throwing weapon!'

They assured him, and he stood suddenly, facing the direction of his plains and saluting with a meaty thump.

'*Grukust-a vah varsi,*' he rumbled, his dark eyes glinting in the early dusk. There was silence for a moment. Torches were being lit around the garden, and Karland understood with some amusement that no one here realised that orcs could see well in the dark.

They spoke a little longer, and Darus, squatting back down, looked troubled at many things they told him. Karland perhaps said more than he should have, but he did not consider Darus to come under the general ban of information. After all, Grukust would have been with them to the end, if he had not sacrificed himself. He believed he owed Darus as much as he could give.

'Will you ever stop calling it the axe of your brother?' he asked eventually.

The look Darus turned on him wasn't quite a glare, and Xhera almost gasped. Karland held up his hands, talking quickly and trying to explain. 'No disrespect to Grukust. But it *is* your axe now.'

Darus smiled slightly, and ran a finger up one tusk, relaxing. 'Perhaps. But until I earn my *kappanim*, I am considered between child and adult. After that... I may call it my axe then, but I think perhaps it will now always be the Axe of Grukust.'

Karland felt his nose sting slightly inside as tears threatened and nodded. That seemed fitting, certainly more than the small cairn of white stones on the mountain that he had painfully helped make. He felt brief embarrassment at his paltry gesture. Then another thought occurred to him.

'You said Grukust won this from a Dwarven champion. The axe is *huge*. It must have been nearly the size of the dwarf! I've carried it. It isn't that light. How would he wield it?'

Darus shrugged. 'Dwarves are strong, the axe is lighter than it looks. Even a dwarf would tire soon if it was normal steel, I think, but it is not. It is their most valuable alloy. *Titan*. I have heard that the elves call it the *grey metal*. This would have been a weapon to bring a shield down and break bones through armour, and the edge would slice through mail, chip and part other blades, even cleave through plate without easily losing its edge. When you fight many foes armed and armoured, a large axe is a formidable weapon, although it is unusual to have two blade heads. It would not have been a weapon for close quarters. For a dwarf it would be like a polearm.'

'Why haven't you earned your *kappanim* yet?' asked Xhera, curiously. 'You know a lot about battle, and you are nearly as big as Grukust.'

Darus laughed, his bark familiar as well. 'All young orks know a lot about battle, Xhera. We fight before we can walk.'

'But still. Why haven't you earned it yet?'

'I am still young,' Darus replied. 'Traditionally we do not quest until our fifteenth summer, when our growth slows. And the past year and more have been... busy.'

Karland looked at him in astonishment.

Darus is the same age as us?

Although he wasn't human, Darus looked like an adult man of his people. He was enormous, near the height his huge brother had been if not quite the breadth, and Grukust had easily topped seven feet. A few orks were even bigger than Grukust had been; the gigantic Murlok, who had looked like an ogre, must have been more than a foot taller than Grukust.

Then Karland remembered something Rast had said to him.

'You live different spans to humans, don't you?'

Darus nodded. 'We rarely reach fifty summers of age. Before our fifteenth summer, we have reached adulthood. Once we are ready, it is time to prove our worth with a great deed. Often this will be combat with a skilled warrior, a demonstration of strength or power before all, or a great feat for the tribe, but sometimes the one who seeks their *kappanim* chooses their own path, of danger and the unknown. So did my brother; so do I.' His voice held no bitterness or regret. 'Many of those do not return.'

Karland also remembered that, although orks slowed their growth when they reached adulthood, they never stopped. Grukust might have reached eight feet tall and many hundreds of pounds if he had survived into old age, he reflected. Rast said orks didn't suffer from ailments of age as did humanity. Their bodies simply wore out and began to stop working. They would walk to the plains to die alone with honour or carry out one last heroic charge and fight until killed if they could. They supposedly had loose units composed of their oldest, most cunning warriors that would inflict horrific damage on a foe and fight until they were killed to a man. It had always seemed insanely suicidal. Now he understood why.

'Is this your *kappanim* quest?' he asked slowly.

Darus glanced at him slyly and pursed his lips, then burst out laughing. Xhera giggled, in appreciation for Karland's quick wit, and at Darus's response, so like his brother's.

'Maybe. I will know when the time comes, when *Rakkata* wills it. May I be equal to the task.'

'I heard you mention something like that before,' said Xhera. 'Rakkata.'

'*Rakkata* and *Grikkala* are the Gods of the tribes. He strides the world for all to see, and judges all orks who would pass to the Great Plains beyond. *Rakkata* is the god of War and Honour, huge and fearful. From his balls flows all courage at birth. If you cannot meet his gaze at your life's end you are cast out, a witless fool, to wander the grey lands for all eternity.' His tongue ran up the side of a tusk reflectively.

'*Grikkala* is the mother of the tribes, the goddess of mating and plenty, hidden in shadow under the mountains where we came from and where we return to. She rides a giant *rinok* with many teats, and watches over the young. Our souls spring from her moist loins at our birth, and she gathers us to her great breasts at the end, when our bodies are spent, our last embrace into darkness.'

'Grukust never mentioned them,' said Xhera. 'They sound terrible.'

Karland privately thought they sounded disgusting.

'They are. Foolish is the *Urukin* who goes against their teachings,' said Darus. 'My brother... believed, but he did not have the tongue for praying. He knew his strikes were prayers to *Rakkata*, and he always said that if the god did not listen, then he had no time for him; he would prevail nonetheless.' A sad smile brought his tusks further out. 'As he did. *Rakkata* must have saluted his end. His tribute would have made the Gods stand to receive him. Never have I heard such a *nurmi valveilla puhelu.*'

Karland remembered the eerie manner in which the orks had raised their deep voices in threnody. The sound had vibrated through him, and the volume had been incredible. Every ork had simply stopped what they had been doing, literally in their tracks, and added their voices in an expanding ring from the centre, which had been Darus. They called to wake the plains for all their dead, but Grukust's call had made the mountains tremble, even before Györnàeldàr had added her powerful voice in surprising tribute.

'Are all your names something *-us* or *ust?*'

'It is the *suknim* of my tribe, the great tribe of *Us*. Many Over-Chieftains have come from my blood. But there are many tribes; *Lo, In, Ru, Va,* many others.'

'But Grukust ended in a *t...?*'

'The *suknim* must be in the last three of the name. The names may end in another letter if two carry the same name. There is a *Grukus* in our tribe already. Sometimes the last letter is the one replaced by the *kappanim*, or it is used at the end. It is the choice of the one who earned it to name themselves, though none may place it at the start. That would make their name no longer their own and remove them from their tribe.'

There was a certain logic there, but it still bothered Karland. 'That doesn't make sense though-' he began, trying to work it out.

'It is how things are.'

Well, that puts a spear through the throat of that conversation, thought Karland. 'What about Brukk?'

'Brukk was once Brukus, born Bruus. He changed his name when he became Over-Chieftain. It is tradition - so that the Over-Chieftain is of no tribes and all tribes.' Darus smiled, his dark eyes glinting over his yellow-white tusks, slightly longer than his brother's and a little narrower. '*Ogrefist* is a human name for him. In orkish he is called *Jättiläinen-nyrkki.*'

'Did your brother have a name like that?'

'Yes. Those worthy of the greatest of deeds have earned these names. He did not use it, and did not like our people to. It was *Käärmekirous, Serpent's Curse,* but he was better known as *Suurisydän.*' He lapsed into silence, perhaps considering his brother's deeds, and there was silence for a moment until Darus translated, his voice deep and soft.

'*Great-heart.*'

That fitted Grukust well, thought Karland. Better than a name for the wyvern he killed.

'So, now you are here,' asked Xhera quietly after a moment, shooting Karland a cautionary look, 'what will you do? I mean, after you speak to the Council.'

'I will stay a while,' answered Darus, reanimating. He had far more patience with all the questions than his brother would have had. 'Once I have given Brukk's message, my duty is done. I will spend time speaking with your Council if they wish, but as Karland has guessed, I am on name-quest. I think it is destined to be fulfilled with the friends of my brother. If you travel, I will go with you. I do not think you will stay in one place for long.'

Karland wasn't sure. They seemed likely to study at the University until they were adults. On the other hand, they couldn't ask for a better companion if they did travel again, not if he was anything like his brother.

They spoke of other things then, about the Gardens and the city, and the Tribes, and later Grukust - not his victories, but his character. Finally, Karland and Xhera excused themselves to study and sleep. Xhera promised that she would come back and see Darus every day she could, echoed by Karland. He could see that his resemblance to Grukust still struck her deeply, and hoped that, in time, she would adjust and accept Darus without old ghosts.

TWELVE

The next morning Darus rose as the sun did, as was the custom of his people. Rast found him squatting straight-backed in the dawn's light, careless of the dew on the grass and the tiny finger-long thread-snakes moving through it searching for small insects. The Gardeners had introduced them to control attacks on the Garden plants. In the morning cool they were torpid.

He wondered if orks ever caught a chill.

Steam rose faintly from Darus, his body temperature higher than a human's. Rast could see Welcomer Guards ringing the garden, more than normal, and four heavily armed Onyx Guard waited nearby, their matte black armour dull in the morning light. Ostensibly these were a high honour for a visiting functionary; in actuality, they were probably best equipped to face Darus if he were to attack anyone.

Rast stepped forward into the light. He had been up much of the night and had spent only one and a half hours in his recuperative *dônaethar* trance. As ever, he was as rested as if he had slept deeply for seven hours. His human mastery of the Elven technique was one of the most valuable skills he had ever learned, he knew. It left so many more hours to do necessary things.

He saw a carved symbol in precious wood in the ork's hand and remembered the *Gropak* Grukust had left with Aldwyn's body for protection.

He had not had it with him when he died.

'Good morning,' he said, banishing old memories.

Darus turned his head slightly, the light catching the side of a tusk.

'*Uuden aamun lahja*, Warrior Tal'Orien.'

'Did you sleep well?'

'The ground here is softer than the plains.' He rose and grinned slightly down at the big man. 'I hope I do not get used to it.'

Rast smiled slightly in return. 'I believe the Council should be ready in an hour or so; they have rearranged their morning for you, apparently. A great honour.' He knew how busy the Council were with the remnants of the refugees and the incessant arguing over a war footing. He had not expected them to see Darus for another day.

'It seems I am interesting,' said Darus. 'The first of my kind here, with news of *urch*.'

'Will you break fast with me?' asked Rast. 'We can have food brought to you here.'

'I was about to ask where I can eat,' said the ork with a chuckle. 'I have already had some trail rations, but that was all of an hour ago. I am hungry. Perhaps you can show me something of… this.' He swept his hand around him at the gleaming yellow-white stone edifices. The Sanctum must be utterly alien to him, Rast realised. He was certainly handling his culture shock well.

He remembered with faint amusement the vast appetite of Grukust. 'This way, Darus.'

They travelled along to the nearest food hall, ghosted by the Onyx Guard. Hardly anyone was around yet; most of the scholars and students would not rise for another hour or two. Some Papered Scholars, those who had earned writs of Mastery in one or more specialist areas, often did not rise before midday; many of them worked late into the night. The food halls served food very early until late. Scholars tended not to stick to a particular schedule in their studies, and even throughout the night it was possible to find tisane and other drinks in the large halls. They never truly closed.

The nearest was the hall of the Academia Linguistica. When it was full the noise was loud, a constant background murmur. Empty as it was now, echoes reflected back from the high ceiling and sounds were sharper. Darus's voice boomed in the large space.

Rast chose one of his favourites - tumbled egg with black pepper and grilled tomatoes. His plate piled high on the simple wooden tray, he turned to Darus, and nearly laughed aloud.

The ork had removed the plate, and was motioning the woman to ladle food directly onto the tray. She cast a helpless glance at Rast, and he shrugged, trying not to grin. Eggs, bacon, sausages, beef, a pie, mushrooms, potatoes, the red *aluki* beans, blood pudding and more, enough for four people at least.

'You can always return,' he remarked mildly. Darus cocked his head at him and grunted. Rast caught the wicked gleam in his eye and reminded himself that, like his brother, Darus was not stupid - and shared his brother's sense of humour. He sighed to himself. No doubt the tales of the huge ork that ate enough for an army would be spreading throughout the day.

They picked a table nearby. Darus was used to using a knife and fingers. After politely trying the fork, he dropped it and used the spoon as a clearly inferior shovel.

Rast inhaled the scent of his hot eggs before eating the first forkful. It was an old habit. You could tell a lot about what you were going to eat if you sniffed it first, which could save unpleasantness. It also made you appreciate the taste more, somehow.

Rast ate more than most men, but Darus put him to shame. He reduced the tray to leftovers not long after Rast had finished his single plate, eating the beans, mushrooms, and some of the potatoes, and trying the tomatoes once before pushing them away. Orks generally did not eat grains and starch, Rast knew. They ate meat, although it was rarely *rinok,* and foraged some greenery, fruits, mushrooms and roots during their nomadic migrations. Most of their food came from hunting the creatures of the plains and foothills, including the wild aurochs and the flocks of *Horātori,* the predatory flightless birds that stalked the grasslands.

Darus wolfed down the eggs, muttering appreciatively, and tore through the meat.

'This food is good,' he said indistinctly. 'I eat eggs raw in the Tribes.' He watched Rast sip his *kaf,* an expensive delicacy here, and made an interrogatory noise. Rast passed the cup over and Darus inhaled deeply, then nearly sneezed. He eyed the cup with suspicion and handed it back.

'Smells like bitter roots and deep, rich earth,' he said. 'It is… interesting. I will not try it.' He sipped his water. Usually orks would have either ork ale or water with food. They had certain infusions they might boil as well, but usually only for illness, and *rinok* milk was used only in ceremonies.

Finally, they were done. Rast picked up the trays and moved to the side of the hall to place them on the racks as a Welcomer Guard entered the hall doors with excellent timing.

'Master Tal'Orien,' he greeted them, 'Darus of the Tribes. The Council awaits your pleasure.'

Rast nodded and they followed him back out into the gardens, up to the tall doors of the Tower of the Dodecagon. A Welcomer Guard bowed low to Darus.

As they entered and walked to sit at the ancient and richly burnished huge circular wood table in front of the assembled Council, the doors swung shut. Darus shifted uneasily, but it did not seem too claustrophobic for him; the Tower was massive, over one hundred and twenty feet wide at the base, and the spired ceiling was almost three hundred feet above them.

Darus seemed mesmerised by the huge chandelier hanging from the spire.

'I hope that does not fall,' he grunted.

Lit every day, it threw a thousand shards of radiance around the tower base from hundreds of tall bright flames, the main mirrors in the centre focusing the brightest light in a circle downwards on the centre of the chamber. Rast had never stopped admiring the exquisite form of the massive light, formed from multiple large hollow glass vials and filled with *paraf*, an expensive clear-burning oil. As far as he knew, it was the only one of its type. It must weigh more than six tons and require daily maintenance.

'Will Karland and Xhera join us?' Darus asked Rast. He did not sit.

'Children have no place at Council sessions,' remarked the dry querulous voice of Whylll Regus from his right, before Rast could answer. He hoped the man did not antagonise Darus.

He wondered exactly at which point Councillor Eremus would.

'Why are they not included?' asked Darus.

'They are young, and not of this Council.'

'They also have other duties,' said Aurelia Brókova with a smile.

'It is partly because of them that I was sent,' replied Darus, frowning. 'Brukk sent warning to you not only because you are most at risk, but because you are their people, and we owe them our lives and our thanks. Of all humans Rast Tal'Orien, Xhera, and Karland are the ones we honour the most.'

'Ridiculous,' Whyll Regus muttered.

Darus went still. Rast put a warning hand on his arm, felt the muscles jumping there under the hot green skin.

'We will be civil to the Envoy of the Tribes,' declared Ulric, glaring around the chairs. 'Let us not forget we speak with the representative of a different people who may take a thoughtless comment... badly.' His brows drew down as he rested his gaze on Councillor Regus.

'We greet you, Darus of the Urukin,' said Mira Lyss into the pause. 'We offer condolences on the fall of your brother. Rast Tal'Orien told us that our quest would have failed without him. It was a noble sacrifice, and many have heard his tale.' Darus relaxed under Rast's hand and thumped his fist softly on his chest. She smiled. 'What news do you bring?'

Darus was probably the most collected ork Rast had ever seen, markedly different from most of his people, but being in a city like this, in a formal council of humans, was clearly something far outside his experience. Nevertheless, he spoke firmly, in the manner of his kind.

'Greetings, Council of Eordeland. *Kiitos* for the honour of addressing you.' He half-turned to face them all in a gesture of respect, and Rast was reminded that, as calmly fluent in Darum as Darus was, he was still definitely an ork. No matter how well he spoke, you could always hear the tonal patterns of his kind and the effect of large tusks on speech.

'I come before you in friendship and honour, for the first time in memory between us. I come to answer your request for aid in payment for warning of the great hungry demon that broke free of the dark woods. I come to warn you.'

A murmur ran through the Council. Ulric forestalled them.

'Many months ago, I sent word.' His eyes swept his colleagues. *'Before* the vote.'

Darus looked at him quizzically and continued. 'I also come on *Kapparin-etsa.* I quest to earn my runed-name.'

Several Councillors nodded, clearly knowing the ritual, whilst others looked puzzled.

'Tell us of your offer,' rumbled Ulric.

'*Hai.* I bear official greeting and friendship between our people from the Over-Chieftain of the *Urukin* Tribes, Brukk Ogrefist. We have suffered much hardship in recent times, and there is much still ahead. Many more of the accursed *Goruc'cha urch* are abroad, in numbers that threaten our people. They hold a great hatred for us. Novin floods our plains with mercenaries. Our game flees. If we are weakened as a people, our ancient foes may find the chance to slaughter us... our children. Against one enemy, we are strong. Against so many, we are not.

'It has been considered... *wise...* to seek more allies. We already have an old compact with the Barbarian tribes of the Sergoth. They are as scattered as we and walk a similar plain. But you; you are the most powerful nation in Anaria, and now you seek aid too. Time and time again in centuries past we of the plains have seen you break greater foes sent against you.'

Including orks, Rast thought.

Councillor Eremus leaned forwards. 'And what would you bring to this... alliance?' she sniffed.

'Might of arms,' was the blunt reply. 'We are fewer in number, but we are fierce. We can guard the plains against your foes, bring word of movement. We can break sieges. We will kill orcs.'

The Councillors muttered to each other, and Eremus nodded slowly, her face calculating.

'That would be valuable... *if* war were coming.'

Ulric thumped his big hand down on the arm of his chair. Rast hoped their argument didn't flare up again.

'An offer not to be taken lightly,' he said. 'They are strong warriors. And we are still missing an army of orcs to the south.'

'If they will keep their word,' someone muttered. Rast looked around but couldn't make out who had said it.

For the first time, Darus showed the temper of his kind, darkening slightly greener as he flushed and baring his teeth and tusks, almost growling. He leaned forwards and his knuckles pressed against the thick tabletop as anger flashed across his face. His chest and shoulders bunched larger than Rast's, and veins stood out starkly against striated muscle. More than one Councillor flinched, and several Onyx Guard twitched slightly. Rast readied himself to intercept the ork.

Ulric leaned forwards, glaring around, and spoke before Darus could.

'Anyone who knows anything about *Urukin* knows that their word is their bond,' he growled. 'Orks have more honour than many men. Do not insult our guest.'

Several Councillors were stony-faced. It had been a male voice, and Rast wondered who had said it.

'Please, Darus. Continue with your reasons.' Mira Lyss gestured.

Darus breathed heavily for a few moments, and then drew a deep sigh and blew it out slowly, relaxing and looking down at his fists planted on the table. When he looked up, the rage had been replaced by a bland expression. When he spoke, his voice was even.

Rast was very impressed. He had shown more control than many humans.

'You are right to question the honour of some of my kin. A Chieftain named Vahkva has been declared outcast; *hylcio.* He wishes to depose my uncle and bring war against Eordeland, against all humans. If Brukk is no longer Overchieftain, many orks would find his voice strong again. Already he turns our people against you with hateful words and lies. He was present when Rast Tal'Orien and his companions were met by Brukk Ogrefist and saw his chance to make trouble. He has little honour.'

Rast remembered that day. He had bested one of their warriors as one would a child, and he knew it had earned him hatred as well as respect.

'He knew that the *urch* we destroyed came from Eordeland, and knows the army of them came here. That you have not been attacked is proof to him you are in league with them. No matter that you still battle them; no matter you also battle the Mercenaries infesting our plains. He blames your realm for the movement of the mercenaries, for the gathering of the orcs, for the deaths caused so far. He has a powerful voice. He says even if you are not in league, you caused our greatest enemies to gather in numbers that could destroy the tribes for the first time in centuries. He hates you nearly as much as he hates them.'

The chamber was quiet as the echoes of the ork's deep voice faded. He heaved a breath and continued quietly. 'His eagerness to see all humans as the same is no different to the way many humans think of us, and he twists many who do not see his subtleties. We are a simple people and prefer action to thought. Vahkva is very clever. He wishes someone to blame, to use against Brukk and the other chieftains. Some of his tribe have been killed and he has used those deaths, too. More than we believed possible have followed him into exile, though still not as many as yet could. This has never happened before.' He shook his head, looking almost perplexed. 'Our people seek allies, not war.' The words seemed slightly hesitant, as if the concept was alien. 'He knows this. It was the reason he tried to split then overthrow the tribes. Vahkva disagrees with Brukk. We do not know what he plans, but you must be on your guard against him. He seeks to lay blame at your feet, to force the tribes to him. He hopes to destroy you. And above all, he desires to be Overchieftain.' He shrugged massive green shoulders. 'Now he is an outcast, he cannot challenge. But if Brukk falls in war no one can stop him naming himself as a challenger.' Darus paused darkly. 'Brukk could fall by the hand of an ork.'

The Council sat for a moment, the words sinking in. It was yet another complication. Finally, Marcus Andragostin nodded.

'We thank you for the warning,' he said. 'I take it your quest and your wish to spend time with Rast Tal'Orien are not related to the Council?'

Darus shook his head.

'Fine. Please, stay here as long as you wish. Learn more about us, speak with Master Tal'Orien and plan your naming quest. You may wish to accompany a delegate or your companions around the city, perhaps? We will discuss the proposal and what path we should take.'

Darus nodded, looking confused. For him, Rast knew, it was as simple as a sworn oath, for mutual benefit. He had never had to deal with bureaucracy before.

'This is how humans do things,' Rast muttered wryly. Darus nodded slowly.

THIRTEEN

Karland stretched in his seat, rubbing his eyes. Days were growing imperceptibly longer, but it was still dark early. Rast was standing at the window like an oaken sentinel, as he often did, his face in shadow and his thoughts elsewhere. From the balcony they couldn't see the camp of Darus in the Garden of the Plains. The fire threw light up out of the seating area, and the low table in the centre was strewn with books and scrolls.

'Aldwyn said that actually the word Dragon is very old,' Karland observed, tapping *Notes on Dragons*. 'It has roots in Old Darum, but it goes back even further. It came from the ancient word *derkesthai*. He says it originally translated almost exactly as 'the one with the deadly gaze'.

Xhera nodded, clearly remembering the first time that awful gaze had fallen on her. To look into the eyes of a dragon was to be transfixed by a supreme intelligence and power far superior to your own. You were judged, stripped to your core. The stories of dragons commanding humans and overriding their will had ceased to be myth after meeting Györnàeldàr. It was said the gaze induced suicidal madness in some, and in two cases he had read about, actual death.

Compulsion did lessen with familiarity, he thought, if you managed not to look into their eyes. He wondered if the intent of the dragon mattered, too - the same way a hostile stare from a human could freeze or startle you, but a kind one would not. He had rapidly felt more able to cope with their huge companion once she had warmed to them. How different to Körànthír, whom they had barely been able to look at until he bowed to them outside Darost.

Their mere presence produced powerful fear.

The only comparable instance was in the Hall of Wyrms, but it had been very different facing the Darkling; their minds had begun to buckle from its very presence. Insanity had crept in. Only the presence of Györnàeldàr had shielded their minds, and later the Greater Dragon. He shuddered to think how quickly they might have gone mad if they had been alone.

Ever since the loss of both Aldwyn and Györnàeldàr, Karland had been unable to stop returning time and time again to his mentor's extensive *Notes on Dragons*. The loss of Grukust had also been keen, especially for Xhera.

For Karland however the loss of his mentor had rocked his world the most. He would never forget the panic, the horrible agony and pain, the fleeing of life and sentience from the eyes of his friend. The snuffing in front of him of one of the greatest minds in Anaria, if not Kuln. The years of knowledge, the work left undone, the care for Karland himself... all gone, as if it had never been.

He had watched the awful moment when the spark of brilliance winked out.

Yet hardly less was the loss of Györnàeldàr, and Grukust. They had been so massive and vital, yet more human in their own way than many men.

Dragons had become almost an obsession for him, as they had been for Aldwyn. He wanted to understand them, to see them, marvel at them, to speak to them, to learn from them, almost as if they were a surrogate mentor. And perhaps they were - Aldwyn's *Notes* said they remembered everything and were of superior intelligence to humans.

Of the Night lurked in the Combic Libraries, where they had begun piecing together references from Aldwyn's books in the evenings. Tonight they compiled them, ready for their return later.

They carried on studying for a while, Xhera poring through Aldwyn's references to Sarthos and past events, Karland continuing with *Notes*.

'When are we going to get the horses?' asked Xhera eventually, putting her notebooks down and stretching. Karland felt guilty. He hadn't thought of Hjarta and Stryke for months.

'We have been busy,' admitted Rast, stirring from the window. Karland was reminded how little he missed. 'Regin will see they are well cared for. Perhaps I will go with the next trade delegation to Deep Delving, if my duties permit.'

'What about us?' asked Karland. He was enjoying his studies, although he could do without the constant attention from Aran, and he still frustrated his tutors with his own inattention. Nevertheless, to see the Arkons again, this time without the pursuit of enemies, and to maybe see even the realm of the dwarves...

'You will not be coming,' said Rast, turning to face them. 'You have much to do here, and you would interrupt your studies. It was a mark of honour to be admitted to the University part-way through the year, and with so little preparation.' He left unsaid how much they would damage by leaving, or the danger, but Karland heard it nonetheless, with some gloom. He already knew that they were now bound by many rules, intimately so. Xhera seemed to function perfectly here, but every time he turned around, he seemed to have broken some minor rule of the campus. He didn't function well with so many restrictions.

'I thought the trade delegations were unanswered?' said Xhera. When they had been there, Regin had admitted that they had stopped trading with outsiders. Still, Darost kept sending parties, as the closest allies of the Arkon dwarves. They were met but not welcomed, and so far had failed to negotiate much more.

'The last three have failed,' acknowledged Rast. 'But I suspect the Council will keep trying until they are plainly told the accord is broken.'

'When is the next one to leave?'

'In forty days.' Rast turned back to the window, plainly finished with the conversation. Karland rolled his eyes at Xhera, who smiled at him, a slight dimple in her cheeks. He was sure she was happy to stay here and study; this was her dream, and she had thrown herself into it with gusto, ranking near the top of their classes in most subjects. Xhera just didn't love to see new places the same way he did.

Karland couldn't study in the fashion she did, listening to a lecture and then memorising notes. He flitted from subject to subject, diving off on tangents and using leaps of intuition and intelligence. He preferred to do rather than hear. The slog of memorisation just wasn't something he could maintain unless he was avidly interested; then he tore through material like a starving man ate food.

He knew the tutors were often annoyed with him. He was hard to measure, often forgetting assignments or scoring very poorly and being told he must make more effort, then suddenly outperforming everyone else in the class. He couldn't help it; it was just how he learned. A few of the tutors realised this and worked with him, guided by Master Darfin, who had become an unexpected ally, but not all. Many were traditional lecturers who were little interested in adapting to the methods of one student.

Frustrating, he was told, did not cover his attitude.

He sighed. It would have been nice to take a break from that and go out into the world again despite earlier reservations, but it seemed that it wasn't likely to happen just yet.

೮෩   ෨ಐ

'I wish we could involve more of the Council, but the plain fact is many of them are focused on other things,' said Councillor Holmson. He stood in his brightly lit chamber, staring into the dancing fire.

'Equally important, I am sure,' Ulric muttered, relaxing back into a chair at the table with a goblet of wine that looked more like a vase.

156

'I'd rather they focused on the economy, the Guard, internal policies - you name it - than got involved with the military and intelligence. To each their strengths.'

'Point.'

Jamus turned to Ulric. 'Which reminds me. I have recalled Garn and his colleagues, along with all surviving Anarian scholars, and most of the *Iterscientiams*. We can't afford to have another leak, or to keep losing our travelling libraries.' He stared at the floor for a moment. 'How one girl knew so many Darostim is beyond me.'

When Dariss Caraway had been tortured, it had torn a breach deeply into the Darostim. She had known far more than the cell she was part of, probably from her forbidden, sporadic relationship with her main contact. The reports of what had been done to her were enough to turn even Ulric's stomach.

'He would be useful. If he had been sent to Meyar instead of Withy-'

'What's done is done, my friend. He is a scalpel where a finger push will do. His solutions tend to be final, at the expense of information. Garn is not as good at earning trust or teachings as many of our less... imposing scholars.'

'Where is he?'

'Last reports put him in Eyotsburg. He was making his way to Meyar before the border closed.'

'The situation is becoming tenuous with Novin. It might be worth sending him there, but he has been in the field for several years now. I think he needs to come back first. Re-centre himself.'

Holmson blew out his cheeks. 'Colridge Garn. He's been responsible for more uncovering and suppression of plots against Eordeland than anyone in living memory. It's been a long time.'

'You think you can still trust him?'

'My friend, he is a fanatic. He believes in Delmatra and The Sanctum, the necessity of what he does, with all his heart. I would as soon distrust you.'

'Hmmf.'

'There is another matter I want to discuss with you. I haven't raised it in front of Eremus, because... well.' Holmson sighed. 'We may have a new problem inside Eordeland. An odd one.'

'*Another* one? What about Colcos?'

'I don't think it's military. There are strange happenings in East Norlund. A small region has gone quiet. Accounts say first one tun, then a village. Now it has spread to five villages and a few tuns.'

'Orcs? Bandits?'

'No… the people are still there, from all accounts, but they act as if in a dream, rarely respond. They don't speak much and just carry on with mundane tasks, reportedly with impressive industriousness. If it weren't for how well they work, I would suspect some kind of drugs, or poison.'

'Five villages,' mused Ulric. 'I wonder if there is anything in the water. Or perhaps a new religion?'

'I will send a delegation from the University to investigate. Perhaps some healers. There might be something in the libraries. It could be nothing serious. We'll need some Guard.'

'Aren't any of Garn's lot available?'

'Most of them are out of the realm, as usual. Two are needed in Darost; we have bigger fish to bake. I'll see if there are any more of his special scholars we can send separately.'

'Let me know as soon as you can. The last thing we need is some new cult spreading in the middle of a war.'

◌ ◌

It was evening in Lodnor. The congregation was long gone from the places of worship, leaving echoes and gloom in the great spired dome of the Church of Terome, only the flickering Lights of Terome dotted throughout giving shadows. Vast candles the size of a man, centred with a thick wick surrounded by seven equidistant smaller wicks, they burned slowly for six months. They were replaced by lighting new from old so the light of the Word would never go dark. It was said that whilst the lights burned, the message of Terome would never die.

Even confessions happened in bright candlelight.

All forms of cleansing within the Church had always ended - one way or another - with fire.

A room panelled with rare, exotic dark wood, gold, and thick Novinian carpets sat at the rear of the great cathedral, high above the floor. Unlike the resonating acoustics of the cathedral's arching ceilings, words within this room were kept within, where seven great seats crafted of precious metals sat against the far wall; virtual thrones. From these the voices of the Church elders, the Cardinals, were raised in argument, all men from middle to late years. Most were soft with wealth and entitled beyond others in the land. To each side along the walls less opulent seats were arragned, the nearest five each side with Primates and the other fifteen holding Bishops. They, too, were arguing, and the chamber was filled with the noise.

158

Teromant Chaplains guarded the doors, elite soldier-warriors protecting the highest-ranking in the Church.

From the greatest chair, the firm voice of an old man dressed in incongruously plain white cloth issued. His voice cut through the debating, and whilst he never seemed to raise it, it was heard clearly, and people fell quiet out of respect.

Sontles found this particularly irksome. His gaze, his mere presence could arrest conversation, and he knew he unsettled many of those around him; he moved through them like a wolf through sheep. His own voice cut through conversation with the dry rasp of sand, and it was effective.

But the Holy Voice of Terome spoke with dignity, quietly in a clear baritone, and people *listened*.

He was speaking now, and the noise quieted.

'Brothers. This warmongering is not the will of Terome.'

Voices rose again, some arguing and some in support. He raised his hand, and his fellows quieted again. Everything about him suggested a man with belief, righteousness, even kindliness, and patience. Those who knew where to look saw beneath this lay political shrewdness, a certain ruthlessness in the name of his faith, and a keen intellect. He was known as a good and kindly man, and indeed he was; the people loved him. But he was also someone keenly aware of his own status and able to use it to further his beliefs. No one rose this far in the hallowed halls of the Church without being a skilled politician. He might have had scruples, but he also would uphold them implacably. There was a charisma born of wisdom about him.

He spoke again, with deep conviction. 'Think on what we propose here. We go against a realm with superior forces. They have our people, our worshippers, in their lands, in their cities. Will they not suffer needlessly? Is our need so great that we must attack a foe a thousand miles hence? What do we gain?

'Brothers. We should be tending our garden closer to home. We have a rot within our own borders. I have heard the tales of atrocities rising, old practices that are not part of Terome's word. I have found men of the Church - *our Church!* - involved in plots so heinous I have been forced to excommunicate them. Our people cry out in need. The Prime Alderman's promise of prosperity for all is simply not working. He has more power now than ever he had when he and his Aldermen were Dukes.

'He gathers wealth with the promise to distribute it to those in need, but we do not see it leave his grasp. He has removed privacy for citizens, he has changed their basic rights, granted by good King Orreld, and he has gambled his country's future on a needless war. Our people starve and become slaves to each other, and our rich become like kings themselves. We have exchanged one for many.

'We must seek to cleanse the dust from our feet before we demand others wash theirs. It will take time, but we can do this. Jarle cries that Meyar must be made great again by its people after the deprivations of Haná; I say to you our land should make our *people* great again, that they have fallen because of men such as him. It is time to realise this, and it will not come from a Holy War. I cannot give the blessing of Terome to this venture.'

Voices rose, and Primate Gilden stood. Sontles had spent much time gradually bringing the man under his sway, and now he mouthed Sontles' words virtually unprompted.

A weak, narrow mind, thought Sontles. *Almost too easy.*

'How do you know that Terome does not bless this venture?' Gilden asked.

'Because Terome has not spoken to me,' was the simple response.

The Primates and Bishops whispered excitedly.

Sontles cursed inwardly, cold anger flaring inside him. His gaze was fixed on the Holy Voice, and he willed the man to change his mind. The man *must* have felt his stare, but he resolutely ignored him. Despite himself, Sontles was impressed. Most men would find themselves doubting, would begin to turn to his will, and would be lost when they looked directly into his eyes. But the Holy Voice was strong-willed, protected by his utter conviction. He was, Sontles realised, a true believer, and that gave him a natural protection to outside dominance.

The man was becoming a rapid barrier to his plans. Already heads were nodding in this room. He was popular and people trusted him. Worse, he could not be bribed; Sontles had already tried several times, from women to gold to land. The man had had the opulence removed from the chambers of the Holy Voice, living quite simply in them. Even his rivals respected him, and many of his views were a common point for all three minor Churches within Terome. He was open-minded, progressive even, and stood a good chance of undoing much of Sontle's work and reuniting the Church.

That could not be allowed to happen.

He sat silent for the remainder of the meeting, alarmed at the turning opinion. It had taken him many years to manipulate events to this level of instability. Chaos and war were almost inevitable - yet this man had begun to reverse opinion in less than a year.

No decisions were made, and the Churchmen left the room in twos and threes, bishops clustering around their Primates. The Cardinals left preceded by Chaplains. Only the Holy Voice remained. He noticed Sontles waiting and nodded, then turned to speak to one of the Chaplains.

As he left, Sontles approached the Holy Voice, who turned and then walked with him quietly through the Cathedral. His muted voice sent unrecognisable acoustic echoes amongst the high arches.

'The Reverend Bishop Aquinas. We have not seen you for some weeks. It is good of you to join us.'

Sontles inclined his head. 'Your Holiness. I have been… unwell… of late.'

'You do not hear the voice of our Lord God,' said the Holy Voice quietly, after a pause. 'I think you care only for your own power, your own game. I see how the Prime Alderman dances with you; you think him a puppet to your ambition. Beware, Sontles. He is no fool, and you will never find your reward in heaven from God this way. I know you favour this war. Repent your sins. I can absolve you, my son.' The sincerity in his voice made Sontles almost wince, but the spark of intelligence in his eyes reminded him that this old man was no fool himself.

'Repent my sins?' muttered Sontles softly, and nearly laughed. 'You know nothing of my sins, your Holiness. I merely… seek to make Terome, and Meyar, greater.'

'Terome does not need your actions to be great,' replied the Holy Voice. 'He already is. And you will not have my blessing for a Holy War without His word. I hear Gilden speak, but it is with your voice. We have always sought to spread the Word in peace, and by example. This is not the way.'

'It is the way of all religion to… spread the word. By war, if peace does nothing,' said Sontles. 'I believe war with Eordeland is inevitable.'

'The Way was never by force. The Church gains power with persuasion and righteousness. Heretics are only punished in extremis, not by default. Why do you hate the Eordelanders so much? I hear it in your voice, Aquinas.'

'You misunderstand, Holiness. I hate all men equally.'

'Even your brothers and sisters of the faith?'

'My concern is power, not conquest or love.'

'Power for Meyar, you mean? Or Terome?'

'Of course.'

The Holy Voice eyed Sontles.

'Terome wants believers, not forcible converts. His teachings are not only concerned with *power*, Bishop Aquinas. I have heard what some of the Teromants do. Their ranks have swelled beyond count. They force and govern where before they were only for protection of the Churches. This gift of the Flame and Inquisition that has continued for years without due process must stop. *Will* be stopped. I will find the ones responsible for this secretive work, and they shall regret the twisting of the Word of Terome. The Inquisition exists to find true heresy, not to expunge those considered less worthy.' There was clear warning in his voice.

'I would never sanction inquisition; surely all in Meyar are believers, your Holiness,' said Sontles smoothly. 'I... do not know what you mean.'

'I fear you do,' said the old man regretfully. 'And I fear your excommunication may become inevitable. But there is the chance for redemption within us all; so, I beg you, while you may... repent and work for the good of Terome, with Him foremost in your heart. Give up this talk of war without need. Terome will provide.'

'You speak... persuasively,' said Sontles after a moment. He had hoped to find a way to change the Holy Voice's mind; to find what he wanted, what could be offered. But now he spoke to him directly, it was clear the man was too pious and focused. He was one of those rare men whom Sontles would never be able to force to his dark will.

It was, regrettably, time to find another way.

'Perhaps you are right. Perhaps we should... discuss this at length another time.'

'I would welcome it, my son.'

By supreme effort of will, Sontles managed to stop his eyes flaring in anger. He had learned that unless he glared or sat in shadow, the red glint deep within his eyes was not noticeable. His habit of keeping a thin-lipped, hooded-eyed expression was trying, but even in such a corrupt society as this he would be noticed at some point if he lapsed his facade. Legend though he might be considered, once he was discovered, he would face danger from the sheer numbers of humans around him, and his plans would come to naught.

After hundreds of years, he knew full well how to manipulate emotions, especially fear, and there were few humans whose will he could not overwhelm in time. He was far more powerful than others of his kind. He had little doubt he could escape if detected and instil the fear of demons into the entire realm.

But he would never escape his masters; he was bound in shadow to them, and he could run nowhere except the shadows by his very nature. The Darklings had no cruelty, no compassion. No care. They would annihilate him utterly if he failed, as if he had never existed, and Sontles had definite plans concerning those he despised and Anaria in general, possibly even the world.

It wasn't even about revenge against those who had bulled and insulted him in life. It wasn't about being better than they were. They were all long dead, and even the vampire that had spawned him was long since dust.

It was about power. Cold cruelty. Control. About hot lusts and the screams of victims, of the fear and craving of women, the subservience of men. It was about being a shark among minnows, a gar-wolf among drugged sheep.

It was about Sontles sating every desire, for eternity, as the whim took him, without challenge.

To such an end, he could keep control of his temper. He smiled his thin-lipped smile instead, and cocked his head, his dry rasping voice carrying barely concealed amusement.

'Would you?'

FOURTEEN

I t was a late Grima day in the city, cool and crowded, when cries were raised on
the walls. The calls and murmurs spread like wildfire.

'Dragon! A Dragon approaches!'

The people of Darost had gone from not believing in the old legends to fierce
pride in the great immortals and an attitude that dragons were somehow *theirs*.
Family crests and businesses had sprouted images of the great creatures, and the
proliferation of taverns and inns with *Dragon* in the name was dizzying. Talk of
adding a dragon to the flag had gained support. A wave of newborn boys had also
been inflicted with names like *Drake* and *Draco*. Rumour had it one unfortunate
young girl had been named *Serpentina*.

Barely behind the calls came a blazing bronze glint. It swooped over the spot
where the statue of Györnàeldàr was raised, circling around the sculpture several
hundred feet up, a long stream of fire erupting and a strident, deep call blaring after
it in salute, before banking to circle the Dodecagon.

Karland and Xhera were already heading towards the centre of The Sanctum,
along with Seom and hundreds of others. Welcomer Guards were streaming towards
the Tower.

Karland reached the Garden of the Plains and stood gazing upward at the fiery
circling form, his face lighting up with the warmth of the answering fire inside him.

For most here this visitor was a curiosity. For Karland, this was a remembrance
of a friend, and a fascination and respect beyond others.

He was jostled a few times in the growing crowd. Someone pushed roughly into
him. He turned, biting his tongue, and saw Aran standing with his friends, pushing
other students aside. Aran turned to him, a supercilious look on his face which
quickly changed to a sneer as he saw who it was.

'They've brought the dragon a snack,' he said to his friends, motioning at
Karland with his lips pursed. Karland stared at him in genuine amusement, and the
grin faded from the larger boy's face.

'You know nothing of dragons,' Karland said, his voice filled with suppressed laughter.

Aran's expression darkened. 'And you do? You're a worthless peasant. None of those stories you've spread to make yourself popular prove anything. Now we'll see the truth.'

Karland felt the desire to argue welling up inside him, and felt Xhera grab his hand, bristling. Although she squeezed it in warning, he could tell she was also about to snap at Aran, and that would just make things worse as far as this idiot was concerned; a *girl* standing up for him. He saw Seom tense, sizing Aran up. Then he thought about how much he hungered to speak to a dragon again, and suddenly his desire to rub Aran's face into the dirt vanished.

He grinned at the larger boy.

Aran looked taken aback.

'As you like,' Karland laughed, the words tumbling out. He felt like he was soaring himself. The bitter anger at the constant goading was absent. A dragon approached, and he would speak to it. The dragons knew him. They didn't know Aran. He had earned their friendship. That was all that mattered.

Aran's eyes narrowed, and he took a step forward. Karland shifted slightly, and then Aran looked up and behind him.

Karland turned to see Rast, a boulder in the stream of the crowd. He was watching Aran expressionlessly.

'Karland. Xhera. As Dragonfriends we are required to greet our guest.' He turned, a dismissal that left a look of both outrage and mortification on Aran's face. Karland knew he had been looking for a chance to appear worthy to Rast. He bit his lip to stop laughing out loud; for a second, the urge to crow was almost irrepressible.

He wondered if realising the stories about him were true would make a difference with Aran, and then shook his head.

Of course they wouldn't.

If anything, it would be salt in the wound.

Welcomer Guard kept the throng well back along the perimeter of the surrounding walkway. Karland could not help glancing back as they were let through. He caught a glimpse of Aran's bitter expression as he realised that Karland really *was* meeting the dragon.

Probably hopes I'll be a peace offering, Karland thought. *Arse.*

He sincerely hoped he wouldn't be, knowing first-hand how volatile the great creatures were.

The dragon sailed overhead, circling the main tower slowly three times, head held high and wings stretched wide, before swooping down just over the right-hand arched bridge to land in the main garden before the doors. Despite having seen and ridden Györnàeldàr in flight it was still as surreal a sight as ever for Karland to see such a huge creature gliding effortlessly through the air.

The dragon landed with a grace that was still surprising, the buffeting wind from its wings blowing loose fabric back on the front of the crowd which was mainly made up from curious scholars of the Universalia Communia and students. The last few beats were a little restricted due to the surrounds, with lack of space between the Cuneus tip bridges and the plants near the tower. It folded the wings gracefully from ten feet up and dropped to land like a cat on the grass. Rumbling, it twined around until its tail threaded under the arch behind it, unrolling in loops. The dragon was clearly trying not to damage the grounds, slithering its supple body until it was settled and looking at the main tower doors, and the group set there to greet it.

Despite its efforts, several valuable bushes were damaged, and the spear-like talons were feet deep into the grass. The scholars of the Sub-Academia Botanica would be in despair. Karland had seen them work night and day for more than a week to repair the damage Györnàeldàr had caused last time she was here. Thankfully it had chosen the opposite end to where Darus had his small camp. The huge ork stood staring at the dragon with guards near the crowd, a strange expression on his face.

'The Council might wish to consider a formal Dragon-ground if visits become a regular occurrence,' murmured Rast, echoing his thoughts.

The bronze dragon did not fill as much of the garden as Györnàeldàr had, being smaller and leaner, but it was still well over one hundred and fifty feet long, its wingspan even wider. Sharp ears swept back into webbed sails, and another spined sail rose at the crown of the head between four dark horns, and then dipped to follow the line of the spine to the tail, from which trailing spines grew out, ending in a wide sail between spines horizontally and smaller dorsal and ventral ones which folded neatly down. Glittering bronze scales with darker burnt umber slashes down the flanks faded to a coppery cream on the belly and throat, and eyes like brown-green lightning flashed under spiny brows, the sharp diamond irises hinting at gold. The crowd stilled where the fierce gaze swept over them.

As with all the dragons Karland had seen, this one was unique and beautiful, utterly different to Györnàeldàr in shape. It looked familiar; he was sure he had seen it when the massed dragons had driven back Yosgaloth from the city. He found himself thinking that it would have been impossible to ride this dragon due to the webbing, and then almost smiled.

Karland had the impression this one was male, for some reason, and given its size was clearly quite a bit younger than Györnàeldàr had been - although that was a relative term. According to Aldwyn, it could still be over a hundred thousand years old - a number he still found impossible to really take in.

The head rose twenty feet into the air on the powerful neck, slimmer, maybe proportionately longer than Györnàeldàr's had been, and it cast its burning gaze around. Several people quailed. Karland shivered at the impact of a gaze so powerful it was almost physical, unfelt since Köranthír left. Even Night or Leona did not have eyes like this.

'I come to speak to the human Council, and pay respects to the Dragonfriends of my Sister,' announced the dragon in a booming voice, paying the gathering hundreds little heed and focusing on the group in front of him. He seemed to be less conscious of his volume than either of the larger dragons had been, and his speech was less archaic - almost modern Darum, in fact. His voice and movements were somehow more agile than either Györnàeldàr or Köranthír, if not quicker.

A squad of Onyx Guard stood formally in front of the main doors to the tower, wary but with weapons firmly sheathed. No one had forgotten what had happened the last time someone had attacked a dragon in The Sanctum.

A Welcomer Lieutenant bowed to the dragon, trying not to look it in the eye and lose his nerve.

'Welcome, esteemed Dragon,' he said clearly, his voice admirably firm. 'We are honoured by your visit. The Council has been alerted to your arrival and are coming immediately to greet you. Normally they would have been ready, but you, ah, arrived much more quickly than many of our guests.' He actually smiled at the great creature, and Karland admired his composure.

The dragon shook his great head and then rumbled with what sounded like amusement. 'I am considered one of the fastest of my kin. Perhaps we should agree upon a formal manner of future visits. The last thing I would wish is to cause alarm.' There was a note of mischief in his voice that made the Lieutenant blink; the dragon was clearly enjoying the consternation it had caused. Karland grinned to himself, remembering Györnàeldàr's surprising humour. 'Bid them hurry, human. My time here can be but brief.'

Even as it spoke, they were moving towards the huge creature, Xhera squeezing his hand again, this time in excitement. She was as enamoured of dragons as he was, and in the texts that they had been devouring in their free time, dragons and their lore had been a subject they had eagerly sought out.

The adroit Welcomer Lieutenant turned to gesture to them with a look of faint relief and announced formally, 'May I introduce those named Dragonfriends by the Saviour of Darost, the great Györnàeldàr.' His attempt at her name was brave, and very nearly right. He bowed slightly and retreated, quite clearly sliding the responsibility of talking over to the experts until the Council arrived.

'Ahhhh.' The breath hissed out in excitement, and the dragon ignored the guard, probably to the man's quiet relief. 'I am pleased to meet you, humans. I am Némaenth.' He seemed excited. 'Our people have much respect for you. Even Kòrànthír, and I never thought I would see him do other than hate humans.' He saw the consternation on a few faces and snorted in amusement. 'Well. I envy my sister her time with you. I would have given much to have arrived in time. She should not have faced the Nameless One by herself.' He sounded sad, and fierce. 'We all face oblivion; none of us should do so alone.' A shiver rolled down him, fascinating to watch as it clattered scales.

'Greetings,' said Rast. 'I am Rast Tal'Orien.'

The dragon looked at him with interest. 'Ah. The human warrior.' He looked at Xhera. 'And this is the human girl child? You all look alike.'

'Xhera,' she said in her clear voice. 'You are beautiful, Némaenth.' She sounded a little awed.

'My thanks,' said Némaenth proudly. 'I am the largest of my colour.' The gaze swung to Karland.

'I am Karland,' he said, his mouth drying. The weight of the dragon's gaze was still like a physical blow, despite his familiarity. Suddenly he felt compelled to say more, remembering Aldwyn's lessons, their meeting with Györnàeldàr, and his study of his Notes on Dragons.

He bowed, feeling his cheeks flush with uncertainty.

'I welcome you, *Nāgā. Hajinamast maitumhi kenko zang neemen vinamra anatur,* um, *vakar... mukar badhy.'* There was a moment's silence from the dragon, long enough for him to be certain he hadn't got a single word right, possibly apart from the honorific, and that pronunciation was dubious. Then he felt his heart plummet at the thought he might have just greeted a female as male.

The dragon reared back, its eyes flashing bright and making him weak at the knees. One of the guards audibly gasped, and there were some cries from the crowd of people. Karland had a split second to realise he might have terribly offended the gigantic being, and then the great creature bowed its head to him, closing the flaming eyes for a long moment.

'Hajinamastë maitumhē kenkyo xiàng nìmen vinamra anatpūr vaka ō mukaeru badhī, friend of the *Zhōng Gúorén Huáng dì Nāgāra.'*

There was astonished silence from the crowd and his friends alike. Karland didn't know what to say. He was not used to being paid such personal respect. He stammered nervously, breaking the silence.

'Sorry, Némaenth. I think I said all the words wrong.'

'You speak *Naga-tō* better than any human I have met,' replied the huge bronze graciously, a clear tone of amusement mixed with something more in his voice. '*You* we were told to be wary of especially, young one, and I now see why. I understand your questions number more than the stars that sing, matched only by your respect for Dragonkin.' It nodded to him, brilliant eyes hooded. He swore the dragon was grinning in some fashion, and for the life of him couldn't tell if it was joking or not. The head tilted to the side, listening. 'I am glad to meet you all. Kòrànthír spoke surprisingly highly of you, given that you are mere humans.' He didn't mean it to sound so dismissive, Karland supposed. 'That my sister gave her life for you says more.'

'Is- is her spirit truly still here?' Karland asked hesitantly.

Nemaeth brought his head down and spoke softly for a moment, his voice a murmured breeze.

'In the higher reaches of the mountain you call Drakeholm Soaring is a valley. It is warm and peaceful amidst the snows, above the clouds. I feel her presence there when I visit. Powerful, proud. Content. She will not leave this world until she decides to move on.'

Karland's nose stung. He felt like crying.

A clatter of guards and feet announced the arrival of some of the Council. Némaenth looked up, and they slowed before beckoning the Serpent to go into the chamber.

Welcomer Captain Jekob stepped forward, looking down slightly, and spoke hesitantly. 'Please, noble Dragon. If you will move to the entrance and speak, we shall bring you a meal. A cow, perhaps?'

Némaenth drew himself up, towering over their heads.

'My thanks, human, but my time is limited. I bear news from the *Zhōng Gúorén Huáng dì Nāgāra,* and the *Próarkhe* themselves. After I deliver it, I must return to my vigil.'

Ulric, Eremus and several others were missing. Mira Lyss was there, however, and she spoke for them, as was customary for the Arbitrator.

'Honoured dragon. I am Mira Lyss. It will not take long to bring them.'

The dragon clattered his wings in agitation. 'There is no time, Mira Lyss. My absence is already too long. I must return swiftly to my watch over the Nameless One. You are our allies, spoken for by Györnàeldàr and Kòrànthír. I come to tell you of a hard choice. To warn you.'

He yawned, his jaws showing shorter sword-length teeth behind canines as long as Karland was tall. Murmurs swept through the ever-increasing crowd. 'We hope our ancient enemy will hide many years in the darkness it has slithered into. It is yet wary of the combined might of Dragonkind and has to recover much of its former strength. It might sleep for a time, but we cannot be certain. One of our kin is already missing.' There was sadness and dread in his voice. 'It may be that they left on their own errand… but we fear the worst. If it is so, Yosgaloth will have grown much in strength. My kin is unlikely to have left without dire cause.'

'Does this mean we are at risk again?' asked Captain Jekob. The faces of the Council were grave.

'We watch night and day, as we promised. We would otherwise watch until we find a way to bind it again,' replied Némaenth. 'But something has arisen that has troubled us greatly and disturbs our vigil. For the first time in centuries, we held Moot. This was the decision I must tell you.' His head weaved for a moment, and he blinked, a flash of blazing green before he narrowed his eyes once more.

'A great shadow grows in the far west. For millennia we have been aware of ill in the world, a feeling of unrest. Of portents. Our sleep was uneasy. But now things have changed. After the Demon of Chaos was revealed in the Hall of Wyrms, and the Nameless One broke free, a great dark power has unveiled itself across the great lands of our world, no longer concerned with subtlety. Its time is come all too soon.

'We fear the worst: the *Suǒbhī nō Qūzhújiànvansaka*, the outsiders you call Darklings. All the chaos they have sowed… unnatural creatures, warping of mortals and beasts, growing war and destruction… it is no longer hidden. One is here, in Anaria; the Dragonfriends faced it for a brief moment. More lie in the lands to the west, which become warped, twisted, making the dark forest in the centre of this land but a pale imitation. Yosgaloth's foul presence changed much there over the ages, but these Darklings distort the very essence of natural order. The dead stir. Foul creatures roam. Mortal races gird for war everywhere. We dread what comes.'

'War?' said Regus querulously. 'We have voted against war-'

'I care not what you have *voted* against, human,' snapped the dragon. 'I have smelled the blood of thousands already shed. I have seen the lands you call Meyar and Novin building their strength. I have seen the tainted ones you name *orc* crawling as a blight on the world. They will all march soon. Unless you have wisdom to add, be silent.'

Regus's eyes bulged in a froglike fashion, but he wisely said nothing else.

'We have been awaiting the arrival of a diplomatic party,' said Adragostin.

'I see far, human, and I have seen no envoys heading here from your enemies.'

'What does this mean for us?' asked Mira Lyss.

The dragon sighed with enough force to blow hair back on the Councillors. The breath was very hot and dry, and smelled oddly of something spiced, possibly the dragon's own scent. It was not wholly unpleasant.

'The Ancient Enemy is a threat to us all,' Némaenth said. 'Loosed, it will scourge this world clean of life, your largest cities first. Your civilisations will end, and humanity will struggle to survive, scurrying in the shadows. But that is not our concern.' The casual dismissal of humanity was jarring. 'The Darklings seek to undo more than just the lives of those on this world, and they march to war. This, you have been warned of already.'

A mutter alerted Karland to more Council members arriving.

'A Seeker is here,' Mira Lyss replied, ignoring them. 'He told us the same.'

Némaenth barked laughter. The echoes thunderclapped around them, thrown back from the stonework. 'Heed him, and the words of my sister. Yosgaloth would not feast for long. The Darkling's goal is to return all creation to the Outer Chaos from whence it came.'

'I have never heard so much rubbish! All these rumours saying the world is ending,' muttered Councillor Regus, standing near Karland. 'Is it really necessary to keep repeating them? Are we to believe beasts and fools? *The dead stir?* Are we children?'

The words were almost under his breath, and Karland heard barely enough to piece it together.

He turned and stared, mouth agape, shocked at the sheer stupidity of the Councillor; the idiot was within seconds of being killed by his suicidal words, and possibly half the Council along with him.

'Be silent!' snapped Councillor Tarqas almost immediately.

Némaenth, capable of hearing a human's heartbeat from half his own body length away, heard every word clearly. He rumbled in real fury. Karland could feel it throbbing through his feet. People in the crowd edged away, sensing the tension, and the Onyx Guard around them shifted, preparing to defend the Council. The dragon could kill the hundreds gathered in seconds; the whole Welcomer Guard could not stop him.

'Perhaps *we* deem it important enough to heed the words of the *Próarkhe* themselves,' snarled the bronze dragon, his great fangs standing sharply from scaled lips drawn back in anger, and his eyes blazing. The whole Council quailed in fear. At that moment he was cruel, arrogant and powerful beyond mortal comprehension. His voice rose to a roar.

'Or perhaps I should not have bothered wasting my time. Do not belittle my words, *mortal!*' Heat billowed out from the dragon's maw along with the words, an almost invisible pop of flame which was more frightening than dangerous. Some in the crowd began fleeing, crying out in fright. Némaenth writhed his head down snakelike and hissed in a terrifying tone, staring full at the man.

'Mira Lyss. Karland Dragon-friend. Get this foolish mortal gone before I fix my teeth in his skinny carcass.'

Whyll Regus went as white as a sheet in terror. Karland swore he heard his bony knees knocking under his formal robes, and barely even noted that Némaenth accorded him as much respect as the head of the Council.

'Lieutenant,' said Mira Lyss her voice admirably steady, although she did swallow first. 'Please escort Councillor Regus away. Urgently.'

Shaking like a leaf in a high wind, Regus did not object. The Guard hurried him from the meeting towards the rest of the nervous crowd gathered out of human earshot.

'Please, Némaenth. We apologise.' Mira Lyss bowed low, face pale. 'We do not mean to doubt you.'

'The time for mortal games is past,' Némaenth said bluntly, the snap of ire in his tone. 'If you will not prepare for what is to come, you will all die. My duty here is done.' He snorted in disdain for them. 'My kin travel west to confront the Darklings. That they have unveiled themselves now means they must consider themselves close to victory. Above all else, they must be stopped. Every dragon is needed. Even the Greater Dragons are stirring. They will soon emerge, and we will find and confront these demons. But there is great risk in doing so.' He blinked, calming slowly. 'The *Próarkhe* can defeat them, but the battle itself could break the world. My people hope that we might aid in protecting the world from destruction.'

'So what are you saying?' cried Councillor Gusta. 'We are on our own?'

'Indeed not,' replied Némaenth curtly with a flash of his eyes. 'Am I not here to forewarn you? We can spare none, but still… we will not abandon our guard of Yosgaloth. What point securing the world if it is consumed as we fight?'

One Darkling had nearly driven Karland insane by its very presence. Now there were four, and he shivered as he finally understood the vision he had been granted in the Portal. He did not doubt the battle could truly destroy Kuln. Yosgaloth also still hungered; Meyar waged war whilst the realms of men dissolved. It seemed hopeless. Looking around at the faces of the Council members, he was not the only one who felt it.

Némaenth slipped his tail from under the arch and almost reversed along his own length, snakelike, until he wove through and reared, looking down over it. Twisting back, his great claws gripping the stone bridge arching from the Segment to the Dodecagon, the great bronze towered over them. The crowd held its breath.

'I can tarry no longer. My people wait. Chaos not only rises, mortals. It is become a foul tide. We must not let it sweep us away.' His eyes sought Karland and his companions, and he dipped his head in salute. 'Until we meet again, Dragonfriends.'

Turning sinuously, he stood high on his powerful back legs and opened his wings with a crack. With a quick glance around to ensure no humans were too near, he brought his fore feet up to the bridge and then leapt up thirty feet or more. His wings caught the air with a slap, and he lifted quickly into the sky, the edge of his armoured tail cracking into the side of the tower. His voice boomed back down to them all, echoing off the stone around them.

'Stand fast, mortals. Look to the skies.' With a blast of flame, he sped back towards the west, and was gone.

ങ്ങ   ഇ

Karland and Xhera had decided that, for the moment, it was better to eat in their room. He had already had one run in with Aran, who had been seething with jealousy, and they were constantly beset with questions and requests. They hoped the attention died down soon.

Seom had visited them, and it was obvious he viewed Karland with a little awe and a great deal more respect - almost as if he were not the same person - after watching his once-unsure friend greet a dragon in its own tongue.

Outside The Sanctum it was a little easier; no one had seen them speaking to Némaenth. Still, it was as if the dragon's visit had sparked wild speculation of anything unusual. Tales that had been scoffed at were now being given credence cross the city.

A few men from up north - further east than where Karland had lived, the other end of the great Northing Woods - had mentioned accounts of strange rare creatures, green and brown, that had been seen lurking around mountains and forests.

'Very odd, they was,' one had said in the marketplace. 'As soon as they knew they was seen they vanished again.'

'Orcs,' nodded one man authoritatively.

'Don't think so,' said the first man.

'Bowers saw one, dintcha?'

'Yeah,' said a heavyset man with a scraggly beard and eyebrows, and oddly full lips. 'Slipped away in the woods. Looked like some kind of creature, but on two legs, like a man. Weren't no orc though. Moved different, smooth-like.'

'Yer seeing things!' laughed the loud-mouthed definitive speaker. 'Orcs been travellin' west, come from them eastern mountains.'

'So how come these ones dint kill no one?' Bowers protested.

'Mebbe they was worried about all yer mates,' said another man with the grin of an idiot who thinks he is making an extremely clever joke.

'Look, this was different. Like a small man wiv rough skin. Skinny and straight wiv these gold-red eyes. I ain't the first. People been seein' them years, now.'

So what colour was they then?' jeered the first.

'Well... Greenish. But they wasn't orcs,' the man added again hastily. He was drowned out by jeers.

'Yahh! Wha'ever, mate.'

'Hahahaha!'

'It was orcs.'

'Drunk, was yer?'

Karland had seen the man's face darken in anger, but he kept his mouth shut to avoid more taunts. He thought the man was telling the truth, personally. He hadn't seemed drunk, and Karland hadn't seen an orc that moved 'smoothly', or that had red or gold eyes. It was amazing how not much more than half a year ago the same men would have jeered at the man for saying he had seen an orc.

Since the release of Yosgaloth, tales of strange creatures had sprung up from all the surrounding lands. Some were simply strange, and some were horrible, telling of death and destruction. The opening of the pass in the Iril Eneth had allowed many unnatural creatures to escape their long confinement, although when he remembered back to the creature that had passed through Hoeven Lake's farmlands it was clear that some had already left.

'This is ridiculous! Dragons? Druids? Elves? Orcs? Demons? Are there any other fairy tales we wish to add?' one young scholar had asked as Karland went to a lesson, her expression haughty and her ringed finger marking her a newly Papered Scholar. Her companion had laughed at her expression.

'If you wish to go and inform a Dragon that it is ridiculous, be my guest. I may even come to your memorial... if they bother holding one.'

Karland had grinned as he hurried past.

People spoke of the dragon for the next week, although many who had not been there persisted in calling him a huge lizard. Karland snorted as he hurried back through the morning crowds. Dragons were lizards the same way a knight's charger was a rat.

He was focused on his thoughts as he entered their rooms. Xhera's voice broke into them.

'You look awful. Didn't you sleep well?'

Karland scrubbed at his eyes. 'Not really. Dreams again.'

Xhera nodded, her face reflective. 'I'm still having those.' Something in the way she said it alarmed him.

'Hoge?'

She shook her head, remembering the Plains Walker that had come very close to raping her. 'Not much now. I haven't thought of him for a long time. I had nightmares for months, but, well. Seeing Rast kill him, knowing I had you there… in time it grew less.'

Karland felt a deep admiration for her. He still woke sweating and panicked from sleep, dreaming about the forest witch who had almost killed him. Usually he lay, frozen, unable to move again as she moved close with that green stain upon her lips, taunting him and teasing him. Sometimes they were terrifying. Sometimes they were discomfortingly erotic. The eerie attractiveness she had about her lingered even in memory. In fact, the events last year had given him a variety of confusing dreams for months afterwards, and they still had not finished visiting him.

Xhera's gaze softened as she gazed into the distance. 'I mostly have nightmares about Yosgaloth, to be honest. I'm usually creeping through tunnels under the mountains, knowing that it is somewhere there, can see me, smell me… and I can't see anything. I'm terrified. I dream of the world… barren, destroyed. The only things left living twisted and horrid. It's… the more I learn of Aldwyn's work, the more I know, the more frightened I am… but because nothing is happening, that goes away a bit. And then it's just this dull unending fear that visits me in my dreams.'

It sounded poetic, but he understood her completely. She shook her head.

'Sorry. What was your dream?'

He smiled his understanding. 'You'd think I'd dream of Aldwyn most, and I do a lot. Sometimes of… Letizya.' He grimaced. 'And Yosgaloth, though the Darkling more. But last night, it was Györnàeldàr. I think seeing Némaenth opened up her memory again. I felt like she was still there, her voice almost speaking to me… it seemed so real.'

'I feel she is still here too,' said Xhera softly.

Karland hoped the dragons were right, that her essence was still somehow here despite the death of her body. She had loved this world.

α   β

Over the next week the excitement died down, and they returned to their studies with Night, who seemed regretful he had missed the dragon's visit. In an overwhelming reversal, the vast majority of the Universalia Communia voted to overturn the original vote against war preparations.

Only three of the Council objected. Ulric was reinstated as the head of the war Council. General Colcos and Rast were now officially involved in helping to prepare for war. An alliance with the orks was agreed on and envoys were sent to Banistari and Morland. A surprising amount was ready in a very short space - almost suspiciously, according to one Councillor.

Eremus had also complained about the cost to Eordeland until someone had suggested emptying the banks of Eordeland as a civic duty, whereupon she had shut her mouth, to general amusement. It was widely known that her family's money lay in managing the wealth of other people.

Karland found it difficult to maintain his composure after the visit. Too many things were matching up in his mind. He had gone back anxiously over what his old friends had said to him in the past, as well as what Night and Némaenth had said. Everything had seemed to settle back into a feeling of normalcy despite the new preparations.

Xhera was able to focus on her work better, and stop worrying, but his mind darted more than hers, considered more things, and he could not stop his impatience from bursting forth.

'We've got this sense of urgency, but no one is *doing* anything,' he complained finally one afternoon.

'Is that what you really think?' asked Rast. He looked up from maps he was considering, sketches of the lands to the west of Eordeland.

'It does seem like it. Earth shaking news, the end of everything, doom and gloom... and then life just carries on.'

'That is how things work outside stories, my young friend. We prepare as we can, but in the meantime, life, as you say, continues. It could not be otherwise. Until we can do something, we must simply go on in the hope that things will not cease.'

'But we should be doing *something*!'

'We are, Karland. And when we know what else to do, we will do more. Meanwhile, we have been warned. Greater forces than we work to maintain the world. All we can do right now is plan. You forget what the Council must still do - they are negotiating with allies, securing the borders and the cities as best they can. Meyar and the orcs are an unknown. They must do the work of a year in months.' His voice showed no sign that he still held frustration over the hurdles they had faced. 'I know we suffered on their behalf, but remember… to them we offered only more questions, not answers.'

With that, Karland had to be content.

FIFTEEN

Finally, something took place that helped take Karland's mind from the impending issues and his lack of answers. A delegation of six elves arrived from the Leohtsholt, four women and two men.

Karland and Xhera didn't see them when they arrived, but after the afternoon lessons they found themselves drawn to anything that spoke of elves. They learned a little of them, finding that scholars were also frustrated by them. Despite thousands of years of living side-by-side, humans had noted little detail of their kind past tales.

Aldwyn's notes said their skin was different, needing no protection from the sun. Karland thought of Seom, and his Morlandish heritage. His tutor had been adamant that men were identical the world over, and the only reason for the colour difference in their skin was down to its thickness and how much sun there was where they originated. Elves apparently viewed humanity's divisions over skin tones with perplexity.

Despite keeping their eyes open, and bothering Rast on more than one occasion, they did not see the elves until one afternoon several days later. Coming back from lunch, Karland saw Rast talking to two of them near a high hallway on the ground floor in one of the Cuneus Atriums.

'There's Rast,' he remarked, nudging Xhera. 'With elves!' He began making his way casually towards them.

'Maybe he'd rather not be disturbed,' she said.

'Don't you want to meet them?'

Xhera shrugged, her eyes on the tall humanoids. Karland sensed a yearning, and a prevarication. She remembered how she had been saved in her vision, and it woke more memories. He knew this wasn't easy for her, and smiled, grasping her hand. It was strange how that felt so natural now; once, he wouldn't have ever dared to even think of it.

The huge man loomed over people passing by, despite being in a corner. Rast could dominate a room from sheer presence, so it was astonishing that at times he could become so unnoticeable. Today, however, even if you did not see him, his companions were hard to miss.

Tall, slim and lithe, they were graceful, moving as if they were hinged slightly differently, more smoothly than humans. Neither were heavily muscled, but rather toned like deer, with a hint of power under the apparent frailness.

As Aldwyn's notes said, they were pale-skinned. Not pale as in races of men, Karland noted, but like alabaster. There were slight differing tints to eye shape and skin tone, but that was as far as the difference went. Either side of a high bridged nose, wide-spaced, almond-shaped tilted eyes with no epicanthic folds sat beneath long, sharp straight eyebrows with a slight upward angle to the edges. Smooth-lobed, sharply upswept ears rose slightly higher than human ears to points with less intricacy of structure. Their hair seemed finer but thicker than human hair, and fell in rich lines similar to a Hadrasian's, straight and long on both man and woman.

Faces sculpted grave and porcelain in repose changed completely when they spoke, blooming into expression like flowers finding the morning sun, and they smiled often. Their soft laughter spoke of much they found in the world that gave them joy, and it seemed to him that they smiled at the unceasing gravity of Castellan James without malice.

There was no comparing them to any race of men. They were utterly different.

'They almost glow,' said Xhera softly.

There was something a little ethereal about them as Rast spoke softly. They replied in lilting tones. The way they tilted their heads and moved said very clearly that they were not human.

A few people were clearly curious about the visitors, but a steady look from Rast kept most at bay. He beckoned the children over when he saw them hovering.

The man was nearly as tall as Rast, if almost a third of his width, and his figure was lean and lithe, with a slim waist. He had light silvery hair that had pale hints of brown-gold leaves in autumn. His hands ended in long delicate fingers, and his eyes smiled under those tilted, tapered brows. His ears swept up and back to bracket a face almost permanently in a half-laugh, as though he didn't take anything the people around him did or said seriously. There was an ancient air to him despite this, as if he had seen many years and many things. He looked barely out of his teens, but in some manner reminded Karland of Aldwyn, despite the lithe muscling his frame held.

The young woman was small for an Elf, a little over five and a half feet tall, although she appeared more petite. Her willowy figure swayed hypnotically when she moved, and even her hands and eyes moved in the same way, with an odd long pause and then a controlled flow to another position. Her hair was milk-white, and large pale blue eyes that were almost silver transfixed him as she turned to watch their approach. Although a small quirk played around her perfect lips, as if she would suddenly smile to break your heart, she was far more serious in mien than her companion. Her figure was tight and strong, with wide shoulders and slender curved hips and small breasts framing a flat stomach above long, slender legs. Something in her reminded Karland of a doe - long limbed, fleet, alert and cautious. Her ears were more sharply upturned than the man's, almost catlike. She was so beautiful she looked somehow unreal.

Neither of the elves showed any veins through their pale skin, or any other characteristics of flaws except her; a perfect half-circle of marks curved on her bare right upper arm's otherwise flawless surface, perhaps a scar.

Karland felt an almost tickling dissonance when he saw her, as if he had once known her. Closer to, their beautifully slanted eyes were not Hadrasian in appearance, but *other*, and noticeably larger than human eyes. Their features were defined, chins pointed and cheekbones high, but without anything being overly sharp, and their teeth were rounded, even and strong.

In fact, they were both a little disconcerting to look at. Until you saw the perfection of an elf, you didn't realise how much you valued the characteristic imperfections of humanity. They almost felt uncanny. Karland wondered if it was the perfect symmetry of their faces.

'Karland. Xhera. This is Galnór; and Lëlylien.' As Rast spoke their names, the elves bowed. They had a way of considering you that made you feel simultaneously their entire focus, yet still a passing event. Both looked ageless, but something suggested that Lëlylien was much younger than Galnór - perhaps a way of moving or holding her head, with a little more vivacity. Serious though her eyes were, they twinkled with what seemed to be contentment.

In fact, that summed them up.

Something. Hints.

Their qualities were hard to define, as much a feeling as visual. Karland could not help comparing them to the elves on the slopes of Drakeholm Soaring. There had been a feeling of darkness lingering around the visage of those, but these two had a feeling of peace and harmony to their movements, faces unmarred by hatred, despair, or scarring.

Although both were dressed relatively plainly in curious light robes, they looked as if they were ready for court. Their bearing was that of nobility, and if they laughed often, you also felt they never forgot that humans were fleeting and chaotic. They were both very polite, wise, serious and amused, their gaze piercing but knowing.

Galnór bowed slightly to them, his arm describing a complex and elaborate arc in front of him that doubtless spoke volumes to the sophistication of the elves but meant very little to Karland. Lëlylien bowed too with a sinuous ease, lower and with even more grace.

The elves were both hunters, he understood from what they said, as well as emissaries. It seemed Elven society did not have roles as humans did, but instead each elf simply did what they were most suited to do, without argument or problem. They had sensed from afar the freeing of the ancient evil, and its turning back. Their keen eyes had seen the skies darken with dragons, something not seen since the terrible Drake years more than two thousand years previously. Even an elf did not live long enough to remember the sorrow of that time, except for the tales of the immortal High elves living in their homeland.

Karland and Xhera stared at them in wonder, listening to their dulcet tones and marvelling at their strangely ethereal beauty.

Finally, Rast excused himself, bowing fluidly to them. 'I must speak with the Council shortly, and Alaria. The day's hearings are almost done. Will you join me?'

Galnór smiled. 'Go, my friend. We wish to speak to these young ones more. Alaria and Tiondél will pass on what you discuss.'

Lëlylien nodded as well, and Rast smiled slightly.

'*Na-senda,*' he said, and left.

'What does that mean?' asked Karland.

"Be at Peace," replied Galnór. 'An interesting human, Rast Tal'Orien.'

'The only human we know of who has learned to focus inwards enough to trigger a *dônaethar* trance,' said Lëlylien.

Galnór laughed lightly. 'It is not really the same, sister.'

'You are her brother?' asked Xhera.

Galnór smiled. 'Through association, not by blood. All elves are family.'

'What is different about the trance?' asked Xhera with interest. 'I mean, when an elf does it.'

Lëlylien laughed lightly. 'For us, it is a waking dream. A human must focus, expend intense effort to rest in the trance. We did not think it could be done until he showed us it was possible. But elves simply pass into a... a waking reverie, if you will. We know humans may meditate, but that is a puddle in rain compared to a deep lake. What Rast Tal'Orien does is... to dive into the lake and hold his breath for a time. It took him many years.' Her gorgeous eyes turned to her. 'We *breathe* the lake.'

They sat and talked for some time as people flowed past, discussing the differences between them. The elves would not answer many questions about Rast's time amongst them, laughingly avoiding the subject and saying only that Rast would tell them more if he deemed it fit. When Karland asked if they knew Rast's past, they sighed with a touch of sadness in their tones.

'Rast is shaped by his past. It is for him to tell you,' said Lëlylien gravely.

'What is Rast?' laughed Galnór, evading both question and gravity. 'The stone against the sea, the sea against the stone. The blade to cut the vegetation, and the vegetation to tear up rock. He is the general and the soldier, the master and the pupil. In some ways the pinnacle of a man, yet something more; and in others a man seeking himself, perhaps something less. You cannot seek to define such a man in one sentence, when he has spent a lifetime, and the sum of lifetimes, to become himself. Rast is like the stars - hidden, distant, cold, pure. But a star close to is a furnace vast and powerful beyond imagining. Our sun is such a star, with Kuln a pinprick next to it. That is Rast.'

Karland supposed that was as straight an answer as he was likely to get from these strange people. Somehow, the elves in stories were less work.

They asked about the children's lives, where they grew up, and about the city and The Sanctum. They seemed delighted by the tales. In return, they spoke of their travelling abodes in the balmy Leohtsholt, where they had lived for three thousand years. They described the wondrous cities made of cloth and woven boughs in the trees, which were nurtured and sung to, and they gradually wove to the designs the elves called forth. They told of their love of working in wood. Very little apart from weapons and some prized decorations were made from metal. They talked of the cities as nomadic, travelling often, but it became apparent that *often* to them was measured in decades, not months.

In winter, when snow blanketed the trees and ground, even elves found less comfort, and moved to warmer lodgings. Elegant wooden housing and clothes thickened slightly from plant fibres were used when the cold came.

Finally, the elves turned the conversation more towards recent events, and asked for a tale of their travels. Lëlylien sighed at descriptions of Györnàeldàr, and it seemed she was enamoured of Dragonkind. They expressed their sorrow over the loss of Aldwyn and Grukust. Lëlylien especially was impressed at the description of Grukust's final stand, and her expression became oddly fierce. Karland, looking at her, realised why Rast had said elves were considered terrible enemies if provoked. She was terrifyingly intense, yet aroused something deep inside him with her fierce beauty.

The confrontation of the Darkling and the Great Dragon was met with a mixture of horror and reverence. They asked less questions than anyone else had, and Karland wondered if this was because the elves already knew of these beings.

What it must be to have such long lives and wisdom, he thought.

'And the *Talénthese?*' asked Galnór. 'This stone portal? I have heard tell of it. I know of one who has also passed within. Will you tell us what you saw?'

Xhera hesitated, and then motioned to Karland. He spoke of his vision of the Great Dragons, and Galnór nodded slowly.

'We long suspected that the *Ruag-dûr* came to our world from outside.' *Darklings.*

'What of your vision?' asked Lëlylien, turning to Xhera. The girl hesitated, and Karland thought she would refuse to tell them, but then to his surprise she began to speak. Something about the elves seemed to reassure her.

'When I was young, I lived in what is now called Valesruin. I was rescued in the forest on a night of green fire by the elves,' she said, her eyes distant.

She spoke more of the terrible events, in more detail than Karland had ever heard before, and it seemed to pour from her. He took her hand after she finished, and she gave it a quick squeeze in gratitude.

'We know your story,' said Galnór. 'How strange that we should meet you, here! One of our Eldar took you back to men, after you were tended by Alaria herself, one of our most respected healers.' He smiled. 'She journeyed with us here. She would wish to see you again. Doródon declined to come; he rarely leaves the Forest of Light. I think the next time he leaves it will to be for his last journey home to *Míthtól.*'

Lëlylien's face saddened a little. 'Elves died that night, and much time was spent tracing the damage to the forest, putting out fires, tending creatures and trees harmed. It was ill chance that the fragment of tainted rock struck your town.'

Galnór frowned slightly, a crease appearing on his smooth brow. 'Doródon did not believe it chance. There has been a Malice at work in recent millennia. Chaos becomes directed.' He looked at Lëlylien, his expression unreadable. Something unspoken passed between them. 'The world moves in ways it chooses. Consider: so many gather here as if by chance. Why here? Why now? It may not be mere chance, but balance asserting itself.'

'I have read much in Aldwyn Varelin's notes on chaos,' said Xhera. 'He says it disrupts balance; that great evil comes from it.'

'Chaos in itself is not evil,' replied Galnór. 'Without chaos nothing would grow, nothing would change. But unchecked, it can seem so. Strife is born from it. And evil lends itself more readily to its influence. Order is less easy to bend to ill use, though it may be... often under the guise of good.'

'Harmony is the key to the Universe,' said Lëlylien softly. Karland looked at her, almost embarrassed by her conviction. Her face was soft and alive, and her eyes sparkled. The way she said the words gave him hope. 'The harmony of life and death, movement and stillness, order and chaos.'

'Our kin have felt the loss of balance in the world. They have grown troubled, heard the tread of war between the realms of men. We felt *Cuil-faikar* move, that which you name Yosgaloth, and we watched powerless from the slopes of Iril Habór as it destroyed Irilview. We remember it of old. Some of our greatest kin joined with the *melkëhlócë* and the *Ældarin* to bind it many lifetimes ago. We sense its contagion and its hunger.' Galnór's face was troubled. 'There is much moving that troubles us greatly. Even the *Ældarin* are wary.'

Lëlylien crouched gracefully, her face equally dark, and spoke to them, almost hesitantly.

'I am most troubled by tales of *mornedhél.* Our kin that... travelled... with *orcs.*' It sounded as if she had to force the words out. 'What can you tell me of them?'

'*Nésa,*' chided Galnór gently.

Lëlylien ignored him, intent on the children.

'Haven't you spoken to Rast?' asked Xhera.

'I have heard his words.' The ageless face was intent on theirs. 'Now I would hear yours.'

Karland thought back to the creatures they had faced, the first elves he had ever seen. They had been like yet unlike these flawless people before him. A sense of discord had flowed around them, and the one Rast had killed had possessed a ritual scarring on his face.

'They did not just travel with them,' he said reluctantly. 'They led them.'

Their expressions did not change, but he had the feeling he had profoundly shocked them both.

He described their encounters as best he could. The elves seemed particularly distressed about the markings on their skin. When he described their deaths, Galnór sighed in sorrow.

'Rast has not spoken much of the elf he killed,' said Xhera, 'but I know it still troubles him.'

'He had no choice,' said Galnór sadly. 'I would have done the same, to my eternal regret. They were lost. Their deaths were a blessing.'

Karland remembered the last elf, the beautiful woman with the same pale blue-silver gaze as Lëlylien. He recalled her quickly hidden despairing fury when Rast had mentioned the loss of her people and found it hard to disagree.

'They felt... lost. Alone. Tragic. Adrift,' Xhera said, as if she were seeing them again.

Although it clearly upset the elves, they questioned Karland and Xhera further. With each query Lëlylien grew more agitated. Finally, and with none of the cracking of joints or groaning a human would display after so long crouching, she flowed to her feet. Elves moving were fascinating to watch.

Her lips, usually set in a semi-pout, were now pressed together. Her eyes looked haunted under surprisingly long lashes, and tears stood in them.

'Elves would never submit to chaos,' she said fiercely, her soft words holding anger. Her voice held denial.

'Remember the tale of Fórnur,' Galnór said gently.

She shook her head. 'This is different.' For a moment her face showed terrible anger, and Karland saw again what it would be to face an elf as an enemy. 'I… must think.'

She moved for the ringway arch and vanished.

Galnór sighed.

'We will speak again with Alaria and the others,' he said. 'Rast has spoken to them at length; we will add your words.' He stood. Karland was surprised to find that they had been seated for hours, and his backside was numb; they had chosen a stone bench, after all.

'Thank you for your tales, Karland, Xhera. We have learned much. And do not take Lëlylien's manner to heart. She is deeply troubled by what you told us.'

'I hope she will be all right,' said Xhera.

Karland stood. 'When do you leave? We would like to see you again.'

'We must decide further what must be done,' smiled Galnór. 'You shall see us again soon. Until our next meeting.' He looked in the direction Lëlylien had vanished with troubled eyes, bowed to them, and was gone.

◌ ◌

Despite Galnór's words, they did not see the elves again for more than a week. During this time they threw themselves into the study of Aldwyn's work. It was a good week; Aran had left him alone and Karland had worked hard with Rast and Darus.

After that, the elves often chanced upon them somewhere in the gardens, or in the high arching halls, or so it seemed; they did a lot that seemed to be random but ended up having purpose. Karland never saw them in the great food halls and surmised that they must be taking food in their rooms.

Rast told him the hot food of humans was not their usual fare. Elves ate no meat at all, enjoying foods that were lightly prepared and cool.

185

Lëlylien seemed troubled, and no longer laughed like her kin, but she still enjoyed their company. Today she had followed Karland and Xhera almost whimsically to the archery session. Erwhist nodded to her, showing no rancour at having an observer.

Aran took notice of the exceedingly beautiful elf maid and did everything possible to make Karland look bad as soon as he saw her speaking to him. Karland's first shot was smooth and good and thumped home just inside the right of the bullseye. His brief feeling of triumph turned to ash as Aran grouped three in the bullseye quickly at forty yards, his finest shots to date, and sneered at Karland.

'Is there nothing I am not better at than you, Dresin? Even the work of a peasant? What use *are* you?'

Karland bit his tongue and refused to look over, although his cheeks heated in embarrassment. He snatched up another few arrows and loosed almost savagely, his heart hammering in his throat.

His shots were poor and eventually he dropped his bow in disgust, having not even come close to the centre again. Sergeant Erwhist bellowed in passing at his performance before moving on. Karland could still hear Aran laughing and boasting about his skill, and Karland's lack of it. He glanced up in frustrated anger to see Lëlylien walking over.

Aran watched with narrowed eyes from behind her, which possibly was meant to make him appear calculating but merely made him look tired. They followed the sway of her figure insultingly, lustfully. He made several comments to his laughing friends, jerking his hips obscenely as he mimed holding her. Karland wondered if he knew how well elves could hear.

Lëlylien squatted next to Karland lithely, like a panther. Her head cocked.

'You let that boy get to you. Why?'

'I don't do it on purpose.'

'But he means so little. He struts like a young cockerel. He has some skill… but I know you have skill, too. Why do his words affect your ability?'

'They just do. They… make me doubt myself.'

'But you have done it before. Surely you know his words are false.'

'I can't help it. They matter. And they make things worse. Without him here, I can do it.'

Karland didn't know how to explain it. Aran's words reached into the hollow doubt at his core, and everything just… went wrong. His muscles wouldn't work properly, he couldn't think straight, he did things badly. It was beyond frustrating. He thought he'd conquered this trouble with Ben Arflun. He was no longer so painfully anxious or self-doubting, but somehow Aran brought it all back, and worse. It was as if he was perfectly designed to tap into the wellspring from which his helplessness flowed to remove all controlling dams.

Lëlylien shook her head. 'Humans are strange.' Her eyes bore into his. 'You do things, yet still doubt you can do them even as you prove you can.' She blinked slowly. 'I know what I can do. And then I simply do it as well as circumstances allow. You must learn to ignore the doubts of others. Elves do not doubt as humans do.'

She reached for his bow, placed a handful of mismatched arrows in the quiver one by one after inspecting each briefly then running her fingers along it, discarding a few. She tested the draw. Then she turned swiftly, nocking, drawing and releasing over and again so fluidly and quickly Karland could hardly follow her. It was beautiful to watch.

Less than ten seconds later she had loosed them all - not at his target, but at Aran's, two over. Her arrows formed a near-perfect ring around Aran's bullseye group of three. Her last had passed exactly between the two most centred, at an angle with hardly any room to spare, ending up pressing his top arrow upwards.

The student archers went quiet, and Aran's boasting was cut off as if someone had slapped a hand over his mouth. Lëlylien smiled at Karland, handing the bow back. 'If those had been my own arrows, I would have split each of his. Believe in yourself, Karland. *You* ride Dragons. Doubt nothing else.'

The silence was broken by a booming laugh. 'Couldn't have done better meself!' chortled Erwhist happily. He took a bow and an arrow from a girl called Grama and loosed it, fast and smooth, though with nothing like the grace of Lëlylien. His arrow hit home a finger's breadth from hers. 'That right there was skill. You can learn to be skilled. But you need to practice and let go of your damned egos.' He glowered at Karland and then handed the bow back. 'Carry on.'

Karland did not do very well for the rest of the session, but he did improve. Lëlylien spoke calmly to him, giving him tips on what he was doing wrong.

'Touch the arrow, if you don't know it. I know my arrows, but an unfamiliar one must be caressed, seen. You must know the shaft, trust it will fly true. Feel the bow. Feel its pull, its balance, let it pivot on your wrist like part of your hand. Do not grip hard… let it float. Do not look at the tip of the arrow; look at where it goes. Trust your body and your eyes. Pinch your shoulders. Pull with your back. Brace with the *v* of your hand and keep the arm straight, elbow out.' Karland tried all this, and she laughed, tinklingly, the first time in days. 'Try not to think about it. Just practice it, feel it. Concentrate on the form, not the results. Let it become natural. Your trouble is you seek to understand too much. You overthink.' She looked at him thoughtfully. 'Your mind is taking control, and that is where your doubt comes from. Your body knows. Do not aim. Loose. Loose. *Loose.*'

Lulled by her words, ignoring everything else, his last few arrows were faster, more fluid, and aimed before he could think. His last three thunked home in a loose grouping into the bullseye.

'There,' Lëlylien said, sounding satisfied. 'Do not lose that feeling. You have felt the connection between you and the target. The arrow is a bolt of lightning following that path. If you tell yourself you cannot do it after this, I will be disappointed.'

Karland looked into the unearthly beauty of her face and decided he didn't want to disappoint her.

After the practise, as daylight faded, he and Xhera walked with Lëlylien. Karland caught a glimpse of Aran starting towards him, then scowling and turning away upon spying the elf maid still with him. He grinned to himself.

Karland was expecting Lëlylien to leave them after entering The Sanctum, but instead they met Galnór. He stepped out of an alcove as they passed like a wraith, behind Lëlylien, who was walking ahead talking quietly to Xhera. Karland nearly jumped at his appearance.

The tall elf raised a finger to his lips and took one step towards Lëlylien.

'If you are to ambush me, Galnór, you may wish to do it when there are no others around. I could hear Karland start.' She didn't turn her head.

Galnór laughed lightly. 'Well caught, I say.' And then to Karland, 'Lëlylien is one of our most talented hunters. Better even than I… in some things.'

She shot a glance back and he grinned at her. Karland laughed.

'Come, I have words to share with you.' Galnór was walking them towards their room. 'Lëlylien must hear them too, though she may suspect them already.'

Although he had been smiling, the words were serious, and Karland began to suspect that whatever the interlude in events had been based on, it might be coming to an end. The words had the finality of a goodbye.

૎ ૐ

Galnór and Lëlylien posed naturally on the recessed seats before the fire, like royalty, or perhaps the subjects of a famous painting. Xhera sat next to Lëlylien before the open balcony door, the sky passing from dusk to night.

'A decision has been made,' said Galnór. 'There is too much afoot here. We need guidance, before our time in the Léohtsholt is shortened.' His eyes grew a little distant. 'After speaking with the Council and Rast Tal'Orien, they are sorely

188

troubled. Never before have any of our kin turned from the Path. We need help. We thought we were incapable of corruption.' His voice softened in almost bitterness. 'So naïve.'

Dark elves, thought Karland, remembering back to the slopes of Drakeholm Soaring. Galnór saw his face change. 'Yes. You have seen them. The disorder to our harmony.'

'We did not think it possible-' began Lëlylien.

'Nevertheless, *nesa.* We must send to our homeland. We need the guidance of the *AEldarin.*' At the look on their faces, he added, 'The High elves.'

'Who will be sent?' asked Lëlylien. Galnór smiled at her. 'You?' He inclined his head and waited. 'And I!' Her voice held a note of joy.

'Lëlylien has not yet visited our grey-cliffed islands, bound by mist,' explained Galnór to Karland and Xhera. 'Our kin will return home, led by Alaria. They have sworn aid to Eordeland. The struggles of humans are not our concern, but… this goes beyond the troubles of men. If Eordeland falls to chaos the other lands will follow sooner or later. If that happens, we shall end up alone, a forest island in a sea of destruction. We will take ship with Rast Tal'Orien from Eyotsburg.'

Karland wondered what that meant for him and Xhera.

A soft knock at the door sounded. The elves looked up in surprise.

'Come,' Karland called, noting their reaction curiously. It seemed they had not heard the visitor approach. He wondered if it were Rast.

The door swung open quietly just enough to allow Night to step through. He hesitated when he saw the elves seated. After a brief pause, he continued. Karland could have sworn that he appeared momentarily off balance, the first time he had seen the calm little man discomfited. He rose and moved towards the scholar.

Night stopped further back than normal, his neither young-nor-old face partially lit in the flickering firelight. The elves looked at him with wary interest, in a way Karland had not seen them study anyone before.

He bowed slightly.

'Greetings.'

His soft voice slid through the chamber. Lëlylien was frowning slightly, as if trying to recall something, and Galnór, usually so affable in his foxlike fashion, was watching Night through narrowed eyes. His nostrils were flaring, and his back was to the light from the fire as his pupils grew larger. Elves could see exceptionally well in the dark.

Then Galnór sprang up with a hiss of realisation, backing away. It was an oddly reptilian noise. Lëlylien was no less alarmed, sinuously putting her hands down on the seat next to her and lifting herself through with straightened legs like a gymnast, sliding them behind her and allowing herself to slither back from the sunken seat. Their eyes never left Night. Neither elf blinked, and Galnór's hand was darting for weapons as if he were unaware of their absence.

The tableau held for another second, and then he spoke in a voice utterly unlike any Karland had heard, somewhere between a rasp and a choke. It was an astonishing noise from the throat of such a normally graceful and dulcet-toned being.

'*Do you not know what manner of creature this is?*' His voice was strangled. 'Stay back, Karland. You are in great peril.'

SIXTEEN

Karland was almost speechless at the elves' behaviour. He glanced at Night, who had not moved.

'What do you mean? What's wrong?'

Night stayed silent, watching.

Lëlylien bared her perfect little teeth in fear, or hate, a bizarre expression for such flawless features. Galnór was crouching like a tiger about to either spring or turn and run for the balcony. He almost spat the words.

'This horror masquerading as a man is undead! A child of Chaos! An unholy aberration, never to walk the light of day!'

'*Vampire,*' snarled Lëlylien.

'Summon the guard and destroy it before it is too late. You are in grave danger,' Galnór said again. His voice was trembling.

'He's a friend of Leona, a Druid - and mine too,' Karland said, turning to Night. He had thought elves and Druids were friends. 'You're a Druid, right?' He was almost pleading with this little man he liked so much to deny the charge.

Night shook his head. 'I never said I was a Druid,' he said softly. 'But I *am* their ally.' He turned his piercing eyes to the elves, who almost flinched. 'If I wished any here harm, surely it would have occurred before now.' His tone carried weariness and regret. Karland's heart thumped.

'You're a... a vampire? Like *Sontles?*'

'*No.*' The words came softly but with a forceful finality that brooked no argument. 'I am not like him. The Order of Illuminus are allies of the Druids and the Darostim.'

'*Illuminus,*' breathed Lëlylien. Galnór nodded slowly. He relaxed slightly, but neither looked any less ready to fight to the death.

'Forming an order of Scholars does not change what you are,' said Galnór, a deep loathing in his voice. 'Vampire.'

'*Vampyre,*' said Night. The inflection was different, the *a* almost a *u*, the *i* drawn out into more of an *ee* sound. 'The older name.' Karland stared at him in dawning horror, and involuntarily took a step backwards.

Night sighed.

'I was born a Vampyre. I have never killed another for their blood. I and my… family… have spent our existence fighting those that do. I cannot change what I am, and I never pretended otherwise.'

Karland stared at the nondescript little man in front of him. Even now, it seemed ludicrous, a mistake, although things were falling into place. His name, the hints about his place of birth, his cold skin; the piercing, almost overwhelming gaze, the silent way he moved and appeared… *only at night,* Karland realised grimly.

The thin-lipped smile-

Almost of their own accord, his eyes were drawn to Night's lips. Night raised his open hands to the side, a gesture more helpless than menacing, and opened his mouth properly, drawing his lips back slightly.

Sharp fangs stood out where a human would have eye teeth, glinting in the firelight. As he watched, they lengthened to more than twice as long as a human canine, slender and razor-edged. A slightly shorter pair matched them in the bottom jaw. They were very white, and possibly the sharpest things Karland recalled seeing.

A vampire.

Vampyre, Karland corrected himself. *But still.*

Night closed his mouth and dropped his hands to his sides. 'Our Order are Vampyres, those who have learned the path out of Chaos. We show it to the Turned where we can. Where we cannot, we cleanse the world of them.'

Even now, describing things in a manner almost like Aldwyn's, he seemed so incongruous that Karland wanted to not believe him. The sight of the teeth had been so surreal Karland almost doubted it had happened. But he couldn't deny the eyes. Their blue gaze cut into him, in a way akin to Leona's. There was something horribly predatory about it, he thought now.

'Is Leona one too?' he asked. He caught a glimpse of Xhera, white-faced and silent, eyes wide.

He heard an almost-snort from behind him, one of the elves, and Night smiled a familiar thin-lipped smile that Karland found faintly more menacing now he knew the reason for it.

'No Druid is a Vampyre. It would be impossible.'

'It… he is correct,' said Galnór, grudgingly. 'A Druid cannot be other than a Druid.'

Karland looked at the elves. They had relaxed into a semblance of normality now, although they still seemed strangely stiff, and appeared to be trying to edge backwards through the wall without actually moving.

Galnór bowed to Karland and Xhera, never taking his eyes from Night. 'Apologies. The… presence of the undead turns my stomach. We will leave.' He looked at the door briefly. 'You should not be alone with this… person.'

Karland wondered, then felt ashamed. The little man had helped them avoid a mob in Punslon, had done so despite his own mission. He had sought them out and helped them study. Rast accepted him, and Karland now felt certain Rast knew what Night was. He knew a major decision had arrived for him, a chance for him to prove his morals and stand up for what was right. He had been alone with Night plenty of times, as had Xhera, and never felt threatened.

He spoke before he could second-guess himself.

'We'll be fine. See you tomorrow morning?'

Galnór studied him briefly, and then smiled slightly. 'You do not lack courage.'

Lëlylien said nothing, but her eyes were serious.

Night bowed slightly, without mocking, and after a second Galnór nodded reluctantly. They left the room, flowing like hunters, never removing their eyes and moving as far around Night as distance allowed. He courteously moved aside to give them as much room as possible.

The door closed. He cocked his head, and then after a few moments returned his gaze to Karland and Xhera. 'They have gone, although they spoke to the guards to keep watch for me,' he said. Karland was surprised; his senses must rival theirs.

'Let's have a seat,' said Karland, managing not to let his voice shake. He was slightly regretting his momentary bravery and personal ethics. 'Would you like some water- well. I suppose not, really.'

Night smiled, a little sadly. 'I can drink it, of course. It simply does little to sustain me.' He moved down into the seating pit in front of the fire and sat in front of them. He really looked no different to usual.

'The first Vampire was an elf, you know,' he remarked as he sat back, near the fire. Karland blinked in astonishment. Night nodded.

'That is one reason they hate my kind so vehemently. She was the brightest star of their age, revered and loved. Ealasaíd is her name.'

Is, repeated Karland numbly to himself.

'She was born from chaos, many thousands of years ago, a chance event that should have killed her. Much changed on Kuln, chaos whipping across the face of the world. Many horrors were born; she was one of the most terrible. The elves did not know what to do with one of their number become feral, violent, unnaturally immortal; a drinker of blood, a render of flesh. She was immensely powerful even before, a true Mage, and the shock of Turning drove all sanity from her, warping her gifts and instilling in her uncontrollable and alien urges. She slew many, some close to her.

'They came against her to destroy her and she fled. For countless years she was simply an abomination. She would sometimes flee the carnage, her nature trying to resurface, but she spread her disease like a plague. Over long ages she slowly regained her reason, preying on anything or anyone that she found. One day, she mastered herself again.' His eyes were sad. 'She must have been the loneliest being in existence... to recover your mind, to recover control and sanity, only to realise what you had become, what you had done... Her husband and child were long removed from her by time and deed. She had tried to kill the child she had loved; she tore her husband's heart from his chest, still beating. Both now were dust. She had no one. It was a tragedy that has perhaps not been matched in the long ages since.

'But she also knew that some of those she had attacked had also become like her. Not all; but enough. The curse had passed on. She dedicated herself to hunting them down one by one, and swore never to lose herself again. At first, she wished only to destroy them, but in time she realised that they could become like her... they could regain control, live lives again, if only they had the chance. So she taught them to remember who they were, if she could.

'Down through the ages the community grew. Most Turned could not be saved. Some did not wish to be; they revelled in their newfound power and lust for blood, and she destroyed them. None of us can face her wrath. She is the first and most powerful of us all.' He inclined his head, as he would to a queen. 'And now she reigns over the Vampyre; those born to become masters of our nature, not the reverse. We have lives and purpose and do not kill like monsters. We do not Turn others. More of us are born now than were once Turned.' He was silent a moment. 'We grow slowly, reluctantly, and like elves we stop after a certain maturity. I was born a Vampyre. I will hunt vampires where I find them, and I will not willingly take a sentient life.'

Xhera's cheeks were wet and Karland felt a lump in his throat, imagining the terrible fate of the elf maiden. Night's voice continued softly.

'We do not desire what vampires do. Our people learned to find more power in knowledge than in blood... we became a race of scholars, if you can call us a race. We count men and elves in our number; the curse does not seem to extend to dwarves or orks. Or orcs, if you could persuade even a vampire to feed on such a foul creature. Their blood is too tainted.'

Karland shook his head. 'I thought you were a legend. Boogeymen to scare children. Even Sontles… I guess I thought he was just, you know. Exaggerated.'

Night shrugged.

'Much legend has a basis in fact.' He sounded awfully like Aldwyn for a moment. 'And Sontles is no exaggeration. If anything, the opposite.' He sighed, something Karland thought must be habit more than anything else. Now he was watching more carefully, he could see Night only drew breath to talk. It was disconcerting.

'Vampyres are the epitome of chaos to an elf,' Night said sorrowfully. 'We represent their antithesis. For a being so in love with harmony, so close to and in tune with nature, and one that by design and choice eats no flesh, a chaotic, undead monstrosity whose nature is drinking the blood of the living, revelling in the wanton death of others, like Sontles… like myself…' he looked a little sad at the wry bitterness in his voice. 'Intellectually, they know me to be different from him. From vampires. The Turned, the once-living. But they simply cannot countenance what I am.' His face held regret. 'I had no choice. I was born to it, and I am thankful for that; a Vampyre can learn to redirect a bloodlust young, to focus on other forms of power.'

'So… You aren't alive?' asked Karland in fascination.

Night grinned tightly.

'To me, I am. I think, I feel, I move. But I have no life as you have. My body works differently to yours. My heart beats blood around my body, but I cannot die. My flesh is cool unless I have just gorged.' Karland stored that fact away in morbid fascination. 'I do not need to breathe unless to talk. I have powers and urges far beyond those of mortal men. My thirst for blood is faint, controlled, but always there. I will heal from nearly anything, and barring accidents I will probably live a good portion of forever. The legends of what men call the *undead* are not all stories. I am profoundly unnatural. But I grew as a child; different to you, to be sure. But there was love, there was community. There was care.

'A vampire on the other hand… consider why they are so terrible. A mortal is torn violently, brutally from their life, in terror and blood. They are damaged in the process, physically and mentally. Then they… resurrect… with faint and confused memories scattered with flashes of searing clarity, overwhelmed and overlapped by animal urges that cannot be controlled, and the realisation of immense power, of immortality… the severing of all ties. Morality, humanity, mean nothing anymore. Mortals lose their sanity when it happens. The urges take over, and that is a tragedy when the person was good. They loathe themselves even as they are driven to their acts of horror.

'But if they are evil beforehand as well... If they invite the chaos in and it rises at the touch of vampirism... Then they become true monsters, revelling in carnage, fear. Violation. Power.'

He was silent again. Karland was envisioning someone destroyed in such a fashion. The thought he could be brutally slain only to rise again and kill someone like Xhera... and enjoy it... was almost too much to bear.

'What...' Karland didn't know how to phrase it. 'What do you eat, here?'

Night blinked slowly. 'There are those that worship our order and offer blood. Not much; just enough. And if not, I can always visit the slaughterhouses and take fresh cattle blood. Not as sweet, but vital. It is a simple meal for me, and I do not need to feed often. Once every few days at most.'

Xhera visibly shivered, and Night smiled sadly.

'A vampire is to be pitied, helped to a gentler path, if possible, but never forget how dangerous they are. One that embraces their curse is to be feared and destroyed at any cost. Sontles is one such as this.' His steady gaze bored into Karland. 'I at least was guided, could learn to subdue that part of me that wishes to kill. My... family... hold self-control above all else. We would be a threat beyond imagining, otherwise.' He blinked reflectively. 'That is why I admire your friend Rast immensely. I recognise his control, the noble desire not to harm despite being so capable of hurting and killing others. *That* is what we seek, and it takes us more than a man's lifetime to fully sublimate our thirst.'

Xhera was staring at him, her face pale. She still had not spoken.

'So that is why you are called Night,' breathed Karland.

'We earn the right to be referred to as lords and ladies, nobility if you will, when we master our base urges.'

Lord of the Night, remembered Karland. He couldn't think of a more fitting name.

'We have formal, powerful primal names,' explained Night. 'Lord of the Shadows, Lady of the Depths, Lady Tempest, and so on. We still have darkness in our natures, so we tend towards the macabre and grim, but not always; there is a Lord of Winter Sun, for example. I am often referred to as Of the Night.' He smiled. 'But the First, the Queen of the Lost, Ealasaíd, keeps her given name in honour of those she lost.

'Immortal scholars,' said Karland wonderingly.

'Yes,' smiled Night. 'We have honour and learning. We have worked with the Darostim to secure knowledge of the world. I would not be surprised if some of them know what we really are. I think once he realised who I was, Aldwyn knew. We are friends of the Druids more than the elves, who hold a kind of icy distrust for us, as you have seen. Druids... Well. They are nature priests perhaps, but they have their own doors to chaos. They understand us far better than the elves, whom I suspect are simply waiting for us to prove our feral side again. It is a shame. After millennia you would think we would trust each other, but then for immortals and near-immortals... It is not such a long time.'

'How do you kill a vampire?' asked Xhera quietly. It was the first thing she had said for some time.

Night shrugged, a smile playing around thin lips. 'We may still be harmed. We do not starve, though we eventually become catatonic. The older we are the more powerful we become, but some weaknesses grow, too. Oh, I can bear weak overcast daylight for a brief moment, but then my flesh yellows and breaks down. Anything stronger and I would truly burn. A painful death, I am told. We are consumed by something in the sun's rays you cannot see.'

Karland tried to imagine what it would be like to suffer the loss of sunlight, to know that the next time you saw it, you would die horribly. He couldn't.

'It must be hard, to lose the sun.'

'I have never known the sun,' said Night.

'So the old tales are true?' asked Xhera. The colour was returning to her face.

'Hot enough fire can reduce us to ash, stop us healing. We can be poisoned by some woods. Wolfsbane weakens, although it kills other creatures of chaos. Pure garlic is deadly to us. It sends us into shock and our bodies stop working.'

'Just from wood and herbs?' asked Xhera.

Night shrugged. 'There are uncounted plants that kill humans quite horribly with which other creatures have little issue. It is the same for us.'

'What about onions?' asked Karland interestedly. He knew the plants were related to garlic.

'I do not like onions,' confirmed Night with a straight face. 'Not so deadly, but still.'

'What about metal? Iron, Steel? Weapons?'

'Weapons do little harm. Even if you removed my head from my body, I could heal if they were brought back together. Even a stake through the heart can be survived. But the purity of silver, ah. Even contact can scar like the worst acid. A wound made with silver will not heal well. If it enters our heart or removes our head... well.'

'Staking through the heart?' asked Karland, fascinated and horrified in equal measure.

'A stake of ash, oak, hawthorn or yew will paralyse.' He grinned slightly as Karland shifted, tensing the muscles in his left torso unconsciously. 'A rowan stake can kill. All of this is relative, in any case; the older the vampire, the harder it is to kill.'

'What about running water? Drowning? Being obsessed with counting?'

'I crossed rivers to get here, Karland.' Night's voice was amused. 'And I do not breathe, so. As to being obsessed with counting, no more than anyone else. A personal compulsion for neatness and order is at odds with our baser natures, but it wouldn't stop us any more than it stops Castellan James.'

'And holy symbols?' asked Karland. 'Could you come in if you weren't invited?' He was finding this interesting.

'Karland, stop now,' said Xhera.

Night laughed quietly. Karland caught the glint of a fang tip; he must have amused the plain little man.

'Half the Gods worshipped by men in the last five thousand years have not been real, and those that exist have better things to do than respond to one mortal invoking them. A name, a symbol does nothing to us. But very often a symbol will be made of something pure and precious, like certain woods… or silver. That *will* cause us pain.' He studied Karland for a moment, and then said quite deliberately, 'And I go where I wish.'

'Aldwyn said he thought there was some kind of… disease, a virus, in your bite. In your saliva, he guessed. If you… if you bit me, would I become a vampire?' Xhera's voice hardly trembled.

Karland wished she hadn't asked that. They were alone in the room with one, for want of a better expression.

Of the Night. Haha.

It didn't seem as funny now.

'We think that is true,' said Night. 'Certainly none but the First became a vampire without being fed upon. It is not certain, though. If you were bitten, you might weaken and seem to die as the curse took hold after that one bite, and then arise again, changed internally. You might simply weaken from loss of blood and recover quite well if you didn't die from it. Some mortals have a terrible reaction to whatever it is, and die horribly, their bodies unable to accept the changes, or become mindless slaves, bound to the one that fed on them and carrying out their orders. The number of mortals that are suited to become a vampire is very small. Most do not Turn. Perhaps the number of feedings change this, or the weakness in the body, I do not know. But we have studied this for millennia without success.

'What we do know is that mortals who are drawn to chaos seem somehow more likely to Turn. It is as if the corruption searches for a matrix and aligns itself.'

'Do the Seekers of Illuminus truly harm no one?' asked Xhera. She was studying Night intently.

He shook his head gently, and Karland saw tragedy buried behind his expression. He must have seen many terrible things in his long, long existence, Karland realised.

'None, outside those who would see our world in ruins, and the vampires we hunt; even there we show mercy where we can. We defend ourselves and cull the feral, no more. *We stand in the Shadows to face the Light.*' The words carried longing.

She absorbed this and smiled slightly.

'I still trust you, Night.'

She moved to him, slowly, and Night stilled, looking at her in puzzlement. Xhera leaned forward and gave him a deliberate hug, and he stiffened, unsure of the contact. Karland was horrified for a split second, then ashamed, then worried. Night's face changed, and his gaze softened, somehow. He patted her awkwardly on the back with a cold hand.

Karland ached for how brave she was. Xhera did not doubt herself as he always did, despite her fright. *She* had shown her acceptance. *She* had given the gesture. She was braver than he was ever likely to be.

'I- we... we're still your friends, Night.' To his surprise, he meant it completely.

Night gently disengaged from Xhera. 'I am... a little uncomfortable, having you so close. I can hear your heart beating, smell your fear. Feel your warmth. I am... not used to it.' He said it kindly. 'But both of you... thank you. It means a lot. I do not believe I have ever been so welcomed outside my people. Your trust in me means much, my friends, and I will keep you from harm, if I can.'

Karland felt a lump in his throat and saw Xhera's eyes shine with tears. Even with his family, his community, Night would always be an outsider from people, especially as he travelled alone. His long centuries stretched out, without warmth or sunlight, empty and forlorn in Karland's mind.

'Come now,' chuckled Night after a moment. 'Let us leave such depressing topics and talk more about Aldwyn's notes. And then, if I may, I would like to know more of the Library of Thingos. You know Thingos believed heavily in interpreting the Prophecies of Sarthos?'

They settled down, and Karland smiled to himself. Night was not just a friend; he was a fellow student - one who knew more than all Karland's lecturers, but still treated them as equals, and that was all that mattered.

α   β

'The elves are everything I expected, yet not,' said Karland the next morning.

He stood with Rast upon his room balcony in the morning light, facing another segment. To their right and below the Gardens opened out around the Dodecagon. For once he had awoken early, his mind buzzing with ideas. Xhera was still asleep, which was unusual; she was normally up before him.

By mutual unspoken consent, he and Xhera had not spoken of Night to anyone. If the elves had spoken to anyone so far, it had not been mentioned. If he were to hazard a guess, they had probably only spoken to Rast.

Night was one thing, but elves were still a mystery.

He tried to continue. 'The stories are…'

'…stories?' supplied Rast with a faint smile. 'I spoke of elves a little before, Karland, but you cannot begin to understand their mystery until you experience it. There is little of mortality about them.'

'All the stories say they don't die,' said Karland dubiously.

'High Elves do not. Others… well. They do, eventually, but to us, it is so long that it may as well be immortality. It is not uncommon for an elf to live more than a thousand years.'

'They are all so happy, but at the same time so… cold. No, that's not right. Distant. Interested and polite, but severe. Inhuman. Sad. Light-hearted in a heavy way. Focused, but not on what we are. Gah, I can't explain it.'

'The word people use for them is *fey*, which means all that and more. I know what you mean, Karland. To us, they live for so long that kingdoms and empires may rise and fall. To them, we are a brief diversion. After they *quicken*, their perception of time alters, and continues to do so. The elder elves, the *Eldar* of their race such as Alaria, are very far removed from humans. Although they find great joy in experience, I think we frustrate them greatly. Humans are so fleeting and chaotic to them, yet all unknowing we experience life in a profound and emotional way they never can. The nature of elves is enduring harmony and peace. The nature of men is transitory, full of passion and conflict. Yet of all the races, men have the greatest capacity for good and evil, and our art rivals theirs.' He sat, head back, thinking for a moment. Karland dared not interrupt; Rast rarely spoke more than a few sentences. Elves mattered deeply to him.

'Aldwyn was wise, and a good friend. I miss his ability to word things I cannot.' The big man shook his head. 'Some time ago he told me that all the mortal races are made of individuals capable of many aspects, but men are the most changeable. I think what he meant was this: more than any other race, humans have their natures in constant conflict for balance. We have scholars and priests who are intelligent and compassionate to nearly rival the most worthy elf; we have artisans and smiths with almost as much passion and skill in their creations as dwarves. We have men who are so evil they may as well be orcs in human skin, but in many ways worse; for orcs cannot help their nature, but often these men act by choice. And yet the unjust can do good things; the just may also be selfish and cruel.

'I am proof of how far a man may go in training himself at war, in ways of harming other men… and still I am as imperfect as any other man.'

He looked down reflectively at his huge scarred red hands, indelibly splashed with the blood of a dragon, as if seeing how many enemies they had ended. 'Elves love changelessness, mourn when it is gone. Aldwyn used to say humans were the strangest creatures on the planet; we desire stability, yet excel at change.'

'I've heard him talk about how we aren't so different to animals before,' said Karland. 'He said we had no right to use animals as we did, but then what could be expected when we did the same even to other people.' He hesitated. He knew Rast had been deeply troubled over finding elves that had lost their way. 'But if what you say is true… what about those elves we fought?'

'Ah.' Rast was quiet, his face troubled. Finally, he spoke, as if still puzzling it through himself. 'What I speak of is in the natural order. What we faced was no natural thing. I have never heard of an elf turning from harmony in that way.'

'Maybe they were half-elves? You know, with human evil or something.'

'There is no such thing, Karland. Humans and elves can be lovers, but they are not able to bear offspring. We are just… too different. These were elves, pure and powerful, but they had a dark aspect upon them.' He sighed. 'Even as I faced them, I loved them. I was nearly undone by the shock. It would be like an orc feeding the poor and tending the wounded from love; it is just not something I thought possible.'

'Maybe not all orcs are evil then?'

'You gamble your life if you think not. Orcs have no feelings for others. They kill and cannibalise without thought. They are driven to it, warped from normal lives. Perhaps the single orc that kills you is not evil inherently - merely doing what all others around it are doing. *Perhaps*. That doesn't make you any less dead, Karland. Chaos has changed much that was good and made it dangerous, but I have rarely seen the reverse.' He watched Karland a long moment. 'It is admirable to judge others on your own morals, your own ethics, but you must be aware that they may not, will not always share them. Orcs consider nothing but their own foul lusts and desires, and think little of the future, and only a little more of the past. Their nature is unnaturally tainted. They live in their own pain and misery and inflict it on others. It is their nature. If you want a good orc, you have one in the orks. In Darus.' He smiled slightly. 'Do not tell him I said that. Orks are what orcs were before their fall from grace. Is it any wonder they hate and fear them so?'

'Do you ever think about this when you fight them?'

'No. I think of nothing but winning.'

'What about the High Elves? The *Ældarín*.'

'They are a deeper mystery. They are like dragons, I feel: immortal, powerful, terrible. Totally alien. No one knows how many there are, or what they are capable of. We must ask their aid, I think. That will mean a sea journey to *Míthtól* where they all live.' He seemed to consider something, looking troubled. 'With one exception. I faced one when we stepped through the portal.'

'A High Elf? You never spoke much of what happened in the portal,' said Karland curiously.

Rast gazed at him inscrutably. 'The message was for me alone.'

'How do you know? Maybe if you talked to some others-'

'Karland.' Rast's voice held a note of warning. 'I may tell you one day. I might have told Aldwyn, were he still with us. All I will say is that I met a High Elf there, in a great hallway. Even to one used to elves, he was... strange. I think they are like lesser Gods themselves, as far above us as a Greater Dragon is above Dragonkind.'

'Lëlylien seems troubled,' said Karland after a moment.

Rast nodded.

'Galnór spoke to me. I know something of her story. She was deeply hurt by the disappearance of her birth sister; he fears she may have been corrupted. Both of them suffered melancholy. Only time will tell if Lëlylien can be healed or not.'

Karland hoped so. Lëlylien was entrancingly, heart-stoppingly beautiful, and something in her spoke to him very deeply. There was a wildness, a sadness that went beyond the other elves. He hoped that she could come to terms with her horror of the elves that had been warped. Perhaps one day she would be as happy as she deserved.

଼ ଽ

The days passed with no decision.

Karland returned from a boring class in the Academia Oeconomica, lost in reflection. Xhera was studying today, but his training with Rast had been cancelled. It would have been just the thing to clear the boredom of numbers from his head.

Now Seom had been permitted to join, it was even better. His friend had been overjoyed to train under the legendary warrior, but had been a little dismayed to find Karland was more advanced in many areas than he was.

They both felt odd about it. Seom had always been the far stronger and more skilled out of the two of them.

However, his friend's surprise and admiration for Karland was as nothing compared to that he had for Xhera. He had badly underestimated her skill with a knife and ended up at her mercy more than once, as had Karland. She committed, was strong and quick. Seom was adjusting though and was well-practiced. He would be an accomplished warrior.

What Karland had been thinking about more was how many times he had seen Rast massaging his knuckles. He hoped the burn from Györnàeldàr's blood wasn't hurting him.

'Hang on, Karland!' called a voice. 'Wait!'

He turned to find the small, fine-boned form of Bradwr Hallt. As ever, the boy had seemingly boundless energy. What seemed bubbly at first Karland had realised was a result of an innate lack of social grace, a curious blankness deep within. He understood not fitting in all too well, but with Bradwr the adulation of others was his obsession.

Xhera was not particularly fond of the young man and had said more than once she found him dangerously vain. Karland privately admitted she might be right but felt almost protective of him.

Bradwr seemed grateful, though sometimes a hint of what Xhera saw seemed to shine through - he was often thoughtless in what he said and did, as if he didn't care about others, although he seemed instantly contrite when pulled up on it, and was prone to dramatic upsets and hurt. Nevertheless, he and Karland had become very close, and Karland valued much of their time together. They had interesting discussions, and Bra agreed with much of what Karland said. Karland saw the imperfections in him, but it wasn't like Karland was perfect either.

Bra was actually several years older than Karland - nearly nineteen, although he looked and acted younger. Karland found him almost beautiful to look at, with a fine, almost sharp bone structure. He panicked easily when things did not go as he expected, and had a lot of fleeting interests, usually coinciding with what other people liked at that moment. He worked hard to be popular and was liked by many as someone fun and bubbly.

Bradwr found the topics Karland studied interesting, at least at face value, but more than once Karland had the impression that he couldn't care less and was showing interest for his own reasons. He often boasted he was mature and grounded but was quite happy to emulate dizzy breathless energy when it suited his purposes. The inconsistency was faintly irritating, but he put up with it, knowing it was Bra's way of coping with uncertainty.

Bradwr had tried hard to get Rast's attention; all the students wanted the honour of training with him. Rast was polite to most, yet he ignored the youth completely.

In less charitable moments Karland wondered if Rast simply thought that Bra wanted reflected glory. He was just far too sporadic and competitive to be asked to be a serious student of his mentor's, and Rast had no time for people he deemed interested only in their own self-image.

They walked clockwise around the Garden of Harvest, chatting about the possible upcoming war. Bradwr was more interested in how he could turn it to his advantage. Karland, having seen some of it closer up, was of the opinion that this was short-sighted and required Eordeland to work together. Bradwr nodded reluctantly. Karland could tell from his pinched expression he was not happy with the statement. He rarely was when Karland didn't immediately agree with whatever he said.

They talked instead about dragons - never a dull subject for either of them, but one that inevitably left Bradwr jealous. He had never seen one up close.

'Perhaps we can go to the Libraries next week,' Bra said off-hand, glancing around and paying little attention to Karland, as usual. His attention was on a nearby group of female students. His fun attitude and youthful looks seemed to be very appealing to many of them. 'I really want to see more of them. There must be lots of books on Drakes.'

'All right,' agreed Karland, biting back his annoyance at the other's lack of attention. The Garden-facing Cuneus libraries of each Academia were huge and varied, fascinating to explore. The Apprentice Scrolls were helpful and knowledgeable, not as forbidding as those in the Combic Libraries.

No one even got into those without express permission. Karland and Xhera found much of them off-limits; very few had full access. Even Papered Scholars could generally only explore their Academia areas.

Still, even the Librariums held much. Karland and Bradwr had found amazing artwork, including fantastic bestiaries, though Bradwr had not been pleased that he had shared it all with Xhera too. There was definitely a jealous streak in his nature.

Karland sighed, looking at his distracted companion. His energy was sometimes infectious, but more often it felt desperate and forced, making Karland feel sorry for him. He was so desperate to do things *with* people he never did anything *for* them.

On occasion he was almost embarrassed for his friend, but he genuinely liked Bradwr despite his flaws, putting it down to inability to express himself. Bra just seemed so lost behind the face most liked of a fun popular student.

Only a few weeks ago, some students - once friends of his, apparently - had called after him as he walked with Karland. Like him, they were from Aegland, the small island off the coast of Eordeland, and their complex multi-syllabled language gave a lilt to their Darum.

'Look, it's the *hunanolhawl!*' one had laughed nastily. Most of the others simply stared coldly. Karland had heard the nickname they used for Bradwr before but had never found out what it meant. Karland hated bullying.

'Come on,' he'd muttered. Bradwr had seemed to shrink in on himself when he realised his companion was not going to confront them on his behalf. They had moved to the gardens. Karland had worked hard to cheer him up, and by the end of the afternoon they had been laughing and chatting as usual. He had asked what it was about, and Bradwr had shrugged and looked upset enough that Karland changed the subject.

'Maybe tomorrow I can join you for practice with Rast,' Bradwr enthused now, his attention sliding back. Karland sometimes got the impression Bra didn't listen to a word.

'Um… well. I said before that wasn't my call, Bra,' he said uncomfortably. 'Rast doesn't want other people joining.'

Bradwr looked upset. 'But, Seom did!' he accused.

'Yes, but… he's a recruit,' said Karland, feeling a little wretched at the evident bitter disappointment.

'Xhera does too.'

'She always has.' He sighed. 'I don't make the rules, Bra. You know that.'

Bradwr's face became unpleasantly pinched. 'Fine. Meet me for the Combic Libraries instead, then.'

'You *know* I can't take you in there,' Karland said. 'But any Librarium? Let me know when and where.'

'Ok, fine. Whatever,' said Bra snappishly. He seemed distracted again, looking elsewhere. Karland sighed inwardly.

'Look, I have to go. I'll see you later.'

He hurried back to their rooms, knowing he had delayed more than he should have. He wanted to catch up on his studies.

Xhera cocked an eyebrow. 'Where did you get to?'

'Oh, I ran into Bradwr.'

Xhera nodded, forming an *Ah* with her mouth. Something in how she did it was so superior it irked him more than usual, and he almost snapped at her.

'What it is with you?'

She turned blue eyes on him. 'I don't like him. I told you before he wasn't worth my time.'

'Why not? I mean, he's never done anything wrong.'

'Hasn't he?' She bit her lip. Karland stared at her and finally Xhera relented.

'You remember a little while ago, I wouldn't tell you why I was upset?' she said quietly. Karland nodded after a moment. 'Bradwr was with some friends I've not seen before - people who I think know Aran. The ones you don't like, maybe. I was already feeling down - we'd been talking about Grukust the day before, you remember? Two months after we held the vigil, just before the celebrations.'

Karland nodded. It had been a sombre few weeks, having the official Drake's Day announced to commemorate Györnàeldàr and the dragons. This celebration came with the announcement, after the rebuilding, but henceforth the twenty-first day of Weod would be in remembrance of all who died.

The day the Dragon fell.

For most it was a time of celebration, a rest. For the three survivors, it was a time of loss that reminded them of the deaths of all their companions. They had avoided the celebrants.

'I was feeling desperate, adrift. Vulnerable, I guess. He saw me alone and stopped, said something nasty to one of them. They blocked my path. Hemmed me in. It was a power thing. He started mocking me, mocking my upset, and you've obviously talked to him quite a lot, because he knew why I was upset.' There was no accusation in her voice. 'He needled and needled, and I just,' she shook her head, angrily, 'couldn't take any more. I burst into tears, and he stood there, with his friends. Just watching, as if they'd done a job well. I don't know how I didn't knock the smug smiles off their stupid faces.'

'Why didn't you tell me?' asked Karland, aghast.

She shook her head. 'You wouldn't have believed me. It's not the only time, though he usually tries more passive-victim stuff. I think he's jealous of our friendship, wants you to himself.'

'Well, he can't have me. You're my best friend, you and Seom. Bradwr is… fun,' Karland allowed, 'but being fun was never the sole basis of a real friendship.'

'You know Seom loathes him?' asked Xhera, changing tack. Karland shook his head, surprised. 'A lot of people are taken in by his *fun* side, but not Seom. Bradwr's hollow, Karland. False through and through. He manipulates everyone for his ego and lies reflexively. He hates it when you don't agree with him, did you know that?' She sighed, genuinely sorrowful. 'You see the good in people too much. You're not stupid. You know he's rotten, but you won't stop giving him a chance to prove himself. And that will be your undoing.'

'I just wanted to… help him be the person he's capable of being. He's smart. Bra could be someone with real worth if he's given the chance.' Behind the automatic defence, Karland now felt a deep anger at what Bra had done to Xhera.

Xhera shrugged. 'I hope you aren't disappointed.'

SEVENTEEN

The time had come for Sontles to begin consolidating his hold on the Church. That the most unholy of creatures could infiltrate and subvert one of the largest faiths on the continent held no end of amusement for him; that he was rising in it so fast and tainting it so much was as much a testament to human greed and weakness as it was to his own power.

After realising that the Holy Voice was too strong to force to his will, Sontles had begun working on his guards and supporters. Most of the cardinals had no real defence against him, softened by greed, rich living and sycophancy. They didn't have the mental armour and strength of character their master did.

Unfortunately, Primate Gilden was breaking down mentally. He had been exposed to the vampire's powerful will for years, and his mind was degenerating into servile mush. It had come on quickly; soon he would only be good for feeding on. It was an annoying by-product of enthrallment; over time resistance lessened, but sanity departed.

Yesterday evening he had announced shakily that he would be stepping down and had nominated Sontles as Primate of Lodnor in his place. Tonight he had retired to his house to rest, leaving Sontles to plot.

Another of the Cardinals was open to bribes, and Sontles had some hold over much of the Church leadership now through either blackmail, agreement or enthrallment. He still faced opposition, but no one knew the extent of his influence. They all assumed that, even if he gained some ground, he was still some way off accessing true power. He was, they believed, merely another, newer player in their game.

Sontles knew better. He was far older and more cunning than any of them. His biggest threat now was the Holy Voice. He cursed the day that Gilden had failed to gain the seat.

To be Holy Voice was to interpret the word of Terome for all of Terome.

Sontles had slowly come to realise the man wasn't manoeuvring politically. He genuinely believed in what he said, with a clarity that made Sontles want to bare his fangs in public.

He had developed the vampire's manner of sparing smiles and tight-lipped speech that made him seem curt and angry, despite emotionless words and voice. It would be the undoing of all his work to be discovered as an undead monster. His dark thoughts seethed with hatred of this man, of all men, especially those who had gained power without the terrible fate that had awaited him.

Something that worried at him like a worm in an apple was that this Holy Voice had such brilliant faith it almost made him squint. It focused his mind and will to a point where he could not sway or corrupt him. Combined with a mind sharper than any of his other political foes - something Sontles hadn't discovered until too late - and the love of the people and Church, it meant he was uninterested in bribery, immune to manipulation, and frustratingly difficult to discredit.

It irked him.

Sontles brooded. Sometimes he felt that the man sensed his corruption, heard the lie in his words. As he moved up the ranks, the Voice would watch him ever more closely. With his most recent nomination, he had to be extremely careful. He had a foe that could disrupt, possibly even blunt, his entire work in Meyar.

A foe that could unmask him.

There was one bright line on the horizon. Sontles knew Terome was a hollow God; one that didn't exist. The whole religion was founded on a lie.

There was no power in Terome.

For all The Holy Voice's influence and incorruptibility, he was not only merely human, but old.

It was, perhaps, time. But first, he needed to make certain.

۩ ۩

Eonder Jarle sighed deeply, feeling the air fill his lungs satisfyingly as he moved down the corridor towards his suite. He was approaching forty-seven, and still felt in his prime, but he had never been hugely active and felt his years as a man ten his senior would.

Eonder tended more towards activities of the mind. He had developed a paunch, but was still rounded in the shoulder, with thickset arms and large hands. His face, he knew, tended toward the rosy-cheeked under bristling eyebrows. A sharp nose took some softness from his face.

He had used much of this to his advantage over the years, both as an advisor to the King of Haná and in his rise to the most powerful man in Meyar. Many had underestimated him, seeing his complexion and his bluff exterior as signs of a privileged upbringing, a general vaguery, even stupidity; a red-cheeked man, almost comically broad, who blustered and blew when he wasn't sitting quietly to one side. Too late, many had found out he had a keen intellect, that behind his exterior he was sharper than they.

Jarle lived for politics. He had never cared what people thought of him as long as it brought him power, and for him power lay in manipulating the fate of others as much as money and adulation. It lay in playing the game and winning. It lay in lying and people believing his truths. He was as adept at engineering long term strategy as he was at delighting in petty revenge. Jarle was not a man to be taken lightly, and he knew it.

People were stupid and easily distracted. They usually thought only of what directly affected themselves. Even those in the places of power often thought a single level deeper, to the manipulations of others. Jarle was a master of deeper thinking still, seeing a far larger, more complex picture that moved with the gravity of Kuln itself.

There was little point in being a King. There was less power than people thought; being a figurehead had disadvantages, and you eventually became trapped in tradition, a target.

Often, greater freedom - and as much power - could be held a few steps behind the throne… or by removing the throne altogether. No, being a ruler alone was not the best way.

Being the first amongst equals, now. That gave you power.

He had studied politics, learned what worked best for him and what could be discarded. Even now Eonder was a more dangerous man than anyone except his fiercest opponents knew. He had taken the basics of Eordeland democracy, mixed in the Banistari caste system and the Noble House structure and serfdom of Novin disguised as government, and gradually introduced it all to Meyar, usurping the original and fairly simple monarchy.

Haná had once been a land governed by a King, with a tenuous if marked separation between the extremely powerful Church and the politically focused state. It had worked, and the King, Orreld, had been remarkably fair and progressive, working to give the people more freedoms and equalise the country in the hopes that it would become a greater power.

Haná had a trading fleet and fertile farmland, with prized crops that were found nowhere else. Orreld had wished to build a trade empire, gifting his people much to encourage them to work for themselves. That this would diminish his own power somewhat did not concern him; he and his family were adored, and devout followers of Terome. They would maintain influence whether he wished it or not.

He introduced basic rights and medical care for a healthy workforce. He encouraged individuality and creativity. He taxed people according to their means.

Orreld had been lauded by Eordeland as the fairest ruler in Anaria. Even Eyotsburg had withdrawn their long-standing suspicion and become valued partners, a doorway to the south of the continent. His people and land prospered.

None of this sat well with the Prime Alderman - Duke Jarle, then - or many others in the court. They were furious that they paid more taxes than commoners. They were angered slavery had given way to indentures. They did not wish any hint of equality to creep into the land. They had spent decades gathering wealth to themselves and governing their duchies closely, as had their forefathers. They had their own armies, loyal of course to the crown overall; they had their own laws inside the generalised ones laid out by the King. Many of them had perfected the process of bleeding their vassals dry and gathering their coin.

The King's plans would reduce their power and wealth, emasculate them. He treated *women* as if they were equal to men, and punished rapists even if they were noble! The populace was becoming more educated, beginning to demand reparation. Terome forbid, they might even have had to give it. The power of life and death, the wealth, the honour and traditions of their families, all stood at risk.

Some of them had seen murmurings of the problems on the horizon, like a distant thunderstorm. Only Eonder Jarle had understood the true depth of the King's work.

Orreld had been his finest adversary - a match for his wits, he reflected.
Almost.

Orreld had believed them to also be friends. Eonder had supported the King fully, publicly and in private, but in the background had begun laying plans. He sent much of his wealth out of Haná, storing it in the great monetary houses of Eordeland, and began persuading his peers to do likewise, all without the King's knowledge. When it came time for taxes, and as the demands for reparation crept in, they had nothing they could answer with. The King looked closely but had to admit that they didn't have the funds. He worked hard to understand what had happened, taking at face value the protestations of his most trusted advisors that the people were not producing enough. Faced with the lack of results, he felt he had to resort to harsher laws for the eventual good of the people, never dreaming that the resulting monies were being sent from the kingdom itself.

The King suspected many, but never Eonder Jarle. He relied on his counsel implicitly. When the people began to rise up, stirred by lies and misinformation, he relied on Jarle to help him calm them, and when it became worse and he felt his family in danger, he trusted his oldest friend to hide them.

Only at the end had he realised his truest enemy was the closest to him. Eonder Jarle had taken great satisfaction watching the numb shock as the pieces fell into place, each revelation more and more damaging. The final knowledge - that even now assassins were at his family's hiding place, and his daughters and wife were at that moment being raped and butchered - had broken him. Orreld was a large man, had been once a warrior with a will of iron, but he had begged in tears on his knees in his own throne room to at least let them survive.

Jarle had been fascinated. He would never have believed that this intelligent, forceful man would unman himself so in front of another. Any respect had vanished, and he had turned and left the throne room, careful to let people see him leave, the doors open, the King alive.

After all, it would not do for suspicion to fall upon him.

The doors had closed. The King had risen numbly and slowly sat, enthroned and surrounded by guards; guards who were no longer his.

Somehow an assassin had managed to creep up to the rear of the throne and had yanked the King's head back, raggedly cutting his throat, and leaving him to claw and writhe on the seat of his power at the moment of his deepest despair. Blood had stained the carved wood, left to dry; the bloody throne was now kept as a monument to the horrors of monarchy.

Meyar was split along old duchy lines. The dukes became Aldermen, to allay suspicion of a ruling class, loudly proclaiming that they were casting off power for the good of the people while they gathered ever more of it.

Aldermen. The old name for mayors. Men who would sit in council for the good of the nation.

The people would be represented fairly, Jarle and his fellows said, as Eordeland's were. Instead of a Council of Twelve, they would have an Assembly of Ten, one for each Territory, split along the old Duchies.

He was voted as first among equals; once, the Privy Councillor and Duke of Lodnor.

Now, the Prime Alderman.

Never again, the people were promised, would one man dictate their lives absolutely. From now on the kingdom would be named Meyar after the disciple that sat at Terome's right hand to dispense justice and fate, because thus it was; the reign of kings was over, the unfair ways cast out.

There were riots and anger. Not everyone had been fooled, not everyone had lost their love for the old King. The country was divided. This would not do.

They had blamed Eordeland; for tainting the thoughts of their King, their neighbours. For removing traditional values, diluting their proud land. They blamed the Eyots for damaging their trade on the water. The Nassings were chased away, beaten, treated as little better than sly folk who stole anything they could.

The Eordelanders were stealing their identity, they said. The Eyots were stealing their money, food, trade. The Nassings just stole; babies, livestock, women.

It was all so easy. One by one he introduced laws; laws he had tried many times to push through when Orreld had lived, but had blocked. Orreld had not known it was him, of course; he had been too subtle for that.

Laws changed so outsiders could be imprisoned or killed outright. Anyone foreign was suspect. Pay went down, production demanded went up. People were proud of throwing off the shackles of monarchy, with an automatic pardon for killing a royalist. People accused anyone they had discord with. Lynch squads purged the old loyalties. Anarchy reigned for months.

The Church was the easiest of all to whip up in a fervour against their former partners, up until the old Holy Voice - a man full of fire and brimstone to all that was not Meyar - had died.

And throughout it all, people still believed the true danger lay outside. They were told Eordeland was their greatest threat. Progressive voices were shouted down - or silenced. Money was recalled from Eordeland's banks. Trade died off.

And all the money flowed once more into the coffers of the deserving.

A year ago, Jarle had introduced the Citizen's Watch. People were rewarded for seeking out dissidents, spying on each other. Neighbours became enemies. If you could produce even a little 'proof', you could be pardoned for murder. But it couldn't get out of hand again, oh no. There were more laws than ever. Laws made people feel safe.

People in the south of Meyar had it worst. Entire farmsteads vanished nearer the mountains in the central regions. Wild creatures moved in from the wildest regions, and people died. Orcs and worse crept in, though now there was an *arrangement*.

Yes, he reflected as he walked towards his rooms, he was satisfied at how his plans had unfolded. He had not only won the game; he had rewritten the rules and made himself the game's master.

Jarle nodded to his personal guards as they opened the door to his suite. Tonight, he had told his seneschal to forgo the young women eager - for the most part - to be in the bed of the Prime Alderman. He wished to think, plan his next moves. The most delicate touches were required to move the responsibility onto his fellow Aldermen, whilst retaining the control for himself; with a few exceptions, they were not stupid, but he took satisfaction in the fact that only one or two suspected how deeply he had been involved in events, and how long his reach really was. He knew several had their eyes on his position, and so was instantly suspicious when the main reception room was dark.

The fire should have been burning and well-tended. The candles should have been lit as soon as he was seen coming. He could smell the tang of recently extinguished wicks. Jarle turned and seemingly ambled out, away from the door, and muttered to one of the guards.

The young man came in with a lit taper from the sconce outside and coaxed the fire back to life before lighting the nearby candles. His fellow verified the other rooms were clear.

Eonder Jarle grunted. Something didn't feel right, and he fingered the exquisitely made spring-loaded dart gun he kept hidden at his belt for emergencies. No one knew about it or the venom it carried, and no one would live to remember it either, if he had his way.

The guards left, and he uncorked a bottle of Hanári brandy. The limited stock meant it was extremely costly.

'*Eonder Jarle.*'

The dry voice came from a chair in the shadows near the window. It was familiar.

He started and looked around, his eyes darting.

'Eh? What? Who's there?' His hand crept downward.

'I would speak with you, Prime Alderman.' A shadow moved, someone rising and moving forward, and the almost emaciated form of Sontles Aquinas was revealed by the light. He was above average height, but his stark frame and stoop made him seem a small man nonetheless. For a second, Jarle could have sworn his eyes held a hint of red, like a faint ember.

'How the bloody hell did you get in here, Aquinas?' Eonder snapped, recorking the brandy. The nearest window to the ground was twenty feet up. This man didn't look like he had the strength to easily walk that, let alone climb. The fringe of hair and the protruding upper lip that spoke of very slightly buck teeth just added to the overall physical image of weakness and insignificance, but they were at odds with his eyes, eyes that pinned you to the wall and saw your every secret. The small mouth never smiled, ever, and his dry and husk-like voice sounded somehow hollow. You couldn't hold how he was born against a fellow, Jarle often thought, but there was something decidedly unnerving about the man.

The warm fire emboldened him. 'And how did the guards not see you?'

Eonder Jarle was wary of Sontles. The Churchman had crept into view some five years ago, and was very rarely seen, although emissaries of his carried letters constantly. He was very smart, especially with figures and patterns, and had an uncanny knack of putting together things others had not, of knowing things he should not.

'They let me in earlier. I cannot imagine… why they have forgotten to tell the new… guard I am here.'

There was that irritating pause he affected, as if he stopped at an uncanny moment to consider what he said before finishing the sentence. It was quite unlike any other speech pattern Jarle had heard, and it was a little jarring.

'What is of more import is *why* I am here.'

Jarle motioned him to a chair nearer the fire and sat. He felt cold more easily these days. 'Do tell,' he said, sipping his brandy casually. He was damned if he'd show how disturbed he was at Sontles penetrating his personal sanctum.

'We have long been of an accord, you and I. I have watched your… machinations… with interest. We still wish the same things.'

Jarle grunted. Sontles had been very helpful to his plans. The Churchman had gained much power in recent years and had engineered the weight of the Church behind Jarle more than once. They had introduced conscription for the Church, and Jarle enjoyed the protection of Teromants, the only non-Churchman to have it. The building of the sins of Eordeland had been raised in the Church by Sontles, and the levers which had been used to mislead the public had been co-manufactured with him. The upcoming war against Eordeland would not have been possible without the man.

And, of course, there was this hidden army that only a few knew about.

Jarle had taken much persuading about this, but the benefits had been clear. Theirs was the only realm no longer plagued by constant raids from these creatures. Instead, they provided criminals and dissidents as placatory means to the orcs in the southern range.

Sacrifices to greatness, Sontles called them.

The Bishop also managed the alliance with the horde in the Dimnesdair.

The arrangement was efficient.

Jarle was no fool. Against any of his fellow realms he would have been mad to wage war alone, and Eordeland was far stronger than Meyar. But they were diplomats, talkers, thinkers. If they could avoid or put off the issue, they would, and it took longer to discuss things in a committee than a decision from a ruler.

Destroying Eordeland by opening it up to the orcs ensured his greatest opponents to ruling would be gone. Their blasted religions - their good-natured insistence that Terome was a man not a God - would be crushed. Jarle wasn't sure how much he believed in Terome's origin, but he believed in God enough to beseech his aid before actions.

It was a delicate balancing act. The Aldermen were wary of the Church gaining too much power; some would say it already had too much. People in Meyar believed, or devoutly proclaimed their belief. The Church was once revered. Now it was greatly feared, and it had an army a full quarter the size of Meyar's. This wouldn't have been a source of concern for the Aldermen if it hadn't been peopled largely by well-trained fanatics. Teromants were the secret police, and to be feared, seeking out corruption at any level.

Most of his fellow Aldermen still referred to themselves as Dukes privately. The nobility structure was still very much in place. It was a great game, Jarle knew. Oppress the people, blame the symbols of the elite, and present the real elite as those who spoke sense.

His fellows also plotted against him, as they always had, and assumed he did the same. Eonder Jarle found this amusing. He expended precisely as much energy as was required to keep them at bay, and no more. He *wanted* the full council of Aldermen. Each allowed different reliefs, so no one could say their lot was truly worse than another Territory. The people had a council of people who they elected. It was all fair.

Of course, this was rigged; how could it be otherwise?

Their biggest problem at the moment lay with the newest Holy Voice. The old man was shrewd and much-loved, cut from a similar cloth to the king. You could spend your entire life weeding and preparing fertile ground, Jarle thought bitterly, and still deep-rooted weeds sprang up.

He had come in on a popular vote, no one entirely sure how. The system for selection of the Voice was supposedly nominated by the bishops based on the voices of the priests and the rest of the Church, which carried a lot of weight. Jarle suspected that it had been a mixture of their clamour, and other bishops and Primates moving to block Sontles' rise to power. His influence was a threat, and he was a cunning adversary.

In response Sontles had moved to take the reins of Inquisition, the arm that sought to persuade the straying back to the fold.

Centuries ago, the Church of the Smithing had almost supplanted the rest of Terome's worship. It had been short-lived, brutal, bloody, against the grain of the true religion. The leaders had been tried for heresy.

Now Sontles was achieving with his subtle machinations what the Smithing had failed to do - the forced conversion of the populace.

Other religions had been forcefully cast out from Meyar almost everywhere. Some priests of other orders had been lynched. But still there was an undercurrent of tolerance from many of the Teromens, a tolerance that was slowly dissolving in fear and the attentions of the Inquisition.

And yet here stood this Holy Voice, whose fervent belief and compassion was beginning to undo the plans of both Sontles and Jarle.

Nobody outside Meyar knew the depths of their plans. One day all Anaria would fall to Meyar. To achieve that… he had to rely on the advice of this dangerous and elusive Bishop.

He did not trust Sontles Aquinas.

'Over a year ago, an Eordeland scholar was murdered. Do you remember?' The dry voice rasped through his thoughts.

'Of course. A right hue and cry about it, too.'

He'd been very annoyed. Kelpas Withy had been a valuable advisor and had facilitated many breakthroughs in the creation of a government; had in fact spent several years advising Jarle personally. Jarle had been aware of the old man's smooth manipulation as he guided the transition, trying to limit the damage being potentially wrought on the people during the process. It had become something of a game for Jarle. He hadn't trusted the old Eordelander, but he had realised his depth of knowledge. Withy had been extremely valuable.

'Indeed. He had… taken something of mine. But he was also on the verge of reporting back to Darost your plans for war.'

'What *are* you talking about?' Jarle said, wondering how the hell the old man had known about them. His plans were long term, had been in motion for years. '*You* had him killed?' His anger rose sharply.

'Kelpas Withy was a spy and a thief, sent by Darost to impede you and learn what he could about your plans,' said Sontles bluntly. 'He tried to report back. I… prevented him.'

This did make a certain amount of sense, thought Jarle, still gritting his teeth. Withy had been given relative freedom, although he had been kept away from anything important, but he had not been stupid. It *was* possible he had overheard something. One of the strengths that marked Eonder Jarle, however, was an unctuous and measured response that never admitted anything, no matter how angry he felt.

'D'you have any proof of this?'

'Enough,' replied Sontles evenly. 'We found reports that he had been sending to Darost. That old man knew far more than you realised, Jarle.'

'And you waited all this time before telling me?'

'Well. The matter *had* been... taken care of.'

Jarle grunted sourly. It was long done. 'What do you want?' he asked again, uncharacteristically blunt.

'It is time for us to work... together once more,' said Sontles smoothly. 'If it comes to pass that the Holy Voice is sadly replaced, I wish you to... throw your weight behind me. If you wish your plans to gain more ground, you will need me with more power than I have now.' A lizard-like blink. 'As a start, I need you to bring a vote to support Church interrogation rights in any state under Meyari law. In return, I will ensure I am the... ranking religious advisor sent with the army. I can coordinate with our... allies. With luck on our side, we could be at the walls of Darost inside months.'

'Don't mention *allies,*' hissed Jarle. His eyes darted to the door the guards stood outside. He sat back, raising his voice again.

'Anyway, after Politikus Belen returned, we promised them a new ambassador,' he remarked. 'He pre-empted our strike, although if his assassinations had paid off, we'd have been that much closer to destabilising Eordeland. The fools still believe a new Politikus is on the way, as if we'd give them a hostage. Belen plays them well. If we're to have any chance of catching them unawares, we will have to march sooner than we thought. What you suggest could upset the delicate balance between Church and State.'

'We discuss this in chamber tomorrow night,' said Sontles. 'This new law would allow us to force conscription as an alternative to execution as a heretic. Working together, for the... common good.'

'I thought the Holy Voice was against war?'

'He may decide that war is inevitable. We would be fools not to prepare.'

'Fine.' Unlikely, but still. 'If you can do it... perhaps these conscripts should forfeit their land to the Assembly and Church as part of their new holy vows. A penance for their sins. Yes... that should do. I'll inform the criers that this is down to Eordeland's attempts to change our society. We must make the people believe we return to the days of glory we had in Haná - without, of course, the monarchy. And so forth. Yes, I think this will work well.'

A dry rasp not unlike the fast rubbing of shagreen on a boat's hull emanated from his guest. It took a moment for him to realise the man was laughing quietly.

'Surely the people can see what you are doing?' Sontles asked.

Eonder Jarle laughed out loud at this.

'Some do, Aquinas. But they're so easily distracted. So easily lied to. They don't *want* to believe that we tighten our grip, so they refuse to, cattle walking willingly to their own slaughter. In the end they even persecute those who warned them about it

for not doing more. If you can persuade people to forsake learning, facts, truth…
and you can make lies more attractive… you can do *anything*.'

'I admire your skill,' said Sontles. 'I use… other methods to get what I want.'

I'll bet you do, thought Jarle.

As Sontles moved to the door, he added quietly, 'Aquinas?'

'Yes?'

'If you ever enter here again uninvited, you'll be slain as an intruder.'

Sontles's eyes glittered. He inclined his head slightly, although Jarle had the
unnerving impression he had amused the man.

'As you say. Prime Alderman.'

ʘ ʘ

Sontles flitted back to his manse, unseen in the shadows, satisfied.

He had never attempted to overwhelm Jarle's will with his own. The Prime
Alderman was too clever, too used to manipulation. If he suspected Sontles of
anything untoward he would try to remove him. It would become messy. And the
man was eminently useful.

Anyway, dominating the will of the weak was very temporary. People reasserted
control quickly unless their minds began to break, as Gilden's had, and it left them
confused and angry.

Too many of his kind had not been subtle with the use of their skills and been
discovered. More powerful than any human they might be, but numbers and
knowledge would overwhelm a vampire eventually unless they fled. It only took one
blade with silver on it, one person to remember the old tales about fire or garlic or
sunlight or the right woods.

Vampires that stepped outside the shadows got burned.

Besides, he had a greater purpose here. This petty struggle, one nation, one
religion, one church, meant nothing. Sontles knew true power; the power of blood,
of life and death, of dominance in both. He wanted more. His masters had laid the
path to destruction, and Meyar was the easiest and fastest route. These petty fools
meant nothing to him. Jarle's threat had been so paltry it had been all he could do
not to laugh in the man's fat face.

More than seventy years had passed since he had found the way to the Darklings
in the hidden tablets. It was ironic that the artefacts had been taken as the five
commandments of Terome without their true purpose being known. More amusing
was that they searched for them still.

218

Sontles had walked the face of Kuln now for more than three hundred years. He had revelled in his power, his lust for death and revenge, but the latter had faded once everyone he had known was dust, either by his hand or age. Vampirism had found an echo of darkness within him, despite his humble beginnings. In life he had been relatively ineffectual, but deep down, he had cursed those stronger than him, richer than him.

Life had been unfair. It had afflicted him with a weak form, unheroic in his own eyes; weak-visioned and bald by the time he was twenty, with only a fringe of hair around his head, his skinny frame lacking strength, nothing to attract women. He was left with little defence against tormentors, with no riches, with a family who cared nothing for him. His hatred had run deep and futile behind his quiet exterior, hidden because he feared reprisal.

When he was Turned, he found freedom, and visited his wrath upon all those he felt had slighted him, those he felt might. His remaining family had paid in gibbering fear for their disdain. His old enemies had died screaming in terror. He had spent decades in a red rage of carnage, but always remained cunning, careful, and precise.

He still revelled in slaughter, but that too had become a colder satisfaction. Killing one or a few at a time was temporary satiation. Holding power over them, in every way... even giving themselves willingly in a riddle of flesh... that meant far more.

Rather than struggle against the chaotic slew of lusts within him, he instead threw himself into their maelstrom, drinking deeply of their waters, emerging cold, calculating as ever, and supremely powerful.

That power had increased fourfold once he had pledged to his new masters. A piece of the dark seething chaos they commanded - were avatars of - became his to channel, to strengthen his form with.

He had risen in power past his own kind, too.

He would rule - dark and with a flickering crown of chaos - over all others, including this petty and overly ambitious Prime Alderman.

It would be *glorious*.

EIGHTEEN

The rain had fallen for four days, pattering on the sectioned dome of The Sanctum at night and filling the air with moisture and grey puddles during the day. It seemed relentless. Not fierce, but vertical and never-ending. The Sanctum had excellent drains and a vast sewerage system, but still small ponds formed here and there.

The days felt bleak. Grey skies and muted greens in the grounds abounded. It was serene and beautiful in its own melancholy way.

Karland quite liked the rain like this; not being in it, but seeing it without distraction. It suited his current mood. It had been more than seven months since Aldwyn had died, and his friend was still on his mind. Sometimes he still felt the twisting pain of watching him die in terror and agony. He knew that Rast had taken it badly, for all he did not show it.

He stared into the rain when he was not trying to study. Apart from the Combic Libraries, much of The Sanctum was more like a cathedral than a stuffy library.

The reading areas at the tip of each Librarium were wide and tall with large windows. The chains on the books were fine and solid, and the Scrolls were very watchful until the book was back on the shelf, the round metal ring on the end of the chain slotted back into place through the metal pole.

Karland remembered what he had overheard back when he had started his journey, listening to Rast and Aldwyn talk about the troubles they were trying to understand. Something Aldwyn had said about rain like this.

The rain falls like the tears of a god, he thought. *Sadly and wetly, as if trying to wash away all the wrong in the world. Weeping in sorrow that it may end.* Something like that, anyway, and it struck true.

Today his spirits were low. He couldn't concentrate, the pieces of what they were looking for didn't fit, and even his books were annoying him. Rain spattered miserably against the glass of the high windows.

'None of this makes any sense,' Karland muttered. 'What the hell are random fluctuations in the quantum interface, anyway?'

'Something to do with reality being disturbed like a pool of water when you try to communicate between two points, I think,' said Xhera. 'Related to being limited to speaking and writing? I didn't pay much attention. It's all theoretical rubbish Quirnan likes to spout.' Quirnan was one of the more earnest - and boring - lecturers.

She sat opposite him in a deep blue woollen overlay that had slipped elegantly off pale skin, exposing her graceful neck and well-formed shoulder. The effect was a little spoiled by an ink mark on the side of her face, and hair that was unruly at best today. She was frowning at the window as well.

'Come on,' she said, standing. 'This isn't doing either of us any good. I can't focus.'

He was supposedly studying the theory of Gifts, something the University was very interested in, whereas Xhera's most recent assignment was the political makeup of Anarian realms. Neither of them were making much headway.

'Let's go through some more of the references in Aldwyn's notes. There were some interesting ones to do with religions and prophecies. We might as well get *something* done.'

'Might be a good idea.' Karland glanced out of the window at the rivulets running down the glass. 'If I can't see all this, maybe I'll forget about it.'

They left word with the Apprentice Scroll and moved for the long inner staircase to the Combic Libraries. The catacombs had several entrances, but the vast caves were partitioned off by thick rock. The entrance to the Combic Libraries was within the most south-eastern Cuneus which housed the Academia Esoterica, the one referred to unofficially as the fifth, at the end of an extended narrow hallway deep below the ground.

Shallower parts of the extended underground cave system had been partitioned off with thick stone for the city - like the huge diatomite filters that the river water and wastewater filtered through, each thirty feet tall and wider round than a well. They were the main reason Darost had few disease problems. The Sanctum had its own dedicated filters, two of them connected to the large hydraulic rams that fed water from the Eaofer and filtered it before sending it up narrow pipes to communal wells. The Sanctum also had a hidden spring which fed clean, pure water to the twelve atrium fountains and the more luxurious quarters; the water from the fountains was collected by further rams and used for the gardens, parks and other purposes. It was a long and complex system well in advance of anything other realms owned.

Separate to the water sources lay the jakes and waste chutes for The Sanctum - long deep pipes that were washed down every day by staff, and once a month cleaned out using special heavy stone balls which blasted through any blockages. The pits for these lay deep in the catacombs, sectioned off, and the resulting compost could be used for other purposes.

Further out, away from the catacombs, Darost stood on its own sewerage system, the main areas patrolled by Eordeland Guard and rumours of the shadow council patrolling the rest. This had been expanded and added to over a thousand years into its own warren under the city, and its cleaning was the origination of the phrase 'DeadKing's balls' - much larger iron versions of those in the Sanctum which careened down major pipes.

There were also two sections used more traditionally for remains, of Council members and other notaries. The catacombs proper had an entrance in the graveyard in the southwest and were where the bones were laid to rest after many years.

The vast majority of the catacombs, however, were sealed off for the storage and protection of knowledge.

They approached the heavy doors at the end of the corridor, steel-faced in thick ironwood. Directly behind the doors was a four-foot wide trench a foot deep extending into the walls either side, up toward the smooth granite ceiling. They stood open, a squad of Welcomers on permanent watch. Further inside, two Onyx Guard stood, apart from the other Guard, near the mechanisms that shifted the counterbalanced doors.

The elite fighters were still mysterious to Karland; he knew they were feared throughout the city, though they rarely left The Sanctum, and that they trained with Rast on a regular basis. Rast had told him little past them being superb warriors. The protection of the Council and the inner Sanctum was theirs, including the Combic Libraries. They didn't have barracks with the other troops. Only the most highly decorated and skilled Welcomers were considered for acceptance into their ranks.

Little else was known outside the usual rumours surrounding any elite force. They certainly didn't banter and joke with the other troops much. Since the suspicious fire in the Combic Libraries, then Draef Novas and their own Captain-General being murdered on their watch - along with very nearly two other Councillors - they were grimmer than ever. They trusted no one.

The Welcomers nodded to them both as they examined their bags and clothes, as did the Onyx Guards inside, although their faces were stern and watchful rather than open.

They passed through the entrance into the small hall that served as a rest area. Through a narrow doorway lay a huge reading room, with desks and cubby holes arranged throughout, as well as comfortable chairs to allow for long-term research. Two large receptacles stood at the rear; one was filled with brightly glowing spheres which Karland was familiar with, having used one in the Library of Thingos with Aldwyn. These were also scattered around the room, their slightly blueish-white light leaving few corners unlit.

The other was filled with dimly glowing or quiescent globes, needing to be replenished by sunlight. Without light, they were white-filled with some form of chemical, and were very tough and hard to break.

To their right was a long desk, which usually had at least one Apprentice Scroll at it, if not a Scrollmaster. A rope hung from the wall at the back, which would ring inside the Libraries to summon someone for a section.

Behind this sat a locked and solid door. They couldn't go through this until accompanied by an Apprentice Scroll. In here was the first section of the Library, containing general information you could take off the shelves yourselves. There were no chains here, no locks; there was no way to take books out of the reading room, and the Apprentice Scrolls verified their charges daily to ensure they were present and in the correct places. The Onyx Guard checked each person leaving thoroughly.

Each section had at least one Librarian Scrollmaster, with at least two Scrolls underneath them, and Apprentice Scrolls below them. They knew the location and the contents of each book they looked after, and had them noted in the section ledgers kept in the reading room along with a floor plan, which was in turn copied back into the Combic Library so future generations would know where to look.

The catacombs were mind-bogglingly large. The Combic Libraries alone were tended by more than fifty Scrollmasters and upwards of one hundred and fifty Scrolls, each with up to twenty-four Apprentices. Above them all were the six Elder Librarians who answered to the Council. This was the Order of the Scrolls, and the Combic Libraries were its domain. Tertius Librarian Tampas had died in a fire a year before, an unprecedented act in here.

There was no fire permitted. No candles, no torches, none of the Nassmoor matches; no chemicals which could cause fire. No acids. No food, no sharp objects. Nothing but water and library lights were permitted into the reading room.

Only Library lights were permitted past the Librarian's door.

Few in the Council now believed it accident, Karland knew. Many rare and ancient books had been conveniently damaged or even destroyed, including their copy of the Prophecies of Sarthos.

The Combic Libraries contained copies of everything in the Librariums above, but they were not generally accessible. It was not widely known that the Combic Libraries contained much more than simple old texts. Even with the blessing of the

Council, there were many areas they simply could not go. Past the two huge rooms they were permitted in, there were many more. If they wanted anything from *those*, the Apprentice Scrolls had to bring it themselves. In some cases, Scrolls, or Scrollmasters. In one case so far, Tertius Elder Librarian Damok himself had brought them an aging text, his dark-skinned hands caressing it carefully.

The rule also did not seem to apply to Night, who spent most of his time in the dark recesses. As far as they knew, he might sleep here somewhere.

They settled down in the reading room after requesting a list of titles. The Apprentice Scroll at the desk kept a wary eye on them, as if they would start doodling in the margins of the texts.

Gradually Karland's mood improved as he lost himself in the work. Xhera's face developed that habitual and endearing frown that meant she was deep in her studies.

They worked for some time, the only noise the scratching of quills. Finally, Karland leaned back, stretching. He had found a book mentioned in two others that Aldwyn had kept, *Gods and Religions* and *Aprolistic Transcendentalism*.

'Look at this.' He passed Xhera a tome he had been reading, the yellowed pages crackling. 'This refers to the Twelve Greater Gods again, but this time it mentions *The Helper*. According to this writer-' he checked the cover, '*Willa Fenos*, most religions worship the same gods under different names and guises.' He frowned. 'Actually, that makes sense. Think how Isha is worshipped, and then how Conta of the Naga Shon Oha is written here.' He pulled another book towards him and waved it at Xhera. She blinked at the dust irritably and grabbed it.

'Stop that. Yes, that makes sense, I suppose. But what you're saying is that half these religious wars we have had are over which knee we should bend? It's ridiculous.'

'It references someone called *Amon*. And Illuminus. Isn't that Night's Order?'

'He did say it's been around for centuries.'

Xhera read through and sat staring at the final page for a moment, chewing her lip in a way Karland found delightful.

'There are bits of that which…' she shook her head. 'There is so *much* of this. What makes you so sure that this means anything?'

'Aldwyn believed it. We've seen some of these beings,' he reminded her. 'The Darkling. The Greater Dragon.' He rubbed his eyes.

'That's true,' Xhera said, her gaze unfocused. She shivered. 'There's so much more out there than we can explain.'

'Aldwyn tried,' said Karland. 'But even he was often frustrated.' He fondly remembered the time with Aldwyn, and just how much of it the old man had spent penning notes. When he wasn't teaching Karland, he was reading and writing.

Karland had been shocked to see just how many shelves of tomes written by his mentor were hidden in the archives of the Library of Thingos, and even here in The Sanctum and Combic Libraries, where his older notes and even inventions were listed. He must have been one of the most prolific writers of his age.

'Aldwyn said someone unknown will make an important choice,' Xhera said thoughtfully. 'To save or damn us all, if you can believe Sarthos.' Her eyes narrowed as she studied him, then she shook her head. 'Anyway. I wonder if the love of the number twelve in Eordeland comes from these Gods, back in the mists of time?'

Karland considered it. 'Could be. It's clear that our history is much more complicated than I thought. I did some extra reading on the history of Eordeland. Did you know that one of the reasons Darum is a common trade language for all the countries is that Eordeland, Novin, Meyar and Eyotsburg are all linked in the past?' He yawned, and Xhera averted her eyes from his gaping throat.

'Can't you cover your mouth?'

'Sorry.'

She looked at him seriously, but her voice was hesitant.

'What if the visions mean nothing, Karland? What if they aren't related to anything here? What if we're just wasting our time?'

'Aldwyn thought they did,' said Karland stubbornly. 'Even though it doesn't make sense.'

She sighed and half-shrugged agreement.

'Is it meant to? We are desperately grasping at anything. We might never know what the portal meant to show us.'

'Then what was the point?' asked Karland bitterly. 'Did we travel and lose them all for nothing?'

'Life doesn't work like that, Karland. There isn't a point. It just is.' Sometimes, for all her childishness in other ways, Xhera was pragmatically mature. 'Still, I feel like we are slowly getting somewhere,' she continued thoughtfully. 'For all it seems like swimming in syrup, things are becoming more obvious.'

'Are they?' asked Karland morosely. 'Instead of answers, we find more questions. Györnàeldàr told me that the *Talanthese* spoke of what-ifs, or what was, or what may yet come to pass, sometimes in metaphor. How can we understand what is really happening? Will it be in time? Do we even know what time we have?'

Xhera looked at him with her blue eyes, lovely and deep in a pale freckled elfin face, and did not answer.

❧❦

Not long afterwards they were interrupted by an Onyx Guard.

'Someone here to see you,' he said shortly. 'He has Council clearance, but you will be held responsible for him.' He turned to the door and gestured.

A huge green form strode in, looking around with narrowed eyes at the room. Seeing Karland and Xhera, he moved over and bumped a fist to his chest gently. Guard watched from the door, expressionless.

'I have been exploring the University,' Darus said. 'So many people! This place is amazing.' He looked around, not quite nervously. 'I feel… strange… being under the ground. My people left there a long time ago.'

'I remember Rast telling me,' said Karland. 'You left because…' he trailed off.

'Our fallen kin,' said Darus, a little shortly. 'Yes. My people have tried to forget.' He changed the subject, with a sigh. 'I thought I could use the books here to tell me more of my brother's axe. It is old, I know that much. I know little of it past that he won it from a dwarf.'

'Come,' said Xhera, taking his huge hot hand with a small smile, her skin pale white against his green. 'I am sure we can find you something on Dwarven weaponry.'

She led him to the desk, and enquired of the Apprentice Scroll, who had been eying Darus with a mixture of suspicion and fascination. When Darus outlined what he wanted, it was obvious the man was astonished that he could read.

Darus snorted.

'We use hides and basic inks, but we read and write, human. And we get books from traders. Nearly all of us can read some Darum.'

The Apprentice Scroll laughed nervously and scurried away to get the books. He handed them over with a nod, making a note in the ledger as they returned to their area.

The big ork's lips moved quickly as he read the books with interest. He was slightly long sighted and held the book out quite far, but read Aldwyn's scratchy Darost script not much slower than many humans. Given that it was not his first language, thought Karland, that was impressive. Orkish was not in the slightest like Darum; it was based on scratchings and ideograms.

One of the things Darus had always been interested in was the origin of the axe his brother had carried. Grukust had won it in a trial of combat, and Aldwyn had made quite a few notes on it - probably without consulting Grukust, mused Karland. Darus was almost childlike in his eagerness to share his findings with his new friends, and they bore his interruptions patiently, interested and happy that he was engaged.

'It says here that Dwarven weapons have a strange structure,' he said, shaking his head slowly. His tusks, a little shorter than his brother's had been, nevertheless softened the occasional word around their thick roots. 'I wish I had known your friend as my brother had. I suspect Grukust was not… subtle enough to have many interesting conversations with him.' His face was sad for a minute, and then he brightened. 'But Aldwyn must have talked to a lot of dwarves when he looked into this. He says here that they make the weapons from two weaves of different steels, one mild and one hard, with a third of a rare metal called *titan.*' He looked at the others; they shrugged. 'Elves call it *mithril.*'

'There are many tales of weapons and armour made by dwarves being light, strong, and harder than steel,' said Xhera. 'Even I heard them on the farm… usually told for the boys. Heroes and so on. Most of them weren't women.' Her glance made Karland feel as if she blamed him for it.

'This book talks of mild steel, crucible steel, and this *titan,*' said Darus. 'It says elves make what they call *Toldere steel,* this crucible metal. Light, strong, sharp. But even that was no match for the dwarf metal. *Mithril* was prized very highly by the elves. He says the weave in the weapon would hold… where, *missä se on.* Ah.' He held the book up in thick fingers, reading slowly. '*Mag-net-ic?* To do with something called *lodestones.*'

Karland had seen metal and lodestones pull to each other. He supposed that made sense.

'I do not know many of these words. Can you explain them? Oh, it says '*Dwarven weapons break the flow of force when correctly placed, allowing the door to be swung open.*'

'That is very clever,' laughed Xhera.

Karland nodded. 'But what about your axe in particular?'

'The human gave me a list of seven more books that might help. There are notes in this book also.'

Xhera and Karland groaned almost in unison.

'I swear, everything he did referenced something else.' Karland shook his head despairingly.

'You should count yourself lucky Aldwyn did so, or you would quickly be lost,' said a soft voice. Night appeared at their desk, his thin arms laden with enormous books that looked far too heavy for him, yet which he hefted with ease. 'I am consistently amazed at his memory.' He bowed slightly to Darus. '*Urukin.* I am Night, scholar and Seeker.' He added another sentence in flawless orkish and Darus grunted in approval, saluting in respect.

'I am Darus.'

'I know of you, Darus. I knew your brother in Punslon, albeit briefly. He was an interesting person. I was sorry to learn of his death.'

'As was I,' said Darus. 'I am glad you knew him.'

'It seems that Eordeland has been gifted with many travellers of late,' remarked Night almost blandly. 'I wonder when they will finally heed our words. The Council of Twelve take so long to decide things, I fear war will be on their doorstep before they do.'

'War is before us all,' said Darus grimly.

ʘ ʘ

Darus, Karland and Xhera emerged into dull afternoon. Their heads were fogged with study, and they needed rest, fresh air and food. Darus bade them farewell and left for his garden.

As they were walking along to the stairwell to their room, a voice called from behind in an odd tone.

'Karland.'

They turned to see Bradwr standing there, pale-faced and tense. Xhera glanced at Karland, then motioned to him and carried on. Bradwr was staring only at Karland, and it was obvious she didn't want to talk to him. For a moment Karland wished she would stick around this once. He knew his liking of the young man got in the way of his better judgement.

This time felt different, however. The antipathy rolled off Bra in waves.

'I came to the Library Entrance and you weren't there,' accused Bradwr. He was almost shaking in anger. 'I waited *hours*. How *dare* you just leave me standing there?'

The fury shocked him, and he searched back to find what he had done wrong.

'I said to let me know. You didn't,' he said finally. 'We never agreed a time to meet.'

'You knew I wanted to come with you,' said Bradwr hotly. 'We arranged the Combic Libraries.'

'Uh,' said Karland, a sinking feeling inside for a long moment. Had he made a mistake?

No. He shook his head, his memory clear.

'We didn't, Bra. You weren't paying attention. It's a misunderstanding.'

'Um, *no*. I wasted my time waiting for *you*, and again it's all *my* fault. I'm sick of the way you always pretend you're so morally superior. It's *never* your fault.'

Karland gaped, astounded. 'What? The amount of times you haven't bothered turning up when we agree to meet and I've waited for you without saying a word… we didn't even agree-'

'How *dare* you lead me on?' Bra spat, interrupting. A horrible pinch-nosed look had descended onto his face. At that moment Karland wondered how he had ever considered his friend good looking, or why he was his friend. He had seen Bra like this with other people, but always believed his stories that it was their fault.

Now he wasn't so sure.

'Look, you *know* you're not permitted there,' Karland snapped, his temper fraying. This wasn't fair! 'What in the hells is your problem? When you said library I clearly said *Librarium.*'

'As usual, you're full of shit,' Bra retorted. 'You're a coward and a liar.'

Karland narrowed his eyes, icy anger washing through him. 'The one thing I don't do is lie. *You* made arrangements you weren't even listening to. You're trying to get me to give you something I can't give you. What's going on?'

'You always think you're so much *better* than me,' sneered Bradwr, changing tack. Karland stared. He couldn't work out where this vitriol had come from. 'How *dare* you get in the way of my life? You never agree with me when I need it. You can't be bothered to help me. You let me down all the time. You always make me feel like I'm a bad person!'

Karland couldn't believe his ears. He had done an awful lot for Bradwr, giving freely of time and gifts. He felt his face drain of colour, and found it hard to think, the shock was so great. He tried to form a reply. He couldn't.

Bradwr glared at him and then walked off. 'You'll be sorry!' he shouted back, voice thin.

Karland watched him vanish detachedly, his heart thumping wildly.

What the fuck is going on?

He took the stairs up slowly.

Xhera was waiting in the room on one of the chairs.

'Not good?' she said quietly. Karland shook his head, eyes wide.

'I actually do not know what just happened,' he replied, and told her what Bradwr had said.

Xhera was quiet a long moment, and then she shrugged. 'Karland. This isn't your fault. I *know* you. He's lying, believing his own lies.' She blew out a long breath. 'You know what? I think he's found new people to weasel in with and just wanted an excuse to get rid of you. You don't fawn on him or get him what he wants. You didn't get him training with Rast, or access to the Combics. You didn't throw me away in favour of him. And you've lost friends and influence with some of the students.'

Karland laughed bitterly. 'Are you trying to cheer me up, Xhera? I know that.'

'No, I mean Aran has spoken against you more than once, but some of these other things have been, well. I think Bradwr hates you not doing what he wants, that no glory reflects onto him. I think this was coming. He's been saying things behind your back for a while.'

'Like what? Why didn't you say something?' Karland felt like his feet were being cut from under him.

'I only suspected. He does it about everyone. Just things that no one else could have really known except us.' She tried to inject some humour. 'It certainly wasn't *me.*'

'I know that.' he scowled.

Xhera sighed.

'Look, think of it in another way… you've found out who your real friends are.' She shook her head. 'Bradwr will regret this when it goes wrong for him, but he'll blame you forever because he doesn't have the strength of character to admit it's him at fault. He's worthless, Karland. Haven't you noticed how many people eventually see through him? It's just… your turn.'

Sometimes she sounded very grown up, he thought.

'Why is he saying these things?' He couldn't keep the plaintive note from his voice. 'I'd never do this to a friend!'

'Jealousy? He doesn't need your friendship anymore? He doesn't like your honesty and wants to hurt you? He's a worthless liar who ruins other people's lives because he's a dangerous narcissist? All of it? I already told you what he was like, Karland. He isn't worth your breath, your care, or your upset.'

'But I didn't do anything wrong,' said Karland hopelessly.

Xhera hugged him.

'Like I said, sometimes people are just shit,' she murmured. 'Everyone else will work it out eventually. Forget about him.'

Easier said than done, thought Karland bitterly.

ଓ ଇ

Sontles lowered the parchment, thinking. His most useful servant was moving quickly east, and although there was little to report yet, there were some promising leads. He usually preferred Ventran to be close by where he could more easily control him, but there might yet be some benefit to him causing chaos across Anaria.

230

Ventran was hiding something, he was sure. He was mildly impressed at the strength of will in the young man. Most humans would have told him their life secrets when pressed.

The pendant was missing still, but he was on the trail.

Yes, this way was better. Ventran was nothing if not focused on his task. Better the pendant was lost or destroyed than Eordeland find a way to use it.

If Ventran failed, he would regret the loss of a useful tool. If he succeeded, he would reward him well.

A bigger problem lay before him now; the Holy Voice of Terome. All the work Sontles had carried out for years with the Prime Alderman was being slowly unpicked. The build-up to the war with Eordeland was on the brink of collapse. If he caught wind of what Sontles was truly doing with the Inquisition, or that he had sent Extinctor Chaplains and Teromants to Matalaga on his own missions…

No assassin would get to the old man; even within the Church's factions, with all the influence Sontles held, he would be instantly denounced and executed if he even mentioned it. No one within the Church would consider harm to the highest of their order, the Voice of God. The Cardinals might, but any harm would have to come from outside, and it would not get through the fanatical Teromants. And he was in good health.

He could reverse the fortunes of the common people. The Voice was beloved by the country, worshipped and lauded. It was infuriating.

No, something else had to be done. If Sontles played this part of the game correctly, he could remove a problem and save a reeling Church, give it direction.

Sontles was as coldly patient as any spider. Being immortal and unburdened with the worries of the living allowed him exceptional clarity and focus. His plans had been in place for decades.

How to remove him?

With almost anyone else Sontles would have tried to discredit them. Letting an opponent tear themselves to pieces publicly was delicious, but it wouldn't work here. The old man was far too astute at the game, and the zealotry of his flock made Sontles envious. Even the total domination of a vampire over the weak-willed could not last long over too many. The Holy Voice was worshipped by tens of thousands of people willingly placing themselves in thrall.

If he could but remove the man and slip into his place… the Cult of Terome would do the rest.

But how?

He sat immobile in the guttering light of the single candle. He didn't really need it to read at night, but it gave him a strange distant comfort, a reminder of his life and how much he had grown.

There was no rise or fall of his chest, no movement. Anyone chancing upon him would assume he had died in his chair, possible some time ago, but his mind was a lightning storm of possibilities.

For hours he sat, considering his options, calculating probabilities and paths. Finally, his dry lips stretched in a horrible smile. He felt his fangs slip out from them and drew breath to chuckle.

It was bold, and very risky… but it could solve nearly every problem with one cast of the bones.

Yes. Yes, that could work.

NINETEEN

Today, felt Karland, had been a good day. His studies had become easier and his bowmanship had improved drastically under the tutelage of Lëlylien, who was slowly becoming more light-hearted again.

His upset over Bradwr's ending of their friendship had grown into unfamiliar fury as he found stories and lies told about him that could only come from one source, people ignoring him and Aran smirking constantly. He couldn't believe that someone he had trusted would spend so much energy in vengeance of their own minor mistake. For a week, his hands had literally shaken with rage at the injustice.

But over the next few weeks, he had begun to calm, to listen to his true friends and value them more. In a way, it was a relief; a truth. He was learning to care a little less about what did not ultimately matter from people of no worth.

He felt happier. He was training well with Rast. Xhera had fallen asleep on his shoulder the other day.

All in all, life was good.

And this evening, Dorn was introducing them to his favourite game.

'Vingitunis isn't a game so much as a way of life,' Dorn said to Karland and Xhera. 'It's old, but it hasn't changed much over the years. It's also called Spoils of Five.' His eyes gleamed with fervour.

Karland wasn't really much for gambling. He supposed it was some kind of fun, and he did enjoy card games.

'The rules are… well, the *basic* rules are simple. It uses the normal pack of forty-eight cards - Tomes, Coins, Swords and Shields.' He flicked a few of each out on the table, and then started arranging them in suits, Primus first, then two, then three, all the way up to the ten, Lady and Lord.

'Three of the cards in the pack are trumps - Lord Coin, Lady Sword and Primus Tome.' He slid them out a little. 'In Novin it's Lord Sword instead of Lady, and Primus Coin not Tome. Three are *spoils* - Lady, Lord and Primus of Shields.' These were also separated for them to see. The Lord and Lady were skeletons bearing

shields in this pack, and the shields for ten were arranged in a skull. 'There is usually
a small buy-in for the hand. The person opposite the dealer shuffles, and then cards
are dealt. You have five cards dealt clockwise around the table - two at once, then
one, then two at once. That's your hand.'

'So how do you win?' asked Xhera.

'You try to get the highest hand, preferably with one or more trumps. One of
these Shields-' he pointed to the separated spoils, '-can be sacrificed to spoil the hand
if the spoiler thinks someone has a trump.'

'What if they don't?'

'The spoiler 'retreats' and automatically loses the hand. But if they bluffed it and
catch someone with trumps, the sacrifice goes back to the pack and all trumps are
removed from the other player. Then the rest must pick an equal number of cards to
the trumps to lose, too. All those cards plus a matching number of new are shuffled
and re-dealt. Adds a lot of chance to the game, and countering become quite
calculated. Once dealt, anyone can *drop* their hand if they think it is bad. If they
think it is good, or are bluffing, they can up the stakes. To stay in and not drop,
everyone must match the stakes until no more raises are given. Once everyone has
dropped or matched, anyone with a spoil has a chance to use it if they wish. If no
one spoils, hands are shown.

'To win the run, or the tabled game, you either win five hands in a row, a *fist*, or
everyone plays until they agree to stop, bow out, or everyone runs out of money.
Some *Vingitunis* games can go on for days, and a lot of money can change hands.
Entire fortunes have been won… and lost.'

'Sounds fun,' said Karland dubiously. 'Which hands win, then?'

'You have the non-trump hands,' said Dorn, warming to his subject. 'A Sum,
where you have the highest single card; Twins, two of any card; Full Moons, two
pairs; Triplets, and so on,' he began shuffling and laying examples out, 'Child,
Family, Index, Noble House, Quarters. Royal Family is the highest hand, 5 cards in
a row, same suit, with Lord and Lady.'

'What about trump hands?' asked Xhera intently.

Dorn laughed at her expression. 'Karland only looks interested. You look the way
I feel about it.' He glanced at Karland slyly. 'You may have stiff competition here,
lad. Cards are serious business.' He gestured at the cards.

'Trump hands are the same as the other hands, with one or more trumps.
Commander, Two Moons, Two Rulers-' he paused. 'Funny one, that. Any five cards
with two trumps, no non-trump equivalent.' He continued, '-Eclipse, Triumvirate,
Stream, River, ' he laid them out quickly with a trump in each, '-Ducal Hand,

Council, Elders, and lastly the highest single-pack hand, Lord of the Land.' He grinned.

'Single pack?' asked Karland dubiously. It already sounded complex enough. *Lord of the Land, though.*

'If you are serious, you can play with two packs, which doubles the trumps and shields, and allows the final Reign Hands. That you call Reign - or Emperor's - *Vingitunis*. The Reign Hands are King's Realm, made of Lord Coin, Lady Sword, and Primus Tome, plus any other trump. So something like Lord Sword and Lady Coin, for example.' He leaned back in his chair.

'The highest hand is Emperor's Decree. Five trumps in one hand.' He shook his head. 'You don't see that very often.'

'So you can counter any of these with the spoil Shield cards?' asked Xhera.

Dorn nodded. 'Primus, Lord or Lady. That is why when you play you must keep a good death-face. Blank as a corpse. If someone reads your intent, they can bluff you. It becomes very tactical, very intense. It is like war. You need to know when the enemy has strength to attack, and when they are bluffing; when to play your defence, or keep it to turn your own attack.'

'You're good at this game, aren't you?' said Karland, half-admiring. It wasn't really a question. Dorn assumed a focus similar to when he fought when he spoke of the game. It sounded interesting, but there were a lot of hands to remember even before the rules of playing, and it also sounded like a lot of work. Knowing luck was involved didn't make him feel any better, given his own.

'I'm a good player,' confessed Dorn. 'It's like war. I structure my attack and defence. You find a lot of the best players are scholars from the *Academia Mathematica*. They calculate odds and percentages much better than I do. But they are often not so bold.' He shrugged. 'Sometimes, boldness and bluff can take a genius down, and there *is* the element of chance, as long as the game is clean. That's why the person opposite the dealer shuffles.'

'Can we play?' demanded Xhera.

Karland groaned to himself. He *knew* that look.

'Of course,' said Dorn. He shuffled the cards in with a fluid motion, the thick worn card riffling in his fingers. 'You deal.' He handed the pack to her. 'Two each, then one, then two.'

Xhera obediently dealt the cards. Dorn looked at his with no real expression, and then looked at Karland, who hid his inexpertly and fanned them in his hand.

'Be careful not to show them to anyone behind you,' said Dorn. 'It is not unknown for cheats to have accomplices to signal hands to them.' Karland nodded, looking at them carefully. He had the Primus of Shields, nine and seven of Swords, seven of Tomes and the Lord of Coins, a trump. Careful not to show his excitement, he bit his lip and looked at Xhera. She was staring at her cards as if she could see the table through them.

'Anyone to play a spoil?' asked Dorn casually. They both shook their heads. He shrugged, and said, 'Let's see 'em then.'

He followed his words by flipping his cards face up on the table and spreading them. He had two fives, a seven, a Lady of Tomes and a Ten of Coins. 'This hand I would have normally dropped.'

Karland flipped his, and grinned. Dorn nodded.

'Moons, isn't that?' asked Karland smugly. Dorn shook his head.

'No - remember one of the pair must be a trump. You have a *Commander*.'

Karland lost some of his confidence, but then then beamed at Xhera. 'Hear that? *Commander*.'

Xhera scowled at him and flapped her cards down on the table so they slid on their little cushions of air. She had two eights.

'*Twins* as well. Karland wins that hand.'

'Again,' she demanded.

Karland rolled his eyes at Dorn. 'You've done it now.'

They played for twenty more minutes. Karland was quite enjoying it, although he didn't have the patience to memorise all the hands and kept getting them wrong. Xhera did better. Dorn explained where they were going wrong, and how they would be beaten if they made them.

Karland tended to play by feeling - and, if he was honest, impatience. Xhera was the opposite. She played with her head and a sharp focus, and in short order she had trumped them both several times. They were roughly even in hands, and her face was a mask of concentration. Dorn was playing in a relaxed fashion, and it was clear that he was enjoying himself. He was not winning much, but he was not losing much either.

By the time they stopped, Xhera had won far more games than Karland had.

'You don't pay enough attention,' she said to him. 'You get bored and then make these… jumps.' She managed to keep most of the condescension out of her tone, but Karland could tell she was irritatingly smug about winning so much.

Dorn agreed. 'You seem like you don't want to get too drawn in, Karland. Enjoy the game as a casual player, but don't play for money unless you are prepared to really focus. Money is where it gets very serious.' Xhera smirked at him, and Dorn's amused expression turned to her. 'You play well, for a beginner, but your face tells anyone used to playing what you are thinking. You go stiff and glare at the cards when you have a good hand, and you're too cautious. Karland plays in a more relaxed way.' He laughed. 'Combine the two of you, you'd have a hell of a player.'

Xhera looked chagrined; she had clearly been trying hard.

Too hard, thought Karland. He admired Xhera's serious mien and her ability to focus and block out distractions. It was why in many areas she was a far better student than he was. It could also be quite annoying, especially when she got superior about it. He hadn't tried hard enough, worried about committing too much. But it was fun, he had to admit. He and Xhera could play together and hone their skills.

'This was your first game. Don't worry too much,' said Dorn, seeing Xhera's face fall. 'Practice. It's worth knowing to pass the time, and you can make new friends in unlikely places.' He grinned again. 'Or enemies.' He stretched. 'Perhaps you would like to see it in action.' He raised an inquisitive eyebrow. 'There is a *Spoils* table set for a game in the north barracks. Why not come along?'

'We have to study for lessons,' said Xhera. 'There are tests coming up for mid-term in several academia, and we are already behind. The extra work with Aldwyn's notes is hard to fit in as it is.'

'And any leeway we get makes us… unpopular… with other students,' said Karland, wincing. 'Well. I say 'we'. Xhera generally attracts less grief than I do.'

'Must be something about you,' she murmured.

He crossed his eyes at her and then grinned. 'Ah, come on, Xhera. Just for a bit. Do us good to get away from books.'

'We get away mornings for training with Rast.'

Karland waved his hands. 'And *not* get bruises.'

'Well. Yes. I suppose we could go for an hour or so?' Xhera looked at Dorn enquiringly.

'It's been going most of today,' he said. 'Soldiers come and go. It's a friendly affair, mostly. Anyone causing trouble over betting gets clean-up duty… or worse, banned from playing. You'd find games in the city rougher. Why don't we go now, and then we can get back to our duties? I have several reports to write tonight, but I'm in the mood for unwinding.'

He left them the worn pack and motioned them to follow him. They wended their way through the corridors, arriving in the north-western barracks outside a door with a constant excited murmur from within.

Dorn opened the door, and they passed into a well-lit barracks common room where a table had been set up. The room smelled of exercise and people, armour and oil. Surprisingly, there was no smoke; Karland guessed it wasn't permitted in barracks.

The tables looked suspiciously well-arranged for gaming rather than food. A murmur of talking and laughing pulsed around the room, and Karland saw soldiers from a mix of units, Welcomer and Guard both. The room was very full. A cheer went up from the middle of the room, accompanied by the chink of small coins.

At their entrance, a corporal turned to the door and then saluted with a fist to his throat.

'Captain Dorn!'

There was a chorus of thumps in the sudden diminishing noise as soldiers jumped to their feet and snapped to attention. The soldiers at the table placed their cards face down - very carefully, Karland noticed.

'Carry on,' said Dorn. 'Here for a quick game.'

With relieved talking and understanding chuckles, the soldiers seemed to collapse back into their previous positions, as if they had expected this response. Karland caught glimpses of Guard he knew by face, and a few by name, including Kith and Gen, a pair who usually ended up on duty together outside The Sanctum. Their company was currently on City Guard duty, and Karland had spent a lot of time talking to them.

Kith was cat-quick, average in height with straight brown hair and a serious manner that belied a very cutting sense of humour. Gen had dimples bracketing a cheeky grin, and although he was taller and wider than Kith, with large shoulders and a broad back, something about him spoke of a street urchin. He had a habit of referring to people as *my old son* rather than using names, and his rough and ready cocky manner occasioned grins from most. He got away with a lot, but he meant no offence. They were both very easy to get on with.

Gen pretended to stare in comical horror at the children, and Kith raised one eyebrow before grinning and winking, his eyes crinkling. They turned back to their game.

'I have told soldiers to leave ranks at the door for *Vingitunis*,' Dorn said over the hubbub as they moved towards the centre of the room and the main table. 'You sit, you're a player, unless you behave unbefitting your rank, even off-duty. Punishment is harsh, but the troops generally agree being banned from the tables is harsher.'

A woman behind him muttered something, and someone laughed. Karland recognised Gen's amusement.

'Luckily, I'm off-duty and didn't hear that,' said Dorn easily. Someone else chuckled. It was clear that he was well liked and respected by his soldiers. It was very unusual for an officer to join the men, apparently; Karland saw few officers above Lieutenant. Dorn seemed to be a special case, possibly because he spent so much time training with the troops. He was rated as one of the deadliest swordsman in Eordeland, and was keenly sought after by the elite for lessons.

There were eight soldiers around this table, a mixture of men and women of varying ranks, none above Staff-Sergeant.

'Simin,' Dorn greeted the dealer. 'What are the table limits?'

The man dealing was probably of Hadrasian descent, shorter than many of his fellows, and had slightly tilted dark eyes and a thick if well-trimmed Eordeland beard. His shoulders were stooped under his jerkin.

'Penny buy-in, sir; ceiling is a Great.'

Xhera looked shocked, and Karland blinked. Eordeland Greats were silver alloy worth half an ounce of pure. It was a huge amount of money, as much as they would earn in months in their homes.

'A Great? I think we're paying you all too much.' A couple of the players snorted. Dorn shrugged. 'Deal me in.' He glanced at Karland and Xhera and winked. A few of the other soldiers around him had knowing grins. He emptied a coinpurse next to him on the table to provide a pile of mixed pennies, decs and a few silver. Other players likewise had different sized piles of their own.

'Buy-ins,' said Simin. With a rattle and chink pennies were tossed or slid into the middle of the table.

The pale-skinned woman opposite the dealer with a slight squint and spiky brown hair shuffled the worn-looking pack efficiently and passed the cards over. Karland saw white scars on her arms, and the tip of one finger was missing.

Simin dealt the cards with quick flicks clockwise; two, one and two. Some players left them face down and tilted the corners up, others picked their hands up and glanced before returning them. Dorn casually spread his and then dropped them face down in a neat pile. A dark-skinned man further around sighed, shook his head, and slapped his cards down.
'Drop,' he said.

'Shouldn't he turn them over?' he muttered to Xhera, who was watching intently.

'No,' she said distractedly. 'People would be able to see what cards weren't there and calculate what's left. Shh!'

Karland wisely retreated and turned back to the table.

The player to the left of Gen slid five pennies in. 'Bet,' she said. One by one, they matched, apart from Dorn, who slid a dec in, his usually expressive face as unreadable as Rast's. A couple of the others muttered, and then around again his bet was matched. Another player dropped.

'Shields?' enquired Simin. The players eyed each other carefully, and then a chorus of finger taps resulted.

Players flipped their cards and spread them. Dorn had Two Moons; the next highest was a Commander. There were a couple of muted curses, and Dorn swept the coins into his much larger pile.

The games continued, Dorn winning several more hands and losing one. He and his opponents kept up a steady banter, laughing and good-natured.

'Have you ever noticed that people call Dorn *Dorn*?' Xhera asked Karland quietly. He stared at her, almost pityingly.

'Well… yes. Dorn is his name.'

She cast an exasperated look at him. 'Don't be dense, Karland. His name is Dorn *Gardenson*. Shouldn't he be Captain Gardenson?'

'Huh.' Karland hadn't noticed but didn't particularly want to say so. 'He gets on with people pretty well for a Captain-General. Maybe it's that.'

He watched them thumbing the well-used cards. According to Dorn, *Vingitunis* packs were widely varied. The most expensive packs would have individual art, gold leaf, or be made from exotic substances; the most basic in blank cheap fibrous card, recycled from used notepaper that could not be written on and erased any more by soaking in small pieces for hours, then stretching the resultant mush over a fine mesh in a wooden frame. It was common for children in cities and surrounds to make card packs this way, trying to learn and compete in the intricacies of the game. These 'dirty' packs were very susceptible to tampering by sharps.

Rule sets differed from one land to another, even one region, but one thing was common everywhere: *Reign* - or *Emperor's Vingitunis* - was played almost exclusively by the wealthy using large sums of money in play and required two matching untampered packs.

After their hour was almost up, Karland grew a little bored. He was not getting as much from watching this as Xhera was and decided he was going back to the room. Rast was likely back soon, and he had study to do. More than Xhera, if he was honest with himself.

'It's been an hour, nearly,' he said to Xhera. She flapped her hand at him.

'A bit longer won't hurt. I'll stay and watch if you want to go back.'

'If you're sure,' said Karland. He knew she didn't like wandering around on her own later in the evening.

'Dorn or someone else will bring me back. Go on.' Her eyes didn't leave the table.

'All right,' he said, amused.

He waved to Dorn, who winked at him, and chuckled as Gen threw his cards down in disgust and proclaimed Kith to be a cold monster. Kith glanced at him and jiggled his eyebrows as Karland moved out into the dark, shutting the door. The cool air and peace descended.

It would be a lovely evening to think as he walked back.

ڢ　ࣀ

He took some time and an indirect route back to the room, avoiding Darus, enjoying rare time alone with peaceful thoughts. The Sanctum never truly slept, but many of the Academia were not busy in the evenings. He only saw the occasional Guard.

Rast wasn't there, but there was a note on the floor, as if slipped under the door. Opening it, he saw it was signed *Xhera.*

He frowned. How had she returned before him? He knew he'd taken a long stroll, but she must have left soon after him. And why wasn't she here? Why had she left a note under the door? Had she left her key?

He sat down to read it. It was short and to the point, written shakily. He wondered what had happened to affect her normally neat handwriting.

Karland

Something important has come up. I desperately need your help. Meet me alone in the Artem Atrium as soon as you find this. I'll be waiting.

Please.

- Xhera

He stared at it, heart thumping. All his calm had vanished. There was something he wasn't seeing here. Something strange.

Gods. I hope she is safe.

The guards had changed, and they hadn't seen it delivered. Karland raced towards the sixth's Atrium, heart thumping. He didn't know how long it had been since the note had been pushed under the door. She must have been in a real hurry.

Arriving a little out of breath, he found it deserted. Shadows slanted down the sides of pillars and a few statues from the small lights at each entrance. The clouded moons cast intermittent light over the gentle fountain in the middle.

He wondered if he was too late, if she had already left; what could the fearful note have been about?

'Expecting someone?' drawled a voice.

Aran stepped out from behind one of the statues that lined the Atrium. The Academia had less rooms overlooking the atrium then the others due to the Auditorium. What rooms were occupied would often have artists deep in concentration or music, so were proofed against noise.

Anger and frustration welled up inside Karland, battling a deep sense of despair that lurched into his gut.

How could he have been so stupid?

He tried to deflect where he feared this was going.

'*You* sent the note,' he said with a sigh, trying to affect weariness. Deep down he was tense. He should have known it wasn't Xhera.

Why didn't I go back to check at the game?

He turned to leave and stopped. There were four more boys behind him. Two he knew; Fron, and Kixel, whom he had never had a problem with. He swore to himself and hoped they were only there for show.

'I grow tired of you, Karland Dresin,' said Aran quietly. 'You mock me. You ignore me. You take honours and airs you do not deserve.'

'I've never done anything to you,' said Karland. Anger grew within him. 'I haven't tormented *you*, insulted you, or felt the need to bring in a gang like a coward.'

'Every word brings more retribution,' observed Aran. 'Your mere *existence* offends me. You're worthless. You deserve nothing more than to be whipped like the brown cur you are, back-woods boy. My family own estates larger than your *Croft*. You answer your betters back, and you refuse to learn your place.' He bared his teeth.

'I *hate* you; hate everyone like you who dares think they are my equal. Your little friend is attractive enough - in time I'll bed her, one way or the other - but you... do you know what would happen to you in Novin, acting as you do to a member of the nobility?'

'We're not in Novin,' said Karland. 'We're in my land.'

'*You* own no land,' retorted Aran, 'and I represent my house and Novin both. A Noble House, with land, traditions, wealth. *Breeding*. But you... you're a rat. A dirty, uncivilised, stupid rat, depending on luck and generosity. Didn't you know? Novin travels with me.' He glanced around, and smiled, continuing. 'And here, there are no watchers. No one to rescue you from your punishment. Guards are not due for some time, and I have a helping hand. You are not as *loved* as you think.'

'This is ridiculous,' said Karland, his voice trembling. There was a sick feeling in his gut now. 'Don't be a fool.' Nothing he said would change what was to come, he knew.

'In Novin you would pay for your insolence. You'd be beaten, whipped; perhaps an eye put out. Perhaps fingers removed. Nothing drastic. Nothing to stop you labouring, as you should. *Peasant.*'

'Very brave, aren't you? Picking one boy, surrounded by so many bigger boys?' Kixel looked uncomfortable.

Aran's breath hissed. 'I've had enough of you, you arrogant whelp. You usurp my rightful place with Tal'Orien. You take my rightful status with dragons. You insult me with your existence and mock me to my face. You aren't as smart as you think you are. I'll teach you a lesson, and if I hear a word about this spoken, you might find something nasty happens to your friend. Your pretty friend who you're *so* close to. Could happen at any time. You and Tal'Orien can't be around forever. I have it arranged, Dresin. One word.' He smiled with such malice that Karland didn't doubt him. Cold dread dropped through him.

'So that's what this is about,' he said in understanding. 'You're jealous. I've got what you think you deserve, and you desire Xhera… and she despises you. I was accepted to the University without needing to be *noble* to ease my way.' That wasn't strictly true, but caution had left him as anger rose.

'You'll never know,' said Aran. 'You were lucky enough last time, but someone like you will never learn enough from someone like Tal'Orien. He and the girl are as flawed as you are; choosing you when they could have had me.' He bared his teeth. 'Enough. I wanted you to fully understand what will happen and why. Now, you do.' He nodded to the others. 'Take him. But make sure the marks can be taken for training wounds. Don't touch his face.'

'Coward,' said Karland, swallowing though a dry throat. He eased into a ready stance, heart thumping. This was really happening. 'Relying on others. If I'm so worthless, why not teach me yourself?'

Aran twitched, anger blossoming, then smiled coldly. 'I don't keep dogs and bark myself,' he replied. One of the boys looked annoyed. Kixel spoke uncertainly.

'Aran, you said we were only to frighten him.'

'Shut up,' said Aran savagely. 'If you want your money, you do the work.' The looks from the others bolstered his words. Kixel subsided uncomfortably.

Shit.

This was serious. Karland was trembling with reaction. He didn't want to fight; in fact, he couldn't believe this was happening in The Sanctum. He doubted anyone would hear if he yelled. They had chosen their place of ambush well.

He was on his own.

His muscles felt like water. He wasn't ready for this here, where he had thought he was safe. It was stupid. He had a year of intensive training with Rast, but he had no will to fight these boys. He didn't want to hurt anyone.

Images of fighting orcs, of killing in the Dimnesdair welled up. He gritted his teeth.

Two boys moved in, confident. They didn't think they needed more.

A fist came in and he swayed aside, ducking under it. His arm swept over the other shoulder, and he threw his head sideways, trapping the punching arm, and then gripped his own bicep and squeezed. The larger boy jerked and choked, his own bicep cutting off his airflow. At the same time Karland jumped, using the boy as a stabiliser, and kicked out hard. One foot missed, jarring his hip a little, but the other connected solidly with the face of the second boy who screamed and grabbing his nose as he staggered back to hit the wall, blood running.

Desperately, he looked for an opening to run, but there was no way he could escape before they caught him. At least if he fought it was on his terms.

The larger boys were frustrated and angered that they were not overwhelming one smaller boy quickly, but Karland knew he did not have long. They were stronger, and now they all attacked at once.

He saw Aran move in and lashed out. His movements were making it hard for blows to land, and his were counting for a lot more than theirs.

His foot slammed into Aran's groin, and the larger boy shrieked, sinking to the floor. Karland ducked a fist and swung his elbow. It struck Aran hard above the temple.

If I can take him down now… perhaps they would back off if he took down their leader.

Movement from the right. The boy shrank back when he whirled to confront him, but then a much larger form slammed into him and they fell. He lay pinned under a far greater weight, and concentrated on breathing and moving the body off him. If he thrashed, he would quickly run out of steam, and this boy had clearly wrestled. A hand sneaked in to try to clamp over his mouth and nose, and he bit at it, earning him a punch in the head. His ankles crossed around the torso, and he tried to use the boy as a shield against the others, but it was no use. A small foot flashed in, glancing from his shoulder.

Another attacker had joined now, if he hadn't missed his guess.

Harsh fingers pried his legs slowly apart. He butted the boy on him hard in the face and threw himself back, his forehead clipping an eye socket, kicking off a hand, and struggled to rise.

He had to get away. The look on their faces told him that they had moved past teaching him a lesson, and through the anger and adrenaline true fear flickered.

As he hesitated a glimpse of the new attacker came into view to the side. Karland froze for a moment in shock.

Bradwr darted in, his face with that same, pinched-nosed white anger on his face - once a face Karland had thought fine, now showing the true ugliness beneath - and struck, trying to stab his small dog-hafted letterknife into Karland's back. Karland just managed to anticipate the ungainly attack. He twisted and punched, feeling no small satisfaction as his fist thundered into Bra's face, breaking his nose and removing a tooth. The slight form fell sideways, almost insensate. A flicker from the corner of his eye made him spin, fist throbbing.

His shirt was grabbed and he twisted desperately, his thumb finding the boy's eye, not enough to harm but enough to hurt. The boy let go with a bellow, and Karland turned to find himself face to face with Aran, fury in his eyes. He twisted desperately, but unlike Bradwr, Aran was no stranger to brawls, and he knew how to use his weapon.

He came in with a knife, his teeth bared in hatred and pain, and it sank into Karland's side. It did not go far in, and was not aimed edge-inwards but outwards, so it was not intended to kill, but it was agony. Aran twisted the blade, and Karland screamed as the wound was forced open, his nerves shrieking at the awful pain. His side wetted in seconds, his clothes soaking up hot fresh blood.

He felt his arms and legs grabbed again, one boy each, and struggled mightily, but could not break free. His strength was gone. All of them were breathing heavily. He vaguely noticed a smaller form holding its nose, watching from further back, and cursed the cowardice of one he had called friend.

'Hold him,' hissed Aran, blood trickling from one swelling temple. He held up the knife, the first two inches stained with Karland's blood. It was far longer than the desk knives permitted by law, but then Aran paid little attention to rules.

Karland could not avoid the fist that came in, slamming into his jaw. A second came in fast and hard from the other side, into his ribs under the right arm. He jerked and coughed, his legs losing power. A shudder raced through his body, deep inside as his liver was shocked, and it shut down for a second, leaving his mind alert. A third hard strike to the stomach left him almost vomiting. Aran knew how to punch.

'You know what we would do to mark serfs that were *too* insolent?' Aran hissed into his ear as he sagged, his breathing deep and harsh with pain.

I must have really hurt him, Karland thought woozily. *Good.*

Kixel's voice came again. 'Aran, this.. this isn't right. Stop.'

'Do what you are told, Jan,' Aran breathed. 'Unless you wish to take his place. I don't tolerate betrayal.'

The loosening grip on Karland's leg tightened slightly.

'Turn him,' he heard Aran say, and was inexorably turned and held face down. He felt his arse squeeze involuntarily as his leggings were yanked down. Aran's voice continued near his ear, intimate, cold. He struggled again, fear lending new strength.

'We take a knife, and slice into the anus. Then we slowly saw through the muscle, above and below, until it snaps. And *if* they survive infection, they work shunned, outcast, unable to control their dribbling shit. They soil themselves non-stop, worse than animals. Even animals don't answer back.' He spat on the floor. 'It marks them as less than human, as punished, staining their clothes, their souls. Filth must be shown to be *filth*.' He was almost raving.

Karland yelled and thrashed despite the agony in his side. Aran could not hope to get away with this, in the heart of Eordeland. In The Sanctum! Even his diplomatic status would not protect him. This was *insanity!*

'Hold him down,' he heard Aran say. His voice was full of hatred.

With a sense of panicked detachment, Karland realised this was real. His limbs were pulled straight.

'Fucking little shit,' spat Aran. 'You deserve thi-*wh-?*'

There was a second of confused motion.

Suddenly the hold on Karland's right arm vanished, and then his leg. He heard shouts and cries, and twisted to the left, striking out with everything he had. His right foot connected with a face and a burbling scream erupted. The pressure on his right leg also went, and he looked up his remaining arm in time to see a silver blur leap to the throat of the boy so fast it seemed unreal. His arm was dropped and the boy froze, looking down. When he realised it was a razor-sharp sword, he backpedalled so fast he tripped. His head connected with the wall and he fell limp.

Karland sat up to see Aran, held off the floor by the throat against the wall, choking and clawing at the powerful arm of Rast, who hadn't looked so grim for many months. Even as Karland watched Aran's arm swept up with the knife. Karland opened his mouth, knowing it was too late, but Rast's other forearm blocked the knife almost casually, hardly seeming to move, then knocked it from the boy's hand contemptuously. He let Aran slide down the wall and spun him, looping a huge arm around his throat and loosely applying a rear naked choke. Aran tried to break free, lifting his legs to add weight and tugging at an arm that might as well have been an oak limb. He was rewarded with a quick jerk that produced a squawk like a strangled duck.

Captain Dorn was standing to the side looking equally grim, his sword out and covering the other four boys. Three of them weren't moving. Behind him Kith and Gen stood, more forbidding than Karland had ever seen them. Gen looked as if he wanted to actually murder someone, and Kith looked like a fox that had found a crippled hen in the snow.

'The piss-goblin got away,' he reported in disgust.

'You may all consider yourselves bound by Eordeland Law,' Dorn said, steel in his voice. He looked at Aran in disgust. 'You will go before the Council of Twelve for this.'

Karland pulled up his trousers and stood, breathing hard, the scrapes and marks of the battle starting to throb. It was a miracle he hadn't been hurt worse, and it was still all very surreal. He couldn't believe it had escalated so far, so fast.

'How much did you hear?' he asked. He still woozily worried that Aran would weasel out of things. He always did. In his experience, the worst, most manipulative, most unpleasant people would continually somehow twist things to their advantage, and Aran had the intelligence and charisma Ben Arflun had never had.

'Enough,' said Dorn. 'Enough that at the very least they will be expelled. This was no petty argument. I thank the Gods you dropped that note in your rooms when you left... and that we accompanied Xhera back.'

'I told you there was a grudge,' said Karland, trying to keep accusation from his voice. He looked at his silent guardian. Rast nodded, his eyes not leaving Karland's face. Aran still struggled, but he was allowed to breathe, just.

'You did, Karland. I apologise. I knew you could look out for yourself, but this...' he didn't finish. His voice held anger, whether at himself or the boys Karland didn't know.

Dorn nodded in agreement. 'This is beyond anything we thought would happen in The Sanctum. I will take up with Captain Jekob as to how the Welcomers were not aware of this.' Three other boys were standing, shakily; Fron lay moaning, dazed. Dorn motioned to him. 'Pick him up. Don't bother to think to escape; you won't make it from the grounds.'

'If any of you attempt to flee,' said Rast softly, terribly, 'I will find you.'

'You're not a guard,' blurted one boy in fright. 'You can't touch us.'

'If you do run,' interjected Dorn, 'Master Tal'Orien - as an agent of the Council - may officially apprehend you and drag you back by your feet. On your faces.'

One look at the gigantic grim-faced man was enough. They nodded shakily, all except Aran, who alternated between glaring and struggling.

'Are you all right, boy?' Rast asked Karland.

'I... I am fine. None the wiser to fighting many attackers.' He tried to smile sheepishly and failed, then gasped as a small movement stabbed his side under his covering hands. Rast's eyes flicked down.

'Dorn, he needs a healer. That is his own blood.'

Dorn nodded and snarled at the boys. 'Assaulting a student of The Sanctum, a Dragonfriend - and a saviour of the city - with deadly intent? Ganging up on a smaller boy? You pathetic cowards. You'll be lucky if you aren't sent to Kingsgate for this. Get moving.'

'Wait,' said Karland tiredly. 'Where is Bradwr?'

'Ah. So that is who we saw fleeing,' said Dorn. 'Don't worry. He won't get far, the little worm.'

Gen grabbed a boy in each powerful hand, hauling them roughly up and almost dragging them along. Kith came to Karland and lifted his tunic, hissing at the wound and the amount of blood.

Karland glanced down. The wound was almost like a dark eye in pale skin, pointed at the ends and gaping in the middle. It was so dark red it was almost black. He could see layers of skin, and something unpleasantly smooth.

He felt odd.

'Kith?' Dorn's voice was emotionless.

'He'll live. I've had worse scratches.' Kith was trying to sound jovial, but his face said it wasn't a minor wound. He dropped his shoulder under Karland's.

'Come on, lad. Let's get you seen to.'

TWENTY

'Your Holiness, the Prime Alderman is here to see you.' The neophyte stood, head bowed, awaiting the reply.

Rembrandt Articorl sighed inwardly. It had been a long day, and the Prime Alderman seemed determined to catch him at a time when he would be distracted or tired. It was a somewhat disappointing ploy for someone so nuanced in politics.

He had been Holy Voice now for a little over a year, and had been mired in a quagmire of policy, infighting, and the increasing corruption of the state.

He was tired. Most of his energy was spent keeping the power of the Church from slipping to the Cardinals, or even the new government. He had never been a staunch follower of King Orreld, but he believed in Terome and was sickened by the misappropriations of power.

Rembrandt was a hard man, but fair, and faithful. He had left his family and wife behind many years ago so that they could not be used against him, walled his heart off from grief, and spent his remaining energies on trying to repair his country and bring the Church back to its core, knowing full well it could be at the cost of his life.

In his youth, he would never have thought he was the kind of man to sacrifice himself for an ideal like this, but after his daughter had died and his wife had blamed him for it, he had realised that even that which he had thought his rock was formless. If lies and misunderstanding could not repair his life, at least one thing remained to him that was solid, real, unshakeable.

He had his God.

The one true God, according to Meyar, and Haná before that. A God that had succoured them, given them a free land and laws; given them five commandments on tablets of platinum, and nine sins on the skins of devils, and a thick book of parables. A God, he thought disgustedly, whose message now seemed to be interpreted more and more to fit the needs of those in power. Somewhere along the way a rot had set in, quite apart from the overthrow of the Kings of Haná.

The Church itself was sick. The Teromants followed the Word in the Light, but some of them he suspected also followed the words of individual Cardinals. There was infighting and the occasional death, and some Teromens seemed to want to worship in awful rites considered lost to ancient history - and newer, darker ones. Not because of their intrinsic lusts, he thought, but because somehow, they were conditioned to it.

He did not intend to see human sacrifice as a requirement for Terome's favour in his lifetime.

'Please tell the Prime Alderman I shall attend him when I have finished my devotions,' he said. 'Make him comfortable in the narthex.' The neophyte bowed and left, the brand of Terome on the inside of his right forearm briefly visible as he reached for the door.

The Holy Voice sighed again, out loud this time, and massaged his temples.

He wasn't a particularly holy man in the oldest definitions of the word. He was no humble priest, no innocent leading a flock. The only thing that separated him from any other politician was his belief and his love of the Church and country; that, and a lack of ambition. He was already at the peak of his climb.

Life would have been a lot easier if he hadn't ascended in the first place.

He would, without conscience, send men to their deaths to preserve his position and the power of the Church. He devoutly believed that his being in this position was the Church's only hope now. It wasn't the power of money and recognition that kept him here; it was the power to secure the Church for another hundred years.

In the murky waters of the destabilised states of Meyar, he knew several political crocodiles lurked. At the moment he was the biggest one as far as the Church was concerned, and thankful for it. The populace had always been solid believers. Those who dedicated themselves further and passed the coveted Sanction were known as Teromens, the men of Terome. Tens of thousands of people were Teromens, as they had been for centuries. This meant that although the Church was ripe for misuse, set up as it was for blind following of the faith, in his hands it was secure. People saw him as the Voice of Terome, and he was, although in his heart he wished Terome would speak *to* him occasionally and not just *through* him. But 'through him' meant what the Holy Voice needed the Church to say to keep strong. Every proclamation required careful thought, politically and theistically. Rembrandt was no fool.

The Prime Alderman was his main political opponent. Rembrandt suspected very strongly that he was the man who had been behind the regicide of the King and his family; he had come out on top and seized control in a suspiciously smooth and immediate fashion once the dust had settled. The man was an old councillor to the King, and had become a despicable despot, the worst kind of autocrat. Young women were delivered to him regularly, willing or no, and he was deliberately building a system of percentages where out-of-touch nobility made policy for commoners and kept the cream of everything - wealth, goods, laws - for themselves and left the people more and more powerless.

Sooner or later, he knew, there would be revolution, and God help them all when that came.

The one thing that kept them in check was the religion. Terome was a stern God, and the commoners were God-fearing.

The Prime Alderman was a concern, certainly, and always edging for an advantage. The Holy Voice could counter him, though. He had been in politics decades longer, and had the adulation of the states, from people in nobility and otherwise. The Alderman would not gain the power he sought through the Church. This mad idea of waging war on Eordeland was the latest foolishness, although he wondered if it was a ploy to bring people together. It was harder to hate your leaders when you banded together behind them to fight a common enemy, and though he had certainly taken the unlikely stories of Eordeland's decision to invade with a pinch of salt, the people had swallowed it unquestioningly. There must be more to it than that. It was not sustainable, nor in his weighted opinion was it winnable.

He had other things to worry about than a politician who wanted to apportion a little of the Church's power, however. There were other, more immediate threats within the Church.

Anyone who believed that the Church was less political than the Assembly was a fool and would quickly be consumed. Church politics were far worse and hidden behind a veneer of piety. Several high-ranking Church officials had their eyes on his role, and he had won by popular vote fully aware that other candidates had been put up with money behind them as puppets. No-one was to be trusted - but three Cardinals, a Primate and a recent bishop required special observation.

Rembrandt had made sure the Teromants were on full alert around him. The Chaplains were fanatically loyal. Food tasters tested his meals, and he kept a surprise on him in the form of the cruciform symbol of the Light shining from the Book of Terome, long horizontal arms representing His knowledge projecting from a block in the middle representing the open Book. He had a similar symbol on his chest. This was the symbol of his office, heavy and cumbersome, and it could be worn around his neck on a heavy chain.

Few knew the Holy Light could be twisted and pulled apart to provide a small but serviceable dagger in the event he ever had to use it, steel adorned with blessings and the forgiveness of Terome inlaid in silver. The sharp blade was hidden within the long arm of one side, and one edge of the vertical projecting block became a short crossguard. The other arm of the Light was just long enough to hold in one hand.

He fingered it, tracing the deceptive symbols carved in the gold covering which hid the joins, thinking.

One of the Cardinals was quite devout but disagreed with many of his interpretations of the Holy Book. He was also prone to snap judgements rather than long-term decisions, and would not benefit the Church in the long run. The other two were career politicians and wanted nothing more than the power that being Holy Voice would provide. The responsibility was not a welcome addition, and he knew it would be quickly ignored if they were in his place.

The Primate was ambitious but weak. Over two years ago he had ordained another as a bishop, the first in some time, and a surprising choice. Now Gilden had stepped aside and ordained the bishop as his nominated replacement, a highly unprecedented act.

This last was a strange man who gave many cause for concern.

Sontles Aquinas was unknown until his ascension, and already was rapidly accruing power within the Church, producing excellent results with the Inquisition. Rembrandt had resolved to investigate further; rumours had arisen of some Inquisitors straying from the path, the old practices rising. Perhaps his control was not as good as it appeared.

Aquinas was knowledgeable of many old practices that, once better left forgotten, seemed to be gaining ground at an alarming rate among the flock. He seemed to travel a lot, which was not acceptable in a man supposed to lead his flock in one region, and only ever seemed to be free to meet in the evenings. During the day he refused to meet, communicating only by writing.

And then there was that long absence in recent months.

Something about him sent a shiver down the Holy Voice's spine. At least one of his opponents had been backed by this man, so it was clear he had resources. Rembrandt shook his head mournfully. He had to find out if he had real faith, and how it could be used. If not, he needed to be removed before he could do any lasting harm. Either way, his ambition needed to be curbed.

The problem was, he was persuasive. Too persuasive. He had spoken in favour of the return of some of the most terrible practices of the Church, and some new ones. When challenged, he always seemed to have a reasonable excuse. A need. It became hard to argue the results. People seemed almost slaves to him at times. Dry though he was in voice and appearance, he was as adept at squirming as any snake.

Although Rembrandt had no evidence, he suspected Sontles was an unbeliever. Worse, he worried that he was directly responsible for the rising of mob burnings, torture, and the conscription and ambition rising in the Church. Primate Gilden hadn't had the wit to rise further even before his mind had begun to wander, and now all too conveniently the man would replace him.

This bishop was someone to watch. He wondered at what point it would become expedient to simply excommunicate him and have him sent to the southern mines. If he could find evidence of his connection to the use of terrors on the populace, it would be enough to have him both excommunicate and beheaded.

He took a deep breath.

Grant me thy strength and guide me to be thine instrument, O Lord, he prayed, and made the sign of the Book and Light before nodding to the far neophyte.

The Prime Alderman appeared at the door after a short pause.

'Your Holiness.'

The Holy Voice sighed inwardly, prepared for a different type of battle. Both men recognised the politician within the other, and Rembrandt knew he was one of the few who saw the sharp mind of the man behind the façade of a blustering loudmouth.

Rembrandt held out the cruciform symbol out for the Alderman to kiss perfunctorily. Eonder Jarle dropped to one knee puffily, and not happily, to do so.

'What can I do for you, Prime Alderman?' Rembrandt asked.

'I regret to inform you that we have had some reports of attempted uprisings in the south and east,' said Jarle without preamble, rising.

'Surely your troops can put this uprising down,' said the Holy Voice noncommittally.

'They may be heretics,' said Jarle carefully. The Holy voice shot him a sharp look.

'Then I should send the Teromants there in force?' He was half-joking.

'The... reports I am receiving is that they are hard to find. It is well-hidden.'

The Holy Voice raised his eyebrows. 'What exactly are you asking of me, my son?'

Eonder Jarle seemed to pause for thought. He did not fool Rembrandt. 'Obviously, this is the Church's concern,' said Jarle after a moment. He held a hand up, in a fist with only the index finger extended, pointing up and jabbing his arm forward to make the point. 'The Assembly will support any means necessary to aid the Church, but we must think of the country as well.'

'I am glad to hear that,' said the Holy Voice. He wondered what the man's game was.

'I understand you prefer not to go to war, but we must strengthen the borders if you move Teromants to the east. We would be foolish not to be prepared if war were to come to us.'

'Too many here are convinced war is inevitable,' said the Holy Voice. 'I will not condone invading Eordeland, my son. It has not been Terome's way to convert by force for hundreds of years, and at the beginning it was never the way. I will unify the Church, and Teromants will not be part of your army. Terome is founded in the Light of the Book, not in conquest. This crusade is madness.'

'Of course,' acquiesced Jarle smoothly. 'I wouldn't expect Teromants to be part of the army. I merely point out that we are increasing our border guard-'

'You are building an army,' Rembrandt pointed out bluntly.

'You cannot expect Meyar not to defend herself,' retorted Jarle.

'She already can,' answered Rembrandt. 'And the Church will help defend her homeland. But no more. The people answer to the will of Terome, and He Lights the Way. If you cross Him, you will yourself be cast out into the darkness.' The warning in his voice was unmistakeable for all his soft tones. 'Be careful, my son. I speak with His Voice. You have built a war machine, Eonder. All you lack is the support of the people of Meyar, and an excuse. I *will not* give you that excuse, and my children will not support your disdain for their lives.'

Jarle bowed, his jowly face unreadable. 'As you say, your Holiness. I merely informed you out of courtesy.'

Rembrandt smiled. 'I appreciate your coming, my son. Remember, we work together for the glory of Terome, and His chosen land. We do not need to conquer others for this. Many of His followers also live in lands you would war with.'

The Prime Alderman returned the smile, but there seemed to be a hint of regret buried within it to the keen political eye of the Holy Voice.

'We must work together to return glory to Terome's lands, Eonder. But you cannot wield me like any political tool. Remember, Terome is both God and Man. He was the prophet, later revealed as God himself. You know his story; he wandered on foot the length of Anaria, coming from the deserts of Banistari and walking without food or drink through the great plains, surviving savage men and bestial orks before claiming the fertile lands north of the great estuary and dark salt mountains, where once an ancient kingdom suffered a dreadful cataclysm. He told of the God, of the light and life. His followers cried of his meeting God at the tip of the highest mountain in the world, the tip of the Arcian Mountains where no other man could survive. Great scaled beasts of flame paid homage to him there, and he continued in his pilgrimage. Here, in Haná, he fell to his knees in the mud and blessed the earth, and then rose to his followers and said, 'I have prophesied the coming of God. You have followed a man, given the commandments and sins by the God himself above the world in the Arcians, written on tablets of platinum. Now I can reveal unto you that this is to be our new home.'

Eonder Jarle shifted, no doubt impatient. He had heard the Pilgrimage of Terome many times.

'He moved to live in a hut near the sea, which became a house, which became a palace in time, which was the centre of Lodinoriam, the greatest city in northern Anaria. One day, he was simply gone from his room, locked from the inside, and the people realised the truth.

'He was not a man; he was the God all along, ascended. He led us and lived with us. You must believe according to the Book that he will return when we need him, if we keep our faith. If we stay steadfast. Keep the importance of Terome's land and people above all else, my son.'

'The glory of Meyar is always foremost in my mind, Your Holiness.' Eonder Jarle bent to kiss the proffered Holy Light, and then straightened. 'I shall leave you to your evening.' He turned and left, the massively armoured Extinctor Chaplains closing the door after him.

Rembrandt sighed, dropping the Holy Light on its chain on his chest. Right now, it felt as heavy as the world to him.

He knew the Prime Alderman thought of the glory of Meyar - with himself at its head. He had watched the man manoeuvre his opponents, many in the Church, into supporting his dreams of expansion. The country was groaning under the weight of poverty and oppressive laws. Unnecessary war was a cheap, brief way of diverting the populace from their squalor. It could not last, and would make matters worse.

No, the only way was to fix the problems from the ground up. He had to open schools again, reverse this cruel crush and forced ignorance of peasantry. He had to lead the rich to allow their money to trickle down to the poor instead of hoarding it, bring people back to the journey under the Light. Remind them that there was more to life than riches or endless toil. And remind them that their money was safer delivered unto the Church for the good of their souls.

It would not make him popular with the Assembly, or many of his brothers, the Holy Voice knew, but he cared only for the teachings of Terome, the power of the Church, and the good of the Teromens.
He was the guide through the dark lands, as Terome had been before he had been revealed as the very God he preached of, and his lamp was the light of their knowledge. He would help them regain their way, and he would not watch his followers be sacrificed for power.

Rembrandt cared, and Believed, and it was like the sun at midnight. He would not fail them while he still drew breath.

ℝ ℠

Eonder Jarle walked away from the Holy Voice, his mind afire. The old man had shown even more mettle than he had suspected, and if he decreed the Prime Alderman excommunicate, nothing would prevent him derailing the process he had begun. The Holy Voice had compassion for the people where Jarle had none.

He could undo *everything*!

Not that it would matter for Eonder Jarle. He would be forced to leave his power. He cursed to himself; he had handled the meeting badly. The Holy Voice was too cunning to be taken in by a ploy like that.

In a way it was about respect. He vastly respected Rembrandt. He had believed that the old man needed to be given one more chance to bend; he had the feeling that it would not be much longer for events to overwhelm opposition under their own momentum. Once the wheel started rolling, in either direction, it crushed those in its way.

He did not know which way it would roll, and that worried him.

ℝ ℠

It was nearing midnight. Very few Churchmen were around, but one in particular was up. An urgent message had arrived, bringing horrific tales with it.

Sontles knew it had; he knew what it was about, and he knew that the time had come to act.

Despite being forewarned by an informant, he had caught the servant with the message on his return from the Holy Voice too late. Sontles had punched a fist through the man's ribcage and out of his back in a shower of gore. He would never tell anyone if he had seen the contents of the message.

That still left the recipient, of course.

Sontles moved like the wind, a blur, silent and fast. He could climb sheer walls and leap higher than any man, dull the minds of the unwary. The night was his air to breath.

No one had seen him come here; not servants, not Churchmen, nor Teromants; not even the hordes of Chaplains that were thicker here.

There was no way not to be seen at this last, however.

256

Sontles walked around a corner at the rear of the Spiritus Sanctus, the great hall of Terome. This was supposedly holy ground, but it didn't bother him; he was invited, expected, a Churchman himself.

Two hulking Teromant Chaplain Extinctors stood, watching him from outside the ornate door. These were the elite warrior-fanatics of Terome, striking fear into the hearts of dissidents. Three hundred years ago they had been holy warriors that exterminated all heresy; now they were specialist troops. Tall spears stood next to them, and one had a broad-bladed sword at his belt. The other had a flanged mace.

Their matte white armour was the thickest in Anaria, virtually impregnable. Dense curved breastplates with the horizontal cross of Terome in polished steel covered their fronts over high belts; plate tassets hung down each thigh and fell dangling in front of the groin from faulds which wrapped around their hips. Solid cuisses covered their thighs, with poleyns and huge plated greaves and boots below, and a skirt of red and white fell from their hips. Rounded helmets with only small eyes visible above vented slots for breathing sat between two gigantic pauldrons, which reached from the tops of the helms to their elbows, like vast shields wrapping a quarter around their bodies. The right bore blessings and script inscribed and painted by the Church for their holy duties on an embossed open book. The left displayed a carved steel skull surrounded by red flames. The cleansing fire of Terome, and their duty.

Death.

They were massive men. Only the largest and strongest could wear the blessed armour, some of which was centuries old and could lock together to hold the bearer upright for long watches. In battle they were virtually unstoppable against most units as shock troops, the armour almost as impenetrable as that of the dwarves. It weighed half their own weight and could stop bolts at range. Even cavalry was wary of them.

The living war machines trusted no one. They eyed him suspiciously, especially at this time of night.

Sontles stared at them unblinking, his eyes boring into theirs. The shadows of their helms hid nothing from him.

They glared back with increasing hostility which began to fade into puzzlement, and then lack of focus. Strong warriors they might be, but it was easy to overwhelm the wills of those conditioned to obey orders. The pathways of command were already set.

Sontles walked up to them, standing almost between them. Their eyes turned sideways to watch him, unfocused. One of them had a trickle of sweat into an eye, which he could not blink. The will of the Extinctors had simply... faded.

It wasn't like the gradual overpowering of Gilden; this was a paralysis, a hypnosis. They stood, bolt upright, like statues. Their eyes and minds were fogged.

Sontles stood with his head cocked, studying them, then smiled lazily. Turning to the man to his right, he reached out his left hand and gripped the top of the breastplate. His right hand moved with a speed and power beyond any human, almost casually punching the side of the Chaplain's helm in the small space between the pauldron and the head. The helm protected the neck from bending, but not twisting. There was a sharp crack.

The man slumped, his helm dented as if a mace had struck it, his head turned almost round, lolling on his neck. Sontles lowered him almost gently to the floor, the armour locked in place. The smell of fresh shit contained in steel wafted to his nostrils and he hissed in glee. He loved it when men died and lost control.

The other man stood like a statue. He was desperately straining to move, but against his own will, he could do nothing. Sweat ran down his face, and his eyes darted frantically. A whimper escaped his lips as Sontles drew the dead man's sword.

Sontles gripped the immobile Chaplain Extinctor by the gorget, pushing him back then grinding up the wall with a hiss of effort, his feet leaving the floor. The man outweighed Sontles many times over even without the huge armour yet dangled, helpless.

His other hand hefted the blade, then carefully and methodically probed with its point in the flexible gap below the breastplate.

'Ah,' he murmured, and inexorably pushed it in.

The man stiffened as the sharp steel caught in a fold of his belly, and then the pain pushed through the paralysis and he drew breath to scream. Sontles tightened his grip on the rim of the gorget under the helm, pressing the man's neck until only a vague choking noise could be heard. The armoured feet drummed.

He pushed the sword home slowly. The tip sliced through fat and flesh, pulled then tore intestine before puncturing through the diaphragm and on. Blood dripped down the handle.

The man's eyes bulged and he trembled, twitching, his armoured hands scrabbling at Sontle's. After nearly two feet of the sword had slid home, the strength left him from one moment to the next. His gauntlets dropped and he jerked, three times, horribly, his bulging eyes staring at Sontles, who detachedly noticed that one of them had burst a blood vessel in the shadows of the helmet. A pretty hue, thought the vampire. They remained open. Sontles lowered him down, watching the blood pool.

He licked his lips, and dipped a delicate little finger into it, sucking it tentatively. Satisfying; but this was merely an appetiser.

He opened the door gently and stepped through the narthex into the inner sanctum of the Holy Voice. Part of him approved of the asceticism of the chamber; there was a large bed, and a large desk, and several chairs, but that was it. Truly the room of a holy man. Sontles found himself approving.

The Holy Voice was sitting at his huge mahogany desk, facing the door. He looked old, weary, numb. He did not look surprised to see Sontles. In his hand he held a piece of parchment.

Sontles closed the doors behind him and turned.

ನ ਂ

The old man dropped the missive.

'What have you done?' Rembrandt half-whispered through his shock. He felt a thousand years old as his voice echoed in the room, empty of most hangings. The high ceilings threw hints of sibilance back at him.

'What needed to be done,' said Sontles.

'You have been using *Apples of Terome* on people?' His tone was of a man who couldn't believe what he had just read. It dared - almost begged - Sontles to refute it. 'Mutilations. Inquisitions. *Burnings.* Conscriptions of people try to flee. An army has been assembled, supposedly on my orders. Extinctors sent to other lands. You have ordered Nassings killed on sight like hounds! This has all come from your mouth!'

They were the most barbaric and shameful parts of the religion Rembrandt had worshipped his whole life, and this horror standing before him with a faint smile had brought them back. He reeled at the implications of what this Primate had done.

'Why… yes. We must root out the heretics. People would not flee without guilt, and guilt is a sign of Sin. Nassings are… not human. We must have conscripts if we… are to successfully destroy Eordeland. If people are to *truly* believe in… Terome again. Does it not say in the Book that those without the Light must be… shown it?'

Apples of Terome. Not used for hundreds of years, they had been part of the Old Inquisition. A ball half the size of a man's fist, it had a screw at one end. The other part, the globe, was inserted into an orifice - mouth for blasphemers, vagina for heretical women and anus for men. As it was turned, the 'apple' opened out into four metal petals that caused intense agony the more they were opened. As they reached a quarter open, sharp tines began to lever out of the top in the opposite direction, tearing the flesh.

They could be used for pain, or maiming, or even death. Fully open, the expanded petals and tines tore through flesh and lodged. In a mouth they could sever a tongue, break a jaw, strike an artery; in other orifices, they simply tore so terribly through the walls of the surrounding tissue that the victim usually died of septic shock.

They were among the most awful tortures the worship of Terome had devised and had only been used a few times in witch trials hundreds of years ago. This maniac had been using them on normal people.

On worshippers!

'You would take us back five hundred years and sink our land in war! The holy fire of Terome is for their souls, not their bodies! You twist the words of Terome to suit your own agenda. *This is not His way!'*

'War is coming. The people are not going to march with a feeble old man making excuses for them.' The gaunt man's voice almost hissed.

'This is madness.' The Voice stood and moved around the desk, every movement with limbs that felt leaden. He was reluctant to even approach Sontles.

'Guards!' he called, then focused on Sontles. He clapped his hands together in the form of the closed Book, then opened them like covers and drew his fingers wide in the sign of the Light.

'I declare you excommunicate,' he said, his voice powerful, angry, righteous. 'In the name of Terome, be banished from His Light forever. You will never find rest in His grace. You are damned for all eternity!'

Sontles laughed then; not his usual dry chuckle, but a full rasping laugh, which sounded even worse. There was something odd about him.

His teeth…

'You know *nothing* of eternal damnation!'

He took in the gaunt figure again, feeling another jolt, now of fear, as he noticed the eyes were glinting red. A red tongue licked over razor-sharp white-yellow fangs. A memory of tales of monsters surfaced.

The Holy Voice reeled back in shock.

What manner of man was this?

No wonder he had never seen Sontles in daylight. He faced something that could not exist outside legend. Terome should have struck it down where it stood! How was it here, on Holy ground, ordained a Primate? In the Church itself?

How can this be?

He held up the symbol of the Holy Light, knowing that its holy might would repel the undead horror before him. Sontles laughed again and reached out his left hand. He grabbed the symbol in the center and slowly crushed it, twisting and pulling. Rembrandt stared incredulously as soft metal warped in the slight hand.

Of its own accord the hidden blade slipped free. Filled with the fire of Terome, Rembrandt stabbed at the vampire without hesitation. The strike was swifter than many would believe he could move, and true.

Almost lazily, the vampire's right hand shot out and caught his wrist, faster than the Holy Voice had ever seen someone move. His grip was so powerful Rembrandt gasped, sinking to his knees. The bones in his wrist were ground together, to agony and beyond, and a sharp crack sounded as a bone fractured. He gasped.

Sontles studied the knife with interest. 'Silver inlays. My, but that would have… hurt,' he grinned. 'With blessings of Terome himself upon the blade! You poor fool.' He twisted the hand and another crack resounded. Rembrandt went white and the knife fell from nerveless fingers as he cried out, almost sobbing.

Where were the Chaplains?

He became aware that he was babbling, prayers falling from his lips for protection from the God he had devoted his life to.

Suddenly the slender man was gripping his throat. The Holy Voice gasped, choking on his words. He hadn't even seen him move.

'Your faith is misplaced. The tablets were not what you think.'

The grip tightened and the gaunt Churchman leaned back, pulling him to his feet and then somehow off the floor without apparent effort. He could not speak, felt as if his neck was about to break. The hand was cold and bony, not feeling like a man's hand at all, and sharp nails grazed his flesh.

Rembrandt's head was pounding, and his eyes bulged in shock. The strength in the delicate-looking fingers was inhuman. Eyes like burning gimlets pinned his own orbs and he could not look away. His will was draining.

Evil poured from this man like invisible mist, swirling around him.

'I know because I have seen those tablets, pathetic follower of a false God. I have deciphered them, and they did not hold petty human commandments.' The pressure eased off as blackness flecked his vision, and he was dropped in a heap, shuddering with grateful breaths. Sontles looked down at him, and part of the Holy Voice shrieked in terror. There was no humanity in the gaze. No compassion. Just an icy coldness, folded like dark wings around a hot core of awful ravenousness.

'They held a far greater power than the five commandments a desperate hermit made up to keep people feeding him. They held the path to *true* Gods. To power not of this world. Terome could not have read them even had they been in base Banistari, but they were in a far older and darker language than that.'

'*Were?*' choked the Holy Voice, fighting to keep terror from his own voice, fighting to breath. 'What-'

'They are no more, you fool.' Sontles' eyes flashed redder. 'I followed their guidance, and they were… consumed in the process. As, almost, was I.' The dreadful Primate drew himself up, his clothes hanging from his skinny frame. He looked like a cadaver.

'How then did he receive the commandments? How did he receive such priceless, unknown gifts of the platinum tablets, in a tongue no man except he could speak? How did he climb the greatest mountain in the world and have beasts bow to him in the airless void above?' Rembrandt gained strength with each demand. '*How could his power and voice flow through me now?*' For a moment, he felt strength and faith blaze through him.

Sontles rasped in laughter.

'He did not climb that mountain to the east. You think dragons would ever bow to a mere mortal? *He lied.* He was a prophet of his own making, but first he was a thief. Those tablets were held in the royal house of Banistari, long forgotten. How he came upon them I know not, but I know this: he was a fraud. Everything terrible done in his name rests on the shoulders of your so-called Church.'

No, mouthed Rembrandt, sickened, refusing to believe. The words had the awful ring of blunt truth.

'Yesssss,' hissed Sontles, relishing the moment. 'He was a prophet, a man. A liar. Nothing more.'

After several breaths, Rembrandt rasped in denial, 'He was an avatar of God himself!'

Sontles snarled. 'Your God is *nothing!*' His terrible eyes leached the Holy Voice's willpower once more, and he smiled almost lazily. 'Do you know why I tell you the truth?'

Rembrandt was unable to reply. He felt hollow. Sontles leaned forward.

'Because I *love* making men suffer. I delight in watching a man of virtue fail. I want you to have nothing left as you die.' He laughed then, and his lips drew back slowly. At the sight of the fangs, the Holy Voice cowered again, shock pounding through him.

Too late, he realised the Prime Alderman had never been his most dangerous opponent. How could this have happened?

Sontles' voice rasped on, almost hypnotic. 'This continent will be ash, in time. And Meyar will be part of it once I have no further need of it. But for you… the end is here.' His eyes flashed. 'You meddling old fool.'

'May Terome strike you down,' grated the Holy Voice, his voice trembling. 'Though I am carried through the shade outside the Light, I shall not fear evil!'

'I do so love hearing a holy man lie,' grinned Sontles. His hands flashed downward. One frail-seeming fist punched into the Holy Voice's sternum so powerfully it cracked ribs, splitting cartilage apart. Rembrant bucked, gasping, almost unseeing in his desperation to breathe. The leering, unnatural visage of this demon in front of him hovered, drinking in his pain.

He barely saw the other hand, flat as a blade, slice sideways. Nails sharp as talons tore across his throat, the edges catching in the loose skin and tearing through muscle, ripping into his windpipe with an odd tugging before the carotid arteries either side ruptured under their edges.

The sudden loss of blood pressure felt oddly in his mind, the same as squeezing a segment of a juicy orange; the skin bulging to bursting until, *pop*, it released. His mind floated, in a way he hated but could not prevent. A weird white buzzing behind his eyes grew, filling his world, his universe. A roaring rose in his ears.

Before his staring eyes, deliberately, Sontles raised a cupped hand, painted with the ebb and flow of his faltering beats, of hot fresh blood.

His blood.

He watched several fast drips run down and fall from the hand. Almost incidentally he watched the greed of the creature as it sucked hungrily at the pool.

Before the fourth drip had hit the floor, Rembrandt Articorl saw no more.

ڃ ࣟ

The vampire drank deeply of the wellspring of lifeforce within his cupped hand, fastidiously avoiding spilling too much as he watched staring eyes film over.

Sontles was pleased at the suffering he had wrought, but not as happy with the manner of the meddling old man's death. He would have preferred to dismember him, feeding on him whilst he was alive and shrieking.

This was too fast. Too neat.

The things he did for his masters.

He sighed and arranged the body, careful not to touch anything else. He wanted it to look messy, painful, and - most of all - believably assassinated for whoever found him and the Guards.

He picked up the fallen knife from the symbol of the Book and studied it for a moment. The inlays and script did nothing to repel or harm him; only the silver would burn him mercilessly if he touched it.

He stabbed it down into the chest of the Holy Voice and left it sticking out between two ribs. Not much blood welled from the intrusion into the chest, and that which did was thick and dark.

The Holy Voice had been a good man, he reflected, as these things went. He had been faithful and altruistic, despite being a canny politician. But it meant little in this world. All that mattered was power, and Sontles would have more than anyone, alive or dead.

He produced an Eordeland-style tunic from his dark robes and dipped it in the centre of the blood a few times, shaking it, then cupped a little more and spattered it. The tunic was rich and belonged to one of the few Eordelanders left in the city; the Eordeland diplomat had loudly proclaimed that war did not interest him, remaining to sue for trade and seeking the Politikus when his fellows had long since left.

Sontles gripped a piece on one sleeve near the shoulder and then with little exertion tore a piece out. He tucked this into the clenched right hand of the dead Holy Voice, and stood, considering his work.

It was crude, to be sure, but the mindless masses - so well primed for manipulation by the Assembly and the Church combined - would leap to the wrong conclusion. The Eord was already suspect over his continued presence.

He slipped from that place then, cloaked in shadows, his true nature revealed for now. The darkness hid nothing from him as he moved, faster and quieter than a man. He did not stop until he was out of the Hall of Terome, over the wall away from the guards, and into the city. He moved in the darkness, avoiding the light, and no one saw him.

Finally, he reached the Quarters of the Eordeland Ambassador, and he slipped in, climbing the outside of the palace like a spider to an open window. The ambassador lay asleep, limned in the darkness to Sontles' eyes as red, shifting fire, throbbing in time with his beating heart, each one like a pulse of red lightning through his veined form in the limpid darkess.

Sontles balled up the tunic and threw it under the bed, then left, a wraith.

A mention to the right people that he was seen hurrying from the Hall late last night, avoiding sight, would be all it took.

Opium abuse was growing in the cities, a booming business, and people would say and do anything for more.

He despised it - it made people's blood taste bitter and gave him headaches, truth be told - but he understood the desperation of craving, of addiction.

He would use it.

TWENTY-ONE

At the mention of violence in The Sanctum, the Council held an emergency meeting in the Bulb at the pinnacle of the Dodecagon. Ringed by Onyx Guard and Welcomers, Captain-Generals Dorn and Jekob stood to attention. With them stood Castellan James and Rast, who relayed to Dorn what had happened.

When the names were mentioned, a murmur arose, to die out into silence as they described Karland's wounds and the nature of what had been attempted.

Aurelia Brókova was the first to break the silence.

'This is very serious. An attempt made on the life of a student of this University within its grounds, the intent to maim, possibly kill! That he is also a student of Aldwyn Varelin, recognised by the city for bravery in helping save us from Yosgaloth and in the defence of his town of The Croft only makes it worse. This is meant to be the most secure place in Eordeland, yet inside two years we have seen assassinations and violence. And by the favoured son of a Novinian noble, here to secure goodwill between our nations!'

'The second attempt on the life of Karland Dresin in this University,' reminded Rast, casting his glance about.

'Jamus, I thought you had the situation well in hand!' said Ulric, bringing his hand down on the arm of his chair. 'You the Castellan are supposed to be our eyes and ears. How could this happen?'

'I have been focused on events with Meyar,' Holmson said.

'Was Aran under no suspicion, being a high-ranking Novinian?'

'Perhaps this was *linked* to Meyar,' suggested Tarqas. His face was dark with anger. Losing his nephew had been hard enough. This second attack on the student of his old friend had finally broken through his despondency.

'We don't know. His background is clean. I think this was personal,' replied Holmson. 'Other than being checked for collusion, this didn't register.'

'Castellan?'

James cleared his throat precisely and stepped forward.

'I had heard rumours of hostility, of course,' he said in his clipped tones. 'But we often have minor altercations between students, which are resolved or contained by the University hierarchy. The Scholars said it was under control.'

'Evidently not,' retorted Eremus. Rast knew she didn't like Karland, but she didn't like the arrogant Novinian, either. It must be a hard decision to choose whom she disliked more. Besides, neither registered on her political radar, which was all she cared about at the moment. He knew she also deeply revered the University, if not the people running it; to her, this was an affront.

'It was being monitored. But this was unexpected. He slipped any notice with a decoy who looked very similar; several of my staff were also paid to leave early - to run errands, and so forth. They will be disciplined. It was my understanding that the Welcomers were also aware of the situation, but Aran's capability for malice was clearly underestimated. I am appalled at how deep his influence - and pockets - really are here.' He turned slightly to Jekob. 'Perhaps the Captain-General may also enlighten us as to where the Guards were.'

Jekob scowled at the Castellan, although the words had been factual rather than accusatory. 'The Novinian picked a break when Guards were moving away from the area, far from where most people would be. He must have planned this for some time.'

Ulric swore. His voice was cold with fury. 'You would think after the stain on our honour a year ago, we would be more alert!' His glance took in the Onyx Guard, some of whom shifted uneasily. Councillor Draef Novas had been killed under their noses. It had been the first time the Guard had failed, and the first time assassins had attacked within The Sanctum. That it had involved Welcomer Guard was worse. 'Karland Dresin and his companions are *honoured guests* of this Gods-Bedamned city! They are not casual visitors!' A movement caught his eye. 'Captain-General Gardenson? You have something to add?'

'For some reason, that boy has been targeted once too often,' said Dorn. 'Perhaps it is chance, perhaps not. But this marks the third time something bad has happened to him here; an attempted assassination of his teacher, the... demon he encountered on the roof, this attempted maiming. If we consider also reports of previous friction with this student... Whether he should be or not, he is caught up in these events.'

Rast shook his head. 'Once is once too often. Councillors, he has performed tasks for you that others have failed in and suffered great loss from it. He is in danger here as much as at home. Before it was because of the pendant. Now it may be because he was one of those who used it. Meyar may want him dead for what he learned, even though we don't yet know what that was. You owe him your protection.'

'So, what is the answer?' asked Eremus. 'We can't have him murdered here in The Sanctum.' Rast raised an eyebrow. 'I may not like the boy, Tal'Orien, but you are right. He deserves our protection.'

'And our respect,' added Tarqas quietly.

'I do not know,' admitted Rast. 'I have spent much time apart from him here, aiding the Council. Unless you confine him, he will remain at risk. He is as safe with me as anywhere, but I am leaving to travel to Eyotsburg.' He shrugged. 'Perhaps he should join me.'

Eremus rolled her eyes. 'This again.'

'He has travelled and fought well, and stands a better chance of surviving than, say, Councillor Eremus,' noted Rast to the Council at large.

She stared daggers at him.

'It *is* the last place they would look for him,' mused Marcus Andragostin. Mutters ricocheted around the chamber.

'I think we must admit he acquitted himself well the last time he went on a quest for us,' said Mira Lyss. There were nods.

Eremus shrugged, a little grudgingly. 'Although he joined the quest of another.'

'You should pay more attention to his reports from the Scholars,' said Tarqas to the room. 'I think one day young Master Dresin will be a further asset to Eordeland, if he focuses.'

'If he lives,' muttered Eremus.

'I can continue his training, as well,' added Rast, ignoring her. 'He is a good pupil and has promise. He has value; he can advise as a student of Aldwyn.'

'What about his studies of Master Varelin's notes?' asked Nessa Contemus, her wrinkled face framing sharp blue eyes. 'We had agreed that he was best placed to try to make sense of this Portal they found. They have spent much time in the Combic Libraries. Do we waste this?'

'I think it highly unlikely they will find anything,' sniffed Eremus. 'So what does it matter?'

'Xhera has broken more ground there than he has,' Daffydd Gusta said. 'She is extremely methodical and organised. Karland knew Master Varelin better, and learned much, but she applies herself well to the texts. Karland is… unreliable… unless it is directly interesting, according to Master Darfin.' Surprised eyes turned to him, and he smiled. 'They are a fascinating pair. I have kept my eye on their studies. He is definitely unconventional and performs great intuitive leaps. Together they've achieved much. I think for the moment the focus should be on going through the texts they have identified to collate the data, and Xhera, in my opinion, is better at that.'

Rast nodded. 'I agree. The question is… will *she* be safe here?'

'I don't see why not,' Augusta Andragostin chipped in. 'She wasn't part of these other attacks.'

'She passed through the portal with us. Karland also said there are still existing threats against her.'

'None of those involved in this… incident… will be able to enact those against her. No one else has shown an interest in her, and she would be easier to guard. Perhaps we can take her from the curriculum and focus on the texts. We can assign an Onyx Guard to her, and Seeker Night is here to work with her. Seekers are not to be taken lightly.'

'He is but one small man,' protested Councillor Woodhearth.

Nessa Contemus chuckled. 'Seekers are *but* nothing.'

'Karland holds the keys to the Library of Thingos, though,' mused Augusta Andragostin. 'From what I understand. We dare not send those away.'

'I am sure he would surrender it to Xhera,' said Rast. 'And she is perhaps better placed to make use of it.'

'Possibly.'

Ulric leaned back, pulling the end of one thick eyebrow pensively. 'So, we send the boy with Tal'Orien and the elves to Mithtol. Why not send the girl to the Library of Thingos in case she can make sense of this portal thing? And we must also show some regard for our allies in Eyotsburg.'

'Send a company,' suggested Colcos. 'Someone who can assess things and offer diplomatic support. Eyotsburg guards our south from Meyar and our north from Novin. We must aid our allies.' Rast saw a glance pass between him and Ulric.

'That should not take long,' said Tarqas. 'A fast ship-'

Andragostin was already shaking her head. 'Meyar has blockaded the route to the west, and reports indicate some of Novin has aided them. The chances of losing a ship are too high. They know Eyotsburg cries out for her allies. We have lost five in the last month to 'pirates'.'

'Surely they could not catch an Eyoti ship.'

'Possibly not, but the point is moot. Any ships travelling through their waters are attacked, and current word is that there have been no Eyoti ships in Tamismuth or Kingsport for two months. Any ship would have to be one of ours.'

'Can they not sail south?'

'And increase the journey from two thousand miles to five thousand? The risk of attack from Banistari raiders is high, and the seas around the Darkenspire Jut are highly treacherous. And that still leaves sailing up the coast of Novin.'

'What alternatives are there?'

'It's a thousand miles by land, across flat plains and easy terrain,' mused Holmson. 'If the company moves fast and skirts the foothills of Rhe they could be there in forty days. And there is a much higher certainty they would arrive.'

'We cannot risk the sea,' said Ulric heavily. 'Few are permitted leave to dock on any islands of Mithtol, and the risk of interception is high. Only fools dare the Storartar estuary without guidance. If they go further north, there are Poviiri *Avslutas* to worry about.' He referred to the fierce longboat warriors from which he himself was closely descended. They were well-known to be extremely territorial, in an ask-questions-to-corpses fashion.

'Can we risk the delay?'

'Meyar will not be ready to move for another eight months by our estimates,' said Tarqas.

'What about the orks?' asked Rast.

'Ah, yes! We could fletch two arrows with one feather,' exclaimed Gusta. 'Would Darus travel with you?'

'I am sure he would. We can pass word to the tribes.'

'Do we have ayes?' asked Mira Lyss. Every Councillor nodded. 'So which company will be sent? Which commander will be sufficient to provide military and diplomatic support?'

'A Guard Major, perhaps,' mused Ulric.

'Gambeson, Tos, and Dimwal are all stationed here,' said Dorn.

Colcos nodded fractionally. At times, he and Castellan James could almost be brothers. 'Gambeson is known to the Eyots. He is most reliable.'

'Can we afford to lose *him*?' asked Eremus a little scathingly.

'We can't *afford* to lose any of them. I think the question more, is who is most likely to return?' asked Ulric.

'Gambeson knows what we face and is known to the Conclave. He commanded the soldiers that followed Tal'Orien to face Yosgaloth. I trust him implicitly.'

Mira Lyss stood. 'Then we send Karland Dresin to support Rast Tal'Orien, and they travel with Major Gambeson until things have settled. It's a question of percentages, Councillors. We can't guarantee the safety of the boy here for the short term unless we lock him in the libraries, and that is not our right. A company is at risk by ship. Direct travel overland is the safest and surest way. We must focus on the city, The Sanctum, and the Council. Too much of import is afoot.'

'Agreed.' Rast's face didn't change but nevertheless he imparted a forbidding quality to his next words. 'Now. About Aran.'

Mira Lyss sighed. 'His trial is set for the tenth hour of the morning in two days.'

'There is no doubt of his guilt,' stated Rast flatly.

Mira Lyss shook her head.

'None. But this is how we how we must proceed. We are not yet under martial law. We must be seen to be formal and correct. Procurators from Legalis Academia will represent both sides, of course, and we will refer to the Universalia Communia in judgement.'

Aurelia Brókova spoke up.

'I move that this is not a matter for the Magistrates, or the City Court. This occurred in The Sanctum, to a student under the direct protection of the Council; moreover, one who is recognised as a defender of the city and who has acted as an agent of Eordeland. This is a judgement for the Council of Twelve.'

Almost every head nodded, and the *ayes* were overwhelming. Mira Lyss murmured to the Welcomer Guard taking minutes. 'Agreed. With the Council's permission, we will make this a closed trial and verdict. We also have other serious matters to attend to.'

'I do *not* agree,' said Tarqas fiercely. 'The verdict should be public. People must know what happened here, and what it means to act like this.'

'You'd spread word that The Sanctum isn't safe?' said Eremus acidly.

'If it was *safe*, Kel-' Tarqas struggled visibly for control for a moment. 'It isn't. A Councillor and a Captain-General were murdered here. Everyone in the city knows there were traitors within these walls. You cannot quash rumour. These criminals do not deserve to have their deeds go unknown. People must know the consequences of such actions.'

Mira Lyss looked to Rast.

'What do you think, Master Tal'Orien?'

'I believe they have long counted on their deeds going unnoticed, Advisor. Perhaps it is time to bring them into the light... to discourage others from a similar path.'

Mira Lyss glanced around the Twelve. Stern faces nodded, and even Eremus shrugged.

'So be it,' she said. 'Their hearing shall be closed and carried out by the Twelve, and the trial shall be made open to the public as well as representatives of all Academia. And the Novinian diplomat. Nothing will be hidden.'

'I will engage with Castellan James to glean what information we can,' said Councillor Jameson.

'Do we appoint a Senior Procurator from the Academia Legalis to preside as witness of process?' asked Brókova in a tone that suggested it would be wise to.

'Yes. They will be impartial and will carefully consider all evidence,' replied Jameson. 'A reliable witness to events for doubters. I say aye.'

There were no objections, and Mira Lyss nodded.

'Procurator-in-Judgement to witness. The hearing starts in two days.'

ʘ˃

The Council sat in their great hall, the part-circle of their huge chairs looming over the central area. They were robed in formal regalia, the black of Judgement trimmed with symbols of all Academia.

The large round table had been removed, apart from two curved sections in front of the Twelve, with a chair between them, and the floor was patterned with the symbol of Eordeland, twelve flames springing out of twelve pages in the book of knowledge, white on dark green.

To the left sat a male Procurator Accusator, and to the right a female Procurator Defensor. Both wore dark ash robes lined with sombre blue. In the chair in the middle sat the Procurator-in-Judgement, a stern-faced older man with pince-nez and red robes representing a Judge of the Legalis. His job was to witness and legally ratify the decisions of the Council, to ensure they did not circumvent any of their own laws. In a lower court, that of the City, he would preside; here, he was advisory only.

To the left, with a wide view of everyone in the court, sat a designated Welcomer Guard at a small desk with tome, quill and ink. Her job was to record everything that took place, for the discussion before the verdict. It brought home the wider skills and duties the Welcomer Guard had over the normal Eordeland military. Usually, a scribe would take care of this, but in a closed session only the Welcomers were permitted entrance.

Two others sat, one ready to focus on the council and one on the accused, to ensure that no words were missed by the scribes.

Other than that, and the Onyx Guard flanking the Council and the Welcomers around the edges of the room, only Karland, with Xhera as support, Rast, Dorn, Gen and Kith sat on benches before the Council to the right.

The atmosphere was excessively oppressive and formal. There was an undercurrent of tension; this was not a normal hearing. It had been hastily convened at the highest level, with overwhelming evidence against the accused.

Despite knowing that he had been vindicated when his attackers had been caught in the act, Karland was nervous. He knew the Procurator Defensor would attempt to downplay what had happened, not as a personal attack but in the interests of being a demon's advocate. Delmatra dictated justice be even-handed.

Mira Lyss looked around the hall, then rose from her chair.

271

'Proceedings may begin. This is a very serious case, at the worst possible time. Let it be recorded that Karland Dresin, a student of the University and one who has provided service to this Council and Eordeland in general, was attacked by other students with the intent of causing lasting physical harm. This attack was witnessed and interrupted by Captain-General Dorn Gardenson of the Eordeland Guard; Rast Tal'Orien, Advisor to the Council of Twelve; and Veteran Privates Kith Drell and Genin Alfinson of the Eordeland Guard.'

She looked over to the side. 'Procurator in Judgement Fohle sits in neutrality to ensure the letter of Eordeland Law is followed. Let it also be recorded that this is an usual case in multiple ways.' She paused to allow the scribe to finish writing. 'Councillor Aurelia Brókova, formerly of the Academia Legalis, will preside. Councillor.'

Aurelia Brókova stood. In her fifties, she was quiet and firm. Her mixed dark-skinned heritage gave her delicate features and a wide nose; her mother had been a second-generation immigrant from Morland, her father half-Banistari. The patterning on her robe had hints of Morland dress and favoured orange colours. Her wide cheekbones often made her eyes kind, but today they were dark and stern.

'Let it be recorded that the Council of Twelve sits in considered judgment this day, with the blessings of Delmatra the Just, without prejudice or hate in their hearts; only the letter of the Law. Procurators, do you stand ready, clear of favour?'

'We do,' stated the Accusator and Defensor.

The Accusator was the older and more relaxed. He had spent the previous day with Karland and his companions, taking notes and requesting evidence. The Defensor was a serious-faced woman who was more concerned with writing notes than her counterpart.

Brókova turned to the Guard nearby.

'Bring forth the accused.'

They were brought in from an antechamber, miserable and wan except Aran, who still bore a look of arrogance. He looked momentarily dismayed; perhaps he had expected the public, or the ambassador.

They shuffled to a stop in front of the Council, hands bound by manacles with a short chain between them. Aran drew himself up and strode forward, ignoring the Welcomers either side. The Onyx Guard shifted.

'You may not do this to me,' he objected. 'I am a noble of the House of Telemer!'

'You will find we can, and will,' replied Councillor Tarqas coldly. 'Novinian Houses have no standing here. You have abused our trust and the goodwill between our nations.'

'I am not one of these,' he gestured behind him at the others. 'I demand my own trial by noble law.'

'It is a shame,' remarked Gusta dryly, 'that you spent so much time here, yet failed to learn the laws of our land. Perhaps if you had spent more time studying and less time interfering, you would realise there is no noble treatment here, son of Telemer. You are judged as an equal with all others.'

Ulric leaned forwards, glowering. 'Now get back in line, *boy*.'

Two Guards grabbed his shoulders and pulled him backwards. Aran nearly stumbled trying to shrug them off. The look of outrage was still there, but now there was some uncertainty.

Mira Lyss nodded to Aurelia Brókova, and she stood and moved forward.

'I call the Court of Twelve to Order,' she said. 'This is a closed hearing of the accused.'

'But-' protested Aran.

'*Silence!*' bellowed Ulric. His powerful voice reverberated through the circular chamber and up into the spire where the vast chandelier burned. Aran went pale. One of the other boys squeaked.

'It is just possible - although frankly astonishing - that you have not understood the depth of trouble you are in,' observed Councillor Jameson. 'If you will not be silent, you will have sanctions set upon you. Your sentences and punishment are likely to be increased.'

Councillor Brókova waited a moment, then continued.

'Although it is not incumbent upon us to explain, the Council wishes to inform the accused that the hearing will be shortened and closed to the public, for a number of reasons. The trial will be public.'

Karland half-listened, the formal words washing over him. The reactions of the accused were mostly numb, as if they couldn't believe this were happening; the exceptions were Bradwr and Aran, the former showing signs of outraged panic, the latter looking amused and bored.

'Eordeland stands on the brink of war, in the midst of a refugee crisis, at a time when her Council is sorely pressed. Those accused were bound in the act of violence, indisputably witnessed. This act took place in the most protected and hallowed place in our realm, against one who had acted on behalf of this Council.

'Because of these facts, the usual process of Law has been reduced. Justice shall be dispensed as quickly and as fairly as possible. Your Procurator has outlined the procedures of Law to you.'

Procurator in Judgment Fohle cleared his throat. 'Please explain the process in this case for public record, Councillor.'

Councillor Brókova nodded and turned back to the five boys before her.

'In time of peace, the Law has inviolable steps, set to safeguard the accused and accusers alike. In times of upheaval, where the safety of the realm is at stake, Eordeland must, of necessity, sacrifice due process as much as required to survive. In addition, there is no question of mistaken identity in this instance. Thus, this case shall be decided herewith.

'This is a hearing to determine the charges against you, to cite initial evidence, and so you may enter a plea. It may be possible to mitigate sentence if guilt is rightfully admitted. Given the circumstances of your apprehension, you would be wise to consider this carefully. Your Defensor may advise you here if you choose to engage. Do you understand?'

Five heads nodded, and Aran shrugged.

'I require an answer, Aran of House Telemer.'

'Yes.'

Even though he was not in front of the Council, Karland felt a serious apprehension. There was something nerve-wracking and oppressive about this formality every bit as frightening to him as being chased by orcs.

'Following this hearing, a period of one week shall pass to allow for investigations to conclude by the Welcomer Guard and for evidence to be considered by this Council. After this, a public trial will be held, and sentence shall be passed. There will be no appeal. You may present any defence you feel you have at this trial before the verdict. Do you understand?'

'Yes,' muttered the other boys. Bradwr looked around in a panicked fashion, nose swollen, and didn't respond. Aran drew himself up to look at the Councillor. Karland had to admire his courage in doing so; he couldn't have done the same.

'This is unfair. You said yourself it isn't the normal way-'

'We're going to war, boy,' rumbled Ulric from behind Brókova. 'You were caught in the act. You've had the reasons explained to you. There is no debate.'

'Be thankful we explained this much, Son of Telemer,' said Jameson dryly. 'In a time of war or threat to this realm, we could simply imprison you all. We have chosen to follow what Law we can in the limited time we have.'

Councillor Brókova looked down at her notes.

'We are here to have the charges against you read, the initial evidence of wrongdoing presented, and any defence you have against it. You may then speak on your behalf. After this, there will be a short time to allow any new evidence to come to light during investigations before the trial for verdict. A Procurator stands ready to advise you, should you wish them.'

Fron, Kixel, and the two boys Karland didn't know looked miserable, Kixel especially. He had been the most hesitant of the four, Karland recalled. Aran had hardly glanced at them; it was clear he considered them collateral damage. He shot Karland a smug look, confident as ever that he would squirm out of this. Bradwr looked small and harassed behind them.

'I dem- I request the Novinian Ambassador as my Defensor,' Aran said.

Even now, Karland found it annoyingly hard not to admire his poise.

'The Novinian Ambassador holds no legal rank here, nor knowledge of our law,' said Aurelia Brókova. 'Your request is denied.'

'Then I request a Defensor of my choosing. A man.'

'Procurators are picked at random from an active pool. Your request is denied. We make no differentiation here between male or female Procurators.'

Aran looked as if he wanted to curse, but he was not as upset as Karland expected.

'Then I accept their counsel,' he said grudgingly.

The others nodded or shrugged in turn; it was clear they held no confidence of escape.

Councillor Brókova gestured to Dorn.

'Captain-General Gardenson; as the ranking officer involved, please state the case before us.'

Dorn moved out and stood to attention before the Council.

'Karland Dresin left a game of *vingitunis* that was attended by myself, Privates Drell and Alfinson, and Xhera. He left alone, stating his intent to return to their quarters. Xhera left perhaps thirty minutes later, and I escorted her back to the quarters along with the Privates. We arrived immediately after Rast Tal'Orien had returned. He had found a note supposedly from Xhera to Karland asking him to come alone to the Artem Atrium. Xhera denied that this was her note, or even script, and we immediately suspected foul intent.' He related the rest of the tale quickly and in detail, before finishing the part Karland only remembered hazily.

'Rast Tal'Orien immediately interceded to prevent grave harm to Karland Dresin, along with myself and Private Alfinson. Private Drell endeavored to apprehend Bradwr Hallt. Aran of House Telemer attempted to use the same illegal weapon on Rast Tal'Orien and was restrained. Karland Dresin was found to be have sustained a serious wound from the attack, requiring a Gifted healer. The accused before you were bound and taken to a cell. Welcomer Guards awaited Bradwr Hallt's return to his dormitory and he was bound there.'

'Thank you, Captain-General. Let the charges be read.'

The Accusator stood, and moved out to the front, several pieces of paper in his hands. The Defensor moved down to the accused to stand next to each as the charges were read. Karland guessed she had spoken to them last night, as the Accusator had to him, and wondered at Aran's arrogance and risk of alienating her.

'Before the charges are read, may I request the right of the accused to change their plea within this week before the trial?' she said. Her voice was clipped and professional.

Councillor Brókova stepped back and conferred with the others. There were a few shrugs and nods, several shakes of the head. Finally, she stepped back.

'They will be permitted to change from a not guilty plea to guilty until the trial,' she said. 'Once guilt is admitted, this Council considers it binding.'

'Thank you, Councillor.' She nodded to the Accusator who bowed slightly and continued.

'Kixel Jan of Papplewick, East Norlund. You stand before the Council of Twelve accused of conspiracy to Gravely Harm a fellow student; and Grave Harm of said student with the intent to maim if not kill. How do you plead?' The words had a formal, inexorable cadence to them.

The Defensor whispered to the boy. Kixel deliberately did not look at Aran.

'Guilty, sir, but I-'

'There is no discussion at this time. Enter a plea of guilt or no guilt.' Brókova's face was stern. 'Do you admit guilt?'

'Guilty, Ma'am.' He looked miserable.

Aran glared at him.

That wasn't supposed to happen, thought Karland.

The Accusator repeated his question to each boy. Fron's pale face sought out the steely gaze of Aran. He ignored the Defensor.

'Not- not guilty.' He swallowed convulsively.

Javin Otalian listened to the Defensor, his face troubled, and then shook his head and whispered a question. She nodded.

'Not guilty, sir.'

Ton Jonalson threw a despairing look at Aran, then cast a look to Javin and listened to the Defensor.

'Not guilty.'

The Accusator's questions changed for the last two.

'Aran Son of Telemer, of the Novinian Great House Telemer. You stand before the Council of Twelve accused of carrying a sanctioned weapon within The Sanctum; resisting Binding with intent to harm the Binder; conspiracy to Gravely

Harm a fellow student; and Grave Harm of said student with the intent to maim if not kill. How do you plead?

Aran smirked, ignoring the Defensor. 'Not guilty.'

'Bradwr Hunanol Hallt of Aegland. You stand before the Council of Twelve accused of fleeing Lawful Binding; conspiracy to Gravely Harm a fellow student; Grave Harm of said student with the intent to maim if not kill; and intent to murder.' His voice echoed in the high hall.

'W-what?!' stammered Bradwr, his face white.

'How do you plead?'

The Defensor spoke into Bradwr's ear, but he twitched away, his thin battered face on the verge of panic.

'I haven't done anything wrong!' he shrieked suddenly. 'It's his fault!' He pointed, not at Aran, but at Karland, who blinked in astonishment.

'How do you plead?' The Accusator's voice was emotionless and relentless. Bradwr's mouth worked.

The Defensor shook her head and stepped away from Bradwr. 'I believe the accused pleads not guilty, Councillor,' she said loudly, trying to drown out any words.

'Yes! Not guilty!' Tears were streaming pathetically down his face.

Brókova sighed, looking at her colleagues, and glancing at her notes before turning her gaze to the boys standing before the Council.

'Do any of you have anything to add to your defence? You do not have to speak, but what you say will be added to the consideration for verdict. Choose your words carefully.'

Aran threw his head back grandly, speaking as if the others weren't present.

'I acted in defence of my character against the verbal abuse of Dresin. I only meant to frighten him. One of the others had my blade in the confusion; I dropped it when Dresin attacked me. It's possible the blade slipped as they tried to restrain him from harming me. When Tal'Orien attacked me, I acted in self-defence.'

Karland almost gasped at the magnitude of the lie and met Aran's sneer with a steady gaze.

The Novinian's smile was sure. He was clearly not overly concerned, and in fact was so casual that Karland started to worry he had a hidden Primus up his sleeve.

The silence grew. Then Kixel Jan spoke up, his voice small, sounding on the verge of tears.

'I- we- I had no problem with Karland. I was told it was a joke, a prank. Just to frighten him.' He half-sobbed. 'It wasn't meant to be real. I can't believe this has happened.'

No one answered him, and his words died away. Jan looked as if he were in shock, staring ahead of him.

Fron shook his head after a look at Aran.

Javin echoed Kixel's words, only saying that he never believed the stories he thought Karland had spread about himself, and that it would take him down several pegs to be frightened. He seemed honest and regretful when he added he'd never expected events to get away from them so fast.

Ton didn't even look up.

Karland shifted his gaze then to Bradwr. His hands were shaking with anger again looking at the friend he had given so much care to, placed so much trust in. Finding out the friendship was a hollow lie was like a physical blow to Karland that didn't end; he placed such value in friendship.

It had all been so unfair. He had never done anything wrong to Bra; quite the opposite. It seemed Bradwr had simply found no further use for their friendship, almost deliberately sought offence. When Karland had predictably reacted badly to that, it had taken very little for Bradwr to transform that offence into hatred.

Most of the lies he had heard about himself had one source.

Bradwr's face was pale, his gaze darting around, and his nose had that unpleasant, pinched-nostril look again. For someone Karland had once thought good-looking, the hollowness and selfishness blazed through and brought a peculiar ugliness to his fine features. There was nothing even approaching empathy in his actions, or voice, or words, and only the stress of the court had brought this out, dropping the manipulative face that showed whatever anyone present wanted to see.

Overlaid on that was the panic Karland had seen many times; the full-blown reaction when Bradwr didn't get things his way. Once, Karland had thought him worthy of helping. Now he saw him for what he really was.

Hallt was a husk, a shell. A nothing. Someone desperately trying to be meaningful with nothing to provide meaning; someone to whom image and self-serving meant more than anything else. Someone who substituted being fun, needed, having attention for true friendship, feelings, or care. A total narcissist; a betrayer of faith.

All those others had been right. Xhera had been right.

'Aran made me do it,' Bradwr burst out under the weight of their gazes, and then quailed at the look of fury which descended on Aran's proud face - fury which Karland was grudgingly certain was justified. The Defensor was trying to quiet him, speaking urgently in his ear, but Bradwr was beyond reason.

'The others were holding him, they're all guilty, I only saw it and ran away, I was trying to get someone to help-' He caught the looks on the faces of the others, and Karland's steady look, and his face twisted desperately.

'-and Karland's a liar, a cheat, a fraud! He was abusive to me, he threatened me, I was only trying to protect myself, he-' the empty words died, reverberating into nothing, and he looked around. The silence was oppressive, even to Karland. Where Aran had lied with confidence, this had been full of panic.

Hatred.

His hands clenched hard, he watched for the first time as Bradwr's stacked lies ran into a harsh wall of reality and fell apart. The narcissism that drove him could not sustain itself without the validation of those he had charmed.

At that moment, the final parts fell into place. Karland felt himself calming. His hands unclenched a little as he accepted that the friendship had always been a lie from Bradwr's side. It had always been Karland who had given.

For the first time in his life, Karland found he had no care for someone. It wasn't even loathing, as with Aran; it was a horrible emptiness. Bradwr was… nothing.

He wondered if he would act the same way, faced with the choice again - with Bradwr about to be killed by an orc instead of Ben Arflun - and knew with an absolute lack of emotion that he would not. He wouldn't bat an eyelid if Bradwr was skewered. He wouldn't even be glad.

Bradwr was utterly worthless to him.

It was a terrible and wondrous thing. Karland had never felt like this about anyone before. The one thing that mitigated his deep shame was that this had been a clear choice by Bradwr, knowing the consequences every step of the way. The arrogance of ignoring that, out of the belief he was somehow special, had been his downfall.

Finally, consequences had caught him, and he had nowhere to turn. Even Karland couldn't pretend this was his own fault any longer.

Good.

'Noted,' said Brókova into the silence. 'Although this outburst has done you no favours, Bradwr Hunanol Hallt, and will be taken into account at the trial.'

Bradwr's face twisted and he began crying bitterly. The other boys ignored him. Karland could almost sense their anger.

Councillor Brókova nodded to the Procurators, and they moved back to their seats, speaking softly.

'Let it be recorded that of the six accused, five plead not guilty.' She looked at Kixel, who stared bravely back. 'Your courage and decision has been noted, Kixel

Jan. Nevertheless, your sentence will be given along with the others after the investigation.'

Kixel Jan nodded.

The Defensor stood.

'Given the pleas, I request the accused are held separate from each other forthwith for their individual safety and to protect their testimony.'

Brókova glanced behind her, seeing nearly every Councillor nod. 'Granted, and a sensible precaution.'

Karland agreed privately. He wasn't sure Bradwr would make it to the trial in one piece if he was left in a cell with the others.

'Procurator in Judgement Fohle, are you satisfied?'

'Indeed yes, Councillor.'

'Then thank you, ladies and gentlemen. The accused will be removed and separately held pending the trial, to commence one week from today. Agencies from both parties will coordinate to gather what evidence they can and interview the accused individually. May Delmatra's Justice keep us.'

The Council stood, and just like that, it was over. Karland was surprised by how quickly it finished. The others all stood, and he hastily jumped to his feet. As the Council climbed the stairs again and the accused were led away, only Aran looking unconcerned, the Accusator made his way over.

'That went about as I expected,' he said with a smile. 'I suggest we make our way to the nearest food hall, and we can talk.'

TWENTY-TWO

The next week went by quickly for Karland. He wondered how fast it went for the accused; certainly, he could think of nothing else but the upcoming trial. He was vaguely aware of the bustle of investigation around them, from Welcomers and Castellan alike. At least one of the cleaning staff had disappeared.

He was also more aware of the presence of Onyx Guard - and Rast - wherever he and Xhera went. They also noticed a difference with their peers, an uncomfortable mixture of curious fascination and avoidance.

And here they were, on the morning of the verdict. His side itched and stung, and Xhera prowled like a lioness, her serious little face set in a scowl. He found it hard to focus on his studies, wondering what the verdict would be, worried that after all this Xhera would still be at risk.

It was one thing to be told his attackers would get what they deserved but in his experience, life rarely lived up to real justice.

He remembered back to the conversation with Procurator Ild just after the hearing.

'That went well,' the Accusator had said briskly. He had a surprisingly pleasant face in contrast to his colleague's severity, with a slightly upturned nose and a brisk, no-nonsense joviality. Sebastian Ild was renowned for his ethics and was considered one of the finest Procurators Darost had ever produced.

'Did it?' Karland had asked morosely, thinking back to the amount of defence. 'It seemed so fast. And it is as if they haven't even asked what happened.'

Ild had chuckled.

'You have to understand the legal process, Karland. Despite this being rushed through, the Council is making an effort to be as fair as possible, especially as it involves a Novinian noble. Normally this is a much more involved and lengthy process. From binding, a charge is made. A plea may be then entered, and a sentence can be made if guilt is admitted, taking into account the honesty of the plea.

'If guilt is denied, a trial takes place after evidence is gathered, usually a lengthy and intricate process. The trial of an accused is a crucial part of our society, allowing Delmatra to judge through Eordeland Law with justice and logic. That they are before the highest Court in our land should tell you how serious their position is.

'During a trial, the Accusator and Defensor present cases, show any evidence, and call witnesses, before Culmination, where we finish our cases. After this, sentence is passed for each of the accused. Depending on the Court and the crime, there is sometimes an appeal that can be made.'

'But what if they miss something, like the threat to Xhera? This isn't a simple thing,' Karland had said. 'What if rushing this gets them off lightly?'

The Accusator had sighed.

'Look,' he had said kindly. 'The Council has a choice here. They could invoke Council rights under wartime law and simply throw legal process out of the window right now, or they could follow the normal route. They do not have time for the latter but wish to be just and fair in the eyes of the public... and Novin. At the same time, they must not be seen to be lenient here or they risk losing the trust of the Communia, and although we are not on a full war footing yet, it is serious enough that martial law almost applies. Don't worry if they don't answer for every transgression. The punishments are certain to be harsh for those caught red-handed trying to harm a Sanctum member, especially one who has acted on Eordeland's behalf. We'll get 'em.' He had flashed a quick grin. 'I'm all for skipping the small stuff and concentrating on the really big things. After a certain point, young chap, there isn't any value in adding it on, and once they are away any remaining threat is unlikely. Less than a month is almost unheard of for a trial like this. It's only because they were caught in the act, and the Council has greater things to worry about.'

Karland supposed he understood what the Accusator had meant, but he was still worried.

Battered but recovering, a spark of anger was tamped within him. Xhera sat near him, her face pale; she had been terribly shaken when she had found Karland returned to their room with Master Darfin himself attending to him and guards on the door. He had expected tears when she had been told what had happened, and she had cried, but not in worry.

She had been angry; angrier than he, by far.

He had needed stitches, and cleaning. His ribs hurt, his eye was swollen, and his side was pulling uncomfortably against the fire of the stab wound. He would heal, quicker than usual thanks to his tutor's small Gift, but the discomfort would linger.

The events kept replaying over, and over, and he was beginning to understand what Rast meant when he said he committed fully against his enemies. If Karland had taken Aran down hard enough, the rest would probably not have continued the attack. His sphincter twitched uncomfortably as he thought of his near fate.

He sighed, pacing nervously, trying not to scratch his stiff side.

In less than two hours, judgement would be delivered. This time it would be in the great Court of The Sanctum, in the northernmost Cuneus called the twelfth. The huge room could hold more than two thousand people for public trials.

It had been an odd week. Rumour had proven impossible to quash, so he had kept his head down and avoided people where he could. Despite this, he had been congratulated or commiserated with several times by fellow students who had also had run-ins with the Novinian.

He had also been threatened twice, even spat on by a girl he knew was obsessed with Aran. Onyx Guards had pulled the aggressors aside and muttered to them, upon which they had usually become extremely polite.

People would believe what they wanted to believe, whatever the proof of the court. This set Karland's teeth on edge; he had been infuristed at the injustice of Aran's lies and the betrayal of Bradwr.

Bra was worst. He had been inside Karland's barriers; trusted, relied on, shared with. Whatever Aran had done, there was at least a certain brutal honesty in his dislike for Karland.

Xhera sat with him, quiet and introspective. For all her anger and bravado, he knew she had been shaken to hear that Aran had set out plans to harm her.

Finally, it was time. They filed out with Rast and two Onyx Guard, taking a lesser-travelled route to the courtroom, entering from a side door.

It took up a good third of the rear of the northernmost Cuneus. Unlike the base of the Dodecagon, where the Council held their usual meetings, this room was built for witnesses, scribes, judges, procurators and public to all have their place, with a secured holding pen for the accused.

In descending arcs, dark polished oak tables sat before chairs backed in leather. The highest semicircle was a raised dais with twelve high-backed chairs made with iron for the Iron King, oak for Isha and dark green leather for Delmatra, the white symbol of Eordeland embossed on each. They were utilitarian, stern, and spoke of practical authority.

The Council Court was held only for the most serious matters. Procurator-in-Judgement Fohle attended again, sitting at the table in front of the Council chairs the next level down. In front of him was the scribe's table, with four scribes and an array of quills and books. To his left, the Accusator sat; to his right, the Defensor.

Both levels were already filled with an audience. It was obvious that this was the most unexpected and shocking things to happen in the University for some time.

Karland and Xhera were escorted to the left, to a curved table facing the three platforms. The other side of the walkway was another table, seating a severe man in flowing Novinian robes. In the front was a section where the accused would sit; a low-walled pen with Welcomer Guards on each corner. It was only used for serious crimes.

It would be used today.

Row upon row of benches lined the floor facing the court, ending a little way back behind carved wooden fences with a closed gate in the centre. A green carpet split the room in two in a line to the centre gate.

Welcomer Guard faced the audience, lining the fencing and the walls of the chamber. The main doors were closed now, the unlucky turned away.

There was loud conversation in the room, muffled by the tapestries of Eordeland law and history. The room was acoustically very clever, allowing the voices from the dais to carry clearly and preventing too much noise from the audience reaching the court itself.

A Welcomer Guard entered with a ceremonial pike, alongside a serious man in the robes of the Court Chamberlain. They walked to the centre of the floor, the Guard pausing over a bronze metal tile. He raised the weapon vertically and struck the pommel hard, three times. The floor must have been hollow under the tile, as the sharp strike reverberated throughout the chamber.

The talk died.

'The Supreme Court of the Council of Twelve is now in session.' The powerful voice of the Chamberlain rolled forward. 'All rise for the Council of Twelve.'

The room was busy with the sounds of cloth and feet as everyone stood. The Council entered slowly through the same door as Karland, moving up the side steps to their dais. Onyx Guards flanked them. Welcomers with crossbows stood to the sides.

It was only now that Karland realised how formal and grave this was. He took a deep breath.

For better or worse, the process was under way.

☘   ☙

The Council sat, and the Chamberlain turned to the people. 'Be seated.' He and the Guard moved to the side.

Councillor Brókova spoke. Her voice was startlingly clear from the uppermost dais.

'This Court has been convened to pass sentence on those accused of the attack and grave harm of a student of this University. A closed hearing has already passed.

'This is an unusual case. We are on the brink of war with Meyar. We are still reeling from the loss of Irilview and the surge of refugees. Wartime law now applies. The process of Eordeland Law is secondary to this. However, in the interests of justice and transparency for the Novinian Ambassador and the people, the Council has agreed to as thorough a process as possible given the circumstances.'

Procurator-In-Judgement Fohle stood and cleared his throat.

'We find that the enquiries are in accordance with Eordeland law,' he said in an extremely measured, educated voice. 'Due process has been followed, and justice may be meted out.'

'Thank you,' said Augusta. She consulted her notes, and conferred briefly with Contemus, who nodded.

She looked at the Chamberlain. 'Call the accused.'

A different door to the side opened and they filed in, hands chained in front of them and loosely bound to a guard. All six were led to the low pen and ushered in, where they sat.

Councillor Brókova addressed them.

'It was explained to you at a closed hearing what you are accused of. Your Defensor spoke to you prior to that and during the investigation. Normally this trial would be to examine the evidence and base a verdict on arguments from each side. However, due to circumstances and Eordeland's current state of emergency, this Council has taken valuable time to examine evidence on each side as it came to light during the investigation, in closed discussion with all Procurators.

'Therefore, this trial shall examine the known evidence and charges, and render sentence upon this swiftly. Is this agreeable to the Procurators?'

Accusator and Defensor stood. 'It is, Councillor,' they said in turn.

'Do you understand?' she asked the accused.

They all nodded.

'Accusator Ild, do you have any new evidence they wish to make known?'

'Yes, Councillor,' said Ild. 'During the investigation, Welcomer Guards, in tandem with Castellan James, uncovered an alarming number of University and Sanctum staff who had been bribed or threatened at the behest of Aran of House Telemer. Complicity has been verified where possible beyond question and those involved removed from their station. They have all attested of their own free will that what was discovered is true.

'There are witness statements sworn, and statements from those accused, that Aran of House Telemer did order a watch upon both Karland Dresin and Xhera;

that he tried to gain access to their quarters, and more than once gained access to Karland Dresin's equipment and weapons; and that he had in place a plan to forcibly kidnap and hold Xhera at a location outside this University, to be actioned at his demand. In line with the alleged threats against her and Karland Dresin we have heard, and on questioning of those involved by Welcomer Guard, it is clear that this was a very real threat.'

A sense of relief almost like cold water washed through Karland at these words, and he squeezed Xhera's hand. They *had* to take the threats against her seriously now!

'In addition, the investigation has made it obvious that there has been a growing discord between Aran of House Telemer and Karland Dresin. Multiple accounts make it clear that this was not typically initiated or continued by Karland Dresin. It has also been demonstrated to the investigator's satisfaction that the note used to lure Karland Dresin was not in Xhera's script. Bradwr Hunanol Hallt wrote the note that led Karland Dresin to the place of the attack, showing clear planning of events. Given that the accused were bound *in flagrante delicto* by unassailable witnesses, it is unequivocally clear that *actus reus* and *mens rea* should both be accepted.'

'Thank you, Accusator. The Council has seen this extra evidence and agrees. Defensor Garin, do you have anything to add?'

'Nothing in relation to this, Councillor, but I wish to have it noted that Fron Grishold, Javin Otalian, and Ton Jonalson changed their pleas to guilty during the investigation. They have also all, along with Kixel Jan, co-operated fully with the investigation and given full accounts and evidence.' She ignored the hiss of anger from Aran. 'I therefore request this be taken into account.'

'Noted. The Council will bear this in mind. Thank you, Procurators.'

They sat, and Brókova leaned back. The other Councillors could have been made from stone as far as Karland could tell. He was almost quivering with tension; now, finally, everyone knew about the problems he had been facing!

He watched the Council members talking, leaning forwards with their heads close, shuffling notes and gesturing. Finally, Brókova nodded, noted something else down, and leaned forward again.

'The Council has examined all the evidence available, and finds that Kixel Jan, Bradwr Hunanol Hallt, Ton Jonalson, Javin Otalian, Fron Grishold and Aran of House Telemer did knowingly and deliberately plan, cause and attempt to cause further grave harm to a student of this University, for no good reason; further, that an attempt was made to maim, and another attempt to kill, this student; that an illegal weapon was used during these acts; and that plans were set to kidnap this student's companion if he did not allow these acts, with the stated intention of rape and coercion. We do not doubt premeditated murder may also have been contemplated. That this comes after a campaign of abuse and interference shows a studied and deliberate disregard for the basic tenets of not just this University, but the laws of Eordeland and common decency.

'It is… unfortunate… not only that your paths led you here, but that you chose this moment to perpetrate such acts. Eordeland stands on the brink of war, on top of other crises. She does not need acts of violence at her heart from inside, based in greed and petty jealousy.

'According to the statutes of Eordeland law, laid down by Farle Torin the Fair, last King of Eorderland, you shall be judged on each count separately, in order of seriousness. Let it be a matter of record that Kixel Jan, Javian Octalian, Fron Grishold, and Ton Jonalson have elected to plead guilty. This will be taken into consideration when sentencing.

'Under the Eordeland Law of Common Design - that is, the invocation of the Law whereby all involved are charged on the most serious crime committed by one - all parties except Kixel Jan are liable. The investigation and witness accounts satisfied us that he alone attempted to prevent the attack, although he was coerced into continuing.

'However, due to the accused Kixel Jan, Fron Grishold, Javin Otalian and Ton Jonalson to not only pleading guilty but fully complying with the investigation and giving crucial evidence, the Council has agreed to further waive Common Design in each case. Thus, only Aran of House Telemer and Bradwr Hallt will be tried for attempted murder.'

The expressions of relief on the faces of those Karland could see were overwhelming. Accusator Ild had told him there had been a strong possibility that they would all be sentenced under Common Design.

Aran was staring with real anger at them.

'Traitors!' he snarled. The nearest Guard struck the bars and he glared, raising his voice. 'I demand the right of trial by combat! To the death. Against my accuser, Karland Dresin.'

A mutter swelled through the crowd and Karland stared, a dreadful pit forming in his stomach.

'This isn't Novin,' remarked Brókova mildly. 'We do not have that rule here. You shall be judged and sentenced according to our laws.' Her voice brooked no argument, and she turned to his fellow accused.

Karland took a deep breath.

A fight to the death!

'Kixel Jan of Papplewick. You are here on scholarship in acknowledgement of your humble background and your skill with numbers. This University took you in, subsidised you, and gave you an opportunity - one which you have squandered.'

Kixel covered his face and wept. Karland knew the boy had relied on the scholarship money to help his family eke out a living. The shame would be unbearable. He guessed Aran had offered him money to go along with this; he felt sorry for the boy's family.

'On the counts of conspiracy and attempt to Harm a fellow student, you are found guilty as accused. This carries a maximum penalty of five years of hard labour, of which you are required to serve one. We have taken into account your attempts to dissuade the other accused, your coercion, and your preceding guilty plea. You are hereby expelled from this University and relinquish all access to The Sanctum. The rights to scholarship are rescinded; your family will receive no further funds. A messenger will be dispatched to inform them of the reasons why your scholarship is revoked and the removal of their subsidy. We are disappointed in you.'

Jan nodded silently, eyes red. His face was cast in shame and misery. Karland felt a little pity, then; he had made a bad decision.

'Fron Grishold of Darost. You have been involved in multiple altercations at the behest of Aran of House Telemer, many against Karland Dresin. He has in return disavowed you. Ensure you take this lesson to heart and give your loyalty more wisely in future.

'On the counts of conspiracy and attempt to Harm a fellow student, you are found guilty as accused. This carries a maximum penalty of five years of hard labour, of which you are required to serve three.'

'*Three!* he cried. Brókova ignored him.

'We have taken into account your guilty plea. You are hereby expelled from this University and relinquish all access to The Sanctum.'

Fron was visibly shaking. Brókova continued, inevitable as time.

'Javin Otalian of Tamismuth. Until this time you have been an unassuming student with good potential. You have caused this to be wasted. We are disappointed in you as well.

'On the counts of conspiracy and attempt to Harm a fellow student, you are found guilty as accused. This carries a maximum penalty of five years of hard labour, of which you are required to serve three. We have taken into account your guilty plea. You are hereby expelled from this University and relinquish all access to The Sanctum.'

Javin didn't respond.

'Ton Jonalson of Darost. You came from a poor background and worked hard to attain a place here. You accomplished much here, accomplishments which are now meaningless.

'On the counts of conspiracy and attempt to Harm a fellow student, you are found guilty as accused. This carries a maximum penalty of five years of hard labour, of which you are required to serve three. We have taken into account your guilty plea. You are hereby expelled from this University and relinquish all access to The Sanctum.'

The large-framed boy swallowed, despair on his face. A woman in the large crowd somewhere wailed, muted. Karland knew he and his companions had been let off lightly despite the severity of the sentences. He felt a little for them, especially Kixel.

There was a pause, and then Councillor Brókova turned to Aran. Underneath his bored smirk lay suppressed tension.

'Aran of House Telemer of Novin. You are here as a representative at the request of your House. Your goal was to become a Papered Scholar, something which you have now prevented yourself from ever achieving.

'We know that arrangements were made to remove you secretly from The Sanctum if required; that bribes and threats have been made using the name of the realm of Novin against staff within The Sanctum; and that several actions were planned against students here. Your sphere of influence was not expected and has troubled us greatly.

'On the counts of conspiracy and attempt to Harm a fellow student, you are found guilty as accused. This carries a maximum penalty of five years of hard labour, of which you are required to serve five.

'On the count of carrying an illegal weapon in a proscribed area, you are found guilty as accused. The penalty for this ranges from a fine and warning up to expulsion from the University and rescinding of all Sanctum access. The fact you used this weapon heavily weights this decision. The sentence is a fine of twelve Greats and expulsion from the University and Sanctum.'

Xhera gasped. Twelve Greats was a *lot* of money.

'On the count of conspiracy to kidnap another student of the University with the stated intent of rape and abuse, you are you are found guilty as accused. The sentence is two years imprisonment.

'On the counts of bribery, coercion and threat - that is to say, the subversion of Eordeland law and decency and the corruption of staff within this University - you are found guilty as accused. The penalties for these vary; this Council is minded to imprison you for a year collectively for the range and number of offences, and you are so sentenced.

'On the count of resisting Binding with intent to harm the Binder, you are found guilty as accused. The maximum penalty is six months imprisonment or hard labour. You are sentenced to six months imprisonment, and a fine of four Greats.' She paused again and looked at Aran gravely.

'On the grave count of attempted murder, you are found not guilty as accused.' A mutter ran through the chamber, and Xhera's nails dug viciously into Karland's hand. He nearly yelped. 'Although it is clear that you intended Grave Harm, the testimonies of several combat experts - including Rast Tal'Orien - and your tutor's statement of your excellent knife skills have satisfied the Council that your use of the weapon was purely with intention of causing pain and disfigurement, not death.

'However, on the serious count of Grave Harm, in this case with the clear intent to maim for life and with what could have been a life-threatening wound, the maximum penalty is ten years imprisonment. The sentence this Court has unanimously ruled is this full term. Allowing for the multiple offences, the Council has collated the overall sentence to a verdict of fifteen years in Kingsgate prison, the last three of which may be reduced to hard labour should your behaviour warrant it.'

Karland nearly gasped. Several people did.

'You also forfeit all your possessions and wealth here, except that kept in accounts and your personal heirlooms. All weapons apart from any hereditary arms are confiscated; those will be returned to your family. Proclamations shall be made public both here and sent to Novin to make your shame and dishonour clear.'

Aran drew himself up. Paler than usual, he still moved with assurance.

'You may not do that.'

'On the contrary,' said Brókova, her voice cold and her face like stone. 'Under the current circumstances we could have simply imprisoned you until you died, without trial. We are showing good faith with Novin by giving you this much. You have represented your realm very poorly.'

'I demand to be heard!'

'You will be given the opportunity to speak after the last sentence. If you do not remain quiet until then, you will be removed to begin your sentence immediately.'

Aran stared at her. From where he was sitting, Karland finally saw concern creasing his brow. He glanced at the Ambassador, but the man's face was as severe and still as it had been throughout.

The pause ended. Brókova ignored him and turned her gaze to the last accused.

'Bradwr Hunanol Hallt of Aegland.' Her voice rang in the hall and Karland felt anger blossom again merely at the sound of his name. He clenched his hands.

'During the investigation it became apparent that there are a wealth of incidents you have been involved in over a number of years, including the recent suicide of a student of this University. These may be dealt with in a separate court session with additional sentences to be carried out at that time after lengthier investigation. We will focus here on your involvement in the crime against Karland Dresin.

'This investigation has brought into the light a person of the lowest morals and character, and one who has mastered shifting blame to others. You are bright and creative, so it is a great tragedy you chose to funnel your energies into base spite and jealousy. We feel there is something broken within you, but something you could have nevertheless contained and learned from. You failed to do so.

'On the counts of conspiracy and attempt to Harm a fellow student, you are found guilty as accused. Evidence has shown that you were a catalyst for these events. This carries a maximum penalty of five years of hard labour, of which you are required to serve five. You are hereby expelled from this University and relinquish all access to The Sanctum.' Bradwr moaned, looking on the verge of panic.

'On the count of fleeing lawful Binding, you are found guilty as accused. The punishment for this ranges from a fine to imprisonment depending on the nature of the crime. You are sentenced to six months of hard labour given the grave nature of the crime you fled, and a fine of four Greats.

'On the count of conspiracy to kidnap with intent to harm another fellow student, and incitement of Aran of House Telemer to arrange the same, you are found guilty as accused. The penalty for this is six months of hard labour.

'On the more serious count of Grave Harm to a fellow student, you are found guilty as accused. You were an integral part of the attempt on Karland Dresin, from what appears to be selfishness and bitterness, and you enabled Aran of House Telemer to almost carry this out. The maximum penalty is ten years imprisonment. The sentence this Court has unanimously ruled is the full term.'

Bradwr's legs gave way. The crowd was muttering, an ugly sound, and Karland thought he could hear the shriller anger of a woman in there somewhere mixed with a few shouts of what could have been triumph. He wondered if it was one of the girls Bradwr had led astray and cast aside.

Karland remembered back to when Bradwr had spoken of another student who had killed herself, pregnant and pretending the child was his. He had sought much sympathy for how deeply it had affected him.

Karland hadn't known the girl. There were other mutters of pressure, forced abortions, blackmail. He was now utterly convinced Bradwr had lied about it all, that it was his child and that her death was only important for the attention it had gained him.

He wondered now how much Bra had contributed to her mental state.

How much he had *pushed*.

With no small satisfaction, he watched the Guard next to Bradwr haul his chains up over the bars and hold him upright.

'Last, and most serious, is the count of Attempted Murder. Your intent to carry out an attack you knew could kill - in cowardice as you struck at someone who thought you a friend from behind, while they fought multiple attackers - marks you as utterly without empathy or integrity. This court unanimously sentences you to thirty years imprisonment in Kingsgate Prison, where you will have time to reflect on the betrayals and decisions that took you there. You will be humanely branded on the rear of your left hand with the symbol of a murderer-'

'No!' Bradwr shrieked, his face contorting like a banshee's. 'This is my *life*! My *LIFE!*' He lapsed into painful sobbing. 'This isn't fair! I didn't murder anyone! Karland is lying!'

Kixel Jan glanced at him with what seemed some compassion, but the others leaned away from him. Aran wore a sneer of disgust.

Brókova's voice overrode his. 'Let it be made clear that you and you alone are responsible for this sentence and the ruination of a life that had promise. You and you alone chose this path. You must live with the consequences of your own actions.'

Karland waited to feel the familiar concern, the hope, the empathy, and was profoundly disturbed to feel absolutely nothing except satisfaction that finally, *finally*, justice had been done to someone terrible. Someone not honestly and unashamedly terrible, but who hid it beneath a false mask of friendship and care.

'You were unconcerned about removing someone else's life out of spite; you forfeited your own right at that moment. Eordeland law makes no differentiation between murder and the attempt to murder with clear intent. This was not a crime of passion. You are exposed as a manipulator, a narcissist, a liar, and a cheat, not by Karland Dresin but by evidence from others and *your own actions*. In this investigation we have only glimpsed how many people's lives you have poisoned with your words and deeds, and can think of no better place for you.'

Bradwr was being held up only by his chains now and was screaming. The Chamberlain gestured to the Guard, who strode out and slammed the ceremonial pike on the strikeplate.

'Order! Order!' he bellowed. The crowd susurrated while Bradwr continued in hysterics. 'If you will not be silent, you will be removed and your sentence may be increased!'

Finally, a Guard opened the gate to the accused and dragged Bradwr out, bodily hauling him upright in the centre of the court. His cries grew weaker. After a minute Brókova spoke again.

'This Council has passed its Judgement according to Law in the sight of Delmatra.'

The pike crashed down.

She turned to Ulric, who stood as she sat. He waited for the noise to die down. Gradually people stopped talking, waiting for his words.

'These crimes are serious,' he rumbled into the quieting hall. 'But Eordeland is soon to be at war. The Council has agreed that these crimes may be served as sentenced... or by an alternative.

'The accused, apart from Aran of House Telemer as a son of Novin, may elect to serve their time in the Eordeland Guard recruits as conscripts, under observation and with restrictions, to be of some use to Eordeland instead of a detriment.

'They may take up sword to protect their homeland to balance these crimes. They may not be promoted or commended during their sentences, and if they desert will be outcast for life, to be imprisoned or killed. In this way they may yet make something of wasted lives.'

The buzz of conversation was loud behind Karland. Xhera whispered to him fiercely.

'How could they do this?'

Karland tried to view it logically. 'If war happens, they aren't trained soldiers, just basic recruits. They stand a high chance of dying, I guess. Maybe it's fair. I mean, I think Kixel didn't realise what was really happening. In a year, he could redeem himself.'

'You'd make excuses for the Lady of Death if she came for you,' Xhera retorted, but her tone was gentle.

'Do you have anything to say?' asked Councillor Brókova as Ulric sat.

Bradwr looked broken, as if his mind had snapped, and Karland was reminded that for all his manipulations and demands he was intrinsically brittle. The other four, standing apart from Aran, shook their heads, looking defeated.

Aran alone drew himself up.

'Indeed, Councillor,' he said. Even now his self-assurance was startling. 'Whatever my charges, I am a representative of the Great Houses of Novin and hold diplomatic status. I cannot be charged with any crime.'

'Young man,' said Councillor Brókova coldly, 'you mistake both the laws and your status here. You are not here as an envoy. You are here as a student. You have no diplomatic status past the bare minimum granted to a dignitary. Eordeland Law applies to you as it does to everyone here.' She gestured. 'There is the Novinian Ambassador. *He* is the envoy of your nation. *You* can be charged with whatever we deem fitting.'

Aran's face went pale for the first time. He had been so confident he could not be touched. Karland glanced over at the Novinian Diplomat. The man sat with his chin propped on his fist, clearly weary and perturbed. Stone-faced, he was stern and severe, long stubble showing under gaunt cheekbones with piercing blue eyes and sandy hair that thinned at the fore. He wore the full attire of a Novinian Noble.

'So these scum can choose freedom where a noble is left to rot?' shouted Aran. 'Novin will not stand for this outrage!'

'Silence!' called the Chamberlain.

'I will not-' the Guard next to him struck the back of his knee with his pike haft, cutting him off as he lurched. Before he could say anything else, the Ambassador sighed and stood, clearly weighing his words. The buzz of voices dipped. His face was blank of emotion apart from a faint regret as he stepped forward and waited. The Chamberlain gestured to the Council and received a nod. He moved to him, spoke softly and turned.

'The Novinian Ambassador requests to be heard by the Court.'

'Granted.'

The man's tone had the harsh, slightly guttural clipped nature of Novinian Darum.

'I have seen the evidence and cannot deny that Aran, Scion of House Telemer,' acted against the laws of this land and your University,' he said shortly. 'He has undermined my work here, and there is clear cause for his punishment. Although I find his sentence more than fair compared to the penalties he might face in our land, I am regretful to intercede on his behalf.

'I request, in the name of the goodwill between our realms, that you mitigate your sentence. Instead of sending him to Kingsgate, I ask you banish him from Eordeland. I will discuss reparations with you then journey with him back to Novin to face the shame of his House before I return. I ask you this so that we have no misunderstandings between our realms in these troubled times.'

'What?' hissed Xhera in outrage. Karland shushed her.

Looking at their faces, he had the feeling that the Council might have expected this to happen. In fact, with war looming it was probably better to expel him than give Novin an excuse to side with Meyar. It sounded as if they might win a concession into the bargain.

Councillor Brókova spoke with the others, receiving several nods and shakes of heads. The three Procurators were beckoned forward and briefly spoke as well.

Finally, a decision was reached, and she turned back to the court.

'Aran of House Telemer of Novin. Pending agreement, at the request of the Novinian Ambassador and in deference to his years of conduct and in the interests of diplomacy, your sentence is deferred upon your immediate absence from this realm. You are expelled with the greatest of prejudice from this University, The Sanctum, and Eordeland, your only possessions your family heirlooms and weapons. You will be taken under Guard to the borders of our land instead of Kingsgate prison. Should you ever set foot in Eordeland again, you shall immediately be bound and begin to serve the full term of your sentence. We request that, upon delivery of his charge to Novin, the Ambassador return here to take up his duties at what is a crucial time for diplomacy.'

'Is this acceptable to the Ambassador?' asked Tarqas.

He bowed. 'It is.'

'It is only their word!' cried Aran. 'The word of a low-born Guardsman and a wandering mercenary!'

'The word of a Captain-General of Eordeland and a warrior who both advises this Council, and-' Councillor Holmson showed his teeth, '-is known throughout Anaria for his honour. Someone you have on multiple occasions tried to bribe,' he considered notes, 'manipulate, coerce, entrap and outright *weasel* tutelage from, so your words show themselves to be hollow. Their testimonies and deeds are beyond reproof-' Aran tried to shout him down, and a Guard struck him hard in the stomach. He sank to his knees, almost retching, eyes bulging in disbelief. The Councillor and Ambassador ignored him. '-where yours are very much not.'

'I would like to point out that my family are marked in this land for a thousand years and more, and could be considered noble,' Nessa Contemus remarked, her dry voice cutting through the chamber. 'Having noble blood means nothing, young man. It is red, like anyone else's, and is as much as accident of birth as is destitution. Your continued assertion that it makes you somehow better is incorrect; it does not. In Eordeland, your actions are what you are judged on... and, right now, you are in Council Court. I suggest you consider this before your next utterance.'

Aran looked up hopelessly as the weight of the sentence sank in. He looked stunned.

'But, uncle-'

'Silence, boy!' snapped the Novinian Ambassador. 'You have caused me enough trouble. The court is in session, and I support their judgment fully.'

Disbelief on his face, Aran's shoulders slumped. Karland realised that he had been convinced that he would be exempt from punishment.

Uncle!

No wonder he had bragged about diplomatic immunity so much!

'Sentence has been passed. The remaining guilty have until sunset today to agree which path they will each take.' Councillor Brókova gestured to the Chamberlain. 'This matter is closed. Court is adjourned.'

The Chamberlain's Guard strode forward with him and struck the plate six times. The strikes echoed around the room, and then the prisoners were escorted out. Aran stood glaring sullenly, unmoving, and was forced forward by the Guard behind him. He staggered to a halt.

'Don't touch me, peasant,' he snarled, and walked out slowly, head high.

Bradwr turned as if he were the walking dead and stopped as he caught sight of Karland. His bruised face twisted.

'I hate you!' he shrieked suddenly, his eyes wild. 'You did this to me! *You!*

'You did this to yourself!' shouted Karland, not caring who heard. 'You're the worst person I've ever known. You don't deserve anyone's care!'

'You think you are so much better than me! You think your morals are so pure and good! How dare you treat me like this? How dare you get in the way of *my* life!'

'How dare you get in the way of anyone else's!' roared Karland, all the pent-up anger at his betrayals bursting out. He felt ugly doing it, but could not stop himself. Xhera squeezed his hand, in warning or support, he wasn't sure.

Bradwr's eyes bulged, and he lost all coherency as he cowered at Karland's fury. His parting shriek dwindled as he was dragged from the room, echoing in the chamber.

TWENTY-THREE

The uproar over the verdict had started to die down a little, but Karland and Xhera were still shadowed when they went to the marketplace. After the stress and difficulties, he had been given a week off to recover, and Xhera had two days spare. His side was sore and tight, but better than it should have been thanks to Master Darfin. He had more innate healing skill than Aldwyn, Karland realised, if less herblore.

They were both aware of the City Guards tailing them nonchalantly. Ever since the problems there had been concern that Aran had left other instructions in the city, and with the threat of Meyar looming, the concern that agents of Meyar might target them had grown. The city was not locked down yet. Short of casting out every trader and Teromen, until the city fell under martial law the possibility of insurgents remained.

Karland was tired of the attention. For someone who just wanted to get on with his studies, he had gained an uncomfortably high profile, dragged into the limelight over and over. Now he could be at risk from elements of Novin *and* Meyar.

Well, enough. Today they were finally going to the Hoard if they had to swim the wide, dark waters of the Eaofer to do so. It was a special day; Moonday, the seventeenth day of the month of Wher. He had almost forgotten in the upheaval.

Karland made his customary greeting to Györnàeldàr's statue, conscious that this time two Eordeland Guard veterans accompanied them, and they moved off, passing deep into the warren of shops.

He left Xhera looking through clothes and moved off with a particular destination in mind, one of the Guard trailing him. With any luck she wouldn't even notice he had gone.

It took a few minutes, but he found the stall; full of various personal ornaments for the fashionable. There were many for men, but far more for women, from circlets and chains that lay on the hair and forehead to headbands, combs, hairpins and nets. The one which had caught his eye some time previously, which he had desperately been saving money for, was an intricately carved ebony hair comb, slightly curved. Long and winding, it was in the shape of a dragon in flight. The dark colour reminded him of Köränthír, but the shape and poise reminded him more of Györnàeldàr.

Karland wasn't good at bargaining, unlike Xhera, but he tried to look uninterested. The clip was superb, almost seeming alive.

'Genuine Bloch, that,' said the shopkeeper. 'One of his early ones. Couldn't ask less than a Great.'

'A *Great?*' Karland gaped at him. That was insanely high. 'Um, one silver?' He had no idea if that was too much.

'Here.' The man turned it over. The carving *did* look like it said Bloch. 'That's worth four and a half, at least. More'n'at.'

Karland sighed and got down to the bargaining. He finally escaped with his pride intact, having paid two and a half silver, which was almost all he had. He wouldn't get his raven quill now, he thought ruefully.

If it *was* a Bloch it was still not a bad price, and it was a gorgeous piece. He looked at it admiringly, drinking in its form, and then closed his hand around it and wandered back to where he had left Xhera. She wasn't there. Casting around, he spied a serious little face intent on something further up the stalls and moved over.

'I, um. Thought you might like something today,' he said, trying to be casual. It was unfair how easily people like Seom did these things. This was his best friend, yet he still had a pit of anxiety in his gut. 'We can *definitely* visit the Hoard today. You know, spend the day. Together.'

Xhera smiled at him, and his heart skipped a beat. 'That would be wonderful! Just let me finish looking here-'

'I also… wanted to give you something that means something, uh,' his mouth ran dry, and he gave up. 'Well, it is your birthing day. Here.' He held his closed hand out.

'You remembered!'

'Hard to forget it.' He grinned and her eyes widened.

'Oh, you perfect shit! I forgot it was yours, too.' She looked mortified.

He smiled. 'Your reaction is all the present I need.' He waved his hand. 'Are you going to take this, or not?'

'What is it?' she said, as he dropped it into her open hand. 'Oh..!'

Her voice trailed off and she stared at it with a stricken look on her face. Karland immediately cursed himself. Either she hated it, or it had really upset her.

'If you don't like it, I can-'

She looked up at him, her eyes full of tears. When she spoke, her voice was subdued and thick with mixed emotions.

'This is beautiful. Oh, Karland. What would my life be without you?'

She hugged him and he felt tears on his neck. He hugged her back, unsure if he had done well or not.

'So... you like it?'

'I *love* it. Thank you.' She sniffed and let go, blinking. Holding up the comb, she marvelled at its polished perfection again, her eyes tracing the fine work, and then swept the hair on one side back and pulled back through before turning the teeth into her hair. It pulled the hair back from her face on the left, and left it cascading on the right, straight and dark.

It looked amazing. Karland couldn't believe how beautiful she was.

She saw his look and smiled.

'I'll do a better job later with some pins. Shall we go to the Hoard?'

'Yes,' he smiled, looking back to check that their guardians were lurking.

His heart soared as she took his hand and strolled with him, her other hand occasionally rising to touch the comb. It had utterly distracted her from her normal shopping.

'So how are you feeling?'

He shrugged as they walked. 'Relieved. Betrayed. Painful. Like I can't go out amongst the students. Happy it's over. If it is. I don't know.' He blew his cheeks out with a long exhale.

'Aran got what he deserved.' Xhera sniffed. 'Actually, he didn't. He deserved to rot in Kingsgate for the rest of his life.' The vehemence in her tone cut Karland until he remembered what had happened to her seven months ago. Aran's words and threats came to mind. He turned from the memories and shook his head.

'It's not him. It's Bradwr. I put so much trust in him. Treated him like my brother.'

'I thought you were a good judge of character,' said Xhera wryly.

He laughed briefly.

'Well. Mostly. I kind of knew what he was like, you know. Deep down. But... well. I thought I could guide him, help him. That there was good in him if he just had the chance. Never thought it would come back on me, too.'

'I never trusted him. He's a manipulator, a liar, an attention seeker. Even the Council said it. If you ask me, he deserved every bit of what he got. Finally might be of some real use to people. All the self-adulation in the world won't do him any good where he'll end up.'

'I hope he learns his lesson.'

'One way or the other, I'm sure he will. You need to let it go, Karland. He never was worth your care or time. You just needed to admit to yourself how disgusting he was.'

He sighed. 'Yeah. Still, plenty of people who think he is great though. His little crowd. Miscarriage of justice, and all that. I guess some people never wake up. Funny thing is, they're all like he was, interested only in validating each other. Fish of a school follow a fool.' He looked up at Xhera; one dark curve of hair had escaped the comb, dropping out and swooping past her jawline. 'Suits you.'

In a way he couldn't explain, either. That image of her was perfection; meant to be just so. Just the sight sent a tingle through him, almost as if it tickled the base of his lungs. She smiled at him, which didn't help ease it.

He didn't care.

They walked northeast from the square and markets, then north to the edges of the river. They moved over the arching bridge in the centre, watching the huge travelbarges moving slowly back and forth with their cargoes and people. On both banks the long docks and the surrounding crowded streets stretched either side of the main thoroughfare leading to the bridge. Those were areas it was best not to travel alone, but the bridge and main streets were well-patrolled.

The river here was nearly six hundred feet across. The bridge arched high enough that anything smaller than a tallship could sail under it, although Darost tended to be the final point for any large ships coming upriver.

They walked along with the crowds, staying to the left. All day there was traffic over the bridge; The houses of money opened in the early morning, and stayed open until nearly dusk, encouraging people to come and lodge their cash with them instead of leaving it under the floorboards. Whilst the meat and food and general wares shipped on the south bank, the north bank had its own, more exclusive docks for the transfer of fine goods in smaller quantities, gold and silver, and other luxuries. Karland knew from Castellan James that all kohfee came into the north bank.

The Hoard was arranged almost like a tree, with the main street moving north and roads branching off this, with other roads branching off those. There were no road signs; instead, each major bank house had a symbol outside it. Further back in the branch streets were the mansions of the very rich, set in huge grounds; the merchants, moneylenders, and the once-noble. Some of these approached palaces.

Karland and Xhera wandered up and down the streets, looking around in wonder. The richness and cleanliness of the streets was stark in comparison to most of the city.

Not just banks lay here either; exclusive eateries, kohfee houses, even some warehouses lined the streets. Large squares with well-tended parks lay at many junctions. Almost all the buildings had their own security, though the most dangerous-looking tended to be on the steps of the banks. Karland saw a lot of very large men in smart dark red uniforms with a totally different design to the Eordeland Guard. They stood at bank doors and even on street corners near Eordeland City Guard, giving the impression of cold, dangerous professionalism, and watched passers-by carefully.

Several times the brutal-looking men stepped towards them as if to move them along before seeing the Welcomer Guard and slinking back, many scowling. Karland got the distinct impression many were eager to have an argument, and he wasn't sure the Guards would be upset.

'Who are they?' he asked Henne, a stone-faced man with perpetual stubble and a scar on his upper left lip.

'Praetors. Bank Guards, though they patrol the whole Hoard like it's their damn front yard.' He almost spat to the side and then thought better of it; spitting on the streets was forbidden. 'Private bloody army, you ask me. They don't like us interfering with bank business.'

'In the banks they're the law. Out here, they obey it. They don't like that much,' remarked the other guard, eying the Praetors warily.

It was an interesting morning, although they were not permitted into any of the real banks, which were accessible by appointment or invitation only. The gilded doors were rich and thick, iron-lined and solid. Karland caught a brief glance inside one as a luxuriously dressed lady left, catching an impression of high, rich architecture, paintings, and expensive furniture.

They took lunch at one eatery, which served sandwiches, kohfee and tea, and other small meals. The price was astounding, as much as two day's meals in the market. The premises were bordering one of the squares, this one with statues of the founding fathers of two banks lining it.

Tempted as Karland was by the kohfee-houses, he resisted, not really having a taste for the bitter black liquid yet. The most famous was Regimund's, a multi-floor house near the centre. Once supposedly a rich man's dog-fighting ring for the city mongrels, now it was one of the most illustrious places for casual business in the city. It was said deals that changed the world were made there.

Karland couldn't imagine himself in such a place.

The richness of the architecture and quality of the materials was astonishing. Marble, stone like The Sanctum's, granite, sandstone - all abounded, towering into the sky. Behind these were the abodes of the ultra-rich, hiding the huge city walls from sight. It was like being in another world; one that had no time or respect for you unless you already had riches.

In fact, the district was almost monotonous once you had seen the squares, the architecture, the side streets. The people. Everything was designed around showing how much money existed there, a display of material wealth and status. The people who passed them mostly had expressions of aloof busyness, a focus beyond the ken of rabble. They acted as if Karland and Xhera simply weren't there.

It was odd, not to be rich enough to exist.

In a way, it was an overload for Karland. It was so alien, as if they were saltwater fish moving below a bright freshwater world they could never be a part of. It was fascinating, alluring, but cold and impersonal. There were no Gods here except coin.

Soon enough, they decided it was time to go. Karland had ticked off a visit to the Hoard, a name he knew Györnàeldàr would have laughed at; there was nothing here a dragon would be interested in.

Unless it were hungry, he thought gleefully.

It wasn't until they had crossed almost completely back over the bridge that they became aware of the rising noise.

Bells and wailings were sounding across Darost. The great Church of Terome's deep bell was tolling non-stop. To their right, west of the bridge, lay the majority of the temples and Churches. They were surrounded by poorer parts of the city which extended down to the docks. It was from here a faint buzzing noise could be heard, as if thousands of people were speaking.

They stepped off the end of the bridge into a susurration of anger. The crowds were thicker to the west, gathered all along the loose rough borders of the poorer parts.

Guards stood everywhere. More arrived as they watched. No one was fighting, not yet, but the atmosphere was charged. Karland turned to look at one of his shadows, and they motioned him on.

'Keep moving, lad. Back to The Sanctum. This is no place to linger.'

Karland glanced at the massed people, pushing against the ranks of the guards and falling back, arguing, shouting. There must be thousands of them.

He saw one man push through the crowd nearby, shrugging off hands to confront one of the Guards.

The man stared at the Guard for a moment, then spat on him.

'Murderers,' he called, lips and voice trembling. The Guards moved in, faces blank, ready to arrest him, and the crowd shifted uneasily.

The Sergeant in charge stopped them.

'Sir,' he said more calmly than Karland could have, 'I know you're angry. But we didn't do this. If you do that again, we'll be forced to take you in, so don't.'

'Don't come into our district,' said the man. 'I fear for my family.' He raised his voice. 'Murderers! They'll come and take you, too!'

'Go home,' said the sergeant tiredly.

'Walk on, lad,' said Henne softly. Karland glanced at Xhera to see her pale face reflecting his worry. They moved on towards the low dome of The Sanctum.

What can have happened?

૦૩　　ৎ৹

'Riots sparking across Darost.' Councillor Jameson shook his head. The Council had been called to an urgent meeting in the tower chamber. It was late, and there was neither time nor inclination to climb the Dodecagon.

So far, only Tarqas and Ulric had arrived.

'What the hells is going on?' rumbled Ulric. 'As if we didn't have enough to deal with.'

'We have just received word that the Holy Voice of Terome has been murdered. Nearly a week ago. It is said the Eordeland Ambassador did it.'

'Murdered! He was our best ally there.' Ulric shook his shaggy head. 'Is it likely?'

'No,' said Jameson. 'I am certain. The Ambassador was just a civil servant. None of his retinue were assassins.' His gaze flicked around and held theirs for a moment. 'Or otherwise. Although they say he was found with irrefutable evidence against him, I don't believe he was involved.'

'What does he say in his defence?'

'He was torn apart by a mob, Ulric. When the commoners thought that he had killed the most beloved man in the Territories… His Guard were all tortured and put to death. It is hard to ascertain how much the Meyari Government was involved. I suspect they seized an opportunity… or created one.'

'Shit.'

'So, what now?' asked Tarqas.

'We've been condemned at the highest levels by Meyar and used as an example. *Eordeland wants to rule the continent,* they say. *We have struck to their heart, liars and murderers. We will bring war to all the lands.*'

'Other realms know this isn't true. Theon Dorine is the second of our scholars to be murdered there on official business.'

'And they don't care. If we are weakened, we are in serious trouble. We can face Meyar; can we face Meyar, and their Church… and Novin, and perhaps Banistari as well? What if these orcs attack from the Iril Eneth at the same time?'

Ulric scowled. 'Right now, with civil unrest, orc bands, and Banistari sniffing our borders, we would be lucky to be able to split our forces enough to take on Meyar and their Church without serious casualties. If the orcs resurface, we could lose part of Eordeland.'

'There is no debate here,' said Tarqas. 'Our Ambassador was killed by a mob, without trial or intervention. The first time a scholar was murdered - regrettable enough. This time an official diplomatic envoy was slain by the people! Meyar owed him their protection.'

'So?'

'So, there is no way that we can deny we are at war now. We *must* respond. We cannot have anything less than full military control of streets and law. Meyar will attack.'

The rest of the Council began filtering in, and Ulric grimaced.

'Better *you* break this to them,' he said shortly, and stomped to his chair, scowling.

☙　❧

Xhera wandered towards the quarters of the elves the next day, thinking. That morning they had been told that Karland would leave with Rast when he journeyed west, and she felt as if a pit of loneliness had opened up before her. She had begged to go along too but been told someone had to continue Aldwyn's work.

Alaria, the leader of the Elven contingent, had visited her later in her room as she sat staring at the wall, withdrawn.

She was ageless, kind, and wise, and very beautiful, almost seeming ethereal. She looked exactly as she had in the vision from the Portal in the Hall of Wyrms. Xhera didn't really remember her, and it bothered her.

Alaria had touched her face gently, and said she was glad Xhera had grown well. Xhera had felt peace at her touch, but it was tinged with sadness. The elf was one of the only links to that night, and she recalled nothing that her vision had not shown her, as if it had all happened to someone else.

She didn't remember her parent's faces.

They had spoken, and without meaning to, Xhera had found herself pouring out her heart in a way she hadn't done even with Karland. Normally so guarded, it was as if her emotions were a flood. It was cathartic, but it had also exhausted her, and she had cried.

'You were very young,' Alaria had said, stroking her hair. 'I see something special in you, Xhera. Be strong. You have much yet before you.'

They had spoken more. Alaria was pleased her sister was well. 'I repaired her body of the damage that night, but her mind has not fully healed,' she said sadly. 'She will not allow herself to see clearly.'

Xhera had left feeling oddly unsure of herself, wanting to talk to someone who would understand. She had wandered aimlessly, as Karland often did, and ended up at the room assigned to the elves, her thoughts untethered. She wasn't sure why; the elves were mostly out around The Sanctum today. She only knew that she didn't want to talk about it with Karland, or Rast, but to someone who was not really connected with any of it. Darus was training with Rast, and she had no idea where Night went during the day.

Nevertheless, she was here. Xhera nodded to the guards in the corridor and raised her hand to knock, before she heard a soft lilting song. She instead pushed the door open gently and walked in, closing it.

Lëlylien was sitting on the balcony at the far end of the large room, clasping her knees. She was on the wide railing, balancing without even thinking on the edge of the long drop. For a human it would have been dangerous. For the elf, it was as if she sat on the floor.

She was half-whispering a haunting melody to herself. It was one of the most musical sounds Xhera had ever heard, tugging at the strings of her soul, especially at this vulnerable moment. She moved forward, unable to take her eyes from Lëlylien.

Her beautiful eyes were distant. You could almost take her for a statue, such was her perfection of features. Xhera felt a mix of emotions whenever she looked upon the elf maiden.

She was so flawlessly lovely it was painful. The knowledge that Xhera would never, could never look like her, move like her, possess such poise, grace and beauty was like the envious sharpness of a knife thrust into her soul.

The other dichotomous edge was an aching joy to gaze upon her; to hear and see the melody of an elf, to have her life made more, simply by being near her. Xhera experienced it with all the elves, men and women, but there was something lost about this timeless elf maiden in particular that sharpened it. They felt like forever green sunlight through leaves.

Lëlylien continued to sing to herself, and Xhera felt her eyes pricking with the emotion of words she couldn't understand. She was spellbound. Finally, Lëlylien stopped and sighed.

'What was that?' asked Xhera quietly, aware that tears had tracked down her face and wiping them hurriedly.

'*Fórnur a Naeg;* The Anguish of Fórnur,' replied Lëlylien. 'Once to have been the brightest star of our people. All his potential, his life… wasted.'

'He died?'

'Eventually. He was a lost soul long before breath stilled. He should have been the greatest man of his age; an enchanter, a mage, a weaver, call it what you will. All his talents never came to be; he wasted away, half-mad. We have never forgotten the first time chaos destroyed the harmony of our people and changed us forever. Many thousands of years later, we still remember his tragedy; a tragedy like no other in our history.' She smiled sadly. 'Until now.'

Xhera could see Lëlylien had become melancholy, almost adrift. The other elves had changed subtly after they had discovered Night, less mirthful and more wary, but this was different. It was a deeper wound, a depression, almost. Xhera hoped it would heal.

'Do you mean… the fallen elves?'

She remembered them, so like the elf in front of her, yet so different, as if a shadow was across them. The ritual scars on one, the strange armour, the cold, emotionless faces. She wondered fearfully then at the blackness upon Lëlylien.

'Yes. The *mornedhel.* The elves you said were somehow *dark.*' She shivered, but her anger, her distress, seemed distant. 'I was… distraught. When first you spoke of them. It has never happened before, not like this. That my kin could fall… yet still be elves. That perhaps even my sister-' she sighed. 'I have no contentment. I will find them and seek to bring them back to harmony. Or…' she turned to look at Xhera, who nearly gasped at the depth of pain in her eyes. '…or let them go.'

Xhera had been wrong. There was still terrible anger there, too. She fervently hoped that Lëlylien could find harmony again. None of the other elves had reacted like this.

'Humans are lucky, Xhera. You sleep. You lose your pain for a while. Elves do not sleep. We have no way to turn our minds from their thoughts.' She blinked her glorious eyes slowly, and a faint crease appeared on her flawless brow. 'I will seek the council of High elves, on Míthtól. To be in the heartland of my people will aid me, I think. I will discover the fate of my sister. But if it is as I fear… I will never accept it.'

She turned her head back again, her eyes trained on the past, and began humming. This time it was a different tune, less mournful. To Xhera it felt as if it were recalling days long gone, and she left Lëlylien to her reminiscing, her questions unasked. Her problems seemed so much less, now, and she felt she was intruding.

As she left the room, she encountered Galnór approaching in the corridor. He smiled in greeting.

'Xhera.'

'I… I just left Lëlylien. I was hoping to ask you to… look after Karland.' Xhera felt troubled, her concerns split.

'We will.' He regarded her gravely. 'Are you well?'

'Yes. I just… I feel a little lost.'

Galnór sighed softly. 'As do we all, at times.'

'Galnór, I worry about Lëlylien,' she said softly.

He nodded, his face sad.

'As do I. There is great disharmony within her. I have seen elves fade for less. I pray it is does not grow worse… that she does not become that which she hates.'

'She hopes to find peace with your people in Míthtól.'

I pray it will be so, Xhera. And I pray you keep safe here without us, in the company of your…' he looked uncomfortable, '-Seeker.'

'He has protected us before,' she said. 'I sense nothing but a sadness from him. I do not think he is a monster.'

'Perhaps not,' sighed Galnór. 'Perhaps not. But be wary. The elves know the price these creatures have extracted. It was greater than we could bear.'

'I will.' She shook her head, her heart thumping again for no reason.

He regarded her with compassion. 'Find your centre tonight, Xhera. Seek Karland and Rast, and spend your time with them. I know this is not good timing, but… the Council has decided that we leave tomorrow.'

Xhera stared.

So soon?

Her heart lurched. 'Excuse me,' she mumbled. 'I… I have to talk to Karland.' The need to leave was suddenly too great to bear.

Galnór nodded, his eyes full of understanding.

'Tomorrow, then, daughter of Valesgate.'

TWENTY-FOUR

Just after dawn Rast and Karland met with Darus and the elves in the small square before the main Darost gates. Xhera had come with him to say goodbye.

The gatehouses formed two huge towers with battlements extending inwards, the long open bailey set with a wide, more typical portcullis gate the other end that he hadn't really noticed before. The first time he had passed through, it had teemed with merchants and travellers, hiding its length and how sheer the walls either side were. Now he realised how strong the fortifications were. If the two-foot thick main gate was breached - something that seemed unlikely, given how strong it was even without the portcullis - the bailey would be a killing ground for hundreds.

Drawn up in smart squads before the thirty-foot tall ironwood doors were the forces to go with them to Eyotsburg. Karland hadn't realised there would be so many. He had assumed a company might be fifty soldiers; instead, two hundred were lined up in formation, sixteen squads of twelve veterans each led by a sergeant, five Lieutenants commanding platoons of three squads each.

There were sixty pikemen, two squads of which had long oddly-curved blades which Karland thought were war-scythes. They also carried very short swords hung far back on their belts rather than directly at their sides. Next to them were another sixty-eight infantry soldiers with shield, short sword and short spear. Behind those were forty-eight archers with their feared Eordeland Recurve bows and short swords. They each carried two sheaves of long wooden arrows, with more on the supply wagon. Further back stood a squad of the famed Eordeland Crosses and their large crossbows. Short swords and Goat's Feet for recocking quickly hung from their belts, and they carried two sheaves of metal bolts each.

At van and rear were half-squads of Pathfinders in light leathers on hobbies, the delicately-framed horses showing more nervous energy than the dun courser ridden by the Captain and the majestic dark bay destrier the Major rode just in front of them. They carried small, strongly recurved horse bows and a single quiver along with a slim, light straight-sabre. From what Karland understood they didn't really act as a unit, instead trained to independence and initiative.

At the rear were six soldiers in white uniforms. Karland knew that having a half-squad of healers was unheard of outside Eordeland; most armies relied on camp medics for battle injuries, and hoping the soldiers lived when injured. Eordeland's healer corps were specially trained infantry that showed an aptitude for medicine, and were as respected as other specialist units. They cut down field deaths drastically, and although they were as well-trained in battle as any other infantry - indeed, they were drawn from existing troops - their duty was to stay safe and care for those injured.

Centred in front of the wagons and mules was a single squad of sappers. Karland knew they were valuable and would be risked in combat no more than the healers, able to do anything from build war engines to destroy enemy fortifications. They carried two hatchets, one large and long handled and one smaller, the reverse of both flat for use as a hammer. He had heard that they could use these for almost any task needed, from felling trees and shaping engines, to throwing at enemies or butchering them. Many enemies had underestimated Eordeland sappers in combat. They also carried what looked like an ingenious folding spade.

Major Gambeson and Captain Aldine stood at the fore, Sergeant-Major Thorne on a skewbald rouncey to the rear, just behind two large wagons hitched to two huge draft horses apiece. They were almost double the weight of brave little Hjarta, Karland estimated.

One wagon was covered in a frame which allowed white healer's canvas to be erected to cover medicines and wounded, the other holding supplies. A third of the space was taken by spare weapons, equipment, and officer's tents. The rest was taken by the rations of dried beans and sprouts, salted meat, cheese, twice-baked campaign tack and two large barrels of fresh water which should see them at least to the shores of Lake Merrimakea, although the troops carried their own rations too. The wagons were light enough that they were manned by a healer each, the rest of whom were arrayed around them, ready to take turns on the reins.

He looked at Ironwood Company of the Azures. It was the first time he had seen any of the army arrayed, and he thought they looked very impressive and professional. If they had been at The Croft, he guessed the orcs would have been quickly broken.

The commanders sat astride, Captain Aldine's half-plate and leather looking like it was freshly polished, and Major Gambeson's half-plate and chain etched and decorated. They both had longswords and shields, the Major's hilt and lower blade intricately inlaid with silver. His brass-decorated barbute rested on the saddle's front plate, the base flaring out like a sallet and the top forming a small crest at the crown of short blue-dyed feathers. His cloak was emblazoned with the white symbol of Eordeland on his battalion colour, a deep azure. It was impressive, but Karland couldn't shake the thought that the symbolic open book with the pages curling up into flames looked quite like an onion.

Each Battalion had a colour, each company within it having a name and a symbol. They wore that colour in the field, and there was fierce competition between them for honours. Karland had seen some of them in the barracks around The Sanctum - Bronze, Teal, Scarlet and Azure were common, and he had seen others he guessed were Forest, Fire, and Shadow. Inside The Sanctum he rarely saw anything other than Welcomer Guards, whose colour was a cream-ivory trim, and the jet black of the Onyx Guard.

All the troops were fitted with hardened leather armour, the archers having just the chestpieces and bracers. The infantry had formed pieces to protect arms and legs, and segmented steel plates fixed to the leather on the breast, backs and faulds. Karland had been fitted for it. It was heavier than it looked, but not so heavy it couldn't be marched in.

The infantry and pikemen wore steel barbutes with nasals. The archers and crosses had open-faced steel sallets, as did the sappers, who like the healers otherwise wore simple leather armour and no arm guards, only missing the green leaf of a healer on the chest.

Karland caught sight of Kith and Gen, and recognised a few other guards. They were all ready to depart; he felt like a pretender when he saw the horses he and Rast had waiting for them. There was no horse for Darus, who towered over even Rast, but Karland had grown used to orks running alongside horses. Darus would likely be able to travel another hundred miles after the last of them had collapsed in exhaustion, horse or no.

The elves also had no steeds. Rast said they used horses to travel, but they had volunteered to help scout and preferred to do so on foot.

Ulric had turned out, looking slightly haggard in the early morning light, with Captain Dorn.

Captain-General, Karland reminded himself. His heart hammered with nerves again. He wasn't sure he wanted to leave.

Courage, he thought to himself.

They were speaking to the Major and Captain, and Ulric waved Rast over. Karland realised quite finally that they were leaving once more; the stability and companionship of the last eight months would be replaced with hardship and danger, and this time he would be leaving Xhera to her own equally important task.

He heard a gulp and turned to find her standing with her face twisted strangely. She looked so beautiful, so strong, and seeing her so upset was heartbreaking for him.

In an attempt to stop himself doing the same, he dug out one of the keys to the Library of Thingos and the map he had drawn up last night with the directions to get there from The Croft.

'I nearly forgot these,' he said with a shaky laugh, and handed them to her. She nodded and clasped them tightly, then hugged him hard. He felt his eyes prickle.

'Hurry back,' she whispered in his ear, and sniffed quietly. The ebony comb she wore in her hair dug into his temple, but he didn't care.

'I will,' he promised. Suddenly there was so much he wanted to say, but with everyone there, he couldn't find a way to say it. He wanted to tell her to be safe, to not forget him; that he cared for her, that he wanted more than their deep friendship. Her breath was warm on his neck in the cold morning, and he inhaled deeply, realising he might not see her again.

And that was the crux. Was it worth not saying something, when it might then never be said?

Courage, he said again, but this time it was much harder. It took more bravery than it had to face orcs and assassins. Before his nerve could fail, he forced the words out.

'Xhera... I wish... I wish I was more to you.' He finished in a rush.

She drew back to look at him, tears fresh in her eyes, her face puzzled as well as sad. 'You are everything to me, Karland.'

A lump of - self-pity? Emotion? - welled up in his throat, and he stammered, his heart pounding at his own words.

'I mean... I wish I was *more.'* The word held volumes, he knew. Sudden doubts assailed him.

He didn't say he loved her. He couldn't bring himself to say it, and the words didn't seem enough - but he knew it was true. He thought about her here, without him, with other boys interested in her, with the threat of war, and couldn't stay quiet.

'I feel like... if I leave... I will lose you before I find you.' That made no sense. He tried again. 'I... ah. I care about you more than anyone else, Xhera. I wish that... that you felt the same, but I understand if - if you find someone-'

Her lips cut his words off.

They were as sweet as he had dreamed, as soft as he had wondered, and as fragrant to him as the sweetest rose. His own lips parted in surprise, and the tip of her tongue touched his briefly before she pulled back, her eyes shining even more, her face so red it was flaming.

'Read my lips,' she whispered, her mouth quivering. 'You are *everything* to me. Come back. Or I have *nothing*.'

She sobbed suddenly, burying her head into his neck. A tear fell from his own eye, the upwelling of emotion catching him by surprise. The lump in his throat was painfully in the way of him speaking again.

One last muffled sob reached him. Then she was gone, running back towards The Sanctum along the main thoroughfare, her warmth fading with her scent.

Karland didn't know what to say, what to think. Something he hadn't even dared hope was there, but still out of his reach.

How cruel is fate, he thought. *I wasted so much time. If I'd only known before.* His throat throbbed with the lump in it.

He was considering telling Rast he would stay here when a powerful hand fell comfortingly on his shoulder, and he looked up into the big man's face. Grim it might be much of the time, but right now it was also kindly, and there was something else there; something almost like a faint wistfulness.

'Never doubt her care for you,' Rast said quietly. 'Or her admiration for your duty.'

And there it was.

If he stayed, he wouldn't lose her admiration, might in fact have what he had always yearned for with the only person he wanted it with. He had sworn to keep her safe, could stay to do just that - not that she needed it much now. She was as able as him in a fight. But he would still have the respect he had already earned, and no one, not even Rast, would judge him for not going.

No one except Karland himself.

His promise to Aldwyn; his promise to be there for Xhera. What good would staying do if the world fell apart and war killed them both? If he was killed here in front of her? If he trusted her to find in her own studies what would save their people and more, if he could make a difference by going - how then could he not go?

'It is a hard choice, Karland, between duty and living.' The words carried a deep compassion and understanding. Rast indicated the nearby ranks of soldiers, some of whom were watching Karland with grins, others with impatience. Karland felt his face flame and wondered how long everyone had been waiting. 'I take it you are ready?'

Karland stammered, and then caught sight of Dorn and Ulric. Dorn winked.

The tear was drying, and suddenly he didn't give a shit if anyone saw it. It was a mark of his care for her, and by the Gods people could see the damn thing on his cheek.

The lump in his throat had eased somewhat.

'Let's go,' he said firmly.

He kept his eyes on where she had vanished until he was mounted and moving to follow the officers through the gates, and swore to himself.

I will return. I will be there for you.

I love you.

He drew his dagger on impulse and sliced down the old light scar on the fleshy base of his thumb, the one he had made with Seom when they were too young to understand what truly being blood-brothers was about. Blood welled up from the scratch, and he swore his oath on his own vital fluid.

He looked up to see Rast watching. Flushing, he cleaned the blade, and then realised he had no binding cloth ready. Rast leaned over and handed him some he had already taken from a pouch, his face expressionless. Karland didn't know whether he approved or otherwise. It might have been foolish to slice his own skin at the outset of a journey when he had to hold reins, but he didn't care, right then, and this determination didn't feel like the childish resolve he used to feel when going against his father's wishes.

Some things were more important than common sense, and it felt his adult choice to make. He nodded to Rast. An eyebrow raised, and a slight smile appeared, as if to acknowledge his choice.

'I hope the trip isn't too long,' he said.

'South of the Arkons there should be little danger. Darus will speak with the orks; I carry a missive from the Council of Twelve to the Citadel Conclave requesting a fast ship, and Galnór and Lëlylien will help us put the case to the elves of *Mithtól*. We should be there quickly, and our return even quicker. It depends on the elves. Take heart, Karland.'

Eyotsburg lay almost a month and a half distant. From there, it would likely be another forty days or so round trip to the Isles east of Mithtol by Eyotsburg ship. Hopefully the journey back without the troops would be less than a month, but it might be more than one hundred and twenty days before he once more set foot in the city.

They departed Darost more calmly than the last time, in the morning rather than late in the night. There was no lockdown in effect, although there was a great deal of Guard presence. The trickle of people into the city could be cut off at a moment's notice if an enemy was spotted approaching from the towers one hundred feet above the high walls.

Nevertheless, there was a great sense of déjà vu. They were leaving again to seek help, on a quest that no one else could really undertake. At least this time they stood a better chance of returning, as long as they could avoid the massing armies of Meyar.

Although Karland was aware in the back of his mind of the great honours and deeds he had been part of and would always carry - and the dangers that might lie ahead - his heart lay behind him.

He would have thought that finding his love requited after so much childish - and adult - hope would have completed him, finally, and in a way, it had, but it had also riven and shocked him. Part of him felt left behind, hopeless, lost; he knew he would not feel complete again until he saw her, and could finally experience everything he'd ever hoped for.

As he rode, sunken deep into the morass of his inner thoughts, they passed through the gates. He glanced to the left as they moved over the massive drawbridge, remembering the damage to the wall and gatehouse from the impact of Györnàeldàr's fall, now repaired. The large mound of grass was still there, bulging up out of the water in front of the wall. As far as anyone knew, there was nothing of her left there; but despite having marred somewhat the symmetry of the defences, it had been left as a mark of respect, although the statue of Györnàeldàr was mounted in the middle of the great square.

The veritable town outside the gates had been cleared in preparation for war, everyone having been brought inside. There were no stalls or buildings, and the stone-lined moat had been cleared before the great river gates opened either end of the city to allow water to flow swiftly around the foot of the walls, providing a wide moat with a good current.

Underbrush had been cleared away, exposing the huge chains for the drawbridge lying semi-slack to either side, freshly greased. Darost was preparing for war, and the famed defences were ready, even after decades.

Looking back, Karland saw the massive gatetowers which held the twin great portcullis halves on huge steel rods. If released, they would swing down behind the great ironwood gates around the city, themselves virtually impenetrable, and latch together on impact, impossible to part without the keys and winches to release them from inside.

It had been centuries since Darost had needed her defences, but they had been kept working. The Sanctum itself had its own strong fortifications - high walls and cunning weaponry, as well as ways of totally blocking the Combic Libraries and keeping the knowledge therein safe from harm for future generations.

The Greatway west had few travellers on it now. It was clear that in these times many paid heed to the rumbles of war. Oddly, inside the city, many merchants and richer citizens were not only unworried but actually pleased at the prospect; quite a few of them saw chances of profit.

Some of the scholars were keen to see what innovations came from this war, one of the tutors saying it was a sad fact that in man's ever-continuing struggle to find excuses and methods to kill as many of his fellows as possible, many new ideas and technologies that later benefited society arose.

Many others seemed to be unfazed by the prospect of war. As Karland had heard someone say, it was all very far away, and Darost had not come under attack for generations. Even when people mentioned the raids by bandits and orcs in the countryside, they generally shrugged unless they had family out there.

Out of sight, out of mind.

He thought he understood what they meant. If he hadn't been through the battle of The Croft, and seen thousands of orcs, he would have dismissed it all as well. Safety and comfort became habitual.

The journey was set at a fair pace. Alongside the horses ran Darus, with the high sweat and endless stamina of his people, breathing deeply and regularly. Karland knew he could run like that almost until he dropped dead from heat exhaustion.

The elves paced lightly to the side as the party travelled, talking with each other and Rast. Something in Lëlylien's alien beauty and serious face reminded him of Xhera, although they did not look alike. Karland was still fascinated with them; they were flowing streams next to Rast's deep river.

Captain Aldine rode bolt upright just ahead. He seemed quite acerbic and methodical to Karland, although he wasn't unpleasant. He just got the impression that he very much like things to go by the book, and if they didn't, he would ensure they did.

They moved for hours, passing several small villages and turnoffs, and then following the southwestern road toward the plains. The great western road curved up to their right, leading to the markets of Gladsmoor, and beyond that, The Croft and the great Northing Woods. Karland looked northwest, hoping that his family were well, and that they would look after Xhera. He hoped his mother did not embarrass him too much with stories, although he suspected she would. Becka was kind and welcoming, and loved Xhera.

The roads were well kept, level, and in the case of the Greatway leading to the borders, paved with great flat stones in very good condition. Not as many people moved as last time Karland had travelled it, but there were still many merchants and traders. To their right was a wider track; the Greatway had a second trail alongside which was for herds going to the Gladsmoor markets. Herders were fined for pats on the main road. He wondered what they did with horses.

They made good time the first day, stopping at an army outpost some twenty-seven miles from Darost manned by a grizzled old soldier and two reserve privates.

One of the soldiers told him that there were many of these, positioned out of obvious view along major routes throughout Eordeland and capable of housing anywhere from a few to several hundred soldiers for a night. The keepers were generally semi-retired or reserve units, if there were any at all, and they kept a small amount of supplies on hand and passed along news. They also had secure areas for mail, one incoming to the cities and one outgoing; designated couriers for the Eordeland Messengers would collect it when they passed either way. If army units that were en route to a location could take them instead, they did.

Karland considered the process amazing. The letters which he had sent Seom and the replies he had received had all passed through these. Towns and villages would periodically entrust their packages and letters to friend or relatives travelling to a larger town. These larger towns ran their own service to drop and collect mail to the nearest outpost, many of them treating it like a competition. The great sorting house in Darost had direct mail wagons to and from the sorting houses in other cities, and mail was directed to towns, then collected by villages and steadings.

By and large, the system worked very well; it was rare for friends or family to not deliver, and the reputation of towns depending on delivery meant that they were also relatively reliable. The couriers themselves were beyond reproach; it was a serious crime to interfere with mail for anyone, and doubly so for them. They were very carefully trained and evaluated. The Gods help anyone caught tampering with wax seals on mail, packages; even worse, the clay *bullae* carrying money or contracts. Getting to *those* meant you attacked a trained party of warriors.

Messengers were allowed to kill at their judgement to protect the contents and were trained as Guards. In fact, many were recruited to and from the Welcomer Guards themselves.

The upshot was that you could post a letter to a friend in a village the other end of Eordeland and be reasonably sure of a secure reply within a month. It was far and away the most efficient service in Anaria; probably all of Kuln.

He thought of his family, how long it had been since last he wrote to them and felt a large twinge of guilt. He hoped they stayed safe.

He thought of Seom, hoped his friend survived the war he knew was building. Perhaps one day they could sit again, with Xhera, and talk and laugh.

It wasn't much to ask, after all. Such a simple thing.

The distant bustle of the city was removed, the crackle of the fire a counterpoint to the quiet murmur of the soldiers. Karland watched the elves and Rast, and talked to Darus a little, largely about things that had happened before with Grukust, but his mind wasn't on any of them.

He was trying to recapture the feel of soft lips - *had it really happened?* - of serious eyes and skin he yearned to caress, of a mind that challenged and enticed him, and the thought of a pale firm body, only glimpsed before, perhaps - just perhaps - shared with him intimately in beautiful balance to that grim memory.

The thought made him shiver. He turned away from the lust he felt before it caused him physical issues and thought again about the purity of young love.

Right then, the promise of those eyes, lips and heart meant more than breasts and physical pleasure; the promise of having a matching part of his soul found that he had long known was missing.

They were pleasant dreams.

The next morning, he could not focus well on his exercises, and eventually gave up and waited for the basic training with Rast.

'Focus, boy,' the big man said more than once. They worked on evasions of weapons, Rast using a wooden stick. After he had thumped Karland several times, he dropped it and stood patiently watching him.

'You are many times dead this morning, and with little effort from me. Go. Eat. Clear your head. I will not be so gentle this evening.'

છ　　જ

The further they travelled from Darost, the gayer the elves seemed and the happier the big ork became. A small part of Karland felt the same, happy to travel again, but a larger part of him became morose, almost homesick in a way he wasn't with The Croft. He had come to regard Darost every bit as much his home, but his heart lay wherever Xhera was.

He kept replaying their last meeting in his mind. At first, it had buoyed him up with delight, but eventually, as always, a poisonous worm of self-doubt crept back in, whispering.

He had misunderstood; perhaps she had said it to try and make him feel better; even if she meant it, she'd probably change her mind. After all, plenty of better-looking young men in The Sanctum had liked her.

A sick feeling took root in his stomach and gnawed at him every day.

What if they wooed her? What if Seom did?

What if you're an idiot, he thought disgustedly, but the thoughts would not leave his gut. Deep down he knew he didn't deserve her. And what was there to really see in him? Things people had said to him over his life returned to haunt him, reinforcing the sickly little voice.

He wasn't good enough. Worthless. Not attractive. Awkward. Not smart.

He wasn't anything, really.

Nearly half a year was a long time. Anything could happen.

He thought of her every day, and brooded more and more, swinging between distraction, panic, self-loathing and depression.

Eventually Rast sat with him one evening, his presence comforting as always.

'Thinking too much again?' he asked softly. Karland nodded miserably. The big man chuckled and shook his head slightly.

'You are introspective in the worst way, boy. You over-think, as if you are outside yourself looking in. Don't make things difficult by seeing what isn't real. It is hard enough to deal with what is really there.'

'That's just it,' said Karland despairingly. 'What is really there just isn't anything. I've been fooling myself for a while. Thinking I could learn from you when you could have chosen a much better student. That I could be something to her, that I am better than I always thought. But I'll never be what I dream of being. Eventually I always realise that I'm… just *me*. I'm nothing special. Never have been, never will be.'

'You are honourable, and you care about others. You do things generously, for friendship alone. You are a skilled student, with a quicker mind than I. Already you have seen and done things most others never will. She believes in you, as do I. You have great potential, Karland, and worth, if only you would see it.'

His words struck the barrier Karland had formed around himself and slid off. He shook his head uselessly.

'Nothing I do makes a difference, Rast. I try to be good and fair. To achieve things. It doesn't matter. People tear you down whatever you do. I'm not as good as you think.'

'My position to judge these things is better than yours,' said Rast. He smiled. 'We all have doubts sometimes. Doubts and urges are something everyone must deal with. It is what you do despite them that defines who you truly are - not that they exist.'

Karland found it hard to accept Rast had ever doubted anything.

They sat for a while longer, and then the big man sighed. 'You will not thank me, Master Dresin, but I can help. And I will.

'You have too much time to think. I thought it would help you consider the questions we face, but it does not. You are distracted. It is causing you pain. It will endanger you.'

Karland shrugged. Rast stroked his short beard, musing. 'So. Tomorrow you march with the troops, as one of them. A different squad every day. We will train lightly morning and evening. Lëlylien and Galnór have agreed to tutor you as well. It is high time you learned to fight as part of a unit, anyway.'

Karland stared at him, his depression temporarily thrust aside by indignation and outrage. March with the infantry? He wasn't a soldier!

He opened his mouth, and Rast cut him off with a raised hand.

'You still have much to learn. Fighting in formation is different to single combat. There should be little danger, so we will use the time wisely. One day it could save your life. You will march with them, bed down with them, train with them, and obey orders as one of them. You will have little time to brood.'

'You can't make me do that,' said Karland hotly.

Rast shrugged. His answer was brutally honest.

'You swore to do what you could to defeat the enemies of the realm and make your family safe. You swore to continue Aldwyn's work. You swore to protect Xhera. Distraction disrupts all of this and endangers those around you. If you meant those things, you will do it.'

It was unfair. Karland was angry, but he bit his tongue; he couldn't argue with Rast's points.

'Fine.'

Rast rose. 'Get some sleep, boy. Know that I am here if you need me. And consider one more thing.' He leaned down slightly. 'You wouldn't be asked to do this if you weren't able. You can do far more than you admit. Must I prove this to you for the rest of our lives, my friend?'

He departed silently, leaving Karland with his thoughts. It was a long time before he could sleep. Bitterness, anger, and worry battled within him, but at least his awful apathy had lifted.

He grudgingly admitted that perhaps the huge man was at least partly right.
Maybe.

ଓଃ   ଚଃ

The next morning, he awoke early, still annoyed. He hated it, preferring to get every last second asleep, but something made him alert this morning. The sun was rising, and the air had a bite.

Few others were up. He saw only the sentries, and of course Rast and the elves, who didn't really sleep as the rest of them did. Not in the mood to speak to them, he instead moved to a clear spot and began his *Chi'Engo* exercises, stretching and warming his body after the night on the cold ground to ready it for training and then the march.

As he found peace in the movements, his breath misting in the morning cold, he thought back to when he had first started them, and how hard they had been. Now they flowed, revitalised rather than tired him. Removed from the anger of last night, he reluctantly admitted to himself that he was spending too much time thinking negative thoughts. Perhaps he did need something to distract him. He knew Rast meant the best for him.

Facing the dawn, eyes closed, he moved through his positions, holding and breathing into his centre, allowing each breath to stretch him just a little further. The sun shone through his eyelids as he moved, bringing a little warmth to him. He could hear the camp stirring through a state of restfulness and calm unusual for his mornings. His thoughts floated to how much Aldwyn had loathed them, refusing to even speak before he had sipped his tisane, and smiled.

As he moved, he thought he could almost sense other presences moving with him in harmony. It was the first time he had been so deeply part of things, and he observed it with curious detachment.

Finally, a hot hand fell on his shoulder. He stopped and opened his eyes to see Rast smiling at him.

'If you had learned this a month ago, there would have been no need to distract you with training. Come, Karland. Eat. You have been moving for almost an hour.'

Karland looked at him in astonishment, and then around. Where he had felt the other presences, he saw Lëlylien and Galnór. They looked peaceful and calm. He understood then that they had been flowing with him for most of his movements.

'You know *Chi'Engo?*' he asked in surprise.

Galnór laughed in his lighthearted fashion, and Lëlylien shook her head, grinning, her pale blue almond eyes sparking with merriment.

'Foolish human,' she mocked him gently. 'Where do you think your kind first learned its value?'

'Lëlylien, *resse,*' Galnór chided.

'This evening, I will take you through true *Chi'Engo* - the first *shak,* or movements,' said Rast. 'You are beyond the basics now.'

'I thought that *was Chi'Engo,*' said Karland.

'That is a basic set of moves to limber and tone,' said Rast. 'Tonight I will teach you more. You have become strong and flexible.'

'Which you shall not remain unless you eat, human,' teased Lëlylien.

'You don't have long,' added Rast. Karland nodded and moved for the oat pot. 'When you are ready, find Lieutenant Nirrah. She will tell you which squad you march with.'

Karland sighed and waved a hand in agreement.

He swallowed the last of the porridge, which was no longer so hot, and asked for the Lieutenant. He was pointed in the direction of the infantry squads and made his way over. As he moved, he heard snippets of conversation.

'Did you see the lad? He was moving like them elves,' a rough soldier nearly as wide as he was tall said. His armour looked as if it had needed custom fitting.

'Looked like a dance to me,' sniggered someone else.

Another woman hit him on the arm. 'If I could look that relaxed after a night on the hard ground, Ferd, I'd dance every friggin' morning.'

Other soldiers laughed, and Ferd joined in. 'Could have something there, Lil.'

'Don't mind them, lad,' said a bald man with a grin. He seemed hairless, without even much stubble, except for two astonishing eyebrows in red and pepper colours that erupted out over eyes as deep blue as glacial lakes. 'I'm Handfast. Whatcha looking for?'

'I'm not bothered,' said Karland, realising he actually wasn't. He wondered if Handfast was a name or a description. 'I've been told to find Lieutenant Nirrah.'

'Ah. Good officer, she is.' He pointed her out and nodded to Karland as he turned back to his business. Karland followed his finger and found himself face to face with a redheaded woman of about thirty with broad shoulders, small hips and breasts, and a long and strong looking neck. Incongruously, a light dusting of freckles dotted her cheeks and forehead, and her hazel eyes were sharp. She was attractive and strong.

'So, Master Dresin. It's you I've been asked to look after,' she said. She sounded a little peeved in her slightly lilting northeastern Darum, but her face showed no emotion. 'I know what you did before; took some balls, going in the Dimnesdair and seeing dragons and demons and such, not that I'd believe it if I hadn't seen you speaking to them. But there's no cart here; no companions but your squadmates. You've passed no training for march, you carry no gear. You've no experience of fighting in lines. I'd never normally allow training in the field.' She ran her eyes up and down him. 'Had my way, you'd not be here, but Master Tal'Orien speaks well of you, and I have my orders. You march here, it's as one of us.' Her gaze was critical. 'You can join Cowlin's squad, infantry all. They move mid-formation, on right flank. You carry your own weapons?' She looked over his short sword and knife critically. 'Good enough. What combat have you learned?'

'Short sword, a little longsword, bow, stave. Unarmed and knife, too.'

If he'd hoped she'd be impressed, he was wrong.

'No shield, no spear.' Her tone held thinly disguised disgust. 'Collect a spare of each, though we find trouble, you won't be fighting in formation. I don't want any soldiers killed.' His hurt must have shown, as her face softened slightly. 'Sorry, it's the truth. I know you didn't ask to join the ranks for a nine-hundred mile march.' She sighed. 'Collect your belongings and pack them. Meet me here to join the squad. I don't want to see anything hanging off that horse.'

Karland nodded, and her lips quirked. 'Generally, you address a superior as *sir* or *ma'am*.'

'Ma'am.' Karland felt quite self-conscious saying it.

The rest of that day was full of interesting lessons. Karland quickly learned not to rush his pace. Many of the soldiers did not speak much, and when they did it was in low tones. They moved in the fast, loose march called a *tab* but many of the veterans quietly called a *yomp*. Once he had the hang of it, Karland had asked the balding man with a salt and pepper fringe over a thick neck and narrow rounded shoulders next to him what that meant. The soldier had snorted and ignored Karland.

The tall woman the other side of Karland laughed quietly.

'Ignore Gorin, there. He thinks you're a soft banker playing at soldier, like to get us killed.'

Where Karland once might have been offended at this, his lips quirked in genuine amusement. 'My father's a cloth merchant in the country,' he said in amused tones. 'I won't get anyone killed.'

The tall woman smiled at him. Her face was strong-jawed, with a delicate nose and ringlets framing it that escaped her hair-tie constantly. Her brown eyes had hard lines around them, but she was pleasant enough. She strode along on long legs, shortening her stride to those around her.

'I know who you are, Master Dresin. I was on the wall when you spoke to the dragon. Some say you also faced assassins, orcs, demons.' Her gaze was critical. 'Not sure about that, but I don't think you are just some fool having fun neither, or you wouldn't be on this mission. After seeing you speak to that great black creature, and speak to the Council... you ain't a normal lad.'

'Well, I am really. Normal, I mean. I grew up in the north, and just... ended up here.' He hefted his pack. 'It's true, sort of. Orcs attacked my home, and I was nearly killed by a demon. And an assassin. But it's not what you said.' He thought about it for a moment. 'I killed one orc, maybe, and a man who killed my teacher, but it was luck both times.'

'Most of this usually is,' she grinned. 'Training and equipment only take you so far. A large part of battle is dumb luck, and you do what you can. I'm Kirri, by the way.'

Karland nodded. He liked her. There was something strong and tireless about her, a definite air that some might have called masculine, but he thought of as… just definite.

'So why is this called a *yomp*?' he asked as they marched on in their loose formation.

Kirri muttered, 'The Cap likes to call it Tactical Advance to Battle, but after one day on the road, it's Your Own Marching Pace.' She winked and held her finger to her lips, and Karland laughed to himself. Captain Aldine would definitely not like the informal description. He caught the faces of several soldiers around them smirking, and realised there must be several of them listening in.

'Can you really fight?' she asked.

'I've trained with Rast for more than seven months,' he said. 'I can handle myself, mostly.'

'You train with Tal'Orien?' another soldier interjected. He sounded surprised. 'He's the most talented fighter I ever saw. If you have his nod, that's good enough for me.' Several voices agreed.

'Load of horseshit,' came a sour voice from his right. Gorin was marching stiffly, looking ahead. 'I seen nothing but this boy dancin' in the morning. He don't belong with us. And even if he can fight a little, what about formation fighting? Strokes, cadence? Pipsqueak knows fuck all. Like to get one of us killed - or more.'

Karland gritted his teeth at the words and tone. Kirri shook her head at him and replied to the dour man.

'You don't have to like it,' she said cheerfully. 'You just have to do what you're told, Gorin. Same as the rest of us. When he's worse than you were on your first march, then you can speak ill.'

'If we're not dead 'cos of him,' Gorin muttered, and ignored them thereafter.

TWENTY-FIVE

Karland set his pack down and unrolled his blankets with a groan. He wasn't used to the marching. He had assumed that two hundred soldiers might make fifteen miles in a day, but they had covered twenty-five.

Barely had he unrolled everything when Sergeant Cowlin appeared.

'No rest yet, lad. When the squad makes camp, there are chores to set to before rest.' He gestured to several of the others. 'We get latrine duty tonight. Grab a shovel from the cart and dig. Another squad is looking after supplies. You'll be fed after the work is done. And move your stuff over to the squad camp.'

Karland sighed and nodded. He wouldn't eat with them, he knew. The other soldiers didn't have to spend an extra half hour training with Rast morning and evening. It wasn't as hard as usual, but after marching more than twenty miles he was trembling with tiredness.

Tonight, they would start formation work; he had long ago given up wondering how Rast knew so many forms of combat.

He moved over to the latrine detail, fetched a shovel, and began to dig alongside a soldier stabbing a long-tined digging fork into the ground, twisting as he went. His side still hurt; it had been a deep wound.

'A few feet deep, lad,' said the grizzled veteran next to him, noticing his hesitation. 'Straight line, mebbe a foot wide. Only grass here, so the soil isn't too tough once you break it up. With six of us working, it won't take long.'

'Never had to do this before,' grunted Karland. The soldier worked with a solid, steady cadence that was efficient, and he tried to emulate the economical movements. It felt good to move his arms, at least, but his back was aching, more on the left side than the other. His side still twinged. 'What about the other six?'

'They's digging another one. We split 'em, see, one for men, one for women. Women catch ill *down there* easier than men, for all we're a filthier lot by far. Hygiene, see? Oof.' He hit a large stone, and Karland helped him lever it up and wrestle it out of the way. 'Thanks. Lot more to bein' a soldier than waving a spear or sword, lad. Any more than one squad, and you need latrine duty. Them as complains are fools.' He spat at his feet, the spittle covered by dirt as he dug.

'Got to use *sense*. Not like them Novinians as just flush their doin's into rivers and lakes. Dig 'em downwind, mebbe twenty feet behind sentry line, lower down and other side of the camp from the food and carts. No danger of contamination, see? You put 'em in the wrong spot and get some rainfall, bam. Half the unit down with the flux. *You* try fightin' with your trous' round your ankles and your guts running down your legs.'

'Lovely,' noted Karland, sweating. He paused to wipe his forehead. Another ten minutes, he thought, and they would be done. 'Least we're nearly finished.'

'Werl, apart from the drainage ditch round the edge. Stops it just fillin' with water if there is rain or spills. Won't take long, then we can rest and eat. Fill it in tomorrow and move on. We got the easy part, lad.' He leaned on his shovel and laughed shortly. 'Another squad gets to fill it in tomorrow after a full night of company shitting. Three inches of earth at a time compacted down to stop flies, and then mound it up a good foot over ground. That's why we're piling the earth along the side. Easy, like.'

Karland laughed, suddenly feeling better, although he didn't doubt their turn would come. The half-squad finished their trench, slightly ahead of the others from the look of it, and he helped his companion out of the trench.

'What's that?' he pointed to where a private was knocking a stout stake in with a large waxed and boiled leather bottle, stoppered with a wooden plug on a cord. It had an x charred on the side.

'Raw spirits, lad. Not drinkable, and anyone trying gets a lash. Army regs. You use the lats, you dribble that on your hands and wash 'em good. Saves illness. We lose less to that than any other army in Anaria. Skip that and get caught and you're in the shit. Lit'rally.' He seemed to think that was particularly funny.

They dug a shallower drainage line, the exit at the lowest part of the ground, and then the veteran nodded to him. 'What's your name, lad?'

'Karland.'

'Good to meetcha. I'm Den Olli. I know you ain't part of the skirmishers really, but anyone who lends elbow grease alongside is fine by me. Heard tell you speak with dragons and all manner of stories. No disrespect, but you don't look a big hero to me.'

'I'm not,' said Karland. He shrugged. 'I went on a quest with Rast and managed not to die. That's it, really.' He grinned. 'But I *did* speak to dragons.'

'Cor,' said Den Olli. Karland wasn't sure he believed him. He shook his head wearily.

'I have training with Rast now, as it goes, so I won't be eating yet. I know some of the soldiers don't want me here-'

'Like Gorin?' said Den Olli scornfully. 'Good man in a fight, but I think his mother ate a whole bushel of lemons when she had him in her belly. If he aint' complaining, he ain't happy. Likes to provoke them as he sees ain't as strong as him. Show him he's wrong and he'll shut up quick enough.' He glanced around. 'For the sake of all the Gods, don't prove him right, or he'll never stop.'

Karland laughed and moved with him towards the camp.

'Gimme your shovel,' offered Den Olli. 'I'll stow it.' He took it and slapped Karland on the shoulder. 'Don't look so down, lad.' His sharp eyes peered keenly at him. 'Did it occur to you that you might be getting' all this stuff cos they know you can do it? You look like you can do things, you get extra things to do.' He grinned. 'That's why you don't never ever volunteer. Stand out from the crowd, you grow tall or get lopped off.'

'I don't want it,' said Karland hopelessly. 'I didn't volunteer. I just got caught up in things.'

Or did I, he wondered, thinking back to his demands that Aldwyn take him when he left The Croft.

'Better'n worse than you have said the same, lad. Pretty sure deep down every hero in the stories, aside every soldier on Kuln, said the same damn thing. You play the hand you get and learn to play it well. You can do it.'

Strangely, the solid, earthy confidence of the soldier made him feel better, even though he didn't know the man.

'Thanks, Den Olli,' he said.

'Olli to me mates. Come sit with us when you get your food,' said the veteran. 'You're part of the squad, f'r's I'm concerned.' He winked.

That simple offer did more than anything else to make Karland feel accepted. He trudged through the camp and found Rast, who quietly handed him a shield and a stick and set him to movements chopping and thrusting. After the latrine work, Karland's shoulders were moaning in pain. He ignored them as best he could, along with several soldiers who stood watching. The elves were also there, and Darus, his dark eyes inscrutable. Karland would normally have been embarrassed, but in truth he was too tired to care.

'There are three main moves with short sword and shield,' said Rast. 'Everything is restricted and controlled to go between shields. No one is more than three feet from the others at any time so ranks can close. You have a low thrust to the side or under the shield for stomach and legs; a chop, which can be overhead or down between shields; and an angled thrust, which starts low and curves up. That one is for neck or armpit. You do not need a hard lunge. Most of the time you will thrust and twist, thrust and twist. You are used to similar moves.' Karland nodded.

They sparred back and forth with sticks and shields for a few minutes, Karland feeling his way through the moves. His former training with Rast had been intense, and he was finding that he picked up concepts much faster now. It would be some time before this felt natural, though.

They paused, and he received some helpful criticism from the watchers, who apparently had been invited. Gen had appeared and was mugging at him from behind Rast. He would have laughed had he not been so tired. Lieutenant Isra was standing further back with sharp eyes, occasionally muttering to Nirrah.

'You thrust too far,' said a soldier called Hern, who had been introduced as a trainer and master formation swordsman. 'Here y'r a unit, all stabbing at once. We teach recruits a starter's pattern; thrust, twist, thrust, twist, low, low, high, low, chop if you can. Once used to it, we let them feel the moves and stop the pattern. It's predictable to a seasoned fighter. You don't need to go far. Short, quick, controlled moves. Husband your strength.'

'*Only three inches; when he coughs, look for another,*' quoted Gen with a grin. Hern nodded.

'Too right, man. Right out of Combol's Theory of Combat. Any more and they might think you like 'em.' There were several laughs. The elves didn't laugh; it wasn't really humour they understood. Darus snorted, however.

Rast spoke. 'Again. This time, why don't you noble warriors help show him. He awaits his supper.'

There were a few startled looks, and then they collected shields and ragged firewood. Forming two rows of three each, one to each side of Karland, they fell into a rhythm and sparred again.

He started to get the movements, and resisted the urge to exaggerate or extemporise. He gained several clouts and jabs, one of which caught his breath, and a stinging ear, but by the time they had finished, he understood the ideas, and had fallen into the rhythm.

'That's it, Karland,' said Hern. 'Keep that up and you'll get the memory in the moves.' He looked to Rast. 'Quick, isn't he?'

'I've trained him hard,' was the response. Rast held his hands out for the equipment. 'Go and eat, Karland, and then sleep. If you rise and perform *Chi'Engo* we will not train tomorrow morning.'

'We will join you,' added Lëlylien. Karland wondered if that was a threat or a promise.

He collected his meal, Darus accompanying him to the fire where his squad were. It was odd, thinking of them as *his* squad. Kirri waved him over, and Olli waggled his eyebrows. They were curious to meet Darus, seeming amazed he spoke so well. Karland had to explain more than once that orks were not stupid and savage, but the lesson was not brought home until one younger soldier made a caustic remark behind Darus as he spoke to someone.

'Damn snotrag thinks he's one of us now. Worse than the boy.' He clearly thought he had spoken quietly, but it was into an unfortunate lull in conversation and the words rang out.

Darus turned, his eyes blazing, and grabbed the soldier by the throat. Daggers were unsheathed quickly, and Kirri and Olli, along with more than half the squad, turned to face several others, voices raised.

'Hold!' barked Sergeant Cowlin.

No one moved for a moment, apart from the choking soldier. He was slowly turning purple, making gurgling choking noises. He drew his own dagger, despite the command, and Darus slapped it stingingly from his hand. He put one foot out in front to base himself, and with little effort lifted his bent arm, bringing the soldier nearly two feet off the floor to stare into his face. The man's arms batted weakly at his, and the feet scrabbled at his heavy thigh.

'If I were my brother,' remarked Darus quietly, 'I would tear your head off for your insult.' His lips quivered around his tusks for a moment. 'You have luck tonight. I am not my brother. But if I hear those words again, I will be *angry*.' His dark eyes were huge, and Karland could see him holding in his temper with difficulty. 'And then you will see the rage of an ork.'

'Personally, I'd shut up,' advised Karland belligerently. 'Darus is pretty even-tempered for an ork, but you haven't just pissed *him* off.' The ork let go of the young man, and he crumpled onto his face, almost sobbing into the grass.

'This beast-' began Gorin, scowling at Karland.

'SHUT YOUR MOUTH, SOLDIER!' Cowlin roared, veins standing out on his neck, and there was silence across the whole campsite. 'Verrin got less than he deserved, by the gods-'

'Sergeant.'

Nirrah's voice cut him off immediately. Heads whipped around, and all talk died. Karland wondered how long she had been standing there.

'I might have known you'd speak up, Gorin,' said the Lieutenant. 'Anyone who wishes to insult the envoy of our ork allies again will dig and fill latrines for the remainder of this campaign and find themselves severely disciplined when we return to barracks. You are required to act with honour. Is that clear?' She glared around her.

'Yes, Ma'am!' snapped the soldiers. Karland found he'd almost said it as well; military life was definitely habit-forming.

'Allow me to clarify,' said another quiet voice, and Major Gambeson stepped forward, his face stern. Rast loomed next to him, and Captain Aldine, a look of disgust on his face as he viewed both the troublemakers and the ork. The soldiers snapped to attention, and Nirrah saluted. Any number of faces were suddenly blank with military apprehension.

The Major's voice carried out into the campsite.

'Soldiers of Eordeland. We are at war, and we march to support an allied nation. If you insult and attack another ally during wartime, you not only put insult to our realm, but you will go to trial under full military discipline. The *least* you can hope for if found guilty is dishonourable discharge for undermining alliance in a time of war.' He looked around him coolly. 'Are you common rabble? You are *veterans of Eordeland*. Display the honour you have earned, or risk losing it.' He nodded to Nirrah and turned away.

Rast stood looking at Darus for a moment, and Karland wondered if he was remembering Grukust's temper in Punslon. Darus scrutinised him back, unabashed, and Rast smiled slightly and nodded.

Captain Aldine glared around him for a moment, disdain plain on his face, and then snapped at Nirrah.

'Lieutenant. I want every man and woman involved in front of me in twenty minutes. I would expect behaviour like this after hard battle, not on quiet march. Present yourself and the squad leaders as well; we will discuss this lack of discipline.'

She winced slightly. Karland felt that was unfair given most of the unit including the Sergeant had opposed the troublemaker before Nirrah herself had stepped in, but Aldine was not finished. He turned his cold gaze to Darus.

'And you... *sir*. I'll thank you to keep your hands off my troops. It may be in your *nature* to brawl, but I need them ready to defend our *other* allies.' He whirled and marched off.

In his nature *to brawl!* thought Karland in outrage. He knew exactly what Aldine had meant by that. Darus heaved a few deep breaths, nostrils flaring in anger, then barked a laugh and sat. Karland relaxed slightly.

Nirrah glanced at Sergeant Cowlin.

'The whole squad was involved, one way or the other,' she said flatly. 'Get them to the Captain's tent and stand at attention. Now.'

'You heard her,' barked Cowlin, at a lower volume but with power nonetheless, almost before she had finished the last word. Karland jumped. The man's clean-shaven face was red with anger. 'Hefson! In line. Get up, Verrin, or by the Gods I'll boot you to the Captain's door.' Verrin staggered unsteadily to his feet, knowing full well the Sergeant wasn't joking.

'Fall in!' the Cowlin snapped. The squad lined up three deep. Kirri and several others were glaring daggers at Verrin and Gorin, who looked subdued. Karland moved to join them.

'Not you, Dresin.' Nirrah held out her hand. He stopped. 'Squad business.'

The squad moved off, looking straight ahead. Karland felt a little hurt he wasn't included, mingled with relief.

Nirrah saw the look on his face. 'That wasn't your fight, lad. We're under pressure here. Much hinges on defending Eyotsburg, and this war, and we know it.'

'I marched with the squad today,' said Karland stubbornly.

'You're not part of it,' she said bluntly. 'But it does you credit to stand by them, despite what I have heard *some* say about you. You're to rotate between squads, anyway. You march with others tomorrow.'

She left and he climbed into his roll, making sure it was under and around him as Rast had shown him a long time ago. He ached all over, too angry to sleep right away.

He lay there for a time, and heard the squad return a while later. Aldine had not been loud in whatever he said, but he had heard the anger in his voice even from here.

The next morning, the punishment became clear after *Chi'Engo*. Despite Olli's proclamation the night before, the squad ate and then moved to fill the latrine pits. As usual, scuttlebutt had swept the camp, and it seemed they would be taking that shitty duty until told otherwise. There were a lot of sour looks directed at Verrin and Gorin.

Karland finished his breakfast and rose to join them. He picked up a shovel and began work next to Kirri.

'What do you think you are doing, Dresin?' barked Cowlin.

Karland didn't stop work. 'Sharing the punishment, sir.' He had expected another bellow but glanced up to find the Sergeant - and several soldiers - watching him, eyes narrowed. 'I was in the squad at the time. I was involved. *Sir.*'

'Hmm,' Cowlin muttered after a moment, his stare direct. 'Your choice. *Soldier.*' He turned and left.

Kirri hissed at him. 'Stone's blood, but he complimented you there, Karland. You're a thrice-fool, though.' She jerked her head at Gorin. '*He'll* not thank you for it.'

He shrugged and grinned. 'Not doing it for him. I was involved. It's fair.' He couldn't explain easily that unfairness in any form ate at him almost physically like a sore. Far easier to simply do the right thing.

Kirri grinned back and nodded approvingly, and they carried on filling the pit in silence. After they finished, Karland wondered if it had been wise. He was already exhausted from the excess work, but when many of the squad nodded to him or clapped his shoulder, he knew it was worth it. He might not truly be one of the squad, but he was no longer just an outsider.

⋘　　⋙

His sense of fairness had done a lot for him in the eyes of most of the company, he realised afterwards. Gorin, Verrin and a few others were acerbic or outright rude to him, although they were stilted and over-courteous when faced with Darus or the elves. None of them wanted to anger the big ork again. But Karland... he wasn't Rast to awe them, or an ally to step lightly around. He was a young boy, and he bore the brunt of their dislike.

One soldier seemed permanently bored by Karland when he spoke to him, arrogant and dismissive. One young woman with bright straight ginger hair and a self-centred attitude was outright condescending and rude. She was attractive and intelligent, and knew it; just as clearly, she had decided it made her better than the others. Karland was dismissed as a virtual idiot by her, told he was mentally her inferior.

He knew her limitations, so obvious to everyone except her, shouldn't irk him. It did anyway. Another woman with a scarred face simply ignored him, Darus, and the elves whenever they were near.

It didn't matter. The officers and the others in the company greeted him differently now, and most of the troops were at least polite and friendly. He couldn't say what it was, but it felt like they had accepted him a little more. Even Aldine was less stiff when he spoke to him.

Once Karland had proved to his squadmates that he was not a liability and would stand shoulder to shoulder with them in any of the work, he became not just accepted but valued. Only a few soldiers seemed to still rankle that he was *playing soldier*, as Gorin put it.

331

Rast worked as hard and as humbly as any of them, but to many of the troops he was a semi-legend, and that distanced him. Karland became a true companion. There was no preferential treatment; the sergeants still bawled him out at the slightest mistake, and he made quite a few, but he wasn't an outsider.

Over the next week, Karland marched with most of the squads. He made new comrades, gained new insights into what each squad did, and followed the squad duties assigned by Sergeants: repaired uniforms, helped with food, fed and curried the animals.

Every day he helped his first squad dig and fill. Every evening he collapsed into bed, exhausted. Every morning, he trained with the elves, running through a mixture of movements which stretched his muscles and warmed them up. They were more advanced than before, and he finally realised to his surprise that doing the movements regularly for a year had vastly improved his flexibility, strength, and balance.

'You have built a good foundation,' approved Rast. 'Now we must build more.' It sounded ominous.

The new moves were torturous. Some of them involved hardly moving once in the position, or moving slowly for part of the movement in a controlled fashion, and some were virtually impossible. The elves performed them flawlessly, of course.

Practice with Rast now attracted a good number of off-duty watchers from every unit. Short mock battles between squads became a light competition.

Karland gradually felt comfortable fighting with these men and women. His time with Rast had left him stronger, faster, and more tireless than they expected. For the first time in his life, he began to gain some real confidence in his own abilities.

It was different training with Rast; the huge man was an excellent teacher, but Karland knew he would never even approach the level of skill that Rast had developed, and that would always remain a little dispiriting. He truly was almost more than human. Sometimes his stamina and fluid movement reminded Karland of the Elves, who occasionally joined in practice, but even after all their companionship he never stopped being amazed at how fast and graceful Rast was for his size.

The company he could measure his own progress against, by and large. No longer did Lieutenant Nirrah believe he would be a total liability in formation.

Darus laughingly tried to join the fighting, but found his size and demeanour did not suit formations at all. Much larger than even Rast, he stuck out over and around any human shield, and the spears and swords were more like dining tools in his immense hands. He instead showed some of the squads how orks would fight against them. After more than one had had their spears and shields yanked from them, leaving them face down in the dirt as often as not, there was a lot more respect, especially when he showed them how Grukust's great axe could be used to disrupt the line. The beards hooked over shields and his immense strength and surprising speed provided the power to reverse the stroke quickly and cut back in before they could react. In sheer power, despite their lack of shields, facing a line of orks would be very dangerous, Karland realised. Where a human favouring two handed weapons would quickly be spitted, orks had the strength to smash their opponents back onto their companions and break open ranks, shields or no. He knew from experience they could soak up a lot more damage than a human.

The company digested these tactics thoughtfully, and they rippled all the way up to Major Gambeson, who tacitly approved; although they were very unlikely to fight Darus's people, they could face ogres, who were even stronger.

Each evening, the lessons continued after Karland's squad duties.

'Shields must be kept high. Not too close to the body - if they are pierced you may be hit. Lock your shoulder. Feel the strike and drop or raise it. On the call of 'bash!', you lock the shields together and draw in ranks, and *push* hard for three steps, if you can. Hit the enemy as hard as you can. Don't worry about your sword or spear. You will be told to do this to create space, or for Pikemen behind you to strike past you. Shields are the backbone of a formation, and you base your attacks around them.'

Another night it would be spears:

'Here is the *angum*. This can be used for throwing but it is not as precise as a true javelin. The head is long and sharp, with a long shank to stop it being cut easily.' Karland nodded, hefting the five-foot spear. 'There are three uses for this in the ranks. It can be thrown or jabbed to lodge in a shield - the weight helps bring it down, and you can stamp on the haft to pull a shield forwards so you may stab with your sword. It can cause much damage to legs, feet and ankles. Or it can be used instead of a sword, as it is longer and can stab more easily; here - if you tuck the haft under your armpit, you can use more leverage and force than a sword thrust, and the small head can penetrate ringmail if you are lucky.'

'Couldn't you also use it as a stave?' asked Karland. Rast nodded.

'In Hadrasia, they name the spear the King of Weapons; they have many types, from thin shafts to elaborate heads, to one called *the mediator's haft*, with a sharp spade one end and a crescent blade the other. But you cannot fight with staves in a formation. They require too much room.'

'So what happens if you throw it or stab and let go? Don't you lose them?'

'If you win, you collect them after the battle. New hafts are easily made. If you lose... you do not need them again.' Rast smiled grimly.

Another time, sapper weapons, the twinned large and small multifunction war axes:

'These hatchets are chopping weapons, although the smaller can be thrown and both can be used to block. Reverse swipes are almost as effective as warhammers, too.'

Karland nearly sliced his own leg practicing, and ruefully decided that perhaps this weapon wasn't for him. Rast didn't press him, instead handing him to the sapper team to understand the other uses and the basics of the engineering they used.

He learned to strike in a series of chops that could be changed in sequence. He learned to strike left, straight, or right on the shouted commands *winestra, diré,* and *wipra* in time with the whole front rank.

The hardest technique Karland had to learn was the crossbow restringing using goat's feet. The pronged metal levers were designed to allow fast re-drawing of the crossbows even on horseback but took some getting used to. Piter, a quiet and thoughtful man who seemed unflappable, was the one who taught him most of this. Karland was astonished that he had finally found a weapon Rast was not very interested in, although he recalled him firing one back at the Battle of The Croft.

When Aldine objected to the apparent waste of their time, Rast replied, 'It benefits everyone to keep skills fresh.'

Grudgingly, Aldine agreed. Rast seemed to be one of the only people apart from Gambeson who could change his mind.

Karland grew more confident with shield and spear. He wasn't sure he enjoyed crossbow but was impressed at the ability to punch through plate mail that the bolts had. He grew used to the pace and the constant work, carrying his pack and weapons alongside all the others. Even Gorin stopped muttering imprecations after a while.

It wasn't until thirteen days into the march that he realised, reluctantly, that Rast was right. He still thought of Xhera, but he wasn't wasting his energy worrying about it all; he had none spare. He was enjoying the march now, learning new things, and feeling a sense of belonging he had never had, even at the University. He was even aching less.

To his surprise, life was good.

ೞ   ೨

Life came crashing back down to its usual level a few days later.

Karland had begun to relax and enjoy the rhythm of the march. As dusk fell, he visited the latrine to relieve himself. He had stopped being so self-conscious about going amongst the others and was in a reflective mood. He had training later with Rast, of course, but was free for an hour or so.

Gorin was already straddled further down the trench, pissing a very yellow stream out. When he saw Karland, he aimed up, deliberately trying to splash further along. Karland hardly noticed, ensconced within his thoughts; the bulk of Drakeholm Soaring loomed to the north, visible over the rest of the range, and it brought back many memories.

He was belting back up, thinking of other times, when he felt a hard shove. He fell face first across the latrine, barely managing to catch himself. He was lucky he hadn't landed in it, but he had fallen in urine-spattered mud, and for the first time in a long time was suddenly angry, angry enough not to doubt himself, angry that he had been attacked so unfairly at a moment he was elsewhere in his mind. It was almost an invasion of privacy.

Had he been pushed a few seconds earlier, he would have been mid-belt and fallen face-first into the pit.

He sprang up to find an ugly smirk on Gorin's face. Karland clenched his hands in fury as the ammonia smell of urine drifted from his front.

Gorin punched him in the face, hard. Karland reeled back in shock; Gorin had struck exactly as Rast always told Karland to strike. He tried to focus, and a fist thundered up into his gut. It was agony; he felt something tear in his deeply healing side. Karland dropped to his knees, retching and bloodied, moaning. He heard Gorin laugh as he turned away, victorious.

'Here, now!' came the voice of Den Olli. 'Gorin, that's too far. You know you ain't allowed to fight in the ranks!'

'He ain't *in* the squad, nor the army, you idiot,' snapped Gorin. 'He's a little mummy's boy allowed to *play* soldier. Look at 'im. He's no fighter.' Disdain dripped from the words.

Karland shook his head, blood flying in droplets, and dragged himself up. Gorin turned in surprise. He hurt, but he was tougher than they obviously realised.

'What the fuck is wrong with you?' shouted Karland. Blood flowed down his nose and from his split lip, mixing with hurt tears. He couldn't believe what had happened. The others had formed a loose ring around them all in that half-quiet, half-intent fashion of those trying not to attract the attention of authority.

'Whassa matter, little cryboy?' sneered Gorin. 'Can't take a little joshing?' His face was flushed red and heated.

'You don't know anything about me,' said Karland quietly, a painful lump in his throat. He was hurt, angry, and ashamed.

Gorin suddenly threw another punch, determined to finish this. Karland had learned from the first, and he was moving from confusion and hurt to *anger*. He wasn't where it was aimed.

The soldier grabbed for Karland's jerkin and threw a knee to Karland's groin which he barely avoided, taking a punishing bruise on the outside of his leg instead. He grabbed hairy incoming arms, groaning with effort, but the man was too strong for him, and he was forced down.

A thought flashed through his mind. *Everyone's right. I'm not a fighter.*

Gorin grinned, his eyes flashing in triumph. It didn't matter that he had ambushed Karland and struck first; it didn't matter he was much bigger and stronger than the boy. He was enjoying humbling him, revelling in victory.

The realisation and unfairness overwhelmed Karland until his focus narrowed to a pinpoint, and something… exploded within him. He surged to his feet, growling, tears and blood streaming down his face, all pain forgotten as he yanked his hands sideways, hard.

Gorin was unprepared for his strength and his left hand slipped. He had obviously thought tears were a sign of submission, weakness, and was not prepared for this sudden furious defence.

'*You don't know me! You don't KNOW me!*' Karland barely heard himself roaring, each *know* punctuating a strike. He was operating on reflex now. Harder and faster than a boy should strike they flew, mostly accurate and damaging.

He smashed an elbow over Gorin's hand into the man's cheekbone, kneed him in the stomach, and then twisted desperately as Gorin staggered, stunned. Karland spun out from under his grasp, his will wavering.

Rast's deep voice tolled out unexpectedly.

'Karland! Do not toy with him! *Commit!*'

Commit.

New determination welled up. He was tired of people pushing him around. Ben Arflun, Aran, Gorin, so many others; he was *sick* of it. Each time he conquered his fear of one champion of unfairness, there was another; different, worse. If he let there be, there would always be another person to make him afraid, make him doubt himself.

Fuck it.

The noise of the crowd was blurring.

Enraged, Gorin charged. Karland lashed a foot into his stomach, much harder and faster than last time. He was no longer just reacting; now months of training with Rast fell into place. Instinct rose with fury.

Gorin half-doubled, air blasted out of him and shock on his face. Another second and he came in again like a drunken bull, throwing hard punches. Karland evaded the blows, sliding away, Gorin swinging more and more wildly. Karland snapped his foot out, slamming into Gorin's thigh, and then against his knee with a painful click. Gorin hopped forwards and Karland sent several jabs and a cross in, then a thundering right hook to his temple, cutting his brow. Gorin fell to the side, a look of disbelief on his face. It was swiftly replaced by humiliation and utter fury. He sprang up and leapt, roaring.

Karland almost saw it coming, in a detached way; Gorin seemed so clumsy. How had the man ever hit him?

Rast had told him time and time again that most fist fights ended up on the floor. He leaped backwards and Gorin stumbled, overreaching. Karland desperately grabbed the back of the thick neck in a solid clasp and jerked his knee up into Gorin's face, feeling the pull of his retorn side. It wasn't as a solid a blow as he had practised, but it was enough to daze the soldier for a second. Karland jerked his arms hard in, and Gorin toppled face first into the ground.

Karland was on him as he hit the floor, scrambling to get an arm around his neck. Gorin roared, a strangled noise, and reached back with his left arm get to the impudent challenger.

Karland slid his right arm under his throat, and tucked his head to Gorin's tricep, locking the left arm up. With the arm trapped, he just managed to find his left bicep with his right hand. He shrugged in, clenched every muscle in his arms and back as Rast had taught, and put his weight up on his toes. Gorin's choking face slammed down into the wet, foul mud mid-roar and it cut off. The only sound was his own grunts.

'You-don't-know-me!' he grated through gritted teeth as he rammed Gorin's face further into the ooze.

The larger man struggled but couldn't dislodge Karland. His feet drummed urgently, and then hands caught them both, dragging Karland off firmly but gently, others turning Gorin over. He looked up at Rast, chest heaving, becoming aware of an approaching voice shouting in anger. His heart was thumping, and he was shaking in reaction.

'You've made your point,' said Rast.

Karland stood back, chest heaving with exertion. He felt numb, even though he hurt all over.

What had happened?

'My side,' he said thickly. Rast's eyes showed concern, and gentle fingers felt under the tunic.

'You did well,' he murmured. 'He is bigger, stronger, more experienced, but overconfident. You are faster, better trained. But he nearly won. That is why you must *commit*.' The big man shook his head. 'Learn this lesson. You doubt yourself. You fail because you expect to. Let go of your doubt. There is *nothing* but the fight.'

'Stand down!' shouted Aldine in fury as he arrived.

Karland wondered why no one had stepped in as they had with Darus. Maybe it had been a test of his mettle.

Maybe they wanted to see me taught a lesson, he thought bitterly.

Soldiers stood to attention, faces carefully blank. Gorin struggled to his feet, spattered with mud, bruised and hunched in pain, his chest heaving. A trickle of blood described the side of his face as he looked at Karland in shocked disbelief.

Aldine snapped angrily, 'You two again! Anyone care to explain this?'

No one spoke; soldiers did not tell tales.

'I will *not* have fighting here! Everyone involved will report to my tent in five minutes. *Everyone*.' He scowled at Gorin and Karland. Even Rast got a sour look. He turned and began walking away as soldiers dispersed, muttering.

Gorin snarled at Karland. 'I shoulda won!'

Rast stared at him coolly. 'Accept defeat graciously, Gorin. It was unfairly started. You picked the wrong victim.'

Gorin glared at Karland, his face beet red, and turned away. He took one step then whirled, leaping at Karland. His frenzy took his squadmates by surprise.

Karland, still full of adrenaline and resentment, reacted without thinking. He stepped in, holding his fist, and dipped his legs, rotating his whole body out of the way and into the strike. His side shrieked.

His elbow caught Gorin hard under the left side of the jaw as he ran onto it. The soldier collapsed, his legs suddenly limp. Unbalanced, Karland staggered back wearily, hands up, but the fight was over. Gorin's comrades caught him and held him upright. He batted the air weakly as if the fight was still happening in slow motion, his eyes unfocused, his legs refusing to hold him.

'Think you reset his brain, Karland,' crowed Den Olli with obvious glee, holding Gorin under one arm.

Karland massaged his elbow. It was agony. He looked at Rast accusingly, still almost shaking with reaction. Rast would have known the attack was coming probably before Gorin himself.

'You could have stopped him.'

'Do you think he would have left you alone if I had stepped in?'

Karland's reply was interrupted by a furious Aldine, who had whirled at the resumed fight. He bulled his way through the soldiers, who suddenly felt a pressing urge to be elsewhere, and actually grabbed Rast's arm. Rast looked at the Captain without saying anything, and after a second he let go again.

'Your boy wants to be a soldier, Tal'Orien? Then he had best be prepared to be punished like one. Brawling in the latrines, damaging a fit soldier in a time of war, attacking a man again after expressly being ordered to stand down-'

'The fight was started by Gorin,' interrupted Rast. 'He threw a fifteen-year-old boy on his face over the latrine while he was using it. He struck without warning, twice. He chose to continue fighting after your order. Karland defended himself. He has witnesses. Do you doubt my word?'

Aldine scowled and glared at Karland. He seemed to be torn between not offending Rast and his clear growing dislike for the boy. 'No. Keep control of your… *protégé.*'

'Perhaps you should instead control your troops so they do not attack children, Captain.'

Aldine glared, then spied Gorin being helped away. 'Bring him to my tent when he can stand. Everyone involved in this debacle is going to regret it, and I *will* get to the bottom of this. The Major has told you once about this behaviour. Any further breaches will result in court martial on return to Darost. Am I clear?'

'Sir!' shouted those gathered soldiers that had not managed to escape in time.

Aldine left with one final withering look at Karland.

'I did nothing wrong,' said Karland hopelessly. He was bruised and filthy, crusted in mud and piss, and feeling that the universe was against him once more. His side felt unpleasantly warm.

'No, boy. Life isn't fair. I will speak to the Major *and* the Captain about this. There will be no further attacks. You carry the trust of the Council of Twelve, and I take ill treatment of you as badly as I take it of Darus.' He beckoned Karland to him. 'You fought well. He will not bother you again. I think after this, no one will.'

'Aldine doesn't like me.'

Rast smiled slightly. 'Aldine doesn't like anyone. He does not think a *boy* should be anything other than a recruit, doing what he is told. He likes everything neat and orderly, forced into the correct position. You are an anomaly. So am I.' He reached over and unhooked the bag of raw spirits and held it out for Karland. 'Careful.'

Karland filled his hands, closed his eyes tightly, and rubbed it into his face and hair to clean the muck out. Immediately he nearly howled; he had forgotten the split lip and bloody nose. He blindly waved the bag away, using the rest to clean his hands and front. 'Enough. Argh.'

'I did say.' Rast's words were gentle. 'You won against more than Gorin today, Karland. You won against yourself. Come, let's get you to the healers.'

TWENTY-SIX

The company moved through the borderlands between the gullied foothills of the Arkons and the plains on the seventeenth day of their march. Once off the main road, going was slower, although the plains here were flat enough that the wagons still made good time. They hugged the low hills, hoping to avoid notice, four pathfinders in the vanguard ahead and four in the rear, the other four flanking split to north and south.

It was early afternoon, and the march was steady. Four hundred miles from Eordeland, they were on the borders of dwarf territory to the north and ork territory to the south. Darus had spotted signs of tribes to the southwest two days before and journeyed to deliver word from the Council. He had gone alone, saying that approaching thousands of orks with a company of human soldiers might be misunderstood.

Rast agreed.

He had returned this morning with acknowledgement from the tribes, to Rast's pleasure; he was glad the big ork still kept their company. He glanced back to see Karland marching, eyes half closed in the sunlight.

The boy's bruises were fading. He was treated with respect now, and even Gorin grudgingly ignored him. Rast had noticed a new confidence in him, too.

The warrior enjoyed the sun as they moved. There had been no sign of men or orks since Darus left, and the day was bright and warm. The monotony was lulling.

Thunder swelled, rolling across the low hills to their right. Darus looked up curiously, as did several soldiers, but the sky was clear, and it didn't diminish. Rast felt himself starting to tense and relaxed into readiness. Calls of alarm sprang up.

Orders were shouted by the thick-necked Sergeant Major even as a roar sounded and an army of infantry that must have at the very least numbered the same broke over the low hill to their right, running full pelt to engage the Eordeland lines before they could react.

'Novinians,' breathed Aldine. 'What are they doing here?'

There was no time to answer. The bowmen managed one ragged volley before the ambushers had closed with the lines. The crossbows were not left cocked on march, and the squads were in loose formation. No human army should be here - even allies were barely tolerated by dwarves or orks.

The Eordelanders were caught off guard.

Lëlylien smoothly began loosing shafts through gaps with almost preternatural accuracy to strike enemies in vulnerable spots and distract them, but the humans were not so confident, and not many fell.

The pikes were not as effective without the entire line engaged, but the infantry locked shields and the attackers broke upon them like waves on rock. With a crunch and an audible grunt of effort from many mouths, the line held.

The levelled pikes and the infantry in between presented a solid wall. Short spears between and below shields stabbed at stomachs and legs in practiced movements.

The Novinians wore leather and mail, and wielded spears, swords and bucklers. Some of them threw short javelins in the hope of weighting down the shields. Where a shield was pierced, the bearer would fall back and worry it free while the line closed, and one behind moved forward.

It was quickly apparent that the ambushers were completely outmatched, even with the advantage of surprise; savage though their attack was, the Eordeland veterans moved with mechanical efficiency, absorbing blows and interlocking their defence. They struggled for a few minutes, the Eordelanders losing no-one and the attackers losing many. Just as it seemed that they had engaged suicidally, Galnór appeared at a full run behind the fight from the northeast, around the hill.

He didn't run as a human would, legs and arms pumping powerfully. He seemed to flow sinuously - his motion was smooth and every move was designed to push him faster. Far quicker than a human would cover the ground, he swept towards them, his pale angular face holding no laughter now.

Darus stood behind the lines, breathing aggressively, almost growling at the need to fight. He accepted that he and Rast would be better off reacting to any breach, but he was spinning the Axe of Grukust in his grip, the long blades flashing. Rast, standing next to him, just caught Galnór's words.

'Ware!' the elf called loudly, hardly sounding out of breath despite his sprint. 'Riders!' His voice cut through the tumult. He sped for the struggling flank, which had few enemies, and stabbed at backs and necks as he slid his way through using surprise and speed.

'Clear his way!' cried the nearest squad's sergeant, and the soldiers thrust fiercely at the Novinians. Galnór darted through, although not unscathed; a cut on his arm dripped bright red blood. The Novinian that tried to follow and stab at his back was brutally impaled and thrust to the floor to scream through bloody teeth.

On the very heels of his words over seventy armoured knights rounded the short rise and charged at the company in two tight wedges, slightly separated one behind the other and aiming at the flank. The pikes were arraigned forward against the infantry, and the engaged Eordelanders struggled to turn their defences in time.

'MAKE READY!' roared Thorne. 'LANCERS TO RIGHT FLANK!'

He was too late; the charge was seconds from impact even as he called commands.

These were no common mercenaries, no foot serfs; these were knights, led by a Knight-Captain, well trained and well-armed on powerful horses in heavy barding. Baying loudly, large dogs with spiked and plated collars ran behind the second wedge.

The pikemen lining the edges of the column tried to disengage from the infantry and bring their weapons to bear, including the deadly war scythes, but few managed before the first tight wedge of horses smashed into them at an angle with a terrible sound, hurling rows of soldiers from their feet. Lances threw them into their comrades, and one pierced a man's shoulder, nearly tearing his arm off. Splinters flew, and the first wedge turned left through the scattering mass of men and women. Broken lances were discarded seconds after impact. Knights drew large axes, maces and longswords, and urged their horses onwards through the throng, hewing and stabbing. The odd knight whose lance had remained whole thundered towards any foe in front of them, seeking to further break apart ranks, the leverage of the long wood opening large gaps.

In thirty seconds of sheer mayhem, they had brutally smashed their curving way through the men and women of Eordeland and plunged back out further down, their own infantry parting for them. The Guard were attacked from before and behind their own lines, and the charge compressed them, making it even harder for pikes to engage the new threat. Several squads were cut off from their fellows by the plunging horses.

Used successfully, the Novinian charge had broken much larger foes than themselves. Against a weaker enemy, a slow charge built panic and inevitability; against a better armed but unprepared force, they had learned to approach quietly, packed in a dense wall, and strike as hard and fast as they could from the flank. The shock of the heavy cavalry disrupted formations terribly, and their powerful and vicious war dogs would hurtle through the breach and cause further chaos. If the defences prevented a charge, knights dismounted to continue the attack as juggernauts of destruction.

Even at this point, battles rarely saw many deaths, but this was often enough to break the will of their foes. When the enemy broke and ran, the true slaughter would begin.

Both sides knew this, and struggled not to be the first to break.

The ranks of pikes and infantry were sundered. The knights carved their way back out barely twenty seconds before the second wave crashed in. They had timed it professionally. There was no chance to recover from the initial charge before the second swept through already damaged ranks, this time aiming at the centre and the wagons.

The shock was immense. Without having the pikes and crossbows ready, the defence against heavy cavalry was minimal, and the bowmen were reluctant to loose for fear of hitting their comrades. Instead, they scattered, trying to avoid the wall of horses.

The dogs fell on the dispersed Eordelanders on the heels of the second charge. They did not simply leap at soldiers as a wild beast would. They had been well-trained. More than one soldier was borne to the floor by a small pack which tore at the shrieking man or woman, their great jaws ripping at unarmoured throats, hands, and legs as they worried the fallen.

Many companies would have broken already, retreating in panic. But these were Eordeland Guard. Instead of dissolving completely into chaos, their ranks almost bowed, the formations flexing to absorb the terrible impact of the charges. Major Gambeson's company was made of veterans, and their training and experience had been thorough. They quickly recovered despite the losses, closing ranks. Infantry pushed through to counter infantry, and the pike squads moved to bring weapons to bear as other soldiers turned to engage the enemies within. The movement of squads even mid-engagement was surprisingly efficient given the bedlam. Even as the second charge hit, the flanks were stronger, and although the cavalry still carved their way in, this time the charge stalled. Knights were thrust from their horses by pikes with a crash, and the war scythes wreaked havoc amongst them. More than a few horses were struck with spears or had their legs cut from under them, but the Eordelanders tried not to harm them. Injured horses thrashed and damaged friend and foe alike; the riderless horses simply wanted to escape the melee.

The knights that had plunged into the heart of the company were pushed back, more than a few killed. A knot of them broke through, followed by infantry and dogs, bulling soldiers out of the way and aiming for the wagons and healers, hoping to strike at the morale of the Eordeland troops there.

The battle was fierce for a few minutes. Then the powerful voice of Sergeant-Major Thorne thundered through the furore.

'Winestra!'

Without changing pace, the next stroke of the front ranks was aimed not at the foe in front of them but the one to their left. The move caught the Novinians utterly by surprise. The Eordeland soldiers to the right defended their fellows to their left, and the next stroke was back to the surprised soldiers facing them again. More than a quarter of the enemy's front ranks fell to the co-ordinated diversion in two strokes.

The Novinians hesitated. Where they had been ready to rush into a divided and panicked company of soldiers behind the devastating charge of the knights, they were instead faced with grim, implacable rows of veteran Eordeland Guard, standing over their fallen fellows and in close formation. The Eordeland infantry - one of the finest fighting forces in the world - made ready. Wounded and dead were being pulled through from behind to clear the field.

The first wedge had swept around, expecting to charge again into flanks in chaos, but they pulled up, seeing row upon row of pikes. Faced with a wall of points their horses simply would not charge, many knights began to dismount for close combat, leaving their steeds behind their own infantry.

'Bolters, release!' roared a deep voice from the flank.

A deep near-synchronised twang sounded. Many knights fell as if poleaxed; the crossbows had finally been brought to bear.

ك ו

Darus roared at the chance to engage, the huge axe of his brother spinning over in his fist. A knight charged at him, and he waited with the axe poised. As the lance came in, he batted it away wide with little effort, and reversed the swing and pulled as he struck. The beard of the axe flashed back and hooked over the lance arm of the knight, and with a mighty heave Darus yanked him from the saddle, out and over the horse's shoulder. It whinnied and broke left as Darus continued his turn and slammed the man into the floor. The knight's shoulder and neck broke with two satisfying cracks, and he levered the bloody tip of the axe-beard out from where it had pierced the armour joint. He could feel the *baresark* of his people descending upon him and fought to hold it back until needed. He knew that what made orks such powerful warriors also made them vulnerable to human tactics. Berserk rages needed to be used at the right time, something many of his people did not understand, and he knew he might inadvertently kill his allies in his rage.

But his blood was pumping, his muscles flexing, and his mind was filled with the red need to kill these puny metal-clad humans.

He spotted another knight hacking at a sapper, his large blade clanging off the raised hatchets.

Darus thundered in, grabbing the horse almost in a headlock with his massive arm and wrenching it over hard as he fell.

Although the horse was three times his own weight, Darus was over seven feet tall and weighed more than twice a large man, with strength a human couldn't match. With a wild whinny the horse toppled, throwing the knight to the side. His helmet came off, revealing a dazed stubbled face and long coiled hair.

A snarling dog leaped at Darus as he rose. He caught it by the throat in his free hand, staggering slightly, and roared in its face before hurling it aside in contempt. The dog struggled to its feet and ran whimpering, seeking easier prey.

All around him Eordelanders struggled to regroup and fight their foes as a unit. To the side, the thrown knight staggered to his feet, shaking his head to clear it. The man ran at him on foot with a greatsword. He swung, clipping the top of Darus's right deltoid as the ork twisted aside, a spray of blood flying.

Darus responded by sweeping the huge axe up and across faster than the knight had expected. It hit the armour in the centre of the breastplate so hard the knight was blasted back off his feet, to land in a clatter nearly ten feet away. The man spasmed and writhed, clawing at the straps, desperately trying to remove the deeply dented armour that was preventing him from breathing.

Another horse charged past, intent on a nearby soldier, and almost in reaction to the movement he spun and chopped with the axe at the long powerful neck with all of his might. To his surprise, the blade bit cleanly through both plate and flesh, decapitating the beast. The horse fell in a spray of blood, its staring head pinwheeling along the ground, bouncing off the jaw as the body simply collapsed at the front mid-stride. The great neck jetted blood in spurts onto the green grass as the momentum brought the armoured hindquarters up over the stump like a pendulum. The knight didn't even have time to scream before he was driven into the ground by the weight of his steed like a stake, shattering his upper body into incomprehensible ruin.

Darus turned, his chest heaving with deep grunting breaths. He could taste the blood spray on his lips, and red threatened to overwhelm his mind as it streamed down his arm to his elbow.

A healer next to him, sword unsheathed, stared in amazement at the carnage Darus had wrought. He ignored the human, fighting down his urges. These enemy humans fought in formation. If he tore through them in rage and ended up surrounded, he would be killed.

He glared at the attackers instead, planted himself before the wagons, and roared in challenge. Surrounded by their dead and wounded, he shook the Axe of Grukust in one great hand.

Let them come to him, if they dared.

A surge of Novinians poured through in the chaos after the second wedge of cavalry hit, knights and infantry aiming for the supply wagons, their war dogs among them.

Rast saw a dismounted knight moving to attack the healer cart and sprinted at him. The knight saw him, his sword half-clearing the scabbard. The huge man slammed into the knight, who was not small himself.

His hands closed on the scabbard and hilt, and he rammed the sword back home even as he forced the knight to stagger backwards.

The knight looked astonished he couldn't draw his weapon. Rast jerked on the hilt to angle the scabbard and hooked the man's plated leg. With their combined momentum and weight, they toppled, the scabbard pointing at the grass. It struck the ground and jabbed in to half its length before the hard earth stopped it, pinning the knight to the floor by his belt. Rast rolled over the man and flipped back to his feet, straight back into a sprint. Behind him the knight was yelling curses, flailing on his back like a metal turtle unable to roll upright.

There was no time for anything else. Novinian infantry were converging on the beleaguered carts with spears and swords. Rast caught up to a group and simply yanked the spear from the grip of the last one as he passed the astonished man. He whirled into the midst of them, the spear spinning in his grasp and cracking into the throat of one and the legs of another.

They shouted in alarm, attacking after a second's hesitation. Rast wove through the deadly blades, using the spear like a stave. He struck and blocked in a whirlwind at the centre, the weapon a blur, swords slapped from hands and spears deflected, the haft and tip cracking helmets and legs mercilessly left and right faster than they could see.

He used the butt to strike back, crushing a kneecap before sweeping the legs of the man to his side. Even as he hit the floor Rast reversed the pole and broke his jaw.

Three were down now, the others desperately trying to stab him. He couldn't let them get too close. The butt jabbed one in the eye fiercely, and as he spun the haft over and turned, his leg scythed out and smashed into the man's helm, sending him reeling. Two swords came in and he blocked both, whipping the end up to send them high before jabbing the spear through the throat of one, stepping past the second. As he withdrew the jab in a spurt of blood his elbow snapped back into the face of the other, knocking him back.

He sensed the attack from behind. There was no time to block; he bent back under a silver blur, then threw himself forward to all fours as the return stroke whistled overhead. His attackers simply couldn't keep up with the speed and ferocity of his movements. He sprang back up almost in the same move and lunged, his right arm sliding around the man's neck from the right, palm up. Rast trapped the sword arm with his own body, locking his arm around the neck and spinning the Novinian. As he flipped Rast lunged backward and grabbed his right hand with his left, jerking up and back hard. The man's neck snapped, loudly, and his sword fell from flopping hands.

Rast's toes hooked under the spear and flipped it up to slap solidly into his palms. It spun over his head twice as he whipped around before cracking into the neck of the man behind him. Even as he fought, he could see another two Novinians sprinting up from opposite directions. A hard stab into his final opponent's crotch flooded the area with red as the man screamed. He turned and hurled the spear into the mailed chest of the one he had knocked back. The man was blasted from his feet. In the same movement Rast's hands dipped to his *shirka* and he twisted and dropped to one knee, both hands flicking out to the sides. One whirred out to slam into a throat, the man falling bubbling blood through a shrieking gargle. The other *shirka* found the eye of the last attacker, knocking the head back in a spray of dark blood. Both bodies tumbled to a halt, mere feet away.

He stayed there a moment with arms out, ensuring his foes were all down in his peripheral vision, then rose swiftly, glancing quickly around. The battle had been quick, and he had no time. To his right he saw a few squads cut off from the main body behind the enemy, and he gritted his teeth.

Karland had been marching in that section.

He grabbed a dagger from the nearest corpse as he hurtled it to find his friend, catching glimpses of the battles around him.

The Eordeland ranks were beginning to reform after the initial shock, but there were enough enemy amongst the soldiers to cause problems, and they were definitely aiming for the supply wagons and their healers. Off to his left, Darus was wreaking havoc among the knights. Gambeson was engaging another knight on horseback with sword, and Aldine lead a squad of engineers against another two knights near the healers. The healers themselves had accounted for several foes, who clearly did not expect them to be fully-trained soldiers.

He also saw the elves flitting amongst their foes in a similar fashion to himself, taking down Novinians surgically and quickly, Lëlylien with curved daggers that flitted like hummingbirds in her light grasp, and Galnór with a slim sword that licked at throats and joints.

The snarl of a dog behind him made him twist midstride. A split-second impression of powerful jaws aimed at his throat was all he saw as it leapt. Desperately he twisted and threw himself back onto his shoulders, tucking his legs to his chest. He struck with breathtaking impact and slid backwards as the dog landed on him. Rast snapped his whole body up and drove his shoulders into the floor.

His feet struck the beast with terrific force. The jaws snapped shut on the lolling tongue, severing the end, and the dog was hurled upwards in a backwards cartwheel, neck broken.

He flipped back to his feet in the same motion, turning and almost stumbling, and surged forwards into the thicker fight, leaping through the Eordelanders into the Novinians in a frantic attempt to reach Karland's position.

He smashed one aside with his shoulder like an avalanche, swept his arm up to deflect a spear and punched into the throat of another, who staggered back, and broke through the front ranks. A mounted knight with an unbroken lance charged. Rast ran at the oncoming horse, flicking the dagger over to lie along his left forearm. As the lance dipped to impale him, he slid on his knees, bending backwards so it passed just over his shoulder, using his left arm to ward it, leaving a bloody welt. His right held the slim dagger out across him. It sliced down the flank of the horse and through the girth strap holding the saddle on. The horse shrieked and shied sideways at the lancing pain. The sudden movement snapped the few remaining shreds of leather and the saddle rolled under the weight of the rider.

The knight hit the ground with a crash and tumbled twice before lying limp. The horse staggered at the sudden loss of uneven weight and took the bit between its teeth, fleeing the fighting.

Rast grabbed the helmet and slid the dagger cleanly into the gap between the gorget and helm, twisting it and leaving it jutting as the knight jerked and coughed horribly.

A soldier arrived almost at the same time. Rast ducked a wild swing, blocking the arm across with one hand and rotating his body. His hand swept powerfully back as the other arm came up in an uppercut that lifted the man onto his toes. His legs were swept, and he whirled in the air, the sword dropping from nerveless fingers. The Novinian collapsed like a wet rag, and Rast paused, chest heaving, desperately searching.

A shriek rent the air. Rast spotted a mounted knight who had dropped his lance, the end broken and fixed in the ruined stomach of a smaller figure, and sprinted at

him, desperately hoping he was wrong. He leaped high, using the same flying side
kick he had staggered the ogre with in the Dimnesdair.

This was no ogre, although he was wearing plate mail. Rast cannoned into him,
his feet catching him in the back with such force that he was almost catapulted from
the saddle. Because Rast had hit him from the side and rear, one foot caught in a
stirrup; he simply swivelled as if hinged at the ankle, his helm smashing into the
ground with terrific force before rolling off to show a white face with eyes closed,
blood trailing from a nostril. Rast fell to the floor, catching himself on hands and
feet, and rolled away from the dancing hooves above him. He did not know if the
knight's neck was broken, but the man wasn't moving. The horse stepped on him
twice and stumbled before moving off at a panicked trot. The knight tumbled along
underneath him, his head bouncing off the ground.

Rast looked at the small figure. It was a woman. She was dead.

He couldn't stay here much longer. He would be overwhelmed sooner or later,
and against an armoured man he was at a severe disadvantage, but he could not leave
without Karland. He ran towards the remnants of the squads fighting for their lives.

A knight swung his greatsword at him and he ducked fluidly under it, stepping
in close, and punched out hard. The man's helm rang like a bell and he staggered
backwards, visor changing down. Rast sprang forward and side-kicked, his lead leg
punching out and hitting the man so hard he slightly dented the heavy breastplate.
The knight was hurled from his feet, losing his sword. Rast powered after him and
dropped, landing with a knee on each arm to trap him, and yanked the visor up
roughly, exposing a bearded face with gritted teeth. He smashed his fists into it until
the knight stopped moving.

Rast rose and scanned around him. Another dog turned towards him, frustrated
by the line of shields. He picked up the huge sword and waited. It leapt, and he
swayed sideways, sweeping the sword across and up, using the power in his massive
body and arms and tightening his core. The sword caught the animal just before the
hindquarters and hewed almost straight through. An agonised yelp was cut off as the
two halves hit the floor trailing guts, connected only by wet strands, the front half
shuddering. He spun the bloody sword back to guard, then dropped it.

For the moment, everyone else was avoiding or ignoring him. There were dead
or dying men and women on the red-stained grass, and more than a few knights, but
as the Eordeland ranks closed and their defence bit back into the attackers, the field
cleared slightly and allowed him a chance to search.

He couldn't see Karland anywhere.

❦　　❧

350

Karland couldn't believe how loud the impact was. He had been able to see where the heavy cavalry had struck the lines to his left on the flank. Men and women flew, weapons scattering as the first compacted wedge smashed into them like a hammer. Before Karland realised what was happening, the horses had curved through the ranks towards him, cutting several squads off, including his. He saw knights discard broken lances and draw swords, maces and axes. They thundered through the disoriented Eordelanders, striking at heads and faces from horseback before reaching a quieter area on the outskirts.

Just then the second wedge hit the same spot with a roar that made his legs quail. Barely seconds after that the black and rust dogs hurtled among them, snarling. They were massive, with huge shoulders and long tails, almost as big as the great grey wolves of the plains and northern forests. Their snouts were shorter, their broad heads holding powerful crushing teeth.

It was a bloodbath as the horses swept past. One of the men went down with a yell, a lance through the back. It tore out in a spray of gore, breaking. Karland backpedalled, then stopped. He could not leave his comrades to die alone, terrified though he was. His heart thundered in his chest and everything seemed distant.

Three dogs closed on one of the soldiers nearby, and his spear took one in the throat. It was Fin, a man-at-arms with an easy laugh and quick mouth. That mouth was now set in a fearful line. Without his squad to back him up he could not face them all with his shield, but was covered on his left by another soldier.

The falling animal wrenched the shaft from his hand as he fell, and he drew his shortsword, keeping them at bay desperately. His companion jerked sideways to avoid a lance straight into the path of a warhorse, which hit him with sickening impact, bowling him over.

The dogs broke from Fin and fell upon him instead. He regained enough senses to begin yelling, and then one of them tore his throat out with a powerful heave of its neck.

Fin, his face contorted with anger and despair, moved to stab one of the dogs as Karland raced to help him, knowing it was too late for the man on the grass. Karland heard thunder behind him and threw himself to the side. Another horse pounded past, a knight standing in the stirrups. When Karland turned back to look at Fin, he saw a long-hafted axe with an angled blade and long spikes wedged in the angle between shoulder and neck, through the muscles and collarbone. It looked profoundly wrong.

Fin looked horrified for a second, and then all thought left his face as Karland watched, his own horror equal to the dying man's. Fin staggered, the axe jutting. He fell to his knees, gulping and trying to speak, one hand raised as if to gain attention for a question. Blood poured from his mouth, and he fell forward, a pool pumping from his sundered neck.

'Boy!' a deep woman's voice called, and he turned to see another veteran running towards him with only a sword. He regained some of his senses. Anyone alone would die. They needed to regroup to get back to their fellows alive.

'Ware!' shouted Karland, seeing another horse galloping in. Without even looking she tried to dodge, but went the wrong way, crossing its path. The shoulder of the horse clipped her from behind and hurled her into him. Karland went down with her on top of him.

The breath was blasted from his body, and he hit the ground hard, stunned. It took him a moment to collect himself enough to start to push her off him. He didn't know her other than by sight. She was much older than he was, her square-jawed face lined at the eyes and with a mole on her left cheekbone which enhanced her looks rather than marred them. He gazed into her face. This close, he could see the dirt from the road in the pores of her skin, hear the agonised whistle of air past her teeth when she inhaled.

The soldier was more dazed than he was, and whimpering in pain, favouring one arm. It looked as if the impact had dislocated her shoulder. They lay there for a moment, his wits clearing.

Even as she began to try and rise off him, hoof beats sounded again nearby, thudding past. She jammed into him hard, knocking more breath from him, and then stiffened, her mouth in an O, looking into his face as if she had only just seen him as clearly as he saw her, perhaps wished to kiss him. Her eyes were blue-green, with the most lovely patterning in the iris, and they flicked around his face for a second, searching for something. She shuddered, exhaling into his face, and slumped on him. The metallic tang of blood carried on the breath, and a gasping from her throat went on and on as she tried to breath in again with lungs that no longer worked. Karland sobbed at the intimacy of the death. He held her as she shuddered, smoothing her hair to try and let her know someone was there.

It must have been only seconds later that she lay stiller than still, and he knew she was gone. He pushed her off him, tears blurring his sight, an awful gash in her upper back where a passing knight had jammed the splintered end of a lance with punishing consequences. The lance lay thrown aside, the end dark with blood.

Trying to collect his bearings, Karland looked around through his tears. He was cut off from relative safety by the Novinian infantry and dismounted knights were attacking his countrymen with zeal, wielding longswords, maces and axes. More than thirty horses stamped riderless behind him, nervous in the din of combat.

No one had spotted him for the moment. Even the battle of The Croft had not prepared him for being in the heart of this.

Hearing a distant roaring he saw a huge green shape head and shoulders above the Eordelanders, tearing into attackers and hurling them around like children despite the extra weight of their armour. It was swinging an axe he knew well with every bit of skill he had seen from Grukust, and he knew at least Darus was still fighting. He couldn't see Rast or the elves.

'*Eord!*' came a bellowing cry from behind him. The voice was rough and aggressive with a metallic tone. Karland turned to see a knight rein in casually and dismount, leaving his sword in its saddle sheathe. He walked to Fin, placing his foot on the body and wrenching out the axe torn from his grasp with a sickening crack. Fin's body flopped grotesquely.

Karland realised vaguely that no one else was approaching; clearly, this knight was to have his own fun. He was a big man, and his polished steel plate was spattered with gore. A crested close helm was beaked with monstrous decoration in the form of a snarling dog's jaws on the front, a split visor above them. The man raised it to show a clean-shaven, weathered face with yellow teeth bared in amusement.

'Come, Eord. Let us see if you can die like a *man*,' challenged the knight. His voice sounded constricted and a little high, as if his vocal chords were tight. He towered over Karland in gleaming field plate. Compared to Rast the knight seemed lumbering.

That judgment nearly cost him his life. Without further warning, the knight swung the axe with practiced control, swiping left to right in a wicked slash that would have parted Karland's head from his neck if it had connected. After a frozen moment, Karland leapt back more than he needed to, his focus narrowing to his enemy and the axe barely missing him. If another foe had come at him, he wouldn't have even known they were there. The din of the battle faded into the background as his mind virtually shut down in fear, and his focus narrowed dangerously. This was not a fight like the orc he had faced in his village, where his anger and protection of his family had overcome his fear, nor was this facing an assassin virtually falling on his knife whilst Karland was in the throes of grief and rage. This was not Gorin or Ben Arflun.

For the first time in his life, another human was facing him squarely with the intent of killing him in combat on a level field. There wasn't any hatred from his foe - only a cold contempt, dismissal, that cared nothing that he was a living breathing person with thoughts and dreams.

This time, there was no outside emotion to provide the impetus to fight; only the blunt knowledge that he would die, brutally and alone, and be forgotten.

Karland's heart was pounding in fear, and he was only aware of his breathing and the axe. His stentorian breath sounded harsh and rigid, and he found he couldn't move properly, stiff and awkward. The man's movements were fast and sure, his grunts of effort and taunts unnerving. Karland barely heard over his own forced breaths, which were fast and taking most of his energy. He was sweating, his attention totally fixated on the man.

Somehow, he survived the first few seconds, scrambling desperately. Gradually, as he moved, his breathing slowed, and almost unwillingly his body loosened itself from the bonds of his mind. He found his dagger in his right hand, his weight was shifting more smoothly on his feet. He forced himself to breathe more slowly, and the fog and stiffness began to lift. The fear was still there, but it was a neighbouring star rather than a supernova within.

The knight's laughter faded, and his attacks became more focused, angrier and frustrated. Karland couldn't see any way to win except to run, but he was tired. Even if the man couldn't catch him on foot, he could on horse. The armour didn't seem to hinder him at all.

Karland fell back under the swipes of the axe blade, hoping the knight would tire. It wasn't until he almost stumbled into the man's horse that he realised he was in danger of being kicked.

Desperately, he grabbed at a stone at his feet and threw it at the knight. More by chance than design it struck the man in the mouth, splitting his lip but doing no real damage.

With a bellow of rage, the knight leapt forward, swing wildly. Karland would have died then, but he tripped. The axe meant for his head clanged instead off the horse's armoured hindquarters.

The horse, unable to see fully, reacted to the sudden attack by lifting its rear and kicking out as hard as it could.

Karland had a split-second memory of Stryke in The Croft as the hooves slammed into the surprised knight, one hitting his helm with a clang.

The stunned man fell with a crash, his axe landing some feet away. Karland grabbed his dagger and scrambled over to the dazed knight, who was trying to rise. He had a vague idea of rolling him to his back and demanding he yield, remembering stories of the honour of knights.

As he got there the knight rolled to one knee quicker than expected, his moves practiced, and snatched at his rondel dagger. He turned and lunged at Karland, but it was clear his vision was fuzzy. His thrust went wide. Instinctively Karland blocked the plated arm, bruising his own, and thrust his other out without thinking.

Almost of its own volition the dagger he held slipped into the left eye socket. With a crunch the blade slid home into the man's brain, driven by the knight's momentum.

There was surprisingly little noise. The knight jerked, one hand half-lifting as if to pluck at the blade, and then with a sigh that just kept going, he sagged forward into Karland, a small rivulet of blood running from the helm. Karland only caught a glimpse of the ruined face as it went past.

The weight of his enemy tore the firmly lodged weapon from Karland's grasp, and he slid off him to land face-down. Karland knelt, breathing hard, his mind replaying the moment, totally oblivious to anything nearby.

He had killed a man; thrust a blade through fragile and precise brain tissue, turning a living person into something that was just meat in a metal shell. The fact that the man had given him no choice was irrelevant. There had been no hatred here. Only fear, panic, simple chance.

Numbly he stood, preparing to try to reach his comrades through the melee, shaking from the adrenaline and the speed of the conflicting emotions.

A growl froze him. Out of the corner of his eye, he could see a dog approaching. The horse snorted nervously. He turned his head slowly left and saw another three, one with blood on its muzzle, all padding towards him.

Without a second thought he whirled and bolted for the steed just behind him. It hadn't been expecting the movement, and before it could react, he had grabbed the tack and hauled himself up, barely ahead of the snapping teeth of the lead dog.

With a whinny the horse whipped around, Karland clinging desperately. More than the death around it, more than the stranger on its back, the horse was upset by the snarling dogs that usually stayed well clear of it. The snap at Karland broke its placidity. For a second Karland thought it would rear, but then it lashed out with a foot, catching one dog and sending it to the floor with a yelp to lie, whining piteously.

The horse whirled again dizzyingly and bolted, trying to get away from the unknown rider and the beasts which followed it. The dogs pursued, which simply made the horse run faster. Karland gripped with his legs and held on tight. The horse had the bit between its teeth and was not slowing for anything. Behind it three dogs ran, snarling in frustration, the fleeing horse tapping straight into their instincts. At that moment, without a handler to call them off, they could not help but to give chase.

The horse galloped away from the battle, north into the foothills, and Karland clung on for dear life. If he fell, the dogs would tear him apart. He only hoped he could calm the horse enough to coax it back around, that the dogs would break off. For now, he was carried away from his friends, deeper into the unfriendly wilds and surrounded by enemies.

 *

As the combatants separated, Thorne shouted for the crossbows to release. Many bolts punched into horses, causing the armoured beasts to thrash. A few buzzed among the Novinian infantry. As they began to fall screaming in pain, they locked shields forward and rear in a loose turtle, but the deadly shafts went through these too. Wounded horses panicked and started heaving men out of the way.

The knights fared no better. The armoured foes were mostly on foot, hacking at the pikes holding them back from their enemies. Now that the formation of the pikes and war scythes was solid, they were equally adept at keeping horses and knights back, and the scythes were particularly effective, able to slash as well as thrust.

The famed Crosses had patiently cocked their weapons and awaited their opening. As soon as they could, they began shooting over the shoulders of the pikes in practiced synchronisation. Eight armoured knights fell in the same moment as if they had strings cut, several scrabbling at their own shells in agony at the steel bolts that had punched a ragged hole through both metal and the flesh underneath. The rest lay unmoving. Metallic cries rang out from some of the fallen, sounding demonic in the din. Scant seconds later, more shots from another squad twanged out.

Heavy metal bolts skipped off armour at angles, wheeling away, but others penetrated. Knights fell from horses and steeds stumbled as the short metal quarrels simply vanished into them. The huge chargers tumbled in a welter of destruction, slamming their riders into the ground with bone-breaking force or rolling over them, smashing infantry aside in their falls. More than one knight lay in sundered armour like a crushed beetle.

The Novinian infantry had sustained heavy losses and relied on their knights to break the enemy. Instead, their knights were also being decimated, and the defence was too strong to penetrate. They had failed to break their enemies, and stood in danger of being fragmented themselves.

In the space of seconds, the battle turned. The Eordeland company had rallied, and the initial shock of the cavalry was absorbed. Calls sounded from further back in

356

the attackers, then a piercing whistle went up in a complex pattern from handlers behind the Novinians. Almost as one, the remaining dogs turned and pelted back from the fight. Half the dogs were down now. They retreated at full run, their ears flapping and the muzzles of too many bloody. The few that were busy worrying at the Eordelanders were quickly impaled on spears, snapping and whining as their legs scrabbled and their fleeing lives warmed the cold tips.

The front row of knights were decimated by the pikes and war scythes, which knocked them to the ground, or found the joints of their armour and tore through tendons and flesh. Blood ran over silver plate and screams of men resounded. Infantry withered under the steady bolts.

A horn sounded, three times, and yells came.

'Fall back! Fall back!'

The knights disengaged again, this time turning full tail and moving away fast to their horses, covered by the infantry. Their infantry followed rapidly, a few last arrows hissing into them as they fled.

The Eordelanders did not break ranks to chase, as they might have usually, but watched them leave, and shouted in victory until the last had vanished. The Crosses felled two more knights before a shouted command halted them.

As quickly as that, the fight was over.

ଔ   ଛ

'I cannot believe a full company of mercenary knights attacked us so close to allied borders,' grated Aldine. 'Where are the dwarves? This land should be safe!' His voice held anger.

'We have not heard from the dwarves for many months,' said Rast. 'They may have withdrawn into Deep Delving.'

Aldine shook his head in disgust. 'The Novinians retreated quickly. Maybe they were on their way somewhere else and hoped to route us, pick over the wagons with a quick strike.'

'Awaiting word from Meyar?' suggested Rast.

Major Gambeson spoke heavily, his face lined with regret. 'If they had ambushed us with bows, it would have been different. We must be doubly on our guard.' It was obvious he blamed himself for not anticipating the attack. Soldiers had died.

'They were professionals. We were lucky.' Rast shook his head. 'It was an attack of opportunity.'

'Luck had nothing to do with it,' said Aldine with some pride. 'Though I do not know how the spotters missed them. Especially the elves.'

357

'The pathfinders sent north did not return,' said Galnór wearily. 'I went further northwest. I recall I did warn you of the cavalry.' His arm had been bandaged, and he showed little favouring of it. Elves healed quickly.

'Barely,' sniffed Aldine.

'He outran their charge to deliver word,' remarked Rast dryly.

'Tal'Orien is right,' said Gambeson quietly. 'Thank you, Galnór. If it hadn't been for you both, as well as Tal'Orien and the ork, they might have destroyed our supplies, maybe the healers and sappers. Even elves cannot see everything.' He shook his head. 'They approached through the foothills. We were lucky to get the warning we did. It made the difference.' His armour was streaked with dirt and dented in places. The knight he had fought had been skilled. Weariness showed in all of them.

The elf bowed his head. Only Rast appreciated the subtly of the movement, conveying both thanks and profound regret at what the elf saw as a failure.

'How many did we lose?' asked Aldine. His tone suggested that he didn't really want the answer.

'We're still tallying the dead and wounded,' said Sergeant-Major Thorne quietly. 'Thirty died in the battle. No healers or sappers, thank the Gods. Two spotters missing. Lancers, skirmishers, a few rangers. No bolters.' He sighed. 'You said it before, sir. We were lucky not to lose more. We still might. There are another seventeen wounded badly enough to need the healers, two critical. If they live the night, they have a chance. Those bastards cut off three squads with their knights, and nearly decimated them, 'scusing the Banistari, sir.'

'Estimated enemy losses?'

'More than a third of their knights, at least half their war dogs, and almost half their infantry,' said Thorne with some satisfaction. 'They paid dearly. We took fifteen prisoners, some wounded. The others were given field mercy.'

'Strip them naked and turn them loose,' Gambeson said. Aldine muttered. 'Will you kill them in cold blood, or ransom them then? We have no time, Captain.'

'Sir.'

'What news of Karland?' asked Rast, his face impassive.

Thorne shook his head.

'The boy's missing. He's not amongst the dead, and they took no prisoners here. Either he ran from the fighting or was separated during the charges and killed. He was among the squads that were cut off.' He held up Karland's knife and spoke with genuine respect. 'He managed to kill a Knight. We found this through his eye.'

'I cannot leave him here,' said Rast, accepting the blade with a mix of pride and concern. Killing an armoured man was no small feat. 'I have a duty to him.'

'Greater than your country?' demanded Aldine.

'Eordeland is not my country,' replied Rast mildly. 'There are others here who can complete my task. Karland is my pupil, my responsibility. My friend.'

'You would pick that duty over ours-' began Aldine, and then cut off as Gambeson raised a hand.

'What shall we do then, Master Tal'Orien?' he asked quietly. 'You were invaluable today. I accept we will not be caught unawares again, and I know you travel with us by choice, but you know this country. You know the ways into Eyotsburg if our way is blocked. We would have carried the day without you, but our losses would have been greater.'

'My first duty is to Karland,' said Rast. 'It is not a light decision. Darus also knows this country. He can help guide you there.'

'Trust an ork?' asked Aldine, and then shut his mouth, glancing at Darus, who sat calmly watching. They had all seen his defence of the wagons, and he had amazed them with his power. Already the companion's feats were whispered amongst the company. They had gone through the enemy like scythes through wheat.

Gambeson glanced at his second in command wryly, not deigning to answer, and Aldine reddened slightly.

'Master Tal'Orien,' the Major said quietly. 'The Council depends on you taking ship to the elves.'

'They could take this message alone,' Rat said flatly. 'I am here as aid, not envoy.'

'But you are to give your accounts of Eordeland, and speak of the visions in the Hall of Wyrms. Only you can do those.'

'Neither might make a difference. You ask me to wager the life of Karland against a possibility.'

'*If* he still lives,' said Aldine.

'May I propose another solution?' interjected a smooth voice. Lëlylien leaned forward, her silver braided hair falling over one shoulder and her ageless face serious. 'I am the swiftest here, and the best tracker. Let me search. I am his best chance.'

Heads turned to her, and after a moment Rast heaved a sigh.

'You may be right, Lëlylien. You are a better tracker than I. Would you do this?'

'He is also my friend,' she said simply. 'I will search until I find him… or news of him.'

Rast studied her, and then bowed his head in acceptance, face impassive. He let none of them see the turmoil of failing another companion within him.

Gambeson nodded. 'We must bury our dead and restock. We move at first light. Progress will be slower. I will not be caught like that again however safe the land should be. From now on we march in close formation on full battle alert. Those lost are my fault, my error.' His face bore the weight of those losses.

'What were they doing here?' demanded Aldine with the frustration they all felt. 'Attacking us was chancy. They must have known they couldn't win a pitched battle.'

'I think they saw a chance and took it, as Rast said,' said Gambeson. 'It could have paid off. Whatever else they are, Novinians are not ones to shrink from a fight.' He stood, wincing. 'Keep me informed on the wounded, Thorne.'

'Sir.' The burly man nodded. He and Aldine stood and saluted.

Lëlylien also moved to depart. She stopped briefly before Rast, and laid a cool hand on his chest, looking into his eyes, conveying more than words in the manner of the elves.

He nodded, his heart heavy, and she vanished into the dusk.

TWENTY-SEVEN

X hera sighed and stretched, laying down the pencil she had been making notes with. It had been a long, distraction-filled day, and she had a decision to make this evening.

She looked over to the letters she had penned. One for Hendal and Martha. One for Jon and Talas. She had also written one for Karland's family, to tell them where he had gone.

She sighed. Her old life was far behind her, but she sometimes wished to see the lake again where she had grown up. Mixed with that was a desire to visit Valesruin one day. To see where her life had really begun.

Where her entire family had died, apart from her sister.

When she thought about what she had before Aldwyn came, before she lost her innocent view of the world... was her life really better now? After all the pain and horror?

Yes.

She had Karland. She had Rast. She wasn't trapped anymore. She knew the truth of her life. It had been terrible, the fear and the pain and the loss of people she had cared for deeply, but she would never have known Aldwyn, or Grukust, or Györnàeldàr if she had stayed. Despite the hurt of their loss, her life was richer for them having passed through it.

And Darus. Night. Rast.

Karland.

There was more to study. More to find. Her life was meant to be more than it had been there, she was sure, but she did sometimes miss the innocence of the farm days. Even, sometimes, feeding the chickens.

For a farmer's daughter, she had ended up with a lot of responsibility. And despite that, despite putting her studies on hold to help the Council, despite the marvellous information in the Combic Libraries - which she knew she was very privileged to be allowed to view - it was not enough.

She could not do this here. Too much was missing. Aldwyn had been a prolific writer and collector of other prolific writers. Between his own studies and his collection of others, there should have been all the information she needed, but it simply wasn't there.

Karland had been right, she reflected. The rest must be in the Library of Thingos.

There was a knock at the door. She had been expecting it.

'Come in.'

The door opened, but instead of Night, it was Seom, his dark handsome face set in a welcoming smile.

'Seom!'

She was pleased to see him; they had all many good times in the last month or so and had bonded closely. She knew Seom was interested in her - and if she was honest with herself, she found it hard not to respond. He was tall, handsome, and very confident. Where Karland knowingly hid softer features and slight asymmetry, Seom could have been the basis for a statue with his cheekbones and bearing. He laughed loudly and did everything with assurance.

She also knew that it hurt Karland when she responded, and that meant more to her - *he* meant more to her - than enjoying the attentions of an attractive boy.

Seom moved in and closed the door, his dark eyes intent on her face. 'I don't have too long, but I managed to convince my Sergeant to allow me some time.'

'What do you mean?'

'I am posted to a force moving to reserves. For reinforcements. We are told nothing, but I think we may be reinforcements against an attack.' The words came out quickly, unlike his usual composure. He sounded worried. 'A lot of the recruits are scoffing; they say even if it's true no one could stand against us, but I've heard a lot of rumours. People here think Eordeland can beat any enemy. I'm starting to wonder, some of the things I've heard. And people die in battle. I didn't want to go without seeing you.'

'Don't say that.' Her heart plummeted.

He moved closer. 'It's true, Xhera. I'm, I don't know. Just… this could be my last chance to say goodbye. Properly.'

His hand traced her jaw, tilting her head back slightly. She shivered. He *was* very good looking.

So self-assured.

He dipped his head towards her face, and her eyes closed as their lips touched for a moment as her hand slipped up to his. She held it lightly, and moved back slightly, feeling sad, and a little longing, breaking contact.

'I- I like you Seom. A lot. But I...' she couldn't find a way to say it easily, or without regret. 'I can't. Karland is... I care about him. More than anyone.' She tried to lighten it. 'No matter how tall, dark, or... handsome I find him.'

'Ah.' He smiled regretfully, his eyes tracing her face. She could tell he was upset. 'So, this is what it feels like.' His smile was wry.

'What do you mean?'

He shrugged. 'Karland has spent much of his life liking girls who are not interested in him. A lot of them were interested in me, but he never held it against me. I never had that problem, not so much. I guess it didn't help his feeling lonely... and now he has the attention of the lady *I* wish the attention of.' He laughed slightly, embarrassed. 'Sorry. I think I misread something... I knew he liked you, but...'

'Oh.' She shook her head. 'I don't want to get in the way of your friendship with him. Or lose mine with you, either. You, me, Karland; we are friends. Good friends.'

'The best.' Seom smiled. 'Look, Xhera-' He studied his hands a second, then looked up. 'I am glad he found you. And I'm glad you found him.'

She smiled. 'Thank you.'

'Just know that whatever else happens, I am your friend. Always will be. His too. I'm-' he swallowed, uncertain now. 'Oh, a lot of the other recruits are excited at the prospect of war. They boast of how they will defend Eordeland. How they will defeat the Meyari.' He shook his head. 'I'm not stupid. I know this might be a fight that I don't come back from. There are always casualties. I just didn't want to leave without... telling you how I felt.' His eyes were dark and steady.

Even baring himself to her like this, he was so confident. How different from Karland!

She hugged him.

'Come back,' she said softly. His arms tightened around her. Before she could stiffen, they let go, reluctantly. 'For both of us. He has told me so many times how you gave him strength when you were young. His rock, his friend.'

Seom looked thoughtful. 'It means a lot. That he said that. But... I don't think he really needs me anymore. He's very different now. Last time we sparred he had me every time, without trying.'

'Try telling *him* that.' They grinned at each other for a moment, then sobered.

'When do you leave?'

'Tomorrow.'

Xhera nodded. 'Stay safe, Seom. We would be less without you.'

Seom bowed from the waist, graceful. 'As my lady commands. And-' he hesitated. 'Say goodbye to Karland for me. In case.'

'Won't be necessary,' she said fiercely. He drew in a breath, and she sighed. 'I'll tell him anyway.'

A light knock at the door came. 'Xhera?'

'Come in,' she called. Night stepped into the room. 'You asked to see me?'

Seom grinned at her again. 'Didn't know you would have other company.'

'Am I interrupting?'

'No, no. I was saying farewell. We march soon.'

Night nodded. 'Look after yourself, young man. I pray that you return safely.'

'Thank you, sir.' Seom looked back to Xhera. 'You take care as well.'

'I will.'

He nodded, smiled, and with one last lingering look, he left.

Xhera sighed. That wasn't something she'd expected.

'Complicated?'

'More or less.' She shook her head. 'Sorry. I need to ask a favour, I think.'

'What can I do for you?'

'I think I need to continue my studies at the Library of Thingos. Is there any way you can speak to the Council?'

'Interesting.' Night moved to a chair and sat. 'You have reached a dead end here?'

'Not exactly. It's just harder to find things without- without Karland here. You're a great help,' she added hastily. 'But Karland knew him better than both of us. Some things just aren't here. I think they may be there.'

'It is possible,' conceded Night. 'I have long been curious about it, myself. There is a problem, however. I can propose you go, even accompany you, but it may not be for long.' His eyes flared ember red for a moment. 'I expect word of a trail to my quarry, and I have other duties. You will need other protection.'

'Do you think so?' she asked doubtfully.

'Yes. The Croft is nearer the borders. Even though it had been reinforced, there is always a chance of enemy attack; orcs, bandits. No land is truly safe anymore. The Library is a treasure trove of information which must not fall into the hands of our enemies. You need to be protected, and you need to be hidden.'

'Oh.'

'I will let you know their decision. I am confident they will agree this is a good idea.' He smiled. Once the decision comes it will be quick, Xhera. Are you certain you wish to leave The Sanctum?'

'I left the place I grew up; I think I can leave the University.'

A part of her wondered, however. Nowhere else had felt so much like home to her, for all she missed the rolling greens and bounding woods of her tun. She had grown up an awful lot since Aldwyn had first visited. The Sanctum held everything she needed to mould her own life as it needed to be.

Karland felt as if he did not truly belong anywhere, but Xhera had always felt simply more… displaced.

Nevertheless… something was different here. Without Rast and Karland, the huge, bustling building of thousands of souls - the heart of Eordeland - simply felt empty.

She may as well do something significant whilst she waited for their return.

And they will *return,* she added resolutely.

'As you wish.' He nodded and rose. 'Whatever our future, know that you and your friends have made a difference. Sleep well, Xhera.'

ʘ Š

Xhera mooned around The Sanctum for a week, unable to focus on her studies. She didn't talk to many people, took little notice in classes, and got no work done on Aldywn's notes.

The comforting, solid presence of Rast was no longer lurking just out of sight, like a guardian angel of shadow. The huge ork and his booming humour was gone. Seom had left.

Worst was when she turned around, several times in a day, to say something to Karland, only to realise he wasn't there. It was like a piece of her was missing. It just wasn't right if she wasn't annoyed with him for something, or laughing with him.

At least she had Night. He gently helped ground her in her studies every evening, sitting with her as long as she wished. His patience and quiet humour was a boon. But he was reserved, dispassionate, distant as the moons; no replacement for the others.

One evening he knocked on her door, entering only when asked, and sat at the table. He carried no books, coming quickly to the point.

'We leave tomorrow, Xhera. Before dawn.'

'So suddenly?'

Just like Karland.

'The Council agrees with your request; in fact, they had already planned for it. Captain-Generals Dorn and Jekob are still concerned about the threats from Aran Telemer. Although he is gone, and Castellan James and Councillor Holmson have begun to uncover much of his web of bribery, there are still concerns over your safety. I can protect you at night, yet… I am not at liberty to give details, but the instructions left were alarmingly well-planned.'

365

So Aran hadn't been bluffing. She felt a pit yawn in her stomach. It was likely his plans had involved humiliation and violation at least, if not death. Aran had no empathy or care for any others and had long looked on her as a possession as yet unwon.

'There are too many distractions for the Council, and for you; you sit here in rooms empty with memories, and it is affecting your studies. It is simply better to remove you from The Sanctum. The council hopes, as we do, that much of what we wish to read of Aldwyn's notes is likely to be in the Library of Thingos.'

Good.

She could not help feeling she was on the verge of a breakthrough in understanding. It was frustrating; there were large sections of the Combic Libraries she was simply not allowed to go into, and even Night was forbidden some areas, not that it apparently stopped him.

'I'm already mostly packed,' she admitted. 'It will do us good to leave here.'

Until they return, she added again fiercely. It had become her mantra.

'I will collect all the works we may need and then come for you in the early hours. We believe it is best to leave without any notice. Do not be alarmed if I wake you in darkness. Sleep early. I will travel part of the way with you and meet you the next evening.'

Xhera nodded, and Night bowed and left.

So. Now to play my own part.

∾ ∿

They left two hours before sunrise, only Tarqas and Gusta of the Council there to wish her luck. Dorn introduced Xhera to the veteran half-squad who would travel with her. The chance of trouble was low; patrols along the major routes were regular now, and the road from the Croft east along the river Lothian towards Boreamere on Lake Nordling was monitored closely. It had been a major route for orc bands moving west.

Xhera wrote Seom a note and passed it to the Guard on her door as she left. There was a very good chance it would reach the recruits within a few weeks.

The journey up to The Croft was leisurely. Xhera had sent word to her parents of her destination but would not be able to visit the tun. They moved on the main roads west then north to Gladsmoor, then to The Croft. Part of her was disappointed, but a greater part was relieved. She missed her family when she wasn't distracted by her studies, but what she was doing now was what she had yearned to do her whole life.

Xhera was learning and making a difference - and had control of her own destiny.

They camped each night, Night not appearing until after dark. If the soldiers considered it odd, they did not say anything; for all they knew, he spent his time sleeping and studying in the long wagon. It was a pleasant journey, and on Night's advice Xhera continued her break from her studies. She found it refreshing, and looked upon the bright world with renewed interest, but there was a constant itch at the back of her mind nagging at her.

She still spent a lot of time thinking back to Karland. He was so brave, so determined to do the right thing despite his self-doubt. She hoped he was safe, desperately hoped he would return. In a world that had shown her uncertainty, isolation and danger, he was her rock. Her soul's mirror. Apart from her studies, he was what gave her meaning, although she could not find a way to tell him that. Everything she said to him sounded forced, was hard to say. She cared for him deeply but could not find a way to admit it out loud. Far too late, part of her cried in regret that she had not gone with him, not realised earlier. Logically she knew she was best placed to continue their studies, and had been in less danger than he, but they belonged with each other. They defined each other. He was her best friend.

She needed him back safely.

When they arrived in The Croft, she saw differences. The barricade was still there, but this time there were Eordeland Guard manning it as well as town militia. It looked a little more permanent, and was expanded, which was a shame in a way. The Croft was one of the most westerly points in Eordeland, and she knew Dorn had been concerned about incursions from mercenaries or Meyar, but she suspected it had had a much more idyllic quality before. Now the town was growing.

A large border fort was being built to the west, but until it was complete, The Croft would serve as a focal point for the materials and troops. It had given the craftsmen there much more work and attracted many new artisans. A garrison was growing there, further outside the town limits.

Whatever happened, The Croft's quiet isolation was ending.

Some things she remembered; the centre of the town was the same, although a large *Iterscientiam* lay grounded next to the inn. She remembered the wagons at the tun, full of books, making their ways between towns and villages for lessons and learning, bringing books to everyone in Eordeland. They were driven by scholars of The Sanctum, roving librarians with great general knowledge. Too many had been attacked in the last year; they were becoming rarer. Both scholars and books were too valuable to place in danger.

Brin and Becka welcomed her with open arms, insisting she stay there rather than the inn. Night had solemnly said he would stay with the wagon, to avoid questions. They were planning to spend a few days here to resupply and rest before moving on to the Library.

Gail, after shyly avoiding her, had astonished her parents by clinging to Xhera and speaking constantly. She asked about her brother several times; although she clearly would not admit it, she missed him. Xhera found her endearing and sweet, although she also saw the determination and strength of character that had probably made Karland's life somewhat difficult. Gail would be a strong woman.

Xhera had told them much of events, missing out the details of the attack and saying instead that Karland was travelling as an envoy to the elves. Brin hadn't said it, but she could tell he was immensely proud.

She also told them that war was coming, which garnered no surprise. Unlike the inner cities, The Croft and the surrounding towns and villages had smelled the fires catching some time ago. Their only real surprise was that it had taken so long.

They also showed great surprise and pleasure that Seom had become a trainee Guard. Becka had fond memories of him. Brin had liked him, although he had also suspected that Seom had encouraged Karland into a lot of the trouble he had ended up in. From what Xhera could make out, Karland had been constantly in trouble of some sort. She had tried not to giggle.

They stayed there several nights, Brin and Becka putting her up. The squad was happy enough to join the not-so-makeshift barracks and catch up with the Guard there.

They were cautious about moving out until they knew it was safe. A trapper from The Croft had been found brutally gored and part-eaten in the Northing Woods a week before they had arrived, with wounds the Croftfolk could not comprehend. The evening after they had arrived, there had been a puzzling discovery in the woods not far from the most eastern farms. A gigantic, misshapen boar had been discovered a few hundred feet from where his torn body had been found, killed by many slashes from strange blades. It had been the size of a horse, heavier, with bony plates and spines. The tusks that had sliced the trapper in half were ragged and two feet long.

The Guards were on high alert, looking for any traces of whoever had killed the creature. None of their weapons would have left the marks. No one was sure what to do with the body. Even the dogs didn't want to go near it.

Night ghosted out but reported seeing nothing near the town outside the usual wildlife. Xhera could tell the guards were cautious, but Kervala was confident of their ability to handle any threat.

On the third night, Xhera had a pleasant surprise; Hendal and Marta arrived with Jon and Talas. They had received her note, and decided to visit while they could, pleased that they had caught her. They were quite firm that The Sanctum was not their place, apart from Talas, who was uncharacteristically quiet. She was wearing glasses similar to those Aldwyn had worn; Xhera had found a scholar to persuade one of the travelling apothecaries to detour to Hoeven Lake and paid him to make her sister a pair of spectacles. It had cost her everything she'd had, but the letter back from her sister had been heartwarming. Her eyesight would never be perfect again, but they helped hugely. The glasses enhanced her eyes and looks and gave her a much sharper gaze than Xhera was used to.

Xhera introduced her family to Brin and Becka, who welcomed them all for dinner, and they had a fine feast. Brin and Hendal spoke authoritatively about many matters, Jon listening in, whilst Marta gave Becka advice. Gail sat quietly, leaving the room when she had finished; she knew Xhera wanted to see her sister. Xhera knew Karland would never have given his young sister credit for such perspicacity before, but Gail was maturing rapidly.

'Are you well?' asked Talas quietly, the others distracted.

'Yes, Talas.' Xhera smiled. 'I'm doing something important, perhaps; and I'm free to learn. I'm just sad for Karland's absence. And you?'

Talas smiled. 'The tun goes as it does. The family Barstak will look after it for a few days whilst we are here. And, well… you are going to be an aunty.'

Xhera laughed in delight. 'An aunt!' She hugged her sister, carefully, then held her at arm's length. She couldn't see a bump.

'I'm not *that* fragile,' laughed Talas back. She appeared more carefree, as if she had finally accepted Xhera's decision. 'I'm so glad you are happy. And safe. It's been hard for me to accept my little sister grew up.'

'I was always the same, Talas. Now I'm just more so.' She smiled at the odd look her sister gave her. 'Sorry. That's something Karland would say.' She sighed. 'I do miss him.'

'I'm sure he is safe,' said Talas. 'He is with Rast Tal'Orien, after all.' She eyed her younger sister. 'You really have grown up a lot, Xhera. Are you two…?' She trailed off, a *look* on her face.

'No,' said Xhera, her cheeks heating. 'Maybe. I… know he cares for me. He's my best friend. I care for him too. I think we just… need time.'

'Hmm.' There was a wealth of discussion in that word, and Xhera wasn't sure whether it was approving or not. 'He's a good lad. Man, almost.'

'He is.' She was right, Xhera realised. Karland might not recognise it himself, but he was not the same small boy as when they had met. He had grown taller, broader, much more skilled. Had Aran fought him in personal combat in court, he would very likely have lost.

'I'm happy for you, Xhera. Really.' Talas hugged her again hard, the contact saying more than words. 'And I'm proud. We've heard how well you've been doing.'

Xhera hugged her sister back, realising how much she had missed her.

'Promise me one thing,' she said softly.

'What?'

'Your child. Don't... don't stand in the way of their dreams. If you can.'

Talas laughed a little sadly. 'I will try, Xhera. I will try.'

‒‒ ‒‒

They stayed another few nights in the town, Night also meeting their families as a friend of Aldwyn's. They appeared to like him, although Brin, outspoken as he was, did mention that he found him a little odd. Hendal and Marta took him in stride; farmers tended to be more pragmatic about eccentricities. Gail was a little scared of him, although when she realised he knew Karland well, she spoke to him a lot more.

Mayor Bedwin came to greet her and the soldiers, and the rangy smith she remembered from the battle nodded to her when he saw her. Even Ben Arflun waved. Tales of Rast and the Battle of the Croft were still told.

It was pleasant, and they overstayed, but it was finally time to move on. Xhera promised her family to visit when she could, although the thought of travelling back to the tun, the place where she had felt trapped for so long, drew mixed emotions, reluctance vying with a little homesickness. She never felt as displaced as she knew Karland did; the closest she had felt that was after they had left her at The Sanctum.

She also promised to stop in whenever she visited The Croft and visit Karland's family. They would need resupplies every so often, and she intended to return every Endwice. Gail had loved having her and Talas there, and looked forward to seeing her new 'sister' every week.

Xhera thought that some of the stigma of Karland's isolation had perhaps rubbed off on her. Later when Karland had become a minor hero of the town in the Battle of The Croft, Gail had loved the extra attention at first; but eventually she became uncomfortable with it, remembering how it had been before. She had friends, but seemed a little lonely for older company, and that Xhera could fully understand.

They moved east, the twelve-odd miles taken at a leisurely pace. Night had said he would join them there later; only Xhera knew that moving during a sunny day was not an option for him. She had no doubt he would find them with ease.

She checked the map that Karland had drawn her and directed Norla to pull off left. The faint track wound back northwest for a way, then vanished, only worn cart tracks showing where Aldwyn had spent a few years travelling to town. After a little time a clearing came into view, and the ruins of the Library of Thingos emerged from the foliage.

The sun streamed down, turning the edges of the clearing golden-green in places, and a dark glowing green in others. The stone was light grey, and covered in vines and growth, but you could still see the base shapes of several buildings. The most complete one was the taller building set against a rock formation near the east end of the clearing.

The forest was dark and quiet in the distance, feeling almost oppressive, but around the clearing the growth was sparser. Sergeant Cassega directed Pahm and Hilford to sweep the north and western edges and Jimson and Norla the south and east while she and Kervala set up camp and checked for vantage points.

Xhera aimed for the most complete building, the one propped against the large rocks where Karland had fallen and broken his arm, and removed the large, long-barrelled iron key from around her neck. Cassega preceded her cautiously, then beckoned, smiling. The interior was big enough to house all of them. Clearing the centre under the hole in the roof, Cassega pursed her lips.

'Perfect for the fire pit. We'll cover that hole for rain. Where is this library door?'

Xhera studied the back of the room, against the solid rock face. She had been here once before, but it was at night and hurried. She couldn't remember exactly where it lay.

There were two alcoves, recesses that swept to the floor and bore old signs of shelving. Both were slightly different than the rock face, looking like faded stone. She guessed it was ironwood.

It took her several minutes of searching before she discovered that the one to the right held a keyhole, recessed into a natural-seeming crack in the 'stone'. The key fitted and turned with some effort, and the door swung in, more easily than she had expected. It was a good foot thick.

'Best come with you,' said Cassega firmly. She took an oiled torch from her pack, but Xhera stopped her.

'Not in a library,' she said apologetically. She lifted one of the Library lights she had been allowed to bring and unwrapped it, casting a white glow into the room. The fireplace here was old and cold, but everything seemed untouched. Scrolls, maps, and other information lay on the desk and stacked neatly around in alcoves. She could almost sense Karland and Aldwyn here, and smiled sadly as she saw the slot where Karland said the archive map was kept. Then she laughed in delight; her own books lay stacked neatly to the end of the desk where she had left them more than three quarters of a year before.

I had forgotten about those!

They began to explore the upper rooms, Cassega checking every corner.

'There's another door?'

'Yes, where the stables are hidden. The same key will open it.'

'I'll get on clearing that out. Come on, let's see it.' The Sergeant was all business, but Xhera could tell she was curious about this place.

Ê ಀ

Night appeared that evening, silent as ever, startling the Guard. He smiled in apology and spoke for a while, then requested Xhera show him the Library. She pushed open the door, and Night followed her into the study room. The recessed fire was lit now, crackling merrily. It appeared to have some kind of distribution to some of the other chambers; the sleeping quarters had warmed considerably.

'I advise you keep that door locked at all times,' he said softly. 'The integrity of the works in here depend on no creatures or damp entering. The door is remarkably close-fitting.' He looked further into the dark tunnel and cocked his head. 'I detect no small animals. Curious.'

She had not yet gone down to the archive deep under the rocks, so they went together, Xhera holding a Library light.

I must remember to place these in sunlight, she thought.

The tunnel split. To the right were the sleeping quarters with four beds, a small kitchen and larder, and several other small rooms, as well as the tunnel out to the hidden stable area. They moved left to the descending tunnel, following it down until they entered the huge chamber with stacked shelves. It must have taken enormous effort to carve this out from the rock, unless it was mostly natural.

'Ahhh,' breathed Night softly. She looked up at him. The little man's face was peaceful, reposed, and his eyes were closed.

'Night?'

'It is good to return to a place like this, Xhera. It is where I was born. The dry, dark silence throbs like a living heartbeat to me. It is like coming home.' He opened his eyes. 'And look at this treasure we have found.'

Thousands of books, scrolls, and other repositories of knowledge lay on dry shelves. She consulted the shelf map.

'There is so much here,' she breathed, almost itching to take books down. 'Aldwyn's notes are to the left, over here-' the light fell on the shelves, and she gasped. 'This can't be right.'

There must have been hundreds of books of varying thickness, and the covers all had the same hand.

'Might I recommend we remove only a few at a time, and mark them off so we may return them to the correct place?' Night said dryly. 'The Combic system of Scrollmasters is sadly lacking here.'

'Good idea,' she said a little nervously.

This could take *years*.

Nevertheless... Xhera felt that this was where she belonged.

'Let's get started,' she said.

⁚   ⁚

Seom collapsed into his bunk, his limbs trembling with exhaustion. Around him other recruits did the same, with moans and grunts. Many were already falling asleep, but Seom's mind was not quiet enough, despite his tiredness.

Training had intensified and the recruits had heard new rumours that they were no longer merely reserves. Something big was coming.

Some said the recruits would be sent into the heart of Eordeland to gain experience in patrols. After hearing from Karland how horrifying the creatures were, sending raw recruits to meet them sounded unlikely.

They wouldn't be sent south to guard against Banistari, either; the Empire's forces were strong, and the border guard there were all veterans. In the cities, they didn't want raw recruits with no siege experience dealing with hundreds of thousands of citizens, either.

That left facing an incoming enemy. Insane though it sounded, Meyar might attack.

Seom was eager to face the enemies of Eordeland, but he also had a good head on his shoulders. Many of his fellows spoke eagerly of combat, of slaying many foes with their courage and skill; he knew how lacking they all were in both. None of them were ready for battle.

None of them were ready for war.

Part of him wished he was with Karland. He had been surprised by his old friend, shocking Seom in sparring. He would never in a thousand years have picked Karland if you had asked him who would excel as Rast Tal'Orien's pupil. Seom sometimes pondered how much better he would be if he had managed to be chosen through fate. Or - he admitted wryly - if he would have been as good. Clearly Rast saw something in his friend.

As did Xhera.

That was the other area that Seom both admired and envied Karland. Xhera had struck a chord with him, as he knew she had with Karland, but for different reasons. From the moment he had seen her he had been entranced. She was exceptionally beautiful, with a trim and well-muscled form. She was intelligent and capable, funny, smart, well-read, and had taken her turn beating him in sparring as well.

Xhera was everything Seom could have asked for in a woman, and unlike Karland he had experienced many different girls to make that judgement. He knew she found him attractive, too. The physicality was electric between them.

Yet… she had an even deeper bond with Karland. Seom might wish it was different, but he respected it. If Karland had been the type, Seom would have gladly competed for her heart, but he knew his friend was not. Nevertheless, his control had slipped once. In that moment, if she had responded, he would have taken his heart's desire whatever regrets came after.

He had asked to be part of the detail sent north with her to guard her and been soundly rebuffed. Only veterans would go, and he had his training to complete.

Seom was both glad and regretful that Xhera had chosen his friend, but for the first time in his life, he truly envied Karland.

He smiled to himself a little. Unlike Karland, Seom was used to things working out for him.

I finally understand how he feels.

He wasn't exactly doing badly here; the recruit's barracks had been full of boys and girls from all over Eordeland, split by the buildings. Anyone caught fraternising was severely punished, and Isha help the girl who became pregnant.

Seom hadn't been caught, and the girls were good with herbs.

He was also becoming a very good swordsman; that was one of the few disciplines he had consistently beaten Karland at. Unfortunately, it meant extra lessons. Seom wasn't stupid; he could tell he was getting extra responsibilities for a reason. Eordeland Guard only had Corporals in the Recruits - they were only considered effective and experienced enough as units to require a Sergeant once fully deployed, and the lowest full private still outranked any recruit.

He drifted off, thinking of a friend who refused to believe in himself, and a girl with pale skin and blue eyes under dark hair.

They would all meet up again soon, Delmatra willing, and have new tales for each other, as well as bruises, no doubt, but one thing was certain: wherever Karland was, he couldn't feel as sore as Seom did right now.

TWENTY-EIGHT

Karland opened his eyes slowly. His head was thumping under blood dried down one side of his face. His right eye was swelled nearly shut, and he was bound hand and foot so tightly he couldn't feel his extremities.

The last thing he remembered was the headlong flight from the dogs into the hills, rounding a ridge to ride straight into another group of mercenaries; the horse rearing, the sky and the ground swapping places.

A large hand dropped into his field of view, grabbing his bruised head. He groaned, gritting his teeth. His head was lifted, turned. He caught a glimpse of a face covered in stubble with dark bristling brows, and then his head was dropped back. The world swam for a second.

'Welcome him,' said someone. Karland blinked up but saw only shadows before a hard strike left him gasping, his arm numbed. A punch caught him on the cheek, making him yelp, and a heavy boot hit his ribs hard enough that he desperately hoped they hadn't broken. A strike in the kidneys made him arch in agony. His head felt detached, even as more blows landed. Mercifully quickly, he blacked out.

Time passed with vague dreams. Then the world swam back into focus.

'Lord Raelf! He's awake.' The voice spoke heavily accented Darum in a peculiarly clipped fashion, the *w* almost a *v*. It was familiar after a year with Aran. Aldwyn had once told him that despite the distance, Novin and Eordeland shared a common language foundation, although the Darum in Novinian was only half-recognisable.

'Good!' a sharp voice called. The word sounded a little more like *goot*. He dimly heard footsteps approach, thudding into the grass at an offbeat tempo to his head.

Heavy leather and chain riding boots stopped near his chest.

'Look at me, filth,' a cold voice commanded him. He peered up, blinking, and with weary fear saw the face from earlier. The man was heavy-set, his wide chest bound in a simple steel plate-mail breastplate that had seen hard use. It was creased on one side, possibly by a crossbow bolt skipping off it, or a glancing sword or axe blow. He had solid, practical pauldrons and big arms, and his legs were covered in mail from the faulds downwards. The square-jawed face was topped by thin eyebrows and fiery hair which stuck up every which way from the helm which had been removed. A thick moustache curled over his lips, and a wide scar on his chin explained why he had no beard. His teeth were uneven and his hard green eyes were almost brown. A weathered arming sword hung at his hip.

'You. You were in that battle. You ran like a coward, after striking down a bold Novinian Knight.'

Even in his pain, Karland felt the urge to point out that he couldn't be both a coward *and* fight and kill a knight, but he kept quiet. He suspected dimly that his life hinged on offending this man as little as possible.

'You're no soldier. What are you, vermin? Spy? Scout? You'll wish you never travelled these plains. Dare to kill a Novinian? I'll cut your cods from you and force-feed them back fresh and bloody before I open your guts to the spine.'

Without giving him a chance to reply, he swung his foot back and kicked Karland in the stomach, hard.

Karland nearly sobbed with the agony and retched. He couldn't breathe properly, his body in spasm, and he wondered if he would die. He struggled for air, and helplessly watched the chain-covered foot draw back again, this time aimed at his face.

'Hold, Raelf,' commanded a new voice. Karland managed to look up. A tall, austere man with wide shoulders and a stag design upon his tabard moved to the side. He was well-built, his face chiselled but with a badly pocked complexion. He was almost as tall as Rast. There was a suggestion of an underbite in his chin under his black goatee, peppered with grey, and his hair was likewise peppered dark, his eyes darker. His armour looked better crafted than Raelf's, the ornate helm still on with visor up, and he moved with the easy grace of a professional swordsman. An ornate but well-used longsword hung from his right hip, short enough to be useable in one hand but long enough to be devastating on horseback. He stopped, facing Raelf.

'This is not how we treat prisoners.'

'He is an Eord. He killed one of my men, Lord Gyrn. I will watch him beg for death.'

'He will die cleanly, if required,' said the tall man, his face harsh. 'He defended himself well. You know the Accords of War.'

'The *Pferdim* are meaningless for scum like this,' sneered Raelf. 'And the Accords mean nothing for the coming war. Honour is for the weak. The strong conquer, however they will. He is not Novinian.'

'Am I then weak?' asked Gyrn softly. His pitted face was cold. 'The Accords mean *nothing*?' Raelf did not reply. 'Ware your words. He is a worthy foe. Duty and strength go hand in hand; without our Accords, a knight is nothing more than an armoured thug, and Novin would collapse in chaos.' He spat at his feet. 'You wouldn't understand honour. You would change coin in the midst of battle.'

The mercenary Captain's face darkened in ugly rage and his hand dropped to his sword.

'You dare!'

'Do you call me out?' The tall man's eyes gleamed in anticipation. 'If you wish Settlement-'

Raelf stilled, his eyes hooded. Karland thought he saw a glint of fear in them.

'I have no time for petty insults.' He turned to leave.

'He may be ripe for ransom,' Gyrn said to his back, almost conversationally. 'If you kill him without reason and I find he was worth gold, I will petition the King to have your head on a plate to adorn the table of my next feast.'

Raelf stopped and turned his head slightly. Karland saw death in his eyes but could not tell for whom. After a moment the mercenary walked away.

Karland's gasps gradually became easier. The tall knight stared down at him.

'You aren't Eordeland Guard, boy, for all you wear some gear. You're too young and small, for a start. You travel with them, and Tal'Orien. Yes, I heard of the slayer who walked untouched among armoured knights; it could be no other man. Who are you? Some Lordling, for ransom?' His frown creased his face. 'Be warned. If I believe you are lying, I will torture the facts from you and leave you broken, though I will take no pleasure in it.'

'I come from a town in north Eordeland. I'm no lord.'

Gyrn shook his head. His voice was matter-of-fact.

'If you have no value, you will be slain.'

Karland felt panic, and it must have shown in his face. 'I- I've travelled with Rast Tal'Orien for some time. I'm his student. We were going to take ship in Eyotsburg to Mithtol - to the elves. The Council of Twelve sent us to Eyotsburg with information.'

Gyrn nodded slowly. 'Then perhaps you are of some use to us. Your... Council-' his face showed what he thought of such a body, '-would not send just anyone on such a mission. You will have worth if you are Tal'Orien's student. His name is well-known in Novin, boy. Many men would treasure the chance to kill him.'

He looked down at Karland for a moment, and then continued in a slightly quieter voice. 'I am of the *Adel* - the Noble Houses. You would call me a Lord of a

Fief, a Dominus-minor. I am honour-bound to follow the Accords of War for prisoners.

'Raelf is naught but a common knight. He has won his Captaincy through skill at arms, not birth. He cares nothing for honour, though he should; the lack of it may damage his company, in time. Be that as it may, he will not hesitate to murder you and take delight in your suffering before you die.' He shrugged, and a cold smile lit his lips. 'I will not hesitate either, make no mistake, but I will do so cleanly and when needed, not for vengeance or cruelty. If you're of value, you will be ransomed to Eordeland. If you're not, I will give you a quick death, rather than leave you to that dog.'

He shook his head. 'It is so hard to judge value. Your Realm has no Royalty, no nobles, no bloodlines now. You don't control your people. You spread knowledge and independence and free those who should serve you. You take pride in having none of what makes us great. We have great Houses, great Lords, great riches. You have books and empty talk. I do not understand you.'

'We're good at war,' said Karland defiantly.

Gyrn smiled slightly.

'Aye. That I can understand.'

He moved away and Karland slumped. He was tired and thirsty, and his head still throbbed. His stomach hurt badly. Miserably, he wondered if anything had torn internally again from the kick. Spit had dribbled down his chin from the retching, but there was no way to wipe it off.

He tried to calm himself, and after a while he had recovered enough energy to take stock of his surroundings. A form near him told of one of the Eordeland Pathfinders, Erim. The man lay on his side, eyes closed, blood dried on the side of his head and rimming his nostrils. He was pale and still.

From where he lay, he could just see the command pavilions if he twisted his head. Surrounding them were scattered camps of rough-looking men. One of these approached him as he struggled to sit upright, and to his surprise helped him, placing a pack behind him.

'Lord Gyrn says you are to be watered and fed,' said the pale rangy man, who had blond hair and stubble that could be called a beard if you were being generous. He was clad in a gambeson and padded leggings with rust stains from mail. Karland could smell the sharp tang of iron. His piercing blue eyes had laughter lines around them, but he still looked as if he would slit someone's throat for a copper piece. His tone belied his look, however.

'You're tough, boy. Thought you wouldn't wake up from that fall. I hear it was hard. Had to bloodlet the horse.' He held a waterskin up and helped Karland drink until he was done. 'Also heard you slew a knight in armour. His sword was on the saddle. Takes some doing.' He produced a knife. 'Don't make me do something, boy,' he said in warning, and then gently unwound the ropes from Karland's ankles and wrists.

Karland couldn't have done anything even had he wanted to. He gritted his teeth against the agony of returning blood, pins and needles setting his extremities on fire. He groaned softly, and the man chuckled. 'I'll wager you go nowhere, Eord. Enjoy it while it lasts. Here.' He took a heavy sausage from a pouch at his belt and cut it into chunks. 'Eat this.'

Karland flexed his fingers, trying to get some control back. Once he was sure he could grasp the food without dropping it from nerveless fingers, he stuffed it in his mouth, chewing with abandon. It was smoky, salty, garlicky, and delicious. Before he knew it, it was all gone.

'What about him?' he asked roughly, pointing to Erim.

The man shook his head. 'Had his. Won't speak. He doesn't show worth soon, he'll be dogfood.'

'He's helpless,' protested Karland.

'He's dead weight. Behave, Eord, and we will treat you right,' said the man. 'Make sure you thank your Gods Lord Gyrn thinks you're worth something.'

He offered another sip from the waterskin, and then gestured to Karland. 'Piss now, before I retie you.' He didn't need to heft the foot-long knife he held.

Karland staggered to his feet and stiffly moved some feet from where he had lain. His tired mind simply said to empty his bladder far enough from his resting spot to be hygienic. If this had been an Eordeland camp, there would have been latrine pits, but the Novinians either hadn't dug them yet or didn't bother, he was unsure which.

As he urinated, he took the opportunity to look around the camp a little more clearly.

The men were disciplined, and apart from their air of menace were every bit as professional as the Eordelanders, although nothing like the Knights from stories. There were no women, no camp followers, no wagons. The knights had horses tied in groups spaced near the perimeter, and it looked like the sentries he saw patrolled with dogs. He could hear more of them throughout the camp. They were well trained and obeyed the commands of their masters well.

The camp must have held one hundred and thirty knights, strewn in a rough pattern around the central command tents with perhaps ten or fifteen to a fire, and to the south lay an indistinct camp of hundreds more infantry. There were three pavilions, one blue-striped and another red. The last was simple white canvas and lower than the other two. Karland guessed this was the infirmary for those wounded

in battle; there was a lot of movement around it and the occasional noise from it
suggesting pain.

He noticed there were younger men in leather armour moving in and between
fires. The largest group of horses held large, stolid beasts which couldn't have been
war chargers.

Shaking the last out, he turned, wishing for a way to wash his hands as in the
Eordeland camp.

'There are others here?' he asked. The man nodded.

'Aye. Handlers. And Squires.' He tapped his chest. 'We dress the knights for
battle, carry messages, guard the supplies, fashion the war lances, tend the wounded
and hold the pavilions and spares on the pack mounts. After seven years of service,
we may be knighted also. I have a year left. My Lord is in the service of Lord Gyrn.'

Karland had thought him a knight. Still, he was grateful to the man for his care.
'May I have a little more water?' he asked, and cupped his hands. The squire nodded
and poured a little into them. Karland splashed his face and rubbed his hands clean.

'Sit back down, Eord. I will re-tie you. Pray your ransom will be met quickly.
We will send a messenger to your company. Failing that, you will be our guest until
we hear from Eordeland, unless you are deemed not worthy. Either way, we will not
keep you overlong.'

Karland knew what that meant. A knife in the throat, or back, and if he was
lucky, a shallow grave. He fought the faintly sick feeling in his stomach and tried not
to think about what it would feel like to be stabbed to death, feel the foreign cold
steel cleave his flesh and let his blood out. At times like this, Aldwyn's instruction in
caring for injuries made things almost worse; he knew exactly what they would be
doing to him.

The squire tied his ankles and wrists securely, but not so cruelly as before,
nodded, and left. Like Gyrn, he seemed a hard but fair man.

Karland's stomach growled around the sausage, and he burped slightly, wafting
the meaty garlic scent past his nose. He blew out to clear his senses, and wished he
hadn't as the smells of the camp came back in.

He lay on the cold ground, and at some point, dozed. When he woke, it was late
afternoon, and he felt stiff but more functional.

One of the dogs padded past, slowing to look at him. It must have weighed more
than he did, even with its heavy spiked collar removed. Karland shivered,
remembering the dogs that had chased him, and how they had hungered for his
blood, but this one simply grunted quizzically and carried on about its business. He
had to admire the training of the Novinians; the dogs were exceptionally fierce in a

fight, almost like a bestial army themselves, but in the camp, without attack commands, they reminded him more of the dogs he knew.

He still wasn't going to try to pet one.

'They… got you too?' The voice was slurred and painful. He turned to see Erim looking at him tiredly. He nodded.

'Got cut off. On a horse. It bolted.'

'Kill'd mine under me.' Erim coughed harshly. It looked like his ribs might be broken, maybe more, and he had a head wound that needed serious attention. 'Don't hold out, boy. Tell them… what they need to hear. Stay alive.' He coughed with the effort. Karland saw blood on his lips.

'What about you?'

'Know I'm… just a scout.' He wheezed and grinned through bloody teeth. One was broken. 'I'll tell 'em nowt.'

'But they'll kill you!'

'Kill us anyway.' Erim sounded tired. 'Think I'm done anyhow. Somethin' ain't right in me. Beat me bad. Only chance… escape, lad.' He lapsed into silence.

Karland lay thinking of where he was, of where he had been and what he had seen. Of where he was going. Of what, and whom, he had left behind. His thoughts were morose, and he wondered how long it would be until Rast knew what had happened to him. He knew they had been on a tight schedule. They might have left. Even if they looked, they would have seen little tale of his fate. His only hope lay in the company having enough care to barter him, if they were still there.

Rast would, he knew. He didn't think Aldine would, and Gambeson… he wasn't sure. Karland wondered how long his luck would hold with the leader of the Novinians.

As if his thoughts had summoned him, he saw Lord Gyrn approaching on his own. He ignored Erim and squatted next to Karland.

'Eord. I trust the squire treated you well.'

Karland nodded, and struggled up, resting his back against the pack. Gyrn watched him, and nodded once, sharply.

'Good. I would not trust one of Raelf's men to care for you. He is angry with you, boy. He feels you have mocked him.' The tall knight sighed. He looked quite tired in mail and tabard, which he wore in place of his plate from earlier.

'Knight-Captain Raelf is arrogant and stupid,' he said almost distantly. 'He thought your company easy pickings. I spoke to the scouts. They told him that it was a company of foot soldiers and he attacked without further information to raid your supplies. He does not think before he acts. I dare say his shock was complete when he realised he had assaulted a full company of Eordeland Guard with archers, crosses and pikes. He lost many, the fool.'

'They attacked from the hills without warning,' said Karland dully. He remembered the sudden charge, the terror.

'Yes. He lost more than twenty knights, thirty-five war hounds, and near half his infantry is dead or out of action. There was little profit to be gained by attacking you, and much risk,' said Gyrn. 'I wouldn't have, I think, even with all my men and infantry added to his. Our contract isn't for random parties. I would have seen the pikes and Crosses, and known you were Eordeland Guard, especially this close to your land. You weren't worth the risk… as he found.' He sounded almost smug.

'You don't like him,' surmised Karland cautiously.

Gyrn barked a short laugh.

'He's a common thug. No honour, no morals. A pig and a rapist.'

'What did he mean, the Accords will not matter soon?'

'Ah, boy. Do not ask and I will not be forced to kill you.' The man almost smiled. 'I hope that they can pay something for you, I really do. I would regret your death. But we will not long wait for a price from Eordeland.'

'Does everything you do run on profit?' asked Karland. He didn't mean to sound accusing, and for a moment was frightened he had gone too far, but the man simply shrugged.

'Profit and honour, boy. The great Houses of Novin are built on deed and gold. On strength and power. The Accords dictate how prisoners of value are treated, and the manner of loot and pillage. We may contract to fight with any, unless it be directly against our own Kingdom. Once taken, coin is the bargain until after the battle. Prisoners of worth should be treated fairly until ransom is met. They should be killed with honour if not. Torture is the resort of information, not vengeance, unless met in Feud. Settlement of Arms is between champions of honour. Pillage of lands and women are allowed only sunup to sundown on the day of conquest, or the following. There is much more, but that is the core; a set of rules for knights to live by.' He looked pensive for a moment.

'The only exception is blood-feud, what they call *kanli* in Banistari. If that is declared, the Accords are ignored. Vengeance may be to one, or every to every living scion and all his family.' He shrugged. 'We are not a gentle people. Many knights do not hold to the Accords much, or only loosely.' Gyrn squatted. 'I have come to ask you, man to man, what your purpose was here and what information you have. I have treated you with respect, and I ask the same.'

Karland shifted. It was true that Gyrn had been respectful. This was business to him, nothing more. He wondered what he could say.

'I have told you all I know of our mission,' he said after a moment. 'We travelled to Eyotsburg to offer them Eordeland's aid against Meyar, and then on to the elves to seek their advice. As for Eordeland...' he shook his head. 'I know many Novinian mercenaries have been forced from the country, and we are gearing for war. That's all I can really say.'

'And what advice do you seek from the elves?'

'I don't really know. Aid against Meyar.' He couldn't help adding, 'There is more happening than war.'

Lord Gyrn barked a laugh. 'No, boy. Whatever they tell you, it is always about war. The Meyari are fools to believe they can war with Eordeland easily, but as long as they pay us, we are theirs for the battle... if it looks worth our while.' Gyrn glanced at his injured companion and rose.

'Scouts are valued highly,' said Karland desperately. 'They'll pay for us both!'

Gyrn chuckled. '*You're* an anomaly, boy, but a scout is no knight. I might consider it if it were worth my very limited time.' He looked over at Erim. 'Will you speak plainly, scout?'

Erim stared straight ahead. Gyrn shook his head. He turned to leave and called back over his shoulder.

'Be wary of Raelf. He intends to end you, boy.' Then he was gone.

'Why didn't you speak? You told me to speak!'

Erim turned, his eyes unfocused, and Karland could see it wasn't all determination. 'Mm? Ah. Get nowt from me, lad. I know more'n you 'bout our force. You look... after you.' He trailed off, wheezing, and his eyes closed. He was getting worse.

Karland thought over what he had been told. Lord Gyrn was cold and harsh, but had a code, as far as his Accords went. He wished he knew more about them, about the danger he was in. He remembered the look on Raelf's face, and knew that whatever the Accords said, and how formal Gyrn was, he was in great danger.

His mind drifted again, and he wondered how far the company had gone, how many had lived, and if he would see any of them again. He thought of his family, and his little sister. He thought about Xhera's lips on his, and wept, a welling of emotion constricting his chest.

He had promised to see her again. The thought he would let her down almost hurt.

A while afterwards - he couldn't say how long, but it must have been hours - a rough voice brought him out of his thoughts. Another squire was bending over him, thin, with a full brown beard and three teeth missing. He didn't look friendly. Quite the opposite; his teeth were gritted, and he looked as if he wanted to plunge a dagger into Karland's throat. He hauled Karland up roughly, and jammed the waterskin into his mouth, squeezing the bag. Choking, Karland fought to swallow, and painfully gulped air along with it. The fellow didn't hesitate, stuffing several pieces of dried meat into Karland's mouth and leaving him to chew it. One fell to the ground and was ignored. Karland nearly choked, trying hard to get it into his cheeks where he could soften it and swallow. It didn't help that the squire roughly checked his bonds. He was thrown over, frightened he *would* choke. Several times a piece fell into his throat, and he frantically coughed it out.

'My Lord!' the squire shouted at the top of his voice, sending it clear to the pavilions. 'These bonds are loose! I will tighten them.' He glared at Karland, who glared back, finally clearing his mouth. The squire moved behind him to his hands. After a few rough jerks that made Karland gasp in pain, his shoulders wrenched back sickeningly, he felt them pulled together so tightly the rope bit into his flesh, and a few more jerks suggested tying a knot.

The man reappeared, his face dark with fury. 'Just you try to escape now, you snivelling little shit,' he snarled. He slammed his hand into Karland's solar plexus and called, 'Lucky he did not attack the Lord Gyrn!'

Karland nearly vomited the food back up, writhing in agony as the squire turned and stalked over to the other Eordelander. Erim lay semi-conscious.

The man peered down at him and grunted. 'You've outlived your usefulness, Eord.' He placed his boot on Erim's head and drew his belt knife. Before Karland could even react, he inserted the point blade-out into Erim's neck, slowly and cruelly. Erim cried out in gargling pain but couldn't move.

The squire thrust it slowly through the middle then sawed outwards, back and forth, cutting through oesophagus and windpipe with rough jerks. Blood spurted. Erim was choking to death as it pumped out of his ruptured blood vessels, his body convulsing. The sound was horrifying.

'No,' Karland whispered, barely able to speak.

The man wiped his knife on the twitching body and walked away, re-sheathing it. He was whistling.

Karland lay there, angry and terrified. The throb from his beating was subsiding, and the pain and need to breath had receded

Erim.

He stared ahead in shock, wincing a little at pain in his hands, and wriggled his wrists reflexively. He couldn't even look at the body of the man who had been speaking to him so recently.

His thoughts were so distant that it took some time before they listened to what his hands were urgently telling him. He gave another tug. After several moments the rope gave slightly and blood flowed into his hands again, causing him to wince in pain. It distracted him, focused him enough to look over again, his eyes drawn to the corpse.

Erim was just a clothed lump in a pool of blood. Karland was thankful he couldn't see his face. He had liked Erim well enough, but he hadn't really known him.

It sickened him that a man could be slain so casually. Everything Erim had been, destroyed in an instant. That was what would happen to him, too.

A tear trickled down his cheek.

'Erim,' he whispered. 'I'm sorry.'

It was obvious that the second squire was from Raelf's side, although his hatred had seemed very personal. The man had killed Erim like a farmer killed a pig.

Dusk was not far off, and he lay brooding until campfires began to light up around him. Two men came and bore Erim's body away. No-one else came near him. A piercing whistle pattern went up from the infantry camped south, and shortly he saw dogs converging towards it.

It looked as if they were being fed. Tiredly, he hoped it wasn't on Erim.

After a while, Karland shifted uncomfortably. He needed to urinate badly, but the second squire hadn't seen fit to let him up.

Finally, he couldn't hold any longer and relaxed his bladder. With a vague sense of shame, the hot liquid gushed down over one thigh and wetted his leathers.

He hoped pissing himself wasn't disastrous in the eyes of his captors, but it had hardly been his fault. He was uncomfortable and angry. At least the pack was still there to prop himself against. Shifting himself further upright, awkward with his hands bound behind him, he froze in shock.

The rope felt loose!

Cautiously, forgetting the hot soak of urine for a moment, he tested it again. There was give, and as he wriggled it loosened further.

The squire must have made a mistake in his anger, he thought jubilantly. He had seemed furious, for some reason, and the hatred had emanated from him. Perhaps that had made him incautious.

A spur of hope and joy rushed through him. His freedom lay within his grasp, and he made every effort to look as if he was only dozing again.

Should he risk moving now, or wait until later, when alertness would be lower and knights would be sleeping? What if someone came again and he lost his chance?

He decided to keep a wary eye out. If he could wait until midnight, most of them would be sleeping, and if he saw someone approaching, he would try to vanish.

His mouth was as dry as his legs were wet; he suspected that if he were caught, he would be killed.

In truth, he was still exhausted, and he nodded off once or twice. Angrily, he berated himself to focus. His legs were still tied securely but loosely; hopefully he could get the rope off quickly. Thankfully his feet would not be asleep, and with great luck he might be able to steal from the camp - but which way should he go?

His best bet, he thought, was to get out quickly, to the north, which was closest to him, and then head west and find somewhere to hide. The dogs were clustered more to the southeast, apart from those on patrol with the lookouts. Getting past them would be hard, and he would need to move fast once free. He wondered about food and drink; there would be no way to take any. He wondered what was in the pack he was propped on. It felt like cloth, probably garments.

The knights and squires changed patrols regularly every two hours, he thought; it was difficult to tell from where he was. If he could time leaving a little before the change of guards, the old ones should be tired and less alert.

Karland refused to think of what had happened to Erim; if he did, he would never move. He knew the same would happen to him if he was caught.

He glanced towards the pavilions, but it appeared that the Knight-Captain and Lord Gyrn were busy. Candlelight and flickering shadows came from within the tents.

Finally, he could wait no longer. He judged it must be nearing midnight, and hopefully the end of a patrol cycle. The area around him was only dimly light by the light of the nearest fire. It was time.

He started trying to shift his hands out of the loops and had the first halfway out before long. He had freed his feet and was rising when a boot caught him in the back, and he pitched onto his face.

'Going somewhere, you little fuck?' came a rough whisper. He got up as fast as he could, and felt rather than saw an arm come in. He blocked what he thought was a punch, and a line of fire sprang up along his arm. He bit back a cry and lashed out with a foot, clipping his opponent's knee. With a curse, the man drew back, and Karland realised it was the surly squire from earlier. He caught the gleam of the foot-long dagger that had sawn out Erim's throat.

He realised he had been cut. How badly, he could not tell. His hand flexed fine, and there was no loss of strength, but blood ran down freely.

'Caught trying to escape,' growled the man with a sneer. He seemed a little more uncertain. Karland wasn't a simple target, but it was buying him no more than a few seconds. 'You'll pay for my father.'

With a leap of intuition, Karland understood. Raelf had given orders to allow him enough slack to get free. These men were trained mercenaries, and very good at what they did. They were not like the coarse mercenaries from Meyar that had infiltrated Eordeland last year. The man who tied him would be unlikely to make such a mistake.

This had been Raelf's plan all along.

His blood ran cold. He shivered, and mentally kicked himself. He was certain he was right. How could he have been so stupid?

'I thought you had Accords,' he said in a low voice, trying to buy himself time.

'Accords? For an Eord? This is blood-feud, whelp,' snarled the man. 'I will find your family and butcher them all. Mother, father, brothers, sisters. I'll enjoy the women first and think of you, cold in your grave the while.'

There was nothing Karland could say. The squire didn't care his father had been a knight, destined to die in battle, or that Karland had defended himself and survived only by chance. He only cared that an undeserving child had slain his father, dishonouring him, and he would revenge himself.

The man darted forwards, dim in the gloom, and Karland prepared to run for the pavilion. His only hope lay in getting to Lord Gyrn before he was killed by Raelf's man.

He ducked a slash, and then the man had him by a shoulder. Desperately he shucked, dropping his shoulder from the hand in a rolling motion and turning his body to present a smaller target as Rast had taught him. The blow aimed for his heart thrust past him, close enough to almost slice cloth. The man grunted in surprise at the lack of resistance, and Karland threw a desperate elbow into his face.

The squire snarled, reeling, and stepped back. Karland weaved, exhausted. He didn't have much more in him. The squire pulled a sword from his hip with his other hand, and Karland knew it was the end. The sword would be in his back before he had taken three steps.

Something hurtled into the squire from the side, and he let out a mercifully muffled yelp in surprise. With a clatter he fell, the sword spinning off into the night, and a dim shape on top of the Squire sucked a sharp breath in through gritted teeth before slamming fists and elbows into his face. It used its whole body to hurl the fast powerful blows in a way familiar to Karland's tired mind, but it was far too small to be Rast.

The figure on top was spinning, whipping back and forth with hands on the knife wrist whilst the dazed squire struggled to keep up. A knee dropped onto his throat, hard, and he made a horrible choking sound. The shape tore the knife from his hand stabbing it violently down through his ribcage. The squire bucked,

gargling, and the shape tore it out and stabbed again, tearing hard through his guts
and into the ground with the tip. It held the man's hand twisted in a punishing lock,
his knee on the squire's neck.

An awful gurgling accompanied thrashing and clawing at the grass as the legs
tried to reflexively come up around the terrible injury Karland knew had happened
to his stomach muscles.

Finally, he died, juddering, and the shape on top spun off him fluidly; it looked
down, breathing hard, and kicked him viciously.

Karland stood, swaying, unsure what was going on. Bruised and battered, his
arm throbbing along the length of the cut, he peered at the figure dimly silhouetted
by the campfires. It was taller than average and had a suggestion of strength and lean
power.

Karland moved to say something, and a rough hand slapped over his mouth. The
shape caught his gaze, and dark eyes glittered at him. The head shook slightly, and
one finger rose to the shadow's mouth.

Karland nodded blearily, too pained and tired to question his luck. He ached all
over and felt ill.

The man touched his shoulder, and gestured to the north, picking up the pack
Karland had rested against.

Karland nodded. He no longer had the energy to care if this was another trick. A
thought flew past, and he grasped at it.

'Dogs?'

'Not this way,' came the low whisper.

They set off, passing snoring men. His heart was thudding in reaction, but that
aside he was so tired he just couldn't be terrified any more. Karland knew he was on
the last of his reserves.

As they passed close to one fire, he turned his head and glanced sideways to the
man who was rescuing him. Now he could see some features. A suggestion of a
goatee stood out around a stern mouth, under high cheekbones and a proud nose.
He looked to have close-cropped hair, almost shaved on the sides, and ears that stuck
out a little and up sharply enough to suggest something demonic. Yet for all that,
they were human, the close haircut accentuating the effect.

The man flashed a feral grin in the dim light and motioned with his head.
Carefully he helped Karland, and they crept through the sleeping men.

The unknown rescuer kept low, and they edged past a group of tied horses.
Finally, they were at the perimeter. Karland found a sentry slumped face-down. He
groaned slightly as they passed, and the man whipped around, dropping to one knee

and his elbow lifting to ram down into the sentry's head with a powerful thump. The arms jerked up in reflex and the shape fell quiet again.

The man grunted, and beckoned Karland. Hunched, they moved quickly away from the perimeter. A little further out was the body of a dog, an arrow in its breast. The man waved at him to wait. He picked something up and began making obvious tracks away from the camp, running - he thought - northeast, dragging whatever it was. Karland wasn't sure what good it would do, if the dogs could track them.

After a few minutes he returned empty handed, collecting a bow, quiver, and small pack from next to the dog. They began to circle west, Karland following his lead. His mind was clearing with his freedom, and he realised that they needed to move away in a less obvious direction. The man must have had something to divert the noses of the dogs.

They moved around and headed northwest, further into the foothills of the Arkons.

Once safely on their way, the man fell back and whispered harshly to him, 'Can you walk?'

Karland nodded. 'I think so. Don't know how long.' He paused. 'Thank you.'

'Thank me later.'

They travelled for several hours, their pace slowing as Karland fell behind. Finally, with a muffled curse the man dropped under his arm and helped him until Karland's legs simply wouldn't move any more.

After the fight, the wounds, the lack of sleep, the shock and the escape, he was in more of a stupor than he had been in the camp. The man's support was all that kept him on his feet.

At last they stopped. As soon as his rescuer let go, he fell to his knees and pitched forward. Groggily, he tried to rise again.

There was another curse, and he felt himself being dragged, then somehow he was floating upward, almost dreamily, a biting pain under his arms. Then a large shape blotted out the stars to the sound of heavy brush being dragged. Movement stopped.

He faded.

TWENTY-NINE

Karland woke to a grey midday glimpsed through heavy foliage. They seemed to be on a butte topped by grass and low thick foliage, but he had no recollection of how he had arrived there. The man was lying near him, asleep. Karland sat up awkwardly, groaning quietly to himself. He felt as if he had been bruised head to foot. His arm throbbed, and he looked down to see clean, tight wrappings around it. The man had seen to it while he had been asleep.

Unconscious, more like. His head throbbed, but at least his side and ribs only ached.

Glancing around he could see they were in the lee of a large grey boulder, in a tiny niche barely big enough for them both. Two large bushes had been uprooted and dragged across to hide them. There was no fire. Karland lay in a basic set of bedding and wondered through his mild headache if the man had pilfered it during their escape.

'Good. You're awake. Let's talk.'

He looked back to see his saviour sitting bent legged, arms resting on knees. He wiped his eyes, shook his head to clear it and rolled it on his neck, then tilted it slightly back, watching him through narrowed eyes in a peculiar fashion over the bottom lids with a grim expression. It made him look judgemental, but also as if he might leap up and attack Karland with his teeth in a bout of insanity at any moment.

The eyes were dark, the face stern and proud, his lashes longer than expected. The dark brown hair and goatee were short, as he had guessed last night, and the hair cropped almost shaved on the sides. A line of beard traced the jawline back and up in front of the ear. A slightly hawkish nose lay in the middle of a proud, strong face with a hint of cruelty that vied with good humour, giving him an aggressively noble profile, and the high brow spoke of intelligence.

Arrogance - or confidence - exuded from the man. His jerkin was well-filled with shoulders and arms, although he was definitely leaner than Rast, and he was well-muscled and lean, perhaps six feet tall. Several scars were visible on athletic tanned skin with hints of yellow to it, suggesting Banistari descent. The face broke into a fierce smile, and Karland noticed good teeth, the front two slightly rounded on their cutting edges, and one of the bottom ones with a chip on the inside edge. When this man smiled, he did it with his whole face, but otherwise the eyes remained cool, as if he only wore emotion as it suited.

'We're lucky. They have war dogs, no real trackers. It'll take them a while to pick up our trail, but I'm not going to sit around and find out. Want to tell me who you are and why they had you?'

His tone had a slightly odd accent.

Karland blinked, his reactions slow, and tried to collect his thoughts. He wasn't sure how much he should say. Although his rescuer had saved his life, he didn't know what his allegiance was. The man watched him with an air of impatience.

'I was travelling with an Eordeland Company, heading for Eyotsburg. We were attacked by Novinian knights without warning. I got separated.'

'You a coward?' The query was sharp.

'I was attacked by a Knight, took his horse. Was chased by dogs. They were pretty pissed off. I didn't feel like dying.'

The man shrugged. 'Fair. So they caught you, obviously. And you killed the knight?'

'Mostly by accident,' Karland admitted.

Another shrug.

'He's dead, you're not. Why didn't they kill you?'

Karland thought back to the horror of Erim's slaughter and shivered. 'They killed the pathfinder with me. They were going to kill me in the beginning, until another company joined them. Someone called Lord Gyrn. He was... *just*. Said he would ransom me if I had value.'

'And kill you if you didn't,' laughed the man. 'Standard knights. That's Raelf's company. Met them before. You're lucky Gyrn was there. Raelf would have gutted you like a pig. He IS a pig.' He sniffed. 'Still doesn't explain why you were important enough not to kill.'

'I was on the way to Eyotsburg, then the elves, to help speak for the Council of Twelve,' said Karland somewhat reluctantly.

'*You?*' The derision was cutting. Karland couldn't quite bring himself to be angry about it. He sighed.

'Look, I keep ending up involved in things. I travelled with someone important, and I know what the Council wants. I guess that was enough.'

'Hmmf,' grunted the man, unconvinced. He lifted his head. 'So. What's your name?'

'Karland.' He held out his hand. The man touched it briefly, rather than a firm shake. It was the greeting of a man who neither liked tactile contact, nor trusted others.

There was silence for a few seconds, and then Karland prompted him. 'And you are-?'

The man looked at him a long moment. A brief flicker of real emotion crossed his face, and then he shrugged. 'People call me The Green Warrior.'

It seemed an odd name, like something from a child's story. 'Why? What's your name? Where are you from?'

The man shrugged, his gaze far away for a moment.

'How do you know Raelf?'

'We have to get moving, boy. I dragged you up this outcrop, but if we get found, we're dead. Let's get out of here. I'll get you free of them. Then I'm done.'

'You're just going to leave me in the Arkon foothills?' asked Karland. A sense of panic set in. 'Without food or water? There are Novinians everywhere. I'm wounded, exhausted.'

'And?'

Karland stared at him. 'I'll die.'

'You might not. I've done my bit.'

'Why bother? I could have been ransomed-'

'That squire would have gutted you,' The Green Warrior said bluntly. 'Even if he hadn't, you wouldn't have lasted long enough for ransom. If I hadn't come in then you'd be dead now.' He looked, thoughts turned inwards. 'Saw them bring you in. Wasn't right to leave you there. And Raelf can suck my dick.'

'But it's right to leave me now,' muttered Karland. 'Can't you at least help me get to my friends?'

The man shrugged. 'Got more important things to do.' Something about the way he said it was the same way he had said his name.

'Like what? Finding out your name?' He said it half-jokingly. The man didn't answer. Karland had a leap of intuition. He spoke, hesitantly, at first, then more confidently, knowing deep down he was right.

'You're looking for something. Or someone.'

The man said nothing.

'Look, there's more at stake here. War's coming. Worse. Trust me. If you help me get back to my friends, I promise I'll do everything I can to help you.'

'War's none of my business,' said the Green Warrior bluntly.

'This war could end the world,' said Karland. 'Not just one land; everything. And where's your answer then?'

The man looked sceptical. 'How can you help?'

'I can bring you to the University in Darost, introduce you to people who might help, whatever you're looking for. I've studied under one of their greatest scholars. I know many who'd be able to give you more information, maybe even ask the Council. Just help me. Please. I... I can't do this alone.'

In his heart, Karland knew it was true. He was weak, exhausted, hurt, and had no clue where he was. The chances he would die even before enemies found him were high.

The Green Warrior made a moue with his lips, bobbing his head side to side slightly and mulling it over.

'You'll help me?' he asked slowly.

'I swear,' said Karland. 'It must have been hard, trying to do this alone. I'll help you any way I can... in return for your help.'

The Green Warrior looked as if he would refuse, and then he suddenly blew his breath out explosively, nodding. 'Done, and done.' He gave Karland that fleeting, wary handshake again.

'Thank you,' gasped Karland, weak with relief. He hadn't realised how much he was stacking his hopes on this mysterious man. He knew nothing about him really, other than he needed his help. He didn't even know if he would keep his word, though his answer had sounded final.

'Right,' said the Warrior, all business. 'So, they're headed to Eyotsburg? Real shitstorm. Mercs everywhere. I heard the northern bridge is blocked. If they're not careful they'll walk into several thousand Knights near the southern. Best catch them before they try to get through, if we can avoid the mercs.'

'Let's head northwest,' said Karland. 'We can't be that far from Deep Delving. I know a dwarf there who can supply us with horses and supplies.'

I hope, he added silently.

He had no money. He hoped Regin would accept friendship and a promise of gold. He also hoped the dwarf remembered him.

'Hmm. Useful friends,' said The Green Warrior. 'Maybe helping you isn't a bad idea after all. We need to move in the next hour anyway, boy.'

'I'll try,' said Karland tiredly.

'I don't give a shit how bad you feel,' said The Green Warrior bluntly. 'You'll feel worse if they catch you again. *Stop complaining.* We have to move, so either man up and get up or sit here and die. Don't waste my time.'

'Look, I didn't *ask* you to rescue me,' snapped Karland against his better judgement.

The Green Warrior's face stilled dangerously, his eyes cold and unreadable, and Karland wondered if he was about to regret his words. Then the man chuckled, as if caught out in a prank, his face lapsing almost immediately into a grin.

'But you're glad I did. Right?'

'Well.' Karland's ire faded. 'Yes. But don't call me *boy*.'

The Green Warrior tilted his head back, looking at him over his lower lids appraisingly again, and then leaned forwards.

'Earn it.'

ೞ   ಬ

Ventran strode up and down his room, muttering. The beam at the end of it was riddled with holes where he had been throwing a dagger over and over, and every few steps he would almost snarl at himself.

Punslon was a tip. Half the town had been buried when some demon they spoke of erupted from the Dimnesdair, and many of the rich had been entombed alive. The rest of it was in pieces, with many buildings damaged or destroyed. The only reason it was not worse was that the citizens had run like rats fleeing a sinking ship.

They had told him that Tal'Orien had warned them. Lady Emma Rin Bordau, in charge of the survivors, had paid heed, leading them and the children to Capsum. Those few who had stayed had vanished.

Some of the town had been rebuilt, but it wasn't the hub of activity it had once been. The orks hadn't come to the market and the town was feeling the loss of trade. Although many returning had been glad not to see the non-humans, more had realised that they had lost a valuable part of the market, regretting the xenophobia that had sprung up. Without the orks, many traders passing through had not been interested in stopping, and there were few enough of them this year. The only coin spent was by Novinian mercenaries, and they were bringing as much damage and upset as they were profit.

Punslon was becoming a ghost town. It was really an outpost of Eordeland culture, despite being a thousand miles away, although it held elements of Novinian, Banistari and Meyari as well. Their fierce pride at being what they called the hub of trade in Anaria was misplaced, thought Ventran sourly. Even now, they had items from many places you would not find collected elsewhere, but Eordeland had always been the financial centre of Anaria, and Eyotsburg the trade.

He wasn't very interested in anything to do with money or politics, apart from what immediate power they brought him. Only a few inns had survived the emerging of this so-called demon. Ventran was convinced that it had been nothing more than a huge earthquake. Stupid provincial louts, even the surviving rich here. Whatever airs they put on, they would be laughed at in the elite halls of Meyar.

None of them could tell him anything useful about Aldwyn Varelin.

Stupid old fuck!

He had started to feel that the old man was some sort of wisp, always out of his reach. Gods knew he had sent out enough parties and assassins to find the old bastard. It was extremely annoying that Politikus Belen had come closer to killing him than Ventran had. Belen was still a powerful figure, for all he had misstepped with their first ploy in Eordeland. It had cost Meyar a lot of gold to appease the Novinians and bring more of them back on for the main attack, and they had refused to enter Eordeland again; several companies had now been escorted to the borders, without their traditional weapons, mounts, or gear, and forced to walk in shame into the plains. They would find it hard to gain work again as mercenaries. Novin put a lot of pride in the traditions and ancestry of their companies.

Ventran had lost too many men trying; he had travelled half the continent himself to find word. His passing through Eyotsburg had been eyed with so much suspicion there that he had not indulged, but simply moved on. The plains were too dangerous and easy to become lost on to cut through alone; ork tribes and dangerous creatures wandered the grasslands. He had followed the great plains roads instead. Twice he had been stopped by mercenaries, and a third time outright attacked. It had taken quick work to show them the seal of Terome he carried and identify himself as an ally.

He had been in this dump for several weeks now. Several people in Punslon had been quite forthcoming with information, though others were wary of a stranger asking questions.

They had spoken of three men, a woman, and an ork - of all things - leaving town in a hurry with two children half a year gone. From the description Aldwyn had been one of the men, as well as Tal'Orien, who was hard to mistake. One of the children must be that brat he had been teaching, although why and where in the hells the old man had picked up a second one was beyond him. They had stirred up some kind of trouble and a mob had gone after them.

Who the second man and the woman had been he didn't know, but it was irrelevant. The party had emerged from the Dimnesdair and not passed through the town again. A guard lieutenant who had been at the logging camp further into the woods remembered only the ork and Tal'Orien in the chaos. He said they had come from the depths of the Dimnesdair and told of several thousand orcs following them. The camp had been abandoned by three-quarters of the people there. The rest had stayed… and vanished.

He knew whose bellies the remains had gone into.

Ventran had heard tales of those dark woods and knew more of them than these people. Sontles had informed him of their allies. The Dimnesdair was not the only place they lived, although it was their largest number. Everywhere orcs gathered, for the first time in millennia.

Ventran was not naïve enough to believe it was purely at the behest of Meyar, but he knew that orcs moved towards Eordeland. Whatever those prissy fools with their so-called enlightened Council believed, they were doomed.

Tal'Orien's party had fled east on the great plains road skirting the southeast edge of the Reldenhort Plains where the orks travelled. The main logging camp had been razed. Ventran had also heard from one sot that immediately before the demon had broken free of the deadly valley beyond the ranges behind them, a vast army had flowed out, moving north and east along the road before travelling north. He had been out hunting, he said, and shivered as he spoke of tens of thousands of horrible creatures stumbling in the fading daylight, desperate to escape the freed horror.

Ventran hoped this was true. If it was, it meant that the orcs Meyar had allied with kept to their bargain.

He had been curious as to why the orcs would ally with any humans, for any reason. Orcs hated everything, including each other. Sontles had told him that they had offered two things that the orcs could not ignore: free reign to pillage the entirety of Eordeland once it was crushed; and assistance in destroying the ork tribes, whom the orcs both hated and feared beyond all others.

One step at a time, Ventran reminded himself. So far, the orcs had provided their end of the bargain, but having met several Ventran had little trust for them. They were brutally ferocious, but cowardly, with no loyalty. They would throw any alliance away if it suited them.

His thoughts moved back to his hunt.

Time was moving on. Ventran could return, but he knew his master would again ask one simple question - one he'd already been asked after killing his first Darostim in Lodnor.

Where is the pendant?

That *bloody* pendant. Varelin had it, he knew. Him or… one of his party.

Yes. That was likely, Ventran mused. He threw the balanced knife again idly, watching it *thunk* into the vertical grain of the beam.

Varelin had taken the kid to Darost. The boy had stayed with him for quite some time from all reports. Perhaps the old fart had been ploughing him as well; either way, he considered the boy important. He was old, would want someone to carry on his work. The pendant might have been left in Eordeland.

That was the next step, Ventran decided.

They had gone east and north, probably to Darost. Tal'Orien and the children returned, then left again. Varelin must have stayed in Darost.

Ventran had nearly sliced the sot's gullet when he had said they come back on a dragon. He did not like being made a fool of. But enough people had agreed that he had cautiously filed the knowledge under *they came back*, and everyone who had mentioned the tale also agreed that the warrior had said they went on to Darost.

Darost it was, then.

Ventran was starting to hate scholar and boy. They should have been dead many times over by now.

But there was another element to his hunt. Finding this irksome boy and his tutor and pulling their guts out personally was only part of the reward for gaining this pendant, or finding where it lay.

Tal'Orien.

Everywhere he went, people spoke of his stature, his prowess. It was really starting to piss Ventran off. He had been intensively trained by some of the finest warriors Sontles could find and he had not yet found a man he could not best in single combat. Ventran had met bigger, faster, stronger, wiser, older opponents in his time, and despite his relative youth, he had beaten them all. He had a genius for underhand fighting, using the environment to his advantage, fleeing to strike when least expected. He excelled at traps and had been well taught in the use of poisons and blades, although he always preferred the latter.

He was also left-handed and adopted a style suited to his sinewy form, often faking a right-handed style first. Few could quickly adjust to his reversed knife play; fewer still could keep up when he switched to his right again. He wasn't quite ambidextrous, but he wasn't far off.

Ventran had spent most of his life not caring what other people thought. They were sheep, and he was a wolf. The mores and rhetoric of society meant nothing to a man who realised he did not have to obey them. He had a dark charisma that he wielded to get what he wanted, and was bold and arrogant. Confidence rolled off him in waves, and his dark gaze had no empathy in it. When people spoke of love, he didn't even wonder what love would feel like. It was only a weakness. He had nearly laughed in the face of the man who had seriously explained the rules of the marketplace in Punslon, as if Ventran was honour-bound to do what he was told.

The words meant nothing to him.

No, he cared little for what pathetic cattle thought of him, as long as it did not interfere with him getting what he wanted. But to be the man who killed Rast Tal'Orien... to know he had killed one of the greatest warriors of the age... more than anything else, that would assure his place in history.

Unless he became a God, with this pendant.

Ventran laughed to himself, amused. His master was an undead monster, softly-spoken and slight, but with horror and death in his wake. And yet Ventran still had trouble in believing in fairy tales. For him, power to rape and pillage and murder under the very noses of people who considered themselves decent and upright, and the horror and despair he generated, were more important than any godlike powers, imagined or otherwise. The only possible betterment he could imagine was living forever.

He had once wondered idly if it was worth Sontles making him a vampire, but his master had hissed in dry amusement.

'This gift is not lightly received,' Sontles had said. 'It takes scores of years to learn to master your... urges... and you would be totally mine to command. Certainly more than you are now.' The words were wry. Both knew that only Ventran's usefulness prevented Sontles harshly punishing him for his transgressions and ignorance of some commands.

Ventran had not liked the thought, and Sontle's next words had solidified his fears.

'Vampirism seeks a darkness with you, Ventran. And that you have, aha. But it is not all. Most human bodies reject the gift. If I bit you and fed, if there was a reaction at all, the likelihood is your body would go into toxic shock and you would die.' The lips drew back over the long sharp fangs. '*Horribly.* Some people recover, it is true, but very, very few are... *graced*... as I have been.'

Hunched in the darkness, he had seemed to grow, even as his slight form did not change.

'Personally, I care little if you wish to take that risk, but it would be a trying loss of a... *useful* servant.'

That much was true. Ventran had a genius for ferreting out information and doing so hidden amongst the scum of the city. He was reliable in most areas, and easy to please, and more importantly could do Sontle's bidding in the light of day. The vampire would be reluctant to chance someone that he had spent so many years training and nurturing.

Ventran had thought carefully about his plan after that. Sontles had told him that this pendant was the key to power, and even let slip several hints that it gave answers from a source beyond mortal knowledge. If this pendant could perhaps offer him a way to become immortal without the dangers of vampirism, he would take it. If not, he would hand it to Sontles as if he had always meant to.

And he would destroy Tal'Orien.

He hated the idea of Rast Tol'Orien, even as he respected his prowess.

He would hunt Tal'Orien from the shadows, and he would torture information from this irritating ward of Aldwyn's if he couldn't find the old man.

So.

Walking to the pillar, he levered the knife from the wood and thumbed the edge thoughtfully. Normally he would go out to find some sport, but a town of exhausted drunks held little interest for him.

He would get an early night, and head for Darost in the morning.

ಉ   ಐ

Karland had the sense that he was constantly being tested.

The Green Warrior pushed him hard, harder than he would have expected to be pushed given his condition. Despite this, he was recovering. His companion's silent approval was rare but heartening. The man proved to be certain, driven, yet unstable in temperament. He would say or do things that Karland was certain were simply to get a reaction of some kind, and it irritated him that he didn't know what game was being played. He wasn't certain he fully trusted The Green Warrior, for all the man had saved him; he suspected the man would simply leave if he found it suited him more than a half-believed promise.

The second evening they stopped to rest, he was exhausted, stumbling. He gratefully dropped to his backside, ate his portion of dried meat, and then sighed closed his eyes, resting his head on his arms, feeling his body complaining. He ached brutally; the beating he had received had left purpling bruises, and his arm alternately itched and twinged where he had been cut. Everything hurt.

Something about the silence made him open his eyes after a few moments. He looked up to find The Green Warrior watching him with an unreadable expression on his face; not anger, nor derision, but more appraisal.

Suddenly, the man rose. 'Roll with me.'

Karland wondered what he meant. He shook his head, feeling nervous under his steady gaze.

'No thanks,' he said dubiously.

'Get up,' snapped The Green Warrior. 'I need to know you can keep the pace. I don't plan on being caught.' He took a step forward, vital and strong. Something in his approach alarmed Karland.

The Green Warrior's eyes narrowed. 'Come on, *boy*.' He waved a hand, beckoning.

Karland shook his head. 'I can barely move at the moment. I'm in agony. I can't fight.'

'That what you'll tell them if they catch us?' The Green Warrior said derisively. 'I want to know if you can look after yourself. If you're worth my time. Get over here… or I'll come over there and test you on *my* terms.'

Karland stared at him, confused. The man's eyes were uncompromising, the mood swing abrupt. He clearly meant exactly what he said and didn't care if Karland was exhausted and hurt. As the bearded mouth drew down in a scowl, Karland nodded and approached cautiously. 'All right,' he said. 'Just… remember what I have been through.'

'You haven't been through anything yet,' said The Green Warrior ominously. Alarmed, Karland backed away. The man suddenly flashed a hand towards his eyes, then dropped forward onto one knee as Karland leaned back, and drove his shoulder into his hip, scooping his legs. Karland tried to stabilise, throwing his legs backwards, but was driven harder and fell back with the larger man on top. He hit the floor with a yelp of pain, his vision flashing, and the breath driven out of him. As he struggled to escape, The Green Warrior's legs seemed to flow around his defences, foot always hooking somewhere, and then he was on top, mounted and poised to strike at Karland's face. For a second Karland thought he would and shielded as best he could. Peering through his raised arms, he expected to see anger in the man's face.

Instead, his foe was grinning, moving to catch a wrist. Oddly, this close Karland could smell a strong, almost musky smell - not sour body odour, but a strangely masculine scent which was off-putting. Growling, he tried to dismiss his mind's treacherous talent for noticing strange things at inopportune moments. Karland fought back, bucking and moving with everything Rast had shown him while trying to catch an arm or leg and at least get free.

'Good!' shouted The Green Warrior. 'There's an arm there. Take it- take it-' Karland missed, and his adversary grabbed his wrist. Karland barely managed to wrench free and threw a desperate elbow at The Green Warrior's face, which he easily dodged. He realised the man's teeth were bared, and he was laughing loudly.

'That's it. Fight! Don't be soft!'

Karland tried everything he could think of. None of it worked, and The Green Warrior was clearly enjoying this more than he was.

A minute later, Karland was approaching exhaustion. He didn't have near the strength, stamina, or training of his opponent, and he was clearly being played with. His attempt to pull the man's arm down slipped too far across his chest and seconds later he had his own arm pressed across his throat by The Green Warrior's head. His opponent's arm swept under his neck, and he used the triangle of limbs to choke Karland, who gurgled as his air and blood were cut off by his own bicep. Frantically he slapped the man's side. The hold squeezed much tighter for a second, then after a moment where his head began to swim the pressure eased and the Warrior sat up. A brief look of disappointment crossed his opponent's face, but then it broke into another of those disarming grins.

'You've a lot to learn, but that was good. See? Even tired and wounded, you put up a good fight. That's when you *really* get to see what someone can do. We'll condition you. Check your weapon skill too. Where'd you learn? Some interesting techniques, though you need to make them tighter.'

Karland coughed, his throat feeling a little sore. 'Rast Tal'Orien.'

'Obviously knows his shit. Ha. Good teacher, though he hasn't taught you much yet. Like to meet him one day.' His voice sounded wistful, and Karland wasn't sure it would be for the purposes of talking. 'You're not totally useless, at least. Anything else, boy?'

Karland heard the test in his voice and knew that this moment would make or break his relationship with this strange, intense man. He hadn't been sure if he would release that choke hold for a moment, and knew he was being assessed in more than one fashion.

He didn't care; he was tired, sore and angry, and the near-constant air of gentle condescension was irritating him almost as much as the knowing, laughing way it was spoken, which made any retort seem like an overreaction.

'I'm able in maths and well-read. I can read Old Darum and know many works of science. I studied under Aldwyn Varelin.' The man didn't yet look impressed, and a note of irate challenge rose in Karland's voice. 'I know the stars in the sky and the realms of the world, and have stood before the Council of Twelve in Eordeland. I've fought men and orcs. I've nearly been killed by assassins and monsters. I've ridden one of the greatest dragons on Kuln through the skies and been named Dragonfriend. I've seen demons and gods and lost companions who were champions, fought you when I can barely stand, and I know more about the world than you apparently do. If that's *still* not enough for you, tough shit. And my *name* is *Karland*.' He glared at The Green Warrior, who drew down each side of his mouth in that half scowl, half grimace, bobbing his head slightly from side to side as if weighing the claims, and then saw Karland watching and threw his head back, laughing again in his sudden, mercurial way. He clapped Karland on the back in comradeship. 'Most of it sounds like bullshit, but you know some stuff, I'll give you that. You can tell me more later and we'll see if I believe you.'

'What *is* your name?' asked Karland, feeling that he had been accepted as a companion. 'I mean, your real name.'

The man didn't quite look at him, but paused for a moment, then shrugged quickly.

'Dunno,' he said again, clearly trying not to look bothered.

'Really?' Karland started again, aware how disbelieving he sounded. 'I mean, you don't know who you are at all?'

'Can't remember,' said the Warrior shortly.

'Anything? Where you are from?'

'No. Drop it.' His voice now held warning.

Karland wisely took the hint, with great effort of will. His curiosity mounted. He couldn't ask away like he had with Aldwyn; this man was far more like Rast, perhaps even more mysterious, and he couldn't be certain asking wouldn't earn him violence. He wondered what it would be like to not know who you were, managing to stop an expression of pity crossing his face. The Green Warrior would clearly not appreciate it.

They sat for a minute, awkwardly. There didn't seem much to say; the man's temper had shifted suddenly again. Then he appeared to relent a little, with a sigh.

'Look, I'm just not comfortable talking about it much. I remember… images. Random stuff. Snippets. Doesn't mean much. Know I'm from somewhere else. No one else here speaks like me.' His idiom was definitely different, but he spoke with only a faint accent.

'Why *The Green Warrior*?' asked Karland, curiously.

'First word I remembered was *green*. It seemed… important. And I *know* I'm a fighter.' He laughed heartily, but Karland didn't think he was joking. 'Turns out people here think green is dangerous. To do with the second moon. They say dark things happen when it's high.' he snorted in contempt. 'Superstitious morons.'

'So how long have you been here?'

The Green Warrior shrugged. 'Few years? Bit more? Moved around a lot.' His head shook. 'Don't want to talk about it.' He rose, putting an end to the questions. 'Rest up. We rise at dawn.'

They travelled fast throughout that day and the next, Karland being pushed hard. He no longer worried about being caught by the Novinians. The terrain they had travelled was rough and their pace was punishing.

In some ways it was harder than being with Rast. This man's intensity and his refusal to brook weakness or failure was much harsher than Rast's quiet encouragement. The Green Warrior expected him to do as well as he, and if he did, simply nodded as if it was natural. He was impatient at Karland's slowness or weakness on several occasions, sighing and shaking his head, but he was generous with food and rest, hunting small creatures with his bow. Karland realised he was not purposefully cruel, but rather had exacting standards of his own and simply expected others to live up to them. Despite himself, he found he was pushing harder and doing better than he would have on his own.

Ruefully, he swore to himself that he would never judge Rast as harshly again.

THIRTY

The days passed gently, dropping into a flow. Xhera awoke in the mornings, moving through the exercises Rast had taught her and taking breakfast with the Guards outside, then moved into the library and began work, keeping meticulous notes. Aldwyn, bless him, had cross-referenced everything in books, on charts, and anything else he could find to help him keep track of all the things he was researching, and it made her life far easier than it had been at The Sanctum. He had often seemed vague in words as he sorted for information in his capacious memory, but on paper he was razor-sharp. She actually felt as if she were making headway on understanding his work rather than diving into a pool and seeing only the flash of a fish before coming up for air.

It became a habit every Midwice to go to The Croft with two of the squad and have dinner with Karland's family. Becka always invited the veterans in, too. It gave Xhera a much-needed rest from trawling through Aldwyn's books.

Brin still had twinges sometimes from the arrow that had struck him during the Battle of The Croft, but he always welcomed her with a smile. He was very different from Hendal, more precise and with skin slightly dusky from birth, not field.

He was also very different from Karland, who had inherited a little of his mild colour. He was not as whimsical or idealistic, or as creative, and was very stubborn. He was obviously proud of his son, although he found it difficult to be open. She wondered if he were just naturally negative, but when he laughed it was real, deep laughter, and he teased Becka constantly.

For her part, she was caring and proud of Karland, but clearly did not understand much of what he and Xhera had been doing - not from lack of intellect, Xhera was sure, but because it just was not something that fitted her world view. They were good people, but despite their travel and education, in their own way they were less open to change and accepting other parts of the world than Xhera's simpler adoptive parents. Hendal and Marta took the world in their stride; they were eminently practical, less bothered about the realm at large.

Karland's father had a very set view, and Becka simply wasn't interested in the same things as her son and his friend. Anything they didn't agree with was either odd or discounted. She was certain they didn't believe half the stories she told them.

Nevertheless, she enjoyed her time with them. Brin was very knowledgeable about a great many subjects and enjoyed informing her about the history of the town and other things. Becka was both warm-hearted and pleasant, and an excellent cook.

And then there was Gail.

She was a complicated little package. Xhera got on very well with Gail, though it was interesting for her to be the older sister for once and gave her grudging insight into a few of Talas's frustrations when they were growing up. Gail was maturing fast, ambitious and intelligent. In some ways she was harder than Karland - she cared less what other people thought, doubted herself considerably less - but she was also sweet, generous, funny and kind. Xhera occasionally saw why they had argued so much, though. She was extremely stubborn and had an explosive temper.

Gods help the young men here when she grew up.

Or in The Sanctum, for that matter, Xhera grinned to herself. She doubted Gail would be content to stay here forever.

In the evenings the half-squad spoke around an evening meal, outside the Library door, exchanging stories. It was peaceful and comradely. Over the days they ceased being merely companions and became instead friends. She missed Karland being there, but not as often as she expected. Her life was busy and full. She wondered sometimes, amidst the odd spark of guilt, if Karland ever forgot about her.

Night told her and the Guard stories from across Anaria, answering most of her questions. She didn't ask as Karland did, in a constant stream that leapt from subject to subject; rather she focused on one area and strove to understand that as deeply as possible.

When they were alone, he spoke of his people as well.

She found the idea of vampyres fascinating. A family, cold but loving, bound by nature and by fate, hunting knowledge and vampires both. The description had touched her.

We stand in the Shadows to face the Light.

His tales were interesting and frightening both, and he rarely mentioned his own involvement in events. Listening to the stories of the atrocities vampires could wreak was chilling.

One of the most disturbing incidences recurred every few score decades amongst young men and women in Novin, occasionally Meyar. It seemed that a certain type of person - usually, although not always, from the upper classes and money - found the idea of vampires alluring to the point that they emulated them.

Several times in the last few hundred years, it had become fashionable to dress, act as and in general pretend to be vampires. Some of them even drank blood. A few committed murder.

Once, Vampyres had arrived and killed several when they murdered too many and committed terrible acts. They had not wanted them to attract real vampires with their foolishness, which had happened in the past.

Occasionally a real vampire had discovered them and veered between insult and amusement. A few had slaughtered many of them; at least one had formed a Death Cult and begun feeding on them to create a brood.

The Seekers kept a close watch on Novin. Night wished they had focused more on Meyar in recent decades. They might have discovered Sontles sooner.

Mostly Night slept somewhere in the darkness of the library, showing an interesting if uncanny ability to know if it was daylight outside. Xhera felt no real fear of him, even though she knew what he was. After a few instances where he had startled her, he had taken to deliberately coughing and making noise so as to not frighten her in the dark, or carrying library lights. She suspected he slept down amongst the shelves somewhere but had never tried to find out where.

Night had told her it wasn't really sleep, anyway - more of a half-doze.

Something else she found interesting was his ability to light a candle without touching it. He said it was something vampires developed, to do with being able to move small things with his mind. The best way he could describe it was to collect and compress the surrounding heat in the air to one point on a wick, which would flash into flame, or remove the air from the flame, which would put it out. He could turn light pages without touching them, too. He said it was a knack.

She still had no idea how he did it, and whatever it was it didn't work on library lights.

So the days went. Xhera amassed a huge amount of reference and worked her way through Aldwyn's notes in a cat's cradle of connections. Night left her to work at it from Aldwyn's end; she suspected he pursued his own studies and tried to meet her in the middle.

So far, she had learned a lot about Gods and other great forces, but little about the pendant or the portal. One thing was readily apparent however: over the last few thousand years, someone or something had been steering the world closer to turmoil, and the pot was at boiling point as far as Meyar went.

Xhera's world was becoming her studies. She would continue by the soft glowing light often late into the night, there being no windows in the secure library. Night generally did his own thing, seeming to spend much of his time in the archives, but he was always available for advice, and he could hear her call his name even from up here.

Deep down, she knew that this was what she had always craved. Learning, reading, accumulating fact but also having to piece it together, having her wit challenged.

The hard work she had become accustomed to on her adoptive father's farm had shaped her as well, so she could not sit in one place for too long before becoming uncomfortable enough to move. Sometimes she stood, pacing slowly around the top level in front of the fireplace, or switched from the high wingback chair to bed or desk. Sometimes she could stand the inactivity no more and would drop her books and move outside to walk the woods or exercise in the stable yard, often to the horse's snorts of interest.

She learned many things over the weeks that mostly raised even more questions. It was a gigantic task, trying to distil the works of decades of one brilliant mind referencing the works of centuries from many more. Gradually, however, a pattern began to emerge.

For a long time, the world had worked as it ever had, or so it seemed; but almost imperceptibly, there had been a shift. Not the usual shift of human politics and realms, but an almost invisible shift in attitudes, in disasters and calamities and actions, vast and abstract things too big for most to notice.

Something was changing in the world. Accelerating, the frequency increasing. It wasn't limited to the numbers of people showing changes in behaviour, or going mad, or even realms and societies as a whole seeming to switch tack. Illnesses, disasters, landscapes, many things that were at least partially controllable or predictable were also showing both aberrations to the norm, and corroborations with some of the more alarming texts predicting events either scientifically or prophetically. Plague, war, famine, natural disaster all featured.

Xhera could not pretend to be entirely objective to all of this. She had seen and been changed by things that had already convinced her that something was not right. Still, she tried not to justify her thoughts, instead seeking to match them to events.

Aldwyn's thoughts were clear in many notebooks and full tomes of facts. He had cross-referenced in detail against previous texts, his own work and that of others. There was a slow but accelerating shift in how things worked, evident in things as complex as murder rates for regions and as simple as sightings of mythical beasts.

She also came across more and more references to higher beings. Many Gods were shown to be related to each other in name or face. There were many religions in Anaria, and although Eordeland was a land of scientists and rational thought - consequentially having a large number of atheists and agnostics - many still recognised that beings like spirits and lesser Gods existed. It was not too great a leap to then accede that even higher Gods possibly existed.

Nearly every God worshipped in Anaria could be traced back in one way or another to twelve Gods, and there were many hundreds of Gods across Kuln. Aldwyn had stipulated that in fact a high number of the distinct Gods of Kuln were technically Lesser Gods, where these Twelve were the Greater, although to a mortal human the distinction was virtually non-existent. The Gods of Kuln that seemed individual had names and seemed quite generic, more mentioned as powerful beings than avatars, but the Twelve Greater Gods each held some kind of role, the custodianship of a Universal law.

She pulled a much more recent notebook from the last few years towards her, flipping it open. It held mostly religious notes, oddly, and the tone was not as clinical as usual.

There are greater Gods than even the Twelve. I can only guess as to the authenticity of this, but having met the being dictating this in question, something I can never admit without repercussions in Darost-' this went on for several pages, which she scanned. She had become remarkably facile at picking out important information amongst Aldwyn's musings.

His words gave her great comfort, as always. She could almost hear the *ums* and *ahs* of his speech woven through them.

Everything around us exists because of the creator. Exists as PART of the creator. We know, at the limits of our understanding and the abilities of the most sensitive of us, that ultimately everything can be seen as strands of energy, vibrating at different rates. We also believe that at this level, energy cannot be destroyed, only changed. This, of course, is no comfort to one who was alive and is now dead, but it also means that if the creator is omniscient and omnipresent, and is in fact everything, logically energy itself may be the Creator. Whether that means it is sentient in some way, or how we can be ourselves if we are part of a greater being, is open for debate, in some detail (see books reference Religion 13-17, Gods and Religions by Tantaro Gielse, The Philosophies of Acum by Pressor the Didactic).

In case this comes across as a religious text, let me rephrase this into personal and scientific observation: I have spoken to many people of many faiths, more than a few of other races, including elves, and to no fewer than three beings whom I can describe as in more of a position to know than mortal men with powers and abilities that may be defined as 'God-like'. These are creatures with ties to this world, without the politics and faiths of men, without the power structures or belief in miracles (sometimes with good reason) that we are subject to.

Men have faith because we do not know enough outside ourselves, cannot see further than our world, with the exception of a very few gifted mortals. We need faith, whether in ourselves or a greater power.

But Elves… High Elves… Dragons… Greater Dragons… other creatures not bound by mortal superstition and the need for blind faith, who have knowledge of what IS… all have been spoken of as mentioning the Twelve; not in worship, but simple respect, even familiarity. That more than anything suggests they are simply higher-order beings.

The Twelve Greater Gods of the whole Universe, our whole reality, govern everything. Life, death, the past, the future, darkness, light… It may be that Eordeland draws its Council and love of the number from a distant memory of them. We already worship Isha and Wheru, whom we call Delmatra.

Even such balanced powers as they are bound by three dictated absolutes at balance within the universe: Order, Chaos and Time. The Twelve are ultimately powerful, ultimately aware, but only set within a certain set of planes and dimensions. In space, in time, in all the upper and lower realms.

So what lies beyond them? Did they not create the universe together, as many believe? Many more do not even know of them, believing another being bound to their world to be the ultimate god or pantheon of gods. Sometimes this being is a facet, unknown to them, of one of the Twelve. Sometimes it is a hollow god, built from superstition and tradition, never having existed.

A name has been found, an all-powerful being that is somewhat outside our universe. More than one devout follower of one of the Twelve has mentioned that their god has spoken to them of events in Universe, alluding to a messenger: Aprolis.

This troubles me greatly, for if this vastly powerful unbound being is a messenger, the obvious question is… for whom? Or what? What message do they carry? What Herald can be more powerful than the Higher Gods themselves?

Years of study have unearthed a name. Something that is not even a God as such, but more of a concept, perhaps an avatar of what lies outside the Universe itself; a being that may have created this Universe. Perhaps many more. This Aprolis may be a Herald to Gods; the Twelve may be Greater Gods to our Lesser Gods of this world, supremely powerful in their own right; but if this utmost being is truly the Creator, then it truly is the ultimate, the beginning and the end of everything. Omnipotent.

So I find a rare and near-forgotten name, used by the Gods themselves, for what the Dragons and Próarkhe call 'Arkhe', the Ultimate Being.

GAL.

Lord of Lords, God of Gods, Parent of All. Rather than a being like us, or even like the Lesser Gods of Kuln - even, dare I say, the Twelve themselves, the caretakers of Universe - GAL simply is, an avatar of creation itself.

Xhera read on, her head swimming. Several times she had to go back and re-read sections to make sure she was understanding what was there.

GAL is simultaneously everything and the avatar of everything, not uncaring of our plight but simply too grand, too omnipresent to be beholden to one tiny part of Its creations, the smallest speck of the smallest speck of one of an uncounted number of specks which sit spinning in Universe; less so the infinitesimal life they host. How anyone can have the audacity to think such a being should individually judge them and be at their beck and call is quite illogical. If GAL cares at all, it will be for the vast creation of the Universe as a whole.

But it is also said that our Universe suffers a blight: dark chaos, beyond natural disorder, spreading within and destroying it, battering the laws of order and rendering huge sections of our Universe full of horror and despair.

The balance has shifted, it is written, and Its Great Work is in peril. If this is so, then why does our creator, who should love us so, not rescue us from our plight before everything is lost?

Xhera stopped reading, unable to believe the despairing tone that had crept into her mentor's work. She had never heard him sound like that. Frightened, yes. Amused, vague, distracted, annoyed. But never such dull despair.

She sat thinking for a while, making a few notes, and feeling thirsty and tired. She resolved to get outside, drink some water, stretch her limbs.

Instead, she found herself drawn back into her studies, like the urge to scratch an itch ever present.

Eventually after several more books and many hours she sat back with a sigh, stiff all the way up to her head with tension in her shoulders from hunching too long. With a deep breath, she moved on. An hour later she noted something in one of the most recent books, about a boy. Curious, she re-read it.

In the edge she saw a lightly pencilled number, forty-two, with a third number. She was sure she had seen it before. Then she remembered the other notebooks Aldwyn had stashed in his library and snapped her fingers.

Cross-referencing to book forty-two and reference section fifty-six she struck gold.

Unnerved, she read and re-read it several times, trying to make sense of it all.

What is it about this boy? A child, born in this time, is mentioned in the Book of Sarthos, in whose lucid moments nothing was uttered lightly. The date and language were difficult to decipher, but I believe it roughly translates to:

"On the cusp of a night moonless, yet under the moon of the Protector in the four-six-fifteenth year of the Domari rule-no-more; north of the east of the pit of the serpent of doom, in the land yet to come for the protection of troth. Lit by stars alone and the dying light of the sun, a saviour born."

This child will be different. Unique. Will make a choice that will save us or damn us. Must they be protected, at all costs, or destroyed? If they die before they can fulfil their destiny... is all lost?

I cannot tell. There is so much. I think Karland is important, more than just for his own worth.

Do I tell him? Am I even right? How much do I tell the Council?

Will the Darostim allow him to live?

ʘ ʘ

Karland recovered slowly as they travelled, the easing of his exhaustion giving him more time to observe his companion.

The man moved with an assured confidence that Karland had not seen in anyone else, not even Rast, who moved his giant frame like a whisper in quiet control. He did everything completely and uncaringly. When he relaxed, he was virtually lounging; when he travelled, he moved with unbroken stride. When he spoke, his manner was casual but his eyes watchful. Everything he did was simply what he was doing at the time, and he did it with all his being.

If he didn't know something, he would give a casual shrug and a disarming grin, but he was knowledgeable far beyond what Karland would have expected of a mere soldier of fortune. He was clearly also a scholar in some surprising subjects, and when he was in the mood to talk showed an excellent understanding of anatomy and healing techniques. When he spoke it was... inspiring.

They journeyed west through the foothills, aware of the bands of men skirting the plains. Karland spotted a clear gap and suggested changing plans, moving south into ork territory instead. The Green Warrior refused.

'Nah. Too dangerous. What happened to your dwarf friend? Need to stay further north. Raelf still might be following us, and I saw how many men they have in the low foothills as I came up. Anyway, those orks are killing any mercs they find.'

'I know the orks,' protested Karland. The Green Warrior cast a glance askew at him.

'Best friends, huh?' he drawled disbelievingly.

Karland, about to snap a retort, stopped.

Actually, remembering the last meeting they had where Brukk had been frightened in front of the combined clans by a dragon with Karland on her back… and having had the champion of the tribes fall in his defence… perhaps it was better they didn't meet the orks, at that. He didn't have Darus with him now.

'Didn't think so,' said The Green Warrior with a grin.

It was hard to take offence at the man sometimes; even when he was being outright rude to you, there was a cheeky grin, a flash of the eye or a wink which made you wonder if he was joking. By the time you'd made up your mind one way or the other, the moment was past.

Halfway through the fourth day since his rescue they paused to eat lunch. The Green Warrior stopped, listening. He grabbed Karland and held up a hand, then motioned him to set up camp.

'Think we're being followed,' he breathed in Karland's ear. He smelled musky and powerful, thought Karland. There was no other way to describe it. 'You bait them. I'll circle and take them.'

Karland wondered briefly if the unpredictable man was using this as an excuse to dump him, then remembered the risk he had run rescuing him and felt shame. The Green Warrior would be more likely to leap into the fight.

He busied himself setting camp, having no idea where the man had gone. The minutes passed, and then an hour. Karland could not keep his nerves taut that long and began to grow restless. Finally, as he looked around, he caught a glimpse of movement. Wondering if this was his fate, he was surprised to see The Green Warrior moving down from a cluster of rocks the opposite side from where he had left, an annoyed look on his face. He was moving directly toward Karland.

'Just a bear, I think,' he called.

Before Karland could ask if the danger was past, a smaller figure glided out from the rocks behind The Green Warrior, an arrow nocked and aimed at his back.

Karland stared in astonishment. It was Lëlylien.

os so

The Green Warrior stopped not far from the campsite at a terse command from Lëlylien, and then turned his head to glare at her.

'Who the fuck are you?' He looked closer. '*What* the fuck are you?'

'She's an elf. A friend.'

'An *elf*? Are you fucking *kidding* me?'

'Do not move, human. Where are you taking him? You are near dangerous land.'

'We're off the trail to avoid mercs,' said The Green Warrior. 'What land?'

'Fool. You have nearly crossed into *Beinbjörn* territory.' Her eyes flicked to Karland. 'Karland. I am glad to see you safe. I will take you back to Rast, after I deal with this human.'

'Look, you pointy-eared bitch,' snapped The Green Warrior, 'I rescued him. I wasn't sneaking up on him. See? Two packs.'

Karland waved his hands to calm the elf maiden down.

'He rescued me, Lëlylien. I was captured by mercenaries after the battle. He got me out. We were travelling to meet you all.'

'An elf three centuries in their grave could have tracked you two,' she rejoined tartly, and then smiled. 'I am glad you are well, Karland.' Her arrow, however, never wavered, ready to draw and loose in a split second.

'Mind putting that thing down?' asked The Green Warrior acidly, moving carefully to be seated near his pack. After a moment of weighing him with her eyes, she nodded and lowered the bow. Karland breathed a little easier. Since Darost, Lëlylien had been troubled, and wilder. He had wondered if she was going to kill his saviour for a moment. Now she relaxed.

'My apologies, human. I was charged with finding Karland and keeping him safe.' She replaced the arrow in her quiver and moved in carefully. As she reached within a few feet of The Green Warrior, he lashed out, his fist moving with blinding speed as he leaped up. She was already flipping backwards, moving out of range. Her foot slashed upwards, missing his face by a hair's breadth.

He charged after her, lunging for her figure. Surprised by his speed, she didn't quite get a defence up in time. A stiff-fingered jab was avoided, and he got a glancing return strike in on her shoulder even as her foot flashed around again, clipping his mouth. The two combatants danced back, watching each other. She was definitely faster than he was. A dagger had appeared in her hand.

'Stop it!' shouted Karland. 'Stop fighting!'

The Green Warrior grinned, dabbing a hand back to his mouth where a lip was split, his momentary annoyance forgotten. Something about action seemed to delight him, improve his temper.

'She's good,' he said, his nature switching to humour as quickly as ever. He turned to Karland, keeping an eye on the elf. 'For someone with a lot of dangerous friends you sure know how to get your ass handed to you.' He used the Novinian common slang for *arse*.

'Look, I got surrounded by a whole squad-' began Karland, and then stopped on seeing the mocking grin. He was being goaded again. After a moment, he calmed sufficiently to return the prod. 'Looks like you just got yours handed to *you*,' he said instead, grinning back.

The Green Warrior's mouth dropped open wide in a silent laugh, eyes crinkling. Lëlylien looked between them, rubbing her shoulder and scowling, and then her laughter tinkled out.

'Humans,' she said, shaking her head. 'He was quite skilled in his movements, but not skilled enough to fool an Elven scout. Had I followed your trail instead to have come upon you from the south, I would have seen your tracks together.'

'You're a good tracker,' admitted The Green Warrior without rancour. 'Even for someone so young.'

'I would wager a fair bit older than you,' she replied, and bowed her head slightly. 'Lëlylien is my name.' She sheathed her delicately curved dagger smoothly.

The man lifted his head briefly in greeting in a kind of sharp reverse nod, no more. 'People call me The Green Warrior.'

Lëlylien's head cocked at this, but she said nothing else.

'So, what will you do now?' asked Karland. He felt indebted to The Green Warrior, beginning to like him. He knew the man had talked about leaving him, and now he could do so with surety.

He wasn't sure if he wanted to man to simply vanish again, although a part of him admitted that it was wearing being next to such a driven man. Driven not in the way Rast was - quiet and humble, and with deadly focus - but by the force of his nature, his charisma. He made you feel a little more alive by his very insistence on getting things done, by demanding you did them too.

'Well,' he drawled, his wicked grin returning, 'I'm not doing anything else. You promised to help me, and I wouldn't mind meeting your friend Tal'Orien.' He looked over at Lëlylien. 'Anyway, what happens if you're alone in the wilds with her and you find you need more help than some skinny elf?'

Karland snorted laughter, half outraged. Lëlylien was less amused.

'Better with me than a witless human who doesn't know the lands,' she said acerbically. 'He might actually survive.'

'Think a woman can look after him in the wilds? He has a better chance with someone with actual balls.'

'Beware, Warrior,' she snapped, flowing to her feet, her hand on her knife.

The Green Warrior opened his mouth as if to argue and paused, and then laughed loudly. Lëlylien's teeth bared in rare anger. Astonished, Karland saw him *wink* at her.

He couldn't believe how quickly the man had riled the normally calm elf maiden. As The Green Warrior continued to smile charmingly at her, her expression slowly changed, leaving her confused as to whether he was joking or not.

'Is this supposed to be funny?' she said, her mouth a tight line. Her gaze flicked to Karland, who shrugged. Something about the man confused even the elf; he was certain anyone else saying that would have had her knife against their throat in demand of an apology by now.

'I think he's teasing you,' he said.

'No elf would ever be so uncouth,' she said accusingly, her eyes fixed on the man. Finally she sat, not looking at him, and began to whet a blade pointedly.

Karland looked over at The Green Warrior. He had relaxed back, chuckling.

'Don't you ever worry you offend people?' asked Karland.

The Green Warrior grinned at him. 'Nope.' He gestured at Lëlylien. 'Anyway, she can take it. She gets shit done.' There was respect in his voice, and Karland shook his head. This man was so hard to read, even for him. No wonder Lëlylien was finding him opaque.

'She's worth your respect,' said Karland in mild rebuke. 'She's an elven warrior.'

'Never met one before. Doesn't matter who you are; you have to *earn* my respect.'

'I must earn nothing from any human,' Lëlylien interjected mildly. 'Or man.' The rhythmic scrape of her whetstone underlined her words. The Green Warrior winked at Karland. After a second, Karland laughed.

'I think you've made an art form out of annoying people, Warrior.'

The man's eyes twinkled.

THIRTY-ONE

Rast, Darus, and Galnór camped with the Eordeland company to the east of the southern Stonestride, the great part-natural, part man-made bridge across to the island city-realm of Eyotsburg.

'It appears we have a problem,' the elf mused, as he sat with Rast and the Major's retinue.

Galnór had joined the pathfinders sent to view the surrounds. His eyes gave them a great advantage for detail and distance. The slender elf often poked sly fun at Darus, despite knowing full well that the ork could see better in the dark than any of them except possibly himself.

He was not laughing at the moment, however. They were still awaiting word from Lëlylien, hoping that she had found some trace of Karland. Now they cold-camped, watching more than a thousand Novinian troops ringing the end of the southern Stonestride outside the bridge fort standing at the entrance to the high arch of stone, its thick gates closed.

The way into Eyotsburg was blocked.

'We were not expecting this,' admitted Major Gambeson. 'It seems Novin has committed a large force to Meyar's aid.'

'We arrived too late,' said Aldine heavily. 'The Council moved too slowly.'

'There were political considerations,' reminded Gambeson. Whether he agreed or not, he would brook no criticism of command. 'We must find another way. They won't allow us to walk up to the gates, and the Eyots wouldn't open them for us.'

'Are there boats we can hire nearby?' asked Aldine.

'There is no way down from the lake by boat,' said Darus. 'I know these waters. Where the lake exits to your island city, the water falls far.'

Rast nodded agreement. 'There are rapids and many rocks, even without the Lakefalls. Eyotsburg is well-protected on the east. It is from the west we must approach, and they will doubtless be guarding that as well. I suggest we move further west into the forest and see if there is any way we can move upriver, although that will be hard going. There are many small settlements and ship docks along the southern shore.'

'How long will that take?' asked Major Gambeson.

Rast looked at Darus, who shrugged. 'Four nights? Six?'

Aldine sighed. 'Another delay we can ill afford.' He glanced at Rast, not in suspicion so much as query. 'You know this land well, Tal'Orien.'

'I have travelled many lands.'

'No chance of moving past near the Stonestride,' grunted Gambeson. 'We must circle south into the plains, move at night. It will be a forced march if we are not to be seen.'

'What about the other elf and the boy?' asked Aldine.

'We shall have to hope that they find their path through,' said Rast quietly. He kept his feeling of guilt confined. It would not help any of them.

'Lëlylien will guide him,' said Galnór.

'*If* she finds him. Be honest, Tal'Orien,' said Aldine. 'If it wasn't for the elf being a better tracker, you'd be looking for him yourself, whatever the Council asked.' His tone was disapproving.

Rast looked at him steadily. Aldine refused to let it go.

'I swore his protection,' he said quietly. 'The only reason I have not left is because I trust Lëlylien to find him.'

Aldine looked disgusted. 'Despite your duty to Eordeland.'

'You forget, Captain, that I am not of Eordeland, and I have given much already to your realm,' remarked Rast matter-of-factly. 'We all have our priorities. I will do what was asked of me, but Karland remains my first responsibility.'

The officer grunted sourly. 'Well, I am glad our priorities match up at the moment, then. Let's get some rest for a few hours, and then press on. Perhaps Darus and the elves can aid us tonight.'

'It looks like there will be cloud. We will have to watch for sentries,' said Darus.

'I can scout ahead and make sure any that might see us are deep in slumber,' laughed Galnór in agreement. 'I may not see their heat, my green friend, but I will hear them. And I can still see far at night.'

The big ork grinned around his tusks at the elf. For races that rarely met, they seemed very easy in each other's company, reflected Rast. Part of that might have been to do with Darus, of course.

At times he was so similar to Grukust that it was easy to forget. Even after being in his company for many weeks, Rast was still caught out by him. During the fight with the mercenaries it had been almost like fighting alongside the champion of the tribes again as he roared and curved the dwarf-forged axe around - perhaps with less finesse than his brother, but to great effect. But then he would do or say something quietly that reminded Rast that Grukust's younger brother was something of a scholar, and refined as well - not just for an ork, but for a lot of people. He didn't have the same raucous sense of humour and he was in better control of his temper, not being so mercurial.

Grukust had been far from stupid, but his wit had been quick and honest. Darus was more aware of subtlety, more learned than Rast had ever expected to find an ork. They didn't have the easy camaraderie that his brother had had with Rast, but there was definitely respect.

Darus caught his eye as they moved to their bedrolls, and raised an eyebrow, his lip twitching slightly about his left tusk just visible to Rast's night vision. Rast smiled slightly.

'I was thinking of your brother,' he said. 'You are alike, yet not. He was a good comrade. I miss him.'

Darus nodded, his lip quirking in an emotion Rast couldn't quite guess at. 'I, too. We were close as brothers, and he had a truly gentle side. I hope to honour him.'

'He would be proud of you already,' said Rast certainly.

Darus smiled, his yellowish teeth even and pale in the darkness.

'I would like to believe so. But until I have earned my *kappanim,* I will not.'

'Do you have a quest in mind?' enquired Rast. He knew only a little of the naming quests of the orks.

'No,' answered Darus honestly. 'I must prove myself worthy in a manner that cannot be questioned, or die in the attempt; and by my brother's axe, it must be great indeed. There is no other way. I am certain that I will find a suitable challenge on my journey with you.' He looked away. 'I hope my death does not interfere with your own quest.'

And there was where human understanding moved away from orks, mused Rast. He understood honour and duty better than most men; it defined him, in fact, as he had found out to his chagrin in the Portal. But despite his intelligence and learning, Darus would follow the harsh dictates of his people unswervingly to death.

'May I ask something?' asked Rast.

'Of course,' said Darus.

'How long will Brukk hold the tribes?'

'Ah.' Darus shrugged in silhouette. 'That is not easily answered. He grows older, though he is stronger than ever, and may face challenges. To lead the tribes Chieftains must prove themselves superior to their people. Trial by arms is one part.'

Rast nodded. 'Also mind. There is no use having a fool lead us to ruin. We must trust a leader to find us the best paths, to deal with other tribes, humans; to bargain for us where most would not understand the bargain. To be strong enough to lead, to win against our foes. All this.

'I do not blame you for judging him harshly. Age and disappointment, seeing our lands destroyed and claimed by humans who never seem content with their own borders, the falsehoods and bargains even he could not see laden with venom… the shrinking of our tribes and lands and ways… they have worn him. He is a good and honourable ork who is perhaps not flexible anymore, has too many burdens.'

Flexible wasn't really an orkish trait, mused Rast.

'So if Grukust had challenged…' he said.

'He would have also had to fight any Chieftain who stood to do so,' laughed Darus. 'One or all. And I think he would have won, too, and become Grukk, despite our traditions.' He sighed, and must have seen the look of regret on Rast's face in the darkness. After a moment he spoke again.

'He would have hated it, human. He was born to lead spirit, not policy.'

Rast nodded, about to walk to the sentry line, and then turned back, curious, as Darus lay down.

'One more thing?'

Darus grunted assent.

'What do you see when you look at me in the darkness?'

'Colours of heat. But it is as if overlaid on your features, a little.' Darus yawned. 'The elf can see well in the dark, but it is different from what he told me. I see less light than he, but some heat at the same time, and they shift. Like layers of fire. It is hard to explain.'

'It must be useful,' remarked Rast. Ever-attuned to combat, his mind began working out how it could be used - or defended against - in an opponent, as he had in The Croft.

A deep snore answered him, and he smiled, reminded of Aldwyn. He and the ork appeared to have the ability to sleep whenever they wanted, wherever they were. He glanced over at the slender form of Galnór, sitting back straight in repose, deep in a *dônaethar* trance. Unlike Rast, the elf was fully aware and alert even deep within the trance. It was a waking reverie for a being that never slept and could be maintained even while he responded. For Rast, it was harder. He had delays in his response as he reacted, and he needed a good hour to replenish his reserves. Galnór only needed a few minutes at a time to recharge his energy. Elves used beds to rest, and might even appear to be asleep, but they were simply resting, eyes closed, dreaming waking thoughts. Sometimes they could be so caught up in them that they paid no attention to the world, but they were not in slumber. Rast had known elves rest in trance while they ate or rode. Unless you knew what you were looking for, you might never even notice; elves could seem distracted at the best of times.

He ghosted along the lines, some of the sentries not even noticing his presence, and then returned to his pack and settled himself for his own repose.

His mind returned to his missing charge.

Once again, he had failed to protect someone. He had betrayed their trust. Once again, the people he cared for were harmed while he survived.

Once again, his duty - all he had - was still not enough.

I hope you are safe, boy.

೧   ೭

They broke camp not long after dusk, the Eordelanders checking their equipment for noise. With Darus leading them and Galnór and Rast hovering like wraiths around the northern edges of the company with the pathfinders, they made their way their way across the plains in a parabola.

Twice the company had to wait for a small band to pass heading north, Galnór and Darus seeing them far before anyone else. The Novinians were gathering, but they were not being particularly wary. Perhaps they believed that more than a thousand knights and foot was enough to ward off orks or barbarians.

If that is their hope, thought Rast, *they might end up rudely disabused.*

Several hundred plains orks would go through them like an avalanche.

Dawn broke as they travelled south-west of the besieged land-bridge. They had moved nearly thirty miles. Ahead lay the sparse woodland of northern Novin, very different to the thick forests of Eordeland. To the southwest lay the mountains bordering east Novin. No one else was visible on the plains, and they kept moving, heading for the distant dark fringe of trees.

After a six hour rest they marched again, continuing until finally they moved wearily into the fringes of the woods. The company pushed another hard mile before they made camp. Hidden from the eyes on the plains, with trees to break up the columns of smoke above the small fires, Aldine allowed several camp pit fires lit at the deep end of a dug out wedged trench, and the soldiers luxuriated in a hot bean stew. They would recover here tonight, then move on slowly and cautiously.

Rast stood at the edge of the camp, gazing into the woods. Darus did not seem quite as nervous as Grukust had under trees, although the trees here felt less close than the Dimnesdair had. Something was troubling him, however.

Rast had a feeling that the woods might not be as empty as they seemed. None of the soldiers noticed anything, even the pathfinders, one of whom was an excellent

420

tracker and woodsman. He tried to pin down his nagging worry, and barely sensed a presence moving up behind him. There was no noise. The lack of any other stimuli gave away the identity.

'Galnór,' he acknowledged. The elf laughed softly.

'Few are the humans that may sense the approach of an elf in the woods, Rast Tal'Orien. What disturbs you?'

'I am not sure,' the big man admitted. 'I do not think the mercenaries will have penetrated far into the woods, if at all, but there is... something.'

'Yes,' said Galnór, serious now. 'The woods lie quiet with foreboding. Something foul disturbs their slumber.'

'We will move through them as fast as we can towards the main roads,' said Rast. 'Tomorrow we head northwest. If we can find a boat or ship to take us to the city upriver, we can pass the word of the Council over to Eyotsburg and find a ship.'

'And then to *Míthtól?*' asked Galnór.

Rast shrugged.

'Eventually. But not until I know of Karland. Once the party is in the city and safe, I will leave to find him. They may stay and wait, or go, as they choose.'

'He means much to you, warrior.' The elf was faintly mocking. 'I thought Rast Tal'Orien was above such human frailties.'

'I have always cared,' answered Rast. 'But in the Hall of Wyrms we found more than a mere portal. It held... visions. I found part of myself I had long ago forgotten was even missing.' He sighed. 'I have spent so long training and fighting; focused on my duty. I never thought there was anything else for me. I found that perhaps there can be. Karland is my duty. But he is also my... friend.'

'Then you are more complete, *mellon*,' said the elf. 'You have given enough.'

'I will never have given enough, ' replied Rast, 'but the reason for giving is as important as the giving itself.'

'There is great truth in that,' agreed Galnór.

ೞ   ೫

As they camped the next evening Rast and Galnór again felt a sense of dread, of something dangerous about the woods they travelled through. It was not near, but it was there, omnipresent and lurking, and it grew the further west they moved.

The third day the party found a wide trail, and eventually a village. Even the Eordelanders noticed that the villagers were subdued. When they had first ridden up the trail from the nearest trees, they had been met with pitchforks and trembling glares as women and children were herded out of the other side of the village. They re-provisioned as best they could, once they had persuaded the frightened occupants that they meant no harm.

These people weren't Novinian. The great forests had isolated villages and town on the southern fringes of the estuary, although few lived deeper south-west. Much further south, some tithed to the mercenary warlords in Novin as a 'Regal Tax'. Other than that, they were largely left alone and had little care in the running of things. Up here, folk had no real land. Ostensibly Novin extended into the forests, although even they didn't know how far, but these people were their own masters.

Now they were nervous, and unsure what to do. They knew little but their village and the surrounds; still, they had heard tales of creatures that slaughtered with abandon. Men, women, children, beasts. Entire villages slain, they said.

Help from the south had been sent for, but they expected little to arrive. The southern lords were always embroiled with war, and rarely came north. The journey was long and difficult.

Further west they were begged to stay and help as they passed a village. Villagers had poured out in supplication and tried to make them defend their homes, offering anything, the women even offering themselves.

The soldiers were disturbed. This village did not deal in rumours; people had gone missing, and strewn remains were all that had been found. People and animals had been found often partially eaten, killed in a manner than suggested the killer enjoyed the death. Others had simply vanished. The village was terrified.

They gave their regrets, Aldine saying they had business and Rast telling them quietly that they should move east, or find a larger town or city. The people looked at him helplessly, trapped in the realisation that they could either become homeless beggars or stay with their lives and possibly die.

He had no answers for them.

The company hurried on, disturbed by the anger and despair that followed them. Moving ever further upward, they cut across to a main trail west. A little short of a large village less than a day later they halted. Something was not right.

Galnór was the first to pause, raising his hand. His keen ears had detected something, and as they drew near his nostrils flared in distaste.

'Death lies ahead,' he whispered.

The closer they drew, the higher tension mounted. Rast could hear an insistent buzzing now and knew the source. Raucous cries from crows rang stridently through the constant noise.

When they broke from the trees even the soldiers were shocked, several gasping. Rast felt his heart twist in despair at the scene in front of them.

The entire place was still apart from the birds which flew upward, disturbed by the living men, and the smaller scavengers which skittered away in response. Flies blackened doorways and moved in swirls amongst scattered corpses.

Bodies littered the streets, not as many as could account for the houses. Blood was spattered everywhere. People and beasts lay with their guts torn out, throats gaping, bodies half-eaten. Many lay shredded into pieces, some distinguishable as belonging to the same person only from clothing.

One woman had literally been ripped in half, her torso trailing intestines and her eyes rolled back in a pale blue face set in a rictus of horror.

Here and there children lay, some barely recognisable as having been human from what was left, another identifiable as a small boy apart from the absence of a head. Clouds of flies rose at the interference. In one building, the gutted hollow husk of a months-old child lay, its soft body ripe for the ravenous attacker. Next to it, the mother that had tried to protect it was mutilated beyond recognition, her head distended and torn as if it had been crushed.

A fly scuttled along the white rim of a skeletal socket around a dark well of decay.

Life was utterly gone from this place. The carnage was sickening.

Rast was stony-faced, and the usually light-hearted elf was quiet. This was not war, or even vengeance. This was wanton lust for slaughter.

The party moved from building to building, weapons drawn.

Something had razed the people of this village with brutal efficiency and power. It had broken down doors, burst through roofs, left bloody prints and large clawmarks.

'I fear the source of this,' said Galnór, his face troubled. 'Those prints remind me of huge predators, but no forest cat or wolf has the power to tear through a door like this. Perhaps a bear, or a bone-bear, but these clawmarks are troubling. Not even gar-wolves do this. This place carries a seething dread to it. A feeling as if nature itself cried out at what happened; as if it were done in orgiastic pleasure.'

'We must move on,' said Rast shortly. He clamped down on his emotions, which were demanding he find the source of this evil and destroy it. 'There is nothing we can do here. These people have been dead for days.'

Aldine joined them, his face pale.

'We will search quickly for any food left,' he said, and then shook his head. 'And survivors, though I doubt there are any. There were hundreds here.' He shook his head, shaken and drawn. 'This is what lies in store for Eordeland if we fail.'

'This was no battle,' said Rast. 'Not even orcs could do this. These people were rent limb from limb.' He looked at Galnór as he spoke. The elf looked troubled. There were no creature remains; only people.

None of them wished to spend more time in that town than necessary. The buildings were searched, including the town hall, and a small church, the pulpit smeared with blood.

No one was alive, in any cellar or cupboard. The Eordelanders took what they might need and moved on, many cursing under their breath. It was hard to see death, but even veterans quailed at the wholesale butchery before them.

Sergeant Spooner - a rough man near Rast's size with huge shoulders, a prize wrestler who looked like an archetypical dockside thug - spotted something in the turned mud and went to investigate, returning with a look of such grim foreboding that no-one dared ask what he had found.

Spooner tucked a small, sad, half-limp white fabric rabbit into his pack. It was muddy and missing an eye. Half the feather stuffing was gone. The rest was sodden.

He sat for a moment, staring into the distance, and then shook his head. His ham-sized hands and strong fingers clenched and unclenched slowly.

Ignoring the surreptitious stares, he said quietly, 'I got three little girls.'

He could have said more; how he felt terror and fury at the thought of them being harmed, at the fear and agony they would have felt; how no child should suffer the depravities of such monsters which killed for such sport; how he could neither find nor respect all the remains of the children here, and how this was the only gesture he could offer. How he felt like crying.

He did not need to.

They packed and left, the skies grey and the woods feeling oppressive. For the first time the company tried to match the big warrior and the elf for stealth, sensing that it might be wise not to meet what had done that, although not a few of them would have welcomed the chance to even the score.

After so much time and so many visitors from the woods, it was hard to tell where the tracks had led out from the village, but Rast thought they looked as if the creatures had left westward. Galnór agreed and directed them north for a way.

'Lucky for those smaller villages behind us,' he said, shaking his head. 'Perhaps one of them did visit that last village - the one with people missing. But here, there were more.'

'Indeed,' said Rast grimly.

The company moved northwest with purpose, Rast and Galnór flitting into the trees and back in a way the Pathfinders could not match. They moved through the trees as quietly as possible. As the afternoon wore on, the feeling of being watched grew.

As they rounded a thicket and crossed a relatively open space, Galnór whirled left, his hand flashing to an arrow and nocking it in a fluid movement. At the same time Rast moved quickly in a circular motion towards whatever Galnór had sensed, crouching and ready. They had both detected something at the same moment, far closer than it should have been able to get to them. The soldiers drew swords in a rush, prepared to engage. Several also nocked arrows.

'Hold!' called a soft female voice. A tall figure in a brown robe stepped out from behind a large tree with hands out to the side only a handful of paces from them. Moving slowly, she raised her hands and cast her hood back to reveal golden hair tumbling around a strong attractive face, piercing gold-green eyes with a hint of luminous hazel shining out.

Rast relaxed, and Galnór unnocked his arrow.

'We meet again, *Banidróttin,*' she murmured. Her lips quirked slightly. 'It seems I can still catch you unawares.'

He bowed slightly to her, his heart more at ease than it had been for some time.

'Leona. It is good to see you again.'

Aldine stepped forward, his face angry with reaction, sword still in hand. 'Who are you?' he demanded loudly. The figure quickly held up a finger to her lips.

'Quietly. There are dangerous foes nearby. Much further and they would have sensed your approach. If so many find you, they will destroy you. All of you. We must move north. I will take you to our camp. We may speak more there.'

'We should follow you without any information?' said Aldine, a little more quietly. He was still angry and suspicious.

'She is known to the Council of Twelve,' said Rast. 'She has quested with us on their behalf. Leona has my complete trust.' He gazed into her eyes for a moment, something nagging him, something he had remembered recently. 'I strongly suggest you heed her words.' His eyes sought the Major, who nodded slowly.

'I vouch for her also,' said Galnór. 'We are lucky she found us.'

'A lone woman in the woods?'

'She is a Druid. I doubt your arrows would have harmed her.... or that she is alone.' The last words held a warning.

Several nearby soldiers glanced around, looking for potential foes, and Galnór laughed quietly. 'I think you will have little luck trying to see Druids in woodland. They can give elves lessons in stealth.'

'I think there's something out there. I saw a large animal; a bear or wolf.'

'The animals here will not harm you,' Leona said. 'Not unless you prove in need of harming.'

Galnór laughed quietly at the look of consternation. 'Not all animals attack humans.'

'What if it did for that village?' asked one soldier, belligerently.

'It did not.' Leona's voice held a tone that cut off any argument. She looked back at Rast, her deep golden eyes unblinking in her strong face, and then a small mysterious smile played about her lips.

'Come. The camp is to the north. We must go.'

☙ ❧

They moved into a very large clearing atop a low hill with fires to the lee of the mound. Several hundred Druids moved around, talking quietly and looking sombre. They were invited to camp to the northeast, putting the majority of the stone between them and the direction they had come from.

'Be at peace,' Leona said to Rast. 'Our foe avoid this place. It is sacred ground. They become confused and weak here.'

Major Gambeson spoke with Rast and five Druids, one of them Leona. The Druids refused to speak of the nature of their enemy, avoiding or rebutting the questions, but he took their warning seriously nonetheless. Captain Aldine advised stiffly that they ignore the nature priests and move on and was tersely frustrated when his advice was ignored.

'If you leave before it is safe, none of you will see the river,' a Druid told Major Gambeson. He glanced at Rast, who nodded, and reluctantly agreed.

The Druids asked them to wait six nights. They were planning an attack, luring their foe into a trap to hopefully kill them all. When Rast offered to help, a lean Druid had shaken his head.

'Your soldiers would perish in moments, *Banidróttin,*' he said. 'Even you would quickly fall. They are beyond you. We have lost many of our own, despite our powers.'

The third night, most of the Druids vanished, Leona included. A little after midnight, a terrible sound erupted somewhere in the distant trees to the southwest. Howls and roars mixed with shrieks and agonised wails drifted towards the camp. Soldiers snapped awake in terror. The lookouts were fortified by the others; no one could sleep with the hellish sound echoing around them. Many of the company were sweating in fear.

426

The elf was wincing, bow ready. His eyes flicked around the darkness at the edge of the campsite.

'Be calm,' said a small woman, with eyes of pale gold-blue fire. 'They will not come here.'

Rast knew Leona fought out in the darkness, against a terrible foe with great powers.

'Let her return,' he whispered inaudibly to himself.

The rest of the night was long. Almost an hour after it had begun, the noise faded and then stopped. Over the next few hours, a roar or a shriek would rend the air. It seemed the enemy had scattered in an attempt to get past the Druids.

Few slept. Those that did were woken by unearthly mournful wailing howls a little later.

The next morning, the Druids had returned as silently as they had left. They were fewer now. The lean Druid that had spoken to Rast was gone. None seemed injured; only missing.

They refused to speak of whatever battle had occurred. Even Leona would not speak to Rast about it, except to tell him that they had lost more than they could afford.

ʘא ʅɔ

Since the Druids' return, two smaller night-time altercations had drifted through the woodlands, and then nothing more. Rast had just finished speaking to Major Gambeson one evening when he heard Aldine call him.

'Tal'Orien!'

He turned as the Captain exited the tent, eyeing Rast distrustfully. Aldine was not coping well with the tension.

'Be prepared to move soon. We can wait no longer. By now the boy is long dead, likely that elf maid as well.'

Rast gripped a strand of anger tightly inside, releasing in it an inner motion not unlike opening the fingers of a clenched fist, and shrugged.

'Perhaps. Perhaps not. But I will not leave here until I am sure they are not coming. Besides, we agreed to stay two more days.'

'How convenient. Our mission won't wait.' Aldine drew himself up. 'You seem to think you're something special. We have our orders.'

Once there would have been the faint tickling urge to knock the arrogant man on his back, but so many years of battle had changed him. If he had to strike, he would. If not, he would not. There was nothing else. He stayed silent.

'Your reluctance to help Eordeland had been noted. I'll make a full report when we return,' grated Aldine.

'As you wish,' said Rast. There was no point in telling the man again that he was not Eordelandish, or that he had given up more than this pompous fool likely had. 'I will not leave here until I know Karland's fate.'

'We don't march to your beck and call. Your arrogance is what doomed the people of that town,' hissed Aldine in fury. 'If you hadn't delayed after the attack, if we had moved faster, we might have prevented it!'

Rast stared at him for a second. He wasn't joking. The accusation made no sense; a week instead of a morning would have made no difference. They could never have arrived in time to help, and even if they had, according to Leona they would have been slaughtered alongside the villagers.

'How many deaths lie on you?' continued Aldine.

Rast's face dropped all emotion. He thought back to those he had failed.

'How-'

'How *many*?' Something in his voice cut off Aldine's words, for all he spoke softly. 'More than you could know, Captain. Do not take your grief at that village out on me. They were long dead when we arrived. I suggest you follow your orders.'

'How dare you tell me-'

'This discussion is at an end.' Rast turned and moved towards the trees. He heard Aldine pursuing him through the camp and wove quickly and smoothly between men and tents. It did not take long to lose him.

At the tree's edges, he paused between lookouts. They had no idea he was there. Rast slipped into his invisibility like an old cloak, almost automatically moving his form in tune with the nature around him.

'I hope you come soon, boy,' he breathed to himself. 'I hope you yet live.'

He had meant every word. If the soldiers elected to move on without him, still he would wait, until all hope had left.

THIRTY-TWO

The Green Warrior moved carefully up the hillside and scanned around cautiously, not showing himself on the ridge. After some minutes he made his way back down, satisfied that they were not in immediate danger.

'We are somewhere to the southeast of Deep Delving,' remarked Lëlylien.

The Green Warrior sniffed and shrugged.

'I guess.'

'How far?' asked Karland. They turned to him. 'To Deep Delving?'

The Green Warrior moued his lips. 'Half a day? Never been there.'

'Less. We are near the main road in. I am surprised I have not seen the tracks of patrols yet,' said the elf.

'We should stop there, talk to Regin.'

The Green Warrior shook his head. 'I don't like this.'

'They could help us. We could get supplies, at least.' There was a faint sense of having done this before. An idea struck him. 'They still have our horses.'

'Dwarves don't like anyone. Everyone knows that. I say we keep going.'

'We agreed-'

'Changed my mind.'

'I was here nearly a year ago, Warrior. I know some of them. They fought a battle against a large orc party tracking us.' He looked around and a peak caught his eye. 'There. That's Drakeholm Soaring. Their city entrance is at the foot of the mountain southwest of that.'

I think.

Now he knew it was there, he couldn't believe he hadn't seen it before. He must have looked at the mountain every day for a week without actually seeing it. They were very close to the underground city.

'Not interested.' The man moved away with a scowl on his face.

Lëlylien called to him.

'It is worth restocking, Warrior. And they might have news of the company, or lend us steeds, perhaps.'

The Green Warrior's mouth turned down in that familiar considering expression again as he mulled it over. When it came, his decision was as abrupt and absolute as ever. 'Fine. But don't make it too long. We won't catch your party if we don't hurry.'

Karland nodded.

They travelled on all morning, careful to wend their way below the crests of hills. Although the mercenaries had seemed to be mostly near the plains rather than deep in the foothills, there was no telling how widespread they were.

They were also cautious of the creatures living in these hills. Most of the more dangerous lived further into the mountains, but Lëlylien told them that wyverns, gar-wolves, and even what the dwarves called *Beinbjörn,* bone-bears, sometimes moved down further into the foothills.

Karland had never heard of them, and neither had The Green Warrior, but Lëlylien said that even Gar-wolves were cautious around bone-bears. There were other dangers in the deep valleys, too; slashworms, and giant birds that hunted with great scythelike beaks.

Apparently variants of these last hunted in packs across the plains, moving at great speed on long legs and preying on the small creatures found there, scavenging where they could. Their beaks were like axes and a pack of them could chase down a single traveller with ease, but they were cautious and rarely approached uninjured humans. In the mountains, they were much larger.

Then, of course, there were other dangers to be found similar to Eordeland. Packs of wolves were smart enough to know hunting men and dwarves brought death in return, but were still dangerous. Great brown bears roamed, and there were forest and rock cats ranging in size from Banistari lapcats to great creatures heavier than a man. This area should be safe, however. Dwarves patrolled the roads and slopes nearby constantly, and a heavily armoured squad with Dwarven weapons would be a match for most creatures.

Karland hoped they didn't meet anything. He already knew that gar-wolves lived in this part of the world, to his great sorrow. He tried not to think about the bones of his friend lying broken on the side of the highest mountain in the world, mingled with those of the terrifying beast that he had fought.

Perhaps one day when he was older, he would return and look for Grukust.

They stopped to rest at midday and then moved on, the sun breaking through clouds overhead and warming the rocky hills around them. To the north, the range of the Arkons loomed, tipped by the gigantic spire at their centre.

They were rounding a trail corner edged by a boulder when The Green Warrior held up a hand in caution. They stopped, and silence washed around them as Karland strained to hear what had alerted him.

There was the sound of something moving, something large. A stone slipped to roll clacking down the slope a short way, and a snort and heavy breathing was heard. Karland tensed, and The Green Warrior looked around, weighing lines of attack.

Karland's first thought was that it was one of these bone-bears. For some reason, and without having ever seen one, the name had nevertheless stuck in his mind.

Lëlylien stepped out in front of them and moved swiftly with no signs of fear. Her light laughter brought a scowl from The Green Warrior.

'Horses,' she called back softly before she disappeared around the corner. Karland relaxed, wondering at her incredible hearing. They rounded the corner to find her standing with a small dray's nose in her hand, a magnificent cremello stallion standing a short way away eyeing her warily with nose and lips twitching back unpleasantly, and a dark mare trying to hide behind him, nervously watching them over his rump. All of them were unkempt and looked as if they had been on their own for some time.

Karland couldn't believe his eyes. He felt his mouth gaping and closed it. Moving forward, he held out his hand in disbelief.

'Hjarta? *Stryke?*'

The small dray bucked his head up, ear twitching at his name. He turned to Karland, and then with a snort of welcome moved in towards him, butting at him lightly with his head. The elf maid turned to Karland in surprise.

'You know these horses?'

'Two of them,' he said, shaking his head. He took in their condition. Hjarta was thinner and had fading scars down his left rump where a mountain predator had swiped at him, but he was moving easily enough. The mare seemed in good health, although she was slightly favouring a foreleg. Then there was Stryke, who was standing menacingly nearby. His ears were not quite pinned, but he was watching them with threat in his stance, and his tail was snapping side to side. He might have accepted Hjarta's welcome of them, but he was definitely not displaying his own. Karland could guess why the predator had only had one swipe at the small dray, and why Hjarta's injury wasn't more severe; he had seen what the huge battle-trained stallion could do to an enemy.

'Stryke,' said Karland. The ears twitched. '*Hastus Verin*, Stryke? *Hastus Verin?*' The stallion snorted, his teeth baring slightly in warning. 'It's me. Karland. Remember?' The ears raised slightly, swivelling towards him. '*Hastus Verin*, Stryke.'

'I can't believe I'm watching you talk to a random horse in the middle of the mountains like an old friend,' remarked The Green Warrior sourly. 'How the hell do you know these animals?'

Karland laughed. 'He *is* an old friend.'

'I would also know how you know them,' said Lëlylien. 'And who taught you words of Old Aeg.'

'Aeg?' Karland asked. He shrugged. 'It's just what Rast used to say to make him stand, hopefully without hurting someone. Stryke is his mount. We left them with the Dwarves.'

'He is war-trained,' warned Lëlylien. 'A mighty steed. Be wary of this one.'

'You don't know the half of it,' muttered Karland. He still remembered the plate-sized hoof whistling over his head to stove in the head of the orc in The Croft, sending the mangled creature pinwheeling more than ten feet. 'Stryke! Good boy. *Hastus Verin*. Don't kick me. It's Karland. Remember? A friend of Rast. A friend of your master. I can take you to Rast.'

The huge creature whickered, whether in recognition or warning he wasn't sure.

'I'm going to try something,' he murmured to the elf. She nodded, cautious. The Green Warrior was watching with his arms folded and head tilted back, curious. Karland took a deep breath, blew it out gently, and moved slowly towards Stryke.

'Hey… Stryke. It is good to see you again. Why aren't you in Tradesholding where we left you? Are you wild now? I hope not.' He kept up the stream of words, trying to mask his nervousness. 'You look in good shape for being locked out. Did they forget to lock the door? Did you escape?'

All the while, he was moving slowly forward. He hoped the horse would recognise him and not attack. What were they doing loose like this? They had clearly been out for some time.

'I'm sorry we haven't been back before now. We had to go on a dragon. Yes, a dragon.' Stryke whuffed, eyeing Karland warily. Karland extended his hand, palm up, and stopped, seeing tension in the horse. 'Come on, Stryke. It's me. Hastus Verin.'

Stryke took a single clopping step forward and extended his neck to sniff Karland's hand. Karland held his breath.

The horse whickered softly, and stepped forward again, the tension leaving him and his ears flicking up. He nuzzled Karland's hand gently, and snorted. Karland carefully patted his nose, wary of the big teeth.

'You do remember! You do. Good boy.' He turned his head to his companions, not ceasing his ministrations. 'This is… strange. We left them in Tradesholding and travelled on foot. The dwarves were looking after them. We were planning to return for them with a trade delegation, or ask for them to be brought to Darost, before all this - before the dwarves stopped talking to anyone. I can't believe that we found them like this. I don't know why they would be out here on their own.' If nothing else, the mountains were probably a little less dangerous now if anything had foolishly attacked Stryke.

Lëlylien moved forward, stepping lightly, and handed Karland a sad-looking purple carrot from their supplies. 'Perhaps we can ask at Deep Delving. It is odd that we have seen no patrols at all. The tracks I have seen are old. I would have expected challenge by now.'

Karland offered up the withered carrot and Stryke took it gratefully, crunching with enthusiasm. He beckoned The Green Warrior over with Hjarta, and he led the calm dray to his partner, eyebrows raised.

'Good-looking horse,' he remarked. 'Tal'Orien's? You said battle-trained.'

'Stryke's saved my life more than once,' answered Karland. 'And yes, he's definitely trained. Be careful what you say. He's not stupid.'

'What about the other?' asked the elf maiden. Karland shrugged.

Seeing her two companions petted, the mare was edging closer. The elf moved slowly to her, speaking in Elvish, calming her, and led her back. At her words and touch, the mare stilled as if by magic, and Karland remembered how close elves were with living creatures. 'She could have come from anywhere. There is a mystery here. Let us press on towards the home of the dwarves.'

'If we can find tack, it will make our journey much easier,' mused Karland. 'Hjarta at least will take gear, and we can catch Rast and the rest quickly.'

'Good thinking,' said The Green Warrior. He was clearly eyeing Stryke as a potential steed, but Karland doubted that the war horse would allow anyone except himself to mount. He'd be lucky if *he* was allowed.

Lëlylien looked over the horses and pronounced them fit, after removing a small pointed stone from the mare's forehoof. The horse snorted in relief, testing the leg as she cropped grass. After a little persuasion, they managed to sling their supplies over the back of the mare and Hjarta. Stryke glared warningly at The Green Warrior, and although he allowed Lëlylien to approach he would not let her mount.

Leading the horses, they moved on foot out to the main thoroughfare and moved west, the ominous peak of Drakeholm Soaring looming over them all the time. It was odd that it was so much higher than the peaks surrounding it. Aldwyn had remarked once that this single mountain changed the weather for hundreds of miles around it, and was the highest known point in the world, which was strange as the range around it was far lesser.

The horses seemed content to be moving somewhere in the company of humans again, especially Hjarta and the mare. Karland wondered where she had come from. They had been the only residents in Tradesholding, although more than a year had passed since then. Given the Dwarven attitude to outsiders, Karland doubted many humans had been invited in during that time.

Hours later, as dusk began to settle, they came in sight of the trail towards Deep Delving and Tradesholding.

The area gave rise to many memories for Karland. Of the exhausting run from the Dimnesdair, pursued by a barely seen horde. Of Grukust, huge and loyal, intelligence glinting behind his brutish exterior and broken Darum. Of the powerful and alien Györnàeldàr and her overwhelming arrival. Of the Portal, that place where knowledge was unveiled to mortals, whether they could interpret it or not. Of the fact they still did not know if what they had learned was important.

He shivered.

Of the Darkling, and of the lesser God that had arisen to confront it.

Last time, dwarves had appeared seemingly from the very rocks to demand they leave the area. This time, there was nothing. The valley looked much as it had last time, but he could see something odd about the entrance to Tradesholding, off to the side of where he thought the main doors for Deep Delving lay, invisible in the surrounding rock.

He beckoned them onward, and as they drew near, he could see that the tall door to Tradesholding lay open, the matching rock face incongruously cracked wide enough for horses to leave. He remembered Regin using a weapon to unlock the door before moving it only with his hands, despite it being made of rock. If it had been left open, a horse could shoulder it aside with ease.

Aldwyn had said that the weapons and tools that were so integral to Dwarven society were the key to much Dwarven mystery, what the Ignathians called *Dwemmerdin*. His notes had been full of information on dwarves, and he wasn't the only one. The Sanctum held many tomes dedicated to the crafts of the Dwarven folk. It was widely known that their weapons were the keys to their kingdoms, but no one else knew how to make dwarf weapons. Anything made by men simply didn't work, no matter how convincing. They inevitably lost their edge, were not as keen, and mostly importantly could not open Dwarven doors. Karland recalled the book Darus had read theorising that they were forged with steel and *titan* in a certain way that could interface with whatever power lay within their doors when held to the right area in the right position removing or stemming the force that held them shut. The doors were also superbly counterbalanced, enough that tons of rock could be moved by one person. He wondered if each Dwarven city might have a different key.

'This is where we stayed last time,' he said. He recalled the pale, injured dwarf that had let them out as their time neared to meet the dragon, as the orcs had attacked trying to flush out the party. All they had done was anger the dwarves and confirm that orcs were gathering for war, doing in one attack what the party had been trying to do for days - convince the dwarves of the seriousness of the orcs gathering. Until the attack, no one had believed them. 'Maybe we can rest here tonight… as long as nothing dangerous has crept in.'

His fertile mind immediately thought of mountain lions, bears, or worse.

'I will search inside,' said Lëlylien. 'The horses do not wish to re-enter.'

'Why don't we look around,' suggested The Green Warrior. 'Karland can knock on the front door. Someone might answer.'

Karland shrugged, trying not to look happy that he wasn't going into the cold stone town. 'All right. I'll start a fire, feed the horses. See if you can find tack in there. The stables were to the right, I think.'

The elf and the human vanished through the opening. Karland set out the camp quickly away from the entrance, where there was good grass for the horses. He fed them from their ever-dwindling supply of vegetables in the hope that it would keep them near, and said 'Hastus versin, Stryke. Keep these two close by as well. All right?'

Stryke twitched an ear and shook his head. Karland hoped that meant acquiescence. He moved off towards where he thought the main doors were. The ground showed a wide trail right up to the rock face, which looked no different to the rest of the cliff in front of him. Slapping his hand on the rock, it felt solid - just a piece of the mountainside. He could see no seams, no outlines.

He wished he had a Dwarven weapon, and then chuckled.

Even if he had one, to open a dwarf door one had to know exactly where and how to hold it. And no doubt even if you knew all *that*, the instant they opened the doors an unwelcome intruder would be confronted by guards holding their own dwarf-forged weapons, or other defences even fiercer.

'Hello?' he called out. 'Regin? Anyone? We seek supplies.' His words fell flat upon the rocks. 'Hello?'

After calling on and off for some minutes, he bent and found a large rock he could lift and pounded on where he thought the door was as hard as he could. There was a faint hollow sound at the edge of hearing underneath the clacking, but there was no answer.

After half an hour, he had given up and moved back to the camp. The horses were grazing contentedly, but the others had not returned yet.

As dusk deepened, he began to prepare food. Finally, he heard approaching footsteps, and looked up to see The Green Warrior laden with tack and Lëlylien carrying refilled flasks. The Green Warrior dumped his load with a grunt.

'Nothing in there,' he said. 'looks deserted. The horses had cropped all the grass, wasn't much. No wonder they escaped. No food, no supplies. Just the spring in the centre, a cart, and this. Any luck out here?'

'No,' confessed Karland. 'I tried everything I could think of. It's as if they have all just left. But that makes no sense - this is the biggest dwarf city in Anaria. Possibly the world. Why would they just vanish?'

'It is a mystery,' said Lëlylien. 'There are no recent signs of battle. I moved around the foot hill to scout and even there the signs of fighting are old, although there was a large battle there.'

'Yes,' said Karland. 'Last time we were here. About two thousand orcs were chasing us, and they attacked the dwarves to flush us out.'

'Two thousand,' murmured the elf, shaking her head in wonder. 'I can scarce believe those numbers.'

'They attacked in daylight,' said Karland. 'It was near sundown, and a little overcast, but Rast said to me that it was unheard of.'

'They must have wanted you very badly,' said the elf. 'Sunlight sickens them. To attack dwarves in such conditions was suicide. Perhaps they weren't aware they were so near Deep Delving.'

'Maybe. We had something they sought,' said Karland, feeling a little bitter. 'It turned out to only give us more questions.'

'Maybe these dwarves just went deeper in and just won't answer the door?' suggested The Green Warrior.

'Perhaps,' said Lëlylien. 'But even dwarves need to eat, and they like fresh meat. They would not do this unless at siege, I think. There is a faint feeling here, an emptiness. A feeling of some deep dread.' She closed her eyes, giving the impression that her senses probed at something, and then slowly opened them, her eyes refocusing. 'I do not think they hide. I feel they have left this place. That they fled.'

Deep down, Karland thought he felt a little of what she said. It felt barren here, deserted.

'...*Whom unmerciful disaster... Followed fast and followed faster*,' said The Green Warrior softly, with a strange look on his face. Karland looked at him curiously. He did not recognise the quote, though it sounded from an old poem. He wouldn't have thought The Green Warrior was the type for poetry.

By common agreement they had left the little cart that Hjarta had been harnessed to before. Karland felt strange knowing that the cart the original companions had shared for so long - that his friend had died in and left his blood on - was hidden in the rocky fortress before them and might stay there forevermore. As always when he thought of his friend, he missed him. There was a peculiar sense of being here before that was almost surreal, speaking of the loneliness of the place. Karland had always had a strange compulsion not to leave inanimate objects around, as if they had feelings that would be hurt. He knew that the subsequent urge to hoard everything was one reason his father had been so frustrated, as he was eminently practical and not given to the whimsies of his son. Still, in the absence of the dwarves, this place felt hollow and lonely instead of eternal and stolid as it had before.

They ate in silence, then settled in for the evening, The Green Warrior on first watch.

Karland slept, thinking of dwarves and wondering where they could have gone.

‘ ’

Rising early, they fitted the tack to the horses. Stryke would not allow even Lëlylien to fit any, for all she spoke calmingly to him in Elvish, so Karland spent a few tense minutes inexpertly doing it instead. Stryke's tack did not have a bit fitting, instead having a wide noseband and reins that joined at the cheeks. Karland remembered Rast saying he often rode without tack at all. He didn't want to imagine what would happen if he tried to force Stryke to a bit.

Tradesholding had stocked several sets, so the mare was also bridled. Lëlylien rode Hjarta without anything.

The three travellers moved followed a trail south at a good pace, breaking out of the low hills mid-morning two days later to see the plains sweeping before them. There was no sign of men or orks. With the elf maid guiding them they found the trail of the company again and turned west along the line of hills.

'What if there are men in the hills to the north, near the tip of the lake?' asked Karland as they travelled. 'The foothills of Rhe?'

'There won't be,' said Lëlylien.

'So sure,' mocked The Green Warrior. She turned to him.

'Yes. That is wyvern territory. They carry deadly venom in their tails and are fast and plated with thick scales. Wyverns will attack anything that moves during mating season and fear nothing except dragons. It would be suicide for any to travel there.'

'When's mating season?'

'All year except the coldest months.' She smiled slightly. 'When you fight a wyvern you do it in a group, in armour, with care, from a distance. If a wyvern catches you alone, you are dead. They are Dragon-kin.' She was matter of fact.

Karland thought that this must have been where Grukust had gone on his *kappanim*. No wonder he was awarded his name and the championship of the tribes; he had killed one single-handed.

There might be thousands living in the crags, breeding and preying on each other and any creatures near them. Karland kept a nervous eye up after the elf maid had mentioned they could fly for short periods. She assured him they usually did so only to mate, preferring to stay on the ground to ambush prey. They did sound curious, with those winged forelimbs, but he was just as glad not to see one.

They moved much faster now, Stryke tending to lead whatever Karland said about it. Lëlylien would scout ahead occasionally, but they did not come across any more mercenaries.

The reason for this became clear when they passed under the foothills of Rhe at the north-eastern tip of Merrimakea's southern shore. The ork tribes had gathered a little way south of the foothills, and from where they stood the camp stretched south and west. There were scores of thousands of them, and their children and herds were with them. This was no war party; this was the orken nation, nearly all the tribes gathered. Mercenaries would be slaughtered on sight.

Karland suggested that they avoid them, remembering the volatile Brukk. They might have been safe with Darus, but even if Brukk didn't kill them outright as spies, he probably would not be very happy to see Karland again. He caught a mocking glance from The Green Warrior and ignored it.

Lëlylien suggested that they skirt along the shores of the lake at either dusk or early morning, when the change between their night vision and their normal vision would make it hardest for them to see the small party. The Green Warrior was sceptical that they could see heat but agreed that it was the best plan. They camped that night without fire, and the next morning broke from the foothills early and led the horses on foot down the slope along the water.

They travelled that way for several hours, Karland nervously watching the calm lapping surface beside them. He hadn't forgotten the waters in the Dimnesvale, but it seemed that Merrimakea was a more placid lake. Whatever lurked beneath its surface was natural... he hoped.

The lake's far northern shore was just about visible, but it widened as they travelled southwest. Eventually they remounted and rode, stopping for food and to rest the horses. The water stretched away now as far as they could see, and the Arkons were purpling behind them as they faded into the distance.

They travelled as fast as they could for days, allowing the horses rest here and there and a fire for six hours each night near the water's edge, away from the plains where it could be seen for scores of miles. They supplemented supplies with fish from the lake and slept well, Karland recovering more of his strength; Lëlylien was useful to have around. The Green Warrior was very interested in her reverie.

'If only we could do that,' he mused, half to himself. 'Always alert, but always rested. You could get so much more done.'

'I still have to rest,' Lëlylien responded, her sharp ears picking up his mutter from the other side of the camp. 'But I stay conscious.'

The Green Warrior jerked his thumb at her, his eyebrows raising in astonishment at her hearing.

'Aldwyn theorised that maybe you shut half your brain off to let it rest, and then switch over,' offered Karland. Lëlylien turned a cool gaze on him. 'Some animals don't sleep either. But humans die if we don't rest.'

'I would rather you kept comparisons to animals to yourself,' she said. The Green Warrior laughed, and her gaze slid to him. He grinned at her, unabashed, his eyes twinkling.

'No one's perfect,' he said. 'Not even an elf.'

'Of that, we are well aware,' she replied softly. Karland remembered the story that Night had told him, and the reactions of Galnór and Lëlylien; it was the greatest shame of the elves. After meeting Night, he now thought that Galnór and Lëlylien also felt shame for their prejudice against those who were ultimately victims as well.

She gazed at them both another moment, and then laughed, softly, for the first time in a long while.

'Never let it be said elves are the only race with humour,' she said. Her face, relaxed in laughter, was inhumanly beautiful, her top lip doubling back up over her white teeth, large eyes softening. 'Though I think humans could learn subtlety with theirs.'

Karland couldn't recall another woman as perfect as Lëlylien. Just watching her movement produced a delightful frission on his skin. She was mesmerising in motion, and perfection in stillness. In looks, at least, the Warrior was wrong about elves.

Ψ Ω

439

So far Lëlylien had been correct; they had seen no one until they neared the southwestern waters of Lake Merrimakea. Tiny dots of a few distant boats were visible as they paused to water and collect themselves, probably fishermen.

'Galnór and Rast would lead them carefully from here,' she mused half to herself, looking towards the army at the southern gate. She had a habit of rubbing her head backwards gently on her upper bow limb, as though seeking guidance, or comfort. 'If there are as many bands on the plains west, we will have to move only at night. I do not know how Novinians are avoiding the orks. Perhaps they have moved around to the south, nearer the Sergoth, and follow the Plains Road.'

'Why don't we just get a boat here somewhere and move down the lake to Eyotsburg?' asked The Green Warrior.

Lëlylien shook her pale head.

'The island has rapids and dangerous currents as the waters from the Lake move to the river and before that are the Lakefalls, which would smash any boat to shards. It is an effective defence. It would be safer to ride through the mercenary camp in daylight.'

The Green Warrior nodded quickly, his face showing no emotion. 'Fine. What now?'

'According to Rast and Aldine, the north is under siege from Meyar,' said Karland gloomily. It seemed as if there were obstacles everywhere.

'The northern Stonestride will be worse than the south,' said Lëlylien thoughtfully. 'Your Council believe Meyar to be the source of all this aggression. There is only one way in east: a small carriage upon a pulleyed rope which rises to the city from Iblis, the stone isle between the two main falls. With war this near, that route will be closed.'

'Couldn't we take it at night?' asked The Green Warrior.

'We would have to somehow make it to Iblis first, Warrior, and they know it is an entry. It may already be destroyed, and if not… it will be under heavy guard. They could cut it before we were halfway across. I do not plan on learning flight soon, human.'

'Fine.' The Green Warrior thought. 'Right, so we follow Tal'Orien. We should be able to move faster than them, and quieter. Maybe catch them before Eyotsburg, with luck.'

Lëlylien nodded, and Karland shrugged. He felt confident in the abilities of his companions - and, to his own surprise, himself - but they were still in danger. Rast and an armed company would make him feel a lot more secure, if nothing else.

The weather was cloudy for the next two days, and they moved mostly at night. During the day they slept, The Green Warrior seeming to have no trouble falling asleep wherever he was.

The next morning Karland was awoken by angry words from the elf maiden, and genuine mocking laughter from the puzzle of a man they travelled with. He found her standing over a prone Warrior, daggers crossed at his throat. His hands were raised and he was grinning that mocking grin.

'What's going on?'

'This *alasaila* waited until I sat in *dônaethar* and then attacked me!'

To her incredulity, he laughed, as if letting them in on a secret.

'Had to make sure it worked,' he said.

'You *attacked* me!'

'I just wanted to see if you were paying attention.' He winked at Karland, unrepentant. 'Got within a few feet, too. She's pretty fast.'

'I *let* you approach, you- you *human*,' she snapped, then shook her head in frustration, removing the blades. 'The next time you attempt to touch me, I will kill you.'

Karland believed her, and clearly The Green Warrior did too. He rolled to his feet and shrugged.

'Now I can trust you.' He clapped Karland on the shoulder, went back to his bedroll, and turned his back on them.

Lëlylien glanced at Karland in frank disbelief. Karland shrugged. He completely understood her perplexity. He couldn't get a reading on the man, and always felt slightly off-balance with him - how much harder for an elf unused to humans! The Warrior was as mercurial as Grukust had been and possessed of a scathing wit. There was always a feeling of wariness, tension, of possible danger about him. Of being tested.

Karland trusted him, but not completely. He still didn't know what his ultimate motives were. The worst thing was that The Green Warrior probably knew all of this, and simply did not care.

The man was a law unto himself.

ʘ ‿

Fifteen weary nights after leaving Deep Delving brought them and their tired mounts down to the plains under Eyotsburg as dusk fell and rested, preparing to dash around the Novinians.

'Try to avoid confrontation,' Lëlylien said with a stare at The Green Warrior.

He grinned at her disarmingly. 'I can't help it if trouble just finds me.'

'I mean it. We do not need a running fight.'

'Get over yourself. I'm not stupid. We'll get past,' he said. 'You focus on finding the tracks of your friends.'

She considered him impassively, then beckoned them to follow, setting off at a walking pace, leading Hjarta and casting around on the ground. After half an hour of movement, she shook her head.

'A party has come through. Rast Tal'Orien and Galnór will have left few tracks I can find. But there are many tracks, from many parties. A company came through here and moved around south and west. Whether that means we have found the Eordelander tracks, however, remains to be seen. There are too many. The ground is unclear. I will look again at dawn, when I can be sure. We must be well past the mercenary camps by then.'

'Let's move,' said The Green Warrior, kicking his mare to the front and setting a faster pace. His abrupt decisions no longer surprised Karland. When the man decided something, he did it. Lëlylien's eyebrows rose, but since it was sense, she simply moved along with Karland.

He was feeling better than he had for a while, despite the fast pace. He was finding muscles in his core tightening up further from the riding, and he had grown used to Stryke's powerful gait. The horse was surprisingly smooth in motion.

Lunis was almost a half-moon, but combined with full Xoth it lit the landscape well.

Karland glanced at The Green Warrior. The man grew more snappish as they went, something clearly bothering him deep inside. His face looked haggard and dangerous in the green tinge from Xoth, which was high in the sky that night. Rather than fitting his name, instead it gave him an ill, dark aspect, a haunting quality that spoke of inner turmoil. His hawkish face looked gaunt and sad, lines of tragedy carved deeply upon its surface.

THIRTY-THREE

In sight of the trees west of Eyotsburg Lëlylien picked up the tracks of the Eordeland company again.

'How can you be sure?' The Green Warrior asked sceptically.

'Galnór has left me signs,' she said, pointing. Karland and The Green Warrior looked but saw nothing.

'Right,' The Green Warrior said, a grin on his face.

Lëlylien shrugged. 'Believe as you wish,' she said.

A rank smell grew beneath the leafy odour of the trees as they moved further west, moving fast along the recently broken trail. Two villages spoke of the company; it was obvious the elf maiden had gone up considerably in The Green Warrior's estimation. She stopped later that day and drew them north of a large village further west, off the trail and through the trees. They were different to the Northing woods, with many evergreens. There was less undergrowth, but the wood pillars of the trunks had their own curiously oppressive quality as they stretched out, cutting off visibility.

'We should check it out,' said The Green Warrior.

'I will not go,' she said adamantly. 'There is nothing there but death.'

He shrugged but didn't leave.

Not far past, Lëlylien stopped, and hissed through her perfect teeth.

'We are not alone.'

Even as she spoke, a brown-robed form stepped out from the trees. The Green Warrior tensed as Lëlylien relaxed.

'Druid,' said Karland to his companion, with no little relief.

'So?' The Green Warrior didn't look any less wary.

'They're friends.'

The figure beckoned them on, making gestures to encourage silence before vanishing back into the woodland. Another form appeared further up a faint path to the north, and they moved towards that one, too. After this had vanished, the Green Warrior stopped, turning his head.

'Not happy with this.'

'Trust us, Warrior,' replied the elf maiden. 'They are nature priests. They have a long friendship with the elves.'

The Green Warrior jutted his chin up the path. 'She a friend?'

Karland turned to find himself regarded by wild, gold-green eyes in a strong, beautiful face.

'Leona!'

'We meet again, young cub. You finally join me in the green woods.' She smiled at him. Somehow she seemed far more at peace here, if more wary. Wilder, in a way. Lëlylien bowed with a smile, and Leona returned it. Her gaze matched The Green Warrior's for a moment.

'We're trying to catch up to Rast. He's with a company of Eordeland soldiers-'

'I found him,' she said. 'Five days ago. There is danger nearby, though less than when Rast came through. Come. I will take you to him.'

Lëlylien nodded. 'I have sensed it for some time. A dark hatred stalks these woods.'

'We seek to cleanse them,' said Leona as she led them north. 'Our task is almost done, but it has taken the lives of many Druids.'

'What is it?' asked Karland.

'The same abominations I left you to fight. We have driven them back, killed thousands, but they are powerful.' She glanced side to side. Karland caught a brief glimpse of brown robe on the right. 'I will say no more here. We must move quickly and silently. They are not all culled yet.'

ʘ ۽

Two hours later, as dusk deepened towards night, they descended a shallow hill and entered a thick set of trees which hid a large clearing next to a river. Leona pointed ahead.

'I will join you later,' she smiled, and moved gracefully away to several other robed Druids. Ahead two large figures moved amongst men and women in armour around a fire. Karland had never felt so suddenly secure again.

'Rast!' called Karland excitedly, moving quickly into the camp. 'Darus!'

The big man turned smoothly, and his usually grim face broke into a rare smile, even teeth flashing through the short black beard. Next to him the ork snorted in surprise, and waved both hands in greeting.

444

'Karland!' Rast laughed and clasped him in a rough hug, seeking to convey through the pressure the relief he would not express out loud. 'You are safe, boy. I was about to come back to look for you.' His eyes took in the fading damage Karland had sustained but seemed satisfied nothing lasting had been done. Then he saw the horses and his eyes widened. 'What in the Gods?'

Karland was perversely pleased that he had finally managed to surprise him.

Rast moved swiftly to Stryke, who was standing with an eye fixed on him. The great horse flared his nostrils, snorted, and then lowered his nose for a petting in an easy way not even Karland rated. Rast smiled and ran his hands over his flanks, loosening his tack. '*Hastus verin*, old friend. *Quies reliqua.*' An ear flicked, and Karland couldn't help smiling.

A sniff from behind him where the Captain stood told Karland what he had thought of the idea of Rast leaving the mission, but then the man relented and stepped forward. He nodded and said, 'I'm glad you are back, boy, though I'd know how you fared. I suppose we owe the elf that.'

Karland bit back a sarcastic reply. 'I was captured by the Novinians that attacked you. Before Lëlylien found me. I was rescued by… a friend.' He indicated The Green Warrior, who stood back a little, a curious look on his face, glancing around the soldiers and raising his head in greeting to a couple. He'd given Darus a careful look over too, noting his huge frame and dangerous weapon. He had obviously never seen an ork before, and his stare kept drifting back to the tusks and face.

'Friend of yours?' he muttered to Karland wryly.

Then his attention came around to Rast. His face slightly tilted back, a half-smile on his lips, and he shrewdly watched over the tops of his lower lids, his gaze calculating.

Rast turned and nodded. 'You have my thanks. Karland is a good friend.' Darus clapped a fist to his chest in salute.

The Green Warrior considered a minute, then nodded once, shrugging. His gaze was not quite judging but assessing.

'This is The Green Warrior,' said Karland. He gestured to the others. 'Galnór, and Rast Tal' Orien. This is Darus, and Captain Aldine of the Eordeland Guard.'

Rast showed no curiosity at the lack of name. 'You are welcome here, Warrior. How came you to find Karland?' He gestured them to the fire, and they sat, the huge man and the elves with typical grace.

'I was travelling behind the mercs,' answered The Green Warrior bluntly. 'Wondered what they were going east for. Spent some time in Novin, knew something was going on.' He showed no embarrassment or discomfort, for all he knew from Karland that war was brewing.

'You don't look Novinian,' remarked Rast. The soldiers in hearing noticeably drifted in at the dark-eyed man's last remarks, their faces tense. The elves and Darus merely watched, curious.

'M'not,' replied The Green Warrior. He shrugged, making that moue with his lips again. 'Far as I know. I have no memories of where I'm from.' His face showed none of the agitation at this fact that Karland had glimpsed before, but perhaps Rast heard something in his voice.

'You have elements of Banistari,' said Rast. 'Skin and face, a little, but still not. Perhaps part Matalagan; yet you seem as Eordelandish as anything, though your speech is strange. It is curious that you were there at that time.'

The Green Warrior shrugged again, deceptively casual, his glittering eyes sweeping the camp. He was clearly aware of the tension and just as obviously uncaring, although a certain readiness had entered his demeanour. 'I wasn't part of the group if that's what you're asking. Just didn't like the way it took ten men to bind and beat a boy. A squire tried to kill him when he was bound and wounded. Wasn't right.' He shook his head, his eyes not leaving Rast's face.

Captain Aldine was eyeing him distrustfully. 'As far as I'm concerned, Tal'Orien, no one but a spy would be out there. Either kill him or get him gone.'

As quickly as that, the mood had changed. The laughter faded, and faces turned serious.

Karland saw Major Gambeson watching thoughtfully. He glanced at Rast, and back to the man, who grinned, but looked ready to respond to any attacks.

'You think I was hanging around in the middle of nowhere looking for an excuse to trek back to where I started? If your journey was a secret, how would I have known who you were or where you were going?'

Rast watched him impassively, then nodded. 'That is true, as far as it goes.' He spoke to Gambeson. 'I'm inclined to believe him.'

Aldine gave a disbelieving laugh, which cut off when Gambeson nodded slowly.

'As am I. It stretches credulity a little far, Captain.' He turned to The Green Warrior. 'Anyway. Our thanks. So where will you go now? Can we provide you for the journey?'

The Green Warrior shrugged again. 'Dunno. Eordeland, maybe. I don't care about all this other bullshit. He promised to help me find answers.' He indicated Karland.

'To what?'

The Green Warrior turned his mouth down in another one of those grim moues, considering how to reply, and looked annoyed when Karland spoke up for the first time.

'To who he is and where he comes from.' When The Green Warrior glared at him, he said, 'Well? Don't you?'

For a moment the man looked as if he would snap at him, and then in one of his lightning-fast changes of mood he simply shrugged, his ire dropping away.

'Yeah.' He turned his head on his neck to loosen it, rolling his shoulders. 'Not much troubles me, Tal' Orien. But a man should know who he is. Our memories make us who we are, right?' He didn't wait for a response. 'There must be an answer somewhere. Who I am. Where I'm from.' His face showed a second of discomfort. 'What I've lost. Nothing's going to stop me finding them. I have an arrangement with the boy.'

'Come with us to Eyotsburg,' said Karland. Rast glanced at him, and the Major arched an eyebrow.

Captain Aldine glared at the boy. 'Take a civilian who admits he was following the enemy from his own mouth?'

'I said take him with us, not invite him into your secret councils,' said Karland, his cheeks heating. Once he would have simply not argued, feeling foolish, but he was rapidly losing his patience with people like Aldine. 'Leaving him here alone here is like a sentence of death. You heard what Leona said. At least take him to Eyotsburg, where he has a better chance. He saved my life. He can be watched, kept away from whatever councils you have.'

'Don't worry,' said The Green Warrior, clearly angered by the response from Aldine. His dark eyes bored into the Captain, who shifted. 'I'll go my own way.'

Karland felt a deep injustice at this. The man was erratic, but had helped him honourably, saved his life. This was poor payment.

'If you won't take him, I'll stay with him and we'll follow you,' he said.

Rast made a calming motion. 'I think it unlikely that a spy or assassin would be so fortuitously injected into our company,' he said. 'I see no reason that he cannot join until the city island. Major Gambeson? The decision lies with you.'

The Major nodded. 'We do not have much to thank you with but can provide company and food. Once in the city, you can charter a ship, or stay, but I warn you - it is a city under siege.'

'You'll be watched,' said Aldine pointedly.

The Green Warrior shrugged. 'Be nice to get some decent sleep for once.'

'Then take it tonight,' said Gambeson. 'We move out tomorrow.' He looked at Aldine. 'Company is at ease tonight. Limited drinking.' Aldine nodded.

'I will help where I can,' said Rast to the Warrior.

'I, too,' said Karland, glaring at the Captain.

The Green Warrior waved a hand, clearly not wanting to talk about his role in the rescue. For all his laughing about having been a hero, when genuine emotion was involved, he seemed uncomfortable. 'Well, yeah. That would be good.'

Karland realised that, despite his readiness to walk off alone into war-torn plains, his new companion must be lonely. To not know who you were, where you came from, and to have an undefined feeling of deep loss beyond that must be terrible. His pride might not let him accept readily, but even the most solitary man valued some companionship.

'I will place trust in you, Green Warrior,' said Rast. 'You have proved yourself already; helping Karland has earned that much.'

To Karland's surprise, Lëlylien also spoke up. 'I believe his heart is noble… although I cannot vouch for his mind. He is volatile and hard to read, even for a human.'

The Green Warrior laughed in his characteristic way and, to the astonishment of everyone except Karland and Lëlylien, winked at her. 'You're all right… for a skinny elf.'

He seemed to neither know nor care that elves were usually treated with utmost respect. The Captain's face darkened at the perceived insult, and Galnór's was almost comically astonished.

Lëlylien burst out laughing at their expressions, the silver tones ringing through the camp accompanied by Karland's, and that more than anything assured them that this enigmatic new companion was accepted. Many grinned or joined in the chuckles.

'We were about to eat,' reminded Darus in his deep voice, drawing a look of surprise from The Green Warrior, and another laugh from Karland; the stresses of the last few weeks were being released. The man had clearly expected an ork to be a drooling caveman from his earlier remarks. Darus spoke Darostim as well as anyone there, however, and was as fixated on food as his brother had been.

'You expected something else?' remarked the ork dryly, reading The Green Warrior's look. 'Maybe grunts?' He rubbed the side of a tuck with a huge finger and thumb, then chuckled. 'Perhaps *I* should feel offended that you have a name better suited to *me*.' He grinned.

The Green Warrior reached over and clapped him hard on the shoulder, laughing in his charismatic way and nodding in approval at how solid he was.

'The name is mine, you hulking great ork, suited to you or not.'

Loud laughter burst from the ork. 'Hulk! Ha. You never met my brother, human. Better suited to him. Champion of the Tribes! He was incredible.' He returned the clap on the shoulder. 'Let us eat.'

Karland was greeted with cries of welcome and slaps to the back by squads that had thought him lost. Even Gorin nodded to him, raising a drink. Den Olli crowed about the armoured knight they had found with Karland's dagger jutting from his eye, and a toast was raised to a red-faced Karland. The Green Warrior laughed approvingly at his embarrassment.

There would be no more questioning his membership of the company.

As they ate, even Captain Aldine warmed to the man. In company he was energetic and lively, the centre of conversation - a natural relator of tales, most of which were outrageous. Karland found some of them shocking - there was an element of chaos and disregard for people in some of them, and others *must* be sheer fiction - but they were all told in such a fashion that you couldn't help laughing along even so. A few of the soldiers clearly didn't care for The Green Warrior, and some of his stories were quite boastful, but his knowing grin and sly wink or burst of laughter would leave you unsure if it really had been a boast, or even true. The animation and flair The Green Warrior told the story with was such that most couldn't help but laugh along.

He drew amused snorts from Darus. The Green Warrior swore blind that one tale he remembered was of a huge green berserker even larger than an ork - larger than an ogre - who drew strength from anger and was unkillable as a result. Karland thought it likely that he had made it up to tease his friend.

'Sounds like *Rakkata*,' laughed Darus. At the questioning looks, he added, 'God of War and Judgement. *Very* big ork.'

Even Druids drifted over, some frowning at the almost raucous camp atmosphere, but others smiling to see the humans so relaxed.

Rast smiled more than usual, seeming to be one of the few who knew when The Green Warrior was joking and when he was not. Certainly he was not as affected by the man's changeability as others, but then that was Rast; implacable as a mountain.

After a while, The Green Warrior borrowed a lute from someone - a battered affair, not as gay as the one Rast had used with the Travellers to sing the threnody for Aldwyn. He tuned it, and then with an almost disinterested air began playing, his fingers light and flying over the strings. There was no song Karland knew, just changing melody, almost too fast to hear, the strings sometimes bending curiously and the notes blending into each. He was using a thin piece of wood to pick at the strings, and the sound was mesmerising and technically beautiful, but there was no attempt at playing something others could play along with or sing to. He was a master, but he played for himself, not others, as if used to a slightly different instrument.

Finally, he handed the lute back, ignoring the guardsman's downcast look and giving him a nod of thanks before moving to talk to others again. Karland guessed the soldier would never be able to play his lute like that, and wondered briefly at the casual callousness of The Green Warrior for neither caring or noticing. His skill had made Rast's honest efforts seem paltry by comparison, but they lacked the heart of what Rast had put in. Like many things he had seen The Green Warrior do, he excelled at it without giving it soul.

Except combat, Karland reflected.

He lived for the fight.

After another skin of wine had been passed around, they all fell to chatting, The Green Warrior still the centre of several interested parties. He was markedly more animated than he had been with just the three of them, seeming to amplify the camaraderie around him, feeding off it. Karland saw how smoothly he spoke to everyone, despite having been so happy on his own, but he still thought the Warrior lonely deep down. He supposed it must be hard to not feel part of anything, whilst at the same time not caring what people thought and doing what you wanted.

The Green Warrior was a dichotomy.

He listened in to the dark-eyed man vividly describing yet another fight he had had, with some amusing events during it. The handsome, well-built woman he was speaking to was clearly charmed by him, and leaned in, her eyes bright from wine; not drunk, but definitely not sober.

'You speak so well of your experiences,' she smiled, her companions nodding. 'You're very different from us in manner and speech. I'd know more of where you came from, who you are. You truly remember nothing?'

'Nothing,' he said with a shrug.

'You *must* remember something,' she insisted, her eyes on his face flirtatiously.

The Green Warrior stood abruptly and studied her, his face expressionless and his mood soured.

'*Nothing*,' he said shortly, and, unhindered by the wine he had consumed, turned and walked away towards the perimeter of trees. The guard looked astonished.

'I was only curious,' she said, uncertain whether to be guilty or annoyed. Karland shook his head, thinking he should have warned the others how mercurial The Green Warrior could be.

'He's... changeable,' he said. 'He won't admit it, but I think it affects him deeply that he doesn't know his past, or his name. His mood will change back again. Just... don't pry too much.'

She shrugged, looking a little regretfully after him. 'Well. Could use more wine, anyway.'

'You could use getting ready to sleep,' said Gustram Aldine, coming up behind Karland. 'We have had a deserved rest, but now we are all here-' he looked at Karland, and then shrugged with a slight smile, '-we will break camp at dawn. We still have near two days's travel before we reach the estuary.'

With some complaints the soldiers made ready, along with Darus, who liked his sleep nearly as much as Aldwyn had. In the distance Thorne was ordering other squads to tidy camp for the morning.

Rast sat with the elves, talking softly. Karland knew he would slip into his *dônaethar* trance at some point, and the elves would simply not sleep, dreaming awake and scouting the perimeter.

He wished The Green Warrior a restful night. For all his camaraderie, the man was deeply troubled, even haunted behind an exterior that spoke of both suppressed violence and nobility.

Karland felt for the man who was fast becoming a friend.

CB   BD

It was late. Most of the company were deep in slumber under the watchful eyes of the Druids. Karland was rasping lightly in his bedroll; Darus wasn't snoring, but his heavy slow breathing could be heard.

Galnór and Lëlylien were sitting, facing each other, eyes closed, sometimes breathing words to each other or laughing quietly in their lilting fashion. Even in repose their forms spoke of grace and elegance, and Rast thought back, troubled, to the elf he had slain during their flight up the lower slopes of Drakesholm Soaring. To have removed such a light from the world had profoundly hurt him, despite the clearly, shockingly unnatural aura the elf had carried. Every time he believed he had forgotten it he was reminded again. Elves in league with orcs; in league with chaos, with death.

Dark elves. Never even in legend had such a thing been heard of.

A slight whisper of movement came. Leona's low voice broke into his thoughts.

'What troubles you, Rast Tal'Orien?'

Rast glanced aside at her shadowed form, her hair flickering orange-gold in the light from the fire. His reluctance to speak was less with Leona, and finally he sighed.

'In the Arkons, we were faced with an elf. One of the people who helped raise me, train me, who live in peace and harmony and wisdom. Yet... he was evil. Dark.

451

Cold. There was no love or harmony in him. It troubles me deeply, but less than the fact that I slew him.'

'No easy feat,' said Leona, and Rast knew she did not just mean the ability to kill an elf in combat.

'Part of me is tired of the unending slaying,' he said quietly. 'Am I to have no other purpose? Ever duty and battle call me back. Few equal me in combat. Tactics and strategy speak to me alongside the beat of the fight. It is a dance I rarely falter in. I was born to fight, and I always fight to win.' He sighed quietly. 'But no matter how talented a warrior, chance can end him. I have nearly died so many times I cannot count them, and each leaves their mark. One day my injuries will mount, age will slow me. I will not be fast enough, or strong enough.'

'That is something all mortals must face,' Leona said quietly.

Something in her voice gave him pause.

'But not you?'

'Druids age… differently. There is a natural rhythm to living your span and dying in the great cycle, and I often think it ironic that we who hold nature so dear live to a different rhythm.'

Rast nodded. 'Yet you do what you must. As do I.'

'Ah, my *Banidróttin*. What is it you fear?' asked Leona, moving in front of him and looking him in the eyes. Her gold-green hued irises reflected the flickers of firelight as they held his. They looked more animal than human - a reflection of her power as a guardian of Nature, perhaps - but he had no trouble gazing into them. They spoke again to his memory, the back of his mind. They reminded him of the distant past, somehow.

They stood thus for some minutes, her face turned up to his, their mouths close. She was tall, though he still towered over her, and yet there was nothing subservient or supplicant about her upturned face.

For the first time in many years, Rast felt a longing for someone. For an equal. Someone who valued him not just for who he was, but who also saw and comprehended every piece of him. Someone with whom they both could fill a great, untouchable loneliness.

He realised that with Leona, his barriers were less protection than he thought. They had been bastions of his emotional fortitude for so long; an ally now somehow within the gates was impossible to hide from.

Leona was strong and beautiful, with a wildness, a hidden power that would frighten most. All the Druids were like that, each in their own way. He was very aware of her as a woman, of course; he was always appreciative of beauty. But something of her spoke to him more deeply than that. To all the parts of him. She was a woman to match him on every level. As powerful and deep as a great river; as dangerous as a wolf, as gentle and caring as a mother.

As beautiful as a waterfall in sunlight.

Finally, he spoke very softly, scarcely believing his own words. They were a sweet, painful release; words that he had never thought to say to another.

'I fear failing.' He looked away. 'I have failed, so many times.' For a moment, old memories skimmed over his mind; family, a lover, his friends. Aldwyn. Grukust. Györnàeldàr. Others. 'For all my skill, those I care for die. I ask myself sometimes: is it because of what I am? Or am I simply unable to protect them? Am I always to fail to protect others? Am I the source of their danger? I fear this cycle of failure and despair, Leona, where I alone survive.'

She moved to speak, and he stopped her with a finger to her lips.

'I think of the words I received in the Portal from the High Elf. I hear them again and again. I remember my decision, and why I made it. And I know I was right; yet still, I fear to fail.' He shook his head, looked away for a moment. 'Great men have said that you must fail to learn to succeed, and it is true; but there is some failure too absolute to recover from. That which causes the death of those I care for. That which could destroy our world.'

Leona's eyes were luminous. 'We all fail, my friend. Every day. As you say… it is what teaches us. Remember your vision in the portal, Rast Tal'Orien. Look within yourself. Your heart knows the truth. The *Bannidrottin* is what you are, *who* you are, but it is not *all* of you. Take not the burden of other's fates upon yourself. They do not die because of you, but *in spite* of you. There is a difference.'

He didn't answer, and after a moment, she spoke again.

'I named you Lord of Death, Rast Tal'Orien, because I sense it, have seen it; but you are also a gentle man. A bearer of great burdens; duty. Honour. Care. You carry music in your heart, yet will see this great work through to the end, no matter the cost to your soul. You have not yet lost yourself in the love of death; and for you, that would be so very easy. You have a nobility I have seen in very few men. You have failed so much less than you know.'

Rast let the words absorb into his consciousness. He allowed them to flow through him, tried to see how they would counter his dark feelings. Their irrefutability denied the self-indulgence of wallowing in depression, which was all too tempting. A small part of him was amused that even this became reduced to a matter of conflict and counters, of sorts.

He gazed out into the darkness, lost in his thoughts, and Leona waited; patient, comforting.

After a time, he nodded.

'Thank you, Leona. You ease my troubles. I rarely feel so torn, so unbalanced. You are wise.' He sighed. 'I will try to heed your words. They bring me comfort.'

She stepped closer, her breath sweet to his nose. Her nostrils flared, as if she could read him by his own scents, and her eyes swept his face, clearly seeing him in the dim light far better than he saw her.

'Only my words, Rast Tal'Orien?' Her voice was a whisper.

His eyes took in the fullness of her lips, and the beautiful symmetry of her face. How did she so easily see all of him? How did he see so much of her?

Always in control of his desires, nevertheless... he ached for companionship.

Hers.

It vied with his fear; with his regret.

Their mouths almost touching, the wild scent of her and her sweet breath filling his nose, he murmured, 'I am but a mortal, Leona. Is it meet for a Druid to be close to one such as myself?'

'Not to some, perhaps,' she breathed, her hair falling around her face like a curling waterfall in the flickering firelight. 'But they are not here... and I am.'

The tableau held for a few more seconds, and then as softly as a feather falling, their lips met.

ෆ ෨

Morning brought Leona and tea. She received several appreciative glances from The Green Warrior, who hauled himself tiredly from his blankets. It seemed he hadn't slept well after all, but he waved his hand wearily.

'Come on,' he muttered wearily, apparently to himself, beckoning the Druid when she offered a cup of water.

They rose and ate. Aldine was busy instructing the troops, leaving the companions to collect themselves.

Leona appeared again and sat next to Rast.

'*Banidróttin,*' she smiled. Rast smiled back, somehow less grim than usual, and Karland blinked. Leona had that effect on people, but he was surprised it had also mellowed Rast. He looked less severe with the bleakness falling from his face. Ruggedly handsome, even.

'*Banidróttin?*' queried The Green Warrior.

'*Lord of Death* in the old tongue,' Leona said. 'I named him so after he prevailed unarmed against more than twenty assassins. They learned to fear him that night.'

The Green Warrior's ears seemed to perk up with interest. '*Lord of Death,*' he mused, and laughed shortly. 'I like it.'

454

Rast sighed.

'We must decide what to do once we reach Eyotsburg,' he said, changing the subject.

'I thought that was pretty clear,' said Karland. 'We make for Mithtol and request aid from the elves, and the company requests a formal alliance with Eoytsberg so they can lend aid.'

'I will travel north to the banks of the estuary with you and see you to a vessel to take you upriver.' She exchanged a look with Rast for a second, then looked away. 'I cannot stay with you. The creatures have been culled here… for a time. But this forest is vast and they move quickly. Many scattered, and though we killed many, I fear some fled south. Once these forests east of the Skyreach are clear, we will move southwest. There are rumours of more.' She shook her head for a moment. 'I have lost many brothers and sisters, but if we miss even one foe, this could all be for naught; the cycle could renew. We will track and hunt all we can.' She smiled slightly and looked back to him. 'We are warning cities; I will return to Darost. Since you cannot take your horses, I can also return them, if you wish.'

'It would be good to know that they are back safely,' said Rast. Karland nodded, thinking of the adventures the sturdy little dray had been on. Hjarta and the mare snuffled contentedly at the grass, happy to relax, unlike the watchful presence of Stryke. Even the Druids were careful to approach him from the front and without threat, as they would any dangerous animal. Stryke clearly communicated with them in some way but was strangely wary of all of them.

'How far can you come this time?' Karland asked, wincing at what sounded like an accusation. Hearing what was left of some of the villages here, he shuddered to think of abominations capable of this slaughter near The Croft.

Leona smiled sadly. 'I will go north with you and guide you to a boat for Eyotsburg before I run for Darost. It will not be easy; boats are few because of the rumours. That village was one of many.' She looked at them unblinking. 'Too many.'

'I thought that you had an understanding with animals.'

'They are not animals. Or men. They are profoundly unnatural; the most dangerous scourge we have ever fought. Every Druid together might not be enough to keep them from humanity. And if we fail, humanity will be destroyed.'

'So we have Darklings, Yosga-whatever, and now these things. And orcs. And Meyar. And Novin,' said The Green Warrior sceptically. 'That's a lot of shit to deal with.'

'All seems a little coincidental, doesn't it?' Aldine's voice broke in as he arrived with Major Gambeson.

'There is much that is linked by common cause. Chaos is growing. You heard Körànthír, and Némaenth. At the heart of all of this lies the Darklings,' said Rast.

'*I* didn't hear them,' muttered Aldine.

'Enough,' said Major Gambeson. 'Captain, the Council has placed their trust. We follow their orders.'

'Sir.'

'Major,' said Leona. 'You have wounded. You have a choice; the journey will be difficult and dangerous for them, though Eyotsburg offers security. Or they may rest here with the Druids, and we will tend to them and see them home in time.'

'The offer is appreciated, Leona.' Major Gambeson bowed slightly. 'However, we leave no one behind while they draw breath. Their place is with their company.'

'As you wish. We should leave soon; it will take us until near mid-morning tomorrow to reach the nearest dock.' With one last look at Rast, she left. The big man watched her go, a strange mix of emotions on his usually stern face.

છ   ജ

After bidding farewell to the Druids, they moved on following Leona. Marching one hundred and sixty troops and two large wagons through the trees was far slower going than on the plains, and for hours they moved along a trail which seemed to curve from glade to dell.

Sometime after dark, before midnight, they camped in a huge clearing. Karland was still exhausted, and ate mechanically, looking forward to his bedroll. No one had mentioned weapons practice, and for that he was thankful; his wounds were mostly healed, but he was still sore.

The camp was set up as usual, with the wagons at the centre near the largest fire, and smaller campfires dotted around for each unit. Tonight, they would not rest long, so Major Gambeson did not deploy the command tents, bunking down like everyone else. To Karland's surprise, so did Aldine, without any complaint. He kept forgetting they were veterans of many campaigns. Although they had earned certain comforts, they didn't need them.

Leona seemed slightly distracted, spending much time at the edge of the camp talking to Rast. Something between them had changed, thought Karland, although he didn't know what.

Finally, he fell into his bedroll and wrapped it around himself with a sigh, vaguely recalling the first time he had shivered on the ground. Now wrapping the roll under him was automatic.

456

Without the rush and laughter of the night before, his lids closed slowly and he drifted away, dreams catching his consciousness on tenuous hooks and dragging it off into wisps of thought and glimpses of his life.

For much of his sleep, he had fragmented, colourful dreams, vivid and strange, but with a feeling of familiarity. Vast shapes moved about above him, familiar in some way, and around him were faces and names he knew but at the same time did not.

Gradually, darkness crept in at the edges. A darkness shot through with jagged red lightning that was somehow also black, like shards of glass, and nothing to do with electricity; fracture lines along weak points in reality. A hot wind blasted through them, but it was no wind at all, and he shivered, despite the heat.

Was it coming in or leaving?

Something in his mind screamed soundlessly at what lay beyond, what huge and terrible beings directed it with no malice at all, simply a cold, uncaring drive to see everything that he was annihilated. The senses of shapes around him changed, becoming twisted, somehow other, and in horror he looked down to find his own body changing too, unnaturally and in blinding agony. His mouth was forced open, his mind shutting down. At first his scream was silent. In a voice not his own, he began to moan, then cry, unceasingly and begging for air but unable to stop. The sound rose to a shrieking wail, which echoed as if from a great distance.

He was losing himself.

THIRTY-FOUR

Karland woke with a start, the remainder of the wail still sounding in his head. It was just a dream, but his heart was pounding, and he was drenched in sweat. He lay in his bedroll for a few seconds before he realised that he could still hear the sound, only now it also sounded something like a wolf howl. He had never heard anything like it; it had a raw, chaotic, angry edge to it.

The night crept towards dawn, the moonlight bright but waning with the promise of the sun to come. It was full moon; Moonday. Green from the bright second moon tinged everything as Xoth sped across the sky.

The sound reverberated through the trees from the middle distance and was answered from several points both to the sides of the clearing and from where they had come. At once, it seemed the trees around them came alive with the dreadful sound.

Karland shivered at the noise and sat up to find Rast at the edge of the clearing, a silent shadow listening to the cries, and Leona half-crouched a little way from him, the fire at her back. She turned her head at Karland's movement and he started again. Her pupils reflected the firelight like shining golden pools.

Darus stopped his gentle snoring and rolled over; Karland turned to look and saw his huge dark eyes glinting in the low flames. His hand was resting on his axe. The elves had vanished somewhere.

Thorne was flickered hands signals to Lieutenant Isra, who nodded and sent Gen and Kith in opposite directions. Others radiated out from each squad. Whispered commands flew through the camp.

Everyone nearby looked up when Leona spoke at normal volume, her voice sounding strange.

'It is too late.'

Rast hadn't moved from his position. Karland shivered as Leona spoke again, an emotion in her voice Karland had never heard before.

Anger? Hatred? Fear?

'The enemy have found us. We cannot hide, cannot run. They defile the very trees they move through.'

'What enemy?' asked Aldine. 'Orcs? I thought you said this area was safe.'

'Not orcs. They fear the trees.' Leona said, almost tiredly. 'These do not.'

What are they?' asked Gambeson, quietly.

'Shape-shifters. Monsters. Undying abominations. Men call them *Varka*.'

They all looked blank.

'Beastmen? *Werwulf?*'

'*Werewolves?*' Aldine snorted in disbelief, and then laughed. 'More children's tales!'

Leona's eyes glittered.

'They are no tale. I thought them all slain here; these must have skirted us. They have our trail, or they would not have called the hunt. My kin are not near enough to help. They will slaughter us all.' Her face was set in a mixture of hatred and almost... pity, thought Karland.

'Don't sound nothin' like wolves,' a nearby soldier said.

'They are not. All wolves hate and fear them. *Varka* wish only to devour and kill for sport, and will delight in your suffering. They know what they do as much as any man. This pack is many. Xoth is full overhead tonight; they are at their most powerful. They will be faster and stronger than you can believe.'

All around them the howls were growing; they held a peculiar edge, of anger, of desire. They really sounded little like wolves.

Rast glanced around at the camp, which was already breaking the company for defence. 'We must not be separated; keep soldiers in squads. We must watch for the vulnerable. Karland, Warrior; protect the wagons.'

The Green Warrior nodded slowly. Karland's face heated. He thought he had proved himself beyond being a liability. Rast caught the look.

'It is not a question of capability, boy. You are not part of the squads. Help where you can but take no risks.' Karland nodded, loosening his short sword.

Aldine glanced at Rast sceptically. 'Have *you* faced them before?'

Rast shook his head. 'No. I know only of tales, but I've learned to my cost not to discount legend. What do we have that may aid us?'

Leona closed her eyes and breathed deeply for a moment. 'There is a clump of wolfsbane near the clearing, off west.' She pointed to the side. 'It is deadly to them.'

Galnór spoke. 'We can find it.'

'Hurry. They will be upon you in the darkness if you tarry. If you cannot find it, return quickly.' The elves nodded and ran swiftly in the direction she had pointed. Karland hoped they could find the plant.

'The only other things that would help are weapons of silver, and fire.' She looked around at the utilitarian Eordeland weapons and armour, good solid steel.

Major Gambeson smiled his quiet smile. 'I have some inlaid into my blade, and on my hilt.'

Another soldier tugged at her heartfinger. 'I got a wedding ring.' She glanced sideways to a brutish-looking man in another squad who was gazing at her fondly, and her lips quirked. Karland didn't know either of them by name. 'I'm told it's silver. Do you need it, Druid?'

'No! No. Use it any way you can,' said Leona. 'They cannot bear its touch. Silver burns and kills.' She turned to Aldine. 'Captain Aldine - ring the carts and wounded with your soldiers. Darus, Rast – you and I will be needed to run interference, distract. I hear perhaps fifteen calls to hunt. We are in great trouble if there are that many.'

'Do it,' said Major Gambeson.

'Light brands from the fires,' shouted Thorne. 'I want a brand every four soldiers! Get lights out there! Horses between the carts, hobbled! Pathfinders, secure them! Build that fire at one end! Ring 'em, healers and sappers to centre!' Men and women clattered as they raced to positions, making ready. 'This is gonna be tight! Crossbows, cock! Archers make ready. Pikes to the fore! Keep them back! Protect the healer cart at all costs!'

To the side, the Sergeants were bellowing orders to their squads. Soldiers raced out to jam burning brands into the dirt of the clearing all around them, sending flickering light out to the treeline. There weren't enough to light the clearing up, but they could see. Fifteen horses were hobbled with thick fleece-lined leather thongs, all except for those ridden by the officers and Stryke, all trained to guard and attack. The pathfinders positioned themselves nearby, ready to make use of their powerful horse bows.

Aldine called to the Druid over the shouting. 'Is this necessary? We must outnumber them more than ten to one!'

Leona shook her head in exasperation. '*One* of these creatures could go through a squad of your finest fighters and leave nothing but pieces without taking lasting harm, do you understand? Their wounds will heal before your eyes. They are faster and stronger than you. This pack could kill every one of us.' She saw the look of disbelief on his face. 'Do not repeat your Council's mistake by dismissing my words as vapid.'

'She does not exaggerate,' said Rast. 'She is vouched for by the Council of Twelve.'

Leona continued, 'With wolfsbane we stand a chance of slowing them enough to kill them before they decimate the company. When they break through the lines - and they will - Darus, Rast, the elves and I should be able to help where needed.' She looked around. 'Do not underestimate them. These are unlike any other foes you have faced. If you can, hew their heads from them, or strike true with the wolfsbane, but don't be foolish just for the chance. *Gaiá* willing, we may survive the night.'

Darus hefted his axe and snorted. 'I'll make necks my targets of choice. What will you fight with? That stick?' He shrugged his powerful green shoulders, the huge axe of Grukust lying light in his firm grasp and looked at her smooth club with some disdain. In the flicker of low firelight, he looked more like his brother than ever.

Leona smiled coldly, her teeth glinting in the darkness. 'Never doubt that I have weapons. They fear Druids for good reason.'

The Green Warrior moved to help with the fire. He liked fire, Karland had noticed. The others moved to the middle of the circle along with the healers and sappers, Rast unfastening his cloak and throwing it to the side. His black armless tunic and leggings blended with the night, showing arms carved in firelight and a face as bleak as granite.

'No one doubts your courage, Karland, but they need strength and experience in the lines. It falls to us to try to protect the wagons. A mistake could mean another's life. Do you understand?'

Karland nodded. Truth be told, he was frightened. The awful howls and roars which grew closer chilled his blood.

Patting Karland's shoulder with a quick smile, Rast moved away.

Karland prepared himself, although his fear of the approaching creatures was nearly overwhelming. They echoed his darkest nightmares; the fear of the deep woods, the hideous things that chased him in his sleep sometimes and that had harrowed him to waking tonight. He only hoped he could find the courage to strike when the time came.

Someone called out to look aside from the main fire and threw wood and kindling on. Flames flared up, lighting up the grass further out around the other camp fires. Karland knew this would make them silhouettes and ruin the night vision of their foes. It would not be much help. The moons were already bright and full, and cast everything in silver-green.

He drew his short sword as Galnór and Lëlylien burst from the darkness, tunic fronts heaped with three-lobed dark green leaves which looked black in the firelight. They were running in that smooth gait, faster than a man, and they looked anxious.

'Take some! Crush them against your blades and points; rub the juice along the length,' they called as they ran along the lines, passing them out. Leona's nostrils were flaring as if she could smell strong vinegar. The leaves were pungent; her heightened senses must find them overwhelming.

'It is a powerful poison and venom to them. It will slow their healing,' she called. 'If the strike hits a vital organ, it may kill; but it will be slow. Rub anything spare on somewhere you can wipe the blade to keep it potent. Rub the residue on your throats. It may ward them off. If you are bitten, you must tell me.' Karland could hear the despair in her voice; it was obvious she considered their chances slim.

Her words were relayed, and the company hurriedly set to their tasks, rubbing crushed leaves on exposed blades, bolts and arrow tips, sending runnels of dark green juice down them to be smeared across. Not enough would be treated; the ragged howls were very close now, interspersed with faint low snarls. Rast produced his *shirkas,* the slender, slightly curved blades quickly coated in wolfsbane to the hilts, along with a plain, serviceable short sword. Darus had run a few leaves over the axe crescents, and the elves had coated everything they could with quick, sure movements. The howls crescendoed loudly, then died away.

Leona's voice cut through the preparations.

'They are here,' she almost snarled. Karland looked over at a tone in her voice he had never heard before. She was half-crouched in a feral, disturbing fashion that raised the hackles on his neck.

He thought he heard the sounds of heavy bodies moving through the undergrowth; a twig cracked here, a bush swayed there. He peered out between the still forms of the guards and saw several sets of burning eyes gleaming in the trees; they were disconcertingly high off the ground, far higher than a wolf or dog could be.

A low growling laugh came from the darkness. The soldiers shifted nervously.

With roars, dark forms burst from the trees from three points around the clearing. They moved faster than a man, and not much could be seen in the gloom until they approached the flames. The leading figure was mostly manlike, but even as they watched, it swelled, howling in pain as its body tumesced. It stumbled from the writhing agony, and then recovered; the body was more hugely muscled by the second and was sprouting a covering of short fur. The long, still-elongating snout opened in a wicked grin full of teeth that were growing past a length a normal wolf could fit into its mouth. It had larger canines than an ordinary predator, and the jaw dropped open unnaturally wide. The face bore an alien expression of lustful glee. Pointed triangular ears raised high atop its narrowed but powerful head, and the yellow eyes glared in hateful anticipation of death and blood.

Similar forms were close behind, avoiding the fires but making no effort to stay concealed. The smallest was still bigger than an average man and more heavily muscled; the biggest was as large as Darus. They were less a melding of man and wolf, and more monsters accentuating the worst of both. Karland had a fleeting second to wonder how they shifted mass and shape.

'LOOSE AT WILL!' roared Thorne, and shafts and bolts thrummed out to strike the foremost creatures, who stumbled and fell. Many missed in the darkness, except for those of the elves.

Almost dreamlike, Karland watched those that had fallen pull themselves to their feet, shaking heads and snapping shafts embedded in their limbs and torsos. One pinwheeled face first in a tumble that would have broken a human's neck, a bolt almost centred between its eyes. Karland watched incredulously as it tried to rise, batting aimlessly at the bolt in its brain. The healing of the skull pushed the bolt back out and finally it caught it in a claw, tearing it from its skull. The barbs came away leaving a hole, but it seemed to only anger the creature. The wound was closing; the bolt was uncoated.

Those doctored with wolfsbane had more effect. Three of the monsters fell to lie weakly scrabbling, the deadly poison deep in a vital wound. Even then the awful vivacity of unnatural life would not leave them, and they struggled to rise.

Howling, the three groups fell on the party almost at the same time. The sound was awful. The first werewolf leapt snarling at Isra's squad, clawed hands leading. Where a normal creature would have been impaled on pikes, the beastman brushed the hafts aside as it leapt with shocking speed and strength.

Short spears stabbed out, trying to keep the creatures at bay; another werewolf fell, snapping at a pike deep in its chest. It snapped the haft with a convulsive blow, but continued to writhe, shrieking in pain, the wolfsbane eating into the dreadful wound. More spears stabbed into it, and still it would not die. Karland could hear soldiers shouting in fear even as they struck. The scene lasted seconds before a soldier had her shield wrenched downward, and she was jerked forward, screaming. Blood spattered as she was disembowelled, her entrails flung wet and gleaming back at the soldiers, who flinched but closed.

The line, hardened by experience, gave slightly under the attacks, trying to absorb the shock, but this was not like fighting Novinians. They tried to push the attackers back by weight of weaponry. It had little effect. Most of the long weapons had no coating. Pikes and spears were wrenched from hands by incredible strength, leaving only shields and swords. Shields were torn forward or down so hard some lost arms; the luckier simply had broken bones. Taloned arms scythed out, bowling veterans away like twigs, opening huge gaps in the line.

Soldiers fell, thrown into others with terrible force, long dark ragged claws tearing through leather armour and flesh. Such was the power of the attackers that many were dead or dying immediately, throats torn out, guts ripped from their bodies, limbs torn off to leave them gasping in exsanguination.

A yawning pit opened in Karland's stomach as he watched, his hands shaking. He caught flashes of soldiers he knew fighting for their lives. Nirrah's squads stabbed one after the other at a monstrous brown shaggy shape with teeth like picks, Den Olli and Kirri shoulder to shoulder, hacking determinedly. As he watched, a claw ripped into Kirri's shoulder, and she yelled in pain. The return swipe would have torn her face from her head, but it was caught on the sharp edge of a sword by Gorin, his face as sour as ever but with a grimace of effort added to it. The squad was a team, and next to the other squads, they covered each other well. Karland could see why his being part of them, here and now, would have been a deadly mistake.

Although the monsters took no lasting damage, it was obvious the weapons hurt them, even the normal ones. Where wolfsbane was on the blades and bolts, they retreated, more reluctant to engage, glaring and snapping. They flinched back from brands thrust at them, blinded, and where their fur caught, they threw themselves and rolled.

Somehow, the line held. The noise was incredible, much worse than the last battle. Karland could barely hear thumps and strikes, the only sounds of metal coming from claws on weapons. Men and women screamed in agony and fear. Commands were yelled through the furore. Werewolves howled and snarled, snapping and bellowing half-words gutturally though mouths ill-designed for speech. Horses whinnied in fright behind them in the corral made by the main fire and the wagons, the war-trained horses and the hobbles being the only things stopping them fleeing. They reared and lunged in panic, pathfinders trying to calm them, but had nowhere to go except the fire at the other end.

The guards were in disarray, trying to hold formation, but the creatures leapt higher than they expected. They impaled themselves on pikes and spears to get close enough to tear men and women apart, heedless of the damage to their bodies. Even as he watched, a howling monster as tall as Rast pushed its raw, agonised flesh along several hafts transfixing it and tore the shield from a guard called Barrek. Karland knew him, had marched with him; as he watched in shock, the creature rammed a fist full of long sharp talons into Barrek's stomach so hard three erupted from his back. He was lifted on one arm - the strength of these monsters! - and thrown into another guard, knocking him from his feet.

The lines pulled back, shivering in and tightening towards the fire. More were out of action, a stray claw or blow removing them from the fight for a time as surely as death. Even a closed-fisted blow from a werewolf could kill. Guard lay with chests caved in and necks broken next to those who looked as if they had been almost shredded.

Karland looked around, feeling as if his legs would give way. He felt utterly weak. This was nothing like any battle he had been in.

So much blood. So much death.

It had been mere minutes.

To his immediate right, Isra's squads fought two werewolves, the first having pulled itself back, shrieking in pain. Gen struck downwards as hard as he could with both hands as one creature grabbed him, slicing deeply into an arm. He sagged in a grip with unholy strength, tendons standing out on his neck in pain; he had underestimated the creature's speed. Kith spun as if on a wheel and his green-stained sword arced in to hit just off centre of the eyes on top of the head. The werewolf's hold loosened, its skull splitting open with a sickening crack, and Gen jerked free spasmodically. The werewolf roared in agony, twisting so violently the sword was pulled both from its head and Kith's hands, and collapsed forward as fluids leaked from its riven head. Karland saw bone and what was probably brain just before the weight of it knocked Gen off his feet.

Gen disentangled hurriedly, and Karland watched in disbelief as the werewolf twitched and wailed in pain. Incredibly, it was somehow still not dead. One eye was damaged, and it seemed to have little control of its limbs, but as the seconds passed the creature began trying to rise, as if it expected the head wound to be of little consequence.

It was healing, slowly. The creature was finding it hard to control itself; the wolfsbane had clearly damaged its brain. Karland was aghast to think how fast it would heal without the poison.

How was it still alive?

All the soldiers in this company were elite veterans, victors in countless battles and highly awarded. They broke their paralysis quickly and scrambled to brutally hack at the exposed neck, chopping hard into flesh and bone, stabbing to keep the werewolf from healing. Karland could not wait any longer. He drew his sword in a rush and joined them, hacking in a desperate attempt to prevent the flesh knitting. His hands would hardly hold the weapon. The great gashes in the neck closed almost as fast as they hewed, and the werewolf screamed in terrible whining yelps.

They were making a difference, the wolfsbane blades slowing the healing. Blood jetted out onto the ground. Two more chops and its head was almost clear of the body; panting, a soldier grabbed it by an ear as Kith sawed at the last shreds of tissue. All of them saw, impossibly, the good eye roll up to regard them and the lips draw back in a soundless snarl. In a jerk of revulsion, the soldier hurled it out over the other's heads into the wolfmen, who howled in outrage. They had not expected to lose any of their number.

In seconds, everything changed.

Gone was any pretence at playing with their food. They hit the soldiers like an avalanche, co-ordinated now, punching through the defence and bursting behind the lines. Horribly mutilated and dying veterans littered the trails behind them.

In a single heartbeat the enemy were among them, and chaos reigned.

ನ ಂ

Rast saw the line collapse. Werewolves tore into frightened guards like foxes in a henhouse. He sprinted out from the centre, ducking a blow that would have broken every rib and possibly torn out a lung, and leapt, catching one of the attackers in the side of the head with every ounce of power he had. He felt its neck snap through the soles of his feet, and he rolled back to his feet and sprinted on, his sword held behind him, point low. Howls of outrage came from behind him.

There were too many of the foe working their way in towards the wagons. If they broke the company, they would hunt the survivors at leisure, and even the elves and Darus would fall swiftly.

All he could try to do was lead some of the incoming creatures away from the healers - and Karland.

More than once, Aldwyn had told him Karland must survive. This time, he would protect one he cared for.

Duty.

His sword batted an arm aside before lancing through into the heart of the werewolf in a fluid thrust; the creature collapsed, gasping as venom surged through its system. Rast leapt over it at the next, spinning the sword in a half-circle outwards in front of him that took the fingers off his new attacker. He ducked as the werewolf howled in pain and swiped at his head with its other arm, then dipped and spun with the sword out horizontally at belt level, eviscerating the third which had just arrived, following him as he ran. As he completed the move, he lifted his trailing leg and, finishing the spin, slammed the heel hard into the neck of the second werewolf. Large as it was, the impact sent a shockwave up into its brain, and it fell as if its strings had been cut. He launched a thundering hook with his other hand into the

466

temple of the third as it tried to hold its guts in and was surprised when even in its agony, it flinched violently away from his fist.

Rast found a few seconds to himself before they could attack again, and ran further from the main group, into the patches of light where some brands still burned.

Sheer surprise had kept them from him, but he knew that both sides had underestimated the speed of their foe; he had been fortunate that their mistake had been greater.

Rast knew his time was limited. Hitting them was like striking heavy wood. He would likely die here, facing three of the creatures. The best he could do was to damage them faster than they could heal, and unlike them he could afford no mistakes.

He felt the cold brush of breathless lips on his, soft and eternal.

Already the first had drawn a shuddering breath and was rising again. Apart from its slow approach, the blood-matted fur on its chest under the clutch of a taloned claw and the rage in its face were the only evidence of the sword in the heart. Another was also moving in, more cautiously. It recognised in him a foe to be wary of. The third had been distracted by easier prey.

He smiled grimly and crouched, hand out, sword held low and back. The werewolf snarled, its eyes fixed oddly on his hand.

Let them work for their meal.

	

As he stumbled back into the centre near the wagons, Karland found it hard to keep track of everyone in the chaos. It was a free-for-all.

He could hear Darus roaring somewhere, and there was no sign of the elves or Rast. Bodies surged around them. It was almost impossible to focus on any one thing. Then he saw Leona nearby, standing in a gaping hole in the squads and lending her aid. She swung her club harder and faster than Karland thought possible for her frame.

The Druid moved somewhat like the elves; fluid, fast, graceful, but with savagery. Her teeth were bared in hatred, and she looked as if she wanted to throw the club down and set them in the throat of the nearest werewolf. She knocked the great muscled arm of one away effortlessly as it clawed out, then slammed it into the top of its head with a crack like a tree breaking. To Karland, it seemed as if the club struck with something more than simple strength. A clear ripple of sheer force seemed to pulse out from the strike.

Despite its far greater size, the abomination was pitched violently face-first into the dirt, as if she had hit it using a sledgehammer and Darus's own strength. Its skull was crushed, the head heavily distorted. The wound wasn't closing, Karland noticed detachedly. Something in her club must be akin to the wolfsbane.

She twisted sideways, hitting another in the side as it passed and throwing it tumbling from its feet.

Another form loomed from the dark to her rear.

Leona whirled as if she knew what was behind, her, as graceful as either of the elves, and whipped the club awkwardly sideways into the muzzle of a huge werewolf which was reaching for a soldier that hadn't seen it. Its head snapped around at the glancing blow, but it did not fall. Dazed, it turned its muzzle and stared at her. Its nostrils flared and the yellow eyes focused on her. Recognition dawned.

The beastman roared in hatred, half-words in the noise. With an answering roar another immediately diverted its attack from the guards as if they were meaningless and sprang upon her from the side. The move was unexpected, and Karland gasped in shock. The heavy form, many times her weight and size, bowled her over and knocking the club from her hand. Hundreds of pounds of vicious flesh swept the woman away like a wave crashing into flotsam, with only an image of the last expression of angry surprise on her face left in his mind. The first werewolf leapt after them into a dip.

Karland cried out in disbelief at the loss of the Druid, unable to believe how quickly she had fallen. It had been so sudden that she had not been able to defend herself. The monsters were already tearing at her struggling form.

He knew if he tried to avenge her, he would die.

Another roar snapped his attention around. Dead and injured Guard lay everywhere. Even as he watched one of the monsters tore the face off a woman with her sword fixed deep between its ribs, tearing its talons down and breaking flesh, skin and bone. Its talon caught in her jawbone, and it tore that from her skull as well. Her face a ruin of raw meat no longer recognisably human, she dropped in a welter of blood.

The wolfmen counted four truly dead now, but even others injured were slowly overcoming their wounds to attack again, and with every strike the wolfsbane had less effect, diluted and washed off with blood. The situation seemed hopeless. The veterans retreated raggedly in towards the wagons, trying to re-establish a line. They desperately needed to push the monsters back out in front of them.

Not all, however, were accounting so little for themselves.

Karland caught sight of Darus, bellowing, slashing his brother's huge axe left and right so hard that Karland wondered if he would behead one of the guards to either side. For all the discussions they had had about him being less prone to *baresark* than his brother, he was fully enraged now. Werewolves lunged snapping at him but were wary of the powerful axe. Even they would find it difficult to recover if it halved them. Two forms lay nearby, dragging themselves back away from him as they healed. Another lay headless, its head kicked far from the body, which still twitched.

Although he was not quite as broad as Grukust had been, the similarity was marked, and he roared with his own tusks bared in the face of his foes, his snarls matching theirs, deeper if less bestial.

One thundering strike with the axe missed, the werewolf evading the downward strike, but it hadn't expected such a quick reversal and the other head of the axe caught it in the armpit on the upswing. The arm spun around in a spray of gore, coating Darus and the nearest guard, and hung by a strip of skin and hair. There was blood everywhere, spraying over Darus and pumping down the furry side of the attacker; the werewolf whined and snarled in agony, falling back and clutching the severed limb. The creature retreated and clamped its big-clawed hand onto the arm, holding it in place and glaring in fury. It was knitting slowly as Karland watched.

A soldier hit the ground hard to the ork's right, a backwards swipe smashing into his chest. Without pause, Darus stepped over to cover him. The soldier raised his head and a hand, and Karland saw it was Verrin. The man looked up at the ork, expressions fleeting across his bloodied face and his mouth an almost comical *o* of surprise, and then he sank back.

Nearby, Kith fended off two of the creatures, shields locking around him. He yelled as a massive paw closed on his arm, and he was yanked with terrible strength off his feet into the midst of the attackers. Isra shouted next to him and slashed frenziedly at her attacker, trying to get to her comrade, but the snapping jaws kept her at bay. The valiant man held his sword tight and managed a stab as he was thrown violently down. The sword went into the side of one of the creatures twice before long teeth closed on his throat and simply tore the whole chunk of flesh out, blood spraying up over the ecstatic werewolves. He juddered in death, a gaping crescent all the way back to his vertebrae missing from his chin almost to his collarbone.

The horror that bit him suddenly coughed and sputtered, its mouth burning, and spat bloody drool out as it stumbled away, trying to stop its throat from closing in shock at the bitter taste of wolfsbane. In retribution, a clawed fist punched horrifically through Kith's ribs, cracking them open. Karland nearly threw up at the sight but forced himself to step forward, his legs trembling. Another of the monsters bounded through soldiers, knocking them aside like a boulder through sticks, intent on the healer's cart.

Karland imagined Leona having her throat ripped out by one of the beasts, and found the courage to leap forward, gripping his sword tightly in one hand and a brand in the other.

So many had died. He couldn't see Rast. Snarls still came from where the Druid had fallen.

Leona.

۞   ۞

The healers waited, pale with fright, their long daggers and swords ready to stab into an eye socket if possible. The two wagons corralled the horses, with the fire at the other end. Stryke stood before them, snorting, his blood up, the other chargers stamping in fear and anger next to him.

Major Gambeson stood with the healers and sappers, determined to protect the wounded. His was the only weapon with any silver.

His heart bled for his brave soldiers, giving their lives against an unnatural enemy they could not easily harm. He looked for his other allies, spied Tal'Orien dancing impossibly alone with three of the monsters; caught glimpses of the elves sliding through the mess like quicksilver, weakening and aiding rather than attacking face-on; the enigmatic Green Warrior was throwing flaming brands to all and sundry, shouting encouragement to the soldiers as if he were their commander and smashing a huge flaming branch at any of the foes that came too near; and no-one could miss Darus, who had killed one of the creatures alone, and stood in their way like a green barrier, bellowing his challenge.

He shook his head.

What allies to have against such a foe!

He'd seen the Druid fall and was saddened. She had also taken one or two creatures down before her death.

A commotion nearby drew his attention. A werewolf smashed towards the wagons through several squads like a battering ram, ignoring them and intent on the healers. Perhaps it sensed wounded inside; perhaps it hungered to kill the horses. It was hard to remember that these were not mindless beasts; they were also men, able to think and plan and hate, and they were faster, stronger and more fearless than any others he had seen in his long career.

He heard Thorne calling for the breach to be closed; there were too many down. With admiration mixed with despair, he saw the boy, Karland, leap for the gap, along with several healers. He cursed and sprinted for them, knowing he would be too late.

470

The werewolf crouched mid-stride and leapt, sailing just over their heads onto the back of the cart. With a snarling laugh, it tore the canvas and wood aside and plunged in.

Karland stabbed desperately into the shapechanger's kidneys, producing a howl of agony. A healer slashed at the back of the leg, trying to hamstring it, and was rewarded by a lashing kick with claws that disembowelled him and sent him hurtling backwards to lie shivering in a pile of his own shredded guts, numb and bleeding.

The wolfman backed out of the cart, blood on its muzzle and a sword in its throat, choking and wheezing. It scrabbled, a bubbling whining snarl erupting, and was transfixed by several more. It whipped around, pulling them from hands, lashing out and knocking soldiers and healers back. One soldier turned to flee, and it slammed long claws into his back and wrenched so hard his spine snapped in its grasp.

How can we fight this?

A hatchet whirred through the night like a bird, thunking cleanly into its back. Another bounced painfully off its head as another sapper threw it. The attacks were an irritant, nothing more. He saw the evil head swing around to glare at Karland, who looked as white as a sheet, but stood firm.

'Eat this, you fuck!' roared a voice from the side. The werewolf's head snapped around.

The Green Warrior smashed a burning brand into its face with all his might. The werewolf jerked back in agony, its eyes damaged from the flame. The Green Warrior laughed like a maniac and thrust as it opened its maw to snarl. The snarl broke off in a yelping coughing bellow, and the werewolf blinked, choking. A healer took the opening and slammed the sharp edge of her sword hard on its snout, cutting a deep wound. It yelped and shook its head, and The Green Warrior jumped forward, dangerously close, and jammed the burning end into its left eye, his teeth bared.

Where blades were ineffective, fire hurt badly.

The werewolf went berserk, leaping back on all fours and flailing, shaking its head violently, yelping and snarling what almost sounded like curse words as it pawed at its face. Swords and daggers opened its flesh on all sides.

Haraldt Gambeson arrived, sword drawn, and dived through after a swipe, desperate to protect his Guard. The silver inlay on his sword was only worked halfway up the blade length, so he stabbed, sending the long, slightly curved blade up to the hilt into its side, and into what he hoped was its heart.

The effect was marked. The werewolf shrieked in true agony, stiffening. The edges of the wound steamed, seeming to shimmer, and it fell, coughing, its movements weakening by the second. It was a mortal blow; there was no slow healing as with the wolfsbane.

Swords thudded home into it as it lay dying, and it stopped moving, the yellow eyes glazing in death, losing some of their awful light. A mixture of blood and vomit trickled from its mouth.

'That's one out the fight!' shouted the female healer, triumphant. A sapper whooped, and Gambeson nodded at The Green Warrior and Karland.

Panting, Karland grinned at him, and he felt a swell of admiration for the lad. He looked around to gauge the state of the attack.

He saw Captain Aldine shoulder to shoulder with Isra's squad, facing three of the creatures which seemed to be fighting in concert. Two clawed at pike heads and pulled spears while behind them towered an immense werewolf, snarling taunts.

Gram was a prickly man, and a stickler for the rules, but he was one of the best formation fighters Gambeson knew, and despite his cynicism was a fair and reliable commander. Gambeson knew the troops joked about him, often insulting him when they thought they were not overheard, but they also trusted him and his authority. He got things done.

Right now he was living up to that trust, squarely between the two beastmen and calling encouragement between strikes.

Behind him, a Guard threw a brand, managing to send it flipping past the face of the furthest one. Both jumped at the sudden flame, and Isra sliced wickedly at her foe to the right, yelling to hold its attention. Given space, Aldine flicked his sword point at the other's eyes, and then sliced hard across its belly as it flinched, sweeping his sword across in a blur, the blade always moving and darting in tight, rhythmic patterns. His grin was likewise tight, teeth bared and shield fending off the scraping attacks. For another minute or two, he held his foe at bay, searching for a way to end the fight.

Then Isra slammed into his sword arm, stumbling to regain her balance as her foe smashed a paw through her defences into her right shoulder, claws tearing through the chain mail links as if they were wool. The creature fell on the Lieutenant, locking its other hand onto her face in a grip that would crush her skull. It didn't notice another Guard in time and howled in agony as she slammed her long dirk into its face. The point dug a furrow along its nose, and then guided itself into the left eye up to the hilt. The werewolf fell back clutching at the blade awash with wolfsbane driven deep into its brain. Isra clutched her saviour's shoulder to steady herself and smiled her battered thanks.

Everywhere heroics took place. Astonishingly, the veteran Guard were almost keeping the werewolves at bay. Squads were moving back together, slowly. Gambeson ran towards them, seeing something else move.

Both women's smiles vanished in horror at the yell from their left, followed by a scream of pain. Gambeson watched in despair, tens of feet away.

When Isra had been launched into Aldine's sword arm, it had knocked his aim and balance off. To his left, Sergeant Cowlin had joined them as another fell. Aldine's shield jolted him and his feet tangled.

With no time to recover his stance or get his sword in line, he tried to get his dipped shield up. Before him loomed the gigantic werewolf, faster than Gambeson could believe something so large could move. A massive-pawed hand slammed down onto the shield, nearly tearing it from the Sergeant's grasp. It would have done so had it not twisted the straps nastily into his forearm, preventing him from letting go. Another huge-clawed hand grabbed his right forearm just below the elbow, and as he strained against it in sudden terror the grip tightened with horrific power. His radius snapped under the pressure, and the bull-necked Cowlin yelled in pain, his forearm deforming.

Gambeson felt as if he were running in molasses. With Cowlin's arms yanked apart as far as they would go, the huge beast in front of him glared in rage and lifted him off the floor as easily as he would a small child. Cowlin was not a small man, yet he dangled easily in the grip. Even as Gambeson began shouting his name, the werewolf's head shot forward and its unnaturally long canines sank into the Sergeant's right shoulder, snapping his collarbone and ribs, and tearing deep into muscle. Cowlin screamed in agony. Its gleaming yellow eyes stared at them in hateful triumph over the shoulder as its teeth sank deeper, and then the giant werewolf dropped the Sergeant like a discarded haunch of meat and scythed a paw at Isra, the other hand up and ready for her.

Major Gambeson whipped his sword in as he arrived. The creature moved like a snake, avoiding the blow, and then lashed out in a hooking tear, connecting solidly with the left side of his chestplate up under his arm. Sharp claws shrieked off the metal, saving him from disembowelment, one gashing deep into his side. The edges of the plate bent, and the impact into his left side was sickening, cracking several ribs. He lost sword and helm, and flew sideways many feet, landing unmoving. He couldn't breathe, and his vision dimmed.

'It's killed the Major!' roared Thorne from somewhere nearby, rage in his voice, and a yell went up from the tired soldiers. Gambeson heard them furiously redouble their efforts, even as hearing faded.

Momentarily free, watching the healers guarding the wagon and nearby wounded, Karland panted, feeling drained. The Green Warrior was tense, next to him. Lëlylien had appeared from somewhere, her quiver empty, her two elegant Elvish daggers in her hands.

The sky was growing lighter, and the advantage of the flames was diminishing. Soon it would be daylight. Around them lay tens of dead and wounded Eordeland Guard.

He became aware of triumphant roars and awful snarls erupting from the direction of the werewolves which had barrelled into Leona, realised that it had been only minutes since she had been taken. He felt sick.

They must have been toying with her; there was a yelp that trailed off to the sound of furious snarls and what sounded like agonised bellows. After a moment the thrashing stopped.

That's it, then.

Feeling numb again, Karland saw Galnór slicing at an enemy, his sword flickering in a blur. An axe almost as large as he was scythed in from behind the werewolf he was fighting, and tore the head off its shoulders in one slice; it was not a clean hit, and ragged pieces of flesh and bone stuck out of the stump, but the head came off, and bounced away. Darus charged into view from the darkness; granted a brief reprieve, Karland turned to see Den Olli and Lieutenant Nirrah battling a huge roaring form thirty feet away, with Captain Aldine nowhere to be seen, but he hardly noticed; his attention was riveted on the sight of Kirri on the ground some distance away with blood on her pale face, another werewolf leaning over her with a taloned hand raised to eviscerate.

He could not get there in time.

A snarl of fury came from the side, and to his astonishment, a large golden form cannoned into the werewolf.

Leaning over, the beastman had little balance, and it went down heavily to the side of Kirri, who seemed too dazed to move. The two forms rolled and thrashed in blinding fury, the werewolf caught off guard.

Karland blinked incredulously. It was a *huge* wolf.

The golden wolf moved more like a great cat than anything, agile and powerful, easily a match for the werewolf in strength and speed. Both were snarling in hatred.

Kirri finally moved, scrambling slowly over to Darus as he ran up. Karland and the others joined him. They watched in astonishment as the other form rolled on top of the werewolf, its jaws clamped around the monster's throat. A gurgling growl came from the pinned creature just before the huge gold-furred wolf on top of it yanked its head up, tearing out a huge chunk.

The werewolf juddered, gurgling, the claws of one hand digging a deep furrow along the left flank of the wolf, showing immediate rib. Darus moved towards them with his axe half-lifted, unsure of where this other wolf had come from, and then slowed as the bleeding stopped. Slowly, the wound began closing. The wolf was still tearing at the throat of the monster, which was struggling less now, although any other creature would surely have been dead by this time. There was a crackle of bone; then the head rolled free, neck parting under those powerful crushing jaws. The wolf had literally torn its way through the huge neck.

It looked up at the three, its muzzle awash in blood to the eyes, and Karland wondered if it would attack; then it darted towards the howling werewolves surrounding Rast. Karland groped for answers. Didn't wolves usually travel in packs? Why was it here?

Darus roared and followed it, The Green Warrior close behind him. Karland was unsure if he meant to attack it or Rast's enemies.

'Are you ok?' he shouted at Kirri. She nodded, pointing to the nearby enemy. The largest of the chaotic creatures was trying to break out of the ring of Guard around it. Their weapons were having little effect. Karland cast around for any remaining leaves, wiped them thickly on his blade again, then broke for the battle in a run with his sword held behind him, as Rast had taught. Kirri picked up one of the last brands from the fire and staggered after him.

The monster was keeping the Guard at bay with swipes and lunges, and the speed of its healing suggested no one had wolfsbane left on their weapons.

Kirri smashed her torch across its face, and it whirled with a roar, then stopped and jerked roughly. The very tip of Karland's sword broke through the skin just under the left of its sternum; he had circled the battle, and, knowing he could not reach high enough to try and hew the neck, settled for trying to strike the heart.

Whipping around in agony, it backhanded him with a paw that hit him glancingly in the chest, its arm hitting his face like a tree trunk. Karland flew backwards, thankfully unconscious of the damage he had sustained, and landed in a heap.

∞

The sword, laced with fresh wolfsbane, had not quite clipped its heart, but the agony was such as the huge creature had never known in its long existence, even from the other wounds it had received. It could not reach the hilt to withdraw it, and it quickly found it had other problems as the remaining enemies rushed in, humans who shouted and roared as they slashed with flaming brands and stinging swords. It was in a slight state of shock; fifteen in the pack, they should have torn these foes apart. Instead, they had been poisoned, burned, pushed back. These humans had shown remarkable courage and skill. Many packmates had died!

They had not been prepared for elves and orks.

For a Druid.

There was no respect - only fury.

It crashed to the ground as it was hamstrung, and before it could recover, the flaming branch was smashed into its face over and over again, distracting and blinding it. The giant werewolf roared in defiance as it felt the first sword bite its neck, clawing wildly and not connecting, but the healing factor was slowed by the poisoned blood its heart was pumping, and it could not recover fast enough. Not far away two fellows were similarly treated, overwhelmed by these pathetic humans.

They would pay.

Its legs were healing, and it was pushing itself up again, shrugging off the blows, when a new blade arrived.

A sword wielded by a pale, staggering, determined man who could barely stand; one with beautiful inlaid artwork in a metal so pure its very body rejected it, with dire consequences. Even as it struggled, the sword sliced through its guts, cutting an unhealing, terrible wound. The huge werewolf shuddered, its body beginning to shut down from the shock of silver. It felt its throat close, and it shivered and burned, its body feeling like it was tearing itself apart.

It was almost a blessing when the burning blade joined the other swords to finish hacking its huge head from its neck. The evil yellow glare fixed on them in hatred as the huge mouth snapped impotently at the air.

The head, almost as large as a bear's, did not die for a long time.

છ   ૭

Rast tirelessly hacked and sliced in a dance with his blade. He hammered his foes with blows from the *shirka* held in the other hand, as well as his fists, elbows, the sword hilt, and his feet. His form, a match in size if not quite strength for his attackers, moved with speed and grace greater than the wolf creatures he fought.

He knew he was in a lot of trouble. Bruises slowed him. Blood trickled from several near misses. The abominations were healing too fast for him to finish one off. One of these foes he might defeat; two, he could not handle for long. But a third shapeshifter had joined his foes, and he was tiring.

The only oddity was their almost instinctive avoidance of strikes with his hands, as if they hurt more than they should. They seemed to take no lasting damage, but it was noticeable.

He used it.

It had been less than twenty minutes since the creatures had broken from the trees, but he knew his stamina would give out eventually. It was hard to hit them; their sinuous speed belied their bulk, and they fought brutally and instinctively. Already the blood on his weapons had washed away most of the wolfsbane and his strikes were becoming less effective, although the brutes had slowed, wary of being struck by his hands.

Rast fought, feeling the dance of the fight. He thought Karland still lived; hoped. He had heard Darus, and The Green Warrior. He had glimpsed Leona fall and had steeled his heart at the sudden despair.

Not her.

He pushed the thought away. Time had become static, fading into this world of pure focus where he moved and lived and fought, each piece another step in the dance he knew so well. He no longer knew if the others had prevailed or died. They might come to his aid, or he might feel the teeth and talons of more of the enemy.

Then something changed in the one facing him, a hesitation, as if it detected something amiss, and Rast struck again, slicing its throat, kicking it back, trying to create enough room to finish one of them. He looked up to see a huge golden wolf running flat out towards his battle, graceful and powerful, and he found a second to fervently hope it was not coming for him as he ducked a blow from his left.

Seconds later, the werewolf flared its nostrils and snapped around with a growl, only to fold over as the wolf hit it in the stomach like a bolt from a ballista. The ensuing roiling mass bowled off to the side, snarls and yelps coming from it as the combatants snapped in fury at each other.

Rast forced himself to put it out of his mind; he still had two opponents left. With room to manoeuvre, he went on the offensive, lunging and slashing incredibly quickly, the sword light in his powerful hands. As one mouth lunged in, he stabbed the sword straight through it, driving it hard through and out of the back of the throat and neck; he let go, knowing that it was firmly lodged, and concentrated on his other enemy. Choking in shock, the werewolf dropped away and grabbed at the hilt that was level with its front teeth. Shuddering, it began the agonising process of drawing the sharp edges back through its flesh.

The other monster grabbed at his shoulder but didn't get a firm grip. Rast slammed his *shirka* into its neck, shucked his shoulder down under the grab, feeling the talons score his flesh, and slid out to the side, dropping under the snap of the werewolf's maw. He caught himself on his hands before rolling smoothly to his back, pulling his knees to his chest and kicking up with all the force of his powerful body. The jaws snapped shut with the enormous force of his kick, severing the tongue cleanly halfway down and smashing teeth, skewing the jaw out of socket.

As the wolfman reared up, its mouth filled with sudden jetting blood, Rast flipped up onto his feet and slammed a hard kick at the crotch of the wolfman. Apparently, they kept many attributes from their parent races; his foot delved into the hairy tangle and connected with the werewolf's gonads hard enough to turn them to paste. As the werewolf dropped to its knees, all strength and focus robbed, Rast whirled behind it, kicking it in the back so it pitched forwards onto its face. He leapt on the broad back, hooking one arm under its armpit, his hand heating strangely where it held the creature. Rast used his powerful back and stomach muscles to provide the pull as he smashed his hard elbow, solid from years of striking and breaking, into the back of the creature's head, over and over again. Rast was nearly as big as the werewolf; he pounded the more delicate back of its head until the skull cracked and caved in. He grabbed the *shirka* and wrenched, slicing flesh that was trying to heal as fast as he sawed. Still he did not stop, knowing it would begin to heal immediately if he did.

A strange noise made him look up.

The other werewolf had managed to remove the sword, and flung it away angrily, the feeling of its throat healing horribly uncomfortable. It had barely managed to growl, the sound coming out as more of a squeak, before the sight of its packmate, defeated by an unarmed human and apparently being beaten to a pulp, brought it up short in incredulity. Rast leapt forward, ready.

Before it shook off its astonishment, an axe slammed deep into its back, cracking its spine and shattering one of its shoulderblades.

The werewolf pitched forwards, and Darus was on it, wrenching the axe from its back and casting it aside. A massive fist thundered into the creature's misshapen skull, and it rocked, dazed.

Darus grabbed the evil creature from behind and looped his forearms around its neck. His powerful arms trembling with the strain. The healing werewolf reached upwards, choking, and clawed at his arms with razor talons. Terrible gouges on his arms gushed hot blood, but Darus did not let go. One clawed hand slashed for his face, and he turned his head. His ear was sliced, but Rast saw him drop into the *baresark* of his people and summon all his reserves.

He bellowed, the veins standing out on his mighty neck, and wrenched his arms as hard as he could to the side. With a loud crack, his foe's neck broke. The mouth still snapped, but the body fell limp. Barely seconds later it began to twitch back to life, but Darus kept yanking side to side, and then grabbed the head in a terrible crushing grip, jerking and twisting it up and to the side. The head began to turn against the resistance of the thick neck; as more and more tissue tore, it turned further and more easily, blood seeping, then pouring out.

Darus grunted with exertion, and then roared in supreme effort and tore the head from the body with a wrench. Rast watched in amazement, as did The Green Warrior and other soldiers who arrived, weapons drawn. Darus hurled the head away in a spray of blood.

The ork stood, breathing heavily, hands shaking. He was losing a lot of blood from his forearms. If tendons had been severed, he might never hold an axe again. He stared at the ground before him, almost in a trance as he fought his way back out of the *baresark*. Blood streamed down his face. The back of his slightly pointed right ear was ragged and the side of his neck was profusely bleeding from another deep cut.

Rast turned, as his other foe rose again behind him, the snout smashed and bent from the impacts with the ground and covered in dirt. One, they could defeat, although now he was weaponless.

The werewolf ignored them all and roared in hatred, flinging itself sidelong at the golden wolf worrying at the sundered carcass of the one it had attacked and sinking its teeth into its neck. The wolf yelped and twisted, and they fell. There was no way to attack without injuring all of them, and no one wanted to go near the awful maelstrom of fur.

Rast spared him no more than a glance. The golden wolf was under the werewolf, with its stomach in the jaws of the hulking creature. It had crushed an arm to jelly in its jaws, but they could see it was in trouble; its guts glistened wetly through a rent in its abdomen in the slowly increasing light of dawn.

Despite the mortal wound, it was causing massive damage to its attacker.

It tore through the monster's belly in turn, and then as the evil beast hunched over in agony, fixed its long teeth into the neck and ground its jaws together, shaking its head powerfully. There was a snap, and teeth met. The body dropped from its jaws, unmoving.

It stood panting on trembling legs, licking its lips and staring around for other foes. Guts hung from it, one eye was torn and closed, and the fur was more red than golden.

A few seconds later the torn eye blinked slowly open again.

All of the werewolves were down, if not yet dead.

Miraculously, they had survived.

Wordlessly, Rast looked back to the last foe. Whatever this strange wolf had done, the werewolves it had killed were not healing.

A whine from the wolf brought his attention around. Darus grunted and breathed heavily through his nostrils, seeming to awaken. Rast held his hand up, unsure of the ork's intent.

He looked back to the wolf, which lowered itself on trembling legs. He gazed at its golden coat – seeming paler now, coated in drying blood - and its strange gold-green eyes, gazing at him sadly as dawn broke.

Eyes he knew so well.

He breathed out in disbelief.

'Leona?'

The wolf licked its chops, whined, and half-growled, half-yelped. Darus blinked, stepping backwards, and Rast moved slowly towards her, then stopped. Even as they watched, the terrible wounds were beginning to slowly close; the pallor was leaving and the tone returning.

He had thought her dead.

Leona.

'What are you?' he whispered, his eyes never leaving her. '*What are you?*'

THIRTY-FIVE

'*What the fuck? What the fuck?*' the Green Warrior roared in disbelief from behind Darus.

Rast simply stared. The huge wolf rose, painfully, and soldiers stepped back, lifting weapons. Aldine had arrived, along with squads led by Nirrah and Thorne. An all-too human glance at them by the animal made Rast's mind up.

'Lower your weapons,' he said softly.

Some did.

'*Now.*' His voice was harsh, brooking no disobedience. The rest followed, reluctantly.

He watched the last of the wounds close. The golden creature looked closely at the dead and dying werewolves and threw its head back to howl in triumph. The sound echoed off the trees.

The wolf with Leona's eyes looked at Rast and whined gently, turned, and padded for the nearest bushes. No one moved for a long moment.

Then Aldine, flushed, hands shaking, threw his sword on the grass. His eyes stared wildly, a man having seen too much he could not understand.

'What the *fuck* is going on?' he shouted. 'Those things went through us like a dose of fucking salts! And what the fuck was *that*?'

The nearest soldiers looked at each other, wordless, as more came up led by Thorne.

'Fall in,' he said tiredly. 'The Major wishes to speak to us.'

The Eordeland Guard looked around at that, their faces lighting up. Aldine looked up, breaking his stare at the ground, a drowning man thrown an unexpected lifeline.

'He's alive?'

They moved back to the wagons, Rast glancing back twice but seeing nothing. He and The Green Warrior gently urged Darus along, the Warrior carrying his axe. The big green ork stumbled along, dripping blood. His forearms were almost entirely red and urgently needed binding; Rast could see dark slimy muscle under the hot green skin, which looked pale.

The carnage was terrible. The creatures had shredded their way through the experienced guardsmen, leaving bodies and limbs scattered everywhere. The one that had reached the healer's wagon had killed two healers and one of the wounded from the battle in the Arkon foothills before Major Gambeson's silver inlaid blade had found it.

They stopped by the wagons, seeing bodies already being laid out, the horses calmed, the fire tended. Wounded were being set out, their cries and moans unending. In the distance squads were checking the fallen monsters warily.

Gambeson was being supported by a healer and another soldier on the edge of the wagon. He was terribly bruised, eyes unfocused with concussion. From the way he moved he must have at least several ribs broken.

Rast spoke softly to a healer. They were worried that he had internal bleeding, perhaps other injuries. Only his armour had prevented the werewolf's talons from punching straight through his body.

Slow to focus though his eyes were beneath his bandaged head, his voice was still soft, lending the stability they needed. At least his colour was returning. Gambeson looked hurt, but he was alive. From the faces of the men and women around him, Rast knew much had hinged on his survival.

The Major called out to them tiredly.

'Discussion can wait; there are wounded. Let the healers do what they can.' He turned to Aldine.

'Captain.' There was no response. '*Captain!*'

Aldine looked up, breathing shakily. Rast could see that he was still deeply disturbed - perhaps not just by the deaths of his soldiers, but the unnatural affront of the monsters that had killed so many. Everyone had been shaken by the nightmares made flesh. He realised the Captain had left his sword lying in the grass.

'Sir.'

'We need to set up a perimeter. Tal 'Orien-'

Darus interrupted the Major's words. He had been looking down at the deep wounds on his arms, still breathing heavily, his rage receding.

Now he bellowed, making everyone around him jump, then threw his head back and roared at the sky, hands in fists and arms curled out to the sides, his muscles bunched and tense with the effort. Bright red blood streamed down to drip from his elbows anew, hampering the efforts of Rast as he tried to bind them.

'*What?!*' demanded Aldine in a near-scream, his face red in fright and anger. Already on edge, he had jerked away at the sudden noise, his hand slapping to his empty scabbard. His eyes flicked around wildly; Rast wondered if his mind would snap.

Darus took his brother's axe from the astonished Green Warrior and shook it aloft.

'For you, *velki*,' he said softly, ignoring the Captain, his gaze somewhere in the sky. '*Grukust-a vah varsi.*'

'Darus?' queried Rast.

His companion seemed to awaken from a trance.

'No,' said the big ork, turning to him. Despite his wounds and exhaustion, his face was proud. '*Darkus.*'

ʕʘ   κο

The Major had issued more orders before being taken into the wagon. It was clear he was badly injured.

Bodies lay everywhere across the camp, some in many pieces. The slaughter was horrific. The claws and jaws of the twisted beastmen had torn through flesh and armour with uncounterable strength.

Rast moved to examine Karland and found the boy groggy and battered, with a new slice up one cheek that wasn't deep enough to scar and ribs that were only bruised. His nose was broken but would heal straight. He had been incredibly lucky.

The Green Warrior seemed unharmed, in some sort of charmed fashion, as did the elves. Darkus had lost blood from the deep claw-marks on his arms; those *would* scar, but they would be badges of pride. His ear would always be ragged, though, and a deep welt down his neck and the scoring on his back said he was lucky to live, too. Rast himself had bruises and shallow claw marks down his shoulder and arm, not as deep as Darkus's. He had also been supremely lucky.

That left one companion.

One he cared about… one he had thought lost.

He moved back past the bodies of the werewolves to the edge of the clearing where she had vanished and watched the undergrowth, unable to see much. A voice called out from the bushes a little further left after a minute. It was tired, but familiar.

'Could you bring me my robe?'

He moved back to the carts where Leona had vanished when the monsters had hit her, and found the two werewolves lying dead, torn apart with amazing force. Even now one of them had a hind leg twitching, constantly, refusing to believe it was dead, and another was halfway between beast and man, as if it had tried to change shape to escape its fate. In awful fascination he looked at its twisted form, the face mostly human with distended jaws and teeth set in a rictus of agony. Somehow she had torn its heart out, finding it within the form bulging with flesh and fur in unnatural places.

Her robe was badly torn and covered in blood. He picked it up and took it slowly to the bushes the wolf had moved into, wary, unsure what he expected to see.

Leona stood before him, partially hidden by underbrush, dirty, bloody, and very naked. She was scrubbing drying blood from her mouth and looked in desperate need of a long bath.

Rast looked away from her, feeling himself answering physically despite the circumstances. Something in her was wild, dangerous, and desirable in a way he had not known for a very long time.

'I think I need a new robe,' Leona said quietly, hugging it to her front.

He looked at her, uncertain.

She tried to smile and failed.

'Rast?'

'Leona. I…' He shook his head. 'What are you?'

She sighed, her face sad. 'Rast… I…'

He waited.

'I think perhaps I should speak to you all.' She shrugged her robe on, her back to him, and turned, pulling it tight and tying it. Ragged rents in the side showed flesh beneath unmarred by the talons that must have torn into it. 'The others may not understand. But you, my *Banidróttin*.' Her voice dropped to a whisper. 'My *Kérdrottin*. *You* matter. What do you think of me now?'

'I do not know.' He looked fully into her eyes, and with a chill like cold water realised why they were so familiar to him.

His mind drifted back to a time long gone; himself near death. A man. Wolves. His home.

His end. His beginning.

'You are… not human.'

'I am not wolf, either,' she responded. 'I am Druid. I am *varulfur*.'

He searched for something to say. He wanted to ask what that meant; to voice his anguish that something he had felt healing his being had been torn from him in a moment. He couldn't speak the words.

'Thank you,' he said at last instead. 'I was sorely pressed.'

She looked surprised at the change in subject, then her lips parted. 'I never doubted you against one,' she breathed. 'The only mortal I could say that of. But I could not leave you to your fate. Your nature… calls to me. I-' she blinked and looked away. 'I do not wish you to think ill of me.' Normally so certain, now she sounded unsure.

He was silent a moment, listening to the clamour and cries of the camp beyond the trees.

'I do not,' he said quietly, at last, realising it to be true. His emotions were in turmoil, but there was oddly no sense of anger or betrayal. There was only acceptance of what was. 'We all have our secrets.' He held out a Dragonblood-scarred hand. 'Come.'

Hesitantly, she took it, and they walked back to camp. Her hand was strong and cool in his.

People drew away nervously as she approached, and silence fell nearby against the cries of the wounded and movement of soldiers further back. Mutters came from each side. Several hefted weapons.

Major Gambeson was back on the edge of the healer's wagon, bandaged, Captain Aldine standing nearby. The Captain no longer appeared unhinged, his sword back in his scabbard, but he was still distraught as he spoke to Major Gambeson.

'Fifteen! Fifteen of those things killed five times- we, we lost over a third of the company. In minutes.' He looked lost for words. Orcs were one thing, but this was something else. 'Sir-' he shook his head. 'What's happening?' The plaintive appeal in his voice went beyond answers for one battle.

Major Gambeson had none. He exhaled tiredly, shaking his head. 'I've never seen the like, Gram,' he admitted quietly.

'It is a miracle you lost so few, Captain,' Leona said as they arrived.

'*Few!*' Aldine looked as if he would explode, eyes flashing, and Gambeson held up a tired hand.

'Gram. Please.'

'I grieve for the loss of your troops, but if your soldiers had been less skilled… if there had been no wolfsbane… if I had not been here… you would have *all* been slaughtered. It is a miracle any of us survived.'

Gambeson turned to Leona, his expression unreadable. 'I think you owe us an explanation, lady.'

Leona looked sad again. She sighed slightly. Rast noticed Karland sitting nearby, bruised face intent on the conversation. At least the blow had not dampened his curiosity. Behind him he could see The Green Warrior and the elves, Darkus looming behind them.

She gave a small, rueful laugh. 'Now enough mortals know, there is no resealing the mystery.' She looked around at them all, her green-gold eyes powerful. 'You are the first in living memory to know our secret. I am *varulfur*. A guardian of Nature. What you call a Druid.'

'You're like them creatures!' cried someone. Rast turned, his eyes gimlets, looking for the owner of the voice.

'No! No. Not like them.' She cast around for a moment, her mouth working. 'We… share similarities. But they are born of chaos, born to slaughter. We are part of nature. Part of this world. We protect it. From *anything* that threatens it.' A fierce light lit her eyes; the eyes of a predator. 'From *them* most of all. Without us, they would have swept away your civilisation thousands of years ago, killed every living thing in this land. You saw what barely fifteen did. We had wolfsbane, deadly to them; we were prepared. You are some of the finest fighters in your land, and yet so many of you died.

'Imagine an army of them. Hundreds. Thousands. Like a tidal wave. They would destroy every city, every land.' She sighed. 'They do not die. They do not feel fear or uncertainty. They will not stop. *Ever*. Until every living thing has been hunted and killed. Men, most of all.'

The listeners were silent.

'We have hunted them here for near a year. Thousands have been culled, but my people are dying too. We may not be enough. We have always been far fewer than they. More powerful, yes, but fewer. If there are enough of them, or they are lucky, we can fall.

'They spread like a disease. Even one left can restart the plague. Never before have so many arisen. And unlike them, Druids are born, not made. There may not be enough of us to stem this.'

'You mean… you're *all* these, wot, varelfer?' asked a brutish soldier, his face haggard with grief. He held a small silver ring, stained with blood, and turned it round and round in his thick fingers.

'Yes,' she said sadly. Rast saw that she knew of his loss.

The man dipped his head.

''er name was Alorin,' he said dully, tears in his voice. 'Fought together. Loved together. Lived the trail. Always knew it would end, but not like this. Not 'gainst… *things* we couldn't fight.' A shuddering breath heaved in and out. 'I 'ope you kill every last one of them fucken things,' he grated finally, and said nothing else, his face sunken in misery.

'Tell me more of these *varka*,' said Gambeson quietly, his face intent and pinched.

'They arose many thousands of years ago, a result of the Chaos that lashed Kuln. The same Chaos which warped Yosgaloth. It changed much on this world, and its effects are still being felt. Gar-wolves, werewolves, many unnatural things came to be. Vampires, too, it is said.'

'How?' asked The Green Warrior, fascinated.

'It is a full story for another time, Warrior. In the genesis of the *varka* it is said a human was twisted terribly by the chaos, mutated into something neither human nor animal that could shift between both but be fully neither. Its terribly damaged body refused to die, instead repairing itself from any wounds, any aging.

'It somehow seeded the beginnings of the werekin. Its child came to consciousness, vicious and powerful, and tore its way from its mother's belly after consuming many of its siblings in the womb. It was a brutal and unholy birth.'

'What happened to the father?'

'We do not know. Perhaps it met its end at a Dragon. We have heard nothing of it for thousands of years.'

'And you hunt them?' asked Rast.

'Always. They are our bitterest foe. No other creature goes against nature as they do, kills so lustfully, so wantonly, unless you consider the Ancient One. But Yosgaloth is an old god, uncaring and hungry.' Her voice held anger. '*Varka* are evil, hateful. They knowingly spread and destroy. The Druids will always fight those who do so. But there are so many more of them.' Her face looked worn for a moment. Rast felt his heart go out to her.

Perhaps she did understand him, with her unending battles and eternal duty. How long had she been fighting these horrors? Longer than he had lived?

'Enough,' said Gambeson tiredly, his face pale. 'Thank you, Leona.' He motioned Aldine closer. 'Captain. Ensure the troops know Leona is our ally. We cannot afford to lose more to *mistakes*.'

'A wise decision,' agreed Rast.

Aldine nodded and looked at Leona. Rast expected him to glare, but the man looked more lost than anything else. The sense of neat order in the world had gone for him, and he could only react mechanically.

'Tidy the camp and make ready to move at dawn,' said Gambeson, coughing slightly, his lips red-flecked. 'I want every soldier remaining to reach Eyotsburg alive.'

Rast hoped the Major would be counted in that number. A healer helped Gambeson back into the wagon.

He turned and found Leona waiting. Everyone else was moving off; Karland was beckoned into the healer's wagon. They were - as much as they could be, in a camp full of soldiers - alone.

'You, at least, do not look at me differently,' she said, her glorious eyes boring into his. Hope and trepidation weaved through her voice.

He half-shook his head.

'You are still Leona. You have a duty. You sacrifice yourself to it. That, I understand.'

'I know you do,' she said, closer to him. The smell of her filled his nostrils, mixed with blood, and he traced the line of her strong, lovely brow with his eyes, from her nose to her temple. 'I could not tell you before how much I understood of your struggles, *Kérdrottin*. How I... share them.'

He smiled, his hands falling to her strong upper arms and resting there. However confused he was at who, at *what* she was, the connection between them was - if anything - even more intense.

'You called me that before. What does it mean?'

'You are Lord of many things, Rast Tal'Orien. Of yourself. Of dealing death. Of duty.' Her voice dropped and she looked aside for a second, her voice a whisper. 'Of my heart.'

He became aware of his own heartbeat then, a solid, slow, powerful beat, and could feel her own in her veins answering through his fingertips. The dragonblood-scarred flesh seemed hot over his bones.

Suddenly it didn't matter if this Druid was also a wild creature; she was a woman - beautiful, proud, and powerful. His match; his reflection. The doorway in the *Talanthese* took shape in his mind, the choice he had made recalled, and he allowed himself a glimmer of a long-forgotten hope.

He was not the only one to have domain over another's heart.

Her lips parted, and he focused on them, unable to forget their taste. Her voice was like honeyed wine, breathy and low. She looked up at him through long lashes, her eyes holding him still.

'Walk with me tonight. In the dark.'

THIRTY-SIX

Xhera thought back to the green-rough days of the farm often - like today, a grey day where everything felt sodden and damp from rain the night before.

She often found herself experiencing things in an oddly tactile way, as though situations or events had a *feel* to them outside just the visual, and she liked to consider it when she noticed. She hadn't ever met anyone else who felt quite the same - apart from Karland, who felt it even more deeply, and also shared her vivid memory for sight and sound. It was almost as if they experienced something *extra* sometimes. Even reading books came to her in two forms: the recall of the text and how it twisted in her mind, but also a feeling of pages gathered between each finger, many of them, taking her focus. Sometimes earlier in life it had been almost a compulsion to feel them; it drew her attention from their meaning and took her being over to the feel and texture of the pages. Sometimes it felt so weird she could not break away from the feeling, and would fit pages between fingers, squeezing and caressing and stopping because it was too much, then doing it again. Often at these times she would also lose the meaning of words and repeat them over and over, hoping they would once more make sense.

She sighed. The compulsion had lessened as she grew older, had matured into more of this texture of things, where memories *felt* alongside looked. She had enquired in The Sanctum about it and had a lot of information on compulsive behaviour back, but it wasn't quite the same. It wasn't intrusive so much as a different level of experience.

At times, she missed her family. They had never understood her and how she thought, the sometimes overbearing but always deep, almost frantic love of her older sister like a half-moon pressure on her left, Talas's concerned face and furrowed brow from trying to focus her close vision firm in her memory. Despite the vertical crease in her forehead, she was still an attractive woman, and like Xhera was serious, except where her husband was concerned. His gentle rustic demeanour and undemanding love brought out her hidden peace, and she laughed often with him.

Hendal and Martha were an overlay of coarse weave, strong and dependable, the closest to parents she knew. She missed all of them with something like a deep itch near the outside of her chest.

Her free time spent learning and peaceful seemed to have a green, smooth, almost leaflike quiet; her kidnap and near-rape had a texture of distance from other people, tinged with brown-red, scented with dark cold earth to the sounds of her own faint screams. That had faded, with support and time, but it was still there. She shivered, and turned her mind to other thoughts, to how she learned.

Karland devoured books far more quickly and had greater recall for the minutiae. She absorbed them more slowly, made them more part of her. For him they were reference, stepping-stones to more knowledge. To her, they *were* the knowledge.

Coming to The Sanctum - despite, or perhaps because of, the terrible, incredible, sorrowful means of getting there - had given her a sense of belonging for the first time in her life. Home still felt like the land around Hoeven Lake, but the peace there now felt almost oppressive, like a block to living.

Home also, she had to admit, felt like wherever Karland was. Rast gave off the feeling of stone made flesh, soft rock. Aldwyn had oddly felt like a library of books to her; messy ones, with random notes in the margins that all somehow made sense. The old feeling of pages between her fingers had been recalled around him, but not negatively. She shook her head, a feeling of sadness welling up.

Grukust, well. He had felt like clear spring waterfalls and rapids dammed over warm green ice, solid beneath fingers, tumbling and chaotic bursts with odd moments of peace. She knew no one else would have described him thus. His brother, less well known, felt similar, but calmer, smoother, a placid, deep pool.

She badly missed Grukust and his hidden gentleness. For all his brutish demeanour, and the stories of orks, he had been her friend. He had had a form of innocence about him, a purity untouched by the intricacies of society, and he had sacrificed himself without hesitation to protect them. She would have given anything to see him again.

But Karland, well. Strangely there was no texture to him for her. He felt like… the other half of herself. Above all others, he was her match. Her friend, her soul. He always thought she was so calm, so serious, but deep down she held a dread that one day he would leave her, as Aldwyn had. As Grukust had.

As her real parents had.

The one thing that loomed larger in her thoughts than anything was the hidden fear she would lose Karland the same way.

She had always had a quiet tendency to macabre thoughts, and briskly drew a breath, putting them behind her.

Karland would come back soon, and then… perhaps an unspoken thing might become spoken. They had survived not only impossible odds, but had seen marvels and been privy to things that, in stories at least, were only reserved for the great. Rast was the perfect hero for the events happening around them, but she and Karland had also been caught up in them.

There was something about Karland, too. His distance, his loneliness, twin to her own, it all spoke to her, but there was something more. Clearly Aldwyn had suspected something else about him.

'Night? Do you think there is anything… important about Karland?'

Night levelled his gaze at her. She shivered involuntarily.

'Why?'

'It just seems that Aldwyn was watching him carefully. I think.'

'If Aldwyn showed special interest in someone, then it would be wise to assume there was good reason for it. Someone very much like Karland. Someone unique.' His gaze held hers a moment.

'I *know* he was,' said Xhera. 'I think Karland has to do something… or make a decision. There are a few texts, but look-' she gestured to a sheet of paper showing cross references and circled thoughts, 'it's even in the Book of Sarthos.'

'That is telling,' admitted Night. 'I've been around long enough to see many of his predictions come true. Men say he was touched by the Greater God Kwor, and the touch drove him mad.'

'I'm worried for Karland, Night,' said Xhera. 'He always seems to end up in the middle of things. And he *is* unusual.'

'I know, Xhera.'

'Not all of Aldwyn's work was viewed by them, but I wonder if the Council certainly are starting to wonder too. Perhaps he will help the Darostim and bring new understanding. Maybe I should tell them.'

Night was quiet a moment.

'I would do nothing hasty,' he said finally. 'You may have the idea that your Universalia Communia - and especially the Darostim - is made up of kindly old men, which assuredly Aldwyn was. Indeed, many who are purely in the pursuit of knowledge are members, Xhera. But they do not randomly seek technology, knowledge, breakthroughs through altruism. Do you think that over the last several thousand years, men have not found many dangerous things? Other uses for black powder used in mining, more destructive uses? Applications for steam, for automation, perhaps. New materials, new machines of war? All of these and more are prey to the creativity of men. The Darostim actively seek these things, yes, but not always to share them. Sometimes they destroy them.'

'Destroy knowledge?'

Night shrugged at her horrified look. 'They take the information, the making, and erase any knowledge - sometimes including killing those who knew. Who would suspect an old scholar of such things?'

'Aldwyn was no murderer,' Xhera said angrily.

'I am not saying Aldwyn did this himself, Xhera. I am saying that his cause was not only to seek knowledge and share it, but to hide it, for the good of the world of men. The Darostim have acted as a brake on certain learning, allowing only that which they deem, in their arrogance - if often correctly - to be safe enough. They have many more members than old scholars who travel… and learn. Those are just the eyes and ears. Not even the Council knows the extent of their reach.'

Xhera didn't know what to say. She knew there had been a network of these secretive scholars, but what Night was describing was more like a secret society of implacable and dangerous people.

'The knowledge they take is held in the Combic Libraries, in forbidden sections, against the day men have need of it without destroying themselves or others. I have seen it. The Combics are split into multiple levels, not just one. The deeper you go the more forbidden the knowledge.

'Did you know that there is a country in Matalaga that has myths of people who live in clouds? Korin is a medium-sized country there, though it would cover much of Anaria. It has a capable army, and a king who is neither great nor evil. They were conquered by Kharkis, split off again when the Empire fell. Over the years they have resisted all further attempts to be reabsorbed by the ebb and flow of the Kharkistani Empire, which is now more or less even with the Banistari Empire. But they were almost invaded themselves by the Korinians. They were one of only a handful of human races to ever discover the secrets of flight, you see, merely a few hundred years ago. They had great balloons, dirigibles they called them. They filled them with light gases that rise from volcanos and flew them high enough for enemy arrows not to reach with fire or tip. They dropped rocks and explosives. They could scout further in safety than their rivals. They had become quite warlike; I think they would have overrun the continent, in time. The other countries could not easily fight a foe with this advantage.

'The Universalia Communia had agents who infiltrated Korin. Some of the knowledge of Korin was even brought from Darost in trade, to gain their trust. Once these agents had infiltrated, and they saw the danger presented, they destroyed all evidence. The Darostim among them took the information to keep it safe, and the Universalia Communia did not know; there are sections of the Combics that are hidden to all but Darostim. The University believed the knowledge destroyed.

'The blueprints were stolen. The enemies were told it was a trick, an illusion. And the ones involved were murdered. That is the cost of knowing these things; you must take the decision to protect it. Hard choices have been made. I pity any who become special enough to warrant their keen interest.'

'You're saying The Sanctum - the Darostim - are founded on blood!'

'It is founded on learning, Xhera. But it is controlled by those who limit humanity for its own sake - from time to time. The travelling scholars are mostly scholars who love teaching. Some are also Universalia Communia, fully Papered. Some of those are Darostim, and a very few of those are assassins, spies, killers. Do not be so naïve as to think Eordeland a place of purity. They are as humanly corrupt as any country.'

'You make them sound evil,' Xhera said, upset.

Night shook his head.

'No. They are fairer than most realms. It is a delicate balancing act. Eordeland nurtures knowledge carefully. Realms of men have brought themselves to - and on occasion past - the brink of extinction by their actions, in the name of greed and short-term power. It may seem arrogant, even cruel, but Eordeland has kept balance within Anaria - and the rest of Kuln - for millennia. They make mistakes; they are only human. But still, their intentions are good, and guided unknowing by the Darostim. We in turn keep *them* in check. *We* are watched by races such as the elves. So it goes. There is balance.'

Xhera shook her head. 'You're telling me the centre of learning in the whole world is built for assassins and spies.'

'I know this is hard to believe, my friend. But nowhere in the realms of men is free of these politics. Eordeland has, I think, good intentions. The Seekers watch them carefully. I have even helped them in the past. But do not assume that they will not do what it takes to keep secrets of men hidden. I can recall twice that they have taken the knowledge of steam-driven engines from other realms, fearing that men would turn them from progress to war. And they are right. Even the legends hardly remain, but once men use horseless carriages to kill.'

'You approve of what they do?'

'I acknowledge its necessity.'

'So what do you do then, if you are not one of them anymore?'

'I answer to my own conscience, and the code of my Order. And those are heavier than you know.' Night sighed softly. 'Don't misunderstand me, Xhera. Eordeland is old, powerful, advanced. It is also a fair and equal place to live, more so than most realms. But just because there is some shine to it, do not believe the base nature of men is changed. If ever a Council came to power that cared more for money and power than the land - and the older a political system, the more likely that is to eventually happen - things would change. It is the nature of men.'

The words echoed in her head long after he had left.

The nature of men.

ʘ   ს

The company buried their dead the next morning, bitterly and with a certain degree of shock in the faces of the survivors. Less than eighty were left able to fight.

Twenty-six more were added to the other five remaining seriously wounded, most needing the healer's wagon to keep up, though most had wounds of a sort. Too many had died of their awful wounds - and continued to die. Their foe had possessed such power that serious wounds had proved largely fatal.

Sergeant Spooner had lost an arm below the elbow. His shield had been ripped from him so hard it had torn it off. Even as it happened, he stabbed, bellowing in fury. Only the quick actions of a nearby healer with a binding had saved him. He had been lucky to live. Most others injured so badly had not.

Almost every squad had lost someone. Pikes and close infantry had lost the most. The sappers had lost three; the healers had lost two. Three lieutenants had died with their platoons, only Isra and Nirrah surviving. Miraculously, many Crosses and archers had lived, with seven pathfinders; they had tried to calm the horses as they used their formidable recurves. One had been trampled and was bruised but alive.

Seventy-nine had died at the claws and teeth of the werewolves in addition to the thirty-three lost to the Novinians. The Guard were numb, veterans or no; nothing they had ever experienced had prepared them for something like this.

The abominations they burned. Some were still, somehow, alive, and burbled or even screamed in rage and pain, half-words slobbering as they charred to unhealing meat. The sound and smell was awful.

The greatest worry for Rast was Sergeant Cowlin. The solid man had been terribly injured by the giant werewolf, but not fatally, and it had been from a deliberate bite.

He was still breathing raggedly with a high fever, and his eyes were bright in a white face as he moaned and writhed. His right arm had no use, and the terrible, ragged gashes on his back, front, and neck were not healing well.

Leona was moving through the wounded, as she had been through the camp, almost questing. So far, she had ignored everyone, but when she saw his wounds, her nostrils flaring, her expression changed. She moved in, a grimmer expression on her face. Rast stepped in front of her at the look.

'No,' he said, quietly.

'You do not know what you ask,' she said. Her voice was colder than usual. 'If he does not die from the bite, he may begin to Change. Sparing him that is a kindness, Rast.'

'We can try to help. There are healers in Eyotsburg-'

'There is no cure,' interrupted Leona. 'If he is infected - and lives - he will join the scourge. His mind will be damaged. The urge to kill and hunt will drive him to terrible acts. You must kill him immediately.'

'And what if he survives and is not infected?'

'That is unlikely.'

'Yet possible. You said so yourself.'

She looked at him a long moment. 'Rast, if he comes to change in a city, he will cause terror and destruction the like of which they will have never seen before. You chance the lives of thousands.'

Rast nodded. 'Gambeson will not allow the killing of his man. I will take responsibility. We will not be caught unawares.'

Leona smiled without humour at his self-assurance. 'You are the only human I would trust to say that with certitude, but you sail for the elves.' She sighed. 'It is not the silver moon you must watch for. When Xoth rises full again, be wary. The influence of Chaos will call to him to Change. If you fail, you doom many to horrific death. And the Druids will still find him, in the end.'

'We will keep watch.'

'See that you do.' Her hand rose, gently, and brushed his rugged cheek, and then she was gone, searching for others.

They moved on at midday, slowly and cautiously. Leona led them northwest towards the closest village with sufficiently large vessels. They camped early that night, wary, but nothing approached. The elves, Rast and Leona prowled the darkness, and Darkus took two watches beyond the firelight, scanning the surrounds with his huge dark eyes.

It was strange to think of him as Darkus now, but not once had someone accidentally used his old name. It just... didn't fit him anymore.

Leona believed that the pack had been a lone one that had bypassed her people. Her foe was cunning, and knew they were being hunted and destroyed. It troubled her; if one pack had escaped so easily, more might have, and they had been heading east. How many might have slipped through the net? The Druids would have to track them, soon.

The camp was subdued. Moans and cries from the injured carried on the air. The veterans were still coming to terms with a near-defeat at the hands of nightmares out of legend. There was little cheer, and great apprehension. Few people slept well.

Five of the horses had hurt themselves in the uproar of the battle, banging into the corralling wagons and rubbing legs raw on hasty hobbles. A huge draft horse had burned itself in the fire and had to be put down. Most of the injured were the hobbies. One had strained a leg in the hobbles after nearly falling. That one would be lamed, possibly forever. The only reason that more hadn't been hurt was how tightly they had been packed together, and the presence of the warhorses, especially Stryke. Only the concerted efforts of the pathfinder's wolfsbane-laced arrows had dissuaded the monsters from the panicked horses.

Two who seemed relatively unaffected by the carnage of the day before were Darkus and The Green Warrior. They seemed to get on very well, spending much time discussing the best techniques to damage opponents, The Green Warrior demonstrating disabling moves and Darkus slowly showing him axe strikes. He could still grip his axe, painfully; he would recover.

The huge ork and the mercurial man were actually a boon. Where Rast was spoken of in awed tones, as if he were not mortal - what man could face three of the monsters in the darkness alone, and live? - the ork's prowess was lauded, the company aware that his axe was one of the reasons they had survived. His bound arms were healing more quickly than the soldiers' wounds, and he was proud of them.

The Green Warrior, on the other hand, lent the soldiers a charismatic vivacity they sorely needed. Without the presence of Major Gambeson, Aldine was too stiff to give heart to the squads, but The Green Warrior was as irreverent and loud as ever. Slowly a sense of normality crept in wherever he roved. He teased, laughed, questioned, waved aside the negatives. Slowly, he brought heart back to the men and women around him.

They camped again that night. Despite their care, another two soldiers died and were buried at sundown. The company lined up in ranks and presented arms for a count of one hundred from Thorne for all those that had died.

In the morning they packed up again, and moved on, weaving the wagons down narrow trails as gently as possible for the wounded in the healer's one. Hjarta pulled next to a horse nearly twice his size, the little dray taking more steps but living up to his name.

Leona led them unerringly along the paths, and they finally arrived at a village with a large mooring and many vessels.

The estuarine dock was part of a village with fishing boats, two of the large red-sailed barges common to the estuary, and several large rowboats. The people were hardworking and worried, no doubt having heard some of the commotion two nights before. The appearance of a large party of armed soldiers nearly sent them to their boats before they saw Leona and relaxed. Clearly they knew Druids.

Once she had vouched for them, Major Gambeson spoke to the headman directly. His quiet manner did much to allay their fears, and he paid fairly and without bargaining. Eordeland currency was accepted in most places on the plains, and the wagons and horses drawing them could not go to Eyotsburg with them. There was only room for his destrier on board.

'What about your horses?' he asked Rast.

The big man shrugged.

'They won't fit here, but I am not selling them either. Leona said she would take them back to Darost.'

'Could she take Aldine and Thorne's horses too?'

As it turned out, she could.

The headman was pleased with the rest; they would be very useful to them and didn't seem to mind that quite a few were injured; eight well-bred horses were a princely sum the likes of which they would rarely see again.

One of the barges was chartered to take everyone upriver. They were strange looking boats, with large sails on two masts for easy tacking, rowlocks and wide-ended oars to help manoeuvre, and wide, deep bodies that flared outwards, fifteen feet across the beam and fifty long. The boats were designed to move in relatively shallow water near the edges of the wide waterway and take large quantities of wood, fish or grain into the city. By nature of being a citadel on a spire of rock, production of their own food and materials was limited.

It would not be comfortable, but they would be able to get the whole company in the hold and on deck. A day's travel would see them at the large docks at the base of Eyotsburg.

As the company began transferring the supplies and wounded to the barge, Karland realised that his time as part of it was coming to an end. Kirri, Den Olli, Isra, Nirrah, all the people he had come to like and admire would be staying in the citadel; he, Rast, and the elves would take ship for Mithtol. He didn't know what Darkus or The Green Warrior would do. The pair seemed to get on well; perhaps they would travel together for a while until the others returned. Darkus had achieved his name quest, and there was no help for The Green Warrior on the islands of the elves.

He felt sad. It was like the ending of another era, one which had seen terrible bloodshed and horror, but had also seen companionship and bonding. Once again he was experiencing a feeling of disconnection. The Guard company belonged together. But people like himself - and Rast, The Green Warrior, perhaps even Darkus - never seemed to truly belong to anything.

He moved over to where Rast was talking softly to Leona. They were standing very close together, ignoring what was going on around them. Karland slowed as he approached; there was a bubble of intimacy around them that he didn't want to pierce with his presence.

Leona turned, as if she sensed him. She probably did, he thought. Did she detect scent as intensely as a wolf did? Hear as acutely? He wondered how far a Druid's powers went.

Leona beckoned him over with a small smile. Karland smiled back at the beautiful, wild woman and moved closer, seeing Darkus and The Green Warrior approaching from the right, talking intently.

He wondered how much animal was in her. Did she eat meat raw? Could she use other powers as a wolf? And… why did Rast stand so protectively by her?

He moved down ahead of the others and stood just back from the bank, wary of what might lie within. He had heard of the great predatory fish twice his length, and cold-water leeches half a foot long that could paralyse if they bit long enough. Aldwyn had told him of shoals of small fish with teeth which could strip carcasses to the bone, considered a delicacy in Eyotsburg, as well as large turtles twenty feet or more long which journeyed from the Saosea to lay eggs in the mud, large groups of fat placid creatures that browsed the weeds, and many more. But he did not look for these now.

Instead, he gazed across the vast river at the natural curtain of dim rock and snow which hid the architect of much of their woe.

Meyar.

There lay the heartland of the people who had, ultimately, killed everyone he had cared about and lost, and now threatened to invade his land.

Meyari called the river the Relden. It was nearly five miles across at this point, and the snow-topped boundary of the Soltsvar mountains loomed on the far shore. The weather here was warm, but further west the cold major currents from the north brought bitter cold all the way down the western edge of the continent, except where the warm waters of the estuary exited.

Here there were no islands, and Karland marvelled at the size of the greatest river on the continent. Darost spanned the Eaofer, which had seemed wide, and Karland had seen on maps how much wider the river became as it deepened into the Tamis to cut east across Eordeland, but this was something else. He had to remind himself that this was at a narrow point, too; almost seventy miles upriver lay the rocky spire of Eyotsburg, itself in a canyon around two miles across. The mouth of the great river before him lay five hundred miles west, ten times the width it was here.

Despite his sadness, his feeling of once again being cut loose, he couldn't wait to see it with his own eyes.

The skipper of the *Drollfinne*, Jenda, greeted them and set his crew to oversee loading. With only three crew it was better to direct the company to place their equipment. It was lucky that they had stopped here; he was on his way back up from the coast, having delivered his cargo, and the barge was - apart from a pungent fishy smell - empty. The red-sailed barges were excellent close-shore sailing craft and could stop almost anywhere. 'We leave on incoming tide,' he said. 'Slows the flow. Makes it easier to move up'ard. Hereabouts, anyway.'

'Tide? We're hundreds of miles inland,' The Green Warrior objected.

The boatman smiled. 'This'n estuary river, serr. Waters can salt-in more'n two hundred mile on season and tide. Level rises by more than the height of a man twice a day at the city. Seen it go five times that in mid-river. Tis a shame you are too early for the *Vral.* We'd make it there in half the time, if we weren't dashed on the rocks.' He chuckled as if either suited him.

'*Vral?*'

'Means 'roar' in old Eyoti, mor'r less. When yon silver moon *Newa* is full or new we have her, and a great swell rolls upriver all the way to the citadel, with a grumble, so she does. It can be dangerous, but if a captain knows the flow, helpful.' He chuckled. 'But when green *Karni* joins *Newa* in the same part of the sky at equinox, we stay off the river, for then she int a swell but a roaring wave more'n fifteen feet high. *Bravral,* she is. Then she tears boat and house away with her to near the city herself.'

The Green Warrior bobbed his head side to side with a characteristic half-moue which Karland had come to recognise as semi-agreement, or mulling over.

'But how do you sail against the current?' asked Karland, curious.

'You gets the west stiff in sails, or tacks upwind on east, young serr. If that don't work you drop anchor or put in till it's blowin' fair, or you rows, if you can.' He waved at the stowed oars that the barges were lined with. 'Slower goin', though. Trips out from Eyotsburg take mebbe six days, easy with the current over that side.' He pointed out to the deeper water miles distant near the mountains. 'Can take three times that to come upstream, dependin'. And then you got the fun when you draw nigh the 'Berg.'

'Fun?'

'The wider the river the slower she flow, young serr. Closer you get to Eyotsburg, narrower she is, see? Water fast and strong on each bank then, though round the 'Berg they's deep. We'll hafta move inta the centre. Stream-shadow cast by the 'Berg, see. Edges are right perfect for ships leavin' though.'

Aldine set Thorne and the Lieutenants to direct loading by squad. One of the first to go aboard was the Major, with the other critically wounded. The healers put them on deck rather than the hold, rigging the healer's tent near the prow.

Karland caught a glimpse as they carefully moved him on board. Major Gambeson was paler than ever, a sheen of sweat covering his brow. The healers were clearly worried. Karland prayed that he would hold on until Eyotsburg.

He remembered entering the wagon two nights before to have his face and chest seen to. The glancing blow had stunned him but done no permanent damage. Although his nose had broken, it was straight and had not swelled too much. He wasn't sure how he had survived where so many professional soldiers had died.

The Major had smiled at him weakly and said, 'For someone who tries to avoid trouble, you certainly stick at the middle of it, lad.'

Karland had laughed, painfully, his voice slightly nasal. 'That's true, Sir.' Seeking to change the subject, he had asked something that he had long been curious about.

'Sir? May I ask a personal question?'

Major Gambeson had smiled in genuine amusement. 'You may ask, Karland. I do not promise to answer.'

'I was just wondering about your name. Did your family make armour?'

The Major had laughed then, quietly, and then sputtered in pain, before smiling and relaxing. 'Ah, lad. Of all the questions, you ask the one most people would never consider.' He had shifted, awkwardly.

'My name isn't related to armour. My family bred horses; some of the fastest. They were Nassingfolk, once. Their horse's value was in their legs, *gambe* in the old tongue. Eventually my family took the name, and one day one was called Gambe's Son. I believe there are still distant relatives of the Gambe family amongst the Nassingfolk.' His voice lapsed. The words had tired him, and Karland left him to sleep.

'It is his spleen, I think,' one of the four surviving healers had said quietly afterward, as she checked his wounds. 'It is likely ruptured and slowly bleeding his lifeblood into his body cavity. We cannot repair this here. We need a Gifted healer, in Eyotsburg.' She drew him closer. 'Tell no-one, my friend. I tell you only because you are Council-sent. Master Tal'Orien should know, but no one else.'

'Understood,' Karland had said, his heart plummeting.

Today he looked much worse. Karland honestly didn't know if he would reach the citadel.

He watched them all boarding, knowing this was the end of his journey with these people - and once more a goodbye to the Druid.

He felt he understood her much better now.

Leona stood to the side of the wide gangplank. The others had mostly said their goodbyes; The Green Warrior had smiled gently at her, surprising Karland. The elves had bowed deeply. Karland had not worked out if they had always known her secret. Darkus had thumped his chest, very gently due to the thick bandages on his arms, and she had smiled and placed her hand on his smooth cheek, resting a thumb along one thick tusk.

'May your strength never fade, Darkus *Varka*-bane,' she had said gravely. Darkus had nodded, accepting the name.

The Major had smiled wanly and thanked her and her people for their service, loudly enough that many of the Guard had heard. Ever the politician, he clearly wanted them to understand why the Druids were their allies, even as he lay with his life slowly waning.

It seemed to have made an impression. Even Aldine was respectful, and many of the company bade her farewell, aware she had saved them all. Thorne had called a salute to her and her fellows, and every soldier able had snapped a closed fist to under their throat. Karland could see she was deeply touched.

Finally, almost everyone had boarded, leaving the horses and wagons being taken away.

The only exceptions, of course, were the officer's horses, Stryke and Hjarta - and the mare they had picked up. She refused to leave Stryke's side, rolling her eyes dangerously, and Lëlylien was reluctant to allow her to be forced. Leona had smiled when she had found out.

'She trusts him,' was all she would say.

'You will take them back to The Croft?' asked Rast.

Leona nodded. 'They will do as I request. Even if you could take them upriver, when you take ship to the west they will be left again in stables, unknown hands around them. It will be better to take them where they will be known, and it is familiar for them. They have had a traumatic year.' She smiled. 'Anyway, I must travel to Darost with some of my brethren. I told you we warn all major cities of this threat. It should be contained, but as you have seen, it is hard to do so fully. I worry others slipped through the net, and about the rumours south. Men must know the signs.'

She turned to Karland. 'Farewell again, young human,' she said warmly. 'A friend to Druids and a foe of *varka* now as well as orc-bane and Dragonfriend. You faced them with honour, despite your fear.' She looked at Rast. 'He's not a usual cub, is her?'

'That he is not,' replied Rast with a faint smile.

'Take care, Karland.' She kissed him on the cheek, her wild scent filling his nostrils, and he felt a deep, primal longing for a moment.

'Goodbye, Leona.' He smiled, emotions warring within him. 'Look after yourself. Good luck against those *varka*.'

She returned the smile and nodded.

As he boarded, his curiosity won out. He moved to the side and dropped down, turning and peeking out, near enough to hear everything.

Technically it wasn't eavesdropping, he said to himself.

Leona and Rast stood together, alone. With a faint sigh which came from her human side, she reached out and took his blood-scarred hands.

'They are always so hot,' she said wonderingly. 'In spirit as well as flesh. From the blood of the Dragon? No wonder our foe shrank from them. They would have felt its fire.' She was quiet for a long moment.

'Such a short time together, *Kérdrottin*,' she murmured at last. 'That duty should come between us again is bittersweet... until we see one other again.'

Karland strained to hear the reply.

'I will count the moments until we do. You... bring meaning to me, said Rast quietly. 'You fill the empty void within. Take care, Leona. Until we meet again.'

Leona smiled. 'We are more than just duty, my heart.' She leaned forward. Rast bent down, and their lips met, hidden by the fall of her hair.

Finally, they drew apart, reluctantly. Karland felt strange as he saw this hitherto unseen side of Rast.

'I will find you. You cannot hide your trail from me, *Kérdrottin*.'

'Are you so sure you should follow it?'

'Wolves mate for life, Rast Tal'Orien.' She smiled simply. 'So do Druids.'

'You know my... responsibilities,' said Rast. 'But after this is over... when duty is done...'

Leona nodded. 'A Druid does not take such words lightly.'

Karland left then, feeling a little dirty. His suspicions had been verified, but the moment had been so strongly intimate that it simply felt wrong to listen.

Nonetheless, it gladdened him that they had both found something they had been missing within each other.

There *was* more to life than duty.

THIRTY-SEVEN

The Storartar was one of the largest trading routes on the continent. Cargo from Hadrasia, Matalaga and other lands was traded out to the central continent, and the ships and captains famed for their skill called Eyotsport home even as they moved between the major ports on the coasts. When Karland referred to the head boatman as *Captain,* Jenda roared with laughter.

'Kind y'ar, young serr, but I'm skipper of the *Drollfinne,* not Cap'n - though I'm also Master. She's a boat, not a ship.'

It was strange to Karland that the premier ship-going nation with the most powerful navy in Anaria was located more than five hundred miles up a river, at the foot of high waterfalls from a lake. But the estuary was vast, fed from multiple sources; the lake itself was huge, and the deep river cut through an ancient canyon that followed the length of a volcanic range. Hundreds of islands and sand banks dotted its length.

Sheer dark cliffs hundreds of feet high rose at times to more than a thousand on the northern bank, forming a forbidding barrier abutting deep swift water below. Several of their larger rivers exited either via waterfalls or underground rivers. Very few places on the northern bank allowed landing, and those which did left travellers facing a long and dangerous journey across the hostile range to the mud plains of Meyar the other side.

The southern bank was gentler, the treeline coming down almost to the water. Small hills, shingle and sand banks and mud dominated, with areas of quiet water pools and heavy plants.

The country was temperate, wild, and sparsely populated, rich with crocodiles, turtles, birds, and fish. Troops of snapa monkeys moved along the banks, great silt-brown bears that took on white backs and caps in the winter fished and foraged, and rarely seen forest cats prowled, grey pelts and dark rosettes offset by their green eyes. Further out, catfish the size of rowboats and huge predatory dagger-toothed fish that had moved up from the seas roamed. Large octopus called Grabbers lay in deep water and along the banks to snag unwary prey. The carving of a fat smiling dolphin at the front of the barge was matched by the cavorting ones playing around the boat, calling and chittering to the sailors, who laughed and threw scraps.

The vast river was fraught with danger for those sailors who didn't know the route or hadn't hired a pilot from one of the small island-ports at the estuary mouth. The waters could be deceptive, and powerful; the bed could shift near the southern shore and islands, and the water level changed with tides and *vral.* The northern current had dashed many ships to pieces on the unforgiving sharp rocks of the cliffs. There were many bays, caves, and jutting rocks, and two vast waterfalls, but only those who knew the river well harboured there. There were pirates on the river, too, and many hundreds of ships at the bottom of the river, which could reach well over three hundred feet deep in places. Further upriver, there were less dangers and increasing numbers of waterside villages on banks and islands.

They tacked and used the trade wind which blew regularly from the southwest as they moved east. Jenda said without it, trade would have been much harder upriver. When the wind died they rowed, the soldiers taking turns. Karland saw the pallor of the Major when he visited the prow and knew that every minute counted. As it was, another soldier died on the journey, having simply lost too much blood from the ragged wound where his leg had once been. Sergeant Spooner grimly held on, his own bandaged stump seeping.

They passed two more villages, and then there was nothing but the odd dwelling. There were many craft moving downriver near the northern bank, and others ahead and behind; the barge was one slow corpuscle in a great blood vessel.

Eyotsburg had always seemed something of an anomaly. A tiny fortified island surrounded by powerful war-like nations, yet the trading and naval hub of Anaria, and a staunch ally of Eordeland, their friendship reached back almost a thousand years. They had not always had such a smooth relationship with Haná or Novin; Eyotsburg was the most strategic point in the western continent. Without access through the Eyot, traders travelling north or south had to travel almost two thousand miles east around the Arkons.

It was a tempting prize.

Eoytsburg ruled the lake too, which was almost a small freshwater sea with its own tides and weather. The boatmen referred to the lake-sailors as what sounded like *Siyoflottas,* with some amusement. It seemed that the river and sea sailors considered themselves to be the real sailors, 'tasting salt' as they called it.

The water that filled lake Merrimakea - called *Inremere* by the Eyots - was fed by several large rivers from the Arkon mountains, and the western end fell in the Lakefalls. Two great falls and several lesser either side of the stone isle Iblis, they plummeted hundreds of feet before pounding into shallow rapids, sweeping down around the base of Eyotsburg .

The cliffs were high and forbidding; the *Osfors* rapids would tear any boat apart east of the city, and the permanent mist and hammering of the *Norfal* and *Sodfal* waterfalls had never been survived by anyone. Sailors, said Jenda, were not meant to fly, and the flodgást punished men for straying from their path.

There were many of these demigod beings. Some were supremely powerful, like the gigantic *koloss* and *krake*, uncaring leviathans of the deep waters that were larger than ships and could smash them to tinders, executors of punishment from Lamora, Mistress of the Oceans; *nakki* were kind and watchful, in many forms, including the mythical half-human half-fish. Others yet were hateful, specifically the malevolent *nicar*, who also often took the form of mermaids or great fish with teeth that took men in one bite. Some were merely small and mischievous, like the half-cat half-fish *fisska*, which liked to tangle nets and lines underwater and steal fish from hooks. That didn't even begin to cover the spirits of land, of falls and rockslides and bone breaking and mountains; the men said it was best to ask women of those.

Mistress Sea and Master Stone had human avatars, chosen through some complex ritual as representatives of the Gods themselves, and were almost deified, rarely seen. They spoke to the Conclave instead, and the Conclave ran the citadel.

Sailors feared the spirits so much that many had never set foot in water and couldn't swim. They were very superstitious, the men showing Karland various tattoos they had of dolphins to call aid, gulls to bring them home, a rock to give them a secure mooring in life. One had a rooster on the right foot and a pig on the left, confiding to Karland that the gods and dolphins alike kept these particularly afloat, and would help him if he ever fell in the water. On the other's face a symbol of curving tears under a cheekbone represented fellows lost to water, and a symbol of a vast creature with tentacles pulling a ship under the waves was the sign of surviving a wreck. That was why, he said, he no longer sailed the sea. The river was no place for a *krake*, and he felt sure one would find him if he ever went out again.

They travelled into dusk and through the night, slowing, but Jenda and his crew knew the wide river well and took shifts at the tiller. They knew every minute counted for the injured.

Thirty miles east of the last village the southern bank stopped sloping gently down and began to rise from the trees, eventually becoming a sheer cliff hundreds of feet high. The river was narrowing imperceptibly but was still nearly two miles across.

Finally, the wide gorge straightened up and the huge island-spire of Eyot's Berg came fully into view, rising hundreds of feet with sides as sheer as the canyon walls.

The barge moved slowly upstream towards the huge isolated granite plug, a mile across and near two long.

There was only one way into Eyotsburg if you didn't cross the Stonestrides, and it took skill. Jenda told Karland the true wonder of Eyotsburg was the management of the Port, with the flow of ships and boats never ceasing.

The town of Hamnstad covered the brown crescent beach from the base of the sheer cliffs out onto the water, yards and houses on pilings out into the current and walkways everywhere. Here was where the famed Eyot tallships were built, in shipyards on the north and south beaches.

The docks were vast, bigger than Karland could believe. They stretched wider than the base of the rock itself. Three piers with wide ways between them trailed downstream, the central nearly one and a half miles long. The other two were almost a mile each. Half their sections were fixed on pilings nearer the shore, with the further reaches floating out over the deep water to account for tides. Smaller docks lined their sides like the teeth of a comb.

The calmer water of the port came from the huge island and two huge stone jetties which jutted out at an angle a thousand feet into the flows upstream of the complex docks, funnelling the side currents past the berths and giving space for quays on the inner sides for loading and unloading heavier cargoes. Most of the cargoes bound for the mainland went up there to the great western market. Other goods stayed at the docks where a second great market lay and were loaded back out on other vessels.

There were almost a thousand ship berths here, not counting those for small craft, and the masts and rigging looked like nothing more than a small forest on the water stretching before the spired isle. There were small dinghies cutting the water west of the city, and fishing boats were anchored to the sides and upstream. Ships were moving up, down, and cross-river carrying cargo and passengers, many coming in to dock and just as many being tugged out to the side to catch the swifter return currents. The sheer profusion of people and craft was astonishing.

The Stonestrides arched high above them, miracles of engineering; they had required Dwarvish, Ignathian and Eordelandish engineers. The northern was the masterpiece of the age, he was assured, and had stood for six hundred years, curving more than a thousand feet to touch the northern lip of Anaria and nestle in a valley in the mountains. It was matched to the south by one shorter but no less impressive, spanning four hundred feet and sloping down to the plains a hundred feet below the southern spur.

The two parts of the river which split around the huge rocky spire and swept under these were powerful. They rushed past Eyotsburg in a foaming roar, only beginning to lose their white waters just east of the bridges where the water deepened drastically.

The Drollfinne approached in the centre of the river where the current was slower. The bargemen began to shorten the sails, slowing.

'What now?' asked Karland curiously. The soldiers could row the barge closer, but normally with only three crew this would not be an option.

'Now we hove to and wait,' said Jenda. He pointed. Around the docks were identical rowboats, cutting across the calmer waters with ease, big enough for twelve men. One of these cut towards them at speed, the long, wide-blades oars flying with three large men a side.

They pulled up to the front and shouted. In return a long thick line was thrown down to them from the bow and secured to a thick post at the rear of the tugboat. It was turned to point back to the docks, and then the long, wide oars swept down rhythmically, dragging the larger vessel cross-current to a wide loading dock in the northern section amongst many other ships.

The boatman threw a money pouch to one of the rowers; he squeezed it, hefting and listening to the sound, and nodded. They pushed off and unshipped oars, sweeping away towards another incoming ship.

'Welcome to the 'Berg,' Jenda grinned.

Thorne started shouting orders into the hold. The company had already packed for disembarking; now they made ready. Those soldiers on deck moved down below quickly.

Rast stood at the rail, looking around. Karland moved up beside him and looked up - and up and up. The island rose five hundred feet, sheer rock on all sides apart from the docks. Wide, steep stone steps to north and south were the only way up other than heavy cargo cranes.

Above this the great citade - the burg - sat atop the island, rising in eighty-foot successive levels, each smaller than the one above. At the centre of the highest stood the Spire of Stormasten, five hundred feet high and slim as a mast. The Eyots called the chamber at the top *Krakbo*; from here it was said the Stenmistresses and Marinmasters of the Conclave could see more than fifty miles in any direction.

The Ordinal Towers sat eighty feet high along the wall at the mid-compass points, with flags to signals across the city. The Cardinal Towers surrounding the spire closer in were of a height with the Cuneus towers of The Sanctum, set north, south, east and west. They watched for danger, but also for signals, from Iblis but also to the west. Along the hostile north bank of the estuary lay small settlements; along the south, posts in the tallest trees. Both were manned for months at a time to pass fast messages from Eyostberg along the river to the *Havsfyren*, the great unceasing light at the vast mouth of the Storartar that shone out each night on its own high rock amidst violent waters. Meyar and Novin had both tried to seize control of it many times in the last few centuries, without success, their ships dashed to flinders on its uncaring foundation.

Any attack on the citadel was foolish at best. Cliffs and wide water protected the docks. The stairs that wound hundreds of feet up to the Eyot could be collapsed and blocked; in an emergency the entire aft docks could be cast adrift to float downriver as a vast hazard. Trebuchets lined the higher levels of the city and catapults and ballistas lined the lower. The Stonestrides narrowed to where two carts might ride abreast while the far end of each had high walls, a garrison, and a thick gate.

Eyotsburg was cautious and over-prepared, as one might expect with much more powerful neighbours around them. The city had never been breached by force. Treachery had once brought the enemy within the walls, but the city had survived, and the navy had taught Novin a harsh lesson in return. Even now, Novinian galleys beat a hasty, lumbering retreat when an Eyotsburg destroyer's sails rose over the horizon. The Eyots were the undisputed masters of the waters.

The barge thumped into the wooden dock. One of the crew leaped across and quickly looped the rope he carried around a mushroom-shaped mooring post, bracing his feet and heaving to tighten it in before looping it and tying off. Other lines were thrown, and he secured the boat as his comrades deployed the wide boarding gangplanks.

The company disembarked, sergeants waving them up the wide dock until they were closer to the base of the huge stairs. The Major's horse was led, tapping its hooves and looking relieved that it was on a more solid surface again. The healers commandeered two squads to help them move the wounded carefully along the dock.

At its head a woman waited with an unreadable expression. Her light blonde hair was in a tight braid over a shoulder clad in workable leathers. In the crook of her left arm was a large book bound in worn leather, presumably for registration of manifests and ships. She snapped her other fingers at one of the children nearby, and the girl ran over and listened to her carefully before scampering off.

Rast and Captain Aldine moved through the ranks to speak to her, alongside Major Gambeson, who was on a stretcher. He was pale and weak, but his eyes were bright.

'Greetings, travellers,' she said. 'I am Jocelyn, Dockmistress of the Fifth. I have no record of an armed company arriving.' Her tone was professional and her manner casual, but they could all see the dockhands and children watching, and the alarm bells strung out along the dock. Behind them, Hamnstad had more people packed in one place than Karland had ever seen before, even in Darost. There were also plenty of soldiers, more of them female than male. Karland guessed one wrong move would see them locked out of the city above, and probably face-down in the water.

The Major smiled weakly. 'Madam, forgive me if I do not rise. I bring word and support from Eordeland, but we were attacked en route.' Even that much tired him. He gestured to Aldine. 'The writ, Captain.'

Aldine bowed in turn and presented the document from the Council. 'Dockmistress; I am Captain Aldine of the Eordeland Guard veterans. This is my commander, Major Gambeson, and Rast Tal'Orien. We come from Eordeland to speak with the Conclave on behalf of the Council of Twelve. '

'Word is being sent,' said Jocelyn, her expression impossible to read. 'We do not often take in armed troops at the docks.' She glanced down, unfurling the writ.

'We need healers. Gifted ones.' The nearest healer turned a beseeching face to Jocelyn. 'Please. Our wounded are dying.'

The Dockmistress hesitated, and then nodded. She snapped her fingers at another child at her back. 'Kin. All haste to the nearest healer.' She turned back to them and said, 'You realise I cannot allow your soldiers off the dock until I'm cleared. Who represents the party? They may travel up and petition the Conclave.'

She was interrupted by the arrival of a tall, brown-skinned and broad shouldered woman with startlingly green eyes. Her slightly curly hair had streaks of grey, but was still mostly naturally red, an unusual combination for her skin colour. She smiled slightly, gold flashing. She was not particularly pretty, and had a hawkish nose, but had an attraction born of strength. More striking than her well-muscled figure was the air of competence and authority.

'Portmistress Quirla,' bowed Dockmistress Jocelyn.

The woman inclined her head. 'Jocelyn. I heard your urch speaking to the Dockreeve. What passes here?'

Jocelyn dropped into half-old Eyoti, still spoken as much as Darum here, handing her the writ from the Council of Twelve, and the Portmistress frowned after carefully reading.

'I'll take responsibility here,' she said to the Dockmistress's evident relief. 'Major, welcome. I recognise your name. Your company may ascend at once. I will send to the Conclave immediately. Your troops are to billet in the third level, in the barracks set aside there.' She looked aside to Jocelyn. 'Cancel your other healer. This is a Major of Eordeland, on behalf of the Council themselves. The Conclave have their own Gifted Weaver. Send down a large platform and clear it of cargo. We must hurry.'

'Thank you,' said Aldine gratefully.

She nodded. 'Normally we have advance warning of state visits at the docks.'

'We hadn't planned on using the port,' said Rast. 'You have a… Novinian problem.'

'Ah.'

A City-Captain approached with fifty guards and city drudges, followed by several large wagons drawn by dock mules. He saluted the Portmistress. A stern stubbled face and dark eyes watching emotionlessly over a polished gorget. Two large pauldrons each side with curved blades running down his arms sat above burnished bronze and steel plates, which overlapped down his torso like the scales of a fish. She nodded to him, speaking quickly in a liquid cadence. Turning back, she hooked her thumbs together, hands flat and palms towards her with fingers spread so they tilted up like the wings of a bird and bowed slightly to them. 'The Conclave awaits.'

Rast and Aldine bowed back, and she left, snapping her fingers towards more dock urchins, leaving upwards of thirty of all ages scampering in her wake. Urch, she had called them. Karland wondered if the Eyots knew it was *orc* in another language.

The City-Captain directed gestured for the Eordelanders to follow him and led them up the wide concourse towards the heavy platforms that lifted loads to the city, his troops forming an honour guard for the wounded on the wagons. To each side, the curving stairs cut into the rock were heavy with traffic, ascending to the north and descending to the south. Passengers, hod-bearing carriers and others moved up and down unceasingly. Sailors with swaying strides walked to and from the docks, children scurried around, and women directed cargo everywhere Karland looked. One man with tilted eyes and thick, hairy forearms beneath a striped jerkin stood smoking a heavy pipe and talking almost unintelligibly. His hands were tattooed so that when they were together, they showed a map of the known world.

At the top, merchants were held back from one large platform, big enough to fit some squads with the wagons and mules. Another platform was cleared for the rest.

Those nearby muttered but fell quiet when the City-Captain glanced over. It seemed the docks, chaotic as they were, were ruled with a steel gauntlet.

Rast looked out as they rose, standing easily near the edge. There was a slight swing to the platform, and the edges were not high; most of the Eordelanders kept well back. Another platform laden with boxes swung downwards nearby. Karland enjoyed the view until he looked down a bit more. The increasing drop brought back the familiar sickness in his stomach, alongside the awful urge to just lean out a bit more, a bit more, look down…

Rast's hand dropped on his shoulder as it often did, the blood-scarred knuckles a comforting and familiar warmth and weight.

'Steady, Karland,' he said quietly.

Karland flashed a faint smile up. The big man knew him well.

'Why did she call them *urch?*' he asked, trying to take his mind off the increasing depth beside them.

'Short for urchins.'

'Ah. So they run errands for her?'

'It is more complicated than that. Quirla would not usually speak to passengers. She reports directly to the Conclave itself and governs over the whole port. Nothing happens in the docks without her approval. She is to the docks what Castellan James is to The Sanctum.' Karland blinked. 'The urchins here are not simply poor like in Eordeland. Sailing and ships are in the blood of those living in Hamnstad. All the workers there are Eyots who started as urchins, running and messaging for food, and then as they become more reliable working, taking charge, more responsibility. No one gains a high position down there that didn't work their way up through the ranks. It means people understand their role, makes it smoother. Everyone can rise, find a position that suits their talents.' He rolled heavy shoulders. 'Some rise further than others.'

'I see.' It sounded fair, and he guessed it ruled out beggars, but Karland could see a few possible drawbacks. He shrugged to himself. *Different culture.* 'And the hands at the end? Is that a salute here?'

'Don't use it. You'll get odd looks. It is a gesture of respect from the women, who tend to be in charge here on the island if you hadn't noticed. It's the sign of the gull; the women revere it and believe the bird will guide their men home. It is only used to show real respect. We are honoured. It can mean many things, but she was really saying that she hopes we find our way.'

ଔ   ଛ

They finally reached the top, nearly five hundred feet up the overhanging cliff. There were fifteen huge cranes with thick ropes running through a complicated pulley system to huge double treadmills, larger than the ones out on the jetties. Some smaller cranes used paired men or mules to turn them, but the largest used teams of oxen. There seemed to also be some kind of counterbalance system in place which could be quickly adjusted for load between the cranes. Karland knew Aldwyn would have been itching to have a look at it.

They travelled at haste through wide streets and a second heaving market towards an open gate. Karland could not tell if this was considered Eyotsburg itself, or part of the Hamnstad below, but narrow streets and high wooden house were

512

everywhere. They passed through thick walls of dark rock, probably brought from the Soltsvar to the northwest. The city used light grey stone for houses and lining the tops of the walls, but the walls themselves were black and forbidding. The West gate was the height of the walls, nearly sixty feet, and could be secured with a pin thicker than Karland, hanging from a chain.

The North and South led to the Stonestrides. The East led to the thick rope bridge and pulleyed platforms which dropped to Inresmere. The eight successive levels above had alternating gates either end, east and west. The city roughly conformed to the elongated teardrop shape of the island but looked more like a diamond. The second level was accessed from the east point; the third from the west, the fourth from the east, and so on. Karland realised this meant any invading army that breached the walls would have to travel the full length of the city to reach the next gate, suffering attacks from roofs and the next wall up as they went.

The squads were left on the third level under the watchful eyes of the Eyots in a huge building.

'Your troops will be billeted here in the barracks,' the City-Captain told Aldine. Aldine nodded and motioned to Thorne.

'You heard the man! Line by squads. Remember we are guests.' Thorne's voice receded as the wounded left the Eordelanders gratefully moving for a building with actual beds, rest and food.

The wagons continued on with the Captain, companions, and three of the healers, the rest staying with the squads to care for minor wounds.

It seemed to take forever before they moved through the final western gate onto the pinnacle. It was less than a third of a mile long and half that across, flat with neat gardens, two pools of water, and the needle-like Spire curving up from a wide base to a point nestled amongst the Cardinal Towers.

'This way,' the City-Captain said, leading them to a building set in timber and stone with wide windows coloured with glass in random patterns. The roof was beautifully set with horizontal wooden slats.

The senior healer joined them as they entered. The healing hall was clean, luxurious, and warm. Tenders moving around, lighting scented tapers.

'Please bring the wounded to the beds,' said a low voice. It was warm and pleasant, not really matching the features of woman it belonged to.

She was short and late middle-aged, large-boned and solid in a robe of deep blue with white trim, tied at the waist. Pendulous breasts pushed out her top above curvaceous hips, low enough to show clear skin. Bright blue eyes and crow's feet lay above a slightly flat nose. A square, manly jaw with a creased upper lip which had almost visible hair on it framed thin lips with broad teeth behind them.

She looked like nothing more than a dowager duchess, bullish, with a solid stare and a regal air, but it was incongruous next to the warmth of her smile and her utterly competent attitude. She exuded welcome and calm, and her tone and her eyes showed her innate beauty.

Everyone had something beautiful about them, thought Karland distractedly.

Her eyes took in the Major, and she glanced out through the doors.

'How many are there?' she asked, pointing to the wounded still on the carts with the healers and snapping fingers. The tenders moved with alacrity, smoothly and with practiced ease.

'Twenty-eight badly wounded, eleven critically including the Major,' replied the healer. 'The critical are stable, apart from him.'

The Gifted Healer eyed the wounded professionally as they were brought in to lay on beds, the remaining healers following. She made no mention of their weapons. 'They have been well tended.' She closed her eyes, turning her face towards them as if seeking the sun.

'The Major is fading,' she whispered. The healer nodded.

'Come. Tell me precisely how these injuries occurred.' The woman moved away, gesturing the healers to follow, and they conversed quickly in low tones. Karland drifted over to Rast, and the others entered. The elves garnered bows of respect, and Darkus a few covert looks, but otherwise they were politely ignored.

As they watched, she ran her hands over the Major, who lay breathing shallowly on the bed. She paused several times, her eyes unfocused.

'I need flesh.'

She sliced back his tunic to expose a mottled, bruised side. Without pause she settled her hands lightly on the area and frowned, her eyes closing as she probed his body with fingers.

'Yes, I see it.' She sighed. 'It is close. There is a rupture to the spleen sack. It has been burst open inside and the tissue is split. There is blood gathering here, and here.' she pointed to the mottled area and another seemingly untouched area. 'His heart is strained; there is not enough blood. I can heal him, but he will require food immediately, and rest.'

Major Gambeson turned his head towards her, opening his eyes, and smiled weakly.

'Shh,' she said tenderly. She laid her hands on his pale flesh again. They were beautifully formed, and without rings or bangles.

The healer closed her eyes and her lips moved silently. Karland remembered Aldwyn's words, saying that they helped focus his mind for healing.

He wasn't sure what to expect, shivering at the suspense.

Over the next few minutes, Major Gambeson began almost imperceptibly breathing more deeply and easily, and his colour began to return a little, losing the blue-grey paleness. His movements began to grow stronger, too.

The healer kept her hands on him. Another couple of minutes and he gasped, and jerked upright, swaying dizzily.

'Easy,' she soothed, her hands making passing motions.

Karland guessed what was happening. Unlike herbs and medicines, unlike Aldwyn himself who had been able persuade the body to heal very efficiently and quickly on its own, what this plain, regal woman was doing with some sense and skill that he could never know was marvellous; she was manipulating the Major's damaged cells and regrowing them, repairing them, sealing blood and organs where they should be, piece by piece. It was plainly skilled and exhausting work. Her voice stayed calm, comforting, but her brow creased over eyes screwed shut in concentration and sweat stood at her hairline. When she wasn't talking to her patient, she was whispering to herself in a cadence.

There was a pause, while she drew a deep breath, and then she let it out slowly, her hands staying still, one over his heart and one over his stomach. The one over his heart flexed slightly as if in time with beats only she could see, almost as if she herself was controlling the smooth strong movements, and her left hand shook. Major Gambeson began to flush slightly, not on his face but all over, very faintly, and sweat broke out on his face and neck.

She moved down his side, over the mottled area, and blew her breath out in a puff. Drawing her hands down over and over, she moved from here to his stomach, as if teasing cobwebs into place, and kept this up for several minutes.

Finally, she sat back, and heaved a sigh.

'It is done.'

She helped the Major sit up slowly and beckoned to her assistants. They approached with water and a snack for her, and cut fruits and a fish broth with crackling seeded bread for him. Karland's stomach growled.

Major Gambeson was normally a methodical and slow eater. Now his hands literally trembled, and he barely prevented himself from grabbing the bowl.

'There are ways to convert the cells in the body to other cells,' the healer said, 'but I am not skilled at that. I could not avoid drawing on muscle and fat for nutrition. You are starving?' The Major nodded, his face looking somehow gaunter. 'Your body has nothing in it. I used what I could.' Her face was tired, and she took the water and gulped it, noting their stares. She drew herself up in her blue robe, and again her square jaw and almost snooty head tilt was at odds with her eyes and tone.

'I will recover in a moment. Detailed healing and forcing a body to create more blood is always hard.' She bit into a dark nugget of something that might have been rolled figs and apple. After she had swallowed, she continued. 'The others will be attended to in a moment. Sealing major blood vessels and growing skin is easier than cellular repair, and they can rest here while I work.'

'What did you do?' asked Karland, fascinated. The dowdy woman smiled at his curiosity.

'I sealed the rupture in the sack around his spleen to stem exsanguination and repaired the organ. I forced his body to produce more blood very quickly. Lastly, I drew the pooled dead blood in his abdomen through the membranes into his upper intestine. It is very hard to draw nutrients that way; it is designed to go in reverse.'

She turned to Major Gambeson, whose cheeks now bulged with bread and broth. 'Your stools will be dark and a little bloody for a day or two. You will have lost strength and muscle, but not too much. Eat to bursting for the next week, sleep late, exercise, and you will recover quickly.' She smiled. 'You should sleep now, but I doubt you will heed me.'

He swallowed, and smiled. Already he looked less pale after his flush receded.

'I must first complete my duty. You have my thanks, my lady.' He finished his food quickly, and was helped to his feet by an assistant. It was clear he was very weak and tired, but it was still nothing short of remarkable.

'I must continue,' said the healer, looking at the others being tended by her own healers, and moved away in a stately fashion towards Sergeant Cowlin. Rast intercepted her, speaking softly. She looked startled, and nodded, waving to several Eyots Guards.

Major Gambeson closed his eyes a moment, then opened them. 'Captain. Are the soldiers billeted?' Aldine nodded, looking relieved. 'Inspect them later and return here.' His gaze swept the room, and his eyes softened as he looked at his badly wounded troops. 'Leave the healers here to aid the Gifted.' He straightened himself, and Karland distinctly heard his stomach rumble. Major Gambeson picked up the tray of fruit almost absent-mindedly. 'I must see the Conclave before I rest. Is my horse stabled well?'

Aldine nodded.

'Excellent. Thank you, Gram.' His tone held a quiet note of warmth. 'Thank you all.' His gaze came to rest on Karland, who felt embarrassed, remembering the battle with the werewolves. His nose still ached.

They exited into grey skies and some wind, but it felt fresh after the quiet of the healer Hall. The Eyotsburg City-Captain stood with twenty men, waiting for them. The wagons had been moved and there was no sign of the Eordeland troops.

Rast and the others fell in; ork, The Green Warrior, elves and Karland, along with the Major and Captain. The City-Captain raised an eyebrow at the ork and Karland.

'They are part of the delegation,' said Major Gambeson, and the man shrugged. It was not his place to argue.

୫ ୭

The spire was forbidden to outsiders. Only the StenMistresses and MarinMasters of the Conclave could ascend to speak to Mother Sea and Father Stone. A low connecting building at the base of the Towers was used instead. As they moved inside through low doors, they entered a long wooden hall with a beautiful stone staircase leading to the base of the tower, white marble steps lined with metal railings. Through two open doors Karland caught a glimpse of a winding staircase of similar design around the narrow inside of the needle-like tower, standing on a relatively wide base which curved quickly to a smooth spire. In the very centre stood something that looked like a permanent, stylised crane with two burly guards beside it. Two lines stretched upwards and another two - probably the same ones, he reflected - came down to the top of a platform with rails and a gate. The sides of the platform lay in rails between two columns, he assumed to stop it swinging and keep it level. He guessed that the two lines ran through a pulley system somewhere above.

There was no more time to view the tower. The Conclave entered through the gilded ironbound door, and it closed behind them. This chamber reminded Karland of a ship's hold in some ways; wooden beams and round windows helped it seem close. He could almost feel the sway of a ship.

Seven came into the chamber, three men and four women. None were young, and all looked serious and stern. The men were almost all leathery-skinned, with a whipcord spryness that spoke of tendons like rope. Only one was large-framed. Once, he must have been almost as big as Rast.

They wore dull-coloured double-breasted frock coats with large, turned back sleeves over a waistcoat and white frilled shirts. Beneath these were trous that were tight to the leg and buckled at mid-calf, and skinny ankles in white socks and brown leather boots. The one concession to finery was thin gold embroidery. Their thinning hair, where possible, was gathered back into a ponytail. There was a lot of stubble, and a moustache on a small evil-looking man who was missing many of his teeth. Two of them had the faded blue tattoos of loss on their cheeks.

The women were more solid, if mostly as old, the youngest with weather wrinkles and generously peppered hair. They wore muted hues of jacket. The cut

517

was practical, allowing for their figures, and under the open jackets they wore a loose blouse that was modest and slightly more frilled than the men's. They also wore trousers, wide-legged and finishing about the ankle, where solid shoes sat. One wore a silver net on her dark hair, another small glass globes from her earlobes which were tied by thin chains to four bars further up her ears.

The impression they all gave was that, despite the fine cloth, they were all ready to start hauling cargo and shouting orders. There was an air of practicability and hard work that was missing from most of the Council of Twelve, who were - after all was said and done - scholars.

The youngest-looking woman spoke softly to the Conclave, and one of the old men replied. There was none of the bickering of the Council of Twelve - only serious words with a sense of tradition. The woman finished speaking and bowed her head as points were made for the others, then made the gesture of the gull. The man next to her shrugged and clenched his fists at waist height, finger knuckles up as if he grabbed the spokes of a wheel, either side.

They turned together and approached. Karland could feel them all eying the party with interest, and wondered how, yet again, he had ended up in front of another council of elders.

The woman spoke in tones that carried to everyone, the others watching. 'We bid you fair welcome, Major, men of Eordeland, and companions.' She bowed and made the Gull to the elves. 'And to the children of harmony. I am Stenmistress Fala. This is Marinmaster Oclin. On behalf of the Conclave, we bid you welcome and rest.'

The old man spoke up, his voice harsh from years of shouting over the boom of the surf. 'We speak for the *Mor-Far*, *Harskarmarin* and *Mastersten*,' he said. 'Our Mother and Father of Sea and Stone. We remember you, Major. The times are dark, but we always welcome our allies.

'Thank you for your healing,' said Major Gambeson tiredly, deep gratitude in his voice. 'And your care of my company.'

'The least we could do. How can we be of service?' asked Fala.

'We come on behalf of your long-term ally and friend, the realm of Eordeland,' replied Major Gambeson, bowing carefully and passing the writ of the Council of Twelve to Fala. He still looked weak and exhausted, but his voice was stronger. Karland was astonished all over again at how thoroughly he was recovering. 'We offer the assurances of aid, and the services of our veteran company-' he grimaced and continued, '-what survives of it. We have healers, sappers, Crosses and archers, and mid- and close- quarters infantry.'

She scanned the text then passed the scroll over to Oclin, who muttered to himself and glanced at them with one eye slightly screwed up, then nodded to the rest of the Conclave and passed it on.

'We welcome you doubly, Major. We are sorely beset. Meyar is attempting diplomatic channels, but they have not ceased their attempts to force their way past our northern gate. Novinian mercenaries gather to the south, and we suspect they are allies of Meyar. War is imminent.'

'Meyar marches to war with us, tens of thousands strong,' replied the Major. 'We saw the Novinians on the way here… and worse. We had to detour around them and come upriver, and we were set upon by terrible foes in the woods to the west. That was where we lost so much of our company.'

'What happened?' asked Oclin in his low rasp.

'We were attacked by myths. Legends. Nightmares. The Druids named them werewolves. Had they not been there we would have all been slaughtered. It seems they have fought these things for centuries. I never knew before now what they did for the realms of men.'

Karland expected the Conclave to scoff, or laugh, as would many of the Council. Instead, they stared at him resolutely.

'There have been rumours,' Fala said. 'And we know of the Druids. The brave may seek their advice sometimes, and find them - or not. It is ill that these rumours are true.'

'I was to assess the situation and lend aid if I can. I am also to send a report back,' said Gambeson. 'But it seems matters are worse than we thought.'

'You will not get anyone through now,' agreed Fala. 'We have much organising to do before we break their blockades at sea.'

'That may be our only option with a guarantee,' Gambeson said. 'We are pledged to lend aid. Had we known you were under such pressure we would have sent more than one company. Meanwhile, we will lend our arms and experience where we can. You know defence better than many, but perhaps we can help with any engineering work or bridge defence and plains tactics.'

'There can be no harm in it, though never doubt we have our defences, should they break through.' Fala looked questioningly at Oclin. 'What of the other part of the letter?'

Rast stepped forward. 'A small party of us request the fastest ship for *Mithtól*.' He indicated the rest of the party. 'We bring grave news and a request for help to the Elven nation. Eordeland faces not only war from Meyari and a horse of orcs, but graver concerns than war that affect Anaria and more.'

'It would not be as easy to convince them without us there,' said Galnór. 'Much moves that should not on the face of Kuln. If my kin join us quickly, we can perhaps prevent war even gaining a foothold. If the realms of Meyar and Novin can be calmed, much may be achieved.'

'Perhaps.' Oclin whispered in Fala's ear. She nodded. 'We see the wisdom in this. We shall grant you exclusive use of a new clipper. I have just the one in mind; the *Eastern Star*. Her Captain is… used to adversity.'

'Thank you,' said Rast.

'She is not the heaviest hull, but none can match her for speed. Breaking a blockade would be hard, but you travel west, on the northwest trade wind. Your journey should be quick. If the blockade is broken by your return, you might go straight to Eordeland.'

Oclin nodded to one of the many guards lining the walls, watching the group carefully. 'The *Star* will be ready in a few days,' he said roughly. 'We give you a house on tier Five and the run of the city. Do you require a guide?'

'I have been here before,' said Rast. 'We will prepare ourselves. There is much to do before we leave.' He sighed. 'Also… one of our wounded must be guarded. He was bitten by a werewolf. If he worsens, he must be secluded and the Druids must be called. Do not leave him unwatched.'

Fala nodded. 'It will be done. Our thanks for your warning.' She and Oclin stepped back to their peers. The City-Captain moved up and stood to attention, and the Conclave bade them farewell as one, a sense of ritual about it. The women bowed over the sign of the Gull, and the men made the sign of the Wheel. The party bowed, and the old Stenmistresses and Marinmasters moved back to the tower doors, and were gone.

THIRTY-EIGHT

Karland slept well for the first time in weeks, though it felt odd sleeping on such a soft bed after the hard ground. The house allocated to the companions was rich and expansive, tended only by a caretaker.

Breakfast was different here. Eyots ate oats and berries mixed with cold water, a small dense bread with seeds in it, and drank a black kohfee-like hot drink made from *chaga* mushrooms from the southwestern forest with drops of fish oil in it. The taste was… sweetly fishy. Odd, not unpleasant.

As they ate Karland queried their host, a woman called Kennard. He was curious about the reclusive rulers.

She told him Father Stone and Mother Sea had no other names, having been ceremonially washed clean of them in the rapids when lowered from the heights of the island. Some died in this process, he was told, and were considered unworthy.

To Karland this seemed strange, superstitious and a little savage, but the feeling he got from the Eyots was of serious people with strong beliefs. They rarely smiled in public but were not as unfriendly as they appeared.

After eating they had visited the wounded. They did not stay long; the healer had performed miracles, and was resting, but the hollow stares and touching of where a limb had once been, were discomfiting. The wounds to their psyches were deep still.

Sergeant Cowlin's fever seemed better. He was able to respond now, and weakly eat, but the wounds had not healed well even with skilled help. Heavily armed guards stood without and within.

Karland prayed he had avoided the curse of the *varka*.

They also visited the company on the Third. Karland spoke with many, but mostly with his first squad. Kirri had hugged him, and Den Olli had cheered and slapped his back. Nirrah had saluted him, a small smile on her face. Gorin had nodded to him. Slowly, the veterans were dealing with the horror of the battle.

He also spoke with Gen, who was quieter than Karland had ever seen him. Kith's gruesome death had affected him terribly, making him listless.

He hoped Gen would recover.

They had spent the morning with them, sharing a subdued lunch. Now they explored the western market.

Rast led them to a small wooden door set back three streets from the dock stairway which led to the main citadel spires. The sign for a Morlandish healer hung above it, and though the front was small it was well-tended. He knocked, the door opening moment later to show a young man's face. He was dressed in a cream robe with a green patch on his right shoulder. Tall with swarthy good looks, his face had small cheekbones and pert, easy-smiling lips. He paused in surprise at the sight of the ork and elves accompanying the humans, then shook himself and beckoned them inside.

Karland wasn't sure why they were visiting another healer. He knew there would be a difference from the Gifted healer at the Spire; she had a rare, otherworldly power which was clearly highly valued by the Conclave, though he was unsure if she had been Morland-trained. Aldwyn had told him they had a disproportionate number of semi- and fully-Gifted in their race. The Daktarim could guide an emergent Talent better than anyone.

This was different. Although the Gifted healer - and now Karland realised that she had not had time to give her name - had been pleasant and her staff efficient, something here spoke of more homeliness, more personal interest. It was hard to explain. He just felt less nervous and more comfortable here.

The inside of the hall was much larger than the outside had suggested. It had a high ceiling with many skylights and windows and hanging lights with positional mirrors for night. Benches and pallets were arranged neatly throughout the room, with frames to draw screens of white cloth around them if required; a few at the far end were occupied. One wall was entirely covered in jars, pots, and small chests of various herbs and unguents, whilst another had bandages and wrappings in all manner of shapes and size. In front of each was a work surface with pestles and mortars, an inset bowl for water, and various implements. One had rolls of sterile cloth and a sharp knife, where plainly a healer had been cutting new bandages. An open fire with a grate cast warmth around the room.

There was also a small bookshelf fronted with glass. It was completely filled with books, some looking quite old to Karland's eye. Steps led up and around a large upper room to a mezzanine section, and a door the other side of the bookshelf was closed and locked. Two more doors stood beyond that.

Several other healers moved around the large space, busy with lotions or writing notes, two without the green patch on the shoulder.

'Welcome, serrs. And dam,' the healer added, looking at Lëlylien. 'I am Jos. Do you have urgent need of healing, or might I prepare medicines for you?' He cast another covert look at the large ork.

'Greetings,' said Rast. 'I am looking for Mirembe.'

The man smiled. 'She is very busy, serr. Can I not be of help? May I ask your name?'

'My name is Rast-'

'Rast Tal'Orien,' a musical voice chimed in from the mezzanine. Karland looked up to see a woman with the darkest skin he had ever seen, a dark brown that was almost black. She was smiling. 'It's all right, Jos. I always have time to see *that* one.'

Jos nodded and glanced respectfully to Rast. 'Apologies, serr. I have heard your name.' He bowed and withdrew to continue his work at the unit in front of the dressings shelving. A couple of the other healers murmured to him in curiosity as he passed.

The woman disappeared, reappearing at the top of the staircase and descending smoothly.

She was tall and slim, and moved in a stately fashion. Her eyes were wide-set and very dark, and her complexion was flawless apart from a dusting of darker dots under her eyes and across her nose. This added to her striking looks rather than detracting from them, bringing attention to kindly wise eyes with a few barely visible wrinkles at each corner. She had dangling bright red earrings set with dyed feathers in her ears, and her tightly curled black hair was cut upwards at the forehead, peaking slightly. At the sides where it was regally grey around the temples, it was tightly braided in upward sweeps to the back of her head, where the hair was shorter. A small flat nose with wide nostrils and a wide bridge sat between two high full cheekbones. Her lips were large and full, and her teeth looked very white in contrast to her skin. She wore no official healer's robe, but instead a white linen dress that fell off her shoulders, baring them and her arms. The contrast between her dark skin and the white cloth was striking. Wide pleats unfolded from a clinging narrow waist, and the hem ended at her mid-calf. The cut was simple and demure, but still would not have looked out of place at a noble's ball. Her feet wore soft, wrapped sandals.

Rast moved to the fascinating woman and took her hand, smiling warmly. He bowed his head over it, touching his forehead to the back, and then returned to his usual imposing height.

'Mirembe. It is good to see you again. I was passing through and thought it past time for a little maintenance. The healers in Darost are not your equal.'

She snorted in a distinctly unladylike fashion, although her eyes were warm. 'Maintenance my hips. You need a top-to-toe, and no change there.' She turned his hot hands over, tracing the glinting red under the skin. 'What have you been doing to yourself now?' Her eyes travelled to the others, showing no surprise at the non-humans. 'And who are your companions?' Her Darum was perfect, although there were a slight cadence to her words where she stressed them differently. Karland liked the sound of it.

Rast introduced them one by one, and Mirembe shook their hands in a businesslike fashion which surprised Karland, who had thought to bow over her hand as Rast had. Her grip was astonishingly firm. He felt that she was looking at him with more than just casual eyes; she seemed to be taking in everything about him.

Karland tried not to stare back, but he found her entrancingly exotic, even compared to Seom. The elves bowed deeply, Darkus clapped a fist to his chest, and The Green Warrior nodded, an oddly gentle smile on his face. She smiled back, and her face looked younger.

'I am Uzuke Mirembe. You are all welcome here. If you have any ills or injuries, I will care for them. I have an old agreement with our silent friend here and owe him much.' She looked amused. Rast raised an eyebrow. 'He trusts me to repair him, and I would be more than happy to do so for you all.'

'Our thanks,' smiled Galnór, 'but our physiology is different to humans. We practice similar techniques amongst our people.'

'I know more of elf anatomy than most humans - you are not so different in many ways. The choice is yours, of course.' Mirembe inclined her head. The elf bowed back politely. Karland could tell he didn't entirely believe her. She cocked her head at Darkus. 'As for you, you *would* be the first of your kind I have treated, but I can see if I may be of help.' Darkus grunted noncommittally. 'I will have refreshments brought for you all. This will take some time. Come upstairs, please.' She turned to her apprentice. 'Jos - Khalim can take over slicing bandages.' She cocked her head at Rast. 'If you have no objections, he has begun learning advanced techniques, and I would like him present.'

'Of course,' said Rast.

Mirembe called in another tongue to one of the other healers, pops and clicks dropping into the words. Karland couldn't even begin to work out how she did that. The healer, nearly as dark as she, nodded and moved off.

She led them upstairs where they found more beds with partition sheets, although these seemed different. They were well padded and higher from the ground with a hole cut where the face could go. Karland thought they looked like torture devices. At the side there was a small office with a desk inside. The walls were packed with books, scrolls and ledgers.

Mirembe gestured them to perch on the strange beds. 'The healers will prepare you and massage you ready for your treatment when it is your turn,' she said. 'Two at a time. I can see you are in some discomfort, Rast.'

Karland expected him to brush the comment off as he normally would, but to his surprise the huge man simply nodded. He couldn't see anything different in his companion.

The other healer arrived with a tray of water and fruit. Jos accompanied him with a tray of small, dark red drinks that looked like fruit juice. It appeared that the green patch signified apprenticeship, as the other healer didn't wear one.

'Please drink this,' Mirembe instructed as Jos handed the glasses around.

'What is it?' Karland asked, curious. The smell was sweet, savoury and powerful, with a hint of dark tart cherry.

'Magnesium, chamomile, cherry, small hot pepper mixed with ginger, birch, willow, demonsclaw,' Jos said with a grin, ticking off the ingredients, 'with crushed gotu kola, horsetail, goldenseal and echinacea.'

'Oh.'

Mirembe nodded. 'A muscle relaxant and mild analgesic. Very strong. It will help you relax and heal. Gifted healers can enhance the effects of their healing with its nutrients.'

Karland sipped cautiously at it until it was gone. It had a very strong taste. He almost coughed as some pepper made its presence known.

'We can talk as we work,' Mirembe said, gesturing for Rast to remove his garments and perform a series of movements whilst she watched, occasionally placing her hands on him.

The Green Warrior looked around at the rest and rolled his eyes. 'Come on,' he said impatiently, pulling his tunic off and then his leggings, leaving him in his undergarments. 'They can't work you if they can't see you.' He took a bite of fruit with relish, nodded, then drank some water and lay face-down on the odd bed, his face fitting into the gap and his arms dangling over the sides. 'You're in luck. I heard this type of healing's costly. Enjoy it while you can.'

As the others sat, curious, Karland measured the two men. The Green Warrior had several scars, a couple quite deep across collarbone and pectorals, and like Rast he had fewer on his back apart from a slight twist lower down. His right calf was smaller than the left.

Rast had silvery scars all over him, and a few knotted masses. The one on his leg was particularly bad, angry and stretched. Mirembe clucked when she saw it.

'You are a mess,' she said. 'Worse than usual. So much for untouchable. I can see we have a lot of work to do.' She sighed. 'Jos, please cancel the rest of my appointments for today.'

Her apprentice waved up another and spoke to him, then moved to The Green Warrior.

Karland sat on a nearby cushioned bench with the others. He could see a bowl of water with flowers floating in it under the hole in each bed, and for some reason it made him want to laugh.

Mirembe and Jos dipped their hands in bowls of scented oil and began gently working the muscles, going deeper and deeper on each repetition. She regularly quietly spoke to Jos, who nodded each time.

Karland hadn't noticed before, but her shoulders and neck were much more defined than her slim frame would suggest, and her forearms were disproportionately powerful. He could see the corded muscles ripple as she worked.

She muttered to herself, shaking her head as she felt the damage to the big man. 'Second rib, pulling through neck and twisted shoulders, jaw slightly out as well. Right scapula has a huge knot underneath. Lumbar vertebrae twisted, slight hip cant. Pulling in calf through the large tendon. Hips out of line. Scar tissue deep in leg, going to need to break this up. Fibula out of line. Tendonitis in six separate places. Muscle tear in forearm. Lower vertebrae slightly off. Too many new scars. Whatever is going on with your hands. Honestly, Rast, you never cease to astound me with what a mess you make of yourself. You must have been in discomfort for some while.'

Rast grunted. 'Some. It has been a busy time.'

She sighed. 'Do not do anything heavy for a few days after I repair this. Please. This is worse than usual. Let it heal, let the inflammation go down. I will call the *Mganga* healer to set it quickly.' She laughed suddenly. 'I almost dare not ask. Who in the names of the Gods have you been fighting?'

'Ogres, demons, orcs, men. The leg was a crocodile. There were also dragons.' He sounded resigned. 'The blood of one I called friend is the stain on my hands.'

There was a pause, and then she shook her head.

'If it were anyone else, I would know it as a jest,' she said, but her tone was fond, and more. There was a real care to it. She began working deep into the leg scar, eliciting a quick grunt of pain from Rast. 'This must be broken down before I release the soft tissue. I see you have worked it yourself. At least you can do something right.'

Jos frowned as he moved down The Green Warrior's back and whispered something to Mirembe. She exchanged patients and moved to The Green Warrior, rolling his hips in a manner Karland thought was a little obscene, then probed and frowned, digging her fingers in.

'This is an old injury,' she said. 'You have problems with your back?'

He grunted, his mouth turning down. 'Comes and goes.'

'You must be hard up when it comes. I will do what I can. There is some old damage to the disc between the vertebrae, and the muscles and bones are in the wrong places. It has affected the leg. There is nerve damage.'

'I had it fixed up by a healer. A... *talented* one. Cost me a lot.'

'They repaired the disc, so they had skill, but they didn't know what they were doing with the rest. Fools, some of these Talented. You have to put everything back and fix the whole body; making one thing work again isn't enough if everything else is still compensating.' She sighed. 'Some rely too much on their talents with healing and not enough on the supportive work of the body itself. Sensing energy is no substitute for knowledge.'

'I thought Gifted healers were the best?' asked Karland curiously.

Mirembe laughed softly.

'They have a Gift most of us do not. A Talent, in our tongue. In Morland we call them *Mganga*. It is beyond my skill, but it allows them to do things no others can do. That does not mean they are the best healers. I know some who can virtually bring the dead to life; others who can do specific things well but feel no need to refine their skills when they can weave such repairs. Some know everything about melding torn cells together deep in a body, yet could not give a man medicine to stop a simple case of indigestion.' White teeth flashed in a grin. 'You can do much even without Talent, if you are educated.'

'What about the Gifted healer here?' said Karland as she felt The Green Warrior's back, kneading with strong fingers.

'Mistress Corvath? She is skilled at mending flesh and bone, but she does not see the body holistically. She sees detail in a series of systems.' She prodded at the man and changed tack. 'These muscles are all out of place and have been for a long time.' She grimaced. 'It would normally cause you problems for weeks as they grow used to their correct positions again, but it needs doing. Sit up.' She cast her eyes over the rest of him, shaking her head.

'You're as bad as Rast. Worse - at least he knows how to repair himself. Neck trauma, collarbone, lower back, rib unseated, shoulders tight, scars aplenty. You two should start a school or something.' She tapped his lower back. 'This needs fixing first. Ready?'

He shrugged.

She turned him on his side facing her, lower leg straight and upper leg bent over it, and pulled his lower arm out so he was partially twisted. Clasping his hands together, she leant on him and used her elbows to stretch him. 'Breath in,' she ordered. He did. 'Out.'

As he exhaled, she jerked hard down, twisting slightly. Her arms pressed down and apart, and she grunted with the effort. The Green Warrior's breath exploded out with a snort of pain as a cacophony of pops reverberated from his lower back.

'Good,' she said, rolling his hips experimentally. 'Other side.'

After a few more torturous moves she stood The Green Warrior up and made him twist and turn and bend. 'Much better,' she said. 'Freed up. It will continue to heal as long as you are careful for the next week. You will need the *Mganga* too, if it is to settle and be permanent. He can persuade your body to do a month's healing in minutes. I warn you though, you will feel it for a long time. Next time, you come and see me as soon as you can. How did you do it?'

'Um,' said The Green Warrior, sounding uncertain for once. He shook his head. 'Dunno where most of these came from.' He twisted and nodded, pulling his shoulders back. 'Feels much better.'

She looked at him closely, as if about to ask more, then shrugged.

'You are lucky,' she said. 'That back injury should have nearly crippled you when it happened. Wouldn't have taken much to finish the damage. That Gifted healer saved you from life as a beggar.'

Jos was still working on Rast. Karland chuckled to himself, watching Rast's face. Jos's elbow had sunk deep into his leg, and was carefully and gently probing, it seemed almost to the bone. Rast was frowning in pain, his eyes closed. He breathed deeply, almost exhaling the pain away. Karland had no doubt he would have been screaming by this point, but it was interesting to finally watch the big man react to something.

Another healer brought up strips of white cloth, smearing a sticky wax on one side and passing them to Mirembe. She wrapped them tightly over his shoulder, arms and leg, holding the skin in certain directions.

'What do those do?' Karland asked.

'Help take pressure off. Lymphatic healing. He will lose any hair removing them, which is less than he deserves.'

'I don't know what you're grinning at, young man,' Jos added, amused. 'It's your turn.'

Karland and Darkus ended up on a bed each. Mirembe worked into the healing scars on Darkus's forearms before bathing them in an unguent and oiling them. Darkus grunted in satisfaction.

Karland hardly noticed, but the pain and pressure was worth it when the release came. He had lived with a few problems long enough that he hadn't even realised they were there.

The massage afterwards was sending Karland to sleep. He told himself he needed to do this more often.

A small man came up the stairs, slightly effeminate, wearing a dark red square-cut robe with darker red square designs. Three white lines striped down over his left eye from brow to cheek.

He muttered to himself, smiling at them all beatifically. One by one, he shook a small rattling wand over their heads with his eyes shut, chanting softly, then ran his hand slowly over their skin, still rattling and chanting.

The man talked to Mirembe quietly in Morlandish as he worked, and she replied, guiding his hands occasionally as he nodded. His hands paused over Rast's leg, and The Green Warrior's back and calf, making him gasp. When he reached his throat and collarbone, he paused over an old scar, whispering to Mirembe, who looked surprised.

'He says there is old trauma here. And Dwarven metal, in the bone.'

The Green Warrior shrugged. 'How?'

She shook her head. 'I do not know.' Her dark eyes assessed him carefully. 'You are missing memories? I am sorry, child. We cannot help you with that.'

The Warrior nodded slowly.

When it was his turn Karland felt a chill on his skin like fresh cold water which was at odds with a deep, intimate warmth underneath it. He felt his heart speeding up and his scalp prickle with sweat.

This must have been what happened to the Major with Mistress Corvath.

The *Mganga* continued, lingering over Karland's old break, side and nose. He frowned a little at Darkus's arms, but when he took his hands away the crusted scabs were flaking off to reveal darker, better-healed scars underneath. When he was done, he bowed and left, looking tired.

'Pretty good, right?' said The Green Warrior, rolling his neck and twisting gently. He looked more at peace, though he kept scratching at his lower back. Karland realised he felt refreshed, rested, and had no aches at all. Then he laughed; where the damage had been he also itched incessantly.

Aldwyn's healing had been a slow, faint echo of this.

'That was amazing. I've never felt magic before.'

'It wasn't really magic,' smiled Mirembe. 'He just spoke to your body and guided it to repair itself properly. Ch'uma has been known to bring people back from near death and heal diseases, but he can only sense the body's energy and realign it as intended. He's no mage, and does not well understand the body's working above that tiny level. He heals differently to Mistress Corvath. She directs repairs instead of encouraging the body's memory and disdains any other healer help, though she is perfectly polite. Ch'uma accepts I know more than he does about the mechanics and prefers to work in symbiosis for full healing. I tell him I am his *shuluwele*.' She smiled.

They were moved to loose robes and reclined wicker chairs where they sat sipping chilled fruit juice. Mirembe sat with them.

'Thank you, Mirembe,' Rast said, looking more at peace. 'We had many badly wounded with us, but they were taken to the Eyot healer. I would have brought them here, but I did not wish to offend the Conclave.'

'I am treasured by the Eyots for my skills, Rast, but they prefer their own countrywoman for their Conclave and Military healing.' She shrugged. 'She is skilled at triage. I am better at rehabilitation and other damage. We work at different things.' The captivating woman stretched like a cat, entwining her fingers and inverting her hands.

'You are lucky, Rast. I am not so busy at the moment. It is good to see you again.' She chuckled, glancing at him. In that moment, Karland realised that she had deep feelings for his friend. 'Despite the damage you have done to yourself again.' She changed the subject. 'How is dear Aldwyn?'

'He is dead,' said Rast softly. 'I am sorry.'

Mirembe sighed, her face stricken, then nodded slowly.

'A great loss. That is one who *did* have a vast knowledge of healing energies and bodies. We learned much from each other.' Her face had lost some of its vivacity. 'How?'

'We were ambushed by bandits. Assassins. He was struck by an arrow. It was quick.'

'I am sorry.'

'Karland was his student,' said Rast. 'We have seen much woe this last year. Aldwyn was seeking answers. Realms march to war. There are other forces moving, forces beyond men. At first I did not believe, but I cannot deny it any more. A darkness is spreading.'

'You have only to look around to see that,' she replied. 'Eyotsburg remains proud, but if Novin and Meyar ally, the Eyots will be hard pressed. If they managed to blockade this far upriver, it might only be a matter of time.'

'It is not just Novin we must worry about,' said Rast. 'Meyar allies with orcs.'

Mirembe stared. 'Are they mad? *Shetani-watu* do not care for the politics of men! They will betray and murder them.'

Rast shrugged. 'Nevertheless.'

Mirembe sighed. 'Would that I could leave here and aid you, Rast, but I am getting too old for the burdens you bear. I cannot leave my healing school.'

'But… you're not old?' protested Karland. 'I'd guess you at forty. At most,' he added hastily when she raised an eyebrow.

The Green Warrior guffawed. 'Never try to guess the age of a woman!'

Mirembe smiled.

'Bless you, child. I'm near sixty.' Somehow it wasn't insulting when she said 'child'. She certainly didn't look it.

'Mirembe has always looked the same,' said Rast. 'As long as I can remember.'

'Oh, hush, big man.' She looked pleased. 'Plenty more lines since then.'

'Mirembe practices Vinvasa Chi'Engo. It is said to keep you young.'

Galnór laughed in his quiet fashion, and Mirembe pursed her lips ruefully. 'Don't give a lady's secrets away.'

Another apprentice healer with the green patch came to collect their drinks. Karland found it hard to keep his eyes off her voluptuous figure. She was more of a girl for all she must have been twenty, and certainly closer to his age than the others. She moved in a wonderful swaying fashion. Her dark skin and bright teeth and eyes were beautiful, he thought.

The Green Warrior saw his eyes following her and snorted, viewing him sideways.

'Come on, Karland. Not with the *natives.*'

Talk ceased. Karland blinked at the derision in the man's voice.

'Keep a civil tongue in your head,' warned Rast softly, face suddenly severe. Jos looked shocked and the girl retreated, staring daggers at the man.

The Green Warrior shrugged, hands open in acceptance.

'No offence meant, Tal'Orien; Mirembe.' He actually did sound genuinely apologetic. 'Old habits. I think. Sorry.'

'See you use that head of yours for something other than fighting, Warrior,' Mirembe said reprovingly after a long moment. 'We are as much people as you.' He nodded after a second, and she relaxed. 'Come, Rast. I have been called worse.' She eyed the Warrior again. 'Although you, young man, are trouble.'

'Seems to find me,' agreed the Green Warrior, a cheeky grin on his face.

'I don't know whether to like you or throw you out,' said Mirembe after a moment, and laughed lightly. 'You're a devil.'

Talk turned to other matters, Mirembe asking Darkus about his people, and Karland listened through an odd mixture of energy and ennui. He would sleep well tonight.

The elves wished to see if any kin were in the city, excusing themselves. The others left the healing school an hour later and began to wend their way through the tight, crowded main streets toward the Third. It was dusk, and torches were being lit; they had been there for many hours.

Rast kept moving up, then dropping back, sensing something amiss. The third time he saw Karland look up warily. The boy had learned well.

Rast glanced casually behind them. A figure slowed and seemed to be engaging in discussion with someone in a doorway, but he doubted there was anyone there.

'What is it?' asked The Green Warrior, drawing casually near and glancing around disinterestedly.

'We are being followed,' said Rast softly. 'They are skilled. I caught only a glimpse. There may be more. You two take Karland back, in case there are others ahead. I will find out who our friend is.'

'Take care, Tal'Orien,' rumbled Darkus. The Green Warrior nodded in agreement.

'Remember what Mirembe said about your back,' reminded Karland lightly, but Rast saw his underlying concern. He dropped a hand lightly on the boy's shoulder, noting how well it was filling out, and moved ahead.

'Take this next alleyway. I believe it leads to another causeway.'

The torches at each end cast light some way in, but the middle of the alley was cast in gloom.

They filtered in, Rast at the fore, and then he peeled to the side and fell into the shadows. He heard a grunt of surprise from the Warrior, who looked for him in vain, but they kept moving.

Rast scaled a wall quickly, moving along the rooftops like a ghost, watching his friends move from twenty feet above them. He settled near the far end as his companions neared the exit, but he wasn't watching them.

A slight movement at the other end in the dimness of the alley gave away the watcher. He was checking the surroundings carefully, his attention focused on Rast's companions.

Secure, the figure dropped any pretence of ambling and scooted into the alleyway, covering the ground quickly as they moved out into the main street.

It slowed as it approached the start of the torchlit regions. Rast edged smoothly over the rooftop, hidden in the shadows, and climbed down as the man approached. He was mousy-haired and tall, well-dressed if not flamboyant.

The watcher crept underneath him, and Rast leaped, landing with a soft thump a few paces behind him.

At the faint noise the man froze, tilting his head to assess what had changed.

'May I help you?' asked Rast quietly.

The figure whirled in shock, hand flying to a short sword. Rast caught the man's forearm in an iron grip as it hissed free, his other hand forcing the hilt from his attacker's grasp to land with a clang. He changed his grip, twisting the arm into a lock, shuffled the man to the right, and put his foot out in what was more of a fierce push than a kick, toe embedded in the ribs. A thrust of his leg sent the winded man crashing into the wall further back from the exit. As he tumbled, Rast caught a glimpse of something around the man's neck in the light. It looked familiar.

He leaned in and grabbed the man's jerkin as if to grip him. The man pulled back quickly. With a snap the chain gave way and Rast was holding it.

He glanced at it in the faint light and smiled grimly.

'Terome. You're an agent of Meyar. What do you want with us?'

'I'll tell you nothing,' snarled the man. He looked frightened as he struggled to his feet. It was likely he knew exactly who Rast was.

'Perhaps,' said Rast. 'You would tell the Eyots more.'

'You'll be arrested for assault. I've done nothing wrong.'

Rast stared at the man, ignoring his words. He'd been fast but stiff with the weapon; he was a better shadow than warrior. An Incursor; a spy of Terome.

'You are an enemy agent in a city your people besiege. You would find me more reasonable than they,' he reasoned.

A faint presence intruded.

'He'll tell them nothing,' a flat voice said behind Rast.

Rast looked over his shoulder. A tall figure stood ten feet away, cloaked and still. It strode forward, and Rast turned smoothly, dropped the pendant and holding a warning hand up. He sank slightly into his legs, ready.

'Close enough.'

The cloaked figure stopped a few feet away. 'My fight is not with you,' a low voice said. It was rough and dispassionate. 'This man is an enemy of Eordeland.'

'The Eyots are allies,' said Rast. 'They will deal with him.' He was in a bad position, with the other at his back, and kept his senses alert for any sudden moves.

The cloaked figure shrugged, and turned as if to go, then lashed out. There was a metallic, mechanical *thunk* noise, and a long, thin blade sprang from the back of his right hand, so suddenly it seemed like magic.

Rast was moving even as he saw the hand strike, and his foot connected hard with the wrist. The blade hit the wall next to the man, the tip sending a line of sparks down before snapping under the immense pressure. Even as it did, a hand grabbed his ankle and twisted hard.

Rast felt his balance give, and hopped, then jumped and turned mid-air, using the grip and leverage. His other foot connected with nothing. His foe swayed under it, letting go and retreating. He was fast, and well trained.

Hands flashed at his face as he landed, and he blocked, unable to avoid the following foot that slammed into his side *hard.*

Exceptionally well trained.

Better than anyone Rast had fought for some time.

He moved with the blow, twisting, and lifted his own leg in a hooking kick. It caught the retreating leg, and the man wobbled for a second.

It was enough to blast through his defences and deliver a brutal two-fisted strike to his foe's solid stomach and chest. The man was thrown back, falling. He turned the movement into a roll and swept back to his feet, one hand to his solar plexus.

They paused.

The Meyari's footsteps were already fading as he fled. He would be difficult to find, and Rast could not turn his back to this foe.

'And now we both lose our prize,' he said bleakly. 'Eyotsburg and Eordeland both could have gleaned much from him.'

Faint gleams came from shaded eyes above a short white goatee.

'He knew little. He is part of a sickness that requires lancing. I will not forget you prevented me from my duty, warrior. Have a care.'

'Seek me at your peril,' said Rast. 'I'll not stay my hand again.'

The figure nodded. 'Nor should you.' His hand whipped up, something heavy leaving it. Rast twisted back, allowing his cloak to foil its flight as he fell backwards. A puff of choking smoke billowed from whatever it was. He clamped his lips shut and rolled backwards out of it, away from any attacks or poison. When he flipped back to his feet, the man had gone.

The cloud seemed to have been harmless, a distraction, and was rapidly thinning. Rast moved to the wall for cover and stood poised until he was certain he was truly alone. Glancing down, he found his foot on the broken blade still at the base of the wall. It was thin and of a curious design.

He tucked it carefully into a pouch and grimaced.

He was unlikely to find his prey now. The best he could do was pass his description on to the guard and hope they caught him.

He began to pad back towards the lodgings, thinking of the mysterious attacker.

A new complication.

THIRTY-NINE

Cataract clouds reduced the moon to a sightless, blurred white orb that did little to brighten the island city. The lights from the land and a string of lights around the harbour were bright, but they petered out into the estuary itself. Ships were flanked by enemies on either shore, and no matter how far the enemy, most preferred to run dark until they had no other choice.

Karland stood at the window, looking out down the slope of the city to the lights of the market and harbour. Their rooms were on the highest floor, looking out over nearby rooftops. Further down they were like a short forest of chimneys, broken only by a wall every so often.

The rooms were fine. He still wasn't used to much opulence. Much as he hated it in many ways, being on the road removed many complications, like his constant worry he would damage something and cause some poor server trouble.

He was unconsciously testing his back and hips where Mirembe had said she had fixed issues. It did feel freer, but it ached now, mostly in a bar above his hip bones on the left. According to Mirembe, this was from muscles that had over-compensated for misalignment on the right side. He supposed dubiously that made a certain amount of sense, and he certainly felt better.

He was gazing out at the harbour for some time, his thoughts far away, on friends left behind. Something drew his attention back. He stood puzzled for a moment, then caught a faint flicker of movement from the corner of one eye. Freezing, he turned his head as slowly as he could, dreading what he would see.

There was nothing but a patch of darkness running vertically up a spire on a nearby roof. The surrounding area was also in shadow, and he could see nothing else. He kept still, his heart thudding and his breathing sounding harsh. It was at an angle from the window, off to the right.

There! Another suggestion of movement, and then for the first time he saw it clearly. The suggestion resolved into a crouched form, huge and threatening atop the spire. The movement was in the shadows around it, a hint of wings unfurling, wafting in the light breeze. It seemed to be gazing down into the harbour as well, attentively.

He blinked rapidly, but with each second he was more certain of what he saw.

He must have moved or made some noise, because it seemed to turn its head to look at him. It dropped soundlessly down and swept into the shadows as if they were a doorway to another realm.

He gasped, leaping back from the window and trembling.

Are we cursed? He wondered. *Does it hunt us?*

It *had* to be the same creature from Fordun's Run; the demon that attacked men in the night.

It had been sitting there, not fifteen feet from him, savouring the night air! There was no mistake this time, and since Darost and The Sanctum - where he had almost persuaded himself it was not the same beast - he had been keeping an eye out for it almost without realising. As if, he thought fearfully, he had known it would reappear again.

Or maybe there are hundreds! In every city. That was more likely, but an equally disturbing thought.

He had been paralysed a minute or so. He broke it and moved quickly for the corridor, looking for the next room and Rast. He whispered urgently through the door, knowing the big man would hear him.

'Rast! *Raaaaaasssst!*

The door opened swiftly and quietly after a short pause, controlled every inch of the way. Someone else might have flung the door open, he thought. He beckoned Karland through and closed it with a quiet click. There were no lights in this room, and the window looked out to the right of the small spire. It was cracked open for air, and Rast closed this too before turning to Karland.

Quickly he related what had happened. Rast said nothing until the end.

'You are certain you saw this thing? You believe it is the same as from Fordun's Run, perhaps The Sanctum?'

'Yes!' Karland burst out. Rast raised a quick hand for him to lower his voice.

'I sensed nothing amiss this night.' He raised his hand again to forestall Karland, his face faintly lit from outside. 'I believe you. I can think of nothing that would hunt us across the continent like this, however. Nothing that *could*. And remember, it did not attack us either time before - assuming it is the same creature, and assuming that there is only one.' His tone reflected Karland's earlier thought.

'Maybe, Rast, but it was there,' said Karland forcefully, willing the big man to believe him. 'It *looked* at me. You wait; tomorrow we'll hear about a group of sailors torn apart in an alley or something.'

'There are enough out there for it to find, if it was of a mind,' said Rast. 'We shall see. I felt no threat, and much moves nearby in a close city like this.'

Karland didn't know what troubled him more: that Rast had sensed nothing wrong, or that the creature had dogged their footsteps.

'What'll we do?' he asked. His fear had receded, but the idea of a shadowy demon haunting him was making him too nervous to sleep. It hadn't followed Xhera. Why him?

'I could search now, but I suspect it has moved on elsewhere,' said Rast thoughtfully. 'Come with me tomorrow, and we will enquire with the guard if anything suspicious has been noticed.'

'All right,' said Karland. He wasn't keen on the thought of Rast vanishing off now. What if it came back when he was not here?

'I shall be vigilant,' said Rast. 'Fear not, my friend. I suspect whatever it is means us no harm - if it did, it has had more than one chance to strike.'

'I'd feel better knowing what it wants,' groaned Karland softly. Rast smiled slightly.

'Sleep on it, Karland.' He opened the door, checking the corridor.

Karland left and moved carefully along to his room. Before he could open the door, a figure materialised from the gloom further down, and he nearly yelped.

'What's going on?' The Green Warrior asked softly.

'Eternal hells,' Karland growled. 'Could you not *do* that?'

'Man up,' suggested the form, and he *knew* The Green Warrior would be grinning at his discomfort.

Karland quickly filled him in, sensing rather than seeing the sceptical head tilt.

'Really? A demon. That follows you. For years. Without doing anything.'

'*Yes.* Ask Rast tomorrow, if you don't believe me.' The last of his residual fear had vanished in the sharper heat of annoyance. 'I'm going to bed.'

'Right. I'll keep an eye out,' said The Green Warrior doubtfully. '...you sure it wasn't just your reflection?'

'Oh, shut up,' snapped Karland, knowing he was being needled. The sharp-eared shape merely shrugged and moved off. Sighing, he shut his door, latched it, and glanced back out the window again. Nothing moved.

'They both think I'm a nut,' he groaned as he lay down. He was there a while thinking thoughts before sleep took him.

೮೩   ೮೦

Two days later Rast and Karland met the Portmistress at the northern docks. The ship was almost ready to depart, and Rast was to meet the Captain. Despite careful queries the day before, no one had seen any night demon. That didn't make Karland feel better.

Portmistress Quirla strode through the docks with absolute authority towards them, barking orders, and then beckoned them after her. They walked for many minutes through a profusion of sails and masts, past huge twin-masted barques, large triple-mast frigates bristling with sail and armament, smaller corvettes, barges and huge haulers dotted amongst the sleeker war vessels. There were ships from many other lands, too. Dragon-headed longboats with square sails and low gunwales from Poviir berthed next to slope-decked dhows with high sterns. It seemed that most considered Eyotsburg a free port in terms of docking, although Karland saw no Meyari or Novinian craft.

She halted near a low, long, tall-masted vessel, handsome and gleaming dark brown under cumulus sails.

'You're lucky to get the *Eastern Star*', she said. 'She's a new Eyotsburg Clipper, well-built and well-manned. You must be important to get a ship of the line during war - she can carry enough troops to do some serious damage, but she is one of the fastest we have and can run any blockade Meyar or Novin might set.' She saw Karland's expression. 'I wouldn't worry about the Rats or Sea-Cows. On their galleons you'll find pressed and untrained crew, and variable stores. They have navies of convicts, jobless, the unskilled.' Her voice rang with professional disdain. 'Eyots are sailors and marines first.' Quirla grinned through surprisingly good teeth, one incisor gold with what Karland guessed was a tiny sea creature pattern on it, although he found it hard to see in detail.

She gestured to the end of the dock where the ship sat, gently bumping large knotted rope-ball fenders into the wharf wall. The wharf was long enough to have several high wooden jetties along its length. A stocky man stood casting a close eye over the side of the vessel, arms crossed and one hand stroking an impressive jutting beard.

'Old Captain Rosso there used to be a pirate. He knows how to keep men in line, but he is a well-liked - and sanctioned - captain of the fleet. Canny sailor and marine.'

'Used to be a pirate?' enquired Rast.

He didn't look much like a pirate in stories, Karland thought. More neat brown hair and gruff competence, less parrot and vehemence, and a distinct lack of sword.

'Well, yes. One of the best out there. A very good thief and a shrewd judge of men. And honourable - didn't kill just for the sport. When they finally caught him, he was given the Choice - the Lakefalls, or Privateering and paying it back as a captain. He took the latter. He knew his time was over. I think he only did it for the excitement, anyway.'

'Didn't that make him unpopular?' asked Karland.

The Portmistress laughed.

'He's hardly the first, or the last. His men trusted him well enough to elect him for more than ten years. It took a quarter of the fleet to catch him in the end. We ambushed him in the estuary from five directions and only caught him when he ran aground.'

'He was elected?' Rast asked mildly in surprise.

'Pirate Captains usually are, Master Tal'Orien,' the woman replied in amusement. 'Our sanctioned Captains have more authority on their ships in theory, but they answer to the Conclave, not to the crew. Pirate captains aren't quite the villains despised by their men that the bards sing about. They're shrewd businessmen and normally popular with their ship.'

'So how long is it to the eastern ports of Mithtol?' asked Karland.

'It's a careful trip down the estuary. There are hazards, a lot of of traffic. But don't worry, once in the open seas nothing can beat an Eyotsburg clipper under full sail. About fifteen days at most. Closer to ten if the trade wind gets behind her.'

'That's not too long,' Karland mused. He thought about the next time he would see Xhera. He found himself missing her again. 'So we formally request aid from the elves, then come back?' he asked Rast.

'That's the plan,' said Rast with a shrug. 'With luck, we shall not be much over forty days, if we can convince them quickly.'

'What if we can't?'

'We stay until we can,' the big man said quietly. 'Or until it is clear our cause is lost. The elves have their own battles.'

'Then I can travel back home. Help Xhera,' Karland said. He also missed his family, and The Croft, although it now seemed like such a small place. His town of birth was forever changed for him after the battle with the orcs, but it still held nostalgia. Deep down though he felt strangely unhomed, as if he no longer belonged anywhere.

'After bringing the answer to Darost, yes,' said Rast. 'I will travel with you if you wish. Until I am no longer free to.' His hand briefly gripped Karland's shoulder. He left unspoken that he also had another claim now in Leona.

'I'd like that,' said Karland. He felt deep emotion at the loyalty his friend showed him. With a twinge of shame, he remembered when he had shied from Rast because of his brutal dealings with the men who had attacked them in Fordun's Run. The only thing that could prevent Rast from his duty was a deeper duty. He was a solid rock in the shifting flow of the stream of humanity.

Karland took in the ship. She was slim, not the largest by far, her deck all one level, but she had the tallest masts in the dock, and there were three. White bundles were furled on the booms and a carving of a crying eagle opened its beak on the prow. It looked fierce and joyful. He also noticed how many sailors moved around her and saw one thing that was definitely different to Eordeland.

'How come there are only men there?' asked Karland. He had seen both men and women of many nationalities rubbing shoulders on ships that were preparing to sail to the east down the Eofer in Darost.

'In Eyotsburg, men rule the sea and women rule the land,' the Portmistress grinned. ''Tis bad luck for a woman to be in charge or work on a ship, and on deck men are kings, the Ocean their Mother and jealous love. There's no place there for us. The ship is a lady and the sea is a mistress; that is more than enough for them. But when they make port, well! The women deal with Father Stone. We nurture him, govern him, guide him. Men who try to make decisions on land do not fare well, except for the Guard. Once they set foot on my dock, even Captains had best heed me, or find their timbered lady landlocked for a while.'

'And you govern over all the harbour?'

''Tis a heady thing, to have power over so many other ladies,' she smirked, gold tooth glinting. 'Come. I'll introduce you to the Captain.'

He was stockier close up, with a weather-worn face.

'So, you're the passengers that have the Conclave's lines knotted,' he said, nodding gruffly. His voice was rough and powerful, sounding as if it would rather be shouting, and his eyes peered a surprising blue from his face, one held more open than the other as if he was used to squinting through thick eyebrows. Despite his gruff demeanour, they twinkled in his face.

Barrel-chested and thick of neck, he hid his balding spot with a peaked cap. He held his large square-fingered hand out, and Karland noticed that despite his brown beard, shot through with grey and ginger, the hairs on his wrist appeared more golden.

With a grunt, he shook their hands, Darost-style, but with a curious motion. He held his hand out ready but cocked back, a little up and to the side, and then like a striking snake it snapped forward and grabbed Karland's. He nearly jumped, and then had a moment to try and return the pressure hammering down before his hand was let go and the man turned to Rast.

The Captain could have crushed spars with his hands for a living. Karland guessed it was from a lifetime of hauling thick ropes as he flexed his fingers.

There was a marked *pock!* as Rosso's cupped hand slapped into Rast's, and a look of surprise as he met a grip as great as his own. He gave one firm shake with an approving nod, and then let go.

'I've a good ship and crew, Master Tal'Orien,' he said. 'She'll get you there quickly. This must be important, to come from the Conclave themselves.'

'You are beset by the Meyari to the north,' said Rast. 'And Novin are in their pocket to the south. There is worse abroad in Anaria. The sooner we speak to the High Council of the Elves, the better. We could use their aid.'

'Aye,' said Rosso, his mouth firm. 'I'm worried about my island home, here. My only consolation is if they ever take the Citadel, we shall all become pirates, and they'll find the fear of the sea put in 'em.'

Again, thought Karland, seeing quite plainly the man almost relishing the thought.

'How long will the voyage take?' he asked.

Rosso pursed his mouth, his fingers rising to his chin.

'Oh, I'd say might be twelve days there with the current winds, if they hold and we catch the tide. We land on the Eastern Isles on a protected inside port. Mayhap fifteen days return, a bit more. How long'll you be there?'

Karland shrugged. 'No idea.' He looked at Rast.

'A week at most, I hope,' said Rast. 'We have two elves with us to speed our way.' He gauged Rosso carefully. 'One of the passengers may be an ork. I hope that is no problem.'

'An ork,' repeated Captain Rosso. He chuckled. 'Big lubbers, they are. No, no problems from me, or my crew. You sure that plains mover will have none at sea?' Rast shrugged, and the Captain nodded. 'You'd be surprised what we have seen in Eyotsburg. Shouldn't do more'n raise a few eyebrows.'

'That is good,' said Rast. 'There may be six of us. Our errand is urgent; when can we leave?'

'Soon,' said Rosso. 'She's unladen and being checked over. Say, the day after tomorrow on the ebb of high tide. Just past midday?'

'You have tides this far up?'

'Oh, aye, every twelve hour or so, regular as clockwork most of the month. That's why the water is so mucky for much of the river. Full of sediment, when the water is exchanged. We get a good twelve feet rise where the estuary slows, and the pilings on the edges of the harbours are for warping ships in. Dangerous business, unless you know your way or hit high tide. That's why we have pilots stationed inside the mouth, for foreign vessels, if they wish the safe route.' He wrinkled his seamed face in a smile, clearly happy with the fact that amateurs were not encouraged to sail in. 'Been even harder in the last few months. Flood tide brought some bloated bodies. Horrible grey-green skinned things, didn't look like men. Scores of 'em, clear out to the sea, as if whatever they were tried to cross, whole tribe or something. The skin reminded me of orks, but they didn't look like none.'

'Beware any mention of that to our plains friend,' said Rast. 'They are distant and hated kin. I would guess they were trying to cross into Meyar unseen.'

Rosso nodded. 'So. Are we agreed?'

'Done.' Rast shook his hand again, as did Karland, wincing at the odd quick grab. It felt as if the man's hand was a leather bag stuffed with rocks.

∛ ∛

That night they visited a tavern, down on the lower Hamnestad. Mirembe joined them, saying it had the best river and sea food in Eyotsburg for hungry travellers. It was boisterous inside, not as reserved as the upper city, but they served good dark ales and a light fizzing wine made from the fruit of a freshwater river tree.

'Watch yourselves in here,' said Mirembe. 'River taverns are not places to be careless.' The bouncers nodded to her, smiling, and she smiled back. People knew her well here.

Rast nodded, and she sighed. 'You've been here before. At least remember you are still healing.' She led them to a booth table big enough for five.

The elves had declined to come, instead climbing onto the roof of the house and sitting to listen to the stars, as they put it. They seemed quite happy, at least.

Rast ordered fatflank, a steak-like dark fish resembling a shield from the river which was dusted in black pepper and salt. As usual, he inhaled the aroma carefully before lifting it to his lips. Mirembe ordered freshwater octopus, roasted and heaped with lemon and crisped bread, along with a slender metal stem of the fizzing wine.

Darkus had listened in suspicion to the descriptions of the food and then ordered a whole grilled salmon which also came with lemon slices. He shuddered when he saw Mirembe's chunks of tentacle, and then spat and coughed when he bit into a lemon wedge. He looked as if he had just been attacked, and his expression reduced Karland to fits of laughter and caused The Green Warrior to suck air between his teeth, thump the table, and laugh a silent, open-jawed laugh as he looked around to share the joke.

Karland showed Darkus how to squeeze the lemon lightly over the fish. With no small trepidation he tried some and his face relaxed into a happy smile.

'It's good!' he proclaimed with a full mouth.

542

The Green Warrior and Karland both ordered the specialty of the island - a large white-fleshed fish called *tepiya* from the sea, skin removed and fish covered in crispy batter and fried in oil. A dark vinegar was sprinkled on it with salt; alongside it came thin salted potato slices and a strange green paste which turned out to be similar to peas. It was absurdly good.

As they ate and drank, they talked. Karland had a full tankard of ale bought for him by The Green Warrior, which Rast studiously ignored. The mood was light and happy, and Karland felt lightheaded quite quickly, deciding one ale was enough. The taste was odd and dark but very clean; Mirembe said the Eyots ran it through fish scales to purify it. It complemented the fish well.

This, he decided, was what life was about; travelling with good companions and eating fine food. He only wished Xhera and the elves were with them; she was more than a thousand miles east, and Galnór and Lëlylien ate no flesh.

As they spoke, Karland noticed that Mirembe touched Rast's arm often, laughing with him, and fuzzily decided she was in love with the big man. It was just something about how she was around him. Rast clearly cared about her, but not in the same way he did Leona.

He turned his attention back to the talk.

'The world's full of some strange shit,' The Green Warrior was agreeing.

'Like what?' asked Darkus, belching.

'I heard in South Novin, right, a whole village of people started arching backwards, then crawling on all fours like that. Lost the ability to speak words, just mewled. Still managed to get their work done and have a life though.'

'What happened to them?' Karland asked, fascinated.

'Other villages killed them all. Men, women, children. Burned them all alive.'

Rast sighed. 'I heard the same tale. The things men will do in superstition and fear… if there is even truth to it.'

The Green Warrior stretched and then poured the last of the fourth ale down his throat. Karland wondered how he could sit and just drink, but then the Warrior was a mere apprentice next to Darkus, who was pouring ale after ale into his mouth as if they were water.

They chatted a while longer, Mirembe and Karland remembering Aldwyn. Darkus laughed at some of the tales, but The Green Warrior seemed bored.

'Back in a minute,' said The Green Warrior eventually, standing and heading for the jakes at the back. Karland felt the ale making its presence known as well and stood to go with him. The Green Warrior moved off without looking back.

଼ଃ   ଓ

543

Karland knew The Green Warrior's mood had changed. It wasn't exactly soured, but he'd seen how, sometimes, a devil rose up within his companion. He relieved himself and waited for the Warrior, who stepped out moments later, looking around carefully.

A man with slightly gapped teeth bumped into him as he stepped sharply back from the bar and turned with a muttered apology. The Green Warrior stared at him belligerently for a moment, then waved it away, but the man had seen the look.

'Whassit?' he said, staring back at The Green Warrior. His companion was a woman, Karland with long golden hair in two braids. She was glaring at them.

The man held up his tankard, an Eyotsburg-style affair with a capped lid to prevent spillage and carvings of fish on the side. Eyots brought their own drinking receptacles with them, Karland had learned.

'Have some,' he said. Karland couldn't tell if it was a peace offering or a demand.

'No,' said The Green Warrior impatiently. He made to move past. The man slapped the tankard into his chest, spilling beer on his tunic.

The Green Warrior's eyes went dangerously flat.

Shit, thought Karland.

'Don't touch me,' said The Green Warrior with what Karland thought to be uncharacteristic patience.

The man blinked.

'Eh? Whassup?'

He patted The Green Warrior's chest again, deliberately, spilling more beer.

'You look like a rat, and I don't want you to touch me,' growled The Green Warrior. 'Get that piss away from me.'

The man squinted and leant forwards, then stuck his chin out and prodded him in the left pectoral with a hard finger. The Warrior bared his teeth, and the man tried to dash the tankard in his face.

The Green Warrior ducked, sweeping upwards into an uppercut which lifted the other man off his feet. As the man hit the floor he turned to go, and the woman leapt onto his back with a shriek, tearing his tunic as she clawed at him.

Karland tried to grab her, but The Green Warrior twisted and pulled her in front of him. He crossed his arm before him and lifted his open hand, glowering at her, poised for a second. Before Karland could protest, his hand whipped down, backhanding her hard across the face. With a yelp she fell to the floor, and he turned to go.

'Are you serious?' said Karland incredulously. A movement made them both turn; the man was coming back in, this time with a knife in his hand. Dimly through the commotion, Karland heard Rast shouting.

'Warrior!'

The Green Warrior ducked under the strike and grabbed the man's legs. He pulled up, lifting him off his feet and propping him on his hip, and then pushed and thrust, tipping the man upside down and driving his face and neck hard into the floor. It was a curious motion, as if he were thrusting a spade's blade into the ground, the man's own weight and momentum doing most of the work. The attacker tried to rise, his nose spread sideways and his back kinked, then staggered and fell groaning even as the woman leapt a second time. This time her nails tore the Warrior's tunic open and drew bloody welts down his chest.

He roared and dragged her around again, glaring down the length of his nose. Her anger collapsed as his arm was raised across again, the back of his hand ready. Karland watched, astonished. Everyone seemed to pause in disbelief.

This time The Warrior hit her hard enough to spin her as she dropped.

Silence descended as if someone had cast a spell. The whole fight had taken moments. Chairs were thrust back as patrons leapt up, looking at them. Several drew knives.

'Best get out of here,' observed The Green Warrior, almost cheerfully. His mood had improved.

Karland groaned. This wasn't good.

At that moment Darkus arrived and grabbed The Green Warrior's arm, his bulk giving those around them pause.

'Come on, Warrior,' he rumbled, and pulled him back towards their table. Rast had risen and was speaking to several men who were approaching, pitching his voice for the incoming bouncers.

'Serrs. We are not looking for trouble. Please. My apologies for our companion.'

'Speak for yourself, Tal'Orien,' laughed The Green Warrior, peering around the ork, who was trying to quiet him. 'Some of these ugly faces look like they need a bashing.' He looked for the rat-faced man, who was nowhere to be seen. 'Maybe already had them.'

'He fucked up Klin right proper, and he were only mindin he own business,' one of the men yelled. 'Tried to offer a friendly drink. So we show this *flot* the same cursty, like.'

Two men moved forward and Rast stepped to meet them. There was clear warning in his face. Darkus moved to intercept another, and they stood, uncertain.

'We do not want to fight,' said the huge ork in his deep voice.

Karland blinked. He was certain this was the first time an ork had ever said *that*. Grukust would have been joyfully knocking heads in seconds.

A gasp sounded before the clatter of a knife, and people turned to see a man who had been sidling towards Rast in the crowd with his arm twisted by his bent hand; Mirembe held it casually in fingers Karland knew were deceptively strong. She jabbed stiff fingers into his shoulder, and he hissed in pain. Letting the deadened arm flop limp, Mirembe motioned to the owner. The bouncers were clearly debating approaching Rast and the ork.

The owner called. 'All you lot stand down. I don't want breakages. Take this outside if you must or sit your arses down.'

'Break up now, lads,' one of the bouncers said. He was a big, bald man with a quiet voice and a tattoo of a trident on the back of one hand, the shaft going up his forearm. He motioned them back to their seats. 'Appreciate it if you get your gear and leave.' He sounded regretful. 'Apart from you of course, Mirembe.'

Mirembe held up her hands. 'A misunderstanding,' she said calmly. 'I will see the man who was hurt free of charge and set everything to rights, from this or otherwise.' It was a generous offer, Karland knew, having experienced it. He'd been horrified to hear how much she normally charged per hour of treatment, and that was but a fraction of what Mistress Corvath charged.

The Green Warrior opened his mouth and Darkus clamped a gigantic hand on his shoulder.

'Warrior. Calm down,' the ork said. 'You place our quest in danger.'

'So?'

'If you go to the local gaol, you will be left behind,' said Rast shortly.

'It wasn't my fault,' the Warrior protested. 'Trouble just finds me.'

'Conveniently,' said Rast. His voice was calm, but Karland could tell he was not amused. 'You could have avoided that whole fight. This is Eyotsburg. *You do not hit women.*'

'They attacked me first.'

'You knocked a woman senseless!'

'Look what the bitch did,' said The Green Warrior, gesturing to his deeply scratched chest. Rast waved it away.

'You are skilled enough to have stopped them without serious harm. We are here with Mirembe, and you embarrass us... and her.' Karland couldn't deny Rast's words; The Warrior had been looking for a fight. 'Our mission is vital. You imperil it.'

'So you're on their side?' demanded The Green Warrior, shrugging off Darkus's hand with a smooth movement and moving back. 'So now I know how much I can trust you, is that it?' For a moment he looked as if he would attack the next person to approach.

Karland had never actually seen Rast exasperated before. 'We are not on any *sides*. You are our companion. Can you not see you endanger us with these games?'

Hoping his companion would listen to him, Karland added, 'Look, Warrior. Can't you just apologise? Say it was a mistake?'

'Oh, I *meant* to hit him.' He saw their looks and laughed, unrepentant. 'I didn't do them any real harm.' His expression was so innocently disingenuous even Mirembe coughed a laugh, although she still looked annoyed.

'You have cost me money, Warrior. You owe me.'

'I'll pay,' he said, suddenly totally serious. 'I mean it. Sorry. Look, sometimes I go a little crazy.' He smiled a hopeful little smile, and even Karland didn't know if he was in earnest or playing further. He had certainly never expected to hear him apologise.

'That is an understatement,' rumbled Darkus. 'You should be an ork. Except you're too dishonest.'

The Green Warrior winked at him, and the ork snorted, throwing his heavy arms up in a strangely human gesture.

Rast sighed. 'Mirembe... my apologies.'

'Oh, Rast.' She touched his face fondly. 'Ever honourable. It was not your fault.' She glanced at the Warrior. 'But I think you need to keep a close eye on this one.'

She led them out under the watchful eyes of the bouncers. Mirembe passed a token to the owner of the bar, who followed them out.

'Truly, that was some of the most amazing food I've ever had,' said Karland, and the owner smiled gratefully, his lines of worry fading. The others concurred, and The Green Warrior clapped the startled man on the back.

'Best food I can remember.'

The owner nodded uncertainly. 'Serr... you're clearly from out-town. You mayhap don't realise some customs. When Klin knocked you, he was offering you a sip in apology from his personal drinker. That's an honour, see? For peace. And when you refused it was an insult. He shulnt ha hit you, right enough. But also... you don't hit women here, serr. The other ladies would ha taken care of her. When women stand on Father Stone, he takes exception to men laying hands. Same comes from women hitting men on boats. It's bad luck for all.'

'Right,' said The Green Warrior, nodding. 'Won't happen again.'

The owner sighed. 'Give it awhile afore you return, and I'll consider it done.' He turned to Mirembe and bowed. 'Mirembe.'

'My apologies again,' she said.

'None needed, Mistress. It was an outlander mistake, and you made amends. The rock has dropped.' They went back in, the bouncers nodding to them.

Mirembe gave a small laugh.

'My reputation is secure, it seems. Warrior, you owe me a half-day's work for what you did.'

'You'll have it,' he promised. 'What'd he mean about the rock?'

'When a rock drops into water, it sinks and is gone. Done is done.'

'Fair.'

ڨ   C)

Karland woke later the next day and spent a rare morning relaxing and doing some light training with Rast. They were resting on the first floor when the light was eclipsed, and their huge green friend came in. Darkus's skin was flushed darker than usual. He sat, heaving deeply.

'Are you all right?' asked Karland, concerned. Rast moved over.

Darkus shook his head, and then burst out laughing, his frame shaking with the force of it.

'That lunatic human will be my death,' he finally managed, wiping tears from his eyes.

'What has he done now?' asked Rast in a resigned voice.

'I wished to see the Stonestrides. He said he would take me in style and left, returning with a cart and a small horse. I do not know where he got them.' The ork snorted briefly, and then managed to go on. 'We got on it and he drove it around towards the northern gate. It was shut. He said we would see the southern. I was unused to riding but he seemed in fine spirits, so I rested. We were on the way when a wagon loaded with cargo slammed us from the side. It tipped us and kept going.'

'And?' Karland asked, fascinated.

'And… and...' the ork gulped. 'And he ran after it, shouting. The driver was swerving the beasts left and right and ran them right into the front of an eatery. The Green Warrior caught it and grabbed the reins from her.'

'Are you telling me he hit another woman? Is he in gaol?'

Darkus was shuddering with laughter again. 'No, human. No. The driver fled into the eatery. I think she was trying to escape but she was staggering like a baby *rinok*. I am sure she was too drunk to see.'

548

'So what did he do?'

'He… he…' Darkus was actually hiccoughing. 'He grabbed her wrist and yanked her arm up, with her hand at her neck. She looked like an outraged chicken with a folded wing. And then he sh-sh-shouted, ah, *vannon sen,* he shouted, '*Citizen's arrest!*' and marched her out the door again.' The ork bellowed with laughter, thumping the seat so hard dust jumped from it. '*Citizen's arrest!*' he nearly howled.

Karland was laughing so hard now he couldn't breathe. 'What does that even mean?'

'I have no idea,' said Rast, and Karland looked up, breathing hard, to find the big man grinning and laughing quietly to himself. 'So where is he now?'

'He dragged her to the nearest guards. They took one look at her and shackled her,' said Darkus weakly, sprawling on the seat. 'The customers eating had never seen anything like it. The staff were cheering for him. He was laughing like a drunken *Uruk.* We got the cart righted and he brought us back here to the inn next door as if demons were after us. He vanished at the back of our lodgings as I sat outside, trying to… recover, and some skinny human ran up shouting about a thief that took his horse and cart and demanded to know how it got there. The Warrior came out of our door as if he had been here all day and told him some story about seeing a cloaked figure. He is still out there, the other human believing every word.' The ork shook his head, still laughing. 'Ah. You humans are too strange.'

'One of us is, anyway,' said Rast wryly. 'I take it back. We dare not leave him behind. There may be no Eyotsburg left to return to.'

Karland grinned, but his reply was serious.

'He has no-one else, Rast. We can't leave him here; I made him a promise, and he's my friend.' As he said it, he knew it to be true. The Green Warrior was as much one as any of the others now. He was struggling with his loss of self, cast adrift. It would be hard for anyone.

His humour bubbled back up. 'And if nothing else, he doesn't let life get boring.'

Rast smiled gently. 'You are right, Karland. He is volatile, a man of dark moods. But he is also steadfast, loyal, and true. You could not ask a better friend. He would take a blade in the heart for you. For any of us, I think, though he will not admit it. And we owe him much. He faces great uncertainty.'

'I think he is right though,' mused Darkus with a chuckle. 'Things *do* happen to him.'

Karland was also starting to wonder if that wasn't true.

'Thank the gods we leave tomorrow,' said Rast.

෪ ෨

They bade their goodbyes to the surviving Eordeland Guard that evening. Eyotsburg was grateful to Eordeland for the offers of aid; the sappers were already at work on projects to enhance the defensibility of the bridges.

There were too few of them, thought Karland sadly. Two hundred and twenty-one had set out from Darost, not including the companions. Only ninety-seven remained able, the other twelve crippled. Mistress Corvath had not lost a single one, but many of them would never fight again. Too many had lost limbs.

It seemed there was a limit to what she could do.

They were lucky that Eordeland looked after its wounded veterans; many realms didn't. Right now, they were trapped in a foreign land far from home with war at the bridges, recovering from the battles and the horrors they had faced.

Karland felt guilt when he looked at them. Many had fallen keeping foes from him. He would add Kith to the lengthening list of people he vividly remembered dying, though his had been worse than most. He had faced many nightmares of that fight.

He wouldn't ever hear his straight-faced quarrelling with Gen again.

Sergeant Cowlin's fate was not yet known either. With Rast leaving, the City had moved him to a secure ward. The Druids had warned that they would search for him. If they found he was tainted they would kill him immediately, and anyone else they suspected. In this they were resolute; to allow him to live would cause a great many more deaths. Mistress Corvath had said she could detect nothing untoward in him but couldn't explain why he wasn't healing properly.

The companions would have been in much worse condition but for Mirembe - who had worked miracles despite her protestations at not having a drop of what the Mors called Talent in her body - and her *Mganga*.

They had to reach the eastern isle port of Rhuntol, which the elves referred to as *Rhuneyatól*. Galnór and Lëlylien said there would be high-ranking elves who could send word to *Míthtól*. They would not be allowed onto the island itself; no other race had ever set foot on their homeland, but the elves would come to them.

Galnór held no doubt that they would swiftly arrange aid for Anaria. The troubles there would spread, if the elves did not already face their own. No matter if the might of the Eldar kept their foes at bay; if the rest of the world fell to darkness, even Mithtol could not expect to last forever. Not if demons of great power moved on the face of the earth. Not if Yoysgaloth roamed free. Eventually even the isles of the elves might be found and cast beneath the waters, and the wails of the lost would be their only voices, wisping on the wind.

All throughout Eyotsburg rumours already ran; the lands across the great oceans faced troubles too. Matalaga was dissolving into fierce wars sweeping westward, and Hadrasia held faint whispers about some kind of scourge.

'Do you travel with us, Warrior?' asked Rast as they stood at the gangplank to the clipper the next morning. 'You have your own quests, but you are one of us.'

The Green Warrior shrugged.

'You lead interesting lives, Tal'Orien. You could use my help. Anyway, Karland made me a promise. So, I'll make sure he gets back from where he's going.'

Darkus's lips peeled back from his great tusks in a comradely smile as they looked to him.

'My people have never been to sea before,' he said. 'I will rejoin the tribes soon enough. Let us visit these isles and see what the elves make of an *Urukin.*'

Galnór laughed. 'Why, Darkus; my kin will find you wondrous and enigmatic, the very plains come to life. If nothing else, they may be interested in your axe... and your ability to drink Elven wine.'

'You boarding?' roared a voice from above. Captain Rosso stood, one boot on the railing, looking down at them. 'Tide's a-turning, serrs and dam. All aboard that's coming aboard.' He grinned evilly, and Karland recalled the Portmistress's story of him being a former pirate lord.

They boarded and stowed their gear, then came back up on deck. A tug heaved them north slowly, towards the northern current. The water was placid west of the jetties but livened up as they slid into the current's grip. The long clipper turned anti-clockwise, the tug disengaging quickly and making for the gentler waters in the middle. The water grabbed the tall ship like a giant's hand, and they accelerated almost imperceptibly downriver, sails unfurling to catch the wind.

As they left the docks, one lone boulder soared out from the northern wall, landing a good half-mile from them. Rosso barked a laugh.

'Meyari siege engine. No chance in the seven undersea hells of hitting a ship with that thing. Waste of a good rock.'

For all his talk of travelling carefully downstream, the ship moved with an easy and practised speed, and the banks flowed past.

FORTY

Captain Rosso, it turned out, *did* have a parrot. Once they were out from port, he let it fly freely about the ship. He'd claimed it from a Matalagan sailor on a ship he'd raided fifteen years ago. The man had sworn blind it knew ten languages and knew when men were lying. After letting the man go, he had realised that the parrot not only spoke no languages except its own, but if it knew when men were lying, it certainly didn't care.

They saw many other ships in the distance, but few approached a ship flying the colours of the Conclave. The estuarine river was big enough for them all, widening slowly, and they stayed to the northern edge where the river was deepest and there were few islands.

With the powerful north current and an experienced pilot for the nights, it took only four days to wend their way down the mighty Storartar.

The *Eastern Star* cut west out of the mouth of the estuary, the shores far enough apart that they were lost to view. A faint dark rock to their far left with a tower marked the domain of the *Havsfyren*. The weather was fair, if colder than on the river, with sun lancing through wisps of cloud. Karland felt freer than he had dared, knowing that the wiles of Meyar were behind them.

At least for now.

The spray of saltwater around the bowsprit and the boom of the hull as it slapped ruts in the waves became a rhythm. Karland watched in fascination as sailors swarmed all over the ship. Slowly he began to see the different roles they played. Several members of their party who clearly knew shipboard life offered to work with the crew in shifts, which Karland found out was considered polite in Eyotsburg and made the passengers something more than just cargo. Without any surprise it seemed that Rast knew exactly what to do to help, and he only had to show The Green Warrior once. Rast worked as stoically as usual and The Green Warrior with energy and a laugh. Both were extremely competent men, thought Karland, but in different ways.

Rast worked humbly and with economy, seeming never to make an error. The Green Warrior on the other hand seemed to delight in his skill and knowledge, easily sharing it and laughing where he went wrong, but equally happy to point out where others did, too. Rast's strength and methodical approach was impressive, but despite his skill and agility he couldn't scramble about quite as adeptly as the lighter-built Green Warrior. Both were experienced climbers.

The elves were both at home, too, moving around the desk and rigging as if they were on flat ground in a way none of the humans could emulate. Karland never saw them lose balance or slip.

He tried to help but felt shy, both at his companion's capabilities and the fact he knew nothing about what needed to be done. He had never been on a ship before; as usual, he worried about looking stupid.

Xhera had told him more than once that his concern over what others thought and this constant awareness of what he looked like limited him. She was right, he thought with a sigh, then caught himself wondering what it would look like if anyone saw him sitting and sighing.

Even Darkus had joined in, willing to learn. The Green Warrior had become fast friends with him, cheerfully showing Darkus what to do, and was very complimentary about the huge ork's strength. Karland was seeing yet another facet of the fascinating man. It seemed that he was less intolerant than he liked to appear; more based on a lack of skill or drive than race or species. Again, he wondered how much of it was real.

In the end it was The Green Warrior who got Karland working the lines. For a man who had such a frightening focus and anger at times, he could be so charming and persuasive. Yet always behind it was the sense that he was watching, both calculating and laughing at something only he found amusing. Karland found his hands grew sore quickly, and had to forcibly quell his companion's pressuring when he tried to get Karland into the rigging. He was still terrified of heights.

If The Green Warrior had one weakness with people, it was that he genuinely couldn't understand why others couldn't or wouldn't do what he did with ease.

The clipper flew across the Grey Sea, her slender hull slicing through the waters at the demand of her huge spread of sail. The cloth was angled to catch the northeast trade winds, and they made good time for the first two days. The Captain gave them another week to reach Rhuntol if the wind stuck.

Karland made fast friends with the ship's boy, a sprightly blond-haired lad a few years younger than him named Sam. The younger boy confided in Karland as if he were an older brother. They got on very well, Sam reminding him of Gail in some ways.

He hoped his sister was all right. He found himself missing her, and his parents.

They settled in well, becoming something more than mere passengers, and ate with the Captain every evening. Rosso's parrot refused to talk and muttered to itself constantly. It frustrated Rosso no end, but he kept it mainly, he admitted, because it seemed expected for an ex-pirate captain.

The bird was both surly and highly intelligent. However much the captain vainly yelled at his crew to call it Pip, they referred to it universally as Evil Bastard.

Karland quite liked it. He swore the bird was obtuse on purpose. The crew pretended to hate it, but secretly were quite proud of the eccentric creature, which was older than the Captain, if rumours were true.

He had taken its recalcitrance as a challenge. So far, he was losing.

Rosso would try to tease it into speech, but it would neither talk nor stay on its perch - and it was banned from his shoulder at mealtimes, which of course were often the only times it would deign to try to alight there.

Instead, as they ate, it would often pick a random chair back and sit behind the person, muttering constantly and staring balefully at the food as they tried to eat, then refusing all offerings. Karland been left with tears in his eyes when the parrot chose Darkus one evening. The ork hadn't known how to deal with it and ended up muttering to himself about the stupid creature. The Green Warrior had laughed raucously, pounding the table, and even Rast hadn't been able to stop grinning as the two muttered about each other, seemingly unaware of the echo.

On the third day out, the morning was slightly clouded, clearer than the day before. Shortly before eleven of the clock the wind abruptly switched direction, coming from the southeast instead of the northeast and causing the boatswain to change the rigging with a curse.

'Step lively!' he yelled. 'Rig for full and by!'

The wind was now to the fore and starboard, and they would need to tack or turn and run south until it changed again.

'The air is charged with intent,' remaked Lëlylien cryptically, her delicate face grave.

Galnór was rubbing his temples. 'This is not natural. Something is happening. A great change comes.'

As the crew was re-rigging, the wind died entirely. The ship slowed, rolling in the swells. Her belly slapped the sea a few times as the surface calmed.

Karland was nervous, looking out at the endless water with no land in sight. He had enjoyed the journey until now, having natural sea legs. Now the water was ominous, a foreign environment he could not survive in; indeed, one that had claimed so very many lives. The ship seemed perched over an abyss, with the unimaginable depths heavy beneath them. The parrot, perched on a capstan, let out a nervous screech and sailed towards the cabin passage. Several wary mutters passed amongst the crew.

The lookout cried from the crow's nest.

'Clouds, Cap'n! Ox-eye as I never seen afore!' He waved his arms at full stretch. 'Out o' nowhere!'

Karland followed the man's arm, saw the ominous dot of dark cloud seem to pulse out and descend. It must be a trick of the perspective, he thought, but it seemed to be swelling out to cover the whole sky. Out of the unearthly calm wind started to pick up, growing stronger by the second. The boat began to pitch, waves swelling and dropping deeper with every motion.

'This will be bad,' called Rast, barely audible above the wind. 'Make ready. You should all get below.'

'All hands! Secure loose gear and portholes! Batten the hatches!' Cries came over the growing noise, the rough voices showing little of the concern they must feel. 'Strike topsail! Reef the mainsails! Rig for storm running!'

Knowing their jobs, sailors already swarmed aloft into the rigging, chased by the commands of the bosuns.

Rosso bellowed, "Move, you rats! Boatswain! I want nothing but bare poles with trysails fore and aft!'

He turned to his passengers, all deference gone in his anxiety. 'Get below. We must run and ride this out as best we can. I've not seen a storm come up this fast or strong before, and I've seen a few typhoons in my time. Never one here, nor like this. We don't have the cargo or ballast for it. Shouldn't be possible in these seas.'

'The world is out of balance,' said Rast grimly, motioning the others to the cabins. 'If you need our-' his words were stalled by a massive blast of air which heeled the ship over to port. She listed heavily before righting and they all staggered, The Green Warrior catching himself with his hands, teeth bared. A sailor fell screaming to deck and hit with a thump, his cry cut off. The Captain whirled, bellowing.

'Flake that mainmast cloth!'

'Fitting's twisted!' was the despairing cry from aloft.

'Cut line and douse it if need be, but get those sails *down*!'

Another blast of wind hit the ship from another side, accompanied by a sudden heavy downpour of almost horizontal rain, and she tipped badly, throwing them all to the deck and against the rail. The narrow ship, built for speed, was in serious danger of capsizing if struck by any stronger gusts broadside.

An even stronger one struck the ship like a physical blow, this time from the front. The ship sat back on her stern, tilting and rotating to port.

A sharp crack cut through the rising blasts of wind, and the Captain's face went white. He ran towards the helm to take control as men threw themselves desperately out into rigging and began to slide down, but not enough of them in time.

'She's taken aback, Cap'n!'

'Clear the rigging!'

With a deafening report and a recoil that jarred the deck from under their feet, the mainmast snapped under full sail as hands dropped to the deck. The ship groaned in agony as the mast dropped to port and slammed down, the rigging catching briefly before the weight pulled the mast over the ruin of the rail. The lookout was flung from sight as if from a catapult.

Rast leapt at Karland, bearing him along the deck and landing with a thump. The Green Warrior and the elves had sprung aside, a loose line whipping the back of The Green Warrior and leaving a welt through a torn shirt. Darkus was nowhere to be seen.

The mast swept crew screaming and broken into the sea. Two sailors lost limbs, lines whipping around the flailing extremities and snapping them cleanly off. Water sprayed everywhere and the ship wallowed badly. Rigging snapped and the mast pulled itself overboard, trailing off the boom. It left a splintered mass where the railing had been, and a jagged stump seven feet high amidships. The ship shot back to level, throwing hands to starboard. Many had held tight, knowing what was coming, but Sam was hurled overboard, his thin scream cutting through the storm. His grip had not been strong enough.

Karland leapt for the rail in horror, nearly pitching over himself, but could see no sign of Sam, or Darkus. With tears in his eyes, he searched urgently for survivors, looking for a small boy or a large green form. He didn't even know if orks could swim. He knew Sam couldn't.

There were only a few men visible, some striking out desperately for the ship, others unmoving. The tethered mast slammed into and out of the water as the waves churned, and with dull shock he saw several limp bodies tangled in the rigging being submersed over and over. One was still struggling.

A roar from the stern erupted, where the Captain had ducked the destruction and surged to his feet.

'Drop the rest! Rig those bollocks-bedamned trysails!' he screamed at the bow over the wind, which was still rising. Waves were already rough enough to dip the narrow ship heavily. He helped the dazed helmsman force the ship around so that the wind was astern, their bow pointing north of Mithtol. The rest of the crew scrambled to

cut lines on all remaining sails, dumping the wind they held, and the ship stopped listing so badly and began to turn.

The Captain swore as the mast thumped against the hull. 'Cut her away!' The wind whipped through the tethered sails above with a crack, and the storm jib caught, pulling them with a lurch. He swung almost in the same breath. 'Belay that! Cut all except the longest lines and lengthen 'em out! We'll use her for a brake!' His eyes sought his most powerful passengers.

'Tal'Orien! Get that ork over here and help lay that mast behind! The way this storm is piling, we'll run too fast and founder. We need a storm drogue, keep her stable and stern square!' He turned his soaked face toward the destruction. 'Bosun!' There was no reply, and he cursed volubly. One or both must have been lost overboard. 'Quartermaster!' He continued bellowing out commands interspersed with curses.

'What about the crew?' yelled Karland, pointing at the men trying to stay afloat, or free themselves. 'And Darkus!'

Several had managed to reach the fallen mast. Captain Rosso followed his motion and a brief look of despairing sorrow crossed his face, chased by resolution.

'Leviathan's arse, boy, if we try we *all* die!' he shouted back, the agony clear in his face, and deliberately turned away again, his shoulders stiff and his jaw resolute.

'Get below!' shouted Rast at Karland through the wind and noise.

Karland shook his head dumbly. 'I can help!' He nearly pitched over the railing again with the rolling, then stumbled backwards as two huge hands clamped onto it. A pale green Darkus dragged himself back over it, soaked and shaking. Karland couldn't tell if he had caught himself as he fell, or climbed the trailing lines from the water. He was just relieved he wasn't lost to the roiling seas.

'What *is* this?' the ork's deep voice bellowed. He looked terrified.

'Hurricane!' Rast shouted. He grabbed the ork and pulled him. 'Need our strength!'

Darkus steeled himself in the drenching spray, gritting his teeth so hard his tusks dug starkly into his cheeks below his eyes. They moved back to the stern, Rast's superb balance helping them both, and together they worked with the crew to lift lines over the rails and allow the broken mast to trail the stricken craft.

The ship dove from vast wave to vast wave, the bowsprit plummeting through dark walls. The crew and passengers lashed themselves to the ship to avoid being swept overboard, and the captain stood with the helmsman, grimly gripping the helm. Rast stood with them. Darkus crouched low near him to rest, hooking a massive forearm around a nearby railing and gripping his own wrist like death. Karland stayed up top; he refused to face his fate unknowing.

The elves' superior agility was proving a boon. Neither was lashed, but their grip was strong even in water and their weight light. They moved carefully between sailors, offering help where needed as the hands manned the lines on the trysails, listening for the boom of surf in case they were driven aground, using their vision to watch for land. More than once they saved a man as his grip loosened.

All they could all do now was let the storm spend itself. There was no way of knowing where or how far they would be driven.

Up in the bow lay the strangest sight of all. The Green Warrior had lashed himself alone before the foremast, and Karland caught glimpses of him in flashes of lightning, laughing like a maniac into the wind and spray and roaring as the ship plunged into each soaking abyss. His dark eyes glittered, and he seemed to be challenging creation itself as he bellowed into the teeth of the storm around them, shouting words that were snatched by the wind. Karland couldn't tell if he was angry or afraid, but his intensity matched the that of the storm, and he was a little awed by a man who would so disregard fear to challenge the power of nature - though there was little natural about this.

Even in extremity the crew eyed The Green Warrior with a mixture of amazement and alarm, clearly thinking him touched by the gods.

Karland recalled when he had heard Aldwyn tell the Council of Twelve of the tsunami that had destroyed towns in the great Banistari Bay of Nestus, flooding the swamps. That had also come from nowhere. In the powerful sway of this hurricane, he finally truly understood at a visceral level what imbalance in the world truly meant, what rising chaos was doing to natural order.

He hung on grimly. The only thing he could think of past the dark, soaking, pitching hell became seeing Xhera again.

୦୪ ଛୠ

For hours they fought the wind, every hand labouring. After a while even the terror was numbed by the incessant motion, the violence, the immersion in a struggle where there was little room for thought. The crew trimmed the trysails constantly, manning the braces and trying to keep the ship in line enough not to heel over. The sea drogue slowed and stablised them enough that they didn't run too fast for the hull or turn to roll broadside and capsize. Every moment brought the possibility of foundering. The *Eastern Star* had not been heavily laden due to the quick mission, and the lack of cargo had the ballast spread thin. She simply didn't have enough weight in the hold.

After an indeterminate time that could have been hours or could have been days, he heard the Captain roar through the wind. 'We pass Mithtol! Driven nor'west! Watch for rocks!'

Karland saw hints of a distant island to their starboard through the lashing rain and grey skies, and wondered what the Captain meant until he remembered that Mithtol was not present to their port unless by the will of the High elves. The islands north were receiving the full fury of the storm, but Mithtol would not be, twisted through time and space as it was. Galnór had journeyed there, though Lëlylien had not yet, and had said that the weather was always mild. The land was held out of reach; no storm or enemy would find it.

They were driven unseeing along its north border and towards the Hadratic Ocean, powerless to turn and seek shelter without being driven upon rocks or rolled in the huge waves. The ship did not pass through the eye of the storm, but was impelled through the edges before beginning to move southwest, lost again in the grey maelstrom.

At some point through the rain and noise, Karland thought he caught vague distant glimpses of something huge rearing out of the sea in almost slow motion, stuttered by lightning. It was half-seen, and later Karland wondered if it had been his exhausted imagination, but he thought a vast creature had lifted itself to clash against a massive flailing mass of tentacles, the huge leviathan's maw slamming onto a kraken-sized lashing monster. Everything was grey, and they looked unearthly, as huge as dragons. The violence of their colossal battle was epitomised in the storm around them.

Do they fight because of the storm? Does the storm come from their battle?

The ship rushed on, curtains of water hiding the vision from view.

They stumbled in groups, holding on, snatching sleep where they could, pumping water, always on the brink of death, always fighting to stay alive. Their lives became nothing but the hurricane.

Finally, the storm began to blow itself out south. The waves reduced gradually, and the skies began to clear. Rain fell in patches now, and the noise of the wind started to abate.

When the sun emerged, it was as if the storm had been doused. The wind dropped back down. After the boom and roar of waves, the shriek of wind and crack of lightning, the silence was as loud as the storm had been, almost painfully so.

The crew and passengers stiffly tried to relax, letting go of lines and pawing numbly at lashings. Karland was shaking with fatigue, as were many of the crew. Darkus and Rast looked equally tired, and even the elves moved with weary care.

'Where are we?' asked one of the hands, his teeth almost chattering now that the physical effort had subsided.

'West of Mithtol,' answered the Captain. 'Far off course. We're lucky she held true.'

'Aye,' came mutters, and Karland heard whispers of thanks to their ship and various gods, mostly those of luck and the sea.

'Call a headcount,' said the Captain. 'I want a full loss and a full damage report.' His face was tired and sorrowful. Karland knew he felt responsible for all his men. The decision to turn his back on those drowning had not been taken lightly.

'Aye Cap'n,' the Quartermaster said. He was pale, left arm broken and an open cut on his brow. 'First mate! Secure the ship. Damage report. Jeffers! You're acting Bosun. Get me a count of heads.' The ship's surgeon muttered in his ear, and he nodded. 'If I'm indisposed, report to the Cap'n.'

The reports came back quickly. Out of a crew of fifty men, they had lost twenty-three, with another nine injured, some badly. It was a serious blow to morale and ship running. The sudden fall of the mast was bad enough, sweeping eleven sailors into the sea to drown, but several others had been killed outright and the rigging had caused even more ruin.

Nearly half the crew was gone from the calamity. The passengers had been extremely lucky to survive the fall and the subsequent storm. The parrot had emerged, battered and muttering, from the Captain's cabin.

The one miracle was a sailor who had somehow managed to cling to the storm drogue, using rope to lash himself upright. The rest had gone.

Delirious with thirst and hunger, he was half-drowned and had lost a lot of skin to salted water rubbing on rough ropes, some of the wounds terribly deep, but he was alive. Galnór had dived into the water and swum back towing the exhausted man. He might die yet; drinking saltwater could kill.

The ship was badly off. The trysails were battered, and she had shipped water through several rents in the deck from the mainmast fall. The figurehead of a great eagle was gone, and half the rail was missing from the port side. Seams had leaked. The rigging was a mess. Without wind, they were stranded.

It wasn't long before someone noticed that this wasn't, in fact, entirely true. The ship was moving west at a surprising speed, and the trysails were catching a little wind, but not enough to explain their velocity. The Captain cast his eye out professionally.

'We're caught in the great western current,' he said, shaking his head. 'No chance we can break out of this and sail east, crippled as we are. It'll take us clear to Hadrasia. We can dock there and repair, if we're gifted fair weather.' He left unspoken the fact that if they faced another storm, they wouldn't go anywhere but downwards.

Numbly the passengers helped the crew patch the ship as safely as possible. They were all exhausted. Karland had never felt so ready to pass out, but grimly they all continued; their lives depended on the ship's seaworthiness.

They all keenly felt the loss of the carpenter. He had been one of the best wrights out of Eyotsburg. No one else onboard came near his level of expertise.

It took three hours to patch the holes and pump the water taken on board. All but the largest cracks in the hull had been sealed with spare planking and pitch. The worst had also required a spare sail, coated in pitch and lowered into the water over the hole. The pressure had sealed it against the hull, and she had almost stopped shipping water. There was more to do, but it could wait.

Assured of survival for the moment, they all rested in shifts, a few seamen left to keep an eye on the water and a hand on the helm. They were to assemble at the dawn watch for last rites and prayers for those lost, and then make ready to hoist as much sail fore and aft as safe to speed them on their way. The only ones not present were the ship's surgeon and the four men with serious injuries, one of whom would probably not wake up again after having his head cracked by a spar as the mast fell. The sailor who had clung to the mast was dying.

Captain Rosso's face was haggard as he stood on the gently rocking deck, near the splintered rail. The loss of his men was as keen to him as the damage to his ship. They had a lot of work to do before the *Star* was as seaworthy as they could make her, and the mood was as bitter as the waters around them.

They mourned the passing of the irascible old carpenter Gert, nineteen able seamen, both bosuns and the bright-eyed and chipper cabin boy, Sam. Many had perished when the mast had fallen, some of them caught in the rigging. Others had been swept overboard and left behind to die a slower death in storm-tossed seas.

'They gave their lives to our Mistress at the whims of Lamora,' said Rosso, bitterly, 'all too soon. From Foam to Form; from Form to Foam. So it is for the men of the Seas.' He cupped his hands to his forehead, brought them down to his heart and then slowly swept them forward and out, as if spreading water to the horizon. 'May their land and loves never forget them. May the waters of salt shrive them. May their souls sail home.'

'*Sail home,*' came the rough whisper from many throats.

Karland felt the bitter grief, recognised it. It was an old companion, returned from Aldywn, and Grukust, and Györnàeldàr. It wasn't as acute this time, partly from exhaustion and partly because he had not known the dead as well. The passengers had been lucky to have no losses, but his companions had proven hard to kill. The worst for him was Sam, who had been so friendly and bright-eyed, so scared of drowning. Although he knew he couldn't have saved him, part of him felt that he *should* have. It seemed beyond unfair that he should die in that fashion. The thought of his battered corpse floating face down, blond hair waving in the water, made him feel great sorrow.

He clamped down on the thought. Rast said there was no fairness in life. Things just *were*. All the living could do was remember those lost.

Once the Captain had consigned all their souls to the briny domain of Lamora, Mistress of the Oceans and fickle daughter of Mother Sea, they all turned back to the ship and her needs. If they were to stand a chance of making port, they still had a lot of work to do.

Karland thought back to Xhera, and hoped she was all right.

That he would see her again.

He was no longer sure if he would.

∛ √

Xhera stood listening to the rain patter on the canopy around the clearing. Outside the library, under the cover of one of the old buildings, she could hear the murmuring of Jimson and Kervala somewhere behind her, quiet and comforting. For some reason it felt like it rained a lot more here, although it was only a hundred miles or so northwest of where she grew up around Hoeven Lake. The woods felt heavy, dark and green.

When her head was too full, she needed to escape the stony gloom, to find some peace. Whether it was in the sun shining down, the patter of rain on leaves, or the sound of the wind in the trees, it soothed her buzzing mind.

The sheer amount of work Aldwyn had had access to was staggering, and the further number of his own notes represented decades of work. She was certain that some of what lay protected by rock and earth below was of equal, if not more, value than anything in The Sanctum.

At the thought of dark earth and stone, her thoughts skipped to Night and back. A lot more made sense now, but she still saw the slight, shabby man she had first met. He had been gone several days, traveling to visit a contact in the east, and was not due back for another halfweek. She missed him too, now he was gone.

How Aldwyn had remembered so much was beyond her. It was clear now why he had seemed so distracted all the time.

Apart from the exercises Rast had given her, which she did every morning, she tended to study all day, occasionally moving around the library to find or replace notes. The Book of Sarthos gave her chills when she read the words, which bled madness. It lay ever by the desk in the main room, with notes of reference to pages on it. She was very careful with it.

Today she had not been able to bear it anymore. Growing up on a farm had accustomed her to the outdoors, and this morning she had felt that she could not stay inside another minute. Moving out and greeting the Guard at the camp, she had decided to walk in the woods, for all it was grey. She felt on the edge of a discovery in the notes and needed a fresh mind.

Trailed by the wiry man and the brawny woman, she had circled the camp, trying to see how much impact they all made to the surrounding woodland. The guards were quiet out of habit. The draft horse was happily back in his little enclosure behind the ivy-laden wooden gates, awaiting the next trip to town. Once a week she visited for supplies and dinner with Karland's family. Gail was growing up fast and was like the little sister she had never had. Gail could be annoying, but was also a funny, smart girl with a sharp sense of humour. Karland wouldn't recognise her, she thought.

She walked slowly, smelling the scents of the wet woods around her. The canopy made the day even dimmer, and unlike the coppiced and pollarded edges of the woods near The Croft, here the trees and undergrowth were wild up to the clearing and the ancient ruins of the library.

Xhera had moved further out from the clearing, despite the uneasiness of Kervala, who was very protective of her. Apart from the odd wild animal, it was unlikely she would encounter anything dangerous here, but she had not forgotten the tales of madmen running into the woods, or the attack of the orcs when they had last visited Karland's hometown. She was not too worried, however; she also recalled how much the creatures feared old woods like this. Leona had said the trees themselves hated the creatures, and although they could not move to destroy them, the hatred permeated the woodlands. Things happened to orcs in woods, she said, and they avoided them as a result. The only exception seemed to be the Dimnesdair, and that place was fey and chaotic - perhaps less so now Yosgaloth had torn its path through and widened the pass onto the plains. That was another reason to take some care; many of the fell creatures that had lived there had now spilled out and travelled to other lands.

Karland and Rast should be requesting help from the elves by now, she thought. She sat on an old tree trunk, covered in moss and with a small cluster of yellow mushrooms at one end where it was shaded. After close inspection, she left them alone. They were False Chanterelles, and she didn't fancy being ill. It was a shame. Mushrooms were a delicacy she loved.

Occasionally, a droplet that had made its way through the gauntlet of green leaves above would deflect off her raised hood. Her cloak was made by Karland's father, thick but not as heavy as it looked. Around her the patter continued lightly, soothingly.

She could see Jimson further down the slight trail she had followed, standing attentively with his hand resting on his shortsword. His Eordeland recurve bow was strung despite the rain, the wax making the string shine where it was slung over a shoulder. She couldn't see Kervala.

Her thoughts turned to Karland, as they often did. She hoped he was safe; her task seemed far more boring without his leaps of intuition.

Even now she wasn't sure what good it would do. From the beginning, searching for answers - even finding the portal - had given dubious answers at best. Nevertheless, she continued her studies, hungrily taking in all the information she could. She had always dreamed of being able to do just this, and she had made a promise to Aldwyn's memory that she would continue what he had started. Privately she thought neither she nor Karland were very worthy successors. The more she read, the more she realised Aldwyn's brilliance. He hadn't been much for poetry and description, but his understanding of philosophy, psychology, and multiple sciences surpassed many others even of the Universalia Communia. In The Sanctum many of his books were revered, some used as de facto curriculum books for advanced classes. He had invented theories, contraptions and methodologies that were still used or debated by his peers, and his notes were detailed and surprisingly simple to understand for the most part - although she had encountered some that were virtually incomprehensible.

A mixture of politics, jealousy, and his absence had contributed to his being ignored by many in The Sanctum. She sighed inwardly. It seemed that no matter the contributions of people in any field, human nature would always find a way to interfere with progress and enlightenment. Aldwyn had been useless with anything to do with the arts, though; he had no appreciation apart from music, and had been about as musical as a dropped pot from what Karland had said.

Once a fortnight a messenger would arrive with news at The Croft, and would carry any findings back to Darost. Several of the Council of Twelve still wanted to send other scholars, or even gut the library and bring the contents back to the Combic Libraries, but for now there was stiff opposition from those like Tarqas, who felt that having a separate secure location was no bad thing. Many of them also felt that extra scholars would only confuse matters; Xhera knew more about Aldwyn's notes here than anyone sent from The Sanctum would.

Her mind full of these matters, she barely saw a flicker of movement out of the corner of her eye. She turned her head to the right, her mind still absent, and a glint of orange-yellow and a flash of green made her frown. Focusing, she stared at the area curiously before apprehension sank into her with icy claws.

Freezing, she swept the area with her gaze, flicking her eyes to where Jimson was.

She could not see him anywhere, and Kervala was still missing.

Her heart beating, she was beginning to breathe in short panicked breaths. Something or someone was out there. Her mind shot back to the glint and flash of green, and she went cold. If there were orcs out here, she was dead.

A slight movement came again, from slightly to the side of the original movement, and she raised her head slowly, eyes wide. Her neck hurt with tension.

The movement was odd, unlike anything she had seen. It was quick and smooth, but then stopped utterly. Even Rast did not move quite like this. He always held a sense of... relaxed tension, was the only way she could think of it. Controlled violence *in potentia*. This was different - as if whatever it was stopped moving and would simply stay in that position indefinitely.

The creature was only twenty feet from her. How it had got so close was a mystery, she thought, before recalling how far away her mind had been.

Bright orange irises filled the eyes, layered with an even brighter yellow interior. The pupil looked as if it were almost a cat's; not as sharp, the centre approaching the circle of a human iris, but the top and bottom moving to points. It was not the eye of anything she knew of. A thick pink nictating membrane flickered partially out and back as eyelids narrowed slightly.

The eyes were set mostly binocular in a face that looked almost human except for a covering of light green-grey scales. A slightly accentuated snout pushed out from where a human nose would have been, again not so much that she couldn't see a basic humanity in the features. Two widespread wedge nostrils sat above a wide mouth. She could not see any ears, as the creature had a hood on that dropped to narrow shoulders in an ash-grey and brown rough robe that ended at the elbows. One four-clawed hand rested on a thick branch, the delicate fingers tipped with light short talons opposite a stiffer thumb which sat central in the wrist rather than to the side as a human's was. The fingers sat two to each side slightly so that a thumb could curl in between them when the hand was closed. It must give a surer, more balanced grip than a human grasp, she thought distractedly.

The limbs were slender and wiry, and the creature stood little more than five feet tall. The body and feet were hidden, and Xhera only glimpsed the appearance of the creature as she realised something in astonishment.

She was looking at a lizard! A *lizard-person*, in fact. She stayed frozen, her heart pounding, wondering if it meant her any harm, and the lizard creature stared back, not blinking.

A crashing behind her and a woman's shout distracted her, and Kervala burst from the brush, sword drawn and teeth bared. Without pause she leapt past Xhera, who looked back to find the creature gone. Kervala vanished between the trees where it had been as Jimson appeared from where he had been on the trail, arrow nocked to bow.

'What is it?' he asked, his gaze darting for a threat. Xhera shook her head.

'I don't know. Some creature.'

A tense moment later, Kervala re-emerged, a grimace on her face. 'I don't know who it was or where they went. Hard to see.' She sheathed her sword with an annoyed thrust. 'I told you it was dangerous out here, Xhera. We're going back to camp. *Now.*'

Xhera stood, moving with Jimson towards the distant clearing. 'It didn't do anything, Kervala. Just watched.'

The woman grunted. 'Bad enough. Could be a scout. What in the name of the Iron King was it? I only saw a robe, but it didn't move like anyone I ever saw.'

Xhera nodded. They would have to be on their guard. Perhaps they should leave here and journey to The Croft, or even back to Darost. 'It was some kind of... well.' She pursed her lips. 'Lizard.'

Jimson shot her a stare, and Kervala barked a half-laugh, half exclamation.

'A *lizard?* It wore a bloody robe!' She shook her head, glancing around alertly.

'I know what I saw,' said Xhera hotly. 'I was staring right at it. It seemed more curious than anything else.'

'I'm really looking forward to reporting we saw a lizard in a robe watching us in the woods,' muttered Kervala.

Xhera flushed. 'I seem to remember no one believed in orcs until about a year ago,' she rejoined tartly. Kervala grunted but stopped muttering.

Their pace was fast. They emerged so abruptly into the clearing that they were met with drawn swords from the others.

'Saw a... possible scout, in the wood,' said Kervala shortly in answer to the questioning looks. 'Unsure of origin.'

'Could be someone from The Croft,' suggested Sergeant Cassega.

'*Definitely* not from The Croft, Ma'am,' said Jimson with a straight face. 'Can't say if it was an enemy.'

'Right. Set camp back outside Library entrance tonight. I want a watch in four-hour shifts, two per watch. Xhera, we'll talk later. I want you to think back carefully, remember every detail before we make any decisions. For now, inside, please.' She clapped her hands at the squad. 'Hop to it.'

Already Xhera's mind was questioning the surreality of it.

Had it really been a lizard?

She sat to write out a report before she lost any details, jotting notes of what she had noticed. After a quick attempt to sketch the creature, she grimaced and threw the paper into the mulch bin.

Finally, she sat back in the tall leather wingback that Aldwyn had near the fireplace. Perhaps, she thought, there were answers in the library somewhere. She would have a quick snack, and then start searching to see if there was anything she could add to the report. The messenger was due in three days, Night in four.

There must be some mention somewhere of a race of lizard people.

FORTY-ONE

The battered ship cut west across the Hadratic Ocean, swept along by the major warm western current that curved towards the east coast of Hadrasia in a loop before moving north up the coastline. Their food had been supplemented by the skills of the sailors in getting some fish, but scurvy would become a problem after the tiny, potent Morland limes the sailors called *calamansi* ran out. The elves had their waybread, which was nutritious and would last some time, but they had to keep it for themselves - a shame, as it was delicious, but they did not eat flesh.

Karland was getting sick of hardtack, which supplemented every meal.

Water had also been less of a problem than it should have been, although everyone was on short rations. Astonishingly, the gleaming copper desalination still on the stern was undamaged. Large and efficient, most days now it did not even need heating. The sunny days with sporadic clouds warmed the water enough to evaporate a little inside, although it needed heating at night. It wasn't a huge amount of fresh water, but it was enough to survive relatively comfortably.

The fact remained that they needed landfall for repairs, soon. The spare mast that they could have tried to lash in place of the mainmast had been torn from them in the storm, and the raw wood and iron that might have been used effectively were far less useful without the skilled carpenter.

The mainmast's stump sat woefully in the centre of the ship. Whilst the remaining masts were taking the strain well, Captain Rosso was worried that they would damage in higher winds. The mainsail had been ripped to shreds, so the crew was busy balancing the wind between the two remaining masts - which now at least had the repairs to the staylines finished. His remaining precious cotton sails could come dangerously close to splitting under full wind. The Captain had ruefully admitted that whichever way they looked at it, leaving the main trade current would leave them relatively becalmed and in danger of eventually starving.

The wind was against them; they would run out of supplies well before making it back to Mithtol with what little sail they had. There were few fish in the midst of the great oceans. Their only choice was to pray for the good weather following the storm to hold and to make for Northern Hadrasia, running before the trade wind and the great west current.

Rast was as inscrutable as ever. Karland could recall little that had ever surprised him, and he never complained or seemed to feel uncomfortable. His dragonblood-scarred fingers looked painful, redder in the sun, although he said that they felt fine.

Karland himself had grown leaner. After clinging mindlessly to the ship throughout the storm and seeing seasoned sailors lost to the water, he was merely thankful to still be alive. His few belongings were still with him, and most of his time was spent working the ship. There was plenty to be done, and The Green Warrior cheerfully shared more than his lot as well.

The one who suffered the most aboard ship was Darkus. Although he had greater strength than even Rast and was more than happy to lend it and his incredible stamina when asked, his orkish heritage brought a set of unique problems for him. He spent most of his time in the shade, taking watches at night when it was cooler. He hated the confinement of the ship, and was afraid of the endless water, though he would not show it.

Darkus still hauled longer and harder than anyone, but he had to rest in the cabin from time to time, sweating profusely in the manner of orks. His dark skin was slick with it, and he drank constantly when he was working. When one of the crew objected, Rast had shaken his head.

'Orks overheat quickly. He needs more than you. We have enough.'

They were not in dire straits, not yet, but they were all thankful for the current which sped them west, and they harnessed what they could of the trade wind to make them move even faster. The ship fairly flew along even without a main mast, the waters generally calm, although the captain had muttered darkly about great hurricanes which could brew in the peculiar clockwise whirl of currents and winds between the equator and the north horse latitude. Karland found himself periodically scanning the sky anxiously, but the mother of a storm which had driven them off course seemed to have sapped the energy from the skies and seas.

The sooner they sighted northern Hadrasia, the better. They were aiming for the city of Ho-Lam but would set no records for the time between Anaria and Hadrasia. The usual journey between Eyotsburg and Ho-Lam for a clipper like the Eastern Star was around thirty-five days.

It looked as if they might take more than forty-four days, the loss of the mainmast meaning they averaged six knots in the calm swells and currents. Even crippled as they were, they would spy land in good time - provided, of course, that nothing else happened.

'Pray the Gods that nothing else comes up in thy weather,' Rosso remarked
dourly. He had lost his joviality since the unnatural storm. 'A great grandmother of a
storm, that one. Never seen the like before, and I weathered the great storm of
twenty-six year gone. You expect a hurricane or two out in the Hadratic, but never
in the Grey Seas.'

Eighteen days into the journey and the monotony had set well and truly in. The
day had much more cloud than usual. Karland had felt a stir of concern, but the
sailors seemed to think it normal weather, so he tried not to pay too much attention.
Not long past noon, he was reminded of current events as he talked to the Captain
about Darost. The man had visited every seaport in Anaria, but never been to the
capital of Eordeland, and as he put it, his grandmother's city.

'Cap'n!' came the cry from the foretop.

The captain looked up and called, 'Aye! Danger?'

'No! Summin in the skies! Look like birds! All goin's west, like!'

'Birds,' he muttered. 'What is he, bloody bored?' He called up again. 'So?'

'They's big buggers, cap'n. A lot of 'em. Passing above us to the north. Land may
be near!'

The captain shrugged. That was true, although by his calculations they were
nowhere near the coast. There was a vast mid-oceanic sea north of the great current
known as the Siaosea, nearly twelve hundred miles long and a thousand wide. Red-
green weed floated there, and the deep waters were a dark clear blue, unlike any
others. Major ocean currents circled it.

It was wise not to wander from the flow. Men who had returned spoke of
migrating birds, great clumps of floating matter and small mysterious floating islands
bordered by extremely deep water. More than one ship had mistakenly found
themselves becalmed in it - there were false currents that deposited flotsam there and
little wind.

All manner of dooms lurked within the Siaosea, Karland had been told. There
were tales of men pulling up to an island and getting out to investigate, only to have
it submerge, stranding sailors who often could not swim. Great turtles, twenty feet
and more across, often dozed there on the surface, feeding on the weed. Other tales
of empty ships wallowing without sail after losing their crew to an island, starvation,
or some other calamity were rife. Men entered the Siaosea rarely and with care.

Rosso pulled out his brass scope and looked up. He harrumphed to himself,
frowning. Karland looked up too, and Rast stood further up in the prow, watching
the dots vanishing in and out of view in gaps as they passed far above the lowest
clouds. Something about their outlines and the way they moved was familiar, even at

this distance. When the captain muttered about them not looking like any birds he knew, Karland realised they were not.

They were dragons, and much higher than the Captain thought.

Rast had clearly reached the same conclusion. He called up to the elves.

'Dragons?'

The elves laughed as they slid down ropes and dropped to the deck.

'Many dragons. Never before have we seen such a sight,' said Galnór.

A few sailors eyed them sceptically. Others muttered and made blessing signs, most of the god of the sea. The Captain said nothing, looking thoughtfully up through his scope. As faint cries reached them in Dragon-tongue, it didn't take long for the sailors to notice the difference. The cry went up again.

'Ware!'

'Drakes!'

'Dragons! Here be Dragons!'

Karland turned to find the captain standing next to him, collapsing his brass telescope with a snap.

'I'd bloody thump that halfwit for such a joke if I thought the bugger could read enough to understand it,' he remarked sourly. '*Here be Dragons,* indeed.' He looked down. 'So your tales had truth? They don't look like no birds through my 'scope. If dragons they are, no telling what they want, lad. May be they'll ignore us.' His voice held a note of trepidation.

Karland bit back a laugh. 'I think we'll be safe,' he said. 'They're heading west.' He noticed a curious swirling in the clouds moving in the same direction as the dragons.

Rast moved over.

'One has changed direction,' he said with impeccable timing.

The Captain cursed in alarm.

As the dragon spiralled down to the boat from a dizzying height, the passing creatures filled the gaps in the clouds. There must be many scores, Karland thought.

The clouds almost directly above them bulged, coiling apart, and part of a vast form erupted into view, the source of the trail of disturbance. It was moving fast despite almost stately wingbeats and carried the suggestion of a glow. The tiny dots of dragons around it confirmed the immense scale.

One of the Gods of Kuln had taken wing.

The Lesser God moved far above, many miles high. The great wings moving slowly but powerfully, sending vast gusts of wind that changed the very shape of the clouds, even the weather it flew through.

Karland simply could not see how it was flying. This was a sight he was aware no other mortals had ever seen before.

There had been no true sense of scale when he had been amongst them in his vision. Here, there was; the form of one above Darost had been only a shadow of this. He was suddenly certain that the great creature here above the ship was the same one who had honoured Györnàeldàr, who had spoken to them in the Hall of Wyrms. He wondered how it had got out of the Hall… and if there was any of the mountain left.

The Greater Dragon must have been far more than twenty thousand feet wingtip to wingtip; if it had turned on its side, it would have only been half its body length from brushing the water. The Gods only knew how much it weighed. Millions of tons? Billions? Its presence was staggering.

You simply couldn't understand that scale until you saw dragons, many of them approaching two hundred feet, swooping around it like butterflies around a horse.

Words and work died. For the first time, everyone was speechless. The captain stood with mouth agape as if he had forgotten everything else. Seeing dragons was a shock but seeing them next to the behemoth hanging suspended above them as if the sky had become solid was too much. The huge creature passed slowly above them, glowing slightly even in the day. For a long moment, it eclipsed the sun, and they sailed silently in dragon umbra.

The incoming dragon reached the ship swiftly and spiralled around it, gliding easily as the rest continued. It glinted a deep iridescent green, with a very light brown underbelly that faded to near white. With wings spread, the membranes were light brown and ribbed, with webbing trailing down its sides and many short horns running down its back in three rows, the middle slightly longer. It was very nearly the length of the ship. Sharp orange eyes glared down at the human vessel.

Now there were belated reactions as sailors panicked. The parrot had cast off its usual antics and was shrieking in terror as it fluttered frantically around the deck.

'Shit! Shit! Arr! Shit! Lubbers! Shit! Bugger me! Evil Bastard!'

Karland wondered if that was deliberate, or just a selection of words it had stashed away. It would appear the bird was more than capable of speaking. At least Captain Rosso would know now that it was just living up to its name.

Darkus came up on deck in curiosity, moving to stand with them at the gunwale. Lëlylien called up to it as it passed in Elvish, and it answered boomingly in the same language, with a blast of flame. At the sound of its voice, the parrot gave one more startled squawk and mercifully shut up.

Then to Karland's astonishment the great creature folded its wings and hit the water from fifty feet up, sending water everywhere and causing a swell. There was less of a splash than he had expected. The dragon entered like an arrow, neck extended, and legs and wings tucked in.

It surfaced with a snort closer to the ship in a spray of salt water. Sailors to shouted in alarm as the ship rocked. The dragon moved alongside and kept pace with sweeps of its body and long tail in a sinuous motion. It fixed its burning gaze on the deck, its head higher than the railing, as at home in the middle of the ocean as in the air.

'Hail, Dragonfriends,' it rumbled loudly in archaic Darum, looking at Karland and Rast. Its voice rattled the railing. Karland wondered if every dragon knew who he was now. Then he remembered Aldwyn's description of their perfect memories. If this one had been at Darost, it would know exactly who they were.

'Greetings,' called Rast, and bowed. Karland bowed as well, as did the elves. He caught the look on the Captain's face from the corner of his eye.

'We wondered why a damaged ship drove for the great west, far from land. Especially one carrying friends of our people, one a mortal marked by the blood of our kin.'

Karland's excitement at seeing the majestic creatures again was strong within him. He remembered their incredible eyesight. 'Némaenth came to Darost to warn us. Eordeland decided we need to seek allies in this fight. We sailed for Mithtol.'

'You are far past those lands,' observed the dragon.

'A storm such as I have never seen drove us past,' said Rast. 'It was sudden and violent. We are damaged and caught in the great western current. We aim for Hadrasia for repairs.'

'We saw that storm. A great wrong in the world. It disturbed countless beings, killed more. Many of your ships and settlements were lost in it,' growled the dragon, and it snorted a great huff of air into the salt water, spraying droplets in a glittering mist for a moment. 'The danger in the west is great. Greater even than in Anaria. We seek a dark nexus of shadow that rises; the genesis of this darkness. A great evil has been growing there for tens of your millennia. Now it spreads faster than we thought possible. There may be a confrontation with the Great Enemy, and it could decide our fate.

'Every Dragon on Kuln comes to fight, bar those few we must set to guard the Nameless One. We may yet fall. And more: every Greater Dragon comes too, lest the confrontation break the world.'

'What if Yosgaloth should break free?' asked Galnór. Karland knew the horror the elves held the creature in.

'If the Nameless One breaks free, still might it be contained again. But if we fail here, our world is forfeit… and more.' The words were blunt.

Karland remembered the horror of the brief confrontation in the Hall of Wyrms before the portal, where a Darkling had briefly confronted a lesser God. Györnàeldàr had said such a battle could break the very mountains around them.

In Hadrasia there could be a confrontation of far greater powers against more than one. Such a battle could bring about an apocalypse. Would Kuln itself survive the confrontation?

He had a brief mental image of miles-long titans flying to the continent they headed for and wondered for a moment if it was really a great idea to continue.

Well, it isn't as if we have any choice.

'We aim north,' said Rast. 'To the city of Ho-Lam on the inland sea.'

'That is well,' said the dragon. 'Darkness lies to north and south of those lands. These demons of chaos and shadow can travel the depths of gloom, where darkness is in fractal disarray, but they must materialise once their journey is complete. The *Zhōng Gúorén Huáng dì Nāgāra* search for them. We hope to find them and bind them without too great a harm to our world.'

'We wish you luck,' replied Rast.

'And we you, mortals. This world is still swept by strands of chaos, though the rent in creation is long-passed; there have been many such unnatural disasters that have no true birth in recent times. You were lucky to have survived. Had we more time we would bring you from the current and set you back to your lands, but none of us can be spared. Be careful, mortals. In all the lands there are forces aligned against you. You must guard yourselves. We cannot aid you this time.'

What are you called?' called Karland as the dragon drifted away from the boat.

'*Rahonamasú.*'

They all bowed, except Darkus who clapped a fist to his chest, ork-fashion, and The Green Warrior, who nodded. He had quietly observed, head tilted back and a small smile on his face.

The dragon bared sword-length teeth in what Karland hoped was a smile, dipping its head in reply, and then snaked away from the boat, swimming effortlessly. It turned its head and called, 'The darkness spreads, mortals! The tide rises. Be not swept away.'

When it was far enough, it unfurled its great wings, curving them to keep them out of the swells. Swimming fast, using the impetus of the great western current to aid it, it beat its wings hard, cupping forward to pull it even faster. The wingtips dipped into the sea in little splashes, until the wings caught the air and pulled it out of the brine, saltwater pouring from the flashing scales.

The dragon circled higher and higher with every beat, becoming another dot and eventually joining the migration in the wake of the Greater Dragon, still easily visible as it slowly beat its way west, and was lost to view.

'That dragon was different from the one the tribes met,' mused Darkus quietly. He had simply observed in his introspective way. Karland was struck again by how similar yet how different he was from his brother.

'They are all different in form,' Karland said. 'All unique.'

He looked behind him to the sailors, who were blessing themselves or shaking their heads, relaxing again. The expression on the face of Captain Rosso said it all.

'Bugger me,' he remarked, shaking his head in relief and astonishment, and then cast a wry glance at Evil Bastard. 'And bugger you, too.'

The parrot muttered to itself and waddled off.

⌒ ☓

The current swept them west. Although the skies greyed on the thirty-seventh day and the wind and spray rose, there were no storms. Karland had grown to love the leap and jump of the ship; there was something primal, powerful, unstoppable and immense about the ocean. Sometimes dolphins leapt about their prow, easily keeping pace with the ship. According to one of the old sailors, who regarded them fondly through scrubby whiskers, the creatures could keep up with the ship under full sail for a little way. He confided to Karland that they were held to be the souls of the dead, looking after the ship as it went. They weren't fish, he said, for they breathed air, and tried to talk to men atimes in their own tongue.

The elves had a different view. To them, the creatures were highly intelligent, with a complex language. Their keen hearing could go much further into the frequencies dolphins used, but Galnór understood little past a few basic concepts.

'They don't really use words,' he said. 'Those sensitive to such things have said they use a kind of sound we cannot hear which maps the world around them. Unless you can make these noises, and hear them, you will never understand all of their language.'

'They can speak?' said Karland in astonishment. He'd thought the old sailor to be pulling his ear.

'Certainly,' said Galnór. His glance was amused. 'You humans have the strange idea that thumbs and a love of gold are required for intelligence. Yes, they speak, though not in the manner of men or elves. Our complexities are meaningless to them, and in some ways, they are simple and joyous creatures, as are we, although-'

he turned his laughing almond eyes to Karland, '-I would not suggest to elves that they are land-dwelling dolphins.'

Karland grinned at him, remembering his description of the *dônaethar* trance to Lëlylien. She must have mentioned it to Galnór.

'Our people have known them long,' said Galnór. 'Ever have they been happy creatures, full of life and play. They have helped men and elves in times of trouble, too, although like any intelligent creature they can be fickle. Many lives have been saved. They can learn to speak some words, with effort, but although they are more than equal to the great ravens of Ignat in intellect, the birds have the ability of the true speech of men. Even our greatest adepts cannot find a way to truly understand the speech of the great souls of the sea, the whales and their kin, but they can see how they discourse. And as you humans say, actions may speak louder than words. We live in harmony.'

It was fascinating to Karland. The dolphins leapt high, some approaching the gunwale of the ship, and more than once he saw an eye above an upturned smile regarding him curiously before the creature dropped to slip smoothly into the waves once more.

At was several days later that he saw another fin tip break the sea off the port side of the ship. It was different, more triangular and larger than the dolphin's. The creature was clearly a fish, moving side to side with powerful sweeps, and it lifted its head out as the ship went past, showing a greyish pointed nose and a huge mouth filled with the tips of terrifying teeth. A black eye stared up, and then the head dipped, and the fin sank alongside the boat again, vanishing down. Karland could see its shadow just under the surface. It was bigger than the dolphins, more than twelve feet long.

'Devil, he is,' said the old sailor nearby, spitting over the rail. 'Them things follow ships... Swim up rivers... Take anything they can. Some of em get much bigger'n that one, too. All shapes and sizes. You meet one int'water, you're dead. Seen em bite through small boats.'

'That was huge,' said Karland.

Darkus leaned out over the rail, fascinated. Karland felt his stomach lurch.

'Don't do that,' he said nervously.

'What was that thing?' asked the ork.

'Shark,' said the old man. 'Means *villain* in old Novin tongue. Evil fish, them.'

'They follow the dolphins,' remarked Galnór as he moved up alongside. 'Large shoals of orange-fin *ton* keep company with the dolphins, and the sharks hunt the *ton*.'

'I guessed it was a shark,' said Karland. 'I read about them. It said they were vicious predators that have eaten many sailors. You get them in the estuary.'

The elf laughed. 'I am sure many men have been eaten, for they will eat anything if there is nothing else, or they mistake men for their usual food, but I don't believe they really like the taste. They often let go after one bite, fatal though that can be. They prefer their natural prey.' The elf shook his head. 'They have no evil in them. You must simply know and respect them. Like most natural creatures they will kill to survive or if threatened, but they have no concept of evil.' The elf sighed. 'Only races capable of thought are also capable of evil. Greed, madness for power, hatred, revenge... Death for the sake of it. That is evil. This is just a fish, a curious one at that. But what I have seen humans do to such as these... wanton killing and torture, for fun... killing in revenge, or sport... there is far more evil there, I think.'

'I don't think I would swim with them,' said Karland. 'Lurking under the water, ready to kill.'

'I have swum with them in the water, and they have left me alone,' said Galnór, smiling. 'They are inquisitive creatures, like huge dogs, in a way. But their habit is to test things with their mouths. It is a shame their bite is so strong the test can kill, and once they smell blood they may give in to their hunger. Land creatures don't really taste very good to them, I think. But we all eat what we must to survive.'

'Killers,' muttered the old man stubbornly. 'Et many a fine sailor.'

'Have they eaten elves?' asked Karland. 'You seem to know a lot about them.'

Galnór smiled. 'I do not believe so, but ever were we more in tune with nature than men. We do not visit their domain often for food, anyway. We do not eat flesh. But I love the sea and the shores. Some of my kin prefer the forests and trees, and they have their peace... but the restless sea has her own majesty. Her own call.'

The old sailor nodded at that, his seamed face squinting out as his deft hands continued their work. 'That she do, serr.'

Karland knew a little of what they meant. In the last month he had learned much about life on board, the powerful ship merely a mote tolerated at the whim of the sea. He had become used to the pitch and roll of the ship, the balance and the fresh sea air.

The companions had been working solidly. The Green Warrior was a very quick study, and pushed and encouraged people constantly. Karland had helped where he could, and Rast's and Darkus's strength had been a boon to repairs. The elves had spent most of their time using their incredible eyesight to watch the horizon and help with rigging repairs, dancing high above the deck on the ropes and beams with perfect balance, to the envy of the sailors.

Karland watched Rast now, helping haul new sail aloft, and wondered at the big man's story. He was so stoic, such an intriguing mix of competence and humility. He never complained, and his focus was always on what must be done.

A laugh caught his ear, and he saw The Green Warrior beckoning a sailor in the rigging, feet hooked through. As much an enigma as Rast, that one. There was something quite pure about his drive and focus, but there was always a sense of wariness in being around him.

The ship moved on, and all they could do was wait.

⚘ ⚘

Cassega had sent Pahm to town on hearing Kervala's report. To her credit, she hadn't snorted when told what they'd seen, but smoothly suggested they ask if anyone else had encountered anything odd.

'Turns out quite a few people have seen something,' reported Pahm when she returned. 'But no one has caught more than a glimpse or been able to approach whatever it is.'

The plain-faced woman looked none the worse for her fast move to town, for all she was not as tall or fit-looking as the others. Xhera knew the half-squad had been picked for their skill and were all veterans of skirmishes, but she always felt a faint surprise at Pahm's capability. She wouldn't have looked out of place in a bakery.

'So it's scouting?' asked the Sergeant.

Pahm shrugged. 'If it's the same one. Might be more of them, Sarge.'

'Good point,' Cassega conceded. 'How long have they been seeing it?'

'Months,' was the reply. 'Mostly lone people in the woods, seen something vanishing. Doesn't seem to have approached groups. No one has been harmed. They seem to come from deeper in the woods, but no one's sure. Never been seen before this summer though.'

'I think we're overreacting,' said Xhera. 'One creature doesn't equal a threat. I felt it was curious more than anything. Perhaps it is a scout for something, but it seemed more shy than wary. I've written a report for the Council, anyway.'

'Do you know what it is?' asked Kervala, a faint scowl on her face. It was clear that whatever its intentions, she wasn't happy with the thought of an unknown being lurking around the woods. Six of them might be some defence against a few of these things, but if there were more, they might be in trouble, and she had quite plainly mentioned this to Xhera.

'No,' said Xhera.

'I don't feel qualified to make a judgement on this without more information,' said Sergeant Cassega. Her seamed face was reflective. 'Xhera, please gather everything you need for up to a week. We'll fall back to The Croft and await the messenger.'

'But I need everything here,' objected Xhera. 'I can't leave the library.'

Cassega's face was stern, although her tone was polite if firm. 'With respect, it's our duty to keep you safe, ordained by the Council themselves. The library won't go anywhere for a couple of days. Please do as you've been asked. We leave at first light.'

Xhera bit her lip to stop herself from arguing. The Sergeant had always seemed like a kindly woman, albeit one in armour, but she was now seeing the implacable nature of a decorated officer in the Eordeland Guard. With a sigh, she nodded.

Was it one of the ancient Kreel? she wondered as she began packing the books she needed most urgently. If so, where had they been hiding? And more importantly, what would it mean that they had reappeared now, when Yosgaloth was freed and destruction threatened civilisation? Questions nagged at her, distracting her from her previous studies.

The one thing Eordeland could do without was another enemy.

FORTY-TWO

Xhera shut the book with a sigh and reached for a scroll held down with a paperweight.

They had cautiously returned from the Croft after several days, having found no evidence of hostility in any of the sightings. Xhera had pointed out that she needed to continue the studies set by the Council. The Sergeant had reluctantly agreed after sending a message back to The Sanctum.

The woods were glowing green in the sunlight around the clearing of the ancient library today. Earlier she had walked among them under the watchful eyes of Kervala, listening to their sounds and the quiet language of the trees rustling. If she was honest with herself, she had also kept a sharp eye out for a greenish human-shaped creature, and had been so intent she had accidentally squashed one of the large bugs that had crept out to inhabit the area now, leaving a yellowish mess inside a bright blue carapace.

She had explored the ruins with interest, making notes. A map of the original layout of the buildings showed the part which held the hidden library had actually been designated as a storage building on two levels, with a small stable and outside storage at the back. The normal library had been a separate building, almost diagonally opposite the storage, but that was now the most gutted and decrepit of the ruins; when the site had been attacked, it had clearly been with the intent of destroying all the works within. The building had been gutted by fire and virtually razed. Only a single piece of wall and the stone outlines of the library remained, with a few rusted chains from the bookshelves. The living quarters had fared better, but after several hundred years little was left but stone.

The storage was the most untouched, backed up against the huge rocks rising out of the forest. It was into and under this that the tunnels had been laboriously carved, where the most precious works had been stored.

Aldwyn had collected various histories of the day when the Library had fallen. She had read them carefully. Thingos had been slain with his family and fellow scholars, the library razed. There was nothing to suggest he had been Darostim, but Xhera suspected he had been. She couldn't think of any other reason a collection of scholars would have been hunted; not just slain, but their very works removed from existence.

The fact that they had created a decoy of a library on the surface suggested he had known that one day this fate could catch up with him. That fate had been terrible, but the storage building and the library underneath it had endured, protecting more than two thousand precious items of knowledge. Paper and parchment books, vellum and reed rolled scrolls, other collected tomes including some rare books little more than ornate boxes with loose sheaves of parchment in them in order, all lay hidden behind an ironwood door nearly as hard to breach as iron itself. Harder, in some ways. Ironwood would not bend or fatigue like iron, and it didn't catch fire easily. Without special tools, it was nearly impossible to cut through before they were blunted. Aside from that, every building in the site had been designed with beautiful architecture. Arched doorways and windows abounded, and alcoves backed with ironwood were sunk into the surviving walls of the storage shed. Some even had shelves. Ironwood would last longer than oak when dry, and a few had endured hundreds of years. The door was well-hidden.

Now she was back behind it, in the glow of the blueish library light. Xhera brought her mind back to the contents of the book. It was dotted with strips of parchment covered in notes, between leaves. There were cross-references to other tomes, including the Book of Sarthos, which she handled with a mixture of reverence and loathing. One of the last in the world, it needed to be copied; she had already sent word to The Sanctum.

It was headache-inducing and part insane, a collection of visions and thoughts that seemed random in chronology and reference. There were careful notes in Aldwyn's neat script in the margins against important events, and not just in the places she had expected.

The eruption of the huge volcano-island Gorudrum around three thousand years ago had detailed descriptions in the Book of Sarthos, although the text had been heavily read and interpreted; it had come in the form of a poem, in another language. Apparently Sarthos hadn't spoken anything except his native Old Darum, but had somehow written in flawless Poviiri, Banistari, and a few other languages, a fact Aldwyn expressed as 'curious'. Xhera could almost hear his voice as she read the word, and smiled sadly.

The fall of Haná was clearly marked, and she had found a horrible section that she had a dark suspicion referred to the release of Yosgaloth. But there were hundreds of other things as well that she tried not to be distracted by, many of them noted by Aldwyn as irrelevant, or untrue, and even more without notes at all. Did that mean they were not important? Or that he simply hadn't found a reason to study them yet? A diamond-headed axe, the crowning of a person both king and queen, a hilt that *channelled*. Something about two spirits, the destruction of something that could be an island or a whole realm, it wasn't clear which; discussion on the thoughts of a sea serpent, the world as a creature of which mortals were an extension of its own awareness and intelligence, descriptions in calculus of the *grey road through reality*, whatever that meant, fifteen different ways to open it that made no sense (Aldwyn had noted next to most of them that they were delusional), and more and more; and this just in the Book of Sarthos alone. The book was infuriating.

She had dark pits under her eyes and her brain felt as if it would evaporate at times. Xhera knew she was pushing too hard, but she couldn't shake a sense of there being something important, hidden right in front of her, that she *had* to discover. She blew out her cheeks and rubbed her eyes. She wasn't sure she had the stamina or focus for this. She took a sip of water from a stone cup and carried on thinking.

Her studies the last two days had led her to the current writings which somehow moved onto the deep mysteries, but in more depth than the University had taught.

There are many unseen forms of power within the Universe, but two of them are greater than the others, more present than anything else.

The major of them is a formless energy, dark and unseen. It pervades everything; the elves call it the Great Skein, perceiving it as countless binding filaments of the same thread. Others call it the Great Lattice, still others the Unseen Ocean. It pulls the Universe apart against its natural inclination to come together and is limitless in power.

The other is a great power in its own right, a weighty and invisible matter extending threadlike through reality like a web. It binds the Universe together, and once was greater than the energy winding around it. It is less thought of, but has been called the Vast Web, the Prime Matrix, the Hidden Currents.

Together with reality they form the multi-dimensional Greater Weave, the Pattern, the Fabric of the Universe, with the energy the warp and the matter the weft, and reality the pattern upon it; everything else lies within their caress. The Greater Weave is what makes all of reality. Flexible, in constant motion, but binding together; strong, unseen.

There was much more, about detecting and using the powers being a sense most simply did not have, about how a conduit could tap into and shape them. There were eight scrolls after this one. Interesting though it was she couldn't see how it related to the directive from Eordeland to find out how all the troubles in the world were somehow linked. She rubbed her eyes and pushed the parchment back under the weight.

Aldwyn had been a kindly old man, vague and frightened of his own death, but he had ranked foremost amongst Papered Scholars. Notes, references, studies, calculations, correlations; it was amazing he had found time to eat, looking at the work representing decades of brilliance. And that, of course, was the crux. It seemed like an incredible amount to her, but she was trying to decipher nearly sixty years of parts of his work in months.

It didn't seem relevant to her search for answers to the visions they had been given in the Portal, but there was something he came back to time and time again. Things she had read in many of his notes hinted that he had been searching for someone, scattered in references to signs that she had found the more she read his notebooks.

One section from Sarthos in particular was scored with pencil marks, and the words underlined so they stood out from the wall of text on this particular page. They were part of what seemed a stream of consciousness, and not all in sequence, but underlined and read in turn, they formed their own sentence.

The choice will come to one unsung, to one unknown and unaware... Unsure, yet certainty must come... Strength from weakness... cursed with a different sight, a third sight, a judgment on themselves, a clear gift to all mortals... One who must find balance, in balance, who brings balance, balance, the balance of the past and the future on the fulcrum of the present... chooser, unwilling but willing... Themselves within, choose they belief or not... Unique of all, common as all... Born in the age of tipping, strife unchecked, the lifting of wings on the fifteenth day of the hundredth year measured by Isha's boon... Chaos! Order! Neither! Both! Chaos must be kept at all costs! Fire! Fire, the fire of rage. Anger of the Gods... the hunger! The hunger! The sun blots! The great serpent eats the sky! Ahhh!

The words started relatively sane, and then began to lose coherency. The last few underlined sentences had frustrated question marks against them, all except the date. Next to the word *boon* was the word *grace* and some reference to a miraculous aversion of something, perhaps a famine. She put that aside for later. The date also had several names of places in northwest Eordeland, the last being Gladsmoor, and the cryptic phrases *the one who makes a choice?* And *Giver of Strength?* next to it. There was also a note and a number.

It had taken Xhera weeks to realise that this referred to one of Aldwyn's notebooks, and a fairly recent one. In here she had found much more detailed notes, clearly referring to a single person that had to do something.

Something what?

Something important but unspecified.

Following the text down, she had realised that the date range mentioned had actually been around Karland's birth date in the year twenty-four eighty-two.

It all snapped into focus. Why had Aldwyn moved to this library? Surely not just for his studies, an old man on his own. Why had he shown such an interest in Karland? Why had he been so cautious?

She re-read the text again. *Unsure, yet certainty must come.* She knew no one else who doubted themselves as Karland did. Perhaps everyone did in some way - she doubted herself from time to time - but Karland wore his self-doubt on his tunic, as Hendal would say.

One special, thinking they were not. One different, seeing things very unusually, always an observer. Someone good, someone who believed in balance. In fairness? Someone pure. Someone *different.* Who saw the world differently to others. It was hard not to read meaning into these words. Her skin raised in goose-bumps.

Karland. Karland is the one who must make a choice, of some kind.

It all fitted. She couldn't believe it.

Aldwyn had been watching Karland as carefully as he had watched her. He had taken him with him on a perilous journey. He had asked Rast to protect him, to teach him to protect himself. He had visited him with a specific purpose. Karland had made a difference even in the hallowed halls of learning. However much Karland thought he was involved by accident, he often ended up in the middle of a critical juncture of events. She had seen that with her own eyes.

He was trying to prepare him for something.

Xhera felt a deep chill. She had always known Karland was special, in some indefinable way. Having an ancient text and a pre-eminent scholar spell it out was quite surreal and frightened her in a deep and primal way. There had been no doubt that Aldwyn had loved the boy deeply. Now she could see much more behind it.

The way Aldwyn had written the script was as if this was a life-or-death decision, something of utmost importance. Not only that, but he had noted it in such a way that a casual reader would never think he meant Karland - including Karland himself, if he read it by chance. The only reason she had made the connection was her sheer amount of research… and luck.

Suddenly, she hoped desperately that he was safe. If her reading of everything here was correct, it could be even more than the life of her friend that was at stake. It could mean the fate of them all, somehow, and she needed to find out how.

Xhera pushed the next scroll carefully aside and rubbed her eyes. Her legs were stiff; her hamstrings felt tight from sitting too long. She knew she would have to run through Rast's forms to loosen up before bed tonight.

It was lonely work, sitting at the Library of Thingos in the Northing Woods without Night. They were a half day's ride from The Croft, and although the half-squad led by Sergeant Cassega remained camped in the sturdiest ruins outside the entrance she usually stayed inside the library.

There was so much information in here she couldn't read it in a lifetime. Although the Combic Libraries held far more, there was more work here from Aldwyn, explaining other esoteric texts.

Of them all, the one she liked least was the Book of Sarthos. More than ever the tome made her skin crawl to read. The ravings were laughing and knowing sometimes, clear and cool at others. It matched up too closely to events in history after it was written to be much comfort.

It also cut off not far into the future from now, as if everything stopped. She hoped that meant the author simply couldn't see any further.

Rolling the scroll back up carefully, she replaced it in the rack of them near the doorway and exited the library to eat with her protectors, taking the proffered bowl of stew distractedly.

'*Chaos must be* kept. *Chaos* must *be kept,*' she muttered. The phrase tugged at her mind. What did it mean? They were *fighting* the chaos that was sweeping across the world. Night had said that the realms of men were on a precipice from which they would not return if disorder swept them over the edge.

Aldwyn's notes referring to this suggested he felt that Sarthos was losing his battle with the chaos overwhelming his mind, but which gave him his gift. She was not so sure; later several fragments of his visions spoke of the battle still ongoing.

It was an oddly out of place phrase. *Chaos must be kept at all costs.*

Aldwyn was never more missed, Xhera thought. The Council never should have sent him. On one old man had lain the fate of everyone; and that old man had died.

Chaos MUST be kept.

'You alright?' asked Kervala, looking at her oddly. Xhera realised she had muttered the phrase out loud.

'It's just this odd phrase in the book of Sarthos. I don't know why, but I feel it means something important.'

'Sounds like something the Sons of Havoc would say,' muttered Hilford.

Kervala shot him a glance.

'It does sound odd. You sure you're alright?'

'I'm fine,' she said. 'You wouldn't believe how much odd stuff is in these texts.'

'*That* I can imagine.'

ভ ৪০

Ventran sat back, pursing his lips thoughtfully. He was in a dockside tavern on the south bank of the Eaofer in the east of Darost and had been in the city for over a month. It was a rough, poor area, which suited him fine. He had avoided the soaring Church of Terome; he was well known to Sontles' sycophants in Meyar.

Ventran could find nothing out about Aldwyn Varelin. It was as if he had vanished, probably into the vaults of The Sanctum. He had heard a lot about the vast complex of segments making up the Dome, even ventured inside several times.

It was risky. The first time had been during the day. He was lucky he had left his knives behind; he was searched thoroughly both times.

The sheer amount of people had given Ventran pause. Finding someone in there was next to impossible, especially since there were heavily patrolled areas and an ominous presence of Guard. It was a city in itself.

Silently, he had cursed Belen. He was certain the Politikus had not helped matters.

He had begun hanging around the food halls, and had finally chanced to hear talk between students of an attack… and the name Rast Tal'Orien. Ventran had charmingly interjected, introducing himself as an Eyot. The students were happy to fill him in on the gossip. Ventran had nodded and vanished to ruminate.

This boy with a girl friend who was watched over by Tal'Orien *had* to be Varelin's student. He was on the right track.

He had come back in once more during the day. Despite the bureaucracy, these people were amazingly easy to distract and fool. Unless you sought to see the Council, getting through the gate required only a permit or knowing enough to manufacture excuses to visit one department, even in such troubled times.

Through stolen snatches of conversation, Ventran had learned nothing more than the fact that the boy and the girl were somehow helping Varelin with studies. He might never even get close to the old man.

There was an alternative, though: his student.

Dresin. Karland Dresin.

They were strange, these Eordelanders. They took surnames, so they could be easily taxed and identified by their rulers. And they accepted them; were *proud*.

Ventran was *his* name, and if he met another with it, he would take their head; there should be only one.

The only Meyari with excess names were those granted franchises by the Conclave of Aldermen, or aristocracy, who had grown a Name over a long and often illustrative family tree. Commoners in Meyar held one name, and that was how it should be. It was largely the same in Novin.

Sontles was the only one outside this order who had another name, and that bespoke foreign origins - unless he was old Hanári nobility, which Ventran doubted.

Sontles had not spoken much of his roots, but Ventran knew more than most. The vampire had been a lowly bookkeeper for a baron, centuries gone, and a dark visitor one night had taken more than simple shelter. Sontles still spoke with venomous satisfaction of having killed the Baron's daughter soon afterward. He had long desired her, and finally found the strength to visit every pent up urge on her before she died. Then he led the vengeful father and his troops to the hiding place of his progenitor, watching as they discovered him, staked him, burned him. It was unusual for a new-born vampire to retain so much control of themselves, so much cunning, but Sontles had been a dry, logical and methodical man in life, if his current self was anything to go by.

Ventran's thoughts returned to the boy.

It was very likely that Dresin held news of the old man, perhaps even the pendant Sontles had sought for so long. If he could find out where the boy came from, maybe he could add extra control over him. Family or friends, perhaps. He might even be able to use the boy to retrieve the pendant if it was locked away in the vast domed University.

He had to be careful here, though. The city of Darost was locking down, and he didn't know it as he did Lodnor.

Ventran slunk through the streets, watching The Sanctum. What he needed lay within, but it was too risky to go in again.

The last time he had entered had been doubly so. Ventran was an expert at stealth and had managed to penetrate The Sanctum at night. He was there for less than two hours, skulking to find ways to enter libraries and rooms, but to no avail. Patrols were too frequent.

As he scouted a segment's rooftop, he had been challenged by a Guard he hadn't seen. Ventran had worked fast to prevent him calling more, jumping and kicking out with both feet. The Guard had pitched over the balustrade and landed hard eighty feet below.

Ventran had beaten a hasty retreat. It was unlikely the man had survived, but he couldn't risk going in again without a clear target. Guards swarmed the buildings like ants.

For four more days Ventran prowled Darost, growing bored and annoyed. He had kept a tight rein on his impulses against a growing pressure from the darkness within him.

If he could catch one or all of them away from their fortress...

In the end, he didn't have to.

He had noticed a sullen young man, barely more than a boy, hanging around in the marketplace before the doors with an expression of anger and hopelessness over the last several days. He seemed to be studying the guards around the square.

Ventran couldn't believe that they hadn't noticed this brooding amateur skulking around. It was obvious he had reason to hate the University.

He sensed an opportunity and approached, uneasily moving out of the way of the statue's implied dragon flame and skirting the Guards standing nearby. It wasn't the most detailed statue he had seen, but something in its design spoke of actual life more than any finely-carved features; truly a work of art.

The youth didn't wish to speak at first, but after a few judicious comments about The Sanctum and how difficult it could be for some, Ventran tapped an outpouring of vitriol against the University, and especially against Karland Dresin. The boy's cousin had been convicted of attacking Dresin and was bound for years of hard labour.

One of those in the attack! This was a gift.

'I've heard of the little shit,' Ventran said. 'He knows where something of mine is. I'm looking for him too. Maybe I can help.'

The youth gave his name as Keva. More relaxed now he had an ally against Dresin, he took to boasting about knowing people who could right the wrong by any means necessary.

What a fool, thought Ventran with disdain. He had no caution. Anyone walking past could hear his words, report him.

'I can get to him if your people can get me safely inside,' said Ventran. 'If you can help me, I will take care of your little problem.'

'I must ask the others,' said Keva nervously. 'They make the decisions.'

'Then take me to them and I will present my offer.'

The youth's face twisted in indecision. Ventran had obviously impressed him, but now more than words were required he was frightened.

Finally, he made his choice. 'I'll take you to them now. But if they say no, you must leave.'

'Of course.' Ventran had hardly been able to contain his glee.

Of all the luck in the world!

& &

Ventran followed the boy north-west from The Sanctum gates into the poorer dock district just east of the Temples, away from the central streets and into territory that

Ventran felt intimately familiar with. This was his first time here, but nevertheless he knew these streets. They were old, and violent.

Ventran carefully watched for any followers on the way, seeing none. His guide was so oblivious a marching squad could have trailed him.

Eventually the boy paused outside a warehouse several hundred feet from the main docks. It was an industrial area, with few houses nearby.

'These people are dangerous,' Keva said. 'I'd best go in and tell them who you are, or they might hurt you.'

'You do that,' said Ventran seriously. The boy nodded and rapped on a door then whispered his name before slipping inside.

Ventran almost laughed out loud.

Finally, the boy popped out again and beckoned him in.

'I put in a good word for you,' he said.

Ventran entered the dim warehouse to find six men waiting. Four of them looked like dock workers – hard, rough men. One was sucking a lit cheroot. Another looked like a reasonably well-to-do merchant. The last bore a resemblance to Keva.

'This the one, Kev?' he said. Keva nodded.

'Yeah. He knows what that shit Dresin did, dad. Said he has beef with him, too.'

'What's the story?' asked Ventran.

Keva's father gritted his teeth. 'My nephew has been given a choice between years of hard labour or death in the military over a minor disagreement. This bastard Dresin thinks he's special. He has the sponsorship of the Council. Of course they weren't going to find fault with him.'

'Seems a little unfair,' Ventran noted noncommittally. The man nodded vigorously, but Ventran didn't miss the questioning look the merchant aimed at him. That one bore watching.

'I wanna even the score. If I can't see Fron free, I want Dresin to pay. Ever since he showed up there have been problems.'

'Dragons!' barked a huge man to Ventran's left. The merchant jumped. 'Evil, deadly beasts! And the Council fawns on 'em like dawgs.'

Two others rumbled in agreement.

'Not just dragons,' remarked the merchant slyly. 'Meyari, coming here, taking our ways and our religions. Novinians. Mudskins from Morland everywhere. *Orcs*. Dragons killing innocent men. It's like it's not even our country anymore. Look what it led to! War. Terror. People slaughtered in the streets. A *demon* nearly destroyed this city!'

'Aye!' shouted another of the dock workers. 'It's all been going wrong since they came back on that monster. That demon never came here till no dragon came. It *led* it here. It *killed* good Eordelanders. Scores of em, they say.'

Another spoke up, his face red with rage. 'That red devil killed me brother! Flamed him down in front of everyone, and him a *Welcomer Guard.* The Council did nowt.' He spat. 'In thrall.'

'Prolly dragons behind the taxes too, makin' us poor. Dragons like their trasure. You heard the tales. They hoard *gold.* Like to be where to rest of my money is,' said the second.

'I ain't payin' for no fuckin' lizard,' sneered the first man.

'The Sons of Havoc will disrupt these invaders,' said the merchant smoothly. 'We are everywhere in the city. Dragons; foreigners; filthy heathens come here, kill our people. Take our money. Supplant our gods. Lead death to our doorstep. Bring their own laws with them. They endanger our way of life. We were fine before they came. Darost is for Eordelanders!'

'S'right!'

Ventran laughed inwardly. This was the same message that was being spread in Meyar; it had taken root here too. He was willing to bet that it had been nurtured by Incursors of Terome. An amusing irony.

'But there are only six of you?' he asked.

The merchant glared. 'Of course there are others. Hundreds of us. Don't be a fool.' He stared closely at Ventran, who wasn't deceived. For all he acted as if he were a large wheel in the machine, the merchant was a bit player.

'So what will you do?' Ventran asked, sinking back into the shadows a little.

'This boy is at the core. He needs to pay. Maybe there will be less dragons here without him around. Maybe these scum won't come here if their devil beasts aren't here.'

'That's a lot of *maybe.*'

'You don't get to question me!' snapped the merchant. 'We still haven't heard what you are supposed to do for us!'

'You have a problem with this Dresin. If you can get me inside The Sanctum, I can find him,' said Ventran. 'Eventually, kill him.'

'I can deal with that brat myself,' snapped Keva's father.

'He's too well guarded. You'd be better put to shaming him, turning people from him. Get him sent from the city, the beasts will follow. You turn him into a martyr, we'll get another bloody statue alongside that pifing dragon,' said the merchant.

'Or the serpents might attack *us,*' added another.

It was an interesting issue. For a moment Ventran allowed himself to be distracted by it.

'You need to get more organised. Distract guards, then strike. You could lure them from that statue, for one. Then smash it up.'

'It's a start. How you going to do it?'

Ventran was growing bored with these fools. Their badly organised rebellion would not aid him. It was time to leave.

'I'm not here for trifles, merchant. I'm here for Dresin. If you can't help me, move aside.'

'Why?' asked Keva's father. 'He's mine.'

'Does it matter how he falls?'

'And who in the hells are you, anyway?' the merchant said softly. Ventran heard the danger in his voice. 'You don't speak like one of us. What is that around your neck?'

It was his symbol of Terome; they must have seen the chain.

The red darkness spoke to Ventran, whispering the end of this. He grinned, anticipation building like the desperate need to urinate held those few seconds more; awful... enjoyable.

'I'm *not* one of you.'

'You sound... foreign,' Keva's father hissed.

'The man asked what you got round yer neck,' growled one of the dockers. Ventran glanced sideways. They were moving around him. Three at least were reaching for weapons. He put his hands behind his back.

'Who did you bring us, boy?' Keva's father asked. Keva shook his head.

'Death,' whispered Ventran, his half-lit face in a rictus.

Both hands whipped out, a knife leaving each. They hit the throats of the two dockers in front of him vertically, spurts of dark blood erupting as the men staggered and choked, one dropping the belaying pin he had picked up.

He ducked fluidly under the grab of the larger man behind him and twisted, elbow up. It hit the man in the jaw, catching the tip of his tongue as it slammed shut. The man howled, and Ventran pulled one of his close-work knives out. The blade was short but deadly, curving forward. There was no hilt as such; the tang was slim until it ended in a ring which fitted around a finger.

He slipped his index finger through it and closed his fist around the tang, the curved blade starting back just after his palm, and sliced upward, turning, opening the man from gut to chest through his dirty clothes. Although the razor-sharp blade was barely longer than his longest finger, it was enough to carve through the muscle and spill out slippery intestines.

He sprang forward and rolled as the man toppled, regaining his feet to ignore the last docker, who was coming in roaring, and leap at the merchant, who wasn't looking so smug now. His feet connected with the man's face, breaking his neck.

Hands closed on him, a crushing grip he would not break. Without even looking he struck backward once, twice, again and again, the knife stabbing into muscle and fat. The man gasped over and over, but did not let go. Ventran grabbed his wrist, inserted the blade and twisted. Two fingers spun away into the shadows and the man wailed as his grip fell away, slumping forward, a bubbling wheeze coming from him. He would die soon, Ventran knew.

Breathing deeply, he faced Keva and his father, both of whom were frozen in place. He could feel blood sprinkled over his features, revelled in it.

'Ahhhh!' he breathed in satisfaction.

'Wait,' begged Keva's father, panicked. Ventran cocked his head.

'All right,' he said reasonably, lowering his knife and stepping forward. 'What is it?'

Relieved, the man opened his mouth.

Ventran slashed the edge through his throat in a blur. It was so easy when their guard was down. Hot blood sprayed and the man tried to gulp convulsively through a severed throat, his tunic flooding black at the front.

Keva screamed at the sight of his father choking and bolted for the door. Ventran danced to the side and scooped up a fallen belaying pin. He hurled it as hard as he could.

It struck Keva in the back of the head, felling him like a tree. Ventran winced, half-laughingly; that must have fractured the boy's skull at the least.

He walked over, casually, listening to the sounds of the dying around him forming a dreadful symphony. The youth was face down, stunned, blood all over the back of his swelling head, moving slowly and mewling. Ventran picked up the heavy wooden club again.

'Never leave a job half done,' he cried gaily, and smashed it down again and again, pulping the back of the boy's head until it was little more than a broken face on an empty skull. The youngster's limbs jerked spasmodically and brains spattered.

Breathing heavily, Ventran dropped the gory wood and glanced around to make sure none of the others had moved. The man he had stabbed wasn't breathing, pink froth drying on his lips. The one he had gutted was breathing shallowly, watching in an uncomprehending daze. The others were dead.

He collected his knives, then cocked an index finger in friendly farewell at the slowly dying man and left.

This *had* been fun.

આ ચ

Night dropped a thick tome down with a slap on the desk in front of Xhera, making her jump. As usual, the small man moved like a silent breath of air; she hadn't heard him come into the room. He had been back for two days, listening carefully to the tale of the lizard before resuming his studies. He had found no signs but seemed to think it little threat.

'I suggest you read this,' he said now. 'This is one of three copies I know about, and only two of your Librarians knew of it. That copy seems to have been destroyed in the fire that claimed your Third Librarian in the Combic Libraries. Za'Amon is a Seeker of our order who has researched the origins of our Universe extensively. I doubt if most scholars will even know of her work or acknowledge it. Nevertheless... it may give you some answers.'

'Huh,' grunted Xhera tiredly, reaching out and running a hand over the thick leather. 'This looks pretty old.'

'Nearly two thousand years,' said Night. Her hand paused. 'Not this version, of course. This one is barely two hundred.'

Xhera looked the book over thoughtfully, waking up a little at something new.

'*Is* a Seeker? You mean, *was.*' She chewed her bottom lip reflectively, then stared at Night. 'How could she still be alive?'

'You do not question that dragons are immortal? Why then show so much surprise at her long life? She is not like you, my friend. Remember what my Order is. She is old, and knows much of our world, and beyond. I am not even sure she is of this world, Xhera. I believe she has spoken to First Ones, even Gods, to gain her knowledge. Aldwyn would have enjoyed talking to her very much, I think. She is one of our foremost scientists and historians. I suspect she may be almost as ancient as our Mother Ealasaíd .'

'Why didn't you mention this to the Council?' asked Xhera.

'I had forgotten most of its contents,' admitted Night. 'It is old, and the original is kept in our tombs. Immortality does not give you an infinite well of knowledge, or we should not need to write anything down. Information fades and is replaced. I doubt it has been studied in the last five hundred years. Our conversations brought it to mind again - and you *are* the official seeker of Aldwyn's knowledge of events. I did not know this copy existed.'

'You keep books in *tombs?*' she asked.

'Yes. We don't need light to read, and it is the safest place to store parchment, scrolls, anything written on fragile materials - as long as damp is taken care of.'

Night shrugged. 'Darkness, earth and stone are an effective shield for delicate objects.'

'What about the bodies?' asked Xhera, fascinated.

'Ah. The residents don't mind.'

She felt instantly stupid.

He flicked over to a point about a fifth into the tome and turned it to face her. 'I know this starts well into the book, but you might need this chapter, titled *In The Beginning*. I can't say precisely how accurate it is, but it is the culmination of centuries of research, and pieces of the information supposedly come from some of the Twelve themselves, or beings that are themselves considered gods. I would say it is as accurate an account of the genesis of reality as you are likely to find.'

'I'll read it later,' suggested Xhera. 'I don't want to lose my place in these-' she pointed to a stack of notebooks. Her eyes roamed the page. The script was precise, and for all the scientific description had a religious feel to its cadence. Words caught her eye that even Aldwyn had only touched upon, and many others she did not know. Xhera knew she was going to have to look up a lot of new concepts after reading this.

'I have my own research to pursue,' shrugged Night. 'I would caution you, Xhera. Sarthos's book is hard to read and even harder to understand. The events within are very easy to misconstrue, and many are based in madness, not prophecy. Perhaps reading this first would give some structure to what you look for, give your mind some needed respite.'

She nodded, and he left as silently as he had arrived. Maybe he was right, she thought, looking at the stack of notes, then the new tome.

Settling in, Xhera pulled the heavy book to her and began to read the chapter.

FORTY-THREE

I n the beginning, before the concept of Time was even a twinkle in infinity, there was a Void.

A Void of Darkness, for as yet, there was no light; the Void had no need. But, still, It was there, and indeed It would have been impossible not to exist, as the Void was everything.

So It was, infinite and infinity; alive, and sentient; omniscient and omnipresent. After an immeasurable period, for, as yet, there was no Time, the Void decided to implode part of Itself, to form a milder version. And in doing so, the Void also formed a God, and this God was the personification of the Void, and had the power of the Void within It. The God named Itself GAL, and was moved to create.

So GAL created; It decreed that there should be a profusion of life, and that this life should live in its own manner, unaided, growing in its own way, and it would be of an infinite variety of sizes, shapes, and composition. So GAL imagined large, fierce, bright bodies that shone with the power of the Void, and teased from them the essence of worlds; this It set to coalesce around their stars, elements to their nucleus. And so it came to pass that the concept of worlds formed around stars, spinning in unity. But, held within the infinite possibility of the Void, they remained as they were made – the ideas of GAL, chaotic, unstable, unable to support such delicate life forms as GAL envisaged, and essentially dead unto themselves, enriched as they were in the infinite Power of the Void. Even the stars were merely a manifestation of the power around them. Nothing truly existed.

The Void was Everything.

And thus it happened that GAL perceived a use for the gentler void; gathering up Its unborn children, It conceived Reality and placed them gently together within it at the centre of the mild void, each of Its children with an initial form from which to grow.

GAL saw this, and was pleased, and, naming the milder void Universe, created a helper to care for GAL's worlds while It created anew. This helper named Itself Aprolis and set out to nurture and teach the children of GAL.

Seeing that Universe was frail enough to submit to the Void's intrinsic chaos and thus destroy Its works, GAL set three Laws in the mild void; Time, to swing to and fro and govern Universe without the greater Chaos of the Void by setting rhythmic flow; Inner Chaos, to prevent stagnation and to spark change and evolution; and Order, to prevent chaos from destroying Its creations, to bring stability and causality. Equilibrium came unto frail Universe; pressure within to balance pressure without.

As Time began to flow, it marked the beginning of the First Aeon and the First Age of Universe, the Age of Genesis. The children given form were set free, accelerated out in all directions in an infinite explosion where, over the Aeons, they gradually became what GAL had dreamed; something more than just images in the Great Void. From nothing, yet everything, there was All.

But even here the children of GAL were still chaotic, though yet slowly beginning to awake; taken out of the potency of the Void they gradually became alive unto themselves, but they were yet unable to support the even frailer life envisioned by GAL. In the parts of Universe where reality wore thinnest, many of the children of GAL took strange and wondrous forms unable to be found elsewhere, and the myriad works of GAL grew.

Aprolis saw that they were unaware of each other and linked everything in Universe using a higher level of energy, vibrating into and around the firmament GAL had conceived, allowing evolution of more than mere physical bodies, granting spirit to anchor substance. Now as they became aware of themselves, the worlds became aware of each other, and found themselves dancing with their stars. So the children of GAL developed, and danced their intricate Dance of Life, led by Aprolis the Star Dancer. Every twelve thousand years the Dance came to a Conjunction, where all creation rejoiced in tune.

The children were born, died; they met, split, begat companions and comets, asteroids and all manner of countless forms; new stars evolved and begat their own children, and an unending cycle of creation began, to each child a destiny, its path its own. The stars in turn lived and grew, died, evolved, and danced their own dance out into the reaches of this new void, forming galaxies beyond number. As they collapsed the largest sometimes expended so much energy that the fabric of Universe bent. GAL guided this accretion of energy and mass to naturally vent back into the Void, to prevent damage to Universe, and thus these deaths formed massive singularities, an escape of energies back out into the Void along an infinite curve; galaxies acquired gigantic holes in space and time at their centres and excess power leaked safely back out of Universe. Balance was struck.

Thus was marked the end of the first Aeon of Universe.

As the dance turned, GAL's children grew anew, and finally began to slowly bear forth the frail dreams of GAL as life upon their surfaces, in all their complexities and infinite varieties. This, the birth of the first of GAL's children's children, marked the beginning of the Second Age of Universe, midway through the fourth Aeon.

And so it came about that the dawn of the Second Age found Universe balanced and unsullied by any hint of Outer Chaos, a time later called the Golden Age. To ensure that this continued, GAL then created twelve equal Gods, to balance and protect. To aid them in this, It gave them great power within Universe - the ability to touch the power of the Void to some extent.

To Zol GAL bestowed the governance of Order, the duty of events happening in the fashion ordained, to ensure effect followed cause, to create harmony;

Zaax was given the theories of Chaos to ensure evolution, unpredictability and change;

To Quen was given an understanding of the instincts of all life and the emotion that grew with them;

To Wheru was given logic, knowledge, self-awareness and wisdom, free sentient thought unbound;

Dúras was created to care for the plane of Spirit, the dimension of energy linking all aware life and allowing souls to move and anchor;

Retilá came to care for the firmament and substance, and all matter connected by the Spirit Realm;

Jerad was given the hot flames of Light to banish the darkness and illuminate, the essence of the bright power of the Void remembered;

To Ashta was given the freezing depths of the Shadow, the darkness that binds all between the stars, the cold of the Void as it was and is;

Isha took up the mantle of birth and life, the creation and keeping of beings countless in number;

And Xagón arose to assume the trappings of death and destruction, to all things a time to end;

Rescha took up the reins of the Past, governing Time, keeping what was as what is;

And Kwor came to mark the Future of all things, ensuring that Time continued to flow.

Each God worked with a balance. As one with Universe, they worked with it, in it, through it. To Order, Chaos, that all might change amidst stability. To Instinct, Intellect, that life might truly live as well as survive. To Substance, Spirit, that all who danced might be luminous beings, not merely crude matter. To Light, Darkness, that there might be a time for fire, and a time for ice; To Life, Death, that all might dance as one with the cycle and have their time; To the Past, the Future, to be balanced on the ever-changing fulcrum of the present;

Equilibrium in all things.

GAL looked upon Its custodians and was pleased, seeing Universe becoming self-sustaining with their guidance. They sat cradled in the darkness on thrumming tendrils of hidden power and enthroned on unseen matter, ensuring that everything within Universe flowed correctly. The power within Universe was present on all worlds; the Life that had begun coming forth from the worlds soon after the Twelve were created had powers touching the cradle of the Twelve, in the manner of the worlds that bore them forth. These were lesser gods, defined by the worlds that begat them, many unique to each parent.

These lesser gods had not the power of the Twelve, but neither were they part of them, and they too became individual beings, attending their worlds carefully. The Twelve spoke to all the lesser gods, and taught them of GAL.

GAL saw all that happened, and was pleased; Its dreams were realised. GAL swore that It would abstain from delivering aid to any of Its children again, so as to let them live in their own manner. It knew that too much guidance would ruin life in Universe, and make it no more than an extension of Its own will.

GAL withdrew from Universe, leaving with Its blessings to grow as it might, unhindered, unforced. Observing from afar, It was no longer part of Universe, and eventually began to create anew. Aprolis watched the Dance with pride for a while longer, but eventually followed GAL.

Aeons passed. Eventually some worlds noticed a biogenesis of life that they had not conceived. The favourable conditions of organic materials from both space and the planets themselves, freely available energy, and water on some hospitable worlds gave rise to organic monomers which slowly combined to produce more complex polymers. These developed in ways the worlds had not thought of, independent to the whims of their parents. In time they began to form more complex molecules from the simple ones, and eventually became simple cells, forming a primordial soup of sorts. Over the next Aeon these learned to use the power of the stars which their parents circled, and the worlds became aware that they were being changed subtly by this tiniest of life, developing biospheres and increasing the beauty and diversity of its parents; to each world different forms.

They saw that it lived, died, and changed with incredible speed. Its very existence had been unforeseen, its beginnings unnoticed, and the chances of it failing incredibly high; yet it was tenacious. Marvellous in its ability to adapt and change, its very frailty was its greatest strength. Seeing this, the worlds eagerly tried to help this curious new life along, then seeking to create their own special children, as had GAL. In this they succeeded in part; their new works grew from an amalgamation of the simple life that had begun to evolve, and a shaping of the stuff of Universe by the worlds themselves, albeit to a far slighter degree than the lesser gods. These children they nurtured carefully, leaving the evolving life to its own devices.

This first true life, born from the tiny atoms of organic material and undetected by their parents for long ages, finally fulfilled the visions of its ultimate creator and grew according to its own whims, unique and free. Evolution took the life through uncounted changes, carrying on almost unnoticed alongside the slow conception of the First Ones; those who were both created and organic.

Eventually the worlds noticed that they were becoming resplendent with flora and fauna not of their own devising, a myriad of teeming life, and were pleased; their own children were almost born after long ages of creation, and would have a living, breathing world to exist in.

As the Aeons passed, their children developed alongside the untamed life to become creatures on worlds that lived and breathed, but had not grasped true mortality. Powerful, yet comparatively frail and alone, the First Ones did not evolve so much as they were guided to the forms envisioned by their parents.

And so the First Ones arose. They quickly developed their own cycles, living within and hunting the frailer life, gradually learning full awareness. Alone in sentience, perfect and unchanging, many of them considered other life to be subject to their whims; some were even resentful, believing they were the only true life to exist and that all else was transient and flawed. It was impossible to ignore the fact that this new life was changing quickly and giving rise to some creatures that were powerful in their own right, some even coming to provide a challenge for the First Ones. Few of them acknowledged any of the companion organisms as worthy of their respect.

The lesser gods gently rebuked them, saying that this new life was to be nurtured as they had been. The new life was frail, and imperfect; it would require guidance in one form or another. In ages to come it might become as great as the First Ones in its own way, and was the ultimate goal of GAL's creation, whom they called Arkhe.

This did not sit well with some of the First Ones, who resented that this weak life born of chance might be equal to or even greater than they in the eyes of their ultimate creator. Jealousy was felt for the first time, and sometimes the frail life suffered at the mercy of First Ones because of this. However, for millions of years this new life and the First Ones existed in harmony for the most part, the First Ones never ceasing to be astonished by the way the lesser life evolved and diversified. Plants and animals spread and grew and changed, providing infinitely diverse environments for the First Ones.

Their own births were very rare and of great consequence, and their numbers increased only slowly. Unlike the rapidly changing life about them that lived and died, they remained immortal, and they slept apart from the world for great lengths of time.

Nearly halfway through the eighteenth Aeon, sentient creatures began to arise more widely, to slowly develop and learn language and culture, to raise themselves from the level of the creatures from which they had evolved over only a million or so years. In time they discovered the First Ones, and worshipped them as gods. As learning increased they also found the Lesser Gods, and even the Twelve above them, and understood a greater kinship with the First Ones.

Resentment reignited for some, especially those that enjoyed being considered as gods themselves, yet others rejoiced that they had more purpose. No longer were the First Ones alone; no longer was the life that had grown just a challenge, just competition, just there. The unchanging Gods and the slowly changing First Ones gave of their wisdom to these new frail children, and the dance continued on.

As it had since the very beginning of all time, every twelve thousand years a conjunction of all the life in Universe occurred; everything bonded, mind, being, and soul, in a wondrous harmony that recalled the touch of the great hand of GAL Itself.

Slowly the First Ones had unravelled many of the mysteries around them, and with the teachings of the Lesser Gods and their intrinsic link to the lesser powers of Universe they learned to create tunnels in the fabric of Universe which took them between the worlds, where they discovered wondrous new places and encountered many like themselves; however different or strikingly similar, all recognised a kinship, although there was often strife as well as the First Ones met others of their own power. The First Ones began to spread throughout Universe to worlds that agreed with them, using methods to bend and move space and time they named wyrmholes, rifts, pathways, tesseracts of reality. The lesser gods that had taught their use more often remained bound to their worlds, neither wanting nor needing to travel.

The other sentient life began to unravel some of the powers around them using the teachings of the First Ones and the Lesser Gods, and also came to use the network of portals that the First Ones had created with the help of their greater kin. Thus, the proliferation of life exploded throughout Universe, throwing new life to the furthest stars. This was not without its repercussions; many beings came into conflict. Life forms that were never meant to meet found foes as dislike or competition grew into hatred, and then hatred grew into warfare and annihilation. Yet, many more had no interest in others, or even explored and settled worlds agreeably, and the webwork between the worlds grew; all war and death was balanced in some way by harmony and peace.

No longer were the races of Universe confined to the worlds on which they were conceived; instead, they spread unto the farthest reaches of Universe. Thus, the already complex dance grew ever more wonderful and intricate, and the natural cycles of Universe adapted to these changes and continued on, as GAL had foreseen.

Cultures, empires, entire species rose and fell. Events moved according to the dictates of Chaos, with Order giving stability, and Time swung above it all. Other life continued to evolve and follow the pattern, and the Twelve governed, fascinated by the profusion of countless beings; even so supreme within Universe, some of them yet felt drawn to the frailty of evolved life. Zol and Xagón were particularly drawn to intelligent life, though the latter was the end of all things great or small, never failing its duty, and Isha found as much interest in the birth of the tiniest creature as the mightiest star. Zaax delighted in life that was in turmoil and displayed great potential for chaos, so different from the unchanging heavens, and found that of all creatures the intelligent were capable of the greatest unpredictability. Wheru and Quen felt the ebb and flow that was tied to the act of living and thinking free thoughts. By nature, Dúras was connected to the spirits of all living things, and Retilá was privy to the ever-changing energy within their flesh down to the smallest being.

The rest remained mostly aloof; whatever affinity they felt for evolved life that conformed to their duties was small, and did not affect them. So, Universe was in balance, and the dance continued down to the smallest living thing, meeting in the Great Conjunction every twelve thousand years.

Finally, it happened in the manner of all things that the Second Age, the Golden Age, ended. One of GAL's first children made a misstep in the dance, only a few millennia after a conjunction sometime in the midst of the eighteenth Aeon.

A great star shining forth in every spectrum stumbled in its movement, many tens of thousands of times bigger and unusually hotter than its siblings. The reason was unknown to all but Chaos; the star was an anomaly, should not have been possible.

Falling out of the dance, it careened into a nearby quasar. Ancient and immense, it perished before its time in a sleeting cataclysm of energies; simultaneously collapsing and pulled apart, it died in an unprecedented explosion so powerful that it tore a ragged gap through space-time before it could collapse into the safety of a singularity. This sparked a chain reaction in the young galaxy that even the supermassive singularity in its heart could not contain; instead, the tear merged with it and ripped it open even further with the opposing forces, swallowing innumerable young stars and pulling them into the rift before they even had the chance of life. The flow of energy through the colossal singularity abruptly reversed in a cataclysm greater than a hypernova; the astonishing energies released were greater than the sum of other stars in that one instant, outshining all else in Universe a trillion times for a brief moment.

All Universe reverberated at the detonation. Life on countless worlds was sterilised by the radiation spearing randomly through the stars from the detonation, sterilised in instants in arcs curving through Universe from the detonation.

After the initial eruption, the sum of the energy did not expand out into Universe, nor did it leak safely into the Greater Void. Instead, it jammed into the rift in reality as it collapsed back down to tiny proportions. Holding it open and feeding it, it formed a conduit between the Void and Universe that did not heal. This stretched through dimensions, leaking raw Outer Chaos into Universe and pulling matter outside in nullification, and the awful tear in the fabric of creation was blasted back on its course into the heart of the expanding galaxies by the instantaneous release of the incalculable power held within the suns that had died.

Such holes had formed before, white-hot outpourings that spilled raw energy into Universe; the converse of the invisible dark holes at the centre of galaxies that sucked everything in to vanish forever. Sometimes, a smaller singularity would even form, perhaps from a gravitational collapse, not powerful enough to open into the Void. This would instead link not to the Void, but elsewhere within Universe; but always before, these energy-spewing holes evaporated after a time.

This time, the powers of an entire forming galaxy had poured into holding the hole open.

This wound in reality hurtled through Universe; anything that fell into the open rip was flung from the dance and destroyed, instantly rent asunder into the Void. Surrounding this small rift was a vast swirling miasma of chaotic energy, an aura of anarchy; a ripple in the fabric of Universe. By nature it did not destroy; rather, it warped and changed without prediction much of what it encountered, distorting parts of the dance and those that danced it. The stars and worlds themselves were rarely greatly changed by the ripple, but the frailer life they contained had no defences and suffered terribly. Even life touched by its fringes was often changed; sometimes twisted, although not always for the worse. The changes were truly chaotic, creating entirely new species, changing the genetic codes of others, wiping out others completely.

Almost the entirety of the tenuous webwork of portals throughout Universe had snapped at the initial blast, stranding races permanently over countless worlds. As the ripple swept through Universe, life that had been identical across worlds became vastly different.

The Twelve felt the hammer blow to the dark fabric that cradled them; GAL Itself sensed the damage and diverted Its attention back to its children. The Twelve watched in horror and confusion as they witnessed the unnatural deaths of innumerable of GAL's children in the overwhelming blast. However, restricted in their roles and part of creation as they were, they could not see the tear in reality that hurtled through Universe; only the changes wrought by it. The gods felt something was terribly wrong, but could not correct it, and so continued with their tasks. They focused on the arrival of the next conjunction, hoping that it would correct the faltering dance.

Ten thousand years passed, an instant, an age; the conjunction arrived. The Twelve joined all life in it as they had for countless ages; but this time they felt an immediate sense of harm. This time there was no peaceful joining, but a great wrong felt by all life. Whilst all in the dance were held immobile for the brevity of the conjunction, the ripple reached the Twelve themselves; unable to sense the rift, held in its path, the concentrated *energies swept through them as GAL and Aprolis looked on. Dúras, Retilá, Xagón, Isha, Kwor, Jerad, Wheru and Quen escaped exposure to the warping energies.*

But though the others were not destroyed, they were changed.

Zaax and Ashta felt the lure of the Outer Chaos; predisposed towards it, they realised that it was the beginning, the end, perfection; everything that had come to be was an aberration, the greatest of which was Order. They saw that Universe had ruined the perfection of Outer Chaos, and that all should be returned to the ultimate entropy of the Greater Void.

Zol and Rescha felt the horror of Outer Chaos, predisposed towards Order as they were; it represented the death of everything GAL had tasked them with. They saw that Order was the ultimate evolution of all from the Chaos from which it sprung, unchanging and perfect, and all Chaos must be expelled from Universe to once more achieve the perfection of a conjunction; one that would never end and bring peace to all life.

The Eight that were untouched saw this and knew fear. They saw the raw seething power Outer Chaos lent to the Two and knew they must struggle to maintain a balance; the power of the Void was such that even so few were enough to destroy equilibrium, and thus all Reality. Their Chaotic brethren had become unknown to them and could not be reached, beginning their work to return Universe to the Void. The imbalance in Universe would act as a growing oscillation which would eventually tear all of creation asunder.

In their despair, they realised this Third Age was to be that of Strife.

GAL saw this and knew that It could not directly intervene without destroying everything and leaving Universe lifeless once more. If once It reimposed Its will, Life would forevermore lose its unique individuality over its fate - the goal for GAL's creation.

For the first time ever, constraints were imposed on Its power. It looked ahead on the tachyon flows and saw that there would exist few chances to avert the coming annihilation before the last hope to restore Universe, whence it would be forever lost.

All those part of Causality were bound by it to some extent. All but one; the random, complex life which had arisen all but unnoticed in the beginning. GAL saw that, in the end, the frailest life, unbound, would save or damn everything.

Aprolis, likewise constrained, could only attempt to lead the dance back to its true path. Correcting the dance where possible, It knew that it would only wander once more, and knew also that the dance would shift further and further as Chaos grew.

GAL understood that the chance for repair could only come from within Universe itself; any outside interference would destroy everything. GAL directed Its servant Aprolis therefore to distract the Four that were changed, to try and lead them back to their duties, yet knowing that this would fail. Calling Dúras, Isha, Xagón, Kwor, Jerad, Wheru, Quen, and Retilá alone to the very boundaries of Universe, GAL then spoke unto them, giving them wisdom and foresight to use the few chances of salvation, and Its blessing for the struggles ahead. Even GAL could not foresee which future would become truth; dissolution, or continuation. As the Eight began to set in motion the last fail-safes for balance against the bitter struggles of the Four, Gal withdrew with Aprolis, to watch his creations live or die in the freedom of their lives as they would.

Initially unnoticed in the mayhem, raw Chaos had manifested in the wake of the ripple, and some of the form of Universe was altered slightly in the offbeat of the conjunction, randomly teasing copied elements of life from those beings affected. This manifestation was drawn to the deeps and Outer Chaos, and slowly followed the ripple which fed it. Gradually it shifted, melding destructive Chaos and the cold of the depths between galaxies with an impression of the life touched by the strands.

Eventually four elements coalesced and gained a form of awareness between the stars. The Chaos gods sensed the powerful essences drifting in the darkness and sought them out.

Ashta gathered them in his beloved darkness, helping give them form and guiding them to sentient awareness - one, but many. Zaax fed their natures, and they hungrily absorbed his teachings. These entities of Chaos entered the fray without any previous ties to Universe, only the urge to destroy, and Ashta was pleased. These demons were dark messiahs that moved outside the limits of the Twelve.

The balance swung ever further out, random, unpredictable, and the oscillations of Universe itself began to slowly tear at reality.

No longer working in unity, it took the combined efforts of the Eight and Two to prevent the other Two from destroying all. The Twelve now strove against each other; those lost to Chaos attempting to change many things using their Darklings as agents, with the others united to prevent them, striving to maintain balance.

As the struggles surged back and forth, there were repercussions on all worlds. Life already twisted and warped often had an affinity for Chaos, and so unknowingly worked toward its goal; other life fought to survive, or in hatred of Chaos. War and death erupted across countless worlds, far beyond what had gone before; a scale of obliteration and hatred not included in the laws of nature, and never before experienced by any species.

For the next fourteen millennia, the Twelve struggled. If Chaos could corrupt enough worlds to tip the balance too far, Universe would quickly unravel. It was far easier to corrupt and imbalance than maintain equilibrium, especially with the four unnatural embodiments of Chaos hidden from the eyes of the Ten in the dark infinite emptiness between the stars.

World after world became empty, desolate, stricken places, where the restless entities who lived and died there mournfully haunted those few still living, dreaming of the Age that was. Countless worlds were ravaged or even destroyed.

The Gods bound to Order countered this by imposing complete Order on many more. By the supreme efforts of the untouched Eight, as many worlds were held steady according to the dictates of GAL, balancing delicately on the tip of natural law; balance proved ever harder to reach than extremity in this.

By this time Universe was almost unrecognisable as GAL's dream. War-torn worlds of ugliness and death spun near to worlds of wonder that had retained the light of hope. Many of GAL's children had been struck from the dance, to wander, lost and alone, barren planetoids and dim stars crying out for their places in the once-harmonious order of Universe. Others were destroyed utterly.

With each new conjunction, the dance was even more disrupted; instead of a wondrous bonding with the powers in Universe, most beings felt an unbearable sense of wrong, and many died of woe, in anguish for the lost harmony. Conflict reached a frenzy in the times of conjunction, and countless trillions of beings were lost from the dance unnaturally.

Chaos disrupted much in Universe, fed by the constant influx from the Void, and Order and Balance desperately worked together to keep Universe in existence. All of the Twelve began to realise that the worlds left untouched by any were rapidly waning in number; it became obvious that soon, there would be few left; then none.

Gradually, the last few worlds fell, taken by first one side and then another. Prophecies set out by GAL were fulfilled or lost to hungry Chaos.

After much sacrifice and blood, the Eight and the Two of Order had managed to win enough of the remaining worlds to balance chaos and slow its encroachment before the last bastion of hope was lost. Universe was left in temporary, fragile balance.

The fulcrum lay within one small terrestrial world, known to its intelligent species as Kuln; the last world in Universe untouched by the conflict, unconquered by any in the struggle; the last free world in creation.

The ripple in reality had passed across Kuln, yet it had survived mostly unscathed. If Kuln were corrupted and destroyed, Chaos would triumph; Universe would be obliterated under the weight of its own instability. The entirety of existence - all possibilities in every dimension - would cease to exist as if they had never been.

Thus it was that the natural powers of Universe were overwhelmed by the turmoil of Outer Chaos in an attempt to destroy Kuln, and, failing that, implant agents to ensure its fall. The Chaotic gods saw a random chance and exerted all of their power; bracing against dark strands of matter and energy, they forcefully violated natural order in a blaze of destruction.

The Lesser Gods of Kuln, forgotten by all, awoke in fury and rose to meet this threat. By supreme efforts they thwarted it. But an Evil came to their world as they fought, and they were unable to stop it entering.

Chaos was kept at bay; the Twelve awaited the next move in this endgame, and all living gave praise that they were spared… for now.

Thus Universe continued in its dance; and Chaos waited.

- *Excerpt from the ancient scrolls of Za'Amon, Seeker of the order of Illuminus*

FORTY-FOUR

'We have some kind of killer loose in the streets.' Dorn's voice was tired and grim. He had been running close to burnout, Ulric noted, but there was no chance of letting up just yet.

'I've had several reports in the last day,' agreed Councillor Holmson.

'That demon?' Ulric asked.

'No,' mused Jamus Holmson. 'I have heard little of that for a while - the odd report, but nothing substantial. Besides, despite its reputation, there were few deaths. This was different. Wholesale slaughter. A man, I think. A very skilled one.'

'One man?' asked Ulric.

'Everything at the scene suggests it, Councillor,' said Dorn.

'Shadow Council?'

'I don't think so. They usually send an obvious message with their killings. And there have been other deaths. Several Shadow Council Hitters have turned up dead in a similar manner, in fact. Looks like they've taken an interest in his work. I imagine they'll send further men.'

'Well, you know what you're looking at, Captain. Perhaps speak to any contacts you have with them. It's to everyone's benefit to capture this killer.'

'Are we sure Rast Tal'Orien has left the city?' asked Ulric wryly.

'Sir?' asked Dorn.

'Don't joke,' said Holmson. 'Whoever did this is a master. Tal'Orien wouldn't so wantonly kill even if he weren't a thousand miles from here by now. We have a new player.'

'Who were the victims?'

'Four dock hands, a successful merchant who had been peripherally linked to the Sons of Havoc, and a man and his son. The last two are interesting - Dinall and Keva Torrin. Keva was cousin to Fron Grishold. His killing was particularly brutal.'

'Really.'

'Yes. Dinall had petitioned the Council more than once on Fron's behalf.'

'Interesting. You think it is related to the Telemer business with Karland Dresin?'

'My gut says no,' said Dorn. 'The others are a factor that make no sense. The only thing tying them was the current discontent in some parts of the city. But we don't know enough yet.'

'Could have been wrong place at wrong time.'

'I would rather find fact than conjecture,' suggested Holmson.

Dorn nodded and left.

Ulric grunted. 'Do we inform the Council?'

'I think the last thing we should do is to distract the already distracted Council with non-war issues. Not until it is necessary. With any luck the Shadow Council will find this person and save us all some trouble.'

'They haven't done well so far, Jamus. And the Guard have more important things to do than hunt through an entire city.'

'True.'

'Do we have other options?'

'As a matter of fact, I think we do. I'd like to know what this person is doing here as well as stopping them. Why now? I think we need more information than a Guard can give us.' He pursed his lips, then sighed. 'I propose we send out Garn. If we'd had him here when Telemer was causing the problems... never mind. He's been sitting idle for over a month, and that makes me nervous. He's a fanatic, Ulric. It makes him obedient and reliable only to a point.'

Ulric nodded. He hoped Garn didn't complicate things further.

૏ ૐ

Unlike Lodnor, the seedy underbelly of which was filled with rival street gangs of thugs, it seemed Darost had a Guild headed by what they called the Shadow Council. Ventran hadn't anticipated how well-organised they would be, or how much interest they would take. They had uncovered his footsteps far faster than the Guard had, and last night two of their representatives had entered his inn room silently, armed with knives and garrottes.

The bodies of the two Hitters had been left on the floor. One of them he had killed immediately. The other had talked... eventually. Their orders had been to find out what he was doing here and eliminate any threat. The Shadow Council didn't like loose operatives in their city.

The killers had been better trained than ordinary street thugs, but clearly they hadn't taken him as seriously as his work warranted. He had gained a lot of information about the city, although nothing about Varelin or Dresin.

Afterwards he'd taken his belongings and left through the window, leaving the door bolted. Once those two were discovered, others would come. Ventran did not plan on a running street war in unfamiliar territory which he would quickly lose through weight of numbers.

He was certain the Guard were investigating the killings, too. Another attempt had been made on him in a dockside area, resulting in a body which may or not have been just a common thug.

One way or another, his time here was now limited.

In desperation Ventran entered The Sanctum once more in daylight. This time the questioning at the gate was far more intensive, and although he was finally allowed in, he dared not risk it again. He was certain they would watch all unusual entrants closely.

He ventured into one of the libraries, supposedly seeking knowledge about ancient Haná. To his delight the Assistant Scroll who served him was an attractive younger woman called Ysa, almost still a girl, and he chatted to her, gauging her responses, and then turned on his full charm.

They spoke for far longer than Ysa should have. He turned his talk to what he had learned from the ill-fated Sons of Havoc, probing.

Ysa had seen the great red dragon, but not the terrible Yosgaloth, though everyone in the city had heard it. She spoke of the flights of dragons that had driven it back in longing tones, clearly entranced by them, and of the great bronze that had visited and spoken to the Council, and Karland Dresin.

Ah!

He prodded deeper, asking little so as to not give his lack of knowledge away, and she didn't disappoint. She knew Karland and his friend Xhera, had helped them collect some study work. She hadn't seen him for some time, although she knew Xhera had left for the north two months before. Probably, he had gone with her; those two were almost always together and had some sort of Council dispensation.

She was also certain that Rast Tal'Orien had left the University. She confessed that she had watched him many times practicing in the yard - not from anything other than admiration for his skill, she hastily assured him, she found him a foreboding man - but he hadn't been there for more than a month. Rumour had it he was on another mission to the west for the Council.

Ventran pondered what this meant. He knew Tal'Orien protected the old man and the children, but the Council wouldn't have sent them all out again, would they?

What made more sense was the Council trying to find the meaning of the pendant Kelpas Withy had stolen and sent away. Both Ventran's agents and the scores of mercenary bands saturating Eordeland a year ago had failed to prevent Varelin from taking it to The Sanctum, but Ventran also knew that the old man had another place he lived in. A hidden one in a northern town.

Yes, that made more sense. In a city gearing for war, sending the old fossil out with his charges to help him study was what Ventran himself might do. Tal'Orien could well be a decoy. They'd been attacked more than once, and he was a very obvious target, after all.

Well, he wouldn't fall for their tricks. Haring around Anaria after the warrior would gain him nothing. But if the scholar and the children *had* left, with little or no guard… then he could take whatever he needed.

Information, pendant.

Enjoyment.

A call from further within the library made Ysa start. She asked him if he would be back and Ventran promised disarmingly to meet her that evening at a *kof*-house in the Hoard, knowing full well he would not. Silently he grinned at the knowledge that she would never know how lucky that ill-fortune would really be. Another time he would have been delighted to spend a… productive evening with her.

North, then. He had seen several names in reports that bore investigating: Gladsmoor. Fordun's Run. The Croft.

Time to leave this city and hunt once more.

CR   SO

'You sent for me?' the cold voice of Colridge Garn came from behind him.

Jamus Holmson turned.

'Garn. We have a killer on the loose in Darost. We don't think it's Shadow Council.'

'You suspect a ploy against the Darostim?' Garn's voice was almost a hiss. He had been difficult to control when he had found out that many Darostim scholars had been exposed and murdered, Holmson remembered. Anything that threatened them must be dealt with immediately and terminally as far as this man was concerned.

610

'We don't know. It's possible this could be related to the recent unrest. The killer is far too skilled to be a common thug.'

'Do you suspect anyone?'

'No. There have been several Novinian and Meyari visitors of late. No Ignathians, and the blade play would have made them a prime suspect. They are extremely skilled. One man seems to have visited the University more than once; if he comes again, we will hold him, but if not, you will find him. If it isn't him, keep searching.'

Garn nodded. 'What… dispensation do I have?'

'Trace him wherever he goes. Find out what he is doing here. Interrogate him, but keep him *alive*. We do not wish a death, Garn - we wish information.' Jamus punctuated his words with a finger before the man's merciless eyes. 'Once you have found him and dealt with him, hand him to the Guard.'

'As you wish.'

Garn had full access to the network. Hopefully it would not take long to find his prey and return. Holmson noticed he was still waiting.

'Is there anything else?'

'I was blocked from my duty in Eyotsburg by a large warrior. I believe it was a man named Rast Tal'Orien. He could be problematic.'

'Tal'Orien is no threat, Garn. Do not engage with him. He is on Council duty and a friend to the Darostim.'

'He prevented-'

'You are not to engage him. Does the Council make itself clear?'

'It does.' Garn's voice held no emotion.

'Then good luck in your hunt. May you find this killer swiftly.'

♋ ♊

Night woke Xhera a few hours before dawn. The light was low enough that she could see a strange red glint in his eyes. It was unnerving, faintly horrifying, and for a second, she almost panicked. Then she calmed, her heart hammering. Night's voice was as calm as ever, and it soothed her. She knew he could sense her fear and probably hear the blood pounding through her veins, but he did not react as her heartbeat began to slow and she shivered.

'Xhera. My apologies for waking you.' He uncovered a Library light, washing the room in blue-white. 'I must leave. My quarry has left his sanctuary. My time working with you has ended.' He shook his head and sat for a moment on the edge of her bed. His hand was strangely hesitant as it briefly touched her leg through the

611

cover; not in a sexual way, but more as if he were seeking comfort, or perhaps trying to awkwardly give it. There was a faint longing in his expression. For a brief second, she wondered if he regretted never having known life.

'You do not need me now. You are better placed than anyone to unravel the thoughts of Aldwyn Varelin, and you have helped me greatly in my own studies. I thank you for your dedication.'

'Must you leave so soon?' she asked. A deep melancholy began rising at the thought of yet another friend leaving her. Other people sought belonging with like people; her friends were all unique, different, yet she belonged with them as much as with anyone.

'I must gather other Seekers and find Councillor Ulric. He leads the Eordeland troops out to meet their foe, and they are stronger than he thinks. Never before has this realm faced so much upheaval inside and out. Eordeland could be broken, and if that happens it is the beginning of the end. Something greater moves across the world than men. Already, I may be too late.' He rose. 'I hope we will meet again, Xhera. Whatever happens, it has been my honour to call you and Karland friends.'

He smiled, fully for once, the white tips of long fangs glinting, and then he was gone, more silently and completely than Rast.

Xhera covered the light and sat with her back to the cool stone wall until her neck became stiff.

FORTY-FIVE

Sontles lay swaying in a trunk carried in a great wagon set with symbols of Terome. The massive creaking wagon had two rooms, a main meeting room for planning with the officers, and a room not accessed by any except himself and the others of his kind. It had taken much searching to find other vampires. Vampiric risings were rare, even with the number of victims he fed on, and the newly Turned were often confused and feral, showing signs of insanity, erratic and hard to control. He preferred older creatures that had grown in power and cunning. Most hadn't refused his offers of alliance.

In a way, the holy symbols were a source of comfort to him, if anything could comfort his dry existence. Terome had no power to harm his kind. Terome was an empty religion based on a misunderstanding. One that, soon, he would ultimately control.

After the murder of the Holy Voice he had sent hundreds of men with messages throughout the city. While the Cardinals were still reeling in shock, he had already broadcast that this was the work of Eordeland and incited the people to gather at the Temple the next evening.

He had come out as early as he had dared as dusk deepened and spoken to the huge crowd outside the Temple. His lack of social grace was countered by his hypnotic charisma for those nearest. It had taken little to whip them into a frenzy, Meyari, Teromens and Teromants all, Chaplains alongside common folk. The emotion that had roared past him in return was like a tidal wave. He could almost fix his teeth in the hatred.

He had promised to lead them to victory against the people that had killed their holiest leader.

It had been easy to have a servant step forward with the evidence; the discovery of the Eord Ambassador's rich tunic rent with blood on it had needed no other catalyst. The mob had stormed the diplomatic quarters and brutally dismembered the man as he sat for dinner.

The Cardinals had come out, too late, in time to find a swelling crowd with fresh blood on them demanding war. Still numb with shock, they had realised anyone disagreeing would be ignored, perhaps torn apart themselves.

At first, Sontle's proposition to go with the army had suited them. Although nominated and accepted as the new Primate of Lodnor, he had not yet been formerly elected and his absence could be used to their advantage.

They had scrambled to place several of their Bishops alongside him under a highly respected Primate, little realising none of their spies would represent the Church for long.

The Cardinals had been pleased; the powerful man would be removed from the Church, allowing them time to recover and consolidate their hold, and he would be watched carefully by an equally powerful Churchman.

By the time he had left after two months of frantic work, he knew they had only begun to realise that his victory would make all their plotting meaningless.

Sontles now had an army under his control, including those spies, and could wield it as he saw fit. It would return without challenge to Meyar. If he chose, with the goodwill of the people, he could march it to the very Temple of Terome itself and bring down the Cardinals.

He would be a prophet; a true prophet, unlike the old faker who had established the Church and then run away.

His lips stretched in a smile.

He would be the last Holy Voice. He would never grow old. In time, the people would believe the god had blessed him with eternal life. He would ascend past that petty office to create his own.

The Nassmoors were mostly empty now. His army had bypassed the northern Stonestride and the second Meyari army attempting to force it and marched along the road parallel to the vast lake Merrimakea. Along with the lake, the Arkons and the Stonestride were a frustratingly effective barrier. To keep the troops in practice, Sontles had given full permission to hunt any Travellers they found on the way. Seven camps so far had been found and slaughtered without mercy, the men and dogs burned, the women taken for use by the troops, and children flung screaming into fires or the lake.

Many new conscripts had balked at this. Fewer had complained when several of them followed after having arms and legs severed at elbows and knees. The Teromens had been very active, repeating as writ that such unworthy people were unbelievers, not even human. They played on the old tales of baby theft and stealing, of luring young women and murdering travellers. They deserved death, as did any that showed pity to them. They were known cheats, liars, baby thieves and wastrels, identified by their weather-darkened skins and bright colours. They were infidels and heathens. The world was better rid of them and their offspring. It was a cull of the inferior, nothing more or less.

Many of the Travellers had spread the word now and the nomads had moved north en masse to the coastal gathers or out into the plains. Only the most foolhardy talked still of following their 'road' and kept going.

Sontles ignored them. When they returned there would be time to hunt them all down.

Eordeland was the key to Anaria. The most advanced, one of the richest, and probably the most powerful, it would be the hardest foe to conquer. If they could break its might, they could destroy its rich farmlands at leisure, ruining much of its wealth. Even if they could simply damage it sufficiently that others would take the opportunity, it would be enough. Other lands would fall one by one, until Meyar ruled the continent.

Already Terome had infiltrated many other realms, sowing dissent and finding many followers. They were beset with uncertainty, divided and weakened. Following up with war was a logical step. Once lands were under the rule of Meyar, the Church would spread even faster, and chaos would spread its influence with it. Fear would rule the land, and terror would feed Sontles and his power.

From such violently disrupted humble beginnings, from such a vile little coward frightened to put action to his disgusting lusts and desires until his rebirth into undeath, Sontles now stood to become a deathless God-Priest over the continent, holding it under the sway of his dark masters. For all Terome had started as a peaceful religion around a simple prophet, giving rise to an indifferent aspect of a hollow God, the real Gods of Meyar had now become the Darklings.

As their prophet he wielded true power. The prayers and terror rising in his wake fed their nature, and it was glorious. Unfettered by a normal human lifespan, he harboured no doubts that in time, all of Anaria would be his.

His thoughts turned to his masters. Their wish to bring the world to the death and destruction of Chaos suited his nature. Of all the Turned he was one of the most suited to its urges, lusts, wanton desires. Keeping the darkness and hatred in his heart as a child instead of letting it out had done nothing but repress it, concentrate it. When it had finally burst forth, even men deemed evil had found his deeds horrific.

Still, you could not make a realm coherent without social structure, justice, making them believe that the atrocities they committed were for the greater good. Even chaos needed some structure for him to have the control he desired.

Thus, the shell of the Church was critical; it turned neighbours into heathens, dissenters into blasphemers, and was invasive and insidious. He had never truly appreciated how religion could control men as effectively as politics before he had infiltrated Terome's order. Far more effective and absolute was using both together.

Now the Holy Voice was dead, there was a vacuum. The five Cardinals had yet to decide whom would become the Holy Voice; fear was a factor, given the demise of the last with such horrible butchery, unheard of for such a well-protected man, but they also had the traditional mourning time honouring Terome's wandering in the barren lands to observe.

When the preceding Voice had won, the benefactor he had hoped to control had become bitter, accusing Sontles of misleading him. He was no longer a concern; Primate Gilden was retired now, drooling into a bib as his mind broke down more every day.

Sontles held influence with many of the senior Churchmen in one way or another, but there were still many in the Church opposed to him; men who wanted power for themselves. Killing them all was not the answer, not if he wanted the Church to function… or to not be discovered.

He had already taken a great risk with the Holy Voice; if the holy fanatics ever suspected a vampire lurked within their order, they would tear it apart to find and destroy him.

It was a delicate balance, like an Ignathian puzzle-box twisted to find a combination of runes on each side.

He tapped his cold fingers against his thigh as he swayed, dreaming lightly in his coffin. Where many of his kind would dream deathlike in lust of rivers of hot blood, he had learned to sail them in his thoughts, considering other matters as the surging urges buffeted him.

The matter of a vote was delicate. Four of five Cardinal Princes had to agree, forcing the co-operation of the last, which could take months, even years if history was any judge. Each of them were supposed to consider the thoughts of the Primates under them, and they in turn took a collected vote from the Bishops they headed.

This was the chance he had patiently awaited. On his return they would have to allow his promotion. In the circumstances it was likely the people would demand his becoming the new Voice.

It was more likely that the Cardinals would try to prevent his return. There were probably assassins hidden in the men he marched with.

They would not be prepared for *him*.

Something intruded on his thoughts. The sense of a foreign presence during the day where there should be none was sharp, even in his coffin. He doubted his four companions had noticed. Vampires tended to be oblivious during daylight hours. It was how his progenitor had been trapped and destroyed.

There was a prolonged faint scratching, metal on metal, as he swam back up towards consciousness. A click came as the complicated lock gave. The heavy door creaked, and he felt a stir of interest. Someone had gained entrance to the chamber!

Long sharp teeth bared in the coffin-like chest. If he had had any breath, it would have been bated in anticipation.

CR   SO

Regeld finally caught the last tumbler with a sigh. Sweat dotted his brow; that had been hard.

He pocketed the picks and pushed the heavy door open, picking up the candle.

The soldier had waited some time before he pushed chairs back and emerged from under the meeting table. The men had been very curious about the lumbering conveyance, and several had bragged that they had seen inside. Rumour was the Churchmen stayed elsewhere, and this held a fortune in treasure. It was certainly ornate.

Just like a Churchman, thought Reg sourly. He had managed to sneak in as part of the detail this morning. For a minute he had been alone in the meeting room and had suddenly wondered what else they had in here. If he could find something worth pilfering, he would stand the balling out he would get from the corporal later.

He was quick with excuses, and usually managed to avoid punishment. Being missing for a whole day would take some creativity, but he was sure he could cobble together enough of a story about being seconded to sudden work that it would be more trouble than it was worth to discipline him. They were on a march to war, after all, and every soldier was needed to keep the conscripts in line.

There it was! He had noticed some conscripts trying to desert, and had forced them back in. If needed, he could always pick some and say they were lying. Enough had tried to leave despite the indoctrination that there had been executions.

If there was anything good enough, perhaps he would even desert himself, and live out his life away from all this. Being a soldier had been fun when it was civilians he could abuse and sluts he could force himself on, but with the prospect of facing actual trained armies - Eordelanders, too - he was no longer so keen.

It had been the work of a moment to hide himself under the table, hearing footsteps as the last cleaners returned. He had almost hissed when a chair was rammed into his ribs, but the detail had left without a backward glance.

617

Now he pushed cautiously at the heavy door, opening it with a creak lost in the vast wagon's own movements. He gently moved it an inch at a time, trying to peer in. It was pitch black on the other side, and he could hear no breathing or movement. Hoping for a glint of something precious, he waved the candle at the gap, but saw nothing.

Carefully he pushed it the rest of the way and stepped through to stop with a curse of surprise.

There was nothing in here of worth, he saw with vicious disappointment. Nothing worth the dressing down he would likely get despite his story, if he could get out unseen. His superiors knew him well, after all.

Instead, there were seven elaborate rectangular long wooden boxes lying bolted to the floor. They were arranged three to each side, with the last at the far end, and were more than six feet each. The side ones were plain, but the last was carved and trimmed in Church red.

A sudden thought occurred.

Not likely to leave any loot just lying around, are they? he thought. *These look like chests!*

Rifling through other people's chests was a favoured pastime of his. He looked around them again, picking the one at the centre as the likeliest for the most valuable items. No longer bothering with stealth, he walked over, placing the candle holder on one of the boxes behind him. It swayed flickering in the motion of the wagon but seemed secure enough.

Looking closer at the centre chest, he realised it was more like a trunk. It looked quite thick, and was ornately made, but had no hinge he could see.

Chest, trunk, whatever.

'You're mine,' he whispered in triumph, heaving up on the heavy lid and pushing it back with a grunt to tumble to the floor.

His eyes widened in shock, his hands gripping the rim, ready to grasp at the treasure inside. A pale, gaunt man with a slightly receded chin and a bald head ringed by a fringe of hair lay surrounded by lavish cloths of a senior Churchman, his head on a soft pillow. His delicately tapered hands were loosely clasped on his stomach, and he was dressed in loose robes that were richly inlaid. It looked like Primate-Nominate Aquinas, but he had rarely seen the man. Had he died on the journey?

Before he could react to the bizarre sight, one of those pale hands snapped out with inhuman speed, gripping his neck. In panic he tried to rear back, but he might as well have been gripped by a granite statue.

The man's eyes snapped open, the shock of their gaze making Regeld gasp. He grinned, showing pointed fangs from myth and horror.

'Wrong,' he hissed. 'You're *mine.*'

Regeld scrabbled, trying to break the grip, and then shrieked as the hand tightened impossibly and pain shot down into his limbs under the inhuman grip.

'No... no... no, *no, no, NO, NO! NO!'* he sobbed hysterically, and then was jerked brutally downwards. There was a frenzied gurgle and a bubbling thrashing followed by several violent spasms, his shadow playing out the tumult in flickers on the wall. A lashing foot caught the candle.

Darkness descended.

ʘβ   βʘ

Excitement pulsed through Darost. Elves arrived, people whispering of many more camped outside in an elegant town of cloth. They advised the Council and moved through the streets in small groups, prompting awe. The city prepared for war, echoed across Eordeland.

Surprising word arrived from Banistari in the form of ten thousand soldiers, three thousand of which were their famed light cavalry, the *Rashim* Lancers. Armed with light spears and bows, they were fast and disruptive. The rest were footmen, armed with scimitars and round shields and fierce courage.

Eordelanders were historically wary of their fierce, warlike southern neighbours. Despite their history of attacking Eordeland periodically and carrying off women, it had not happened for more than a century, and it was said that if you took salt and kohfee with a Banistari who gave you his word on his lineage, you were his friend. If you drank sacred *ayran* together, he would die for you as a brother.

Thankfully the area south of the Iril Eneth where one of the great cities of Banistari lay was surrounded by swampland, so invasion up past Valesruin and the Leohtsholt in any great numbers was difficult - especially given the superstition the Banistari had about the Elven woods and the pale folk in general. They would not move within sight of the trees. It was also close to the borders of Morland, and *everyone* treated the Morlanders with respect. They were powerful despite their few numbers and were the oldest civilisation known on Anaria, possibly Kuln.

Moqaddim Jiran al-Maftuh Raml reported to General Colcos and was welcomed to the Council of Twelve, having left his black-robed decalegion under the watchful eyes of half the Eordeland army on their southeastern borders. Unexpected as they were, they brought with them a far greater and more unexpected gift: just over a thousand dwarves.

Tall and lean in the dark blue Banistari robe and wide trousers befitting his rank, the *Moqaddim* had a proud nose and a long goatee tied off with silver beads, the rest of his beard being short. Beneath black hair and tanned skin, dark eyes glinted under a curving brow and a high forehead enclosed by a loose hood stitched with black trim. He was accompanied by a powerfully built bearded Dwarven warrior, just over five feet high and with a long beard jet black apart from distinguished silvering around the jawline and in a wide streak down the centre. His face was like granite, unlike the *Moqaddim* who broke into a smile after a ritual obeisance to the Council and elves.

'Peace be upon you, honoured leaders, *In šā' Jerah*. I come with news from my blessed rulers King Ahmadil and Queen Mer'Isha, may they live a hundred years and be blessed.' He touched his hands to forehead, lips and heart, then spread them wide. 'We have not always been close allies, but the beloved rulers have heard your words, and agree that this threat to you is a threat to us.

'So I bring you three thousand *Rashim*, and seven thousand of our finest *Jundi*. We wish to assure you that we do not seek to step onto your soil at this time as anything beyond loyal friends.'

The unspoken meaning of *at this time* was not lost on those present. The armies of Banistari reacted to the whims of their rulers, and the King and Queen were fickle enough that, had they remained aloof, they could have decided to invade whilst Eordeland was weakened. However, they would never betray once their word was given; by sending Jiran, it was a pact.

'I bring with me a representative of the *Quz'ah* nation from the *Jabal Haram*, the mountains you call Darkenspires. We were approached with a request that they be given passage through our lands to yours.' He bowed again to the dwarf, who stood quietly to the side. 'May I present his reverence Dúfr sur Hámarki.'

The dwarf grunted and nodded distractedly. He showed no other deference before he spoke. Even for a dwarf, he appeared dour. His Darum was excellent, if a little accented.

'I greet you, humans of Darost. I bring a full *Bardapúsund* of ten battle groups, one hundred dwarves in each. We hail from the city of *Dökksteinn*. Perhaps it is not so well known to you here, nor as large as *Khazâ-dí Djûpur*. We know you had a good relationship with our northern kin, and we have seen them but rarely… until recently.'

'They have communicated with you?' asked Mira Lyss.

'Of a sort. Without warning, they began arriving at our gates, seeking refuge. Then many thousands arrived in a flood, the remnants of a kingdom. After that only a trickle. A terrible Doom has come to our people, and their city lies locked and abandoned.'

There were murmurs of surprise from the Council. Councillor Holmson spoke up.

'No wonder we have heard nothing from them lately. We had hoped to rely on their strength and skill. The coming struggle will affect us all.'

Dúfr nodded. 'That it may, but you will receive no help from them. We are debating what to do to retake their halls, but meanwhile this battle thousand is all we can spare for the coming struggle.'

'It is welcome,' rumbled Ulric, who looked a little like a larger version of the dwarf. 'A thousand Dwarven warriors is a gift beyond compare in any conflict, and we thank you, and Darkstone Dale. What happened to Deep Delving?'

The dwarf's face was grim, and his voice was harsh.

'They fled a terrible Bane. We had warning from them of a vast army of *Rühk-villazhū* on the move, and prepared for them, strengthening our gates, guarding our treasures. Each Dwarven city has been readying for conflict. Orcs are at home in the bones of the earth almost as much as we are. But when evil came to them, it was from within, and it was not those foul ones.

'We have ever been careful of delving too deeply, especially in the Arkons where there are some things better left resting in the roots of the world, but it mattered not. Something invaded their tunnels.

'A dwarf went missing here or there. *Rühk-villazhū* were assumed, on the heels of the warnings. But then entire patrols disappeared without trace. Then a full battle group.

'At first it was only in the deepest, largest tunnels that dwarves went missing. Slowly it crept in towards the city. One day the King himself was travelling with his sons. The city should have been secure, yet a main gate in the depths was rent asunder. Something came through that gate. It left nothing but charred scraps. Our royal family is gone, humans. It is no more and cannot be replaced.'

His words were heavy. For longer-lived races like dwarves and elves, any deaths were a terrible loss. For royal family with children to vanish was catastrophic. The Council were silent.

'Foul breath came on the deep winds, reeking of charnel and gore, and those who wandered died horribly. Men, women... *children*... were carried away without trace. A terrible light scoured up tunnels, bringing death. There is a terror there we cannot face. For the first time in our history, our people fled. Deep Delving lies abandoned, and we may never return.' His words were harsh with bitterness.

There were mutters around the table, and the word *Yosgaloth* was heard several times. The dwarf's head rose.

'You know of our Doom?' Dúfr asked. He looked around the Council, his eyes direct. 'Tell me.'

'Our enemies freed an ancient evil from the Dimnesvale. It followed the mountains here and caused great destruction before being driven back. It took sanctuary in the Arkons,' said Ulric.

The dwarf showed his teeth to him.

'You did this to us?' he accused, his eyes hard.

Mira Lyss rose, raising her hands to those who had started to their feet to object, and turned to Dúfr. Jiran stood to the side, all but forgotten. His eyes watched everyone in turn, his face unreadable. Three elves also watched, saying nothing.

'We had a city called Irilview,' she said quietly. 'This demon followed a vast horde of orcs northeast. It found our city in the night and levelled the walls, consumed everyone it found; few escaped. We lost forty thousand people, Dúfr. Men, women, children. The power of this creature is beyond imagining.

'After Irilview it came north, seeking us. The only reason it did not destroy this city was the sacrifice of one of the greatest dragons on Kuln. She saved us; you see her statue in the square before The Sanctum. Still we would have been lost, but for the arrival of every other dragon in Anaria, and it took all those hundreds to drive it back.

'They came, not for us, but because Yosgaloth will consume even them in time, and it had to be halted. It will not stop before its hunger has taken every living thing in this world. Our enemies counted on it to destroy all of us.'

Dúfr said nothing, but his eyes were fixed on her. She continued softly.

'The demon fled but would not return to the Dimnesdair despite the efforts of Dragonkind. It took refuge under the Arkons, and they promised to keep watch. They could not follow it into the darkness, but they hoped it would remain quiescent so close to a sleeping Greater Dragon.'

'We know of that being,' said Dúfr slowly. 'It is one of the reasons we curtailed our delving.'

'We sent word to all our allies, Deep Delving among them,' said Mira Lyss sadly. 'Not all of them believed, but we sent word. Our message may not have arrived, or been turned away. I cannot say, Dúfr. Deep Delving has not spoken to us for more than a year.' She shook her head, seeing the pain in his stony face. 'We are sorry for your loss. Truly. We share your pain. Please believe me: we did all we could to warn your people.'

The Council regarded the dwarf soberly as he chewed his lip, letting the words sink in.

'I must think on this,' Dúfr said bluntly. 'I have heard your words.' He nodded to her, and turned, leaving the council chamber. There were a number of indrawn hisses of breath at his rudeness, but Mira Lyss spoke up, seeing anger on many faces. Her tone was strained, but level.

'I would remind you they have lost their greatest city of a handful. They are few in people; now they are less. They are *not* to be judged on our terms.'

Ulric nodded. 'This is hard for them,' he said. 'And yet they have still sent us a full tenth of their combined army. We must understand.'

'And what if he decides that blasted worm was our fault and takes them back again?' demanded Marcus Andragostin.

'Then we make do with what we have. But I think he will see sense. It was not our fault. Give him time to leave his bitterness aside.'

'Time is something none of us have.'

'Nevertheless, Councillor. We give him what we can.'

☙   ❧

Two days later, Ulric stood before the rest of the Council wearing his grandfather's conical helmet, the eye-rings framing his bushy brows above heavy mail and half plate.

The great bronze Dragon Némaenth had swooped down on a courier near the borders three days ago and sent the frightened man pelting back to Darost with reports of an army forty thousand strong, moving swifter than expected, already well past the Foothills of Nassar in the Nassmoors.

They were out of time.

The border guard along the Iril Eneth to the south had been strengthened heavily, but it worried Ulric. There was still no sign of the orcs.

Eremus had also been strangely quiet in his opinion, but he did not hold out any hopes of her admitting she had been wrong. She could twist a sword into a corkscrew, given time.

'You represent the Council of Twelve on the battlefield,' said Mira Lyss. 'We know you will not fail us.'

'Let us hope that is so,' said Ulric. He caught Eremus's eye briefly. Her expression gave him nothing.

'Is it really necessary for you to go? Surely General Colcos can undertake any major decisions. He has the full confidence of the Council,' said Nessa Contemus.

Ulric looked at Colcos. He stood in his straight grey unadorned uniform, his austere, almost skull-like face pale under iron-grey swept-back hair.

'He directs our strategy. We need someone to speak for Eordeland with our allies,' Ulric returned. 'There are too many things we do not understand.' He turned to Holmson. 'What news from Tal'Orien and the homeland of the Elves?'

'We have had no word. Either the elves have been blocked from our lands, or Tal'Orien failed in his quest. I fear that means he may have perished.'

'We have heard nothing from the orks either. Their envoy may not have reached them.'

'Perhaps they arrived but the elves declined?'

'Nessa, they should have returned themselves by now, or sent *some* word. We can look for no help further than that which the elves have already offered.'

'The troops are ready to march,' said Dorn. 'And word has reached us that Morland healers will be with us by this afternoon.'

'Is it wise to have three senior commanders in the same army at once?' asked Whyll Regus.

'We can't underestimate the seriousness of this. We haven't had war in centuries,' said Ulric.

'I believe it is crucial,' General-Marshal Colcos said in his clipped, educated tones. 'Now is not the time for complacency. The remainder of the Guard is barely enough to man all the cities for defence and still maintain peace and security between them. We must keep the land safe outside cities and secure the border with Banistari. The loss of Irilview has taken ten thousand veteran soldiers from our ranks. We are taking a huge number of our troops beyond our borders to face a foe twice our size and cannot be sure of total victory. We need every advantage we can get. Dorn is inspirational, a natural leader. We need his spirit, and we need Ulric's… diplomacy.' Someone chuckled.

'Gods help us all,' Eremus muttered almost inaudibly.

Colcos indicated a square-jawed man with a serious expression who looked as if he planned every chew of his food. 'General Vierce will secure the cities. General Neider is on patrol at the moment securing our borders and countryside. You will be as safe as possible.'

Mira Lyss leaned forward. 'I hope it is enough. Too much time was lost before we could prepare.'

Smoke that, Eremus, you dried trout.

'Councillor Ulric, we wish you luck and the speed of the Gods. May you all return safe and victorious.'

'May we return.' Ulric turned after his abrupt rejoinder and left, hearing Colcos and Dorn following him from the Dodecagon chamber.

He waited until Colcos caught him.

'Dannon... do we make the right choice?'

The ascetic man smiled slightly.

'You are there to bind the allies, Ulric. I am there for the strategy of our troops. Vierce is extraordinary at defence, and will serve the cities well, especially Darost. Neider... the last real mistake he made was as a Captain, and he can produce great efforts from men. Eordeland is well guarded in our absence, old friend.'

'Mm.' Ulric glanced at Dorn.

'You need someone in the front ranks to show them how it's done,' grinned Dorn. His hands caressed his twin swords.

Contrary to old stories, he rarely used both at once; it wasn't an effective way to fight even for an expert. Ulric had seen him beaten only once, and that was when sparring with Tal'Orien, winning a round each. He wasn't sure that man was wholly human. Dorn Gardenson would lend much-needed spirit to men battered by internal conflicts and the loss of a whole city.

'In Wheru we trust.' He caught Dorn's amused expression. 'Delmatra, then. Whoever.'

'The troops are ready. I have recalled the recruits to march with us. We'll need them.'

Ulric nodded. 'We march in the morning, then. Say your farewells.'

FORTY-SIX

The army snaked its way out of Darost at dawn, sixty Company Captains under four Battalion Commander Majors beneath a single Regimental Colonel. Coloured bands flashed on arms; Fire, Emerald, Carmine, Teal. Only a few of their companies left in reserve, they had a forced march ahead of them, but rest before the battle.

Colcos wondered how many of them would return.

Some of the people assembled cheered them; the criers had done what they could to generate an air of bravado and triumph. Many more did not. The streets were not as full as he had expected, either; many Eordelanders simply didn't believe war was coming. Others had protested war, accusing the Council of aggression.

The fault for that lay at the feet of Eremus and Regus.

Darost centred on trade. Many nations had merchants visiting, and many more came for the centre of knowledge at reputedly the only University in the world. This had meant that, no matter how hard the Council of Twelve had tried, inevitably information had filtered in of events in the world, and people had put two and two together more often than not. Some had come up with four; some had come up with five.

Some of the populace had fled the city, moving towards more eastern cities in Eordeland. Others believed they were fools; Darost hadn't seen invaders for more than a century, and it had never been breached. It was constantly upgraded and repaired, but the army, well trained though it was, simply hadn't faced a real enemy in numbers for some time.

There were always skirmishes, of course. Troops were drilled and deployed as far as Novin. Soldiers were circulated to ensure they saw action. Even Eordeland had a fair number of organised outlaw bands. Battalions hunted them regularly and men saw action. Some of the bands were large. General Colcos was a firm believer in mock battles, too, and tested his soldiers and commanding officers hard.

More than thirteen thousand Eordeland Guard left the city, the tromp of so many feet together somewhat hypnotic. Proud, old companies marched; Emerald Eyes, FireFangs and Poppies marched across from the Beautiful Sixth, Teal Jackanapes and Blackcircles.

Sixteen hundred elves and a thousand dwarves awaited them outside the gates, accompanied by ten thousand proud Banistari alongside four hundred Morland healers rightly feared for their abilities to kill or cure.

It would have been the mightiest force assembled for centuries if reports hadn't put Meyar's at nearly twice the size. Almost twenty-six thousand free people marched to preserve the sanctity of their lands.

Colcos led the army seven days southwest to the borders and there waited for the pathfinders spread out into the north and south plains to send word. Two days later, they moved out at a forced march.

The latest reports had shown that the enemy had turned south around the Arkons. They meant to drive down towards the plains then strike east to Darost along the Greatway - the fastest, easiest route in.

It was incredible folly. If they took the city, Eordeland would have its head severed, but no army had ever breached Darost. An army twice their size wouldn't threaten the city and its powerful defences; with his force behind them the Meyari would be thrown into a meatgrinder against the walls. Either they were fools, or they had another plan.

He suspected he knew what it was.

Meyar had lured them out as much as they had lured Meyar. If they could annihilate his force - unlikely, but still - they would be able to strike into Eordeland without serious opposition until the two Major-Generals co-ordinated an attack.

His main concern had been that Meyar would strike along the north coast into northern Eordeland, down past the Northing Woods and past Gladsmoor. They could destroy crops over a quarter of Eordeland and cut east to strike at the rolling plains communities to destroy even more, splitting the realm. They wouldn't even have to approach cities to ruin half the wealth of Eordeland, but it would be slow going with difficult terrain ripe for guerilla strikes and sallies.

He had balanced this carefully, trying to look like enough of a threat to force them to deal with him, yet a tempting enough prize to be worth it.

Colcos knew some of the Meyar commanders by reputation. He thought the odds were good they would engage and crush him first given the chance.

He was offering that chance.

Meyar only had one border and no powerful neighbours, so could commit to a larger force; Eordeland had many borders and two powerful realms nearby. They couldn't afford to empty their land and cities of troops in the same fashion.

Win or lose, war inside the borders would be ruinous to Eordeland. There was no question in the minds of the Council that the enemy would defile and destroy instead of occupy, and with the destruction of Irilview, Darost was already being pushed to bursting with refugees. They could not permanently lose so much land and so many civilians.

They moved into the foothills of the eastern Arkons at dawn six days later, fortifying lightly so they could recover.

Dannon Colcos had a strong force, for all its relative lack of numbers. If he could position them well in the Arkon foothills they would be hard to defeat. He needed somewhere defensible for the command, with height and visibility for archers, but with enough flat land that the cavalry could move unimpeded - especially the fleet-footed Banistari *Rashim*, who were very difficult to fight at full gallop. He also needed to have defences at his back, and the foothills would serve admirably here. It was impossible to get a significant armed force through the mountains.

He needed to tempt them into attacking while at the same time channelling and meeting the enemy to break them up, allowing the infantry to destroy and demoralise the Meyari as efficiently and quickly as possible. The faster they could break their attack and spirit, the less would die and the more likely the other army would retreat, broken.

Colcos finally picked an area in front of a sheer hill rising up to the low mountains, giving them protection to the rear as they faced east. There was a rise in front of this face, gently sloping down to east and south, with a couple of steeper points which would deter the whole front from rushing them and a vertical face ranging from twenty to forty feet high running to the north backwards into the foothills and crowned by pines. They had a clear view out to the northeast and the borders of Eordeland.

The approaching Meyari force wouldn't be able to get many men up that face, and those that did would find themselves facing elves in woodland. He doubted any would get through there. The main force could be loosed upon from the ridge as they approached, and with luck they could channel the lines of attack; one to one they were more than a match for the Meyari. They would also be rested and dug in, while the enemy had been marching for weeks.

They would need every advantage they could get. The speed of their march had precluded bringing any artillery with them, and although they were protected on two sides and had high ground, they were completely open to the south and east.

They wouldn't be able to effectively channel the incoming mass of men to meet their troops on even terms; once they crested the hill it would be bloody work.

Dotted sparsely around the northern rise were the woods, not thick enough for true cover but enough to allow the elves to harry the enemy with the main Eordeland recurves. The crossbows he would reserve until plated knights were about to engage with his troops.

The dwarves had informed him that their fighting wedge would attempt to split the incoming Meyari in two, allowing each side of infantry to crash upon them and hopefully break them quickly. If they could instil an early rout in the poorly trained enemy they could carry the day quickly, in the north at least. That didn't account for the Teromants, though.

They would be much harder to break.

The *Rashim* light cavalry would circle the edges, keep the enemy off balance with speed and confusion and peppering the flanks with their short recurves. The key was for them to not stop harrying the front; once surrounded, and he had little doubt they could be, they would become compressed and less effective.

Reserves consisting of crossbows and several battalions of infantry and pikes would rest in formation to the west, away from the fighting. They would be cycled in to replace troops in the southern and eastern fronts and allow them to rest, a vital tactic to be able to sustain battle against such overwhelming numbers. If his reports were correct, the men at arms would be outnumbered by nearly five to one unless he could whittle them down before they engaged.

The north then was covered, as was their back. The line of retreat to the northeast to Darost if needed would rely on them punching through the enemy.

And where in the bloodied hells are those orcs? Colcos thought, worried.

It was too much to hope that horror had consumed them all. If they *did* exist, they could overrun the southern border forces of Eordeland, striking up into the heart of the realm and murdering thousands while the army was engaged here.

They could attack cities; block reinforcements.

The problem worried away at him like a loose tooth.

⊗   ⊗

Two months after leaving their borders, the Meyari army rounded the upper reaches of the Arkons and prepared to move south.

Every night prayers went out, Teromants at each campfire preaching. Even foul creatures would rise against the godless foe, the Primate told them, the conviction of Sontles in his voice. Even Hell rose up against Eordeland.

Sontles listened to the generals argue about the upcoming attack. The tales of Darost's unbreakable walls were legendary. A vast army of Banistari had broken against them more than seven hundred years ago, and they hadn't lost any of their endurance since then.

It was moot, anyway. The scouts had reported that an Eordeland army had moved out from Darost towards the foothills south of them as expected, but far earlier than planned.

Somehow, they had known of the attack.

They couldn't risk leaving this army at their back. Although it was a far smaller force, Eordeland Guard were a dangerous foe. The commanders argued the best approach.

Sontles considered. They needed to distract Eordeland; regain the element of surprise. It was time to send word to his allies… to raise the legions of hell against this green and rich land.

He beckoned one of the Turned over. She drifted gracefully to him, her skin so pale it seemed almost light blue over dark blue veins and her eyes blazing in her face like a snake's.

'Go now,' he said very softly, knowing her unnaturally sharp senses would pick the words up. 'Alert the Novinians to the south to make for the Arkon foothills, then find the *orq* and tell them to attack. If you can, observe the enemy deployment when you return.' His eyes glinted red in warning as he saw the hungry look on her face. 'Be an unseen shadow.'

She nodded and almost blurred as she left.

Sontles turned back to the arguing humans, satisfied.

The army of near fifty thousand orcs to the south would strike hard. They were barely a cohesive force anyway and could roll along hidden paths at a shocking speed.

Eordeland wouldn't know its doom until the *orq* were amongst its people.

FORTY-SEVEN

'*Land ho!*' the *Eastern Star's* lookout cried from the foretop, pointing port and ahead. Karland rushed to the rail, his sun-browned skin warm. He ended up amidst several sailors who stood muttering and making obeisance to Lamora.

'I can't see anything,' he said.

'Below the horizon,' said someone. 'Give it a minute, lad.'

Gradually a dark blur began to coalesce just above the horizon. It seemed to float, the wind ahead blowing crosswise to the current and leaving a line of deep blue under a lighter line of sparkling sun.

'Ready sails!' roared Captain Rosso. 'Balance the pull fore and aft! Catch that easterly wind! We need to make that land!'

'How do we break out of the main current?' asked Karland.

'Gots to catch the wind and pull port,' said the sailor who had spoken before. 'Better done early than late. If we drift out to t'edge, we c'n use the push to move out quick, like. Be slower going in, though.'

'But we can hardly see the land?'

'Current's swift, son. Be near enough afore you know it. With Lamora's luck we c'n break out only some miles to go.'

'Is the port nearby?'

'No,' said Rast, moving up alongside. 'It is a few days upriver, to the inland sea of Jamis. They call it the Giver of Water in northern Hadrasia; on the surface it is fresh, but underneath it is bitter. This is the centre of the Zuun Empire. We must make landfall soon, anyway; we have run out of *calamansi.*'

Barely an hour later, as the coastline drifted past, the ship listed port and moved out of the current, her sails billowing under the watchful eyes of her Captain. Stricken though she was, still she moved with grace, cutting through the gentle swells with her sleek hull.

Not long afterwards, they entered the mouth of a large river - nothing near the Storartar, but miles across as it entered the sea. The land around them was lush, vegetation and sand battling for the water's edges. The sea was warm, and surprisingly clear for an estuary. Large, bulbous creatures moved through the waters, both in the river and out to sea, browsing on vegetation between sword-like reeds as thick as wrists. They were at least as large as a *rinok*, a strange pink-grey with wide, almost stalked eyes, huge gapes lined with jagged round tusks as long as a man's arms and fleshy wattles. They seemed to almost gallop through the water, short paddle-like tails helping them manoeuvre. They ignored the *Star* as she pushed slowly against the current, but Karland thought they might be very dangerous for a rowboat. He spotted a strange looking crocodile, smaller than the ones in the Storartar - perhaps ten feet long - with a very long thin snout filled with saw-edged teeth, and a long sail-like tail with webbed spines at the end sticking up far above the water. He wondered what it ate.

The sun seemed reluctant to cloak itself in cloud; swarms of insects flitted around them and out onto the water, looking like tiny dark waterspouts in their swirling numbers. There were less of them further out into the river centre, but they definitely sucked blood, as he discovered ruefully.

As they moved inland the river narrowed only slightly. Jungle grew up, tangled vegetation rising in odd-looking trees. Coconut palms hung over short grasses, vines looped around everything, and huge wide-boled squat trees spread like tables, their tops eighty feet across over a gnarled squat trunk it would have taken the remaining crew to link arms around. There were hints of the jungle they had passed through in the Dimnesdair, but this felt older, more natural. A flash of movement on the south bank hinted at a large cat of some sorts, tawny, with large dark squares clouding its form. Darkus called out in surprise at what he thought a group of orks moving through the trees but were in fact great apes larger than he was, silver-grey with black stripes curling down from their heads like an inverted palm silhouette. Wise dark faces watched them almost sadly under huge and heavy brows, although they looked less tragic when one yawned, revealing teeth a panther would envy.

Here, too, were familiar sights; fish swayed in shade, and twisted trees stuck out into the water, string-like roots propping them. A herd of small antelope with fantastic curling horns drank nervously at the river, one with head up and alert watching for predators. Birds flew past overhead, striped in incredible colours. Parrots in a riot of regalia flew from bank to bank, arguing in raucous voices with what looked like great silver-headed crows with black-striped wings.

One parrot landed on the railing, red-feathered and looking around with curious eyes before leaping away in a fearful cloud of feathers after an outraged screech from Evil Bastard, who clearly considered the ship his property. A small flock followed the ship for a few minutes, calling insults. The evil-tempered bird drew himself up at the stern and shouted back, interjecting a few choice actual words for once, before turning and defecating down the rear railing. Having shown what he thought of them, he retired below decks, happy in a job well done. Darkus's howls of orkish laughter trailed back as the ship moved on.

Finally, they broke out into a sea. Boats and ships dotted the horizon, and the waters were gentle. They could not see the far shore north or east; to port lay fields and less wild low woodland, with villages and towns littering the landscape.

They had found civilisation again.

Another day of travel took them to the great port. The city glittered in the distance like a jewel, rising dark and stern on a hill next to the sea's edge. The water was incredibly clear; it was sweet, too, as promised, and marvellous. Much deeper down the occasional large form could be seen moving, creatures from the sea trapped uncaring under a layer of unsalted water. Other fish flitted just above them, out of their reach in water that would not support them; very few fish moved between layers, although dolphins were abundant. Karland saw a group of whitish sharks with very long pectoral fins tipped in red doing so, their dorsal fins breaking the surface to travel alongside the ship for long moments before sinking back down as they returned to the depths. For all their slender build and smaller size - not much longer than he was tall - they looked dangerous.

'We are here,' breathed Rosso, seeming to relax for the first time in a month. The great port of *Jamis-iin oron zai.*'

'Home to the *Zuundaichid* Kingdom,' said Rast quietly.

'Have you been here before?' asked Karland.

'Once. I was a pilgrim here.'

'You've been to a lot of places,' said Karland.

The big man shrugged. 'I have travelled far in my life. I sought answers.'

'To what?'

'Many things, my young friend.'

The ship drew nearer to the port, and buildings and the city began to resolve. A dull grey high wall almost as high as that of Darost circled the city, with strangely-tiered towers rising from it adorned with what looked like snakes curling from the corners. The city itself was almost all angular and coloured a bright, light yellow interspersed with red, the roofs and walls inset with coloured glass that made the entire city sparkle like light on waves. A huge palace dominated the centre, rising far above the rest with four ornate towers to each corner. The city was larger than Darost, with a town surrounding the walls, itself ringed by a lower wall less than half the height of the city's. It lay with gates open, curving around the vast dock areas of the port. Unlike Eyotsburg, restricted by available space, this harbour sprawled for miles.

It was almost surreal, after so many weeks at sea. Safety, land, food, all lay nearby, and for the first time he dared wonder how they were going to get back to Anaria. The remaining crew were leaner, though they had not yet begun to show signs of scurvy from the lack of Morland limes. The fish and tack diet had kept them going, and the copper still had saved their lives. Rosso had sourly remarked on how much cleaning it would need from the build-up of salt, then muttered to himself at the other costs to repair the ship despairingly, sounding more than a little like his parrot.

They had taken unceasing turns bailing the ship where the mast had sprung leaks in the planks. It would be a pleasure to not have to do that anymore, Karland thought.

His mind drifted to those they had lost.

Wish you'd seen this, Sam.

'Thank *fuck*,' said someone beside him, breaking into his thoughts. He turned to find The Green Warrior watching the approaching port, a frown creasing his face.

'I'm looking forward to being on land,' Karland said fervently. He felt that sense of surrealism he always felt in new places where everything was so dissimilar.

'Won't be any different,' growled The Green Warrior. 'Look.'

With a sinking heart Karland realised he was right. The city they approached geared for war. There was a growing army encamped outside the open gates. The docks were thick with soldiers in a dark blue armour that looked strangely insectile. Every ship around them flew a five-coloured flag of silk, a white line bordered above and below by dark blue, then green, then red, then yellow.

'The Warrior is right,' said Galnór. 'This place prepares for great battle.'

They came into the docks to be met by a company of soldiers. Their faces were hard and grim, with tilted eyes and that strange insectile armour. Strangely wrought pikes and curved swords were in their hands.

'Be careful,' Rast advised them softly. 'Life is cheap here and they are on edge. Let me speak to any who come to us.'

The gangplank was dropped and the sailors that had leaped across to moor the ship were surrounded, a barely withheld threat of violence evident.

A flat-faced bald Hadrasian with flowing grey mustaches which only seemed to fall from the edges of his upper lip stepped forward. He barked a command in a musical language Karland had never heard before. Rosso replied haltingly in the same language, and the man's face broke into a sneer.

'Anarians,' he almost spat, the *r* sounding strangely soft to Karland. 'What you want here? You have trading paper?'

'We were blown off course heading for Mithtol. We had no choice but to continue here for repairs.'

The man grunted. His eyes and face were empty of emotion. His skin was slightly darker than Karland's, who would have killed for his cheekbones. 'We at war, Anarian. Trade, repair ship, go.'

'I would pay my respects to the *Khaan* of *Zuun Khaant-uls*,' said Rast. The man looked at him in surprise. 'The *Daichin-Khaan* knows me of old.'

The bald man looked at him closely, then nodded. 'So. *Daichin.*' He gestured for them to follow him. Rast waved to the ship, and the two elves danced lightly down the plank after them, leaping the final seven feet with ease and landing with perfect balance. They were followed by Darkus and The Green Warrior. Muttered curses ran through the ranks of the Hadrasians and weapons were readied.

'He is a friend,' said Rast, raising empty hands. They didn't exactly lower them, but they seemed less liable to use them. He looked to Rosso. 'Captain; I do not know how long we shall be gone. We will send word.'

'Aye. Take care.' Rosso was already looking at the ship with a frown.

As the four of them moved away, the guards fell in about them.

'Let me speak,' warned Rast softly. 'Their ways are different. They react badly to insults.' He directed his words with a stare at The Green Warrior, who shrugged.

Karland opened his mouth to ask a question and received a stone-faced glare from his nearest guard.

Maybe it could wait.

೧   ೲ

It was a long trip to the palace through winding streets. Darost had seemed chaotic to Karland, but it was quite mild compared to the poorer areas here in Ho-Lam. Rickety markets dotted the streets like bird's nests, full of squawking vendors who carefully ignored the party. People hurried here, moving along streets so thickly populated it was a wonder they could pass. Two-wheeled carts pulled by men holding long handles passed at a run, some with passengers and some with cargo. Citizens casually spat at the street sides or blew snot from a nostril as they walked.

The noise was incredible, people shouting everywhere in the tonal tongue of the land. It sounded like a thousand arguments, but Karland could see many of them calmly talking despite the yelling. Perhaps it was just how the language was spoken, he thought.

635

No matter how heated or what was being discussed, the people's faces were mostly blank of emotion. It was curious, not being able to read people as easily as at home. Part of that might have been the presence of guards everywhere, staring into faces and expecting people to get out of their way.

When they passed into the central, richer areas, the carnage was cut off as instantly as if a thick portcullis had separated them. The noise was fainter behind tall houses and another thick wall; the streets ceased winding and expanded, becoming cleaner, clearer. The centre sparkled.

'It's so clean!' he marvelled, especially after the dirt and mayhem of the outer city.

'Anyone littering here is put to death,' said Rast softly. 'Commoners can be jailed for simply setting foot here.'

Death?

Karland stared at the big man. He wasn't joking.

'Hadrasia is terrible,' he said.

Rast shook his head.

'They also hold personal honour in highest regard and will die to uphold a debt to you. Besides, you cannot judge a continent by one people. Their southern neighbours are the *Sinhala* - and a more honest and friendly people you may never meet. They revere the great jungle tigers, and fight like them, but if you are not an enemy, they will treat you as family. The *Zuun* are proud and warlike. It is strange that two such different peoples lie border to border, and not always peaceful.'

They passed fountains and far higher quality shops. People here were more relaxed, would actually look their guards in the face; yet for all that, they seemed even more alien. Their faces and voices had little of the movement and volume outside the city. The blank, mostly olive-skinned expressions on faces with defined bones and tilted eyes were matched by careful movement, and a sense of perfection. There were less guards here in their insectile armour, and those visible seemed more of higher rank, their colour grey. They were also noticeably polite to the residents, unlike those in the outer city.

In the centre of the inner city stood the gigantic palace. Hundreds of feet high, it spread in all directions, with battlements on a curtain wall and domed turrets

Closer to, the palace looked like a beehive. People in bright silks flowed in and out without interruption, each knowing their place. It looked extremely efficient.

Huge doors swept up twenty feet. In a curtain wall they looked impressive, but on a palace they looked gargantuan.

The party was led down the main passage, the ceiling soaring above them. They were handed to another guard detail, and then another. Each time they seemed to be higher-ranking and more respectful.

Finally, they reach large twin doors, flanked by two guards in lurid crimson. Another stepped forward.

Karland did not recognise the insignia of the Guard in the bright red segmented armour. He wondered if he was equivalent to a captain, or like the Onyx Guard. He wore a tall, smooth helmet with an almost T-shaped shadowed visor, his armour smooth apart from sharp jutting pauldrons. A red cloak fell from his shoulders.

He removed the helmet and passed it to another guard, then walked down their ranks, requesting their weapons in thickly accented Darum. He glanced over them quickly and professionally, handing the weapons to another guard.

Darkus must be getting used to this, Karland thought. He had handed over his axe without comment.

When the Guard reached the front, he bowed shortly to Rast.

'Master Tal'Orien. No point asking weapons. You do not need any. Please give word of honour you do no harm.'

'The *Ezen-Khaany Khamgaalalt* have my word,' said Rast, bowing.

'I thank,' said the man, sounding sincere, and bowed lower.

The doors opened into a large chamber which held trappings of state and a desk with a map held open, bounded by red and blue silks. In the far reaches an opulent bed lay, covered in a chocolate-coloured silken sheet. The room was warmed by a long, low fire. Lanterns dotted the room, made from thin hardened leather.

This was no throne room; it was private quarters.

Before the desk stood a large figure, almost as large as Rast, tall but not as muscular, though his shoulders were huge. He wore the long dark robe Karland had been told was called a *deel*, clasped in six places on the right with gold and made from thick dark green silk, with brocade that Karland could not decipher. The bottom reached to the man's mid-calf, widening slightly outward from the hips, with two side partings to upper thigh with strips hanging down the back. The arms were long, widening towards the end, and the collar was high. Creases on a shoulder and one side suggested a sheath of some kind was often worn.

It fitted his figure well, cinched at the waist by a wide silk band wrapped around the body seven times in orange. Over this at about waist height was a broad leather belt with an ornate buckle in the shape of a stylised cow skull with horns.

His hair was long and dark, bound up in a leather thong, tied into a tight knot at the back.

His head did not move at their entrance, and he spoke quietly and precisely in the fluid language Karland had heard at the docks.

'*Nadad evgui baidald orokhgui baisan.*'

'*Khussen myanga myangan, Daichin-Khaan,*' said the red-armoured Guard. 'Anarians arrive at docks. One you know.'

The imposing man turned with exceptional grace to study them with the same lack of expression that marked his people. None of them ever seemed surprised, thought Karland.

'Rast Tal'Orien,' he said. His voice was smooth and balanced, reflecting the man himself. Karland would bank money on him having studied similar fighting arts to Rast and was somehow unsurprised that he knew his mentor. 'You arrive, unannounced, as you left. It is… good… to see you again.' He bowed very slightly, and Karland heard surprised mutters from his guards.

'Bal'Hon,' said Rast, bowing. 'It has been many years.'

'It has,' the man replied, eyes flicking to his companions, especially Darkus and the elves, then to his guards. '*Orkhi!*'

For a second Karland wondered if he had recognised Darkus, but it was a command. The guards took a step backwards with their right foot and bowed with their hands up, touching their foreheads to the heel of the left palm with elbow to knee, and left.

'Come forward,' he said, clasping his hands behind his back. 'You arrive at a bad time, Rast Tal'Orien. Or a good one.' He gestured around him. 'We are soon to march to war.'

'Against Sinhala?'

Bal'Hon laughed shortly. His face looked less alien with emotion upon it.

'No. Far south of the dark peoples. Great armies are said to be marching north. Already they have decimated cities. The Tri-Cities themselves are under attack. They grant no quarter. We hear tales even of… sorcery.'

'War rises everywhere,' remarked Rast. 'The lands of Anaria are similarly out of balance. What sorcery?'

'First it was great beast men. They moved north, skirting the jungles of Sinhala and finding our great plains. They invaded the roaming grounds of our cattle and joined their herds. At first we killed many, but they were no real threat. We think they fled something else - this force moving north. The brutes low to each other in deep tongues, and are much stronger than a man, but they are stupid. When we have leisure we will drive them back from our herds, but for now we will destroy the force that defeated them.'

'With great respect, Bal'Hon, we must return to Anaria as soon as possible.'

'Of course.' The man gestured. 'Stay here. You and your companions. I am curious about them, especially this great green warrior. They must be of significance to accompany you. You may visit city as you wish, but you will remain guarded in the outer city. For your own safety.'

Rast bowed after a short pause. 'We would be honoured.'

'It is done.' Bal'Hon studied Rast's face. 'We will also speak of our time together, and how it ended.'

Karland had never seen Rast wince, but he swore his friend did without actually doing so.

Bal'hon clapped his hands, and the door opened.

'*Tednii kheregtseeg kharaarai,*' he said to the man who entered wearing a tall black headdress. The gaunt face with arching cheekbones held a small jaw underneath long dark eyes, and his face almost cried out for the thin pointed beard and long moustaches it wore. His skin was much paler than his master's.

'My vizyer will house you in noble quarters,' Bal'Hon said. 'He speaks excellent Darum. Tell him if you require anything. We shall speak soon.' He turned away, dismissing them as if they had ceased existing.

'Come,' said the vizyer with a bow. 'This way.'

He followed them from the room, snapping his fingers at several servants who stood nearby.

'*Omnod ordond zurgaan saikhan oroog beltge. Dars ba jims avchir.*'

They scurried away, gazes fixed on the floor. The vizyer turned to them and addressed them all.

'This way, please.' He led them at a stately pace. 'You are fortunate. *Daichin-Khaan* Bal'Hon shows you great honour.' He smiled slightly, his face relaxing. 'It is rare I am asked to perform such a mundane task for him. You must be noble guests.' His voice was very cultured. He noticed Karland's surprise and smiled a little more disarmingly.

'I studied at the great University of Eordeland, young *ezen*. Many noble *Zuun* do. Your language is the common trade tongue on three continents.' It wasn't quite an insult. 'May I ask how you come to *Zuun Khaant-uls*?'

'A great storm drove us off our path,' supplied Rast. 'We were on an urgent mission from the Council of Twelve to *Mithtól*.'

'Ah. The fabled pale demons.' The vizyer's eyes creased and he bowed to Galnór and Lëlylien. 'I jest, of course. Your kind do not often come west, but we know of you. In a city of stone surrounded by plains and seas with fibrous trees, your hard wooden art is highly prized.' He cocked his head toward Darkus. 'And you, *ezen*. Might one enquire who you are?'

'*Ezen?*' asked Darkus, his deep voice reverberating from the walls.

'Merely an honorific. Similar to Lord.'

'Oh.' The big warrior grinned. 'I am an ork, human. I represent the tribes of the great plains. My uncle is Over-Chieftain.'

'Ahhhh.' The vizyers eye's flashed, and he nodded. 'Yes. The fierce warriors. I have heard tales of your strength. I would be interested to see if it matches one of these beast men. They are of a height with you, and stronger than any man I have seen.' Karland could not tell if he was aware this might be taken as an insult. 'We must show you our plains. They are hot and dry. The plains of Anaria could be lost within them.' There was another pause. 'I am certain they are inferior to yours, however. Ours contain only cattle, skinpigs and earth-lions.'

It was hard to tell if he was deliberately being supercilious or not. Given his education and intelligence, Karland guessed he knew exactly what he said, but the people here spoke differently. He was not even sure it wasn't a subtle sense of humour.

Darkus hadn't seemed to take offence.

'I would like to see these plains. What are these beast men troubling you?'

'They are giants, of your height, but slower. They speak no human tongue; they are barely more than animals. Despite the number we killed, they moved past us and joined with our herds roaming the plains. Curiously, they seem to find kinship with our cattle and have not harmed any. Not yet. We have time to deal with them later.'

'Why not leave them with the herds?' asked Karland.

'Our herds must not be interfered with,' replied the vizyer.

They continued walking through halls and courtyards, talking, until they arrived at a set of doors shaped like shells, flanked by guards in the chitinous armour. The vizyer, for all his strange looks, was actually distantly pleasant. He seemed genuinely interested in them. Karland wondered if he missed his days in The Sanctum.

The doors opened into an octagonal courtyard with eight doors. Six were open, with rich rooms hung with silks and tapestries visible inside.'

'Please, these rooms are yours. Rest for a few days. The *Daichin-Khaan* will send for you when he is ready.'

He bowed, turned and was gone. The shell-like doors closed with finality, and the companions looked at each other.

'Pretty plush, for a prison,' remarked the Green Warrior with a shrug. It was the first thing he had said.

છ   ૭

It wasn't quite a prison. The shell-like doors were not locked but stepping outside meant instantly being shadowed by palace guards.

For three days they rested, exploring the quarters. Each room was opulent, with soft beds and scented fireplaces. By comparison, the luxury quarters in The Sanctum were austere.

Boiled water, food and fruits were brought three times a day, servants stood on call in the courtyard, and twice the vizyer visited them to talk.

No word came from the *Daichin-Khaan*, which Rast told them meant *Warrior-Emperor*. He counselled them to accept their current status as honoured guests and warned against angering any of the *Zuun*. They were still strangers in an uncertain land, and their hosts could as easily kill them all and take their ship as aid them. Despite the clear history and respect between him and Bal'Hon, it was as obvious that he was not entirely sure it would hold.

On the fourth day the Green Warrior decided he had had enough of the same walls.

'I'm going to the city,' he announced. 'Maybe check the docks.'

Darkus snorted. 'I had best come with you then, or you will end up causing trouble.'

'I had best go with you both,' remarked Rast dryly. 'Orks are not renowned for avoiding trouble, either.'

The matching grins from both warriors made Karland snort with laughter. Lëlylien's tinkling laugh filtered in from the side.

'We will stay here and explore the palace gardens,' added Galnór. 'I hear they are extensive.'

'Karland?'

'I'll just - you know. Explore.'

Rast raised his eyes. 'What did I do to deserve three of them?' He shook his head. 'Stay out of trouble, boy. I mean it. Do what you are told. Avoid attention. It might be best to stay here, or at least not go far. Why not go with the elves?'

'I might,' conceded Karland.

'Mmm.' Rast's voice was dubious.

ca   so

Karland ended up with one shadow, and decided some time alone was needed. He wandered the halls, trying to find something like a library. His guard was unresponsive past a grunt, either because he didn't speak Darum or didn't want to, and servants avoided him as if were furniture. They swept around the corridors like brightly coloured flightless bees, faces emotionlessly intent on whatever tasks they were doing.

Unable to find anything familiar, he decided to at least see if he could climb high enough to see the surrounding lands and docks as the sun reached mid-afternoon.

He climbed a set of stairs up the inside of a curtain wall, his guard following him up, breathing heavily in his armour. Karland reached the top to be challenged by a harsh command.

'*Zogs! Ta khen be?*'

A spear was lowered towards him. His guard reached the top, waving his hand and speaking urgently, a little out of breath. Karland guessed he was saying they were allowed to look around, but the wall guard did not look convinced.

'*Ene khuu bol ezen yum uu?*'

'Is there a problem?' asked a young voice in flawless Darum. Karland turned to find a darkly dressed boy with perfect bearing looking up at the guards. He must have been a year younger than Karland at least. His clothes were rich silks, in simple black apart from beautiful work across the shoulders and upper back. His long straight black hair was held in a top ponytail with a gold clasp, the hair pulled back from a high intelligent forehead. His tilted brown eyes held long lashes. Something in his features was familiar.

The men made obeisance immediately, dropping their right foot into a backwards lunge and bringing the heel of their left palm to their forehead.

'*Ezen-Jinong.*'

He ignored them, focusing on Karland.

'You are one of the Anarians.' It was not a question.

'Yes,' said Karland. As usual, he felt the need to explain. 'Our ship was damaged by a huge storm. We were driven here from Anaria.'

'So far,' the boy murmured. He inclined his head slightly. 'I am Bal'Jin.'

'My name is Karland. I'm pleased to meet you.' Karland held out his hand. One of the guards hissed but stopped when Bal'Jin looked at him.

'My hearth and herd are yours,' he replied, and took Karland's hand in a firm grip after hesitating slightly. '*Tavtai morilogtun.* Be welcome.' He smiled slightly and let go, for a moment seeming his age. 'This is the first time I have shaken hands the Anarian way.' It was something between a confession and a statement.

'You did well,' Karland smiled, then hoped that didn't sound condescending. 'How do you normally greet?' He noted the guards had not moved yet. The boy flicked a hand to them to rise.

'Nobility bow from the neck. Commoners bow from the waist. Criminals bow from the feet.' Karland couldn't tell if he was joking or not. Bal'Jin gestured to the walls. 'Would you care to share the view with me?'

'Thank you, Bal'Jin.'

His shadow hissed again. The other guard almost screamed at him, raising his spear.

'You will address the *Ezen* as *Jinong!*'

'*Chimeegui bai!* The Anarian has my *express* permission to use my given name,' snapped Bal'Jin. '*Shuudan ruu butsakh esvel sakhilgyn asuudal nuurle!*'

The wall guard turned like a spun wheel and almost ran back to his post. Karland's shadow hesitated, already being at his.

'Leave us,' said Bal'Jin.

The man hesitated another second, agonising.

'*Orkhi!*'

He virtually ran back down the steps. Bal'Jin sighed.

'My father no doubt told him to keep you in his sight at all times. I do not like to force indecision on the guards, but I sense no harm in you, and I would be alone.'

Karland realised why he looked familiar.

'I can leave as well-' he began.

'Is it not obvious I wish you here?' said Bal'Jin sternly. He moved away, clearly expecting Karland to follow.

They moved up to the next level, Bal'Jin ignoring all the guards, then the next. Two hundred feet up, they could see out to the harbour. There were no guards here, but Karland sensed many eyes from below.

'I often come here alone,' Bal'Jin said after a moment. 'My mother loved it here. She used to bring me and whisper to me. The docks are busy and dirty, but from here they glisten with the promise of adventure. Of freedom.' He sighed. 'I was young, but I remember.'

'What happened?'

The pause was long enough for Karland to wonder if he had asked too much, and then Bal'Jin spoke distantly.

'She cared for my father, and he loved her dearly. But her heart was another's, I think. She often spoke of freedom, but she did not have it. Nevertheless, we were a family.

'Almost ten years ago there was an uprising; my uncle, who we believed dead, tricked the Sinhala. He attacked and slew one of their royal family under peace oath, then led the vengeful army to my father as he travelled near the border under light guard. Believing they had found the killers of their prince, the Sinhala fell upon the train and slaughtered nearly every warrior. They captured the women and servants, and my father, leaving my uncle clear path to the Throne of Bones. My mother was killed during the attack, thrown from her horse.'

'I'm sorry,' said Karland, knowing how inadequate it sounded.

Bal'Jin lifted his hands. 'It is, and will not change. I do not blame the Sinhala, unlike my father.'

'How did he survive?'

'One man survived the raid unscathed. He tracked the party back to the main Sinhalan army, and then stepped forth to make a deal with them. They knew and respected him. He told them what had happened; he had been scouting before the attack and seen my uncle ride past. He had returned, but the attack began before he could speak. He regretted slaying several Sinhalans.' Dark eyes met his. 'You arrived here with him.'

'*Rast?*'

'Rast Tal'Orien.'

'That man gets everywhere.'

'You disapprove of him?'

Karland half-laughed. 'No. So they listened to him?'

'They did not attack him. Rast Tal'Orien is held in high regard in their land. He asked them not to take my father to trial, which would have ended in swift execution. They told him that they would not if he could avenge their prince, or produce proof, before the next dawn.' He laughed shortly. 'It is more justice than the *Zuun Khaant-uls* would have given them.'

'Which did he do?'

'Both. He took horse to my uncle's camp, entered unseen and confronted him. Bal'Dar had been his student, along with my father. My uncle admitted the deed, thinking it would not matter. He planned to kill his teacher.

'Rast Tal'Orien slew fourteen of his elite guard, many with their own weapons, and returned with my uncle bound across his shoulders. His horse failed from being forced to twenty-six *mym* in sixteen hours. He told the Sinhala what he had heard and cast my uncle at their feet.'

'How much is a *mym?*'

'Oh, perhaps six of your Anarian miles? I am not exactly sure.' Bal'Jin turned to look out to the harbour again, his excitement at the old battle evident.

'I do not know how much of the story is a tale, Anarian. Fourteen elite guard! I was told he set his exhausted horse free one *mym* from the Sinhalans, unwilling to ride it to death, and ran the rest of the way with my uncle across his shoulders.' For a moment the youth's face animated with admiration, and Karland realised how handsome he was.

Karland shook his head. 'I saw him defeat eleven armed mercenaries with his bare hands. Two had bows and their leader was an elite warrior. He killed them without effort and saved my life. I believe everything you said. That is what he would do with the horse. He is my friend, and teacher. I have never met anyone so noble, honourable, or deadly. In Anaria he is called *Banidróttin*.'

'Really!' Bal'Jin actually grew excited. 'You are his student? I always wished to study under him, as my father did. I would be honoured to meet him.'

'I can introduce you any time,' said Karland.

'I... thank you.' The words sounded little used. He breathed out for a long moment, studying Karland intently.

'I feel things sometimes, Karland. Things I cannot tell my father. He cherishes his isolation. I do not. I... *feel*... you understand what I mean about being alone. I would like us to be friends.' There was something terrible and noble and forlorn about him. Karland caught a glimpse into how lonely and trapped he must feel.

He knew that feeling well. How much worse must it be for a prince with no mother and a distant father?

'I think we already are, Bal'Jin.' He smiled. After a moment the prince smiled back and bowed his head slightly.

'It is done.'

The words carried more weight than expected. Karland wondered what that meant.

'So what happened to your uncle?'

Bal'Jin lifted his hands, which seemed to be the Zuun equivalent of a shrug, then clasped them behind him.

'My father demanded the right to kill him by trial from the Sinhalans. He will never forget their attack killed my mother, but he knew at whose feet her death lay. The Sinhalans agreed to the trial but forbade killing. They wished to bring my uncle to justice in their own court.

'Bal'Dar was a powerful warrior, as was my father. Both were hurt and exhausted, my father worse. They fought for many minutes, nearly killing each other. Eventually they were separated, and my uncle was taken away. Bal'Dar laughed at my father, and taunted him about my mother even as he went to his death. My father was furious that he had not been allowed to revenge himself upon his brother and broke free.' Bal'Jin's eyes were distant. 'He broke Bal'Dar's neck. Rast Tal'Orien barely stopped the Sinhalans from killing him; only their respect for him prevented it. I think my uncle wished to die an honourable death, but also cause much disruption. He hated the Sinhalans.'

Karland thought about how having a student murder another would be for Rast. Surely as terrible as realising he had trusted a friend under truce.

'So if Rast saved your father's life, why does he seem strange with him?'

'My father offered Tal'Orien riches and honour, but he spurned them. He said he carried the burden of not being there to prevent the attack and told my father that although what Bal'Dar had done was unforgivable, my father risked the lives of countless of his people in war for personal revenge, which was almost as bad. He said he was disappointed.

'My father was… angry. Rather than fight his friend, Rast Tal'Orien vanished. My father never liked being thwarted, and he was furious. He felt disrespected.

'I think the worst part was that my father knew he was wrong. Given time he would have calmed. He never had the opportunity. His respect for your teacher has warred with his fury, and my father does not temper his fires quickly. I do not know now what his actions will be. I am sure he will offer your teacher no harm; I hope he will respect you as his companions, too. But he may demand reparation in some form.'

'Oh.' That didn't sound good.

'I tell you this as my friend. I would request you not repeat my words to anyone.'

'Of course.' Karland felt that Bal'Jin had bared his soul, and that he should do something similar. He was comfortable with him, for all he could not read him well; there was something there that he held in common with Xhera and Seom.

He told Bal'Jin, then, about his own isolation growing up, and what he felt he could of Xhera's.

'I am honoured that, well. You are also becoming one of my friends,' Karland finished. He didn't know Bal'Jin well, but he knew what he meant by *feeling*. He did not fully trust the prince, not yet, but he felt a bond with him nonetheless.

Bal'Jin smiled.

'I knew I was right about you, Karland. You *do* understand.' He glanced at the sun, low to the water. 'I cannot stay much longer; it is almost dusk. Let me have my thoughts here. I will visit you tomorrow, and we will talk more.' There was more than a little of his father in that.

Karland nodded.

'Later,' he said. Bal'Jin nodded briefly, his eyes gazing east.

At the bottom of the last steps, he found his shadow lurking. He half-expected the man to glare at him, but to his surprise the man bowed lower than before and escorted him back to his rooms.

The others were there, talking in the central yard. As he entered, Rast raised an eyebrow, and Karland shrugged.

'How were the docks?' he asked.

'Full of ships and stink,' said The Green Warrior. 'How was your day?'

'Meaningful,' Karland said. He thought back to his last vision of the black-clothed prince standing looking out at the docks. 'Definitely meaningful.'

❧

Bal'Jin visited Karland several times over the next few days for an hour or so at a time. Each time Karland wondered at how isolated he must feel, but he valued the visits. Bal'Jin, for all his strangeness, seemed to be fitting into a space left next to Seom and Xhera. They were fast becoming friends.

It was clear he wished to avoid the others for the moment, and Karland said nothing. He was grateful to have someone his age around, truth be told. Bal'Jin said only that he was not yet ready to meet his father's tutor.

The young prince was old beyond his years, used to power. They made strange fellows, but he genuinely loved hearing Karland's stories, and told him much about the city. He was very reserved much of the time, but as they grew more comfortable, they laughed and swapped information.

When Karland told him he had studied with Rast for a little while now, Bal'Jin had smiled with the same confidence Karland had seen in Aran. It was momentarily off-putting, although they were completely different people.

'My father has spent my whole life training me to carry on in his place,' said Bal'Jin. 'I would match skills with you one day.'

'That would be interesting,' allowed Karland, hoping his new friend would forget about it. He wasn't sure what would be worse - being beaten in a culture where respect could be lost by losing, or beating the crown prince of an empire during a fragile new friendship.

Bal'Jin's determination to train with him was dimmed from an unexpected source. Emotionlessly he told Karland on his next visit that his father forbade him to do so and refused to hear any discussion from Karland on the matter.

Karland was fascinated with what he learned about the empire, though it was constantly brought home to him how terrible and alien it was in many ways. His biggest surprise came when he asked how Bal'Jin spoke such perfect Darum.

'A quarter of the city speaks some,' replied Bal'Jin. 'Most northern lands use it. It is a very simple language, well-suited to trade between cultures.' Karland blinked.

'Did you learn it in The Sanctum?'

'I have never left this city for longer than a few days,' the prince replied. 'We have an extensive library here, with many works. Even some in Darum. It is the finest library in the north. I wager it even equals your University.' His voice was proud.

Karland doubted it. 'A library! I looked for it the day I met you.'

'We have had scholars visit from Eordeland for many decades. They often run the library for a while. One is here now, a Papered Scholar. He teaches the nobles Darum and political knowledge, and in return may study our texts. I will take you to him tomorrow.'

ʕ ʘ

Bal'Jin was busy the next day, but he sent a servant to guide Karland to the Library. It was soaring and filled with books but didn't come close to filling one cavern of the Combic Libraries.

Sitting at a table was a skinny man with a lined face and an oddly bulbous head which was balding on top. The rest of his hair was mostly white and stringy. His nose was slightly ratlike, but otherwise he looked venerable.

Karland introduced himself as a student of Aldwyn Varelin and of The Sanctum. The librarian, who introduced himself as Tames Sacrev-Tatintone, carefully placed his pen and ink down and peered over his glasses.

'Aldwyn? Aldwyn Varelin? Ah, yes,' The man said, wrinkling his brow. His diction was perfect. 'Tell me, how is The Sanctum? Still teaching the cream of Eordeland?'

'Students from everywhere are welcomed,' said Karland proudly.

A fleeting expression of distaste flickered across the man's face.

'It is not always a good idea to dilute knowledge with the unskilled. Morlanders, for example, are simply unable to learn the same way as Eordelanders. Their brains are different; not as capable. Tell Varelin he should teach you that,' reproved Tames. 'I recall his efforts to convince sensible scholars that old stories were true. Made rather a fool of himself.'

'He died on a mission for the Council of Twelve. They believed him,' said Karland, feeling a spark of anger inside.

'Truly? A shame.' He made it sound like anything but.

'Which Academia are you from?' Karland asked, pushing down his upset at the remark in the hope of finding some form of shared interest.

'I am from the Academia Mathematica.'

'Numbers aren't my strongest point,' admitted Karland. 'I find them a little boring. I'm better with language.'

'Numbers are very interesting, dear boy. They are a puzzle which requires intelligence to solve. Immensely satisfying.' He managed to give the impression he found Karland limited, and at the same time made it perfectly clear that as far as he was concerned, they shared nothing but air.

Karland, disconcerted, felt the smile fall from his face.

'Oh. Of course. Well. May I view the library?'

'I am afraid these books are far too valuable for the untrained, young man. They are worth more than you realise.'

Karland struggled to keep his composure.

'Bal'Jin said I could-'

'The *Jinong*, meaning *Crown Prince*, who of course is never referred to by casual name? Of course he did, my boy. But rules are rules. After all, you wouldn't be allowed to simply traipse into the Combic Libraries, either.' He looked over his glasses and down his nose at Karland. 'Mmm?'

It was obvious he was making a huge effort by being polite.

'Actually, I have Council permission to study in them.'

'Come now, boy. Really!'

'Feel free to send them a missive.' Karland was growing angry.

'You know perfectly well it would take months to receive a reply, based on names you might have heard anywhere,' said Tames superciliously. 'No, no, I am afraid the rules must stand.' He smiled insincerely, waiting to get back to his writing. Karland felt like a bothersome child who should be neither seen nor heard.

He thought he'd go mad if he couldn't read a book soon. He desperately gripped his anger and tried to find any way to salvage the situation.

'Your book must be interesting,' he began, then cursed himself. Of course it was, or the man wouldn't be writing it. Why could he never say the right thing?

'Obviously,' Tames echoed his thoughts, sighing that the intrusion was not yet over. Irritation with Karland warred with wanting to talk about his work and lost. 'It is a record of my travels and adventures. I am going to send it off soon. Perhaps with your very ship, if it manages to repair in a timely fashion. It is sure to become a staple for lectures. It covers my travels on three continents, my works and theorems, and the kingdoms I have been advisor to.'

'That's amazing,' said Karland, meaning it. He had some idea of what went into writing a book, and this looked thick. The man must have a wealth of experience, however condescending he was. 'Aldwyn always said it was very hard to get a book published in the University for curriculums.'

'But I don't care,' said Tames quickly, sounding irritably as if he protested too much. He removed his glasses. 'I don't care. It will be written, and worthy of it.'

'I just meant it will be some time before I can even think of writing a book about what I've done.' Karland laughed self-deprecatingly. 'I've only been to two continents so far.'

'But what can *you* have done, hmm?' asked Tames. 'I have had a *far* more interesting life than you will ever have. I have eaten with one of the four *Chóngs* of Kharkistan. I have travelled Matalaga and met tribes unknown to Anaria. I have seen the *Mau-Ti* and found a dead *krake* washed up on the shore, as long as a street. I am a Papered Scholar of The Sanctum and part of the Universalia Communia. I have been an advisor to kings. *You* will never do those things.'

For a second Karland was astonished. He might not do those things, it was true, but he would do others; perhaps more monumental. In fact, he was pretty sure he already had.

He opened his mouth to ask why Tames was writing a book to be used if he also didn't care if it was published, and how he could assume Karland would never equal his achievements, then subsided.

This man would never admit anything that made him feel inferior. He only wanted to be told how worthy he was, show how much cleverer he was. Nothing anyone else had done mattered.

He was very different to Aldwyn.

'I've already done things,' Karland muttered.

'Oh? Such as?'

'I've met and ridden a dragon,' Karland said. He couldn't help it; he had to say *something*, and the truth *mattered*. It was like The Green Warrior all over again, except this time he wasn't being tested but deliberately insulted. 'And I was gifted a vision in a portal in the Hall of Wyrms.' He shook his head. 'It was overwhelming; beautiful. Like nothing I'll ever see again.'

The way the scholar looked at him under raised brows with chin tucked - pityingly, judging, as if he had made it up just to top his own stories - made Karland grit his teeth and resolve not to say another word.

'I think you are a very serious young man, and it has been an absolute delight chewing the cud with you.' Tames raised the glasses to his face again and turned away, dipping his pen and beginning to make notes. After a second Karland realised he had been politely, snootily, and completely dismissed.

Arsehole.

He stood for a moment, then left.

FORTY-EIGHT

Seom drank thirstily, watching his squadmates. They were bearing up well under the pressures of the rigorous training. Not every squad of recruits had been so lucky.

Of the thousand that had marched in companies to the northern border of Eordeland, then marched to meet others with the army at full speed, seven had died. Three had been from weapons accidents. One had been executed, which had shocked them all; he had raped another recruit. All the way to the noose he had begged and cried, but in a time of war punishment was swift and harsh. Several others had died from illness.

One poor soul had died horribly from the pace, pushing too far, too hard as they journeyed. Over the course of a week his muscles had died, twisting his legs terribly. The rest of the squad had had to carry him on a stretcher.

The young man had moaned in excruciating pain for days, soaking himself in dark brown urine before he died. The Daktarim healer at the main force said his kidneys had failed.

Recruits were always pushed hard, but this was too much, thought Seom. They weren't supposed to die!

'Corporal!'

Seom turned and snapped a salute. He proudly displayed the slashes on the left breast, a symbol of the trust his fellows placed in him. He hoped he didn't disappoint them.

There had been additions; one of them had been Kixel Jan, conscripted in by agreement to begin his three years. The boy was quiet and followed orders well. Seom was growing to like him. It was a shame he'd ruined his life by joining those attacking Karland.

He had also seen several others, including Bradwr. Seom was glad *that* one wasn't in his squad. A whining narcissist who complained about everything would disrupt morale terribly. He'd already been punished twice.

Lieutenant Dolvich stopped next to him.

'Inspection, Corporal.'

'Sir!' He turned and snapped to his squad. 'Fall in!'

It still felt odd.

They dropped everything and fell in, standing to attention with stiff arms down. Seom stared straight ahead, hearing other squads around him doing the same.

'*Saluuute*!' roared a Sergeant nearby.

He raised his right arm and put his hand at his throat, flat and palm towards him, fingers straight towards the left shoulder, hearing his squad do the same. Recruits weren't permitted armed salutes, where a fist or a weapon could be used.

'At ease,' rumbled a voice. Seom relaxed, moving his hands to his sides, and looked over. This was no normal inspection; the bearlike form of Councillor Ulric, leader of the War effort, stood nearly in front of him, glowering at them all under his heavy brows. He was heavy-set and broad in his vast chainmail vest and furs. He looked like a northern raider. A heavy war-axe with a spiked back hung at his side.

Behind him stood the tall, slender form of General-Marshal Colcos. His grey thinning hair was swept back, and his sharp cheekbones stood out under sunken eyes and over gaunt cheeks. There was something skeletal about him, but also an implacability; a ruthless drive to conquer.

To the other side, Captain Dorn stood, looking unusually solemn. Seom had met him at many of the training sessions with Karland and Rast.

He caught Seom's eye and very slowly winked. Seom suddenly struggled with the urge to laugh.

Something must have shown on his face. General Colcos leaned forwards, eyes as bright as an eagle's.

'A new Corporal?' His keen gaze took in Seom and the squad. 'We have pushed the recruits hard, Lieutenant. Will they be ready?'

'As ready as they can be, sir,' replied Dolvich.

'I'll wager they'll surprise you,' drawled Dorn, smiling slightly.

'Good,' grunted Ulric. 'I hope they surprise Meyar, too.' He raised his voice. 'From now on you are all marching with the main force. We need every soldier with us. Consider this your test. Your job will be to support the main Guard.' He turned. 'This is General Dannon Tarkin Colcos.'

'We must not fail to hold them,' Colcos's clipped voice came. 'You all have the opportunity for greatness, and I *shall not* fail Eordeland whilst I have breath in me. Ensure you do likewise.'

'Where the fight is thickest, you will find me,' called Dorn. His name and skill were both known to the recruits. 'We stand against the incoming tide. Strong! A rock Meyar will dash themselves against. We will endure! *You* will endure!' His voice rang out, and Seom felt excitement grow in his breast. He knew this was deliberate, had heard cheers from other units, but it happened anyway. 'We will turn them back. I will stand between them and our land. Will you stand with me? Will you *fight with me?'*

Seom was surprised by the roar that erupted from him, echoed by a thousand throats. It went on and on, the recruits forgetting the pain and danger.

As the noise died, Ulric raised his arms, and bellowed, his voice rolling out across the ranks.

'Be ready, sons and daughters of Eordeland! They will come soon. Trust in your hearts. We will crush our enemies… and drive them before us!'

Cheers erupted again. Ulric dropped his hand to his axe and unhooked it, raising his fist to his throat with the axe held vertical in front of his face in armed salute. The scattered sound of a thousand feet stamping and arms snapping up to throats to return the salute was heard as the roars died. The commanders moved on, Dorn nodding imperceptibly to Seom.

The recruits hummed with excitement.

The enemy could come today. They could come in a week. But when they did, they would find an army ready for them, even down to the recruits.

ં ઠ

It was a calming sight to see the Morlanders practice every morning. Some of them did it individually where they had camped, but many would congregate, and their flowing moves were oddly in time. Clearly, they had been performing them for many years, the dark-skinned men and women moving in unison.

It looked like a dance. Some moves Colcos could see would be of use in combat, although they were far too slow. Others he could not fathom.

Morland had many rituals. The fact that they were open-minded and focused on healing did not offset some of their rigidity. He hadn't seen a single one of them eat before praying, touching head, heart and lips before raising face, eyes up, muttering.

He turned his head at a movement and saw Uzuke Asha'ne approaching. He had never quite worked out if it was a title. Asha'ne was tall and his red robe had no sleeves, the hem with a darker red square design around it. His muscular arms looked as if a sculptor had carved and burnished ebony in perfect form. His face held a high forehead and a broad nose, with large eyes so dark they looked black, and the three vertical white ash marks of a *Mganga* healer down over his left brow, eye and cheek. Colcos thought the man to be about forty, but it was hard to tell. He moved like a panther, and his hair was short and tightly curled.

'You watch our Chi'Engo, General,' he said, his smooth deep voice holding a slight cadence to it. 'You should join us one morning. There is great peace in the movement.'

'My own meditation is with the spear,' said Colcos, smiling slightly.

'Ah! The Lover of our weapons. We fight with it, hunt with it, court with it. Its dance is beautiful.'

They stood watching the flowing forms in cream and red, synchronised amidst the bustle of the camp. General Colcos didn't believe in remaining aloof from his men; the soldiers flowed around their spot closely, talking.

One man caught his attention as he shaved, gesturing to the moving forms. His words drifted clearly over to them. Colcos held up a hand in apology to Asha'ne and motioned a nearby Guard.

'Bring that Lieutenant to me.'

The guard left and arrived back with a puzzled-looking Lieutenant, young, with half his whiskers shaved.

'Did I hear you call our allies *mudskins*, Lieutenant?' asked Colcos in a quiet voice.

'No sir,' snapped the guard, eyes forward. His jaw rippled with the lie. Colcos stared at him, then nodded.

'I would be *ashamed* if one of my officers were to refer to our friends and allies in a derogatory fashion.' Asha'ne's protest was waved aside. 'Since we agree, I am certain you will have no problem travelling to each campfire as you are, before you eat, and publicly thanking the Morlanders there for their efforts to ensure the soldiers know their value to us. You will also bring me a full list of soldiers who are… intolerant, should you notice anything.'

The soldier opened his mouth, and Colcos said, 'I should carefully consider anything you might say, Lieutenant. And I shall be receiving reports on your progress with interest.'

'Sir!' said the officer, saluting, his face red. He turned and marched away. Colcos nodded to the side, and another soldier trailed after him.

'I apologise,' said Colcos.

'I understand,' said Asha'ne mildly. '*Mudskin* is not the worst I have heard. We have people much the same; they name you *white savages* and laugh at what they call the scrabbling of your young realms to assume prominence, without understanding that their derision lessens their own.' He shrugged. 'It is easy to fall into habits. We once lived in tribes, thought as you do. Your nation is young yet. In every land people distrust the different, and they fail to see the difference between a darkness in souls and a shading of skin. In realms like Meyar, that fear is harnessed. *Mgeni, devils, foreigners. Monkeys, shitskins, shadowers…* worse. Next to these, *mud* is hardly an insult.'

'Nevertheless,' said Colcos. 'It is the intent, not the words.'

'Did you know that light skin is a mutation?' asked Asha'ne conversationally. When Colcos raised an eyebrow, he grinned, his teeth white against large, perfect lips in his dark face. 'It is true. The first men were even as we are now. I tell you this not to be superior; it just is. The skin of our people did not lighten until we left the brightness of mother sun and travelled to new lands.' The way he spoke made it clear that he considered all men one people.

'Really?' said Colcos, interested despite not believing a word of it.

'Oh, yes. Skin is dark to prevent harm from sun. When you do not need so much protection, the skin becomes light. This you know. You, with your fair skin and blue eyes, are transmuted, my friend, and all the more human for it.' His eyes crinkled. 'Diversity is why the race of man succeeds.'

'My eyes are a mutation as well?' asked Colcos, amused.

'Of course. Mine may bear the brightness of the sun better, you can see perhaps a little better in the dark. The difference is extremely small.' The Morlander sighed. 'We are an ancient nation, General; the oldest civilisation. We went through three Empires before Kharkis even began to gather his armies. We have tried every version of politics, philosophy, and rule, and we know the hearts of our people.' He shook his head. 'We have numbered three Magi in our long history and have trained more Talented users in healing than any other land. The Daktarim have plumbed the secrets of the human body even down to the tiniest parts that make us and have records matching your Sanctum libraries on healing. We have studied people in health and death from every known realm, and so I can promise you this: underneath our skin, we are all the same creature. Oh, there are minor regional or inherited differences, but we know one simple truth: there are no races of men. There is simply *Abantu*.' He smiled. '*The People*. It is our duty to look after each other, whatever land we inhabit.'

'Would that all men understood as you do,' said Colcos regretfully.

FORTY-NINE

Bal'Jin arrived in good spirits three mornings later. He strode into Karland's room, smiling. For the first time his demeanour was almost casual. Karland spied several crimson-armoured guards in the distance nonetheless; they were never too far from the *khaanku*.

'It is impressive, is it not?' asked Bal'Jin. 'The library is one of the marvels of my father's Empire.'

Karland told Bal'Jin what had happened with Scholar Tames, and the smile slid from the prince's face to be replaced by the usual distant impassivity.

'I see,' he said. 'I had not realised that a wandering scholar's word held more weight than the *Khaanku.'*

Karland tried to speak, dreading he had done something wrong. Bal'Jin raised his hand to forestall any words.

'We will speak of this more later.' He changed the subject. 'I wish to know more of your lands; what they look like, what creatures are there. Tell me more about where you grew up.' He sat on the nearby cushions and gestured for hot tea. A servant bowed and moved to the kettle. 'I cannot picture these tall forests of yours.'

Karland spoke of The Croft, and the deep woods nearby, with the river and the fields around it. Bal'Jin had trouble imagining the bear.

'Such a huge, powerful creature,' he marvelled. 'Our earth-lions are large, but not that large.'

'Earth-lions?'

'Great cats on the brown plains with long manes running down their spines. They are more than a man's weight, and often hunt in prides of ten or more. Be very wary of flat plains with drab bushes, my Anarian friend. They are quick.'

They spoke of for a short while. Bal'Jin was wary of the elves - there seemed to be some superstition here of them - but he had seemed unsure how to deal with Darkus until Karland had spoken of Grukust's sacrifice.

Bal'Jin had looked momentarily fierce.

'Honour above all,' he said, almost in a mantra. 'I had no idea. I must speak to this brother of your friend. I would hear more of these dark woods and these giant elephants, his plains and rinoks. If we had those, we would be unstoppable! Elephants here are furred and live in the north. They cannot live outside the snow.'

'It is a day in the telling itself,' Karland said, not liking the sound of that. Bal'Jin was still the proud prince of a cold warrior nation, and he was constantly reminded how different they were. 'Creatures exist there that are not natural. Although, I have seen strange creatures outside Anaria - like the fat creatures in the river to the sea.'

'Ahh,' said Bal'Jin. You speak of the ones with the huge mouths? Like trunkless elephants in the water?' Karland nodded. 'Those are *hippotatamus,* my friend.' The emphasis was on the second *ta.* 'Best avoided. They are short tempered and more dangerous than any creature hereabouts. Sometimes they attack boats. Thankfully they prefer the river and the ocean. They rarely come this far into the Sea of Jamis.'

'I saw a crocodile, too,' said Karland. 'I think. Big tail, like a sail.'

'*Nuruumatar,* ' supplied Bal'Jin. 'Mostly they eat fish. We serve them at feasts.'

Karland wasn't sure a huge scaled lizard was high on his list of delicacies. Another thought occurred. It had tickled him for a little while.

'What's a skinpig?'

'Ah, the skinpig.' Bal'Jin actually grinned. '*Arisgakhai.* You have seen the pink, wrinkled creatures on the plains west of the city? Larger than a goat, big feet, long ears and tail? They eat termites, ants, other insects - I have seen them catch flies on the wing with their long tongues, and their snouts go deep underground. We eat them at feasts, too. And any other time. They are very good.'

'They don't sound dangerous.' Or tasty, he admitted, though he would reserve judgement.

'They can disembowel a man with their kick, but they are cowards, and stupid. Many houses keep a skinpig or two as pets to keep the pests down. They breed incessantly. You will never get precious wood eaten by termites if you keep a skinpig.'

One of the guards bowed and motioned, and he nodded and rose.

'I would speak again later. When do you train with Master Tal'Orien?'

'Evenings.'

'I may watch you. My father said nothing about not attending.' He sounded wistful.

'Until later, then.'

Bal'Jin nodded and left, his usual reserve fading to the fore again.

CB   SO

'How are things with your new friend?' asked The Green Warrior that evening. They sat in Karland's room on plush furnishings, eating fruits and meats. Karland was now constantly checking his to see if he could detect skinpig in it. Uneasily, he recalled the last time he'd eaten unidentified meat.

He remembered back to training with Rast a few hours earlier. Bal'Jin had watched closely, almost fiercely, then left without a word to anyone.

'Bal'Jin is lonely, I think,' he said. 'He's different, but decent. He answers most of my questions.'

'And asks many more,' laughed Galnór. 'Remember young human, he may be younger in years, but he is decades your superior in politics. He gains far more from you than you from him.'

'He has told me many things,' Karland defended. 'Not just about the lands, but about his father.'

'Indeed,' said Rast softly. He sighed. 'It will come to a head sooner or later. Rosso sent a message saying that it will take some time to source enough true wood. He cannot mix palm with oak. We might be months. And there is the matter of payment. The wood we require for the ship costs more than gold here.'

Karland's heart sank. Seeking to change the subject, he shrugged. 'I don't think he shares his father's view entirely,' he said. 'Maybe even his father doesn't.'

'We shall see.'

'Well. Anyway, there is another Anarian here. And a library! They are very proud of it, though it is small. The librarian is a Papered Scholar.'

'Hmm. He will be Universalia Communia, if not Darostim,' said Rast thoughtfully.

'He didn't seem like Darostim,' said Karland resentfully.

'In what way?'

Karland told them what had happened.

'Did you bash the arrogant prick?' asked The Green Warrior. He sounded genuinely interested.

Karland laughed. 'No. I mentioned it to Bal'Jin this morning. Scholar Tames has apparently been told that I have full access to the library, and if he stands in my way again, he will be thrown onto the plains to grub alongside the skinpigs. Bal'Jin was angry that he assumed more authority than the crown prince.'

'*Skinpigs?*' asked Darkus.

Karland grinned and relayed what he had been told.

'Skinpigs,' mused Darkus, then roared with laughter and slapped his thigh with a sound like a wooden board hitting a side of beef. 'I like this word.'

'Do not let it go to your head, boy,' said Rast, drawing his thoughts back to the subject. 'We can ill afford to lose any allies here. It is unlikely Tames is not Darostim.'

'He did not act like our ally, Rast. He's a pompous prig who delighted in throwing me out. He doesn't care for any of us.'

'Nevertheless. Not all Darostim are like Aldwyn. Unpleasant this man may be, but he is still a direct link back to The Sanctum.'

Karland nodded slowly. 'Anyway, Bal'Jin asked if I wanted him on his knees, begging forgiveness. I just wanted him to not be an arse, really. I said no.'

'The *Jinong* is a useful friend to have,' remarked Lëlylien.

'He will not go against his father's wishes,' warned Rast. 'Do not place too much import on your new friendship. I am certain it is real, but remember he is not Anarian.'

'I know. But he is becoming more relaxed, I think. He wants to meet you all tomorrow. Unless you have something better to do.' Karland was getting a little annoyed with all the warnings. He wasn't a complete idiot.

'I think we would be wise to extend every courtesy to Bal'Hon's only son,' said Rast. 'We need all the help we can get. I can only hope that the Council sends another mission to *Míthtól*. Eordeland may need the elves if what we fear is true.'

'What will happen when we don't arrive back with word?'

'Others will be sent. But it may be too late. We must hope that Major Gambeson gets word through to Darost in time.'

No one said anything for a moment.

'War cannot be far now,' said Galnór softly into the silence.

α   β

Bal'Jin met the companions formally the next day. He was extremely reserved, clearly still in some awe of Rast.

Gradually he had relaxed, unlike the six crimson-armoured imperial guard that accompanied him. Strangely, of all of them, the charm of The Green Warrior had begun to work on the *Jinong*. The Warrior could be as likeable as he could be aggressive. Karland had shaken his head; the man was as much a mystery as ever.

Or perhaps Bal'Jin recognised a distance within the Warrior similar to his own.

He spoke with Darkus of the tribes and plains, asking many questions. Outside the line of direct questioning, Karland saw how adroit he really was at getting information, but Bal'Jin was also surprisingly forthcoming.

The elves he practically ignored until Lëlylien rose to get water. Karland didn't miss his glance toward her hypnotically graceful movement and grinned to himself. When she returned, he drew her into the conversation, and Bal'Jin was comfortable enough to begin responding to her and Galnór.

With Rast, he was attentive and respectful, and very measured throughout. Finally, he rose.

'I… thank you, for your welcome of me,' he said, surprising Karland with the honesty in his voice. 'I have little chance to speak to interesting people, and now there are many at once. I hope my father can see you soon. I… enjoyed our discussion. One day perhaps I will journey to Anaria and see your homes for myself.' There was a faint longing in his words. He nodded, flashed a slight smile at Karland, and left.

'A complex boy,' observed Galnór.

'He is truly alone,' said Lëlylien sadly. 'I see it in him.'

'Not the only one,' The Green Warrior replied almost too quietly to hear and did not speak again.

ଔ   ଌ

A few days later a summons finally arrived from Bal'Hon. They were collected by the vizyer, who had stepped back a little when Bal'Jin had taken an interest. He spent several minutes asking Rast their ancestry and titles, then beckoned them on and retraced their original route, this time to larger, more ornate doors with many guards outside. They opened to show more guards inside. The chamber within was five-sided. Karland knew that four was considered an unlucky number here. He also took care not to step on the peaked threshold of the room, which he had been told was ill-fortune.

The ceiling soared, almost perfectly domed, and a dais made of moonstone rose polished from the marble floor. The throne that sat upon it was incredible.

The Throne of Bone was where Bal'Hon ruled from. Rather than gruesome, it was extremely well-crafted, but the bones were quite clearly human. At the ends of each arm Bal'Hon's hands rested on a human skull wrought into the chair. The sides and back were built of interlaced femurs, with ribs arcing from their ends. It was an impressive monument.

The bones were polished and coated in some kind of lacquer, browning them slightly, and they had been ornately carved to fit. Above it was a large round window which shone a circle of light onto the ruler.

660

To each side there were advisors, and further back other members of the court stood, some talking quietly. The vizyer walked to the left hand of the throne and turned, speaking Darum.

'*Daichin-Khaan* Bal'Hon of the *Kuun Khaant-uls*, Lord of the Inland Sea of Jamis from which sweet tears flow, Emperor of the Great Plains from horizon to horizon, *Ezen* of the vast herds of the *Kuun*, Defender of the North, Master of the East, Great Dragon of Hadrasia;

'I present those known as The Green Warrior; Darkus, Envoy of the Anarian Plains Ork Tribes; Galnór and Lëlylien, of the elves; Karland Dresin, student and scholar of The Sanctum; and Rast Tal'Orien, warrior and honoured friend to the *Kuun*.'

Bal'Hon nodded, emotionless.

'You are welcome in the court of the *Kuun*.'

Karland wondered why they had been brought before Bal'Hon was finished, then realised that it was likely for the benefit of the court. There were curious glances from the ranks of nobles and whispers in the tonal language. Most were directed at Rast. It was obvious some here remembered him.

Bal'Hon rose.

'*Noyon. Bid busad bukhnees iluu khuchtei baidag.*' He spoke more words in *khel*, mostly aimed at the twenty-five or more noblemen at the front. When he finished, they bowed. A gong rang, and the collected nobles made their gesture of respect one by one and began to file out.

When they were gone, Bal'Hon descended from the throne and gestured them to follow him. Six guards closed in, three of them around him and between the Anarians. They walked to the other side of the huge chamber and entered a room with a large table. Many maps and scrolls were pinned on the walls; more lay on the table, along with small features and rectangles representing differing units. It was the first war table Karland had seen.

'I have demanded the nobles bring their troops before the city, ready,' he said. 'It will take many days; the *Tumetu-iin Noyan* command ten thousand troops each. I intend to do several things here, Rast Tal'Orien.' He put his hands on the desk and leaned own, staring at the field.

'I will crush this pitiful foe. I will remind my *ezen* who rules here. And I will gain respectful concessions from the Sinhalan Empire.' He breathed deeply. Karland realised he was probably exhausted but suspected the man would drive himself to collapse rather than look tired in front of anyone else.

'This is a difficult time,' Bal'Hon confessed. 'The Sinhala are being pushed back into their jungles, and loathe as I am to ally with them, I cannot call them cowards. We may require their help to destroy this enemy completely.'

'What do you face?' asked Rast.

'Rumours put these combined armies in the millions.'

'That is absurd. No armies could be that large. Past twenty thousand, a campaign cannot last more than a few months. The logistics alone-'

'Indeed. It cannot be larger than the armies of the *Zuundaichin*.' He said this last with a wry twist of his mouth. 'Ours is the largest in Hadrasia. What I do know is this force has been moving inexorably north for almost a year. It has not slowed or stopped, except to besiege cities. Many it has surrounded are said to have fallen eventually, but it is hard to get information. In the southwest, the great Tri-Cities of Tola themselves have been under attack for some time. It is a scourge, and like any other it must be destroyed.' The Lord of the East exuded extreme confidence. He turned to Karland's mentor, and his features relaxed a fraction, his voice becoming more human.

'Come, Rast. Lend me your wisdom. You are the greatest warrior I have known.'

'You do not seem sure of the figures,' said Rast. 'How accurate are the reports?'

'I do not believe them,' Bal'Hon said firmly. 'Hysterical farmers and peasants. There exists no army in Hadrasia we cannot destroy on open ground, no two lands that can jointly equal our numbers. Even the Tri-Cities of Tola - powerful and strange as they are - do not challenge us on the plains. Where others are weak, we are strong. We shall not fail. And Sinhala has sworn to strike from the flanks when we engage.'

'They can be trusted if they gave their word,' said Rast slowly, almost unwilling to be drawn in. Bal'Hon nodded reluctantly. 'What is your current force?'

'I have almost two hundred thousand men ready without leaving any cities below siege strength,' Bal'Hon answered. 'And I can conscript more. We have set up caches across the country. Herds have been thinned, crops have been dispersed. The outlying regions have been preparing for our march south for months. Logistics are not a problem for as long as it takes to get there, and some time past, including our return.'

'But to do that, you would have to strip your kingdom bare. Your people could starve. It is not sustainable.'

Bal'Hon said nothing.

'Bal'Hon,' said Rast. 'I will lend you what advice I may. But you must know… there is more at stake than war between nations, on any continent. Greater forces move on Kuln. We *must* return to Anaria as quickly as we can.'

'But how will you get back unless it is on your ship?' The *Daichin-Khaan*'s smile wasn't quite cruel. 'I can lend you none of mine. They are needed for war supplies. I cannot build you one; the wood required is rare and costly and it would take a year or more. The only answer is to repair yours.'

Rast said nothing.

'Is Anaria truly the only place great things may be decided? Come now, my friend. It is a small land. You are owed a great debt for your courage; it is likely no other could have done what you did for me. My life is yours... but I have heavy responsibilities.' His stare was direct. 'I offer you a bargain. I will have your ship repaired by our finest builders, in gratitude, as quickly as possible, as my... gift. In honour of my debt. But this will take time, especially finding a new mainmast. Trees large enough for that grow very far from here.

'Meanwhile, you will travel with me to view this threat. It would be our honour for you to accompany us.'

'Bal'Hon, I thank you for your offer,' said Rast. 'But I must remain with the ship. Our country also lies at war, an Eordeland itself stands under grave threat. Your expedition could take many more months. We do not have that time.'

'Perhaps you failed to accord my suggestion the gravity it deserved.' Bal'Hon's voice was fractionally colder.

Rast studied his face, then bowed slightly after a second. 'As you wish.'

'And these others, your companions. They will come also. I have heard much of their talents.'

Karland shifted uneasily; he had probably heard the details from his son after Karland had told him of their travels.

'The boy should stay here,' Rast ventured.

'He is a good companion for my son. Bal'Jin finds it... difficult... to have true friends. Your student will accompany him. We move out in four days.' He stood. 'I do not expect to be gone long, old friend. We will view this rabble, perhaps even crush them quickly. You will be on your way home within the month. Come now, can you tell me you feel no thrill at exercising your greatest skills once more?'

'I am tired of fighting, Bal'Hon. It has lost me everyone I have ever cared for.'

'Not everyone, surely.' Bal'Hon's flat gaze took in Karland and the others.

Rast sighed. His voice was soft.

'Not yet.'

FIFTY

Ulric pored over the latest reports by library light with Colcos as Dorn inspected the evening defences with Colonel Hargreave.

Three or four more days at most and the Meyari would come into view from the north; the main force of more than forty thousand had moved far out in advance of their supply wagons, bringing only a huge wagon pulled by a team of oxen and several other odd wagons drawn by heavily armoured bulls.

From the opposite direction, pathfinders watching the Reldenhort plains brought more ill news; a large force of heavy cavalry moved north around the Arkon foothills at good speed towards their position. More than four thousand Novinian mercenary knights would crash into their flanks as they tried to channel the Meyari coming up the hillside.

They were likely to hit from the gently sloping south right after the main Meyari force hit from the east. Colcos would have to split the army to prevent them being flanked by the heavy cavalry and the war dogs they rode with. It was a solid pincer they would be caught in, but there was no way around it and they should be able to limit it to the two neighbouring fronts.

The real danger was being hit hard enough by one attack to allow the other to slice their forces in two. If that happened, they could be surrounded and destroyed piece by piece.

The main shock damage would come from the Novinians. If they could be hemmed in from the west as they rode and stopped with pikes and war scythes, they might even be able to push them east and deal with the whole enemy on one front, but they would need luck.

Both forces were alarmingly synchronised. When they arrived, the allies would be hard pressed.

This morning they had offloaded the last of the supply train's supplies around the command tents on the crest of the hill and sent it back to Darost and safety.

They had enough to last them a month, long past when this campaign should be over.

Ulric was tired. He was younger than Dannon, though not by much, but governing as a member of the Council took its toll at the best of times. He moved to sit in a chair and glanced over to the General, who was frowning and muttering to himself, half-turned away. The other advisors had retired to their Battalions, leaving the two to discuss updated positioning. The map was laid out flat with rectangular pieces representing a thousand men each set out in formations and estimated incoming lines of attack.

Their strategy was good; their troops were the equal of either force - both if all went to plan - and Colcos was one of the finest Generals in Anaria.

Then again, plans only ever lasted as far as the first step.

Ruefully, he listened to the creaking of his bearlike shoulders as he stretched. As he finished, a surprised grunt from outside reached him. He had barely caught it against the general sound of the camp and wouldn't have if he had still been looking at the maps and reports. His tired mind dismissed it, and he wearily moved to rise from the chair again.

Another soft sound caught his ear and then he froze as an incredibly pale woman appeared from outside. She hadn't appeared to move into the tent, yet there she was, the tent flap falling behind her. Shorter than average and plump with dark hair, she would have been quite pretty if she hadn't had a feral, insane air about her. Her gimlet stare pinned him to the spot as blood dripped from her hands and ran down her chin.

He felt strangely weak under her gaze, his muscles refusing to answer, as if his energy was being drained.

'*Dan,*' he managed weakly, and gritted his teeth, struggling to move. The woman tilted her head back and laughed softly, bloodstained fangs gleaming, and her head swung to the General, who was still lost in thought, his back to them.

She moved towards him as he turned, her hands curving into claws, and Ulric pushed through his exhaustion and fear and snapped out of his trance. He grabbed the chair he had risen from and swung with all his strength, the blow smashing the woman to the floor. Colcos started, exclaiming in shock, his hand leaping to his spear.

Ulric's axe was at the other end of the table.

Damn.

With a shriek of anger, the woman threw the remains of the chair off her and lunged at Colcos. The General's spear slid neatly into her chest with his usual economy, only enough to penetrate and kill. She whirled, wrenching it from his hand, and drew it out, hissing in pain and anger. Her eyes locked on his as the wound stopped bleeding and began healing. She flung it aside without visible effort.

Shouts from outside sounded at the noise.

'You'll pay for that, worm,' she promised. 'Before your guards arrive, you'll both be dead.'

Ulric did not doubt her. The speed she had moved at belied belief.

'I think not,' said a quiet voice from the doorway. Ulric darted his eyes over but only saw a dark blur. The woman screamed, moving faster than he could see as she sprang to escape. There was a crunching sound. A splat of blood hit the tent wall, and then, quite absurdly, the little scholar Night was standing with a broken piece of the chair in his right hand, the woman held up by it. His teeth were bared in hatred, and both men could see they were every bit as dangerous as the woman's. He no longer looked like an amusing, slightly shabby man; right then, he looked terrifying, his name holding new meaning for both of them.

The makeshift stake of wood stood out from her back, directly in line with her heart. She choked bloodily, her mouth opening and a look of fright on her face, her hands clutching at his. Night let her sag to her knees, and nodded to the shocked men, calm returning to his face and manner.

'Ash chair leg,' he said conversationally.

They said nothing. The woman scrabbled weakly at his hand, which was reddened where it held the wood.

'If you are going to stab a vampire, general, ensure it is directly through the heart with the right wood. Your ash spear did not go deep enough. Several types of hardwood trees inhibit healing, so a wooden stake from one of these is best, but whatever you do, you must then strike their heads off and burn them, or risk their return.' He gestured for the axe, and Ulric strode forward, handing it to him haft first. Night had no trouble with its weight.

The woman tried to claw and bite him. With a speed that left a silver arc in the air, he sliced once. It went straight through her neck without slowing and her head toppled from the powerful blow. Night wiped the weapon clean on her clothes and handed it back to the general as guards poured into the tent, weapons pointing at him.

'Stand down,' said Colcos, waving his hand. 'He saved us. Take this outside and bury it.'

'If I may,' said Night politely. 'Keep the head separate and burn them both, then leave the ashes for the morning sun. There is no return from ash, and sunlight is purifying.'

Colcos nodded at them. 'Do it. Double the guard. Run a count and see if any more of these creatures have infiltrated the camp. Check with the elves and dwarves, too. From now on, no strangers are to be allowed to approach. No one moves outside pairs, no-one leaves the sentry lines. Dig and fill pits inside them.'

'Sir.' The captain nodded. 'Five guards are dead. Three from Brutes, two Grippers. Carmine skirmishers.'

'How many were fed on?' asked Night.

The captain looked between Colcos and Ulric, and then shook his head. 'Fed on?'

'How many had wounds, probably on their throats, that could have been drunk from by a vampire?'

The guard hesitated.

'A va-? Three... Sir.' He sounded unsure how to address the scholar. 'But-'

'They must be cremated. It is extremely unlikely, but vampires exist only because sometimes the darkness propagates.'

'Do it,' said Ulric shortly. 'Now. Leave the mess here until tomorrow.'

The guard nodded and left with his men, one gingerly and carefully carrying the gory head by the hair and two of them dragging the cadaver. The chair leg was still firmly lodged in its chest.

Colcos turned to Night, his voice surprisingly calm. 'Our thanks, Seeker.'

'Mind telling me what in all the hells just happened?' rumbled Ulric. His tiredness at least had vanished in the spurt of adrenaline. 'And what in the hells you are doing here?'

'Just what you *are* would be a start,' said Colcos, wryly, retrieving his spear.

Night smiled thinly, his teeth hidden again, and seemed amused and resigned at their expressions.

'I think it best if I stand guard here tonight,' he said with a little bow. 'And perhaps I should explain a little more about myself as I do so.'

'Perhaps you should,' said Ulric. He eyed the splat on the wall of the tent, a few drips running down. The piece of chair had not been particularly sharp. To ram it through ribs, heart and body like that with one hand, so hard that blood flew, would take unnatural strength and power. Even Tal'Orien wasn't that strong. And the speed the man had moved at!

'You recall that I sought a man named Sontles?' asked Night, taking a seat in one of the chairs. Ulric nodded and sat on his bunk, Colcos perching on a remaining chair. 'He is one of the few vampires that has slipped through our net more than once. He is powerful and dangerous. Now he has control within the Church of Terome... and a pact with forces which give him more power than any here could perhaps face. But he is not the only one of his kind, as you saw. There may be more, so your precautions about the camp are sound. Your men should learn which old defences work and which are just stories. Religious symbols are meaningless. Sprinkling beans or grains of rice before me might have me reaching for a broom, but no more. Prayers and chants do nothing. Empty words.' He shrugged.

'On the other hand, certain woods and plants are poisonous. Silver may kill. Garlic and sunlight are deadly. Without these, you must inflict as much damage as you can and hope to slow the healing until you can take the head. Even vampires cannot heal from that… unless you replace it.' He smiled slightly.

Ulric looked at the broken chair and grunted with grim laughter.

'What about you?' asked Colcos quietly. 'You saved us, but why work against others of your kind?'

'That requires some explanation of the Order of Illuminus. Vampires are not really my kind, even though we share a heritage. I have never taken a life to feed. Our Order is a family that are not just scholars. We also hunt the Turned. Most people did not choose a violent death and insanity; we try to save them, to turn them back from the monstrous path they follow. Some do. Most do not.' He sighed. 'Suffice it to say that I was born as I am. Our order take the ancient name *Vampyre* and hunt those we cannot save. We will do our best to protect you from those you cannot fight easily. Tomorrow night, you will have to change your orders somewhat, Councillor; more of my kin come, and you will have to introduce them to avoid mistakes.'

'Lucky you came when you did. There was more of a *stake* in attacking us than she realised,' said Ulric. Exhausted laughter threatened to escape for a moment.

Colcos shook his head tiredly, and Night smiled slightly.

'We are few, but the fate of the world is not ours to just record. We must survive, too.'

Ulric felt weary. He had always felt there was something unsettling about the little man, but had assumed that he was a Druid, if an odd one.

'Before we turn in for the night,' he muttered acerbically, 'was there anything else you wanted to tell us that might come in useful? Anything important?' Colcos snorted at his bluntness, but he was too tired to care.

Night seemed to take no offense.

'Perhaps. Tell me, Councillor: what do you know about werewolves?'

Ulric blinked.

'About *what?*'

೧   ಔ

668

Xhera knocked on Brin and Becka's door at dusk. It was second Zoldi, eighteenth in the month of Weod, and the days were long. She wondered why they had asked her to come today instead of in two days at Midwice as usual. Today Kervala and Jimson had drawn duty, much to Jimson's glee.

Brin didn't really know how to talk to tough, capable women like Rene Kervala. He tended to speak more to the male soldiers. Becka had little in common with them, but was always welcoming nonetheless.

This time there was a difference when the door opened. Becka was smiling ear to ear.

'There's a surprise for you,' she said, beckoning them all in.

Xhera heard voices as she entered the living room, one being Gail's. The other was Talas.

'Surprise!' she called, beaming from behind her glasses, and rose. The baby was definitely showing now, Xhera saw. She laughed and hugged her sister carefully.

Dinner that night was an excellent recipe, passed to Becka from a lady from East Norlund. Xhera had never tasted anything like it, chicken and celery with the odd walnut piece in a creamy sauce with quartered hard-boiled eggs. Both light and dark meat were used, and the top was layered with thin slices of potato, fried and salted, with black pepper. The whole thing was baked in the oven and was delicious.

'Karland's favourite. Hot chicken salad,' smiled Becka.

'Salad?' asked Kervala. She hunted between pieces of meat.

'There's some celery in it,' laughed Becka.

Kervala chuckled. 'I could eat more of this type of salad.'

They spoke for some time, Brin offering around a glass of his good red wine. Talas refused, as did Kervala. Jimson allowed himself a small goblet.

Talk turned to Karland, and the work Xhera was doing. As usual, she didn't say too much, conscious that the guards would be listening.

'I'm a little worried,' she confessed. 'Shouldn't they be back by now?'

'Could be in The Sanctum already,' remarked Brin, relaxed in his chair. 'Besides, you said a sea voyage. Lots of delays there.'

'Wasn't there a huge hurricane a couple of months ago?' asked Talas. 'In western Anaria?' Xhera cast a worried glance at her. 'I just mean it might have delayed them. I don't think they would have been in it,' she added hastily.

'Shouldn't think they'd have got there that quickly,' Karland's father said. 'That's right though. Grandfather of a storm, I heard. Swept away whole towns on the west coast.'

Becka exchanged a look with Xhera and said nothing. Xhera could see she didn't like the line of thought either.

Talk turned to other matters, but Xhera couldn't shake a sense of foreboding that had descended upon her. She was convinced it had something to do with the lack of any word or return.

Talas had left Jon at the tavern; he had decided that he had earned a good drink, and would not disturb his wife, who would join him later. This was her last chance to travel and see her sister before the baby was born; there was too much work to do at the end of the season on the farm. They would go back early the next morning. Brin and Becka both insisted that she stay, but she refused.

'I'm sure Karland is all right,' she said as she bade goodbye. She gave Xhera a hard hug. 'And next time I see you, you will be an aunt! Unless you can find time away from the studies to come home… for a while.'

'I'll try,' said Xhera. 'I miss the farm. But I wouldn't stay long.'

Talas gave her a sad smile. 'I know. I understand better now.'

'Thank you,' said Xhera. She smiled, but deep inside the thought of Karland and the great storm remained. It had a… grey-sparked *feeling* that swelled outward from her chest over a churning stomach. She was terribly afraid she had lost her soulmate; that despite his promise, they would not be together again.

They bade farewell. Jimson escorted Talas gallantly to the Tavern, and then returned to meet them at the front. Climbing on the cart, they left the Gates and struck out east from the town along the wide tracks to East Norlund.

As they unhurriedly moved into the darkness through spits of rain that heralded a coming downpour, away from the lights and cheer, Xhera desperately hoped that her fears were unfounded about Karland.

Not because of Aldwyn's writings. Because, for the first time in her life, she had been content, though she had not realised it until he was leaving. Happy. Not alone anymore. She had someone who understood her completely.

She couldn't have lost Karland.

Ê ࠊ

Ventran prowled the shadows in The Croft after two drinks in the Orc's Head, the tavern near the gates. Apparently, it had once been called the New Moons, but after tales of Tal'Orien striking the head from the orc chieftain they had renamed it. He had preferred it to the larger tavern in the centre, the Inn of the Twelve.

He was irritable.

Not only did he incessantly hear stories lauding that bloody warrior, but it was difficult to engage in his hobbies in a small town where everyone knew each other; and however much he kept hearing how large The Croft had grown in the last year, it was still a small town.

And a fortified one, as well. Since the Battle of The Croft - a grandiose name that still brought a wellspring of mirth up inside him - the Guard presence here was high, with a mixture of trainees and veterans. He had to be very, very careful.

There had been no luck in Fordun's Run. He had heard of the fight in the bar, but that was of no use - it was when they had been travelling to Darost, and they had no news since then.

Gladsmoor had similarly disappointed, but at least here there had been talk of a half-squad of soldiers and a girl matching the description of Karland's little friend. One person spoke of a small man who had accompanied them, but no one else had seen him. Had to be Varelin.

The trail had ended at The Croft. They were nowhere in town. It was very hard to ask about them without seeming to pry, and the end of his second week approached.

What kind of idiots had an eight-day week with a rest day on the fourth and eighth days? Why couldn't they have a six-day week with two solid days for debauchery like any normal realm, he thought sourly. All this Midwice and Endwice nonsense was irritating.

He was in what this wretched town considered a decent alleyway at dusk when the soldier walked past with a woman just beginning to show pregnancy. He was lightly flirting, and she was laughing, but it didn't seem serious. An attractive woman, with expensive glasses on her face.

A snatch of conversation caught his ear, and he paused.

Oho.

Ventran crept after them with care. The soldier was clearly experienced, and even chatting lightly kept his surrounds in view, scanning people and approaches.

He heard the name Xhera again and felt like crowing in triumph.

The insubstantial bitch had finally become real again.

At the door to the tavern, the soldier made a leg to the woman.

'Regards to your husband, ma'am. I'll look after Xhera.'

'Thank you, Bem,' she replied warmly. 'I know you will.'

He nodded and watched her move inside. Ventran almost followed her; he was sure she and her husband would be a wealth of information.

Then again, it might cause problems. It didn't follow that she knew this library's location, and access to that might salve Sontle's ire if he couldn't retrieve that damn pendant.

Making a decision, he followed the soldier back. Sooner or later, where he was, she would be. And where she was, that brat Dresin and the old bastard Varelin would be too.

The soldier met another soldier, a capable-looking woman, and Ventran felt like crowing in delight. There stood what must be the girl, outside a house! She waved at someone inside and turned, heading for a cart. There was no sign of the others.

Ventran deliberated. He doubted he could take down two veterans without attracting attention. It wasn't that late in the evening, and this was near a row of shops, so there were people around. A group wandered by as he watched.

He moved instead into the alley behind the houses, looking for an alternative, watching them carefully as they began to move away.

So intent was he on trying to listen to his victim that he was caught by surprise when a heavy footfall landed near him. A rough voice sounded.

' 'Ere. What you doing?'

Ventran turned his head slightly. 'Ah,' he said, and fumbled at his crotch for a moment. 'Just stopping for a piss.'

The man scowled at him. He wore farmer's clothes and had large shoulders and hands. Ventran didn't know if he'd been drinking or not, but he didn't seem friendly.

'Where you from?' the man asked. 'Not round 'ere from yer accent.'

'Out of town,' Ventran said smoothly. 'Can't a man drain himself without interruption?'

'You ain't allowed to piss in public here, mate.'

Pifing fool, thought Ventran. He couldn't hear the voices behind him anymore.

'Right then,' he said cheerfully.

'Hold up.' The man took a step forward. 'You best come with me to the Guards. Just a formality, like.'

'Why? I've done nothing wrong.' It was true. He hadn't even pissed.

'Been a lot of bad people here causing problems. Just register with the Guard and stay out of trouble. And don't piss behind people's houses.'

'I will. And I won't,' Ventran said, turning away. The girl was long gone; he needed to get away from this fool.

The man's beefy hand dropped on Ventran's shoulder, stopping him with a solid grip.

'I said with *me*, frie-'

Ventran spun, hands dipping. His shoulder dropped from the man's grip, and he whipped both hands up one after the other. Each held daggers.

He stabbed in and out alternately, viciously. Every soft slicing impact was accompanied by a gasp from the man and a small spurt of dark blood. Within six seconds he had punctured lungs, stomach and spleen with more than ten thrusts. The last two wounds kept the blades as he let go of the hilts, slapping a hand over the man's lower face and gripping his collar to lower him to the ground. A soft, dwindling shriek was trying to come out from behind his palm, which covered mouth and nose.

He held him there a few seconds more, until he was sure the man's lungs were filling with blood and he could not call.

Ignoring the desperate gurgles, he wrenched the knives out and cleaned them on the man's tunic as his legs jerked.

'Couldn't just fuck off, could you?' he snarled, his anger flaring. All this time being careful, and this idiot forced his hand. He lunged again, stabbing his victim over and over with the freshly cleaned knives, teeth bared insanely. 'Couldn't- just- fucking- mind- your- *business*!'

He rolled the corpse over and cleaned them again on the back. The front was sodden with blood.

Best hide this body and get after the girl. He cursed; he shouldn't have killed this man. In a town this small it announced his presence like a trumpet blast, and he might have just lost his chance to find Varelin.

Ventran didn't like to admit to himself that Sontles might be right about controlling his urges.

He rolled the body back again, preparing to drag him into the darker recesses of the alleyway behind the houses. It wasn't far from the main roadway here. Time to dump him and get out of town.

Dammit.

'Hello?'

It was a young voice. A girl. Ventran froze, crouching lower.

A high gate had opened behind him, leading to a small garden behind one of the shop fronts and houses. It might have been the one Xhera had been in front of.

A small figure stood there, holding an empty box used to throw remains onto a midden heap.

She must have heard something. Ventran, so caught up in his fury, hadn't even heard the bolt draw back.

She could have been anywhere from seven to nine years old in the dim light. She put the box down and walked forward, peering into the gloom. It was obvious she could see part of Ventran's victim; the man's left leg was twitching gently, over and over. He had seen it happen before, but it was remarkably inconvenient now; movement was what people saw in darkness.

'Are you all right, mister?' she said, taking a hesitant step forward. Ventran ghosted around to her right, stepping softly and moving smoothly.

The girl stepped forward, squinting at the leg she could see. As her eyes adjusted, she saw more, including the dark front. It was obvious she still did not understand what she was seeing.

A few more steps and she was there. She leaned over to shake and gasped; her hand would have touched blood. As she drew in a breath to scream, Ventran materialised behind her.

He slapped a hand over her mouth and pulled a dagger out. The girl bucked and writhed, unable to breath, panicking. He cupped his palm in case she tried to bite and dragged her back from the houses.

Turning her to face the lights of the main street, he held the knife up so she could see it, twisted it in front of her eyes, then slowly brought it down to her neck.

'Shhhhh,' he whispered into her ear. 'Stop fighting or I'll cut your little throat, darling.'

At the words and the sharp touch, she went still, her chest heaving. He tilted his hand, so her nose was clear, and the girl sucked air in desperately.

'I'm going to ask you some questions. I want you to answer them immediately,' he purred. 'If you scream for help, you will die like this man here. Do you understand?'

There was a second where he wondered if he had to repeat himself, and then she nodded frantically.

'Good. Now. Nod for yes, and if I think you're lying, bad things will happen to you. Understand, little girl?'

Nod. Nod.

'That girl who left the street with the guards. Do you know her?'

Nod.

'Her name is Xhera.'

Nod.

'Ahhh. Was it your house she was at?'

There was a pause. He laughed, the answer confirmed, and drew the knife a little way, slicing the merest fraction of skin.

What luck!

The girl let out a muffled sob and nodded again frantically. Tears of fright were streaming down her face.

'Think carefully before you answer this, child. Where did she go? And remember: one scream is your death.'

He took his hand off her mouth a fraction.

'S…somewh-herrrre,' she stuttered, crying. He shook her.

'*Where?*'

She shook her head.

He leaned in. 'I know you know, you little slut. I don't care how you know, or who you are. If you tell me what I need to know, I go away. If you don't…' he caressed her throat with the tip of the dagger.

She gulped and didn't respond. Ventran sighed.

Pifing stubborn child.

He didn't have time for this.

Dragging her backwards to the corpse, hand over her mouth again, Ventran reached down. Using the knife, he sliced along a piece of bloody cloth at the front, sheathed the blade, then tore the cloth free. Balling it up, he forced her mouth open and rammed it in, then replaced his hand. She gagged on the taste of coarse cloth and blood. Ventran ignored her.

He kicked her right leg out to the side, braced the inside of her knee with his own leg, then twisted and knelt hard, his knee on the outside of her shin.

He had not broken a child's bone before. It felt… different. Softer, springier. There was surprising give before it fractured, and it felt like a green stick rather than a dry branch.

The tibia fractured and the girl screamed into the cloth, her nose dribbling snot over his hand and her eyes staring, unseeing. She choked on the gag as she almost passed out.

He hauled her upright, holding her as she began to collapse. Ventran grabbed the end of the gag and hauled it from her mouth, then replaced his hand.

He waited until her sobs and chokes subsided a little, stroking her cheek, then spoke.

'That was the *least* I will do to you. Tell me, or I break the other leg… then the arms and hands. Then worse things will happen to you, my sweet young thing. Just tell me where Xhera went. I *promise* I won't hurt her.'

Ventran removed his hand and listened impatiently to the soft sobs. He gave her a shake.

'*The L-Library of Th-tThi-Thingos,*' she managed, hardly able to speak.

He felt a surge of joy. So she *was* there. What a prize!

'Where is it?'

'East, a cart ride, somethi-i-ing!'

'Where *exactly*?' He brought the knife up again.

'*I don't knoooow!*' she wailed. He slapped his hand over the mouth again at the volume, distractedly thinking. He believed her; time to get rid of both of these troublesome problems. He had somewhere to start, at least.

'Thank you,' Ventran purred. 'See? That wasn't so hard.' He lifted the knife to her throat.

'Gail? Where are you?' a man's voice called, worry in its tone. Ventran cocked his head. It was close.

Unexpectedly she bit at his hand, and he reflexively flung her away. She hit the ground and swooned at the pain from her leg.

He heard the calling voice coming closer. At the same time, more voices came along the alleyway; it was obviously used for movement more than those in a city. He had chosen this spot poorly.

'Splint your leg, girl, or it won't heal straight.' Ventran laughed softly, mere feet from his victim, and sheathed his dagger. 'Maybe we'll meet again one day.'

He pointed menacingly at her.

'*Learn to run,* Gail.'

He vanished over the nearest wall. Behind him he could hear her soft cries before a man's voice shouted in alarm. Running feet answered him.

Ventran ran gracefully, leaping walls and weaving through the dark streets like a cat, only stopping when he was several away.

Time to head back to the tavern where he was staying, collect his gear, and head east. Now he knew what he looked for, a few questions about the Library should give him an idea before he slipped over the wall and left.

The distant sound of running Guards and cries of alarm cheered him.

His urges caused trouble, true, but they were satisfying, and that was all he really cared about.

ʕ ʅ

Less than an hour later, Ventran unhooked a horse from the tie post. Spatters of rain were starting from heavy clouds sliding in; the moon was silver-bright as it drifted between them, with Xoth only a green tinge in the sky.

The Library was a common tale in the town, once he knew what to ask for. He had encountered several people on his way into the tavern whose tongues had been well-loosened by drink. Most of them had known its rough direction, and one had described a direct path east to the fabled ruins he had used to deliver supplies from time to time a few years ago, before the woods became too dangerous and the main road was the only safe way.

The cart would have to go south, then east a way, then turn off northwest to arrive there.

Ventran had realised he had an opportunity. True, he could try to chase down the cart, but that only netted him the girl, and her Guards would be alert. But if he could get there first… he might find Varelin and the boy alone.

He couldn't stay here, anyway. It wouldn't be long before people came looking for him.

He had slipped away, moving over the wall and around to the hitching post at the entrance for Guards as the rain got heavier. Now to find the beginning of this narrow trail the drunken shopkeeper had mentioned.

Everything had fallen into place after months of frustration. Perhaps one day he would return to visit Gail, he mused.

When she is older, he reminded himself in amusement. He didn't really hold with interfering with children, but she might be good sport when she had learned to flee.

Yes, tonight had been remarkably fortunate.

He really should have played some dice.

FIFTY-ONE

I t was afternoon. A clear day. Not a day many would think would be a battle for the fate of their realm, and more. Songwriters and commoners always talked about battles in the rain, in cloud and fog, or on a day grey as the hearts of those who fought, as if the weather would suit the mood.

Colcos knew as well as any that battle would take place whatever the weather, and after so many years there was no longer any incongruity in men lying in dappled sunshine screaming with their guts freshly spilled.

Weather was a help or a hindrance, no more.

The army was arrayed as planned, awaiting sight of their enemy, each Battalion with Companies in reserve. Dotted orange highlights gave way to light blueish, bordered by dark red and light vivid green towards the northern rise.

Recruits were excitably nervous; Guard were quiet and watchful. Veterans were pragmatic. Pathfinders reported a slowing of the Meyari; plainly, they were readying themselves for battle. He had half-expected them to wait until morning, at least, but it appeared they were eager to press the attack. He wondered if that was the influence of the church; he had never fought Teromants before.

The command tents lay just past the edge of the pines at the top of the hill. Ringed around them were the stores, then the empty camps of the allies. Next to the pathfinders, healers and recruits, the Morlanders waited, impassive. Although their slender straight swords and short broad-bladed spears were ready, they weren't there to fight; all wore the cream of the Daktarim or the red of *Mganga*.

A thousand Crosses with their unique recurved repeating crossbows lay to the south with Teal and Fire Battalions, near the slope leading west to the steep foothill face backing them. They would wait until the Novinians charged, then loose bolts to break it whilst the main force engaged the Meyari. More stood there, ready for the Teromant Chaplains. Although their weapons weren't as fast as bows, in formation and sequence they could deal a hideous amount of damage to opponents.

Next to them were three thousand reserve men-at-arms, bearing a mixture of spear and short sword and shield or heavy bills in ranks. As the battlefront tired, they would cycle through in squads and keep up the defence, giving their fellows a chance to rest.

Across the southern-facing top of the rise were two thousand more men-at-arms and two thousand archers, ready for the Novinian charge with *Moqaddim* Jiran al-Maftuh Raml and three thousand desert warriors. To the west of them, out of sight around the slopes, lay a thousand Eordeland heavy cavalry and more than a thousand *Rashim*. They would cut around the slope and flank the Novinians to try to drive them east and north into the teeth of the main defences.

The eastern slope was where the hammer would fall from Meyar, where he would stand for now with Carmine and Emerald Battalions. Looking down the slopes were three thousand men-at-arms led by Dorn, with two thousand archers along the northeast ridge and behind the lines. Next to them stood four thousand more desert troops with wicked scimitars. Slightly behind them the wedge of a thousand dwarves waited patiently. They should have the same effect as cavalry, mused Colcos. They would hopefully punch out from behind the troops deep into the enemy lines, allowing the battalions to either side to press in and divide the attackers. The dwarves didn't have many shield bearers, preferring large two-handed weapons, but were so well armoured that few strikes got through. They all wore the grey metal they called *Titan*. Lighter and stronger than steel, it was an alloy that was extremely rare, much sought after, and difficult to make. They guarded its secrets closely.

Throughout the trees, elves silently moved, each skilled in blade and bow beyond most men. They would fight in their own fashion, protecting archers and the ridge and leaving the armoured work to humans. Out of sight to the east the two thousand remaining *Rashim* waited, ready to savage the Meyari infantry.

They were as ready as could be.

The Meyari force arrayed against them was near forty-five thousand strong; they must have almost emptied Meyar. Before this Colcos would have said there was no way they could field so many and still threaten Eyotsburg, but even so they would not be a match for the Guard.

The Novinian force was also a threat. Although small in number, they were heavily armed and experienced knights, accompanied by dogs bred to war. If they could split the Guard, the reserves at the rear would be rolled over. Ulric was planted against them like a solid post, bellowing encouragement to the pikes and scythes there.

All they could do now was wait. One hour, two at the most, and the enemy would be before them all.

☙ ❧

The Eordeland archers loosely spaced through the tree fringe on the ridge had been well trained. Companies knew their range and prime targets, and had a designated master bowman with strict orders.

Lucyn Tamerlane of Fletches Company was tall and strong, a superb instinctive archer. She regularly won the Winter games, and was a ten-year veteran of campaigns in various skirmishes, some against Banistari and their lightning-fast horse archers. A fierce fighter known for not suffering fools, none would draw or loose until she did.

Sergeant Garrels had seen her in action before, fought with her. Even old Erwhist respected her skill.

Pathfinders stood with them, some moving quickly off back to the command tents, through the stakes dotting the edges of the sparse woodland, others taking their place. The squads watched the approaching mass of men moving down from the north, and there were a few soft curses.

'Quiet,' he muttered to the nearest.

He knew how they felt. The rolling low hills leading out to the plains were black with troops. Several thousand heavy cavalry moved beside loose formations of what - to his professional eye - were clearly conscripts. Battle fodder, he thought grimly. People who didn't want to be here in the first place, fouling the blades of the Eordelanders so that the trained men behind could strike down the defenders.

In stark contrast to the disorderly mass, which must have numbered four thousand or more men, the farthest side was composed of rigid ranks of the most disciplined of their enemy. A column of Teromants marched, perhaps eight thousand, and they were trained, well-armed and armoured in half plate and mail with those bright yellow horizontal crosses on standards and armour. Not as well trained as the Novinians, but religious fanatics. The levied would be easy to rout, but the Teromants would not, and they would give courage to the others.

Or fear. The result was the same.

Behind them came those curious wagons, five of them, drawn by the armoured bulls. He guessed he'd find out what they were.

Nothing good.

The main body must have as many spearmen as the allies themselves. The rear was brought up by several thousand archers using Meyari flat bows. Not as powerful

680

as longbows or the Eordeland recurves, but cheaper and easier to use and maintain, they would be the main danger until the cavalry and infantry crested the rise. Hopefully the woods would offer protection, and by that point the heavy bill squads would be staving off the horses while the soldiers engaged the troops. The trees and stakes they had placed would discourage a charge.

The archers were buoyed by the elves in the woods with them, although they were rarely seen. The elves wouldn't be loosing at long-range targets, but would work to engage any enemy that entered the woods.

To the side several thousand of the best recruits stood ready to defend the archers and rise. They looked nervous now, the confident laughter gone. Garrels wondered how many would survive the battle. Even their corporals looked too young.

Faint shouts were becoming audible over the stuttered tromp of tens of thousands of marching feet. The army gradually came to a halt just out of bowshot. The Sergeant heard whispered questions from some of the younger archers who had never been in real battle, asking if they would camp or leave. He shook his head. They were allowing all formations to catch up, fall into place, and run a final check before they took up the attack. The enemy knew where they were, and they also knew, as did every seasoned soldier, the advantage of causing the enemy to wait. Reflexes and senses dulled after a time, impatience set in, nerves frayed. Giving an army with inferior numbers time to appreciate how many more of you there were was a good part of psychological warfare.

Half an hour later, shouts were heard relaying up and down the ranks. In admirable time, the formations began to move towards the hill.

'This is it,' he called quietly, hearing his own message pass along his squad and relay to the recruits. 'Wait for the leading bow.'

The massed ranks moved towards them, and individuals began to resolve. Part of him was screaming to start loosing, to begin taking down the vast numbers as fast as possible, but he appreciated the patience of Tam. Her dark eyes were locked on the approaching army as they began to angle to their right, the cavalry reaching the bottom of the hill and pausing for the drafted men to begin their ascent.

Finally, she angled and drew, her arms locked steady, the bright green tie on her arm just visible. All down the ranks the ripple of drawing bowstrings spread, the archers following the soldier next to them.

There was a second's pause, and then a screeching wail sounded. Her first arrow, designed with a tapered chamber just behind the arrowhead with three holes drilled at angles, described a long high arc with a hair-raising noise before falling. The sound cut off suddenly as it thunked solidly down between the neck and shoulder of a lieutenant-colonel at the fore on a horse. His horse reared in fright as he toppled sideways off it, and the Spear behind milled in sudden consternation.

The arrow was the signal for the Eordeland force to loose. Thousands of arrows left the treeline on the same arc and fell from the ridge as deadly rain. Chaos erupted in the marching force on the right flank. The ill-trained levied troops fought to get away from the arrows, and it took several squads of Teromants to brutally restore order.

Shield bearers were brought up to cover the flank and the archers to the rear returned shafts, most arrows finding only trees. The Teromants were no fools; they hemmed in the panicked foot soldiers and left them only the hill to the front to escape the deadly shafts. Thousands of conscripts charged desperately up the hill into more arrows, the cavalry sweeping around south slightly to come up on the left. A roar erupted from the foot soldiers, led by the Teromants, who slowed their advance; once they had given the courage to shout defiance, they let the commoners scream their way up the hill, following at a measured pace. Many would be out of breath when they reached the top, but they weren't there as skilled fighters.

∛ ∜

General-Marshal Colcos watched them coming impassively from the ranks. He wore his customary light grey tunic under a leather and metal segmented cuirass and lightly mailed arms, his ash-hafted spear in one hand with a plain grey shield in the other. A functional, unadorned nasal barbute protected his head.

Next to him Captain-General Dorn, wearing a more usual full segmented cuirass and a plumed Imperial helm with neck and sideguards, called last minute encouragement to the men. His swords were still sheathed, but he would be leading the defence against the enemy ranks. Dorn was what Colcos considered a true leader, similar to Rast Tal'Orien; both led by example.

Wish we had Tal'Orien here now, thought Colcos, and then his lips curved into a wry smile. *If wishes were soldiers, we'd stretch to the horizon.*

As the Meyari broke into a yelling run, Dorn called to the men nearest him, hearing his orders relayed down the ranks.

'Steady! Not yet!' He turned to the messenger next to him. 'Sound the cavalry!'

The man put a field trumpet to his lips and sent out a three-note call. He repeated it, and second later they heard the movement of two thousand horses at a trot. At a yell and another horn, the thunder of a charge mounted, and the horses swept around the crest to their right.

682

The enemy cavalry moved to head them off, but they were disadvantaged with the incline, and the Eordeland heavy cavalry thundered down the slope like falling boulders. There was a moment amidst the pounding of the hooves when the world seemed to draw breath, and then the forces met with a clash that reverberated off the foothills behind them.

Lances tore into bodies and faces, clashed off shields, snapped and splintered. Both forces shuddered for barely a minute before a horn sounded and the Eordeland cavalry broke off, moving in a curve along and back up the slope, drawing the Meyari horse out. A second time, the tactic of a downhill charge worked as a thousand *Rashim* crested the rise and raced down at an angle, the ululating cries of the horse archers shrill amongst the yells and shouts.

They flashed past the Meyari in a column, their short recurves wreaking terrible destruction on the flank of the charging conscripts and the rear of the cavalry. Disorganised, the Meyari cavalry turned to follow and received a second charge from the Eordelanders, who drove into them and forced them downhill, leaving a jumble of the dying and wounded from both sides.

The disorganised remnants of the Meyari conscripts reached the front lines then and launched themselves at the wall of shields and pikes, the Meyari Spear right behind them. The Eordeland Guard fended the inexpert attacks off easily, wreaking terrible slaughter.

The *Rashim* continued in their gallop without pause, faster than their foes, and raced along the unprepared ranks of the Teromants, who hadn't expected anyone to get past their own cavalry so soon. Protected only on the side toward the ridge, arrows slashed into them in hissing flights. Hundreds fell before the horses were past, wheeling out onto the high plains and coming around to harry the rear. The agile unit was impossible to pin down, and the attack was fast enough that few Meyari turned from attacking the ridge to return shafts.

The spearmen to the rear raised shields, those along the outside locking them along the flank to minimise damage from the ridge. To the left, the better-armoured Teromants marched at an implacable jog, curving left around the hill towards the southeast, crying prayers to Terome and invoking the wrath of God on the non-believers, which ignored the fact that Terome had a well-known and busy cathedral in Darost.

Colcos moved back towards the peak of the hill and the command tents to gain a more strategic view. A full company of spearmen held back to protect their precious archers from the *Rashim*, who had wheeled and galloped across the army back around the hill to the southwest. They refused to come close enough to allow spears to land. Arrows still arced from them, forcing spearmen to shield the archers as best they could. Several Meyari companies broke away to the north as the horsemen left, escaping the carnage, and rounded the curve of the ridge.

Resisting the temptation to meet the charge with one of their own, the bills and men-at-arms of Eordeland stood firm. They were just past the cusp of the rise, meaning every attacker had to run up a hill first with little flat ground when they reached the top.

The main ranks finally smashed together with a sound like steel thunder, the Eordeland line bowing in a few places but nowhere near giving. They held firm, swords and spears carving deep into the Spear, but found their weapons fouled.

Screaming commoners, knowing the only way through was to overwhelm them with numbers and somehow get away, threw themselves bodily into the ranks, trying to open a path. They were cut down without mercy, but the sheer amount of bodies made it hard to stand, and the bodies pierced brought weapons low. The Meyari Spear struck mercilessly through their own men, and Eordelanders fell.

The Teromants curved up and around, cresting the hill in a charge and smashing into the southeastern ranks with a crash as they lowered their long spears, holding shafts between eight to ten feet in length. They stabbed over shield and into the ranks of Eordeland in a one-two motion, staggered up and down the front.

It reminded Colcos of sewing.

Soldiers fell either side, coughing blood, terrible wounds punched into bodies. Although the Teromants were ordered, they also fought with religious fervour, which worked both for and against them. They pressed the attack fiercely, tiring themselves, where the Eordelanders patiently waited, fighting to conserve their strength. The Teromants pushed forward in a narrow front, the waiting fanatics behind them singing prayers. Short sword or spear and shields formed an effective block, while pikes and war scythes dipped over shoulders, taking the religious guards in the necks or cutting into arms, some hooking shields down. Made for use against cavalry, they did equally well against foot soldiers.

For twenty minutes the masses moved up the hill, trying to push the Eordeland front back. The arrows and *Rashim* had slain hundreds, but so many came they hadn't made much of a dent. Cavalry met cavalry, and a sudden break by a large unit of the Meyari horse towards the flank line nearly caught the men-at-arms unaware. If they hadn't had polearms they would have been trampled, but they held the horses at bay. Another ten minutes of bloody work continued to the screams of men and horses, and then a rumbling clatter from the southwest announced the arrival of four thousand Novinians. Huge dogs with spiked headgear and jointed fishscale fore-body armour ran snarling with the horses in packs, trained to protect them.

'Make ready!' called Dorn, his sword red to the hilt and his shield battered. Colcos heard Ulric bellowing from the South as he moved back to the hilltop.

'Pikes set! Scythes sweep! Sound the second charge!' Similar calls cascaded up and down the ranks.

Horns pealed out, and from his vantage point Colcos saw his second unit of heavy cavalry gallop out around the crest of the rise. They were overtaken by the yelling *Rashim* on their agile and nervous desert horses, who peeled to the right and sped past the knights.

Arrows lashed out, but this time the effect was less. The men and horses of the Novinian mercenary knight-captains were clad in plate armour, as were their horses, and most bounced off. A few men and horses and many dogs fell, but the *Rashim* were forced to break off, pursued by a number of warhounds who moved to hamstring the horses. Whinnying in fear, they sped away, arrows arching back at the pursuers.

The heavy cavalry had reached a full charge, aiming at the left flank of the Novinians. No newcomers to this warfare, several companies were arrayed pikes-out, ready to wheel and face them before the knights struck. The unit condensed into a tight front, ready to crash into the Eordeland ranks. Arrows came in again but still didn't break the charge. Crossbows twanged, having more effect. Men and horses tumbled.

Just before they reached the men-at-arms, the Eordeland heavy cavalry collided with their flank.

Excellent timing, thought Colcos, trying to remain detached as people he respected were brutally butchered around him in their hundreds. He called for a summons, and a horn rang out in a series of long blasts.

Men and women screamed as lances tore into them. The Novinians were better armoured than the Eordelanders and were the superior cavalry. The attempt to push them around east in line with the Meyari failed, and the men-at-arms were forced to engage.

The line trembled and deformed further as the knights slammed into it. In several places the mercenaries had formed a wedge as they struck, carrying the forerunners far into the ranks where they and their war-trained horses lashed around them, ready for the supporting knights to push aside and widen the breaches.

Men-at-arms and bills struck back, none breaking. Knights were torn from horses by the pikes and war scythes which slammed into them, seeking chinks in the armour. Many staggered to their feet, dangerous adversaries for any soldier once up. Dogs following the horses tore into the ranks, leaping and snapping. Some were impaled by pikes, but they were a distraction for the knights and their valuable horses. Many of those were causing havoc, going mad surrounded by enemies with no way out, huge hooves stoving in skulls and blunt teeth snapping shut on anyone that came near.

It was carnage. Although the Novinians were outnumbered on this front, they had caused a lot of disruption, and weren't alone for long. The Teromants further east spread their front to meet them and drove forward.

Meyar moved up the hill and spread down around to the south, lessening the number of men exposed to the ridge archers. The secondary archers behind the flank front loosed as well, but as the unit pressed in to attack the arrows arched further out to avoid the risk of striking their own ranks. As the mass of men moved forward the rest of the summoned *Rashim* appeared from the east, striking the rear unexpectedly with their slashing arrows. They had to choose targets carefully; once they were out of shafts, the only replacements were on the field or in the supplies behind a wall of Meyari.

A commotion to the north came, screams and shouts. A pathfinder brought news of companies of archers and spear that had scaled the short rise and charged into the woods. The elves were slaying them in droves, but they had caused some damage to the Eordeland archers and recruits there.

Colcos wished he had found a funnel to shunt the incoming masses through. The south was too unprotected against these numbers. Suppressing his anxiety, he called commands to subordinates for relay and watched as his southern front flexed. He had faith, and it was well rewarded. They held.

Unexpected disaster struck ten minutes later. At five points the strange armoured wagons, forgotten by all in the melee, crested the hill at a charge. Closer to, the bulls were large white creatures, smaller and lighter than the great plains Aurochs but still the height of a man at the humped shoulders with horns curving up and out. They pulled in sixes, two at the centre and the others to each side behind in a wedge, with heavy plate armour covering all but their inside buttocks on each side and chest plate harnesses instead of yokes. They moved as fast as draft horses, charging at a shocking rate, pulling large wagons curved and scaled like insect carapaces with large doors to the sides and the rear. Rounded slitted cabins spoke of drivers pulling thick collected lines attached to nose bits. Goads prodded at the inner unprotected rumps, urging them on.

Trained to toss men out of the way, they thundered in, heads low. The Meyari Spear moved aside quickly, though some not quickly enough, and the massive beasts hurled them aside or rode them down, the heavy wagons crushing them.

They erupted through the Eordelander line amongst Carmine Battalion, the pikes and scythes not finding weak points fast enough, the bulls snorting and lowing in rage, carving deeper ruts into the shocked troops than the Novinians had. Horses didn't like charging armed men, but angry bulls didn't care. The drivers hauled back on the lines, pulling the nose bars, and the bulls skidded to a halt, stamping.

All three doors crashed down into ramps and huge men in matte white armour poured out, ten to a wagon. Colcos stared at them in astonishment; they were enormous, seven feet tall with red skirts falling from their hips. Their armour was thicker than any he had ever seen, and those pauldrons were like curved shields. The steel skull in red flames on one and the scroll on the other bracketed a polished symbol of Terome across their breastplates under a v-guard.

These could only be Teromant Chaplain Extinctors. He had never believed they existed. Old tales of holy warrior-fanatics who took stimulant drugs and were impossible to kill echoed in his memory.

He watched in despair as they smashed into his infantry like beetles into ants. They moved slowly, but the armour was all but impossible to penetrate. Huge weapons were causing havoc among his soldiers, disrupting the squads.

Alone they couldn't do much for long, but the Meyari Spear had poured into the breaches behind them along with the Teromants. The front ranks were suddenly fighting desperately for their lives on multiple fronts.

What shock troops!

He signalled to the dwarves and to Dorn. They had to counter them, and the cavalry were out of reach.

Before anyone could arrive *Moqaddim* Jiran appeared with two squads of *Jundi*, desperately moving to plug the gap. He had fought man to man with a Knight-Captain of Novin and plunged with valour into the enemy at the fore of his men without surcease, despite the Banistari wearing only light armour. Now he had lost his horse and part of his armour but he did not hesitate. He darted forward with his heavy scimitar, graceful and lithe, seeking gaps in the thick shell.

The Extinctor moved faster than expected, forcing him back, and before Colcos could believe it the hulking warrior accepted a slice to the waist, trusting his plate, and threw a powerful oversized left fist into the Banistari General's face, breaking his nose and stunning him.

Ignoring the frantic stabs of the *Jundi,* the Extinctor stepped forward and thrust a long spear through the dazed man's unprotected midsection with an awful jerk.

'No,' whispered Colcos.

Jiran slumped, impaled through the stomach. The spear stayed propped in the ground, holding him above his fallen men. The rest went berserk, swarming the Chaplain, but other Extinctors arrived and drove them back.

A great man, thought Colcos with regret. If he lived, he would carry word of Jiran's courage to the Banistari court personally.

Dorn moved rapidly through the ranks toward the nearest Extinctors, collecting billmen with him. He arrived and roared for the pressed Guard to fall back, the fresh pikes coming to the fore in concert. The Chaplains tried to advance, hacking at the points, but enough pikes kept them back, probing their armour for weak points. One caught in a helm in one of the breathing holes and almost pushed it off. Dropping his huge mace, the Chaplain reached up to secure it and retreated.

One by one the Guard pushed forward, using massed pikes to slow, then reverse their advance. Then the crossbows arrived, and the fatal twangs cut through the furore. Bolts skipped off, but three of them fell. Two more toppled with armour pierced at joints by slicing war scythes, overwhelmed by Guard who held them immobile or hacked at their straps.

Colcos watched with interest as, further away, a squad of dwarves emerged to face an equal number of the hulking brutes. The Extinctors advanced tirelessly, swinging. The dwarves lined up in a wedge, the foremost with a huge two-handed hammer that held what looked like a chiselled spike on the rear. Chanting, they strode forward. Colcos was struck by how much they looked like smaller versions of the Extinctors they faced.

They collided, the men smashing the smaller dwarves aside, but the resilient foe kept their feet and struck back. The Teromants appeared shocked. Dwarves were generally stronger than humans and knew fighting in heavy plate better, and theirs was far superior. They also had weapons of *titan* alloy which were light and strong and pierced steel more easily.

The first dwarf's hammer creased a poleyn hard enough that the knee joint stopped working properly. His return stroke blocked the spiked axe that came in and casually reversed his grip, spinning the haft and striking down with all his power.

The chiselled spike rammed straight through the breastplate next to the symbol of Terome, causing the man to stagger and clutch his chest, suddenly wounded.

The dwarf stepped back and shouted, swinging his hammer up in an arc that hit the underside of the helm with crushing force. The Extinctor toppled back lifeless to the earth.

Beside him a dwarf was hammered to the floor by a mace, staggering back upright and attacking again, though clearly injured. One of his fellows slammed a spiked mace into the face of another brute, felling him with the blow.

A call from the side made them laugh with grim humour; one of them had studied the armour then darted in, sliding a bolted lever. The Extinctor had locked bolt upright on one side and fallen like a tree. Shouts called the discovery over. The smaller folk had more strength and stamina than these giants, able to penetrate the thick armour and now lock it, and the Extinctors moved back, three of their number down to one dwarf wounded.

A horn rang out from the wagons and as one the war machines turned and trudged back, their job done. One of them stopped and directed Spears to pick up a fallen comrade; a Spear argued, and the man almost halved him with his broadsword. The rest picked up the heavily armoured corpse, dashing to the wagon.

The hidden drivers goaded their bulls and turned them slowly, and the shock troops withdrew. Two of the bulls were struck in the unprotected rear, one by a bolt that lamed it instantly.

Despite the damage done, the Eordeland Guard had heroically thrown the Spear and Teromants back, almost closing the breaches again, but they had lost many to the surprise attack.

Colcos chewed his lip bitterly. They wouldn't be caught by them again, but it shouldn't have happened at all.

The battle raged for over an hour longer before men each side withdrew slightly, the Eordelanders moving in orderly squads to replace tired men. The Meyari Spear had far more fresh coming forward to engage. The Novinians had sustained a few hundred knights down or dead but had killed many more. Thousands lay unmoving, blood soaking the earth.

The knights moved back, whistling their huge dogs in and swinging around for another charge. The *Rashim* were still raking up and down the normal troops in long curving sweeps, trying to distract the Spear and having some success. They had only lost a hundred, too fast for most troops to hit, and took the opportunity to restock arrows.

Wounded were passed back to the centre, and the Morland Daktarim went to work, healing as well as they could. There were five *Mganga* amongst them, red robes edged in square designs. Colcos saw miracles performed to save lives and heal wounds that should have killed, leaving men and women once more able to fight, but it was not enough to balance those lost.

The respite was brief; the armies came again, led by the relentless Teromants. An hour and a half later, the fighting was less fierce, the combatants settled into the energy-saving rhythm that replaces adrenaline.

Colcos reviewed his map with Ulric, placing pieces and calling orders to be sent to the horn. He wondered when they would pull back. Battle had an ebb and a flow, which depended on the field, the combatants, the goal, and the course of battle. An all-out attack wasn't sustainable for long, even with overwhelming forces.

Several of the levied squads had managed to escape. In their panic and with their lack of training, they had also impeded the advance of the Teromants and Meyari Spears more than once. The Guard let them run.

The sky was still clear, although the afternoon was waning towards dusk and shadows crept up from the western mountains. Meyar had managed to begin to push the lines back when the Dwarven wedge moved out into their front ranks, chanting and striking powerfully with their fantastic weapons. Much slower than cavalry but inexorable in their advance, the wedge drove into the spearmen as if by a hammer. The stout fighters used weapons sharper and stronger than the enemy's to carve a deep hole into Meyari ranks, opening up plate armour with ease. Cries of *dwarves* and *magic weapons* rose. No cavalry could get through the press to support them, and they retreated.

Once the dwarves were deep into the enemy lines, beset on all sides, they began to expand sideways, becoming a rounded rectangle. The men-at-arms either side took heart at the brief respite, moving up in wings at the barked commands of the lieutenants. Suddenly the enemy were facing a rout there instead of a break in the enemy line, and only the arrival of several thousand more men prevented it. Despite this, they didn't regain all the ground they had lost, and men wouldn't willingly face the dwarves, whose armour was all but impervious to steel and who wielded their weapons with the air of those who ate with them, slept with them, forged them.

The elves had spied more squads of men trying to slip through the trees, including a squad of Plains Walkers, who had bypassed the battle and tried to move around to access the command tents. They were elite troops, experts in camouflage and close fighting, but now they faced elves.

The ageless woodland folk released their deadly and accurate arrows, rarely missing. Where they were closer, they fought with knives and swords, quicksilver-sharp. No elves fell; no Walkers broke through.

They held their enemy at bay on all fronts, men and women performing incredible feats. Their greater training and weapons were telling, but Colcos was still frowning as Ulric arrived back again. He had expected their foe to withdraw and regroup after not being able to break Eordeland quickly. Heavily outnumbered, they still had the advantage of ground, and each Eordelander was accounting for multiple enemies. Yet the enemy fought on, relentlessly.

Something wasn't right.

FIFTY-TWO

Councillor Ulric was discussing strategies with General Colcos in case the attack continued on into the night when an ungodly screeching erupted, and a roar went up from the reserves not far behind them to the west. The burly Councillor bellowed through the chaos.

'What in the *hells* is that?'

A few minutes later a wounded armsman with a bloodied emerald band stumbled into the tent. The man's face was grey with shock.

'Orcs! Orcs come from the west, out of the mountains. They fall upon us from behind. We're trapped!'

There was a moment of stunned silence in the tent, against a backdrop of screams and fighting.

How can that be possible? thought Ulric. No army could move that many through the mountains at such speed. Then his thoughts turned sour.

No army of men. We have underestimated our enemy.

The sun still gave light, but it had dropped further, the mountains beginning to cast the battlefield in shadow. The creatures would not be so hurt or blinded by the waning day.

Colcos caught his eye and snapped orders.

'Send to the battalions to hold them while we prepare to clear a path through the Meyari. Divert Emerald Battalion. All reserves are to hold the rear. Send to the elves and the archers on the ridge to reinforce them. Set the crossbow ranks to fire through the shoulders of the pikes. Keep discipline, it is the only thing that will hold firm against that rabble.' The men saluted and ran. He turned back to the messenger. 'What numbers do we face? What is the composition of the troops? Anything, man.'

'At least as many as the Meyari,' said the man bitterly. 'More. We had barely any warning. It was only luck that pathfinders caught movement as they rounded the foothills from the west. They have hundreds of ogres with them, too. My squad was just back from the Meyari front, and two of those creatures killed everyone. I'm all that's left! We're finished!' His voice bordered on hysteria. Men around him muttered.

Colcos drew himself up, his eyes flashing. His cultured voice cut though the noise to everyone nearby.

'Get a grip, man! You are a soldier of Eordeland. *We will hold.* They come uphill, and we hold a superior position. The Meyari are far more exhausted than we are, and those fresh cannot get to our front easily. Our cavalry is holding the Novinians at length. The next man I hear saying we are finished will find himself on charges.' His expression softened. 'Take heart, private. You have done well. If you think any orc is worth even one of you, you are very wrong. We fight for our homes and families.'

The soldier looked ashamed. 'Sir. Sorry, sir. Heat of the moment.' He brightened slightly. 'The dwarves turned to meet them. Even the ogres find *them* hard going.'

Colcos took heart at that; their allies were known for their dislike of the foul creatures. He nodded to the man's bloodied shield arm. 'Get that seen to before you return. And know that Ulric and I will be behind you.' The soldier's head lifted, and he saluted.

'Sir!'

As he exited the tent through the pinned-back flap, Colcos turned to Ulric.

'About a mile behind him,' grunted Ulric wryly. Colcos ignored him. This was no laughing matter.

'This is desperate, Ulric. We are surrounded by four times our number. We relied on the hills to protect the west.' He pulled his tunic straight under his cuirass. 'The Novinians will be harder to deal with than the Meyari. If we use the dwarves and call to the cavalry to attack, I think we can punch a hole through the Meyari army and move northeast through them. We must withdraw to Darost at the first opportunity.' He sighed. 'I'm sorry, old friend. This should have worked. We wondered where those blasted orcs had gone; now we know. We must make preparations to fall back… if we can break free.'

Ulric shook his shaggy head. He was tired, feeling the aches and pains of combat that he would have brushed off fifteen years ago.

'If our only other option is death, then we must retreat,' he said bitterly. 'We have been out-manoeuvred.'

'We still face a great many of the Meyari,' said Colcos wryly, 'but if we can find a way to make them retreat enough…'

'An all-out attack?' remarked Ulric from under bushy brows. He grunted and bared his teeth in a smile. 'The trouble is the Teromants. They goad the conscripts and have proved hard to break, despite heavy losses.' He muttered to himself for a moment, then barked a laugh. 'Here! They have a Primate of the Church there, no doubt giving proof that their God has decreed this is divine will to destroy us. You saw him earlier, near that monstrous wagon the size of a small house. If we can kill him… they may withdraw enough that we can reinforce the rear.'

'That could work,' said Colcos. He called instructions out to men to relay to the battalion commanders. 'If it doesn't… we are going to lose a lot of good men for nothing.'

'We need something, or we're going to lose a lot more,' said Ulric sourly. 'Can we beat the Novinians back?'

'Perhaps.' Colcos turned to another messenger. 'Sound for both units of *Rashim* and all cavalry to bear on the Novinians. Hold them at bay, drive them back, but free up those ranks! As soon as we free up men on the Novinian front, reinforce the rear.' He shook his head and looked at Ulric. 'This will be tight. If it doesn't work… well. It has been an honour fighting with you.'

'It will work,' scowled Ulric. He clasped the man's arm, and then said, 'Best get to it. I'll move to the west and command the reserves against the orcs. You look to the east. And pray for a miracle.'

ᴄ⋅ᴔ

The Banistari were wreaking havoc in the ranks of the Meyari, the *Jundi* fiercely blocking the the spear and conscripts and the Teromants fragmenting under the arrow waves of the *Rashim* to their rear and flanks.

The dwarves had moved further into the hills, soaking up attacks from the orcs and blocking any attempts to flank by the mobile Novinians, who were learning to give them a wide berth. Calavry had less advantage in the rougher ground, and the dwarves were exactly the wrong army to use horses against. They had long weapons and were heavily armoured enough that even riding down by horses didn't incapacitate. They also chanted war songs as they fought, which seemed to unnerve the horses, and moved in unison, delivering shattering blows to their enemies, breaking charger's legs and smashing through the Novinian's steel plate with alarming ease.

When the orcs had sprung their trap, the dwarves had moved quickly to take the brunt of the attack. Astonishingly, their losses were relatively light so far, and more than nine hundred dwarves met the incoming orcs in a fighting wedge. Normally being surrounded on two sides was a disadvantage, but the dwarves deliberately split the incoming army. The unison of their fighting disoriented the orcs, who were chaotic at the best of times. Once split, the wedge would expand into an advancing front, the sides rushing up and piling through the army intent on the sides of the wedge. This spike and wave motion was repeated and served to thoroughly confuse the badly organised front of attacking orcs.

Even more at home in the hills and gullies than the orcs, the dwarves used the terrain to their advantage, giving ground grudgingly to a foe many times their number. For every dwarf that fell, the orcs fell nearly in tens. Nevertheless, the numbers told, and the dwarves were slowly being overwhelmed.

They had less defence against the ogres, their clubs smashing bodies to jelly even through the wondrous armour.

The rear ranks were being pushed back towards the crest, despite their best efforts to hold. The allies, afloat in a sea of enemies, were being dragged down. The cavalry that could help were busy with the Novinian mercenaries, and that front was depleted as more rushed either west or east. The allies were being compressed. It would be a bitter fight, and the chances of success were slimming rapidly.

Respite came from the Meyari front. They were tired, not being as adept at cycling men as the Eordelanders. A concentrated volley from the archers cleared a space a few tens of paces in front of the Eordeland lines, and several thousand Banistari warriors charged forward, their heavy swords carving a line through the enemy. From behind them punched a block of men-at-arms, two full companies with a few squads of archers to their rear. They split sideways without warning deep within the enemy, disregarding the blades and spears, many falling in agony. They caught the Teromants by surprise, and the men-at-arms battled north fiercely.

The archers took aim, ignoring the blades that cut them down, and sent volley after volley out into the midst of the commanders of the Teromants, raining around the vast wagon. Several were struck, two killed.

The Primate, resplendent in his mitre and heavy robes, was transfixed by several shafts. His horse was struck by many more, and he shrieked in pain and anger before the horse fell heavily, neighing in agony, and tried to roll to its feet before sinking to its side, flanks heaving. A bloody crushed mess to the side spoke of the fate of the Primate, and the nearest Eordelanders cheered and pushed forward.

The Teromants fell back, many cut down as they stared, unable to believe that God had not protected their leader. Extinctor Chaplains boiled out of their wagons, roaring, and charged at the attackers. The few surviving Eordelanders fell back at a horn call, Colcos clenching his jaw in triumph, silently saluting the fallen. He could see the disarray within the religious fanatics, their faith shaken, and the Spears faltered as they pressed forward. For the first time in hours, the Meyari forces began to let up, relieving the east.

Horns called, and the panting troops at the front facing Meyar found rest as squads moved to reinforce the west.

Ê Ë

Colcos left Dorn in charge of the Meyari front and joined the western flank. Next to him Ulric swore violently.

The fiercest fighting was now against the orcs. The creatures had no plans for conquest, no moment of empathy for another like them. They came to kill, to maim, to murder, later to feast. They were feral, ferocious, and brutal.

Still, they were not fighting well. The sky was still light, and their vision and resolve were bad. They had moved fast and far, fresher than the allies, but not by much. Once night came, they would be far deadlier.

Ogres dotted the new attackers, launching dead men with each brutish swing. Some bastard had trained them in squads and armoured them with crudely beaten metal and shields. They were devastating to the Guard around them. Even the dwarves were forced to fall back, and the elven bows were not accounting for them quickly enough.

Even as he watched, one roared in rage and swung a mace up, whipping it down to crush two men into the earth. Blood spurted from their burst forms, and the creature bellowed in triumph. It swung the mace back to strike again and clanged it off another ogre, which swung a slow punch at it in anger, the battle forgotten. Fifty feet away, another stood amongst the press of orcs and men battling for their lives. It was roaring with blood drooling from its mouth as three heavy pikes transfixed it through its ribcage, slicing its lungs to shreds. Even as he watched, a brave man-at-arms darted behind to hamstring it. Halfway through the move an orc caught him from behind and stabbed into his spine, and he fell under his gigantic foe as it toppled slowly backwards.

Surreally, he saw a dwarf launched by a swing from another beast in an arc to crash into several others nearly fifteen feet away; in awe, he watched the incredibly tough folk bounce back to their feet and smash straight back into the fighting, including the injured one, who had somehow held onto his war hammer.

Nearer the trees, an injured ogre bristling shafts was felled by a single elf, who ran at it, springing over a swipe and twisting to lash out with a fine sword, slicing its throat wide open before he somersaulted to land behind it with a roll as it sank clawing at the dark bloody gash.

A shift, a moment, and the battle front swept to their very feet, men and dwarves giving ground smoothly to each side.

Ulric bellowed and lunged forward, burying his axe deep into the neck of an orc trying to avoid the stabbing spears around him, warding others with his thick shield. Beside him Colcos stabbed with his spear with economical, deadly thrusts. To his left, the dwarves were grim-faced and chanting in a constant low rumble, swinging their incredible weapons with no sign of weariness. An ogre lost half a leg and fell crying out in dim terror, a testament to the power of the mountain folk.

Morlanders led by Asha'ne leapt unarmoured into battle to protect the wounded, their slender swords and wide-bladed short spears darting. They were hard to strike, and moved a little like Tal'Orien, Colcos thought. As they fought, they called and sang rhythmically, Asha'ne calling a phrase and his people replying in deep voices.

To his right, three ranks of Guard held firm as elves moved behind them, every arrow finding a mark. Occasional mounds that looked like porcupines dotted the heaving sea of orcs, ogres fallen victims to the woodland folk's skill. Any breaks in the ranks were closed up quickly and professionally, and individual orcs only went near the elves once, hating their bright aspect.

Slowly, almost imperceptibly, the compression of the allies slowed, and Ulric and Colcos moved back, looking around.

The Meyari mounted another attack to the east, but it lacked the spirit of the first, and for now at least the Extinctors were staying back. The Novinians had broken free of the cavalry to the south but had withdrawn a distance and moved more east; Colcos was unsure if they were readying another attack or weren't pleased to be fighting alongside orcs. Novinians had their own honour, bound to their purses though it was.

Then again, they might also effectively block the retreat to Darost from there. He knew from experience that any withdrawal that dissolved into disorder ended with most of the retreating slaughtered. They couldn't afford that.

The fight had been going now for nearly five hours. Colcos couldn't remember the last battle that had gone so long without break, but this wasn't a normal battle. The orcs would fight into the night, their natural element, and wouldn't stop until they had won or been routed.

The allies might still end up crushed between two armies, but the orcs had found a new annoyance in the form of *Rashim,* a thousand of whom were shaving troops from their flanks with arrows as a farmer might shave cheese with a knife for his sandwich. The creatures did not have the discipline of the allies, and were shrieking in rage, chasing the horses only to be run down by the heavier cavalry following them.

The dwarves and elves were blunting them, too, along with *Jundi* and Eordeland Guard.

They could hold for a while, even longer if the Meyari were slow to re-engage. Perhaps long enough to rout one enemy, and if one went, the other might follow long enough for the allies to flee.

There was hope yet if they could withdraw; there were simply too many enemies to stand against. They had exacted a terrible price from all three armies arrayed against them, but had in return lost a third of their own, and were still hugely outnumbered. When they retreated, they would lose many, many more.

Colcos had a moment of regret. Though they had performed miracles here, it wasn't enough. He snapped off commands to those around him, ensuring that the allies and ranks were ready to withdraw if they saw a weakness in the Meyari line.

Tapping Ulric on the shoulder, they fell back to the command tent. Both of them were aching. Ulric was panting and moving a little stiffly. He had accounted for several orcs and helped bring down an ogre, but there had been no storybook heroics, although he had seen countless real heroics that day. No one had broken ranks, the only reason they were all still alive. Recruits had stood shoulder to shoulder with seasoned troops. They had seen them blocking strikes at the Morlanders and wounded, one young dark-skinned corporal killing three orcs.

After today they would all be veterans, Colcos mused.

Those that live.

Very faint noises like thunder echoed through the clamour around them, virtually indistinguishable over the din. Colcos hoped there was no rain on the way, but the sky was clear. Perhaps a rockslide had been set off by the weight of their foes in the hills. The shadows stood even with sunlight now, stretching slowly over them from the peaks to the west.

'We are holding,' Ulric said bluntly, drinking from his flask. The men were being cycled as before, although this time it was from the centre out to three fronts. It couldn't last for long; they were all exhausted, but the Meyari were dispirited, and the orcs had not crashed over them as they'd hoped. The battle had lost some momentum.

'At least until we can find the right moment to cut east and retreat,' replied Colcos. 'There are fewer of them now; we may find our land less destroyed than we had feared when they pursue.'

Ulric grunted. 'None came through the trees to the north.'

Colcos smiled wryly. 'There are elves still in those trees, and ogres seem to prefer room for their clubs. The hillside there is very steep and dotted with stakes. The orcs are reluctant to enter. We were lucky, there.'

'And what if we can't retreat? Can we last until dawn? The orcs will have to leave at sunrise. They had to wait until near dusk to attack. The dwarves say the sunlight makes them sick and dizzy.'

Colcos shook his head slowly.

'I fear if we must stand tonight, old friend, none of us shall see the dawn. We hold our own, for now, but come full night, after hours of battle? I am told orcs can see in the dark as well as elves and dwarves. If we cannot break free in the next hour, Ulric, this rise will be where we meet our fate.'

Half an hour later, a scout brought welcome news, along with the Dúfr. The Dwarven leader looked as if he had been dipped in dark blood, and grimly satisfied by it.

'The orcs pull back to regroup! They try to round up the ogres and work themselves up for a new charge.'

Ulric laughed, a release of tension. 'They seemed dismayed when they could not break our lines at once.'

The dwarf nodded shortly. 'Aye. They have less courage in a direct attack than the humans we faced earlier. You saw their disarray. They have little structure and little to give them heart. Orcs prefer to kill in the night from safety; I think our teeth have put them off.'

Colcos looked over at where the creatures were reforming. The orc ranks were loose enough to hardly warrant the term. Ragged lines of mismatched warriors glared balefully at their foe in the waning day but made no move; the orcs waited for full night. They had lost thousands against the allies, but there were still far too many left. Behind them, he saw the Meyari ranks reassembling, and swore softly. They were preparing to assault them again, presumably waiting until the orcs struck before they also renewed their attack.

It was what he himself would have done.

Without warning roars and shrieks rippled through the orcs. The ones nearest the front stared in hatred, rattling their weapons.

'What are they doing?' asked Ulric.

'Psychological warfare,' answered Colcos. 'Every man they panic with this display is a man easier to kill.'

The taunting went on for several minutes before a new sound came. The noise from the orcs died out in seconds, replaced by muttering and coarse laughter.

A symphony of howls cut through the air, sounding strange and terrible. Men clutched their weapons nervously and muttered, but cries of distress came from the elves.

'Ai! Ai! Ráka!'

'What new deviltry is this?' asked Colcos.

He was answered by a sudden assault from the south, the attackers surging up the hill and engaging his men so fast they couldn't react. A wave of grey, black and brown fur crashed over the ranks of men. Screams of fear erupted as weapons slowed the enemy for seconds at best; bestial snarling and roars of anger resounded. Blood poured from terrible wounds as chaotic creatures tore out throats, ripped off limbs, and left a trail of dead and dying. They were a far greater threat than even ogres and moved with inhuman speed and cunning.

'No,' breathed Ulric. 'What are those?'

Colcos remembered Night's warning. 'Werewolves,' he said disbelievingly.

Cries spread, terror in the voices. Several hundred creatures from the darkest myths of men were made terrible flesh, tearing through armoured soldiers as if they were straw.

The orcs still did not charge, watching and laughing horribly. Men and women had necks snapped, shields bent, throats torn out. They were eviscerated through chain mail, slaughtered by unnaturally long teeth bathed in hot blood.

The werewolves barely slowed when they hit the ranks, their terrible wounds healing almost immediately. They ignored the pain and the horrible gaping holes in their bodies, boring through the ranks in seconds, snapping and snarling and sending seasoned veterans into panic.

The orcs were a horrible foe, something most had thought stories, but they fought and died like men. These were different. They were nightmares, and mortal men couldn't stop them. Only two werewolves lost their heads in frenzied defence; the rest were unstoppable.

Some slowed when they met the dwarves. Even their awful strength could not tear through *titan*, and the stoic squat warriors caused more damage with their weapons than any others. A few were feathered liberally with shafts from hidden elves. Some went down snapping in real pain. Something in some of the arrows and dwarven weapons had wounded them; they *could* be hurt, at awful cost.

'Rally the men!' roared Ulric. 'Drive them back, anything it takes!'

Even as he bellowed, discordant horns sounded amongst the orcs and shrieks of bloodlust sounded as they heard the rumble of a charge. Answering horns sounded from the Meyari troops.

Colcos twisted his lips bitterly. 'We are lost. Those things alone are enough to tear us apart. We must retreat *now*, or there will be no-one left.' He waved the nearest white-faced messenger over to sound the full retreat, but paused, as even over the din a new sound broke through. The ground seemed to tremble, and a horn far deeper than any before sounded to the immediate south behind the fury of the shapeshifters.

'Have we not enough?' bellowed Ulric in fury, his face red and his mighty arms wielding his axe as if to hew the entire field before him.

For the first time in his career, Colcos felt despair. No one could ever say they hadn't faced incredible odds here. He just would have preferred it if they had lived, for the sake of his realm - for his wife and two sons - but there was no running now.

A new foe joined the battle.

ʘ ʘ

The army of orcs shuddered like a great creature, roars of confusion spreading north through the disordered ranks.

'What happens?' cried Ulric.

The answer heartened him no end, and he could see the effects on the Guard as the words came.

'The Tribes! Orks and Barbarians come to our aid!'

Moving as quickly as his bulk allowed to the nearest rise, he looked out and in the fading light saw thousands of warriors, huge orks to the southwest and large fierce men and women in fur and woad to the south. An unearthly chanting call followed them, something between a hum and a bird call. It was interspersed with that incredibly deep distinctive horn, which he knew could only come from the four-foot horn of a great aurochs bull. It rose and fell without stopping, throbbing in the air, and the Barbarians seemed to flow with it.

The orks had only one thing in mind. As one, the huge men and women bared their tusks and roared at their hated fallen brethren. The mighty green warriors tore through the fringes of the Novinian mercenaries, barely slowing in their rage and lust to get to the orcs, their ancient hatred kindling in their characteristic berserk rage. Heedless of protecting themselves, they would have had more losses were it not for the Barbarians, who crashed straight into the ranks of the attackers and covered their charge as they turned to engage the orcs from behind.

They fell upon the Novinians and the werewolves alike, their speed and ferocity countering the mounted companies and their reflexes almost matching the chaotic monsters.

Several thousand orks and as many Barbarians slammed into the enemy like a dwarven hammer into soft clay.

The orcs not confronted by this new attack found themselves at the end of actual dwarven hammers as the reinforcements gave the defenders newfound resolve. The Eordelanders cheered and launched a counter-attack.

Slowly, the allies began to hew the orcs apart, turning their crushing reinforcement into bloody pulverisation.

The orcs had turned to fight their cousins, and despite the vast disparity in numbers looked on the edge of panic. Even the ogres were reluctant to face their berserk brethren as they killed and maimed hundreds every minute. The orks were slamming through the foul army full pelt, roaring in rage.

Many of the werewolves turned to engage the Barbarians, only to find themselves faced with more than just blades. A wordless trilling chanting rose in volume and pitch, a counterpoint to the soaring deep voice of the horns. Scores of the strange and reclusive hooded Sergoth Shamen stood, their voices turning into a shriek, and many of the werewolves paused, clutching their ears in agony. The Barbarians had green-stained weapons which were having a marked effect on the werewolves, the cuts causing agony and slow to heal. They continuously wiped them against sodden green cloth at their belts.

Ulric swore he saw one Shaman, his robe cast back to show a strange bird mask which appeared to have glowing blue tattoos. He threw his hands forward towards a cluster of his people, who immediately struck with such frenzied power for a few seconds that a werewolf was almost dismembered in moments, writhing and snapping. Next to the dwarves, and the arrows of the elves which seemed to somehow hurt the monsters, they were the only army having any real effect on the creatures.

It was a respite only; not enough were being killed. The werewolves were in danger of coring the Barbarians and reaching their Shamen, who seemed to provide a binding spirit and power through their chosen that defied normal human fatigue. If the strange bird-masked figures fell, he could only guess what it would do to the abilities of the Barbarians.

The noise of thunder and a lowing deep enough to split the world were loud now. With a heave, the Barbarians threw their monstrous attackers back in smooth unison that should have been impossible to achieve with so many in the chaos of battle.

They leaped back as the reason for the noise finally became apparent.

The plains cavalry had finally arrived; giant aurochs bulls and the huge brown *rinoks* of the orks, vast powerful flesh that moved with the inevitability of mountains. The *rinoks* swept North like a landslide as the aurochs lowered their heads and powered through the werewolves to the sounds of yelps and crunching bone, crushing many badly under their huge hooves and spearing beasts so powerfully with their horns that some were simply torn in half.

These were no docile cattle to die at the hands of butchers or the claws of lycanthropes. The massive bulls were almost ten feet high at their humped shoulders. They smelled the unnatural predators… and hated.

The werewolves had superhuman hearing and reflexes, but intent on the humans before them, few heeded the signs. They were used to being invulnerable and took less care than those who took hurt or died; but to heal, they had to be whole. If their heart or brains were too badly damaged, their bodies couldn't regenerate them. Nothing could heal like a werewolf, their unnatural cells multiplying and repairing the damage almost immediately, but there were limits to what could be repaired before the spark of life dimmed too far.

A score of the abominations were stamped into mush or torn apart, and their attack on the Barbarians faltered. Several aurochs went down under the weight of the terrible creatures as they reacted to the charge, howling and tearing at the throats of the huge beasts. Ulric could see that if they regrouped, they would be able to avoid the lumbering cavalry. The aurochs had caught them unawares and the charge was unstoppable, but it had slowed, as all charges must.

'Come on,' he muttered to himself. This battle had turned into a complete free-for-all in the space of a few minutes, and not even a seasoned warrior could guess the outcome now, but he suspected that, given time, the werewolves out of all the combatants might be the only ones to triumph. They were too fast, too strong, healed too quickly.

Several packs of the monsters had split off, breaking through lines and ripping at everyone they came in range of. They were making their slow but inevitable way to the command tent, and he felt his mouth dry with fear. The Meyari had charged in but were being held by Dorn; Gods only knew where all the Novinians had gone. Several packs of werewolves were chasing the *Rashim* with a vengeance, catching the rearmost and pulling them and their horses down.

He watched werewolves tearing into a battalion of brave Eordelanders near the base of the hill. They fought to the last man, inflicting terrible wounds before he too was savagely torn apart in howls of bloodlust. They were already healing, several snapping gobbets of man-flesh and howling with laughter, their unnaturally long teeth catching the light. One of them glanced up at the command camp and roared something roughly to the others. They dropped their food and bounded up towards the command section, the remaining light gleaming in their eyes.

Ulric knew he was dead. Dusk encroached, not that it mattered; fighting these horrors in the day was impossible enough. It wasn't sufficiently dark for Night to aid him, and he wasn't sure where the scholars of Illuminus were, or if even they could stand up to a pack of these things. In the dark the werewolves would shred any human they found, and there were plenty here.

Another howl came from the northeast. Ulric glanced over wearily for a second, expecting another pack. He could see nothing, but when he looked back he saw the attackers inexplicably pause, snarls on their faces. There was a brief second for him to wonder what had happened.

Perhaps it was a warning, he thought. *But of what?*

More than ten creatures that looked like nothing more than giant wolves burst from the trees and flew at them. Subtly different, they weren't wolves like the red ones in the Northing Woods either; they moved with a grace and power he'd never seen before.

They caught fifteen of the werewolves before they could escape and tore into them with a violence that made him shudder.

He expected to see the horrors shrug them off as they had all other foes, but this time there was a difference. The huge wolves were faster and more agile than the foul creatures, and stronger than any normal animal on four legs had a right to be. They slashed fangs through hamstrings, abdomens, throats, tore limbs off with violent twists and shakes of their heads and jaws of bone-crushing power. Werewolves screamed in agony, and he saw with astonishment that the wounds they sustained weren't healing. Whatever the reason, these creatures had something in their attacks that prevented the werewolves' unnatural bodies from regenerating properly. Within a couple of minutes, the previously invincible creatures were dead or dying, and the blood-drenched victors were howling in victory, yapping to each other while more and more arrived to surround the rise.

Mutters ran through the ranks of men around him, and they parted as a large man in a light brown robe walked smoothly through them. He moved a little like an elf, but more primally, and his golden eyes marked him as kin to Leona.

Druid, thought Ulric.

A huge golden wolf padded next to him serenely. Several elves accompanied him, and they nodded at Ulric, signifying that they had allowed these wolves and the Druid through the woods.

Ulric found himself vaguely wondering if the Druids had control of these creatures. It seemed incredible, but after today he was prepared to believe anything.

'Councillor,' the Druid said quickly. 'I am-' he broke off as snarls and howls rose again. The wolf at his side whirled with a deep snarl of its own that spoke back to Ulric's ancient monkey origins and made him quail in his middle.

That had been the sound of death.

'I am Jonar,' he continued. At the name the wolf looked up at Ulric, the golden-green eyes searing into his. Jonar smiled. 'We promised, Ulric, to aid you. We spoke for all Druids, the *Varulfur*. We are come. And now you know our secret.' Howls and calls grew from the northeast, scores of them, and a horde of huge wolves of all colours passed around the rise at a full run. Jonar turned, ready to follow. Ulric grabbed his arm, a dreadful, incredible thought occurring.

'Are you-'

Jonar gently disengaged himself from the robe, leaving it hanging from Ulric's hand. His naked body was lean and powerful. 'We must go. We are eager to join our brothers and sisters. Hunt well, Ulric.' His grin was feral. 'We shall.'

He stood, his eyes regarding the man for a moment, and then took a large breath, as if preparing for something he was unsure about. 'It is… hard… to do this in front of the eyes of men. It has not been done before.' His eyes gleamed with wild light, and suddenly he looked less like the calm nature priest and more like the beasts he watched over. 'Tell your men not to harm those who run on four legs. Remember; we are your allies, whichever form we run in.'

He turned and sprang, his arms extending as he leapt, further than any man had a right to be capable of.

As he leapt Ulric watched in amazement. Time seemed to slow, and Jonar's features blurred slightly as he seemed to glow, swirls of hinted luminescence cascading around him. For a brief moment man and wolf existed as one, and then only the wolf landed, a huge black as large as the one next to him.

Ulric had always imagined the change of a werewolf to be horrible, agonising. This had been… beautiful, almost.

Like a fairy tale.

Jonar looked back at the astonished men and dipped his head, then threw it up and howled a challenge to the sky. Around the hill arose the answers, lighter and purer than those of werewolves. An answering challenge full of hatred and snarled words rang out from near the Barbarian front, and then the wolves were streaming towards them, hurtling as fast as their powerful bodies could manage.

The impact as the terrible creatures of chaos and the wolf-Druids met was visceral, both sides exuding a hatred that equalled anything the orks had for their own fallen kin. It was all the more terrible for the snapping and snarling and tearing, animalistic noises that creatures on two legs had learned to fear in the night long ago. Orks and men alike hastily pulled back from the carnage.

Mortals had no place in that fight.

Ulric gathered squads and tore into the orcs, pushing back into the ranks and insinuating himself into their tight weave. Before, the formation had loosened and threatened to dissolve; now the men were once again together.

He didn't know what good even these wolves could do; there were perhaps four times as many of the werewolves. He slowed as he caught glimpses of the unearthly battle.

The Druids - what had Jonar called them, *Varulfur?* - were clearly more than a match for the werewolves despite their lesser numbers. He had already seen them fight, but now he understood how powerful these guardians of nature truly were. They were more than wolf, but not as the lycanthropes were. They had the minds of men and women, but they seemed to have some *other* powers as well. They held the werewolves at bay, and then began to drive them slowly back. The werewolves clearly feared this foe that could destroy them. Although he saw Druids falling under the weight of fur and fang, many more of the twisted creatures fell. If the werewolves would just break-

He ducked an incoming jagged axe, feeling it screech off the top of his helm, and staggered. The man to his right smoothly jabbed a spear through the throat of the orc in front of him with an economical thrust and nodded with a faint smile, then turned back to formation. Ulric cursed himself. That had been an acolyte error, and he would do well to keep his mind on the business at hand. The orcs had broken through again.

FIFTY-THREE

General Colcos moved back to the rise. The original allies were regrouping, tightening their ranks and taking the chance to recover. The Morland healers were working feverishly to save lives around him. Recruits ran ceaselessly with replacement arrows and bolts and other weapons from the dwindling spares.

He could see the entire battle from here, and it was something that would remain in his mind for the rest of his life. Seasoned though he was, he had never seen anything like this.

The Gods help them, they might not even need to retreat.

They might *win*.

He had caught a glimpse of the Novinian mercenaries fleeing a detachment of aurochs bulls, easily outpacing them on their horses, but pursued by *Rashim* on their fleeter ones. They had lost almost half their number, and evidently felt they had earned their money.

The Barbarians hit the Meyari Teromants on the left flank, boring into the religious fanatics along with the *Jundi*, who had been enraged at the loss of their *Moqaddim*.

The Extinctors had reengaged but quickly found that aurochs bulls could ignore even their thick armour. Their own bulls had no intention of facing their larger brethren, and took off north, ignoring the drivers. One wagon was overturned and broken apart, flinging the driver from the wreckage to be gored by his own panicked team.

The Meyari force began to give ground rapidly to the east and southeast, faced with one implacable foe and one violent and primal foe that attacked to the unnerving chanting hum of a Shaman. They were verging on a full rout. Arrows still fell among them from the trees, and there seemed to be some kind of commotion around the house-sized wagon which was now falling into shadow.

To the west the *rinoks*, every bit as large and even heavier than the aurochs, were flinging orcs around like confetti. Even the ogres were outmatched in strength against the creatures, bowled over and badly trampled, bellowing in pain and surprise. One slammed a spiked mace into the flank of a *rinok*, expecting the creature to be knocked down or killed, but the huge animal snorted in rage and dug its long horn under the ribs of the ogre. With a powerful toss of its head, it flung the ten-foot tall creature over its back, nearly knocking off the huge orc woman who rode it. She ducked under it and leaned down to yank the mace head out from her mount, eliciting another burst of angry snorts. Enraged, it picked another ogre, its mind equating the bad wound in its side with the large creatures.

Usually placid, *rinoks* could sustain a lot of damage to their short-furred inch-thick skins, which were hard to pierce, and once they charged, they were as unstoppable as an avalanche. What they lacked in reach to horns of the gigantic bovines they more than made up for in bad temper when roused, and they could soak up a lot more damage.

Orcs were crushed underfoot or hurled tens of feet, their weapons doing minimal damage to the mountainous creatures. They screeched in fear as huge furrows were carved in their ranks, and they pushed and shoved to get away from them. With angry roars ogres were forced back or hurled to the floor and trampled to death.

Yelling, the Eordelanders threw themselves back into the fray, their solid formation holding the foul beings firm as the orks decimated their hated foe. The creatures could not stand against the fury of their kin, and shrieked and hacked with abandon at anything in their frenzy, even each other.

The orc attack was slowly turning into retreat. The Meyari were being pushed back, and the werewolves were struggling in knots with Druids. The Novinian war dogs had run at the sight of the nature priests, fear and awe overriding their training.

Against all odds, the Eordelanders and their allies slowly found themselves winning, and a roar went up again as they pressed the attack. From certain death, there was now possible victory as the enemy retreated on all fronts.

The orcs broke before the Meyari did. Hit by their ancient foe, pushed against an immovable razor-lined wall of trained men, and being carved apart by creatures that vastly redefined the term heavy cavalry, they panicked and ran in ones and twos, streaming back towards the hills. Cries went up.

'They fall back! The enemy retreat west! The orcs flee!''

Another roar erupted as the men of Eordeland gave chase, some even breaking ranks.

The allies pursued their attackers back to their original perimeter - all except the orks, who ignored all others and continued to harangue the fleeing orcs. The dwarves were clearly itching to join them but held defences. Shrieks came from the woods to the north, but Colcos wasn't sure if they held jubilation or spoke of more battle.

The western sky was light, dusk well under way by now. The plains to the south were lit from the west too, and the sky to the east was fading. It would be a beautiful evening.

The General-Marshal felt tense, however. With the enemy retreating, he wasn't sure why; even a second attack in the dark would be well met by the allies, and all the forces needed rest. The night vision advantage of the orcs was matched by the Tribes as well as dwarves and elves.

As if by a lodestone, his eyes were drawn to a shadowed rise to the northeast where the trees ended. His blood ran cold. Hadn't there been elves there?

Even as he thought it, the fair folk poured from the trees, fear on their faces, many weeping. Laments of murder in darkness reached him. They had abandoned the ridge further along.

Several dark figures stood there, one of them with hands held high. Faint shrieks of dark words reached him, and the figure fell to its knees as if under great strain. Black feelers seemed to crackle off his form, like tentacles of night, visible even in the shade of the Arkons.

A low feeling unsettled him, something like a dark bubble deep within. It was subtle but growing. Dannon Colcos had never been a superstitious man, one prone to imagined monsters. The werewolves had rocked him badly, shaken his practicality, and only by distancing himself from his emotions had he been able to view them as just another enemy. The Druids hadn't helped with that, but even they were just one more shock in a day that had profoundly changed his view of the world.

Something felt *wrong*. Something around them, *in* them. The humans felt it; the Druids were howling in what sounded like unrest. Even the orks slowed their rage-filled charge, murmuring uneasily, sensing something. The Sergoth Shamen's low chanting hum rose in pitch and sounded somehow more desperate.

Shadows skittered through his mind, echoed by shadows around them all. Images of jagged red fractures leading to nowhere crashed like lightning through him, and all around him men stood slack-faced, or fell to their knees. Horses were standing trembling or throwing riders. Panic spread, but it was a freezing panic.

Something terrible came.

A great oppression began to grow in the minds of men. A feeling akin to a dark sound vibrating through their bodies dropped through the sub-aural, an onyx pebble sinking into thick, dark oil. The agitation in the armies of chaos increased, the orcs slowing their retreat, seeming emboldened, even energised. The Meyari were much the same as the allies, apart from the Teromants, who were falling to their knees and moaning, praying, unsure if this was the work of god or devil.

Shadows coalesced slowly, gaining speed, many slipping from the hills and mountains to the west and the deeper shadows there, speeding through the men, insubstantial and cold, like living dark silk. Faster and faster they came, while a dull subsonic tone dropped through every being's head.

Wind whipped around them all, hurtling into the dark centre.

A suggestion of a vast crouched figure faded into being to the east behind the Meyari, the shadows slipping up into its form. Men cried and laughed and moaned as their minds began to give way, a few going mad at the presence of the figure, many simply losing their willpower. Weapons drooped. Elves, dwarves, orks and men staggered and moaned in fear.

The figure raised its head slowly, dark horns semi-opaque over canted dark red slits of eyes. A ragged red suggestion of a mouth opened in mocking laughter that reverberated through bodies instead of ears, and a twin-tined tail of shadow lashed sideways.

Cries split the air from those few not frozen into immobility. A few arrows winged their way at it from the elves, who forced willpower into their actions better than the humans. They burned up in flashed of dull red, seeming somehow to fall *away*.

'Ruag-dûr!'

'Demon!'

'Devil!'

'Darkling!' This last was gasped by Ulric, who stood with his teeth bared and veins starting out on his forehead. His axe had fallen from nerveless fingers and dangled on its leather thong; his shield lay at his feet.

Colcos fought the lethargy and terror in his numbed mind, pulling his barbute from his head, unable to comprehend what he saw. The very presence of this creature had disabled his army. He dimly saw Ulric trying to lift his weapon, a fierce look on his face at his own internal struggle. It was between them and safety.

A Darkling!

He had heard the tales told to the Council, but the events they had mentioned held no basis in reality for a pragmatic soldier. Now he faced nightmare made real. A small part of him found a new respect for Tal'Orien and the children who had faced one before; already some of his troops had passed the threshold to madness, gibbering and laughing, as his mind threatened to do. His will and sense of self died, and he felt stretched thin, as if his being and sanity were all too brittle suddenly. One faint hairline crack and he might shatter, never to recover.

The elves were the only mortals not frozen; crying out in horror, some flung down their bows and blades and fled, and others wept and covered their faces. Some tried to protect men stricken to immobility.

The battle chants of the dwarves had faltered, and they stood unmoving. Some sagged, crashing to their knees under the pressure. Dimly Colcos saw orks trying to force themselves to charge suicidally before their courage failed completely, but there was no need.

Their foes returned to them.

Their eyes burning with madness, one by one then two by two, then in whole units, the orcs rushed back in to slaughter soldiers who could not protect themselves. The ogres did not join them; they reacted much as the *rinoks* and aurochs did, throwing anything out of their way in their panic to escape.

Like the orcs, the werewolves went berserk, halting their rush and bounding back, only to be met by the apparently unaffected Druids.

Three dark figures appeared from the trees near the foothill, racing with impossible speed towards the ranks of men and elves.

At that moment he understood what dread the elves had fled. Something in their movement and their appearance only in the darkness suggested to Colcos that they were vampires, like the woman who had attacked him.

They were met by other blurs which sped from the northwest in the growing darkness of the foothill's umbra. With a ferocity and speed matching that of the Druids', violence erupted there.

Dimly, Colcos realised Night had finally joined the battle.

The Darkling stood slowly, savouring the terror and chaos around it. Its head came nearly level with the top of the cliff behind them to the west, hundreds of feet high. Sunlight falling on it seemed to be sucked into shadow. The baleful red eyes fixed on the rise, not on him particularly but on the allies in general, immobile in a sea of chaos. One dark figure was left slumped on the ridge; the one that had called its master.

-*Fools,*- came the crushing thought, the voice rasping through their heads in a mind-quailing tone. The pressure of the words made him gasp.

-*Your time here is at an end. You are a mistake, a marring by the foulness of perfection.*-

It raised arms and cold blackness darkened the air, as if the sun had set locally. The orb was a dim spot in the sky to the low west.

-*I am not bound by any god now. Feel the despair of chaos.*-

Jagged black lines of lightning that seethed with a dull red matching its eyes coruscated out, tearing into ranks of men, dwarves, and orks. They shot in thin, random lines horribly far through the Meyari and their mounts, ripping them to shreds that seemed cauterised and layered in ice at the same time, leaving still-writhing corpses horribly distended and changed. Pure primal chaos from outside reality tore apart their beings, the sheer concentration of it rending them apart as if cut by the finest blade in the crudest fashion. The flickering lines of absolute nothing jagged their way through the Meyari, straight through every unit of the allies in their randomised paths, and into the front ranks of the orcs, then faded.

In an instant, thousands on both sides were dead and dying; or worse, *changed* in some horrible way, mocking and mutant versions of themselves. In some places only one here or there was affected. In others, units were wiped out to a man.

The dark streams had been indiscriminate. They had flashed through the front ranks of the orcs, crackling dully, and hit Druids and werewolves locked in battle. Many orks and *rinok* were also cut down. The results were the same for every creature struck; nothing could withstand such seething chaos.

All except one force.

Some of the outlying and spreading lines reached the Barbarians, but impacted strangely against nothing, a dull translucent blue glowing into purple as a deep note tolled out for a second before fading.

The chants of the Sergoth Shamen rose tonally through the shrieking of men and beasts. It swelled, rolling over the defenders, propping up the pressure slightly from minds under siege from a seething morass of insanity. The Barbarians moved slowly forward into their allies, bringing a cessation of torment.

Madness receded from their minds. General Colcos regained control slightly. It felt as if he were swimming through treacle as he called, but he managed. Soldiers around him recovered their wills to fight, and the mad hatred of the orcs and werewolves slowed. He realised some of them were terribly close. One orc swung towards him, raising a crooked spear and cocking its arm to thrust. Barely two steps from him it met a sword straight to the chest. The weapon punched through at an angle and ripped itself from a dark hand. The orc collapsed, choking and clawing at the churned mud.

A tall, good-looking dark-skinned youth next to him with corporal's bars on his breast bared his teeth, yelling in victory. His face wore strain and tears of fright, but Colcos had seen him strike down several other orcs and survive where veterans had not, struggling against the presence of the demon.

More jagged pulses of black-red lightning tore through the armies again. Men screamed and convulsed a little distance away from him. In horror he watched one woman bulging out of her still buckled armour, her face changing and pulsing into something horrific even as her lower body dropped from her upper. It was clear she was still living and in agony as it happened; he prayed she died quickly.

He called to the Corporal.

'Sound the retreat,' he rasped, forcing the words past numb lips. 'South'.

The boy ran to the emerald-tagged body of a hornbearer and blew a ragged imperfect retreat call on the brass horn.

Men were already trying to flee. The orcs were slashing into the ranks that had routed them not fifteen minutes before. Laughing, the gigantic demon strode forward, its almost insubstantial body still causing visible damage to trees and the ground it stood on. Lines of power radiated out from it, and everything nearby fractured and twisted. It swept up a vast clawful of writhing figures, Colcos couldn't see from which army, and bit into them. Two simply vanished, and several others fell in chunks. One fell whole and screaming hundreds of feet.

Dannon Colcos knew they were all lost. This thing didn't care about any of them, whichever side they were on. It would kill them all. Its very presence warped and destroyed. It was the antithesis of life.

It was the end of everything.

08　80

A strange shriek rent the air from somewhere to the west. The demon paused, almost cocking its formless horned head. The pressure in Colcos's mind lifted further, and the surviving allies scrambled to get back from the Darkling as the darkness thinned, allowing natural light to seep back in. The orks lost no time joining their comrades as their *rinoks* stampeded south, along with most of the aurochs bulls. The presence of the demon was still mind-numbing, but no longer to the point of insanity.

Ulric stumbled up, ashen-faced. 'I never could have believed,' he stuttered. He shook his head. 'We have to retreat. *Now.*'

Colcos nodded. 'We cannot stand here.' *Or anywhere,* he thought in despair at such a foe. *If we can regroup, break their armies…* but what of this demon? Would the dragons help? He wondered what had distracted it.

This was an enemy no man could stand against, and when the spell was broken soldiers ran, helping each other up and moving as fast as they could. A full half of the dwarves were down, their comrades desperately trying to carry the bodies away; strong though dwarves were, carrying more than one comrade was not possible. Several of the *Rashim* peeled off and tried to help, but Colcos could see the bitter face of the dwarven commander, the *Jundi* fleeing south.

The Darkling could wipe them all out. That kind of power was all-consuming. But it was toying with them; enjoying their despair, in its cold way.

Another shriek rose, but not from the demon. It had a strange duality to it, and came again from the west, nearer. With a mounting horror, Colcos began to suspect a new dread. He glanced at Ulric, whose face was resigned, slack in terror.

'I know that noise.' The robust Councillor sounded beyond exhaustion.

A crunching, clattering slither became audible. The demon lowered its arms, ignoring the mortals.

A dual shriek rent the air, interspersed with the agonised screams of hundreds of orcs. Colcos turned slowly to see a sight he had only heard of from survivors of Darost; perched on the lip of the foothill to the north, two vast heads curved around. One glared with a roiling, sickly-yellow orb at the profusion of life it found on the rise before it, and the other was fixed on the huge demon of darkness standing the other side. The eyes were bright in the shadow of the sun, which had nearly set. A tail curled around the base of the foothill, long pulsing pink veins hanging off the end. They were dark with orcs and a few ogres writhing in pain and terror, being sucked dry of vitality. The rest of its bulk was hidden.

Arrows soared in flights as the shifted focus of the Darkling freed the allies to act. The shafts stuck where they would have bounced from the armour of a dragon, but the gargantuan creature didn't even notice the pinpricks apart from flinching its heads back and blinking the yellow orbs in their protective leathern hoods as they weaved.

'Yosgaloth,' breathed Ulric.

Colcos shook his head. It was too much to comprehend. If the ancient demon found its way to Darost again, everything sacrificed was for nothing - his, the dragon's, all of it. Dimly, he heard the blast for retreat call again.

Where are the dragons? He thought desperately.

Then he remembered they had left Anaria.

Six wet air-holes pulsed at the bases of the serpentine demon's necks as it drew in a breath, and then both mouths opened in that horrible shriek again. One whipped sideways and blasted green caustic mist over a large knot of werewolves, then snaked down to snap shut on them as they writhed in agony, their incredible healing trying to counter their bodies dissolving. The other narrowed the orb in focus and a sickly yellow beam burst forth, decimating any living creature it touched. It swept through the dark blurs where vampire fought vampyre and carved some of both sides into steaming chunks, immortality torn from their sectioned bodies.

The armies broke. There could be no survival between these titans.

The allies grimly fled south, ignoring enemies they ran next to. Dwarves moved in an unstoppable trot, leaving their dead with their precious weapons and armour. Orks and Barbarians rode as fast as their steeds would take them, carrying their precious cargo of shamen who had stopped chanting as if afraid to draw the attention of Yosgaloth upon them. Orcs scattered away from the hungry demon.

Colcos and Ulric found themselves running south with the better part of their men. It was downhill and away from trees and the monsters that threatened them all. Elves were overtaking the humans; Druids overtook both.

A beam of light struck the earth with a dull thump and swung through units of Banistari and Eordelanders before continuing through orcs. Pieces of men and horses erupted and hit the ground, smoking and foul. A rolling bank of green mist blasted down the hill almost immediately afterward, and in horror the fleeing combatants saw hundreds of orcs begin to rot to slime with appalling speed, screaming through already frightful faces that were distending like melting candles into a morass of organic goo filled with rapidly-pitting bones. Weapons corroded thousands of years in seconds, save only the grey metal of the dwarves, which fizzed.

Yet it seemed that Yosgaloth was not so interested in those before it. The attacks felt incidental, a precursor. One head remained fixed on the demon, which was immobile, staring at the most ancient being of this world as if trying to judge what it truly was.

Without any warning, the vast nameless horror lurched forward over the lip and down the slope, crushing thousands of hapless orcs. It was aiming directly at the dark form before it.

The air dimmed more as the Darkling appeared to grow and compact at the same time. It hissed and flung its arms forward, far thicker ropes of black-red lighting roared forth than before, horrifying in their intensity. They crackled over the neck and side of Yosgaloth, which screamed in agony and flailed wildly as it was smashed back. The energies left smoking scars, but amazingly didn't have the same effect on the vast creature as on mortals. Whatever Yosgaloth was, it wasn't normal flesh and blood. Ichor tricked thickly from the cracked flesh.

Almost before Colcos could draw breath, the weaving heads had focused on their attacker and two pale beams of light lanced out, striking the Darkling with terrible force. The shadowy figure was slammed backwards, one beam where its shoulder appeared to be penetrating through for a second.

A subsonic wail rose as the twin-tined tail of shadow thrashed, killing hundreds and splintering several nearby trees.

The titanic opponents glared with hatred at each other.

ʘʘ   ʘʘ

The Darkling knew this foe. Its own essence, and that of its siblings, had warped the demon's hunger into something all-consuming and mindless, and through its own agent on Kuln it had affected its release to sow chaos throughout the mortal realms. Never had it considered this nameless demon to be a threat. It was still merely a creature of this world, after all.

The agony when it struck was unexpected and intense, worse even than Dragonfire from that red dragon.

Now it sensed the chaos and power sleeting throughout the creature's form, and realised that this was a being that was more than flesh. It would take more power than it was prepared to use to best this enemy. The Darkling would far rather leave it to continue its feeding and use its own energies elsewhere. Unconcerned with petty victory, it desired the dissolution of reality above all else, according to Zaax's design.

When the universe was rent unto chaos, all would resolve back into pure formlessness, including this creature. But before then, without the dragons and their great kin to keep it in check, it would decimate all the realms of Anaria, leaving the land lifeless.

The dragons had been diverted. All would fall in chaos.

Preparing to leave the mortals to their doom, the Darkling began to dissolve its essence into the shadows.

ʘʘ   ʘʘ

Yosgaloth hungered.

It had sensed the dragons above, had crept through lightless caverns under the Arkons with great cunning. Two had been less cautious than they should and had been consumed. The battles had been great, but each time it had won, as it knew it must.

Feeding on them had made it far stronger, stronger that it had been in many millennia. They were so vital! So powerful. It knew it could not face them all together and was wary of the Greater Dragon dozing above. Mindless it might be in its constant famishment, but its instincts warned it.

It had feasted long and well on the great dwarven city, taking many, and had found many creatures dwelling in the roots of the world. All had sustained it, strengthened it.

Yosgaloth had dozed, biding its time.

715

And then… the dragons had left, and the Greater Dragon above had gone with them. It sensed some remaining, but those few could not track it through its dark warrens.

And then… a great many bodies, a great noise. Blood and death, somewhere above. The prospect of so much life to consume had driven it out of its hole, heedless of dragons above. It had not feasted on so many since the time of plenty, bound in the pit, when hundreds of thousands of men had come to it. Holding off its hunger with difficulty all those millennia ago, it had stayed quiet with cunning, sensing the men entering its domain. When they had entered, it had taken them all, ecstatic with gluttony.

And now… this promised to be a feast such as that had been. It wended its way from its dank hole along hidden caverns, emerging through the foothills. As it approached the scene of the battle, eager to feast, it had felt something *else*. Something far greater. A feast to sate even its hunger.

Warily, it had crested the foothill and seen a dark being of enormous power, enough to make it forget the mortals it had come to devour.

Something within it had felt kinship. Yosgaloth recognised that part of its essence was somehow bound to this thing before it, a thing not of Kuln. It saw not just through eyes but felt its deep connection with the energies running through the universe, vast arteries pumping huge power. But there was more; the ragged darkness before it had a strangely multiple character to it. It felt no emotion, no care, but it also had a deeper bond with something that seemed *outside*. The anarchy within it spoke to the anarchy raging through Yosgaloth's being.

It *needed* to consume, to feast. There was no other purpose. The power before it was so strong, the Nameless One could see nothing else. It had to gorge, to match that chaos. What power this demon would give it when consumed! Power greater even than any dragon.

When the demon attacked with that very essence, it was agony it had not felt since that red dragon had exploded fire deep within its throat before the city. The damage was deep.

This foe might undo it, a forgotten part of itself realised.

The First One attacked back reflexively, causing the shadow etched with red to stagger. The demon began to fade, shadows curling from it, and Yosgaloth knew it fled, leaving it only the paltry morsels scattering far and wide around them.

Caution and hunger warred, and found only one answer.

This dark shadow must be destroyed.

Must be devoured.

Such a meal could not be allowed to escape.

Yosgaloth whipped forward with horrible speed, lancing more beams into the dissolving demon. For a split second, the Darkling lost focus and formed again. It realised its peril then, and blasted all its immense power at the huge form slithering towards it. Dark lightning played over the oncoming behemoth, slashing huge wounds over a head and flank. One giant yellow eye darkened slightly, ichor spilling from it as huge steaming rents were opened in the flesh of the hungry ancient one, and the screams blasting from both mouths were deafening.

The Darkling tried to dissolve again, but it was too late.

The momentum of Yosgaloth was too great to be stopped. Its tail tendrils, pulsing pinkly, lashed forward to aid its movement. Larger than even the Darkling, Yosgaloth crashed into the demon with an impact that resounded from the foothills.

Both demons screamed in agony as they lashed at each other with all their terrible might. Yosgaloth swallowed a claw-tipped arm, the talons of which burst from a neck seconds later as the chaotic crackling tendrils sliced into its being. With a heave it tore the arm clean from the Darkling and swallowed convulsively, gaining renewed energy even as it ate, the terrible wound closing slowly, leaking grey-green putrescence and a dark brown liquid. The Darkling bucked and shrieked in disbelief, chaotic energies like sinews of light spitting from the raw-red smoking crater where the arm had been.

At the same time Yosgaloth's tails whipped around the Darkling, the pink tendrils latching on and sucking power from the huge being, heedless of the dark aura around it. Many of the tendrils froze or were severed, but many more found purchase.

The Darkling's other hand, wreathed in dull red flame, tore deep into the side of the snakelike creature and ripped at its innards, sending anarchic energies into the core of Yosgaloth. The entirety of the Darkling's body seemed also to be harming the great demon wrapped around it, even as it tried to consume it. The Darkling's mouth and eyes were open wide, emitting a deep red smoking light which seemed to wither even the flesh of the ancient hunger. A rumbling roar emanated from it, a bass note discord to the unholy screeching of the hungry god.

The ground trembled. Trees fell. Lancing flashes of red were returned with powerful sickly yellow slices. The power slashed the area around the combatants, stray beams ending scores of those fleeing. A miasma of Yosgaloth's fetid killing breath surrounded the two, but it caused the Darkling no harm.

Dark clouds had gathered, oddly localised, but there was no rain. The air was charged. True lightning flashed an accompaniment to the energy below, striking into the aura of powers tearing at each other and further wounding the struggling giants. A huge rockslide was touched off to the west, its rumble a counterpoint to the monumental havoc the armies fled. Many of them had turned at a distance to see the incredible sight before them, in some cases Meyari shoulder-to-shoulder with Eordelander, their petty dispute forgotten as gods battled in the sight of mortals.

Yosgaloth was wrapped tightly around the Darkling now, like a doubled constrictor. The Darkling in turn had its hand buried in the ichor-stained flesh of one of the necks, holding the head away with strength that matched the thousand-foot long demon. It was bolt upright, its twin-tined tail lashing at Yosgaloth, slicing great rents in the slimy body.

The battle was not merely physical; a vast oppression grew and grew as unseen energies were punctuated with flashes and sparks of incredible intensity, each titan straining against the other in spirit and raw power as well as in body. The clouded darkness around them doubled, tripled, and it was hard to see much except what was shot through by red sparks and the intense yellow light scouring the dark demon. Discharges of energy from both grounded around them as lightning lit them in sporadic stop-motion flashes.

The unfortunate mortals caught too near the struggling behemoths ceased to exist in horrific ways. The closest were simply drained of essence, withering awfully to nothing in seconds, or charring to dark ash. Further back, they were aged, damaged in an instant, horribly warped by the chaotic energies, their lives mercifully almost as brief as the nearer, except for a few who survived at the fringes, changed. As the power met and strained against the other in invisible barriers, some humans and orcs were pinned, crushed to upright smears of molecule-thin redness as if they were bugs between two titanic sheets of glass. Further out, many were driven insane by the pressure in their heads. More than one was blinded by the intense pressure, or had massive damage done to their balance and hearing.

The power grew and grew, each striving strength against strength, locked in a stalemate physically and moving into the realms of pure energy, each trying to gain an advantage. For a second more they held their pose on the east side of the rise, growing more and more indistinct in a coruscation of force, the dark form rigid and ragged in the static coils of the nameless one. The pressure grew to a point where those closer collapsed, screaming, clawing at their own skulls.

Abruptly, there was a soundless detonation of brilliant light which erupted from the titans, temporarily blinding all who watched. Surrounding trees were bent away from the shock. A blast wave threw men and beasts to the floor in a circle for thousands of feet in every direction, expanding out at the speed of sound, something subsonic trembling through them. More rumbles from the mountains spoke of the abuse of the energies not meant to be unleashed. A darkness seemed to leap upward and spread across the sky, to be gone in a blink. A thin wail heard only by the mind seemed to fly west faster than thought.

All was suddenly deafeningly quiet.

Slowly the cries of the wounded grew clear again, and men shook their heads.

Ulric carefully and painfully got to his feet, purple spots in his eyes and ringing in his ears. His beard was full of mud, which he spat vaguely. He helped Colcos to his feet, staring at where the battle had been.

At the epicentre, a thousand feet wide, there was nothing left. No sign of the huge Darkling and its chaotic power. No sign of the vile creature Yosgaloth and its horrible hunger.

The east side of the rise had a huge crater in it. Where thousands of bodies had lain, most had vanished. The tents and supplies were gone. The wounded had vanished. The woods that the elves had been in were just gone, along with the entire top of the hill.

He hoped dazedly that they had escaped.

The earth was bare and raw, scrubbed by fire and energy beyond comprehension.

Both armies were in tatters, ruined. The aurochs and *rinoks* had run, many trampling their own masters. The Barbarians and orks had fallen back towards the plains, far out of the path of Yosgaloth.

They had destroyed one another, he realised dully. Whether they had consumed each other, hunger versus chaos, or had cancelled each other out in some way with the hellish energies they had wielded, the simple fact remained that suddenly, and unexpectedly, both were gone.

ʘ   ʇ

The allies who had not fled were in disarray, surrounded by scattered enemies, who were slowly gathering again. For ten minutes, only the cries of distress from those who were injured or had lost their minds echoed from the rocks.

Most of the humans were reeling in shock. The Meyari were in a worse state, but the Teromants were rising to their feet from where they had been praying en masse. Perhaps their prayers had protected their minds somewhat, Ulric thought. To his grudging admiration, they were regrouping to attack again.

The orcs crept back from the hills to the northwest, seeing that their foes were stunned. There were still tens of thousands of them, and they had not been affected as the allies had.

Neither had the werewolves. Snarls and roars erupted from them as they padded toward the helpless. Druids answered, but they had suffered many losses from the dark lightning.

The armies shuddered independently, stirring and waking to pull back together, the allies coalescing.

Dwarves were already reforming, down to less than five hundred. Here and there he saw elves gathering, many weeping as if their hearts were broken.

The Barbarians were worse off than his own troops, he saw; although they had been further out from the Darkling, the presence of the demons or the energies unleashed had done something to their Shamen, who had mostly collapsed into heaps. He didn't know if they were dead or injured, but the Barbarians had retreated to guard them, and were out of the fight for now.

So were the *Rashim* and the cavalry. Any animals had fled, whatever their riders had wished. A call went up in the desert tongue from the *Jundi*, ululating, and squads of them began to stumble together. Eordeland Guard guided the wounded to the centre, the ranks reforming. Tired, broken, confused, damaged, yet the stalwart men and women of Eordeland made ready.

The orks were returning, their pride overwhelming the lingering fear and confusion, but their berserk rage had gone, leaving them unsure.

Ulric looked desperately around. Of the original allies there might be less than ten thousand left, with no defensive position, no formations.

They had survived the annihilation, but the cost was too great. The allies were broken. They could not regroup before their enemies slaughtered those remaining. They were weary and still outnumbered at least twice over.

Ulric looked up to see great birds circling in the last of the daylight and realised how tired he was.

The vultures will pick our bones clean. How many times has the battle swung?
'What now?' he asked Colcos.

The austere general turned to him, gaunt face emotionless. He stood proudly in his spattered but still perfectly-hung grey uniform and chestplate, his spear in his hand.

'Now? Now we make them pay for each life. Until we are done.'
And then they heard a call. It was one he had heard once before.

૎ ૏

The spell was broken. Thousands of orcs regrouped to charge down the hill and destroy their hated kin, their hunger for slaughter and revenge outweighing the danger. Among them slavered werewolves, laughing and baying as they watched their disoriented enemies.

They were all unaffected by the chaos, and there were easily enough left to destroy the scattered and reeling allies. The orks and Barbarians were weakened; the elves and dwarves fewer. The Teromants called on their God to aid their attack. A few remaining ogres bellowed.

Those left to defend Eordeland were victims.

Both sides knew it.

At that moment, a roar sounded from the distant sky. Not just a roar; a challenge, a call, so powerful it had its own almost physical presence. It grew and grew, and a flash came.

Némaenth dropped out of the sky into the heart of the enemy like a flaming meteor, freed from his vigil over Yosgaloth. Nearly a hundred orcs were pulped under his immense weight as he slammed into the ground. Turning with sinuous speed, his tail lashed out. Over fifty feet long, it crushed more bodies as he scythed a taloned forelimb the size of a cart sideways in a blur.

Orcs and ogres were shredded. Nothing on the field could stand up to this kind of physical power. His searing breath scorched hundreds of feet along a broad cone as he swivelled his head on its long neck, targeting werewolves who shrieked as they blazed like the rest.

Nothing survived Dragonfire.

Hundreds of the foe were turned to ash, their flesh seared from their bones. He spun on the ground again, his tail whipping, and broken bodies were flung hundreds of feet over earth and rock torn up by spear-like talons.

An ogre lumbered up with a huge lance and jammed it into his side as he snapped and writhed, managing to get it between his armour plates with brute strength.

Némaenth howled in anger and pain, and twisted, wrenching it from the beast's hands. His jaws took off its head and shoulders, before tearing the offending weapon from his side. Hot blood hissed and sprayed flinching foes before the wound sealed.

In less than a minute more than a thousand lay dead. His bright enraged eyes bored widely into the enemy's, and they felt their wills being overridden. They froze, unable to move, some even stumbling closer… another sweeping burst of flame so hot it was barely visible incinerated swathes of them.

With a groan, the enemy broke and scrabbled away from him. With another bark of rage which echoed back from the nearby hills, a smaller dragon dropped, almost the grey of *titan* but limned with red-gold fire on scale edges in the last of the sunset above the peaks.

This one swept down into shade in a curve and along just above the ground, wings out, and spread its front limbs wide as it breathed a line of fire that melted armour and destroyed all in its path. It ploughed to a stop through hundreds of enemy, leaving a wide, clear rut on a field black with foes and gathering them to the armoured chest in a hug that left nothing but ragged smears on the light blue underscales. Claws razed out, taking heads and limbs in fountains of blood. The tail lashed with rock-breaking power. Even ogres were hurled scores of feet by the powerful strikes, and orcs rained down in their dozens.

Blazing green eyes cast around in fury and lit upon the Teromants. The dragon leapt, wings snapping out to glide.

The Meyari broke immediately, streaming north around the large wagon. Extinctors ran along with the rest, one at the rear slumping with oily smoke pouring out as his thick armour glowed red then started to melt.

The metallic grey dragon loped after them like a tiger, chasing them in an orgy of bloodlust. Bulls lowed and tried to bolt in the Extinctor wagons, entangling themselves and their partners.

Heedless, the dragon tore the poor creatures out, eating chunks from several. It threw the Chaplain wagons aside, smashing them to splinters with warriors inside, and then its eyes lit on the gigantic wagon halted at the back.

A hundred feet of blue-yellow flame roared out, blasting into it like a fist, killing the oxen and reducing the front to ash as it tumbled the huge wagon over. Two shrieking forms sped out of the wreckage, faster than any human, one burning as it ran. It collapsed after twenty feet, wailing as the flames consumed it; the other, fast as it was, was not fast enough. A gigantic limb shot out. The vampire was punctured by brutally sharp talons and lifted to the face of the dragon.

Spitting and coughing blood, its awful metabolism trying to heal around the terrible wounds, the vampire glared into a green gaze far more powerful than its own.

The dragon laughed, roaring, and snapped the creature in two, swallowing in gulps of its armoured jaws, then turned its head around to target another cluster of Meyari.

Terrified by the visions of everything they had seen, and the realisation their God was not protecting them, the Teromants were running as fast as the rest.

The two winged serpents tore through the enemy. Werewolf, orc, ogre, vampire, or human, none could face them and live. The vast creatures roared in their joy of killing, their teeth longer than the weapons of those they killed. It was like watching armoured men destroy a nest of harmless termites.

Flame bowled over whole ranks, flashed flesh to vapour; armoured bodies tore entire units asunder in heartbeats. Unnatural beasts shrieked as flames consumed them and they were obliterated past any hope of regeneration. Armfuls of enemy were crushed to smears, tails broke scores of them, jaws annihilated anything they closed on. Metal slagged and leather charred to ash. The colour of the dragon's underscales vanished under dripping red-black gore. It was pure carnage.

There was no fighting dragons.

They ran.

FIFTY-FOUR

It was raining softly by the time they were halfway back from The Croft, a fat pattering rain. Xhera was stuffed, and Kervala and Jimson were more than happy. Becka always seemed determined to feed them all to bursting every time they visited.

Xoth added a greenish tint to the dimly lit surrounds from the northeast, less than a quarter the size of Lunis but bright and moving fast. Both early moons were hidden in heavy rain clouds, giving patchy light, but when Lunis shone through the dusk was bright.

Cursing, Xhera realised she had left the ebony clip that Karland had given her at the house. Her hair tended to fall in her face when reading, and it had proved a beautiful and thoughtful birthday gift. She felt uncomfortable without it.

Just have to pick it up next time.

Her thoughts turned to Karland again.

She missed his simple complication terribly. There were things she wanted to tell him of Aldwyn's work - things she wasn't sure she should, but desperately wished to.

Aldwyn had seen something in Karland that had tied into the visions of Sarthos. He had always been marked for more than being the son of a cloth merchant.

Guilt lay there, that she hadn't treated him quite as she knew he wished. She didn't understand why she hadn't responded, either. It wasn't that she found him unattractive, or felt he was like a brother. They just… fitted so well together she hadn't thought about it. And, well…

She had enjoyed the attentions of some of the other boys.

Like Seom.

She hadn't been so popular in her own community. It had been fun, and she'd always had Karland there; her rock, her meaning. Only when he had left, faced with the possibility he might never return, did she fully admit to herself that he meant more, that perhaps she had waited too long.

It was only three days until Drake's Day - the day Györnàeldàr fell. She wished he had made it back to be with her for it.

He should have been back by now.

That was it, she decided suddenly, pushing fears away. *When* he got back, they would answer the unspoken piece missing from their lives. They would fill it for each other.

There, as simple as that.

She hoped.

They slowed as they came to the northern turning and moved into the woods. Another half an hour would see them back at the ruins of the library. Xhera wished that the rain would let up for a while; the heavy woods grew dark, and the grey sky made everything feel close and bleak.

'Strange,' muttered Kervala after twenty minutes. 'Where in the hells is the challenge?'

In the woods the patter of drops amplified, but the cart should still have been noticed.

A few minutes out from the camp, Jimson held up his hand and Kervala drew the wagon to a halt. She grabbed Xhera's arm as she was about to leap off, stopping her in her tracks. Xhera listened carefully but heard nothing but the patter of rain.

'What is it?' she whispered. Kervala shook her head.

'Don't know.'

Jimson looked back at them, and his hand flickered in signals. Karvala nodded and moved left, taking Xhera with her. Jimson moved right.

'Do you think it is the lizard man?' whispered Xhera.

'Be quiet,' was the only low answer.

They moved slowly through the bushes until they reached the clearing's edge. Xhera realised she couldn't hear any laughter. There was a faint smell of smoke dulled by the rain, but it didn't smell like the usual wood.

There was no noise at all. Even the usual small forest sounds were silent. The guards were quiet at the best of times, but there was usually *something*.

She could see nothing. It was grey and bleak, the rain pattering constantly, and the light was low. No guards moved around the clearing.

Perhaps they were inside one of the ruins, as they often were when it rained, but there was always someone on patrol. Always a lookout.

They weren't challenged. The horses were gone.

Kervala was like a coiled spring beside her. Her sword was out; Xhera hadn't seen her draw it. Her breath came in long hisses between the patters of rain.

She waited for minutes, and then slowly moved into the clearing toward the main door of the library, inside the tallest ruin, keeping them behind cover as they approached. The ruin was a dark shape in the rain. No fire welcomed them from the doorway.

They were within fifteen feet when Kervala stopped dead and crouched, a vehement curse spat under her breath. Xhera nearly shrieked when she saw what she was looking at.

The broken form of Pahm lay amongst the rubble, face down.

Karland had once fallen from this roof and broken his arm landing on soft earth inside. Pahm had fallen directly onto jutting broken stone from the old buildings, covered in ivy but still deadly. Her head hung down; Xhera caught a glimpse of a face covered in runnels of blood and water, smashed in on the left side, before she hurriedly looked away. Her stomach lurched.

There was no way she had simply fallen; her body was too far from the roof for that. She had to have been bodily flung from the edge.

Her heart was pounding in fright, and she took a better grip on her knife. Kervala was a veteran guard, decorated and deadly. Pahm had also been a veteran. All of them were. It was such a shockingly ignoble end to the years of training, talent, and survival; to a quiet, fervent woman.

Kervala's teeth were bared, and she was looking around the clearing intently. Xhera hoped fervently that the rest were chasing the horses, or looking for whoever had done this.

Kervala approached the doorway in a ready crouch, sword ready to thrust, parry or slash. The point was unwaveringly at about throat height, the hilt held in both hands low and to the side.

She slid up to the doorway and cautiously peered in. Her body seemed to freeze, but after a moment, she beckoned Xhera to her. Xhera came up and could not stop herself looking inside around Kervala.

Two bodies lay inside. The stink of charred flesh filled the space; one had fallen over the embers of the fire. The heat hadn't been enough to burn the clothes, just to char them and the skin underneath. It was Sergeant Cassega, her face holding a surprised, confused look, and her eyes looking upward in a squint. Her head was tilted up and back, and her helm had fallen off, showing her short, cropped hair. The silver tints were not visible in the gloom. Her mouth was part open, foam flecks on the right side, and a dark feathered dart under her chin showed the entry of the poison which had damaged her brain before stopping her heart.

Xhera gagged. She couldn't see who the other was, but it was enough. Death had found them all. They needed to escape. It must have been a deadly force to have quietly overcome such seasoned foes.

'Xhera.' Kervala's voice was rough with grief and anger. 'Get into the Library. Lock the door. I'll get Jimson and we'll retreat to The Croft for help. Allow no one in unless you recognise their voice.'

'What about Norla? Hilford?' She could hear the fear in her voice. Death had struck in the grey rain, horrible and sudden, and people she had known, liked, lay butchered before her.

'If they're still here, they're dead,' she said bluntly through gritted teeth. 'I saw Cassega kill three mounted and armoured Banistari once, with nothing but her sword. If she fell, they fell.'

Xhera took her key out and moved toward the alcove where the great ironwood door lay, almost undetectable unless you knew where to look. Her hands shook, and a noise from outside made her jump. She dropped the key with a slight tinkle to vanish into the darkness.

It had sounded like a sharp cry.

'*Fuck.*' Kervala's harsh whisper heightened her panic. 'Leave it. We have to get out of here. *Now.*' She grabbed for her arm and dragged her back to the doorway. They peered out but could see nothing new in the downpour.

'Get back to the horse. Cut the traces and ride for The Croft. I'll follow you if we're separated. *Go.*'

Kervala moved through the door, eyes darting around the clearing. Xhera followed, her slender knife in the fighter's grip Rast had taught her. He had praised her prowess, and she knew she was good with it, but she had never killed. She had seen the effect doing so had had on Karland, and knew it was one thing to know how to use a weapon, and another to use it, especially when frightened.

Halfway across the clearing, Kervala swore quietly and brushed her neck. A figure moved out from behind one of the lower ruins, blocking them. His hair was short and slicked down from the rain. His face was attractive, a sharp expression making him look faintly foxlike. His build was lithe and powerful, and the way he moved suggested years of training.

He was lowering a pipe, a look of annoyance on his face. For the most part, he was fairly unremarkable; someone she might not look at twice in Darost, for example.

But his eyes and mouth… they made her feel like shrieking. Something in them spoke to the primal part of her, jubilantly broadcasting horror and death. His eyes pinned her as if she was a butterfly impaled writhing on a pin of insanity, and his smile was the lazy smile of death. He moved casually, but in that second, she felt as though she were being stalked by a dark predator. Buried memories she thought she had conquered of Hoge and his men arose like bile, amplified by the way he looked at her.

As if she were already a victim.

Kervala held up her hand and motioned her back. Her neck had a line of blood on it where a dart had sliced the flesh; Xhera could only guess if any of whatever toxin had entered her bloodstream.

'When I engage, you go,' she said. 'I'll catch you up.'

'But he killed the others!' cried Xhera.

'And I'll avenge them! You think I'm not worthy of their sacrifice? He'll pay.' Her words were fierce, her tone confident, but Xhera despaired. If this man could kill the rest of the veterans then he likely could kill Kervala as well.

And me.

'Give me the girl,' said the man, his grin mocking, 'and I won't shit on your dead corpse. Deal?'

'You fucker!' Kervala's face was like stone, her teeth bared. An almost subsonic snarl was emanating from her, barely audible. The man opened his mouth to mock her again, and she lunged.

Her strike was solid. Kervala had been one of the hardiest fighters of the squad, and her sword moved deceptively fast. It dipped for the stranger's throat, but he slipped to the side. The sword skirled off the flat of his knife, held reversed grip. He danced back, and Xhera noticed with sinking heart that his footwork was excellent, even on wet soil and stone. This was no average combatant.

'Go!' grunted Kervala to Xhera, starting her. Her sword darted and wove, almost a blur, seeking flesh in her unarmoured opponent. He was far more agile than the armoured warrior, but had to move fast to avoid her strikes.

But Xhera could see she was slowing. Perhaps something had been left in the wound. Xhera drew her own knife.

'I'm not leaving you,' she shouted. She moved to circle behind him to attack, but he knew what she was doing, even managing to flash her a wink before he moved around Kervala again. Her attacks were making him focus; she was no amateur, and he clearly respected her skills.

Kervala was heavyset, with a weight and height advantage, but their enemy seemed to flow around her attacks. The sword missed every time, although not by much. His knife skittered off her armour and slashed several times into her arms, none serious wounds. Blood leaked down her arms in rivulets.

Xhera dared to hope they could beat him. She moved behind him again, and dashed forward, ready to sink it into his kidneys. Well before she got there, he changed tactics with Kervala.

Ducking down, he spun inside her next swipe, swiping his knife at her exposed swordhand whilst pulling a poignard from his lower leg. Kervala hadn't seen it, and spun her hand over his in a move that would end with the sword buried in his throat. Her teeth bared again in victory.

He twisted suddenly, moving aside from the blade, the other hand punching forward. It shouldn't have made a difference, wouldn't with his knife; he was too far. But the poniard was longer and sharper on the point than the dagger. At a foot and a half long with an almost diamond cross section, it was so slender it was hard to see. The long needle-like knife was designed to punch through leather.

It hit her directly over the heart, and her own twisting forward momentum drove it deeper. It opened a gateway through the armour, pierced her skin, and slid in.

'Oh!'

It was a gasp, and exclamation, a denial, as they collided, their bodies melding intimately. The man twisted it expertly, probing, and she shuddered. Xhera was standing to his rear right, and his back was to her. She had frozen in horror.

'Xhera.'

Kervala said her name again, but this time it was calm, quiet, almost lost in the sound of the rain. The word asked for forgiveness, signified the cessation of hope and despair, spoke of a lifetime at its end.

Kervala slumped onto the man's shoulder, her mouth working like a fish gasping for air, her eyes fluttering. She was trying to say *run*.

He held her up, looking down at her almost tenderly.

'Shhhhhhhh,' he whispered.

She hiccoughed, spasming several times slightly, and then relaxed, her cheek bunching up on his shoulder. Xhera saw a drop of red-tinted drool fall from her open lips to be lost in the water running down both of them.

He opened his arms and let her fall to the side. Kervala collapsed off him like a puppet, splashing wetly to the floor to lie face up, eyes staring and a dark stain on her chest where his dagger had pierced her heart.

He turned and looked at Xhera.

'Hi!' he said brightly, but she was already moving, her paralysis broken.

He had expected her to run, to scream, to try to escape. He hadn't expected her to lunge, the knife flipping over in her hand smoothly. The thrust aimed at his heart just missed as he twisted, his reflexes superb. A little of how he moved echoed Rast, Xhera noted detachedly as the tip of her knife sliced instead into his pectoral and cut upward.

The cut was shallow but shocking, and his counterstrike to break her hold on the knife didn't connect. She was already moving away, and his other hand shot out to strike her. She tucked her chin and swayed back, her foot rising to strike the outside of his hip as she flicked the knife over to lie along her forearm. Faster than her, his leg rose and caught the foot on the outside of his shin. His next strike with stiffened fingers almost earned him a sliced arm as she moved to block the fingers seeking her throat, but he pulled the blow and instead hooked her heel with his foot and tugged a little. Her foot slid on the wet ground, and she stepped forward, off balance. He jabbed three times in quick succession, and her knife arm numbed. The knife fell from nerveless fingers, and his next kick swept her legs from under her. She hit the ground hard, the breath leaving her body. A toe jabbed her hard in the solar plexus and she retched, winded. Her right eye was already feeling swollen from the impact with the wet earth. Curled up, she couldn't move in time, and knew she was dead.

A hand grabbed her and forcefully dragged her upright as she struggled for breath. Trying to focus, she looked up. Strangely, the young man was grinning at her in a feral fashion, his chest dripping red from her strike. He hadn't even used his knife.

'Trained with Tal'Orien, did you? Not many people get a hit in, bitch. You're good. Won't underestimate you again.' He laughed softly, sounding utterly normal, which made it all the more chilling. 'I've come a long way to find you. I'm guessing the old man isn't with you. Where's the boy? Inside the Library?'

Xhera struggled to focus on his words, gasping as the bruised knot in her stomach unwound.

'What-boy?'

He shook her roughly, the smile never leaving his cold face.

'Xhera. Xhera. That *is* your name?' He chuckled. 'Aldwyn Varelin's student. Karland. He spent a lot of time here, and you've always travelled with him, him and Rast Tal'Orien.' His tone when he said that name was almost thoughtful. 'No one in that little town has seen the old bastard for a year. So. Let's try again. Where's the brat? In the Library?'

'He's not even in Anaria,' said Xhera. The memory, so close to all this slaughter of her friends, broke through her numbness and she felt her eyes sting. The bruised eye was worse. She wished she'd never realised how important Karland was. She wished he was here now; she thanked the Gods he was not.

'Come on,' he chided. 'That's the best you can come up with? I don't know why you and your friends were here - waiting for him perhaps? - but it...' he trailed off as he watched her, and the smile dropped from his face. 'You know, I could almost believe you. When?' The tone was sharp and demanding. 'Where is the pendant?'

'You *bastard*. You fucking *bastard*.' Xhera gritted her teeth. 'Karland left Anaria months ago. And Aldwyn is *dead*. So whatever you wanted, you are too late by a year. The pendant is gone. It vanished when we used it.'

She expected him to react perhaps by killing her, or worse, and tried to prepare herself, although in truth the thin veneer of rage hid a dark ocean of panic that threatened to overwhelm her at any second. She knew he could tell this. Worse, the very presence of him was worse than the actuality of Hoge and the bandits had been when they had attempted to violate her. This man wouldn't even do it for power, or enjoyment; he would do it as a tool and have no limits. He was triggering every flashback and feeling of helpless terror she had had since then, and she had begun shaking uncontrollably.

The handsome, terrible young man before her laughed, throwing his head back, and his eyes flashed in an emotion she couldn't plumb.

'*Dead!*' he shouted. 'And about fucking *time!* That useless old faggot gave me the run around. Everyone I sent to kill him failed. Ha! At least the last fools managed before they died!' He almost doubled over, one hand slapping his thigh, and the other let her go with a small push. The fear had gripped her so thoroughly she had no strength, and fell backward heavily, looking up at him. All the fight had left her; his very presence made her muscles feel like water. Right now she couldn't have hit him if she had tried, let alone lifted her knife. She tried to stand, to run, and managed to clamber unsteadily to her feet.

After a moment he stopped laughing, wiping the rain and presumably tears from his eyes, and watched her take a wobbling step. The mocking grin was back on his face.

'And where do you think you're going?'

She couldn't speak, and just shook her head in denial, in dumb animal panic.

'*No pendant*. You used it! And what did it get you? Ah, I'm sick of chasing the fucking thing. What a waste of time. But not, maybe, a complete waste.' His eyes narrowed slightly. 'Where's Rast Tal'Orien?'

She stammered, all thought of dissembling gone, and finally managed to get some words out. This man's stare still pinned her whenever it fell on her fully. It was not like the stare of Night or Leona, or a dragon; he was just a man, but something forceful in it, something utterly cold and uncaring, robbed her of strength. He didn't seem like any of the soldiers or professional killers or Teromants they had seen before. Xhera didn't know what this man was, but she had never met anyone as horrifying.

'He- he went to Eyotsberg, to sail for Mithtol,' she blurted, wanting only for this man to leave her alone, but knowing that she would die badly. A hidden part of her looked for the knife; not for protection, but to end herself before that happened. Something she had never even contemplated before became more paramount with every moment in his presence.

'No doubt that is where that little shit went, too,' remarked the man with a slight frown. 'If they seek help, they'll return very soon. I hear you're all very… *close.*' He laughed shortly. 'You know what I think? I think that when they come back, they'll come to see you. And if you're gone… Rast Tal'Orien will come after you.'

Suspicion tinged her fear. 'No.'

'Oh, yes,' he laughed, his eyes blinking in the water dripping from his brow. 'You're all such pathetically *good* friends.'

Defiance flared, and she blew water off her lips before she spat at him.

'Rast will kill you. He will break every bone in your body.' Even as she said it, she wondered. She had never seen a fighter like Rast, but this man reminded her uncomfortably of him. He was uncannily good.

'Quite possibly,' the man grinned. 'That's why I'll choose the manner of our meeting, to even things up a little. I don't care for an *honourable* fight.' His eyes drifted down then up her figure. 'And then, of course… there's *you.*' Her heart quailed at his words, and he confirmed her fears. 'See, I think if he knows I have you, he'll follow me. If I kill you now, I am sure he would seek vengeance; but then I wouldn't have his little knife-flipping whore to distract him. To give me the edge. I have heard a lot about that big bastard; *a god among men, no man can match him in battle.* Well, everyone has their weakness. Let's see how well he does with your life in the balance.'

Xhera shook her head in denial, forcing down the scream rising in her throat. She couldn't stand this man's company for a moment longer. She couldn't lead Rast to his death.

'And then there is the matter of what else you can tell me,' he purred relentlessly. 'Where's the key to the library? Where's its entrance? If I can't have Varelin or the pendant, I can have his works.'

'I don't have it,' she said weakly, thanking whatever fate had caused it to fall in the darkness near the entrance. 'Search me if you like.'

'Oh, I will,' he promised, then shrugged. 'No matter. It isn't important.'

'If you stay here the Guard will come looking for us,' she said, desperately hoping the terrifying man would leave now he had failed in his mission.

'No doubt.'

His voice was unconcerned. His eyes grew intent, and the smile that lit his face was like a candle from below, even in the grey mist and dreariness around them. His voice was conversational.

'By the way… have you ever been raped?'

The casual, unrelated question froze her to the core. Her face drained of blood.

'No,' she whispered, although she didn't know if she answered him or denied the question. She didn't even know if it was true after the woods near her home.

'If you wish this to continue to be the case, you will not try to escape. I promise you, I will find you if you run, and I will defile you utterly, in every way you can imagine. You will *beg* me to merely rape you by the end.'

She looked into his oddly dead eyes and believed him. Her guts twisted, bile rising in her throat again, and the returning horrors of her kidnap and Hoge amplified all his threats unbearably.

'Behave, and I'll treat you well enough. It's easier to get information from someone at least a little willing, after all.' He flashed her another grin. She couldn't bear the discordance of his easy-going attitude against the horror of his reality. 'Let's go.'

He dragged her past the clearing's edge where a form lay still. Her breath caught and her heart was suddenly hammering.

It was Jimson. His eyes had rolled up to stare into the leaf mould. His head was bent sharply back, and his throat had been opened so far, she could see the round edges of his windpipe and arteries in the faint torchlight and gleaming silver moon, even a wet glint of the inside of his vertebrae. It was a horrifyingly intimate view of part of the body that couldn't be seen in life. The ground and the underside of his chin was dark and slick, clear tracks of rain streaking them. She heaved, trying to back away, and heard the laugh as her attacker's grip stopped her. She vomited, hot and stinking, part of it spattering onto her arm and front.

'Wash that off in the rain,' he advised. He almost politely gestured for her to precede him. 'We have a long way to go.'

℮ ℯ

It had been an eventful day. Bal'Jin had offered to take them to the plains southwest of the city to watch a skinpig hunt the day before they left for the south.

Karland did not enjoy watching the large animals chased down and speared. One man had been kicked over, hard; the deep scrapes up the abdomen of his leather frontguard were a reminder that these animals could be dangerous.

They had journeyed out just after lunch, Bal'Jin riding a horse and shadowed by mounted crimson. He was not only eager to watch the hunt, but to display the wealth of the people to Karland - the great herds.

Fifty men worked in teams to capture or kill the Skinpigs. Another fifty were there as troops to protect him, as well as his personal bodyguard.

There had been consternation in the city this morning when a dark pulse had seemed to flash across the sky from somewhere to the east. It had been so fast Karland had thought he had imagined it, like the great shadowed flickering of something vast, as if the sun had blinked. It had seemed to curve south and vanish. The sounds around him had paused for a split-second, then continued.

What in the hells was that? he'd thought.

Summer faded and the rains were coming. Karland felt the need to get back to Anaria like a physical twist, twinned against a newfound fear of vast, uncaring waters. He tried not to think of Xhera.

What he had felt before - the feeling of doing nothing - was tenfold here, but this time they had no choice. He hoped everyone back at home was safe.

Karland was also beginning to understand his new friend a little better. Bal'Jin would never come out and admit things directly, but he clearly took every opportunity to get away from the city in general and the Palace in particular.

The *Jinong* had invited him out to watch the sunset and view one of the great herds which was currently near the city.

Karland stood on the hill to the south of the city with Rast, looking west across the brown-green plains. Skinpigs dotted them in small clumps. In the distance a vast herd of the small *Kuun* cattle moved slowly, a great dark mass drifting north with the specks of horse herders moving around them.

To his rear was the eastern sea, a faint blue horizon; in front lay low hills and plains, with a dark green border to the southwest where the deep forests lay and a lighter, more vibrant green south where the jungles began rising from vegetation. This was the highest point in the near plains, the slope down gentle but running for miles, green swells on a grassy ocean.

Bal'Jin stood nearby, silent, shadowed by the two red-armoured Imperial Guards. Further back lay the troops of his honour Guard.

His eyes were closed, light playing across his angular features.

'You hear the voice of the plains,' he said. 'Part of it is the silence. When it is loud enough, it has its own voice.'

He was right. The silence was deadening, almost loud. It was broken moments later by the faint coughing roar of an earth-lion.

The sunset was glorious. The dusty plains of Hadrasia were much hotter than northern Anaria, and even the setting sun was warm. The distant clouds on the horizon had begun to colour themselves red-pink and underlight with orange. He closed his own eyes, trying to simply feel the sun on his face. The warmth penetrated his eyelids, and he tilted his head up.

He must have been there only for a few minutes, finding a rare moment of peace, when Rast grunted. Karland looked over to see him massaging and flexing his hands, rubbing his thumbs deep into the red scars that faintly shimmered under his roughened knuckles.

'You all right?'

'It tingles. As if with faint heat. I felt it on the ship, too.'

Before Karland could ask what he meant, a cry went up from the Honour Guard. Startled oaths in *khel* were harsh in his ears. In the distance, the herd of cattle seemed to pulse, spreading in several directions before moving south in a stampede.

A gasp from Bal'Jin made him turn.

'What is it?'

'Karland.'

Rast pointed upwards. Karland followed his finger.

Glinting almost metallic in the sun, lit like hundreds of beacons in flashing orange-red, first one, then a few, then many flights of dragons were flying south from all different points, as far as he could see. Unlike before on the ship where they had seen only a few of the flights, this time the clear sky was filled with the gigantic creatures. Amongst them were Greater Dragons; otherworldly, glowing, as different to their smaller kin as an eagle to a gnat, almost coasting forward on millennial wingbeats instead of expending effort flying.

Karland counted more than twenty of the Greater Dragons amongst the horde as they moved on. The air glittered black with wings, the red of the sky and the reflections of the setting sun flickering in shards as they moved, great shadows moving across the plains. The sight was incredible, the whole sky seeming to glint and flicker rainbow hues from scales near and far. No wonder the animals panicked.

Faint cries reached them; calls to war.

The calls of the serpents.

The dragons searched for their foes, after countless millennia.

'The legends are true,' said Bal'Jin. His voice held awe and fear, and he was pale. The Guards were muttering prayers to themselves. 'Great Serpents ride the wind. Where do they go? Will they destroy us? Is this the end of the world?'

'They go to war,' said Rast grimly. Directly above them flames spouted, as if in confirmation. He rubbed his scarred knuckles absently. 'As do we... and theirs is the greater peril. I fear this fight is one that may not be won. Perhaps not even by dragons.'

Karland stared out, lost in the mesmerising sight of so many moving at once. They moved differently to birds, slower than bats, deliberate and sinuous and powerful.

'I do not understand.' Bal'Jin sounded uncertain for the first time since Karland had met him.

'When we told Bal'Hon greater forces moved, this was our meaning,' replied Rast. 'They seek dark demons that seek to unmake this world. They have no interest in humans.' His voice was sombre. 'The battle to save us could yet destroy us.'

'We do not know if we'll survive even if they win,' said Karland soberly.

The Darklings might not even be found, and he remembered the dangers of a Greater Dragon facing even one. What would be left of the world, or the life upon it, if the whole of Dragonkind confronted the Darklings unveiled in their full power? That was as great a danger as the Darklings themselves. He thought of the peril they had faced, and those lost to it. His family, his friends, those still left.

Xhera.

'Face the Darklings, save the world,' he murmured, and looked at Rast. Rast said nothing, gazing upwards. He seemed chiselled from granite.

At that moment, Karland's self-doubt, his worries, his fear were absent. Nothing was more important than those he cared for.

Especially Xhera.

There was no choice. They might not succeed, but they would not be lost without trying. He felt a fierce exultation rise within him into the base of his throat.

'Let them come,' he whispered.

Here ends Book Two

Thanks

The Serpent Calls relied on some extremely talented people as I wrote it, both for editing (John Jarrold, Tiffany Chevis) and for honest feedback (*many diuerse brayve soles*). I think it was a good attempt at a first large-scale fantasy book, and set a story in motion I've had bursting to be told since I was young. Tides of Chaos is a much better book, I feel; the world is more alive, the characters more human, and the book simply better written, with lessons learned.

Once again, thanks is required to the talented pool of authors who have inspired me to write these books, some of whom I've now met, some of whom I won't ever meet. Across the great and ever-increasing galaxy of speculative fiction, their work shines brightly, creating gravity in assemblages; the beauty of it is, authors such as myself will each find different ways to navigate using the stars of their work. We all stand on the shoulders of giants, and perhaps that's the only way we get to see the top of the beanstalk.

I would like to thank my editors Tiffany Chevis and Priya Brown for their work on the draft, and will miss Tiffany's excellent feedback going forward. Priya was surprisingly gentle, for which I'm also grateful, along with her friendship and understanding of my personal struggles during writing.

I also had another excellent swathe of constructive feedback from test readers; thank you to Matt Cook, and also to Teresa Osset Ojea, whose deep review, scientific help exploring bases and biological ideas, and support on every level has been profound. The joking and laughter helped more than you know; this book needed you.

Thank you always to Grace (and oh, how life has hit us since the first book) for putting up with me writing and doing all the other things I do, but also supporting me unconditionally despite terrible hardship through one of the worst times in our lives. I will never not be grateful for you.

Finally, to all those others who *believe* in my writing, my world, and the characters that make themselves known to me, rather than are created by me; to all those who loved the first book and the companion stories, and affirmed my feelings that perhaps - just perhaps - I wasn't wasting my time… thank you.

Even if I was… I'd still be writing. That's the terror and the beauty of it.

About the Author

Chris lives in the UK and is the author of the World of Kuln series, as well as other diverse stories, and also writes articles and books in non-fiction and business. He moonlights as a TEDx and conference speaker, coach, and consultant for executives and organisations in complexity, agility, resilience, and human learning. He has too many hobbies – which include scuba diving, climbing, martial arts, gaming, reading,  working out, photography, composing music, and generally learning anything and everything he can – and leads a very active lifestyle as a strong mental and physical health advocate. He reads almost constantly. For him, life is about learning and doing. His brain is… busy.

Chris is atypically autistic (ASD ½ and ADHD traits, with likely dyscalculia and occasional dyspraxia), and has differences in sensory and emotional input, as well as increased sensitivity in all of them, and annoyingly persistent imposter syndrome, so he sees different patterns and linkages in the world. He is very imperfect. A lot of his dreams end up in his books.